DAWN OF THE LAST DRAGON RIDER

Shawn Wilson

Podium

To my wife and children. Without you, these words are meaningless.

All rights reserved. No part of this publication may be reproduced, stored in a retrieval system, or transmitted in any form or by any means electronic, mechanical, photocopying, recording, or otherwise without prior written permission from Podium Publishing.

This is a work of fiction. Names, characters, places, and incidents are either products of the author's imagination or used fictitiously. Any resemblance to actual events, locales, or persons, living, dead, or undead, is entirely coincidental.

Copyright © 2024 by Shawn Wilson

Cover design by Jack Nguyen

ISBN: 978-1-0394-5955-7

Published in 2024 by Podium Publishing
www.podiumaudio.com

DAWN OF THE LAST DRAGON RIDER

DAWN OF THE LAST DRAGON RIDER

1

A Mother's Commitment

Tomorrow. Tomorrow, she would escape or die, taking her child with her either way. She had been watching and waiting for this chance for months.

She watched her brown and copper-colored egg vibrate slightly as Stioks ran his hand along the top of it.

"You should be proud to know your child will be my dragon. When it hatches, we will rule this kingdom and others, all because of the power we share."

Stioks's face cracked as he smiled at Indyn, blood seeping from the small fissure that appeared when he smiled. She saw the damage that she had done to him years ago when he'd captured her. The left side of his face, scalp, and shoulder was burnt beyond all healing. His bloodshot left eye contrasted sharply against the obsidian black section of his face as it tracked her. He never wore his helmet when he came to torment her, more than happy to remind her that her best had not been enough to defeat him.

"Is your collar bothering you, Indyn? I would take it off, but we both know I have not broken you enough to stay where you belong. Yet . . ."

Shaking her neck, Indyn felt the rusty metal collar rub against her silver scales as the huge red metal chains attached to its sturdy loops scraped across the stone floor and connected to the stone walls of her prison. The cave she was confined to had been carved out of the mountain, and a small window with bars was the only source of light in her cell. The stone roof was intentionally low to prevent her from standing at her full height.

Indyn released a bestial roar in Stioks face. She felt the rage and shame of knowing she had been pulled from the skies and imprisoned within the hole she was kept in, hoping she might birth an egg. If she could have, she would have engulfed him in flames, even if it would have cost her child its life, but her collar prevented it. It would have been a mercy and prevented a life of slavery.

Stioks chuckled at her futile display of rebellion. He moved closer to Indyn when he saw the runes on the collar glowing. Standing a few feet from her muzzle, he turned the burnt side of his body to her and gently tapped his chin.

"I think you missed a spot around here," Stioks added. He laughed at his own joke far too loudly.

"Try to enjoy your time off," he called as he left her prison cave. "Juthom and I will return in a week and see if my newest addition is ready for the ceremony."

Finally, those three fools are gone.

Not long after she had been tortured by his presence, through her cell's window, Indyn saw Juthom and Stioks ride to the east. Right behind him were the other three female dragons who worshiped Juthom, leaving the mountain for the feeding grounds. Their complete devotion to Juthom allowed them freedom she would never be given.

They despised her for giving birth to an egg without having to be taken by Juthom. For years, they had freely given themselves each time they were in heat. He had ridden them across the skies, but thankfully, none of them had produced an egg. They revered him because he was a black dragon and a powerful creature who was almost as old as she was.

It has to be the magic Stioks infects Juthom with. That could be the only reason why they cannot seem to conceive. That awful human reeks of death, and everything he does damages the kingdom.

What fool of a man coops four female dragons together? It was a wonder none of them had killed each other yet.

She knew Juthom and Stioks were headed out to ravage the countryside and make kings pay tributes of large caravans of food and wealth to his mountain. Even with all they could ask for brought to their doorstep, Stioks and Juthom felt the need to terrorize the people, fanning the flame that once swept across all the kingdoms, resulting in her kind being hunted for centuries. Men like Stioks were why the world had forgotten the age of Dragon Riders, when men and dragons bled and died together to safeguard the innocent.

That fool was moving them all, anyways. He had a city built for them. For years Stioks had forced the two kingdoms to the east to construct a hall he felt was worthy of his power. He had promised towers for each of them, but Indyn knew what they were. Prisons. They were captives that only had one purpose. To bear an egg for him. A dragon he would bond with.

The three of them disappeared from her view. They would be gone for hours, gorging themselves, hoping against hope it would allow them to get pregnant when Juthom took them.

* * *

Indyn unwrapped herself from her egg and struck the chain near her neck again with her last talon. She had been striking it for half a day, hitting the same spot every time. Two talons were gone already, broken by the magic in the chain. But she could feel the link weakening.

When her last talon snapped off, she snarled in frustration. Testing the chain with her aching nub of a claw confirmed her suspicions. The link was almost broken. So close! It was now or never. If she would get away before the other three returned, or just like that, she would lose her only chance. She strained against the chain, tugging with all of her might. No one would call her weak, but this prison was built to hold her and her alone.

They had believed it was enough.

They had underestimated her will.

She struggled to breathe as the collar began to choke her. Every ounce of strength she had surged through her back legs as she strained to break free of the chain.

It dug deep into her neck, cracking scales that most weapons could never hope to pierce. Blood ran down the chain, but she felt the weakened link failing.

They will not break me! Indyn screamed in her mind.

Her back claws dug into the stone, creating deep furrows as she groaned. She was so close, but the pain was worse than anything she had ever experienced.

Her gaze landed on the egg. Inside the pit of her stomach, her rage roared from red- to white-hot, its fire fueled by a mother's love for her first child. With one last massive lunge, she gave everything she had left and drove her body across the room.

The link snapped, and Indyn crashed into the stone wall beside the gate, shaking the room and causing small rocks to pelt the floor. She lay there, almost motionless, as she tried to regain her breath. Blood ran down her neck, painting her silver scales a rusty red.

She was not worried. She would heal in time.

It was over. Freedom was hers.

Joy filled her heart, replacing the rage, as she beheld her child, knowing they would escape this place. She was carefully lifting her egg in her claws and preparing to leave, when a jolt of pain lanced through her hands where they touched the smooth bronze shell.

Something was wrong with her egg!

[Identify]
Bronze Egg
Sex - Unknown
Ailments
Cursed - ?

Oh no, no no. This can't be?! she thought frantically as she stared, first at that notification, then at her only child.

STIOKS!! She seethed, not daring to bellow her rage, worried she might attract unwanted attention.

Glancing outside, she checked to see if she could spot Juthom's broodmares returning from the feeding ground. When she didn't, she collected her mana and empowered a spell.

[You cast Dispel Curse on [Bronze Egg]]
[Dispel failed - This Curse is too high level to remove]

Indyn flexed her neck, wincing as the collar rubbed against her broken scales. She sighed, knowing what she had to do.

[You cast Transference on [Bronze Egg]]
[Transference Complete]
[You are now cursed - Unable to heal]
[You are now cursed - You are being tracked]

A scream escaped Indyn that was nothing compared to the fire that suddenly raged through her bones. She felt weakened, and her body ached. The effect of the curse was more than she had imagined!

Blinking back tears, she grasped her child in her talons.

We must go now, little one!

Ignoring the pain that wracked her body, she kicked the door with her back leg. The wooden door tore off its hinges and clattered into the massive hallway outside her prison. Together they moved into the hallway and toward the exit of the mountain that had been her prison for years. *They needed to escape now!*

A day into their prison break, Indyn had noticed the three females miles behind her. She had glanced back, as she had every so often, and had seen them as she had been slowly gliding below the clouds. She was trying to decide if she would trust her egg, and her life, with the Dragon Rider she had heard about in the West.

The curse!

Frustration filled her, as she knew that plan would no longer be viable. If Stioks and Juthom attacked the Dragon Rider with these three, he would stand no chance at all.

She beat her wings and rose into the clouds, feeling the cool moisture across her scales as she climbed above them. They would still be able to track her, but she needed to add some distance between her and them while she figured out her next move.

[Activate Flight Burst]

The wind buffeted against her as she surged forward. Her skill launched her across the sky like a bolt of lightning. Her talons gripped tightly around her child as she left a trail of clouds swirling in her wake.

What to do? Where can I go?

Her egg moved slightly in her claws, and she rotated her head a bit as she streaked across the sky and gazed upon it.

I will find you somewhere safe!

By the second day of nonstop flying, fatigue was setting in, and Indyn felt the slow and steady trickle of the blood that ran down her neck. She had been cooped up in the mountain far too long, and the stamina she had once enjoyed when she'd roamed free was gone.

She knew where she needed to go and changed her direction, realizing the only hope her child had was a future without her. The mountain range near Ebonmount would be the safest place for her child. It had been home to dragons ages ago and was her only option now.

Checking behind her was a constant chore, and she had to drop below the cloud level to ensure she could spot her pursuers if they got near. This plan would require everything she had, yet she still did not know if it would be enough.

A predatory smile still remained on her face as she glided across the sky. Hundreds of years being up there had taught her how to fly as efficiently as possible.

Blast those three!

She knew this moment would come; changing direction had allowed them to catch up. Sometime during the early morning, they had appeared miles behind her. She had almost not seen them as they had climbed high into the sky, right below the clouds. Against the red and orange colors of the sky, she had noticed that petty yellow female, Upi. Her youth and size allowed her to close the distance faster than the other two.

Gazing down at the landscape, Indyn calculated the distance to where she needed to be; she was almost a day away. Based on the lead she had now and the time she expected she would need, she would have to wait a while before using her flight skill again.

As the third day stretched on and the sun started to set, Indyn knew the time to make her move had come. The sun would block their view of her as she made her next move.

Fear not, little one. Mother has a plan.

[Activate Flight Burst]

* * *

Indyn's wings felt weak. Four days of constant flying combined with the stress of her flight skill was taking its toll. She glanced down again and saw her small bronze egg nestled gently between her massive claws. She cherished these last few moments she had, caressing her child that was moving inside. Soon she would have to abandon it. Soon it would hatch, and she would rather die than let it fall into Stioks hands again.

Hold on, little one, Indyn thought as she crested over the top of the snow-capped mountain.

Growling to herself, Indyn admitted that bastard Stioks was no fool. The trap he had set on the egg had cursed her. The three females could follow her, and she could not heal. More blood flowed from the cut on her neck every day, weakening her even more. Every second counted now, before she bled to death.

Her eyes were heavy when she spied what she had been looking for. For days she had flown here, knowing a quarry was located in the circle of mountains that dragons once claimed. She hoped it would be refuge enough for her unborn child.

[Flight Burst Expired]

Indyn groaned and tucked her wings as she dove down the mountainside. Using her skill to widen her lead on the three dragons chasing her was draining her mana at an incredible rate. Soaring to the bottom of the quarry at night, she was unseen by the world. No one saw her massive form blocking out the stars in the night sky. There were only a few small lights off in the distance in the town that worked these rocks.

Stupid females for wanting a dragon like that for a mate. Those young ones had no idea what it meant to be free.

Indyn had not seen them since yesterday evening. She had used Flight Burst multiple times to press a lead she knew she needed for this exact moment. Everything was riding on it.

She had planned the details of her escape, but everything had gone sideways when she'd found herself cursed. Now she had to follow this different path. She would save her child, even if it meant she would never see them hatch.

Lost in those thoughts, Indyn ignored the pain consuming her body, the darkness eating her from within.

Status, she thought.

Indyn - Adult Female Dragon
Age - 247 years
Color - Silver

HP - 12,740/30,000
MP - 1358/5000
Ailments
Exhausted - You are slowed and unable to regenerate mana
Cursed - Unable to heal while cursed
Cursed - You are being tracked
Bleeding

Almost crashing as she landed, her wings flopped against her back. This small break would be the only rest she would experience for days.

She found a spot off to the side of some large boulders and quickly dug a small hole in the hard-packed dirt. She needed a place that would work for what she had in mind. She carefully dug out a spot where stones would protect her child. She made a little divot and gently set the egg in the hole she had created.

A massive toothy grin spread over Indyn's muzzle as she drew on her mana again. She had never used this spell, even though she had learned it a century ago. Now she knew it was time and would grant it to her child. Her silver body glowed in the night as the light spread from her whole body to the tip of her nose. She bent and touched it against her egg, and the light left her and caused the egg to glow brightly for a moment before the area faded into darkness once more.

[You cast Nemesis Transference on [Bronze Egg]]
[Nemesis has been set to Stioks]

Indyn sagged from the mana she had expended but knew it would be well worth it for her child. Both her child and anyone who managed to bond with them would be blessed if they ever fought that man.

Someone will find you. Someone will help you! she thought as she pushed her will upon her child. The bronze and brown egg twitched in reaction to the brush of her consciousness. It understood its mother's desire for it, even while trapped within its shell.

Grow strong!

She covered her egg with a few larger rocks, gently setting one against the others. If no one came and her child had to hatch without someone to bond with, it could escape by pushing the rock out. In these woods, it would find game and be able to grow.

Indyn moved a little way from that spot. She quickly grabbed a rock that matched the size of her egg and gently blew a small fire on it. The rock turned a dark brown color, and she hoped it would work for what she needed it for.

Launching herself from the ground, she took off back into the sky. Her wings ached as she struggled to gain height and started the climb to go away from her child. Unable to beat her wings fast enough, she crashed into a few trees as she took off. Her body struggled to fly. Indyn's heart felt broken, but she knew this was better than the alternative. No child of hers should be enslaved from birth.

As she slowly climbed into the night sky, Indyn glanced at the shrinking landscape. Trees, farms, and a village all filled her vision. Up north, she saw the lights of the town called Ebonmount. This was the place her child would call home.

Her eyes snapped open, and Indyn dove as the fake egg she carried slipped through her talons. She had fallen asleep for just a moment as the exhaustion of another day caught up with her. Her heartbeat was weaker, and she felt cold. The blood loss was taking a toll. The ground was rushing toward her at an alarming rate, and she frantically snatched at the rock as it tumbled through the air.

Her claws wrapped around it, and she stretched her wings out to slow her descent and try and regain some altitude.

Focus, you fool!

She was angry with herself. Being weak and falling asleep was not an option. Her child deserved hope and a future, and that required her to push past her limits.

There was still another day before she could reach the final part of this plan. She knew the others were gaining on her, despite not seeing them today. It was nearing nighttime, and surely they must be suffering as she was. Even without a curse, they must be just as exhausted, Indyn made herself believe.

Her lungs were only allowing shallow breaths now. Tomorrow afternoon would be all she needed to make it through. Panting, she beat her wings and gained altitude. Flying this low to the ground would not be good if she fell asleep again.

Pain wracked Indyn's weakened body, and she roared. A bolt of lightning from Upi had struck her.

The fake egg in her talons almost fell from her grasp again. She had not known that carrying the rock's weight in her weakened condition would slow her down this much. Between it and her exhaustion, the three females had finally managed to catch up to her.

Even without that blasted yellow dragon, Upi, barely clipping her with a violent bolt of lightning, Indyn's body was at its limits, and she struggled to stay airborne and out of reach of the three female dragons. Early this morning, they had closed the distance so easily.

"Give up the egg!" Upi roared as she flew a few hundred meters behind Indyn. "Surrender, and perhaps Juthom will let you live to see the hatching!"

Indyn ignored her and the other two. Up ahead, just a few miles away, was what she had been dedicated to reaching this whole time.

The smoke from the volcano was billowing out. Magma peaks never stopped churning lava down the mountainside. No one lived here, due to the poisonous clouds and the unforgiving terrain. Here she would sacrifice herself for the freedom of her child.

[Activate Flight Burst]
[Insufficient Mana]

Indyn cursed. She had used it this morning for a little more distance between herself and her pursuers. Her mana was gone, and she was at death's door. The curse had let them track her, and the inability to heal had left her bleeding this entire time. This chase would end one way or another very soon.

She beat her wings. Over and over, ignoring how badly they ached. Her will was the only thing keeping them moving. They might catch her, but she would make sure it would cost at least one of them their life if they tried.

"After her!" bellowed Upi. "Stioks will torture us if she gets away or something happens to that egg!"

"Let her die! Then Juthom will be all ours!" Vivines hissed. The red dragon struggled to stay near Upi. Her larger body prevented her from being as fast as the yellow dragon. "We will fly her down and snatch the egg from her dead body!"

Upi fired off another shot of her lightning but narrowly missed as Indyn's body gave out momentarily, missing a beat of her wings from exhaustion.

"She will run out soon," Upi roared in exaltation.

Indyn's body had no more to give. She was operating past her limit. Her will to save her child was the only thing keeping her wings moving. Her heart felt like it was going to explode in her chest. She almost dropped the rock again as her talons felt unable to hold onto it. She struggled to resecure the fake egg every time she flapped her wings. If she dropped it now, they would realize she had tricked them and would search for the egg, her egg. Indyn focused on one thing as she fought to stay in the air: knowing her child would be safe.

She was grateful to any gods that might have allowed Upi to miss her lightning shot. Had Upi hit her, she would be plummeting to the ground right now, and all this pain would have been for nothing.

Now, she was just a single mile from the edge of the volcano. She could feel the heat from here. The smoke in the air rose high into the sky and burned her exhausted lungs. She could taste her own blood with every breath.

Smiling, Indyn risked a glance back and saw the three female dragons were closer now, but they were too far to stop her. They did not realize what she was committed to. Had they known, they would have run her down hours ago, no matter the cost.

Commitment to the point of self-sacrifice. You three will never understand this, Indyn declared to herself. This is what separated a true dragon from those mindless slaves that thought they had her.

She tucked her wings and dropped from the sky. Angling herself, she dove toward the opening of the volcano. She saw the molten lava as it bubbled and popped. The red glow of extreme heat would kill any dragon after enough time. It would be her resting place.

"What is she doing?" Vivines cried as she saw the angle Indyn suddenly took.

"Strike her down!" Upi called out, but she knew it was too late.

They were too far away, and Indyn was too close to the opening.

Indyn hit the magma with a blazing splash, and her body plunged deep beneath the molten rock. Her mouth opened to scream from the pain, but hot molten lava rushed down her throat and scorched her from the inside, cutting off all sound. As the last flicker of her life burned out, her last thought was this:

Be free, my child! Live!

2

Treasure Found

"Kaen, get yer arse over here before I shove this pickaxe up it!"

Kaen came running out of the woods as he pulled his pants up. Hess was waving and shouting at him as usual; Kaen often lost count of the number of times a threat of bodily harm came from Hess each day.

"Sorry, sir!" Kaen yelled back with a grin. "I thought I was catching a snake in the woods but realized it was just myself."

The men around the foreman started laughing, and even Hess shook his head and smirked at Kaen's joke.

Men continued breaking rocks while full and empty carts rolled in and out of the quarry. Kaen dodged a cart and arrived, barely out of breath, before the foreman, Hess.

Kaen glanced up at the mountain of a man who ran this hellhole of physical labor. His arms were larger than most men's torsos, and his legs had lifted most of the boulders in this quarry, many considered impossible to move. The fact that he was taller than most men by a full head only added to his boss's impressive size.

"Boy, why do you tell lies about the size of your manhood," Hess joked as he handed Kaen the pickaxe. "You seem to forget I was there when you were born, and at first, we thought you were a girl."

Kaen laughed and hefted the pickaxe over his shoulder. "I wish I had a better answer to give, but then you might make me do more work," joked Kaen.

Hess took a playful swipe at Kaen and brushed the top of his head. "It's a good thing your dad made me promise to watch over you, or I would have fired your lazy ass already."

"Pfftt. We both know you keep me around because I can cook and catch game in the woods. Two things your usual rotating girlfriends cannot seem to do," declared Kaen as he walked toward the section of the quarry he was assigned to.

"Gah, your mouth reminds me of your father's!" Hess shouted as he watched Kaen walk away. "It was not near as nice as your mother's!"

Kaen held up his middle finger as he jogged toward the other boys who were already working on the rocks they needed to break up for today. He loved the man and owed him his life, but that did not mean either one wouldn't tease and joke about the other any chance they got.

"What's this about a grub you found in the woods?" Patrick, a lanky teenager called out as Kaen approached.

"Oh, you know, Hess. He would get upset if I told him I was out there hunting and checking my traps. He already thinks I'm lazy," joked Kaen.

"And by lazy, you mean the most productive member of his workforce besides himself," Cale, Kaen's best friend, said laughing.

Patrick hung his head in mock shame and sagged his shoulders on his lean frame. "And yet, Kaen is forced to carry our slacking efforts," Patrick moaned before laughing and changing his tone. "Thankfully, Kaen does enough work for the three of us."

All three boys started laughing and returned to work on the rocks they were responsible for. Hess was fair with the three of them since they were all teenagers. They had a more manageable workload, and once it was done, they were finished for the day.

"Kaen, you want to take care of that bigger rock?" Cale asked as he motioned to the one taller than all of them. "You're the one with the skill, so you should be the one to take care of it."

Kaen groaned but nodded. He and Hess were the only two in this quarry with a lifestone. He had gotten his lifestone from his father a few months before he had died on a quest. Most men would never be able to afford one. His dad had taken a quest on the promise of one. That job had cost his father his life but had provided Kaen with a future. Someday, he would leave this town, make a name for himself, and follow in his dad's steps.

Stretching a little before he started working, Kaen wondered about his current mining skill.

Skill Mining Status
[Mining 11]

Kaen grinned like a fool, remembering he had achieved a new level in that skill last week. He could now see better where to swing the pickaxe. He knew how to hold it and how to use his core through each swing. It was nowhere near Hess's skill of twenty-eight. That man could split most rocks in half with one swing of his custom-built pickaxe.

Letting his mind go, Kaen allowed his body to take over as he started working on the rock. His lifestone seemed to guide him, and he noticed a slight crack and line running through the rock. Setting his feet, he swung the pickaxe and connected the point where that line was.

Crack

A large piece dropped off to the side, and Kaen moved away from it as it fell.

"I hate when he makes it look that easy," Cale called out as he hacked repeatedly at the small boulders he was working on.

Patrick laughed and kept working on his group of rocks. Both boys knew Kaen did most of the work, but Kaen never complained about it. He loved spending his days with his friends while getting stronger as he thought about the adventurers' test he would hopefully take soon.

Kaen made short work of turning that massive boulder into more manageable pieces for them. He had reduced the rock by over two-thirds of its starting size in less than half an hour.

The three boys continued to joke and share stories as they worked through Hess's assigned pile. None of them ever really felt like it was a horrible job, as the constant conversation made the time fly exceptionally fast. A few hours later, the three of them turned in their equipment. They finished a good hour or more before the other men were done.

"I'll see you later tonight!" Kaen shouted at his friends as he darted off into the woods near the quarry with his bow and quiver.

Cale and Patrick waved as they ran to catch up with one of the carts headed into town. They had finished a lot earlier than expected, and both boys wanted to venture into town and see if they could meet up with a few of the girls they had been flirting with lately. Kaen had blown through those rocks faster than usual, and they had both noticed. Each of them wondered why Kaen was working harder than usual. If he did that all the time, Hess would give them more work, as he always did when it became apparent their current load was too easy.

Kaen ran toward the spot he had emerged from earlier. He had gone into the woods that morning to check a few traps he had set and relieve himself before all the workers showed up. While checking his traps, he found a few trees knocked down at a weird angle. He had stumbled upon them while scouting the deeper part of the woods he had put snares in and wanted to try and figure out what could have caused that damage.

Thirty minutes later, he reached the area of trees that lay on their sides.

Running his hand over the exposed wood, Kaen let out a small whistle.

What could do this?

The trees had been snapped at the base from something brushing against them two-thirds of the way up the tree. Whatever it was had stripped the bark off like sandpaper. Rough, large chunks of the tree were missing. Kaen spent time searching for tracks. He followed the line of trees that had been knocked down and found a small clearing near one of the deeper areas of the quarry that he believed had not been used in the seven years he had been here.

As he looked around, he saw weird lines and a few muddied pools of color in the dirt and on rocks.

Bending down, he used a stick and lifted the substance he'd scratched off a rock to his nose and recoiled at the foul reek of rot and acid.

"Blood," Kaen murmured as he glanced around the area. There was enough blood that something must have been hurt pretty badly.

"Where could this thing have gone?" he said as he looked back at the trees. He slowly backed up and looked at the scene before him from different angles. He could feel his mind working the problem out. His lifestone thumped in his chest, alerting him to what he was wondering.

It flies!

Kaen realized it was something that flew, and it had to be huge to do the damage it had done to the trees.

[Tracking Skill Increased]

Kaen smiled, and his eyes went wide.

"Yes!" he shouted as he jumped up with a fist pump into the air.

He could now easily see the pattern that had eluded him.

Skill Tracking Status.
[Tracking 4]

It wasn't a huge increase in his skill, but it would make tracking things much easier. Kaen could see where it had flown off toward the mountains across the way. He glanced down at the ground and realized he needed to get higher.

Scrambling up the rocks and boulders, he climbed up about thirty feet and saw what he had been missing.

[Tracking Skill Increased]

"Hell yah!" Kaen shouted, his voice echoing off the rocks and mountainside.

Skill Tracking Status.
[Tracking 5]

A dragon! It had to be a dragon! The size of the prints in the ground and how deep they were left no doubt now in his mind. Kaen could see the claw marks and imprints. It had messed up some of its tracks when it turned around.

Kaen peered at the area and wondered why it had landed and moved around so much. Even if it was bleeding, there was no reason to spend that much energy turning around down here in the dirt of the quarry and around all these rocks.

Kaen focused on the ground below him and saw that there was a time when the dragon was close to the base of the rocks and mountainside. He then noticed scratches in the dirt, obviously from its long, sharp talons.

He almost tripped and fell as he started running back down the mountain to get to where he saw the marks. Rocks tumbled and bounced around his feet as he scrambled down the rocky side.

When he got to the area where he had noticed the scratched dirt, Kaen found a burnt area off to the side. The dirt was melted and fused into something he had no idea how to describe. It wasn't like glass or metal, yet it felt hard and would be difficult to break. He had missed seeing that section, as a few larger rocks and boulders had blocked it.

Kaen started to follow the claw marks and found that the dragon had dug out an area underneath some larger boulders. The rocks appeared to be placed on top of the spot the dragon had dug.

"What would a dragon bury out here?" Kaen wondered aloud as he lay on the ground and tried to peer through the small space between the rocks it had stacked up. He could not see anything from that angle, and he was frustrated because he would not have time to dig anything out since he was losing light fast. There were only about two hours of sunlight left, and he still had to make his way back to town.

Rubbing his hand across his face, Kaen groaned. This was an opportunity of a lifetime, and he could not pass it up.

Tomorrow! Tomorrow, he would check this out.

Kaen ran through the woods, dodging trees and jumping over logs and holes. His mind was racing as he ran.

Treasure! It had to be treasure!

The dragon must have gotten in some fight and needed to hide its treasure. How long would he have to retrieve a piece or two of the treasure before the dragon returned? The damage to the trees seemed to be only a few days old, at least as far as he could tell. That meant he probably did not have long to figure out what the dragon had buried.

Hess would have to help him. Surely, he would be willing to help for a little bit of the treasure! They would only take one or two pieces, so as not to upset the dragon and make it want to search for what it had lost.

That would be perfect, Kaen told himself. He and Hess would find out what the dragon had hidden, and then they would carefully take just a little of it. They would be rich, and he could stop working this job at the quarry and train full-time so he could prepare for the adventurers' guild over in Ebonmount. He could easily afford to get his adventurer's token and make a fortune taking on quests and missions. He could then travel to the other kingdoms and make a name for himself!

The light of the day started to fade, and the sky turned orange and red from the sun setting, and Kaen had a new outlook on life as he raced down the path from the quarry back to town. Soon, all his dreams of being an adventurer would come true. He could be just like his dad had been!

Don't go! Stay!

The egg pulsed and flexed.

It had sensed someone near it. It knew there was someone with a lifestone.

I'm here!

The egg shook and shivered for a moment and then stopped pulsing as it felt the presence leave. It would have to wait for their return.

3

A Bargain Struck

Hess slammed his hand down on the table, causing the piece he'd hit with his massive fist to crack.

"Dammit, boy!" Hess shouted as he glared at Kaen. "You are a fool to believe in fairy tales like that! No dragon would come here, and none would bury their treasure out in the open like that!"

Kaen opened his mouth to talk, but Hess held up his oversized hand and stopped him.

"I know . . . I know," Hess said, sighing and shaking his head. "You want to be an adventurer like your dad. I know you think this will give you the money you need to go and get your token, but you are not ready yet."

Hess grabbed his oversized chair and plopped himself down in the massive structure made from thick pieces of wood designed to support his weight. It still creaked as he sat down on it.

"Your dad would haunt me if I let you go before you are eighteen. He knew you wanted to be like him, but please listen to me when I say you are not ready yet."

Kaen shook his head and pointed at Hess. "I think you mean you aren't ready for me to leave," Kaen argued as he glared at Hess. "You don't want me to leave."

Hess picked up his cup and took a drink. He was flustered and upset. How many times had he followed Kaen through the woods, chasing after some treasure or something else he'd sworn he had found? That boy had worn him silly on treasure hunts in the past. He had given in to them when he was young, but Kaen was sixteen, and he needed to focus on the task he had been given.

"Tell you what," Kaen interrupted right as Hess was about to say something. "If you come with me tomorrow, and I am wrong, and there is nothing there, I won't ask you to venture into the woods with me again on some random fairy tale or stupid hunt."

Hess stared at Kaen and saw how he was standing. His brown hair was matted to his head from having run all the way back from the quarry. Even in the light of the cabin, he could see that Kaen at least believed there was something there. The way he leaned forward reminded him of how Kaen's dad acted when a quest he felt they both should do was up for grabs.

Hess moved the piece of wood he had cracked and then returned his attention to Kaen. "You promise? No more calls to go looking for treasure in the forest? You will work till you are eighteen in the quarry, and I'll give you the money you need for your token?"

Kaen laughed and coughed a few times. "How did that last part get added to this? I was saying no more requests to join me in the woods. Why are you adding the last part?"

Hess pressed against the table, making sure to avoid the cracked piece, and stood up. A slight grunt escaped his lips. Even though he was still in phenomenal shape and could easily handle any man in town, all the years of adventure had taken its toll on him.

"Listen son . . . "

"I'm not your son!" Kaen quickly interjected, grinding his teeth.

Hess closed his eyes and took a deep breath. He let it out, opened his eyes, and smiled.

"I know that, Kaen. I do. You feel the need to remind me of that fact even though I have taken care of you for over six years. I have tried to help you become the man I know your father would want you to be."

Hess moved around the table and came to stand a few feet from Kaen. He glanced down at the boy and noticed that Kaen would not look away. His brown eyes were locked on Hess's.

"It is time for you to grow up," Hess explained. "You need to finish growing and getting stronger. Working in the quarry will help you do that. It will give you time to hone your skill with a bow, and I know you will get better tracking as you scour those woods. These skills will help you when you finally get to Ebonmount and sign up to be an adventurer. We have talked multiple times about all this, and you know they have tests you have to pass. It isn't just about the money for the token."

Kaen grunted and nodded. He was well aware of the tests but planned to use his bow to pass that test. He usually had no problems when he hunted game.

"I'll pass the archer test easily. I can hit most of the animals I shoot at," Kaen declared.

Hess smiled and crossed his arms. "Can you hit them when they are running, and you are running? What about when it is attacking you? When your nerves freeze, and everything in you tells you to escape. Can you make those same shots when someone yells in your ear?" Hess asked.

Kaen opened his mouth, but suddenly found no words coming out. He thought about that for a moment.

Skill Archery Status
[Archery 8]

"My archery skill is an eight. That is really good!"

Hess shook his head.

He almost said *Son* but caught himself.

"Kaen, that is an average skill for a boy who shoots animals in the woods that do not know he is there. For an adventurer, you need at least a fifteen or higher. When they give those tests, they will yell at you the entire time. Men will throw things at you. You will have to keep your composure and still be able to hit targets that stand still and move," Hess explained. "I honestly believe that if you took the test today, you would not pass. This is why I have pushed you to stay here till you are eighteen. I could give you the money tomorrow, and I know you would return home a few weeks later, broken and disappointed. I am not sure if you would try again or give up on this dream of yours."

Hess put his big finger in Kaen's chest and pushed a little. "I will not let the memory of my friend, Hoste, suffer that kind of fate. I will not let his son attempt what I know he is not ready for."

Kaen shifted under the pressure of Hess's finger in his chest.

Hess had never explained his reasoning for why he had pushed him to do all this a certain way. It made sense, even if Kaen did not like to admit that Hess was probably right. If he did fail, he probably would not try again.

Kaen suddenly smiled, grabbed hold of Hess's finger, and tried to twist it behind the man. Hess laughed and quickly grabbed Kaen's head in his other hand and pushed it into his armpit.

"It smells! My god, that smells horrible! I give up!" Kaen complained as he fought against Hess's massive arms and was forced to breathe deeply the nasty aroma that came from Hess's armpits.

Hess let go and broke out in a loud laugh as Kaen backed up and wiped the sweat from his forehead.

"I'll accept your offer," Kaen agreed, standing tall and pulling down his shirt that had ridden up. "If there is nothing there, I will not ask you to join me in the woods again, and I will wait till I am eighteen to join the adventurers' guild."

Kaen reached out his hand, but before Hess could grasp it, Kaen pulled it back and held it up with a smile. "If there is treasure there, then you have to let me be off by lunchtime and help train me for the adventurer test," Kaen stated, extending his hand again.

Hess laughed and grabbed Kaen's hand before he could pull it back again and shook it. "I hope for your sake you are right," Hess teased. "Otherwise, you will find your life filled with many rocks to be broken for a long time to come!"

Kaen nodded and grinned. He knew there was something. He was so certain he was willing to bet the next two years of his life on it.

"Tomorrow then! We will go after everyone is dismissed!"

Laughing, Hess walked back to his chair and sat down.

"Tomorrow it is. For now, though, I need someone to finish the dinner they promised and refill my drink," Hess said with a wink. "I don't have a girlfriend this week to take care of those things, so I'll have to let my best friend's daughter do it instead."

Kaen laughed, rolled his eyes, and headed to the cooking pot, where something smelled horrible. Hess somehow always appeared to have no clue how to cook, and his lack of trying to get better was evident from every meal he ever made.

Multiple men commented on Kaen and his work the next day at the quarry. He had arrived early and had started working on the large rocks in each group, even though it was not required of him. Patrick and Cale had both called out to him and asked him why he was in such a hurry. Neither one could understand why he had left them with just a few small rocks to take care of and dashed off to another section to help some older men.

"Kaen, you're going to wear yourself out and ruin your reputation if you keep working like that," Hess shouted as Kaen finished helping a fourth group of workers.

Kaen laughed, moving to get a drink from the water cart before heading to help one more group.

"What has gotten into him?" Patrick asked Hess who, along with Cale, stood in the middle of the quarry, watching Kaen attack a few more boulders.

"I believe he wants to catch up with my skill in mining," Hess joked, even though he knew that wasn't the answer. "One day, I will tell him there is more to that skill than just breaking rocks. I'll have to take him into the mountain and work a few mines as well."

Cale glanced up at Hess, and his eyes went wide. "You worked in a mine? Wouldn't that be really hard for someone your size?"

Hess chuckled, bobbing his head. "It is not always easy being this large, and being in a mine is not my favorite thing, but that is where I got the metal for that pickaxe," Hess stated as he pointed to his pickaxe off to the side. "It is made from a special metal men would pay a lot for."

Hess stared off momentarily, lost in thought as both boys waited to see if he would say anything else about it. When he realized they were still staring at him, he waved them off.

"That is a story for another day. You two are done for now, or you can help your friend, who will probably need me to carry him home based on how hard he is working today."

Both boys groaned and looked at each other. They each had a smirk on their face. They could head home and be done, but they also knew it was because of Kaen that they finished before everyone else each day.

"I guess we will help him and the others," Patrick said and grabbed his pick-axe. "Another hour should be enough."

Hess nodded and watched the boys run off to join Kaen. Cheers could be heard from the men they ended up helping.

"I pray something is there," Hess muttered to himself as he watched all the workers pick up the pace and laugh as they worked.

He knew tomorrow would be bad for everyone, especially Kaen, if something wasn't.

4

A Dragon Egg

"This way!" Kaen shouted as he ran ahead of Hess.

Hess shook his head in wonder. How that boy still had energy after a real full day's work amazed him. Hess easily navigated the forest but took his time: a twisted ankle was no fun at his age. He had his pickaxe strapped across his back because Kaen insisted he bring it because they might need it.

Hess moved faster as Kaen disappeared ahead in the trees. It had been a while since he had been in the woods like this. Now, all his time was spent at the quarry, the bar in town, or at home. Being out here made him realize he needed to be more intentional with Kaen if he was going to prepare him for the adventurer's test.

As he moved through the woods, the trees lying down on their side came into view, and Hess immediately recognized something was wrong with how they faced. What Kaen had described had seemed impossible at first, but now he was fearful Kaen could be right.

Hess jogged toward Kaen, who was standing on one of the trees that had been knocked down. He was pointing to a section of the tree.

"This is where the dragon rubbed the bark right off!" Kaen declared as he pointed and smiled.

Hess approached the tree and almost missed his step for a second. He saw the area on the bark and the notches from the missing wood. He now knew Kaen was right.

"Hairy dwarf balls, Kaen!" Hess cursed, taking in the area around him. His hand instinctively reached for the handle of his pickaxe, but he caught himself and lowered it.

Eight massive trees were knocked over, and half of them had large gouges in them. The dragon had hit them as it had taken off, and the underside of its chest rubbed off huge sections as it gained elevation. These trees would not have slowed the dragon down at all based on the size it must have been.

"We need to be careful," Hess said as he glanced around the woods. "Who else knows about this?"

Kaen frowned and wondered why Hess was acting so weird. "No one but you. Why would I tell anyone else and risk someone taking the treasure the dragon must have hidden," Kaen asked.

Hess nodded, relieved that no one else knew about this yet. He would have to come back later and do something to remove this evidence. People would panic if word got out that a dragon was in this area.

Kaen had hopped off the tree and moved toward the mountain's base. "You coming or what?" he called out as he jogged ahead.

"Wait for me," Hess shouted, running to catch up with Kaen.

I pray the boy is wrong, Hess thought as they came to the clearing at the mountain's base.

"Stop messing with that blood, and hurry up over here!" Kaen implored Hess as he stood over by the bunched-up boulders and rocks he believed must have treasure under them.

Hess stood up and tossed the blood-covered stick he was holding on the ground.

It was dragon's blood. That smell was one he would never forget. Everything about this felt wrong. If there was a treasure, he was sure they should not mess with it. A wild dragon could be a very greedy and vengeful thing. He was trying to remember the last time he had heard of a wild dragon roaming the kingdoms. It had to be at least ten or twenty years. All the time he spent in the woods and away from the adventurers' guild had kept him out of touch with what was really happening in the world. Maybe dragons had returned, but that seemed impossible. They *had* decreased in numbers.

Hess finally made it to where Kaen was standing. Most of the air in his chest left his lungs when he saw the claw marks that had dragged through the dirt.

"Kaen, are you sure about this?" he asked as he looked at the pile of boulders. "If a dragon has hidden something there and they realize it is missing, they will come looking for it. It would not go well for anyone near where it disappeared from."

"No, sir!" Kaen exclaimed. "We shook on it! You know something is here, and we will see what it is."

Hess grimaced and nodded. He had promised. Even if this was a bad idea, he could not go back on his word. "How about we find out what is hidden and decide if we want to take something or just leave it? No point in dying if it is obvious to the dragon that we stole something."

Kaen groaned and looked at Hess. He could see the concern on Hess's face and in how he was acting. Hess was never timid like this. How evil must a dragon be that Hess would be so afraid?

"So, if it is just a few small things, we don't take anything?" Kaen asked, disappointment oozing from his voice.

Kaen walked around the group of boulders and then lay down on the ground again and tried moving some of the dirt with his hand to see if he could see anything back there. "I can't see anything, and the dirt isn't moving."

Hess nodded. "When the dragon dug out the soil, the force of its claws packed that dirt. It will take a pickaxe to break it up. It is like dried, hardened mud."

Kaen groaned, stood, and dusted the dirt off his shirt. Breaking that kind of dirt up was no fun at all. He had had enough practice doing that over the years. "So, can you move the rocks?"

Hess inspected the formation and shook his head. The dragon had picked up rocks bigger than him as if they were nothing but a pebble and stacked them tightly. It made sense if it was hiding something from people.

As he walked around, a boulder that seemed misplaced caught his eye. He walked around in the other direction and kept his eye on it. It was not packed in like the others. It almost looked like it had just been gently rested against the others.

Hess walked over and put his massive hands around the boulder and tried to pull it toward him, but he could not generate enough leverage to free it. It shifted, but he did not want to be under it when it rolled. If he had a rope, that might work.

Hess glanced up at the sky. There was a good three hours of sunlight left. Maybe a little more. They had finished quickly today, and he had sent everyone home early, much to their delight. "How long do you think it would take for you to get to the quarry and get me a rope? One at least thirty meters long?"

Kaen laughed. "I can be there and back in less than an hour!" he said as he dropped his bow and quiver and took off back in the direction of the quarry.

Hess smiled for a moment and shook his head. That boy and his never-ending energy.

Once Kaen disappeared, Hess turned back and looked around. Before Kaen returned, he needed to figure out why a dragon had chosen this area to land and bury something.

Hess heard Kaen running back to the clearing. That boy must have chased off every animal for miles, from the sound echoing through the forest.

Kaen was drenched in sweat, but a dragging rope was looped around his shoulder and along his side, bouncing as he ran.

"That looks like an awful run," Hess teased, watching Kaen stop a few feet before him and drop the rope onto the ground.

Kaen collapsed on the ground and lay there on his back, sucking in massive breaths. "So . . . bad . . . legs . . . cramp . . . " Kaen tried to say between breaths.

"Just breathe. Shake your head when I ask a question, but just breathe," Hess told him as he bent down and grabbed the rope.

Kaen nodded and kept his eyes on Hess.

"You noticed that section of ground that was burnt?"

Kaen nodded and pointed a shaky hand in the direction of the charred ground.

"You notice that the dragon burned something and took it with it? There is a small indent and section of the ground behind it where the ground is not scorched like the rest," Hess stated, watching Kaen's face.

Kaen shook his head and tried to ask a question, but Hess stopped him. "Breathe. You are fine for not noticing that. I spent twenty minutes examining that area before figuring out what I was missing. Now rest while I get this rope tied to the rock."

Kaen nodded and closed his eyes.

It was all Hess could do to keep from laughing. He could smell the boy from here. He had no clue how bad he would smell by the end of tonight.

It had taken about fifteen minutes to get the rope set up the way he wanted. Now, all they needed to do was pull on it, and it should pop right out.

By the time he had almost finished setting up the rope, a new surge of energy must have filled Kaen who had gotten off the ground and was dancing like he had ants in his pants.

"You ready to do a little more work?" Hess asked as Kaen danced around in excitement.

"I thought you would never ask," Kaen said, running over, grabbing the rope's end, and pulling it taut.

Hess smiled and shook his head. "Ok, when I say pull, we pull. It should pop out pretty easily if it is going to come. If not, I'll have to hit it with my pickaxe. I would prefer not to do that if we decide not to take anything."

"That's fine," Kaen declared. "Can we just pull and get this over with? I'm dying to find out what is in there!"

Kaen's heart was pounding fast for some reason. The anticipation, he guessed, but his lifestone was also acting all weird. It was pulsing, and he could not figure out why. Perhaps it could sense his excitement.

Hess nodded. His curiosity was getting the better of him as well. There could be no telling what might be buried behind these rocks.

"On three!" Hess said, wrapping the rope around his waist and arms. He dug his legs in and shifted his heels to get a good grip in the dirt. He turned and saw that Kaen had done the exact same thing. The smile on that fool's face looked downright silly, with his matted hair and dirt-covered face.

"One, two, three!" Hess shouted, and both pulled on the rope. There had been no slack in it before he had said three, but now they could feel the rope stretching just a hair as the rock started to shift.

They both grunted and drove back, using the leverage of their legs, and slowly, the rock started to tip toward them.

"A little more!" Hess grunted through his teeth. He could feel the immense strain of pulling on the rock through his core and legs.

Inch by inch, the rock moved toward them till the center of its balance shifted, and it suddenly toppled over. The rope loosened from the break in the tension.

Hess and Kaen crashed to the ground when the rock fell, causing a cloud of dust to fly up from the impact.

Hess started to untangle himself and saw Kaen dart past him toward the hole that now gaped between the other rocks. "Wait, son! They might shift!" Hess called out, but it was too late. Kaen was already past the boulder they had moved and was standing still near the opening.

"What is it, boy!?" Hess yelled, springing to his feet and running to see what Kaen was looking at.

When Hess stood next to Kaen, he understood why Kaen's mouth was open in shock.

"It can't be!" Kaen declared in disbelief.

"A dragon egg!? A real dragon egg?" Hess muttered.

Kaen looked at Hess for a second before pointing back to the egg. "It's hatching!" Kaen said with excitement.

5

A Boy and His Dragon

"Move!" Hess shouted as he tried to push Kaen away from the opening.

"No!" Kaen protested, fighting back against Hess. "I am not leaving. It is a dragon!"

"Exactly," Hess exclaimed as he grabbed one of Kaen's arms and started pulling him away. "We need to go now! They are dangerous!"

Kaen struggled and kicked Hess in the leg, causing Hess to let go of his arm. The kick had not hurt him, but Hess was shocked that Kaen had kicked him.

"I'm not leaving. I want to watch it hatch. I can feel it reaching out to me!"

Hess froze. Kaen attacking him like a rabid animal and saying that he felt the egg reaching out to him, surfaced a memory from deep in his past.

He turned and glanced at the egg. It was flexing and another crack had appeared in its bronze and brown shell. Years of reading cracks told him that it would soon break free.

"What do you mean it is reaching out to you?" Hess demanded, moving to stand between Kaen and the egg.

Kaen tried to watch the egg, but Hess's massive body blocked the entrance.

"I don't know," Kaen said, grunting as he tried to push Hess out of the way. "I can feel it in my mind. I can feel it in my chest. I can feel it in my lifestone! As soon as I saw it, I felt him say *hello*, and the egg cracked. Now move!"

Hess stumbled as Kaen frantically pushed him out of the way. He watched Kaen move closer to the egg and put his hand on the outside. He saw the egg push toward Kaen's hand when it drew close to the outside of the egg.

"Impossible," Hess whispered.

There had not been a bonding in many generations.

"I'm here," Kaen said softly, running his hand along the edge of the egg. "I'm here. Show me who you are."

Kaen's eyes widened at the enthralling sight before him. Hess suspected that Kaen had no idea what was happening, but Hess knew it would be impossible to pull Kaen away now.

Hess did not remember the exact term for what was happening, but he had heard about it a lifetime ago. Once a dragon found a person to bond with, it was for life. Both could live for hundreds of years. They would share their life force, and both would grow strong enough to rule kingdoms if they survived those who challenged them.

There was a loud pop and a crack appeared. A chunk of the brown shell fell to the ground.

A trilling sound came from inside the egg, and Kaen leaned as close as possible when he saw the golden eye peering at him.

"Hey, Pammon, I'm Kaen!"

"You know its name?" asked Hess.

Kaen reached a hand inside the egg and stroked the top part of the ridge along Pammon's nose. The dragon trilled, and it appeared to be smiling.

"I can hear him. Inside my head," Kaen told Hess, tapping his temple with his other hand.

Kaen tapped his thighs with his hands. "Come on, you can do it! Get out of the shell, Pammon!"

The dragon trilled and growled and flexed against the egg's opening. It pushed, and suddenly, the egg split open and it tumbled out. Slime covered its dull brown and copper scales as it flopped around on the ground, spreading its wings and adjusting its tail until it finally stood.

"Good job!" Kaen cheered. He bent, rubbing Pammon's head and helping to remove some of the egg enzymes from his body.

Hess stood in awe. What would Hoste have given to see his son with a dragon? He could barely believe it himself.

Pammon turned and glanced at Hess and cocked its head. It let out a shriek that seemed so puny for such a dangerous creature.

Kaen laughed and shook his head. "He is a friend. He will not hurt you."

Kaen turned toward Hess and motioned for him to get closer. "Put your hand out. He won't bite."

Hess glanced at Kaen, who was smiling as he rubbed the little dragon's head, and then watched the baby dragon cock its head sideways and return Hess's gaze. He was not completely certain Kaen knew exactly what the dragon would do.

Hess slowly held his hand out, bent down a little, and smiled. "Hey there, Pammon," Hess said. His deep voice cracked a little, and Kaen chuckled.

Pammon slowly stretched his neck and sniffed the large hand near him. After a few sniffs, Pammon turned and looked at Kaen, who smiled and nodded. Pammon then put his head under Hess's hand and moved it back and forth around his fingers.

"Scratch his head," Kaen whispered and winked at Hess.

Hess laughed and moved his fingers around on the dragon's soft scales. He could not believe how soft they felt. He knew one day they would be strong enough to stop almost anything from penetrating it.

The trill that Pammon let out as Hess scratched his head, brought the largest smile to Hess's face he had worn in years. He found himself laughing and shaking his head. Moments ago, he had feared the dragon, and now he was scratching it as if it were a puppy or cat.

Suddenly, Pammon snapped his head back, turned to Kaen, and let out a loud screech.

Kaen grimaced and turned to Hess. "He's hungry, he says."

Hess nodded. He reached into the small pouch on his hip and pulled out some dried meat. He held it out to Pammon, who sniffed it and tossed its nose up at it. He screeched at Hess, then turned back to Kaen and let another screech out.

"He wants fresh meat. Not that dried meat," Kaen said, with a shrug. "I don't know where we are going to get that."

Hess stood, took a deep breath, and then released it. Hess grabbed Kaen's discarded bow after spotting it on the ground.

"We only have a little over an hour of light left. Something will be out there. You wrap up that rope, and I will find something. Hopefully, it will be enough to tide him over until we figure out what we will do."

"Aren't we taking him home?" asked Kaen.

Hess chuckled. He knew that question was coming before Kaen had even asked it. "I am not sure what we will do tonight. We will figure it out, but we need to be careful. Lots of people will want to have a say about him and you."

Hess trotted off toward the woods. "Get the rope and be ready to leave when I get back!" he shouted.

Kaen and Pammon watched as Hess ran away. Turning to Pammon, Kaen smiled and shrugged. "I guess I'll get the rope."

Pammon let out a screech.

Pammon lay on the ground, his belly bulging. The dragon was slightly bigger than a good-sized dog. It had eaten the two rabbits and squirrel Hess had managed to shoot, barely chewing before swallowing both rabbits.

Now he was lying on the dirt with his eyes glazed over, and a low thrum was coming from him.

"I guess we will have to carry him home or stay out here" said Hess.

Kaen nodded. He was overwhelmed with something he had not felt in a long time. For over six years, he had felt partially empty inside. When his dad died, all the joy in his life had vanished. That first year had been challenging. He had been awful to Hess. And each time, Hess would just smile and gently help him do what needed to be done. Hess never yelled at him or struck him.

With this connection to Pammon, Kaen felt a different kind of joy. He could feel the contentment from Pammon, and it made him feel alive.

"There aren't many things out here that would bother us with a fire going, but I know I smell horrible, and we both need to eat. Would you be up for carrying him home?" Kaen asked.

Glancing at the snoozing baby dragon, Hess chuckled.

Pammon opened one eyelid just a little before closing it and starting its low thrumming sound again.

"Out of everything I have ever carried in my life, I will admit this might be the most memorable, as long as he does not claw me to death."

Kaen laughed, and Hess smiled. They both saw the tiny, sharp claws on Pammon's paws and back feet. There was no doubt how easily those could cut someone.

"Ask him if he will let me carry him. If he says yes, then I will do it."

Kaen walked over to Pammon, lifted his head, and tapped him on the skull. Pammon shook his head at Kaen, whining at being awakened.

"He said you can carry him," Kaen said, lowering Pammon's head back to the ground. "He said he is tired and just wants to sleep."

Hess nodded and grabbed the coiled rope on the ground. "Let's get him inside the rope coil so I can carry him. We need to head out. I want to be somewhere we know, before it is completely dark."

Working together, they got the mostly limp dragon into the rope's coils and secured Pammon inside it against Hess. Pammon had let out a few grumbles and small whines, but had gone right back to sleep once he was strapped in.

The trip back to their house had been mostly uneventful. No one was on the road when they finally reached home. The sun had been down for almost a half hour, and the only light came from the stars in the sky and the sliver of the moon that was out. They had traveled on that road for years, so they knew where they were and where they were headed.

Once they got close to town, they stayed on the outskirts of the wooded area until they made it near their place. Having a property in the woods meant they were not in the actual city but close enough to be at the town's only drinking establishment in twenty minutes or so.

When they got to the house, Kaen worked on getting a fire going. Once they had a little light, he fixed up a place on the floor in the small room he slept in, and Hess gently lowered Pammon to the ground. The dragon had slept the entire trip and still had not woken up now that he was on the floor.

Hess motioned for Kaen to join him at the table so they could be near the fire.

Kaen sat down and glanced into his room, where he could see the light of the candle inside it flicker off the dragon's brown scales. They almost looked like copper in that light.

Hess set two wooden cups on the table, pulled a cork from his bottle, and poured a little into each cup.

"Are we drinking alcohol?" Kaen gasped as he watched Hess put the cup in front of him on the table.

Hess chuckled and gently sat down in his chair. Leaning across the table, he held his cup out and waited.

Kaen realized what Hess was doing and quickly picked up his cup and tapped it against Hess's.

"To your new life," Hess said. "Your life will never be the same, and I pray you stay on the path that will make your father proud." Hess tipped his cup back and drained it.

Kaen glanced into his cup and smelled it. He had only tried some nasty mead Patrick had stolen once. It had made him sick for a day, and he had not drunk since then. Surely this must be better, no matter how much the smell seemed to assault his nose.

Kaen tried to drink the alcohol like Hess had. One quick swallow. The only problem was, the second the taste of it hit the back of his throat, he gagged and ended up spewing most of it over the table and the floor.

Hess roared in laughter and shook his head. "It takes many of those to learn to keep it down. I hope you never practice enough to be able to down it in one shot like me," he teased.

Kaen grimaced and tried to smile. His throat burned, and his eyes were watering. "Why did you do that?" he gasped.

Hess leaned forward, and his face turned serious. With his massive thumb, he motioned to the dragon sleeping in the other room and then pointed at Kaen.

"That changes everything for you. From now on, you must learn to question everything someone offers you. Even a friend like Patrick or Cale. A dragon's body is worth a fortune. The easiest way to kill it, is to kill you."

Hess glared at Kaen, and Kaen shifted under the weight of Hess's stare.

"I will do everything I can to prepare you for what is coming, but I am afraid we will not have a lot of time before someone finds out about Pammon. For now, you must not tell anyone, and you must train your dragon."

Kaen glanced at Pammon and then back at Hess. "How do you know these things?"

Hess sighed and leaned back in his chair.

"I learned a lot the hard way."

6

Training a Dragon

Hungry! I'm hungry!

Kaen slowly opened his eyes and saw Pammon staring at him. He jerked back a second, glad it had not all been a dream. When he had finally lain down for the night, he'd passed out immediately.

"Morning, Pammon!" Kaen groaned a greeting and yawned. He reached out and rubbed the ridge of Pammon's head and was rewarded with a small trill.

Hungry! Pammon crooned and started to shriek a little.

"Give me a second!" Kaen exclaimed as he rolled out of bed and looked for his pants. The pair he had worn yesterday was on the floor, but he could smell them from his bed. He dug through the chest at the end of his bed until he found another pair of leather britches. He pulled them up and, as he started to tie off the middle, noticed that Pammon was acting funny in the corner of his small room.

"Don't you dare!" Kaen shouted as he saw his dragon start to hunch its backside.

Pammon turned and looked at him; for a moment, it looked like the dragon was glaring at him.

"Outside!" Kaen ordered, running over and grabbing Pammon's neck, and pulling him toward the door.

Pammon fought for a minute, screeching at Kaen as the two wrestled in his tiny room. His sharp claws dug into the wooden floor, creating grooves when Pammon finally gave in to Kaen's tugging and let himself be pulled out the door and toward the back of the house.

Kaen never let go of the ridge on Pammon's neck, glad the dragon had stopped fighting him. He knew he could not have won that fight. "Just a few more feet, and you can go outside!"

Pammon let out a weird sound that sounded almost like a sigh, but Kaen was more focused on opening the back door than on what Pammon was trying to tell him.

When the door swung open, Kaen realized the sun was barely up. He had not slept that long, but he felt amazing. Pammon darted past Kaen and found himself a spot about ten feet past the porch and proceeded to relieve himself.

Kaen stood there, amazed at what he was watching. The fact that the dragon was real and he could hear it in his mind, was still overwhelming him. He could feel where Pammon was. Closing his eyes, he sensed his dragon watching him. *His dragon.* It was an eerie feeling.

Kaen suddenly felt the need to puke when the smell wafted over to him from what Pammon had just completed. "Oh my gosh, that smells awful!" Kaen declared as he pinched his nose. "We need to bury that!"

Kaen had shoveled a lot of shite in his life: goat, pig, cow, and even human crap. Somehow, the load Pammon had just given birth to made Kaen wonder if some evil entity had clawed its way from the dragon's backside, seeking life in a new world. A sulfuric hint came from it as hot steam rose from the pile. A closer glance showed that the pile contained fur and bones that had not completely dissolved.

Pammon shrieked at Kaen and flicked his head around the yard. He spotted a few chickens roaming the area and took off toward them. With his wings tucked close to his body, the way he ran was almost amusing, except for the fact that a dragon was running after chickens in the country, not far from town.

Food!

Squawks and feathers erupted as the chickens darted and dodged to stay away from the Pammon's snapping mouth. He shrieked and roared—or attempted to roar—as he chased them. When the chickens suddenly changed directions, Pammon also tried to turn but lost his balance, tumbling and fumbling on the ground till he regained his footing.

"Pammon, stop!" Kaen shouted, running after the dragon in his bare feet.

Had anyone been walking along this morning and seen the event unfolding on Hess's farm, everyone in town would have believed them drunk as they described the scene.

Topless and barefoot, a teen boy chased a small bronze dragon who waddled more than he ran after a chicken trying to escape certain death.

After about a minute, Kaen caught up and grabbed Pammon's tail and dug his feet into the ground, cursing at the rocks and sticks thrusting against his bare feet. Kaen growled in frustration for a moment before remembering what Hess had told him last night about dealing with his dragon.

"PAMMON STOP!" he ordered. He fixed his whole mind on that command, adamant that Pammon stop. Immediately, Pammon slid to a stop, causing Kaen to fall over him face first.

Pammon huffed and glanced back at the chicken that was squawking and running off, claiming victory over a dragon, before turning his gaze back to Kaen. **Hungry! Need food!** Pammon whined in a small screech.

Kaen let out a huge sigh and got up off the ground. He looked at his pants and saw all the dirt and junk on them from the tumble he had taken. Perhaps Hess had been right, a dragon was not going to be easy to train at all.

"I know you are hungry," Kaen answered with a sigh. "Let me get some clothes and shoes on, and I can help get you food. It is too dangerous for you to be running around out here. Now back inside the house!"

Kaen stood there, pointing at the back door. Pammon glanced at the door and then back at the chicken standing a bit away, eyeing the two of them. The chicken let out a few squawks and bobbed its head, almost as if taunting Pammon. Pammon let out a blast of air from his throat and started to waddle toward the house, dragging his tail along the ground.

"What did I get myself into?" Kaen muttered.

When they got near the house, Kaen saw Hess standing by the side of the house, watching them.

"How long have you been there?"

Hess came out from around the corner with tears running down his face. "Oh, Kaen, you have no idea how funny that was," Hess said as he wiped away his tears. "The great dragon chasing a chicken and a boy chasing a dragon."

Kaen lifted his middle finger at Hess and scowled. "You could have helped!"

Hess shook his head and pulled a bag from around the house's edge. "I did help," Hess replied, tossing the bag at Kaen's feet. "Give these to your dragon, and then we must get inside and talk. This week is going to be a long one."

As Hess walked past Pammon, the dragon sniffed his hand and trilled. He then gazed at the bag Hess had tossed near Kaen and started to whine.

Eat! Food!

Kaen picked up the bag and looked inside. There were four rabbits inside. When had Hess gone hunting? He pulled out one of the rabbits and held it out toward Pammon.

The dragon started to wag its whole body from excitement and opened its mouth, letting out a trill.

Eat! Eat!

"I know, I know," muttered Kaen as he tossed a rabbit to him.

Pammon leaped forward, caught the rabbit midair, and swallowed it whole. Kaen repeated the process three more times, tossing a rabbit and watching Pammon swallow it whole.

After Pammon had eaten, Kaen returned to the back door of Hess's house and led Pammon inside. Without waiting for instructions, Pammon moved to a spot in front of the fire Hess had started and laid down on the wooden floor.

Hess appeared from the small area where he stored food and put a few slices of dried meat and a few overripe pieces of fruit on the table.

"I'd offer bread, but I have none, and I also doubt those chickens are going to lay any eggs for a few days."

Kaen sat down on his chair with a thud and sighed. "You warned me last night, but I was unprepared for that."

Hess laughed and returned to the food closet. He came out a minute later and put a small pack on the table. "That is dinner for tonight. I expect you to cook it and have it ready when I get home."

"Why do you say it like that?"

Hess sat in his chair and motioned to the dragon dozing on the floor behind him. "You are going to have to train him. If you let him sleep all day, he will be up all night. You need to hunt, so you must go while he is sleeping. You will only have a few hours to make sure he does not wake up and tear this place apart."

Hess leaned forward, tapped the table with his massive finger, and then pointed at Kaen. "You best ensure he does not use this house as a crapper. If he does, you will find yourself and that dragon sleeping outside for a long time to come."

Kaen gulped and nodded. He could not imagine that ball of crap Pammon had dropped in the yard being deposited in here. It smelled horrible outside.

"Remember, you need to *force* your desires on him. Just like you did when you made him stop chasing that chicken. If it helps, remember all those times you knew I was serious about the instructions I had given you. You do not want the consequences for not obeying."

"How long will we be stuck in the house?"

Hess rubbed his chin for a moment as he thought. "If things go well, it will be a week."

"A week!" exclaimed Kaen. "How will I stay away from work and my friends for a week?!"

Hess waved off the question and picked up a piece of meat. His fat fingers deftly rolled it into a tube, and he took a bite from it.

"I'll tell them you are sick and that they need to stay away in case it is contagious," Hess replied between bites. "I'll tell them I have seen something like this before in my travels, and you just need a week to recover. They won't bother you, and most will stay clear after I embellish the story a little bit."

Kaen chuckled, took a piece of meat, and started rolling it up too. "I will work on everything you told me to last night. Any other tips?"

Hess smiled and finished the piece he had in his hand before grabbing an overripe apple from the table. "Do not give in to his cries. He will try to get you to relent and let him do what he wants. You cannot do that. He is young. I have heard it takes a few weeks before a new dragon starts to grow into their intelligence."

Kaen nodded. Last night, Hess had spent quite some time explaining the few things he knew about dragons. He could still not believe his dad and Hess had met a Dragon Rider while working for the adventurers' guild.

Hess stood up and entered his room to prepare for the day. "Tell your dragon to go sleep in your room. Then tell him you will go hunting, and he must stay in your room!" Hess shouted across the house. "You're wasting time sitting at that table!"

Kaen knew Hess was right and quickly grabbed the last slice of meat on the table and wolfed it down. "Come on, Pammon, it is time to move to our room."

Pammon lifted an eyelid, then closed it, and, with a grunt, turned his face away from Kaen.

Kaen scratched Pammon's skull, soliciting a soft trill from him. "If you don't move to the room now, I will not scratch you the rest of the day," Kaen announced and stopped scratching Pammon.

Pammon groaned when Kaen stopped, and Kaen pointed to the room. "Move now, or I will drag you by your tail."

Pammon sighed like an unhappy child and slowly stood up on all four paws. He snorted at Kaen and waddled into the room he and Kaen were now sharing. Just inside the doorway, he plopped down and curled up.

Kaen walked over, bent, and scratched the top of Pammon's head with one hand and his spine with the other.

Pammon trilled loudly as Kaen praised him for moving to their room.

"Ok. Stay here. I need to go hunt so you can eat later. Do you understand?"

Pammon said nothing, just glanced up at Kaen.

"Pammon, tell me you understand. Stay here," Kaen ordered as he pointed to where Pammon was lying.

I stay. I tired.

Kaen laughed and nodded. He hoped Pammon would obey, but he knew Hess was right. He needed to hurry and finish getting dressed so he could go find Pammon more food.

As Kaen was about to leave the house, Hess called out for Kaen to stop.

"We need to talk about one more thing before you go."

Kaen turned and looked at Hess as he finished attaching the quiver to his hip. "What is it?"

Hess sighed, pulled his shirt down, and tapped the spot where his lifestone had been inserted.

"I need you to check and tell me your stats."

Kaen's eyes went wide. No one was ever to ask someone for that kind of information. It was too private. "Why would you ask that?"

Hess pointed to the side of the house where Pammon was sleeping.

"He is going to change yours completely."

7

Learning to Hunt

Kaen took a breath and let it out. Hess had told him how dangerous it was to share this information long ago or to ask someone else for theirs. He knew it was not something Hess would ask lightly. For Hess to ask must mean something had changed.

Full Status Check
Kaen Marshell - Adolescent
Age - 16
HP - 126/126 (5%)
MP - 0/0 (5%)
STR - 14 (5%)
CON - 13 (5%)
DEX - 16 (5%)
INT - 11 (5%)
WIS - 9 (5%)
Blessings:
Dragonbound - 5% current bonus to all stats

Kaen stood there in shock. All his stats except for wisdom had gone up!

"I have a five percent bonus showing by all my stats," Kaen stated excitedly. "Even my health has gone up!"

Hess nodded and put his hand on Kaen's shoulder to settle him down. "Look at me, boy."

Kaen stopped moving around and focused on Hess, who had his *serious* face on.

"Those numbers will increase the bigger Pammon gets. I do not know the complete details, but I know adult dragons and their Dragon Riders can have stats far beyond anything a normal adventurer can achieve. A single experienced Dragon Rider can wipe out an army on their own." Hess paused for a moment before adding, "Without aid from their dragon."

Kaen was shocked to hear that. To know that someday he would possibly be that strong was unbelievable.

"Guard that dragon with your life. Keep him a secret and make sure he learns to obey this week. In time he will be able to make his own decisions, but right now, most of what he does is instinct fed. Which includes crapping in the closest spot."

Hess turned and walked out the front door and down the dirt path that led toward town. "Make sure you get enough food for the whole day and keep him out of sight!"

Kaen watched Hess walk away. He was in shock from finding out that he had gotten stronger without doing anything but forming a relationship with Pammon. It felt unreal.

Kaen whistled a merry tune as he shut the door and started heading toward the forest. He had a job to do.

Stay close, Pammon called out as Kaen left to go hunting. **When you gone, I lonely**.

Kaen paused in the doorway, turned, and went back and gave Pammon a few scratches along his ridge, causing him to trill.

"If I don't go hunting, then you won't have food to eat. I know you will be hungry in a few hours, so maybe if I get lucky, I can find a deer for you!"

Trilling, Pammon nodded and put his head on the floor and glanced up at his person.

I stay, you go. Get me food.

Laughing, Kaen nodded and stood up to leave the room.

"It's only been two days, but it feels weird when I'm gone," stated Kaen as he stopped outside the door. "I can feel you and know where you are, and I want to sit right next to you all day."

Letting out a sigh, Kaen chuckled and smiled.

"If I don't get the chores done Hess told me to, I doubt we will like the consequences."

Blowing air from his nose, Pammon snorted and closed his eyes.

Kaen was right and Pammon knew it. It was obvious Hess was in charge.

The week had disappeared in a blink. Each day became easier as Pammon knew what to expect and learned that Kaen would not be swayed when he gave instructions. By the third day, Pammon stopped testing Kaen and did what he knew was expected.

Pammon had grown considerably in a week and had put on at least fifteen pounds. Then again, he was eating a lot more. On the fifth day, he ate two deer in total, as Kaen had managed to get lucky and find one in the morning and one in the afternoon.

Hess had kept everyone from the quarry away, and no one in town had felt the need to test whatever sickness Hess told them Kaen had.

Kaen and Hess stood outside in the backyard that morning while Pammon did his usual morning duty. It had been seven days since Pammon had joined their house.

"That stuff is fertilizing gold. Make sure you put that in the compost pile with the rest."

Kaen groaned. Each day Pammon's pile of crap grew, as he ate more. Occasionally, it was not solid, and moving it to the compost pile was probably one of the worst chores Kaen ever remembered having.

"I'm not sure that stuff is worth the smell."

Hess laughed and pointed to the garden he had on the side of the house.

"Are you kidding me? Look at those tomatoes! They are growing faster and bigger than should be possible! It makes them grow in a fourth of the time!"

The plants did look better than they ever had, and the apple tree had perked up after Hess added some to the base of its trunk a few days ago.

"If that dragon of yours weren't such a pain to keep fed, I would go into the fertilizer business and get out of the rock business."

"Speaking of feeding him," Kaen interrupted, "are you sure about taking him out today?"

Hess nodded and handed Kaen the bow and quiver.

"It's time. He needs to learn, and you two must get out of the house. It smells like a dwarf's sweaty ball sack in there."

Kaen laughed, attached his quiver to his belt, and took the bow. "What will you tell everyone at the quarry?"

"That you will be back in two days. Make sure Pammon knows how to hunt so he can stay in the woods while you are at the quarry. Now go, I cannot be late today."

Kaen whistled for Pammon, and the dragon turned and looked at him.

Coming.

Kaen led his dragon into the woods at the edge of their farm. He knew something was up with Hess because he had said he could not be late today.

"Be quiet and stay still," Kaen whispered at Pammon, who was doing his best not to move, even though he was flooding Kaen's mind with his thoughts.

Hungry! Kill rabbit!

Kaen nodded and pulled his bow back. He judged the distance and let the arrow fly, piercing the rabbit.

"Now you can get it."

Pammon darted toward the rabbit and quickly covered the distance between them. He no longer waddled like a duck so much as he moved toward his meal.

His running had smoothed out after he had figured out how to hold his wings to help balance himself.

Hess had no idea when Pammon would learn to fly but felt that he should be able to within the first month.

Two deer had escaped because Pammon could not contain his excitement at such a large meal. It had taken multiple rabbits to fill him up.

"We need you to learn how to hunt and fly," Kaen said as he slowly ran his fingers up and down the rugged ridges forming along the top of Pammon's head. "I need to know if you can breathe fire or something else."

Fly soon. Fire later.

Kaen glanced at Pammon. His dragon was sitting still, staring at him.

"You know how to fly and breathe fire?"

Soon. Too weak. Need food.

Kaen could not believe how much better Pammon was getting at communicating. This, however, was a new step in their 'talks.' Before, Pammon only talked when he was hungry or needed to take a crap or sleep. Occasionally, he still mentioned killing the chicken at the house.

"How much do you understand when I talk?"

Most. I sense . . . feel . . . you.

"You know what I want by what I feel?"

Yes.

Kaen returned to stroking Pammon's ridges and listening to him trill with pleasure. He could tell when Pammon was happy, hungry, or upset. He had not considered that Pammon could do the same with him.

"You need to learn to hunt. Once you can do that, I can let you roam the woods near where I work. You can get stronger while I work. Do you understand?"

I hunt. You watch.

Kaen laughed and motioned for Pammon to take the lead. He stayed a few yards behind and watched as Pammon sniffed and glanced around the woods. His brown copper scales helped him blend into the ground as he slinked around the woods.

Rabbit!

Kaen froze and tried to locate the rabbit Pammon was talking about. He couldn't see it, but Pammon was slowly stalking like a cat through the woods. He sprinted toward a few trees, and Kaen saw a brown rabbit bolt across the base of the forest floor.

Pammon ran along the ground after it, weaving around trees and bounding over bushes and other obstacles. Suddenly, he pounced on a spot, and dirt started flying through the air. The rabbit had gone into a hole, and Pammon was digging after it.

Kaen ran closer and watched as a stream of soil flew behind Pammon and started to pile up behind him. He could feel the thrill Pammon was experiencing. A weird urge seemed to drive Pammon on, and excitement at the possibility of his first solo kill seemed to exude from him.

A few more moments passed, and Kaen knew that Pammon had been successful. He could feel the joy coming from him.

I killed it!

"Great job! You did great!"

Pammon turned around, holding the bloody rabbit in his mouth. His face and scales were covered in dirt, but it almost looked like he was smiling. Kaen smiled and nodded at Pammon, who then gulped down the rabbit and let out a loud trill.

Again!

Hess saw the smoke drifting up into the air from the chimney as he got to the edge of his property. It meant Kaen was cooking, and something smelled terrific as the wind blew toward him.

"I'm home," Hess called out as he got to the porch and stomped his boots to remove as much dirt and dust as possible.

The door swung open just as he finished taking his boots off. Hess turned to see Kaen grinning at him like a fool. "How was the quarry?"

Hess laughed and shook his head. "Breaking rocks is a pleasure I miss. I prefer to do that instead of listening to the head of the Franstum house complain about us not meeting our quota last week. I informed him our best worker was out with a terrible infection of *Cramduncunkle*, and he wanted me to personally send you his best wishes to get well soon. If I'm not careful, he might offer you a raise."

Kaen laughed and moved back inside the house. Hess knew that Kaen was cooking more than what he had left him.

"I guess that proves just how valuable of a worker I am and that I deserve a raise!"

Hess rolled his eyes and ignored Kaen's statement. "Is that venison I smell?"

"It is. I managed to get one as Pammon chased it. He did well today. He caught seven rabbits on his own."

Pammon was lying on the floor near the fire, and he raised his head and gave a small trumpet sound from his throat. Hess heard him and laughed.

"Well, that is good to know. Tomorrow you can spend one more day together. After that, you will need to return to work."

Hess took a piece of fruit off the table and bit it. The apple tasted so much better since he had used that fertilizer from Pammon's crap around the tree. "After this week at work, you will hate the weekends. We are going to start training to prepare you for the adventurer's test."

Kaen nodded, went to the fire, and stirred the pot he had sitting off to the side near it. "If Pammon can learn to hunt, he might be able to get us a little extra meat during the week."

Hess sat down at the table and held out his hand toward Pammon. Pammon's head popped up, and he started sniffing the air and moved till his nose was next to Hess's hand.

Pammon let out a screech and started to wiggle in anticipation. Hess laughed as he turned his hand over and showed a red cube to Pammon, who sniffed it before quickly snapping it out of Hess's palm.

Hess reached over and scratched those growing ridges and smiled as Pammon trilled.

"What was that?" Kaen asked.

"It was a congealed blood block. I got it from the butcher in town when I stopped by his place on my way home. He is going to let me get a few scraps. I told him I needed to try and fatten you up."

"Well, tonight we will eat like kings. Fresh meat, a good stew, and some amazing apples!"

"All thanks to your dragon and his magical crap!"

Kaen laughed and nodded.

"All thanks to Pammon and his magical crap!"

Pammon gurgled in delight. He could feel the joy Kaen had and knew they were praising him.

"Stop, Pammon!" Kaen shouted as his dragon chased that chicken around their yard again. "It's been two weeks! Let it go!"

It's taunting me! Pammon shouted as he ran after the chicken. **He says he is better!**

Judging the chicken's path and where Pammon was headed, Kaen ran between the two, holding his hands out and bracing for impact.

Pammon skidded to a halt a few feet from Kaen and let out a huff.

I'm hungry. I want to eat the chicken!

"No, Pammon, no chicken. Now, let's go into the woods and get some food for you!"

Grunting, Pammon turned and moved toward the woods.

Kaen could feel that he was flustered and not really mad at the chicken. His words were improving, yet if Kaen was a betting man, he was sure Pammon had just been terrorizing the chicken for the fun of it.

After hunting until Pammon was finally full, they returned home, and Kaen watched as Pammon slowly trod behind him, his belly almost dragging against the ground.

He had shot a deer that had been foolish enough to be eating at the plot he had planted a week ago in the woods. Pammon's crap had made those seeds sprout in no time.

Tired. I want to sleep.

Glancing at the sun, Kaen shook his head. "You need to sleep in the woods. Don't sleep all day, though, like last time! I didn't get any sleep with you tossing and turning."

Grunting, Pammon stopped moving and sat down and looked at Kaen.

You go to work? Stay with me?

Kaen's heart broke, and he ground his teeth in frustration. The pain of having to leave each day hurt. Even knowing Pammon was growing and taking care of himself didn't seem to fix the pain he felt in his chest when they were apart.

He moved toward his dragon and began to scratch his head and all over the scales of his neck.

A soft trill rang out through the woods and Kaen smiled.

You can go. I be fine. I see you soon.

Pammon turned and took off slowly into the woods, and Kaen could feel him moving deeper until he found the hole and logs they had built to give Pammon a place to sleep that was covered during the day.

Letting a sigh out, Kaen ran off toward the quarry. He would probably be late, yet Hess would not hold it against him. He knew what Kaen was doing.

"Faster!"

Laughing as he shouted, Kaen watched as Pammon ran through the woods. In less than two months, Pammon had managed to begin flying a little bit.

It took a running start, but within ten or twenty yards, Pammon was able to leap into the air and become airborne. He had managed to stay aloft for two hours at a time with a solid hour or two rest in between.

Hess is coming!

Glancing over his shoulder, Kaen saw Hess coming through the woods. His mentor shook his head and smiled as he came, holding a few targets under each arm.

"He is getting the hang of it!" Hess called out as he started setting up the targets at different distances from where Kaen was standing.

"Yeah! Two hours yesterday. I can't believe it!"

Nodding, Hess saw the smile on Kaen's face and watched as Pammon flew right above the treetops over them. This small clearing had worked well for them to let the two of them be together while he trained Kaen.

"I bet in another month he'll be able to fly all day long," Kaen declared as he grabbed the quiver of arrows he had sat down on the ground next to him. "Imagine what he can do then."

"Eat and crap more?" Hess joked.

"Yes!" exclaimed Kaen as he took his bow off his back. "I am having to make sure he travels farther away each day. I can't tell you how long it's been since I've seen a deer. If it wasn't for these food plots, I doubt we would have any close by."

Moving behind Kaen, Hess pointed at the target on his left. "Well, let him focus on flying. You focus on shooting. We need to work on your archery skill, and you still need to practice with a sword."

Groaning, Kaen pulled an arrow out and took a shot at the target, hitting one of the inner rings but missing the bullseye by a good two inches. "I don't want to use a sword. I told you already, I'm a bow guy."

"Stop talking and shoot the other three targets and focus," Hess said, choosing to ignore Kaen's resistance to learn the sword.

Stretching in his bed, Kaen glanced at the empty spot on his floor. He let out the breath he had been holding and groaned as he sat up.

Pammon had outgrown their house and now had a small burrow they had helped him build in the woods. Soon, they would make something bigger, as he had already almost outgrown that. He couldn't believe how fast Pammon was growing.

Closing his eyes, he focused on Pammon and where he was. *I wonder where that silly dragon is.* Kaen thought as he searched for his location.

Why did you call me silly and when did you learn to talk like this?

Kaen's eyes popped open, and he almost fell off the edge of the bed. He looked around the room. "Pammon? Are you here?"

No response came from inside the house.

Tell me why I am silly.

Trying to figure out how to do what he did, Kaen recalled what had just happened. Closing his eyes, he focused on Pammon and then thought about what he wanted to say.

Pammon?

Who else would this be?

Pammon! You can hear me!

Yes, and do not shout. That is loud.

Laughing like a fool in his room, Kaen smacked the edge of his bed and let out a *whoop.*

This is awesome! Why didn't you tell me how to do this before?

He felt the frustration Pammon must have been feeling after he asked that question.

Did you teach me how to fly? How could I teach you to do this?

Fair point. This is so amazing, though! How far are you from me? A few miles?

I am at least half an hour from you and Hess. I am hunting farther away as there is not a lot of food right now near your place.

That is because you have eaten it all, teased Kaen.

Do you need me, or are you just calling me names?

Ahh . . . sorry about that. I was just wondering where you were this morning. You fly off, and I never know where you are or where you are going since I didn't know how to talk with you, but now I do!

Yes, silly boy. Now you do.

Laughing, Kaen got up and started getting dressed.

I need to tell Hess about this, but I am excited we can finally talk more!

A wave of joy and happiness hit Kaen as he felt Pammon react to his thoughts.

I am too. Now, I need to focus. There is a deer I am tracking.

Pulling his boots on and tossing on his shirt, Kaen headed out back to find Hess and share the good news.

"Are you going to help?" Kaen asked as he hammered in another set of nails, keeping the support board secure so he could tighten the rope.

"Nope. It's your dragon's shack. Besides, you need the workout, not me."

Cursing under his breath at Hess, Kaen smiled as he watched Pammon dragging a log he had cut down toward him.

Ignore Hess. We will build my place without his help.

Yes, but I would prefer if he helped as I don't want it to fall in on top of you.

Why would it do that? Are you not skilled in crafting a shed?

Pausing as he tied the rope, Kaen began to laugh and had to finish before he could focus again.

"What is so funny?" Hess asked.

"Pammon and I were talking," Kaen stated as he tapped his forehead with a finger. "He was not excited to hear my shed-building skills are not that good, and he doesn't want to have it fall upon him while he is sleeping."

Glancing at Pammon, Hess saw the dragon looking at him with two big eyes. "Hairy dwarf balls, Kaen," he cursed as he shook his head. "I'm going to end up helping you because your damn dragon gave me puppy-dog eyes."

Chuckling, Kaen shrugged as he waited for Hess to join him.

Nice job with the puppy-dog eyes!

Confusion hit Kaen, and he saw Pammon cocking his head sideways.

Tell me, what are puppy-dog eyes? Are they tasty?

The only thing that prevented the logs standing straight up from falling on Kaen as he bent over into a laughing fit, was Hess and his quick movement to catch them.

"Kids," Hess mumbled as he glanced at Pammon, who was still watching him. "Kids and dragons . . . this is going to be a long few more months."

8

Unexpected Surprises

"Again!" Hess shouted as he started to throw rocks at Kaen.

Kaen ran, letting arrows fly at the targets on their farm with his bow, trying to dodge the rocks while hitting each target.

Six of the eight targets set up at different paces had an arrow in them. He had missed two, yet it was a huge improvement.

"You took your eyes off those two targets because you were more focused on the rocks coming at you!"

Kaen nodded as he moved to retrieve the arrows from the targets. The two that missed were in the woods somewhere. He did not want to waste the time required to find them right now.

"I would rather stay alive than die if those were real attacks," Kaen answered, pulling the arrows from the hay victims. Some were shaped as people, others were just simply round. None of them were wider than a foot now.

"That might be true," Hess answered, "but not killing the two you missed could also spell death for you. Sometimes, you must choose if a small injury is worth winning the battle."

Hess watched Kaen retrieve his arrows. The boy had worked exceptionally hard each weekend, which made the first day back at work extremely difficult because he was so tired. This schedule had accomplished what Hess had intended it to. Kaen had gotten stronger. It was partly due to Pammon and how much that damn dragon had already grown. It was now the size of a horse. Pammon had not been happy about it, but there was no way they could hide the dragon at their place anymore.

"You want to go again?" Kaen asked.

Hess shook his head. "Where is he?"

Kaen momentarily closed his eyes, turned, and pointed into the woods. His finger pointed straight like an arrow to where he knew Pammon was. "He is flying right now. Staying low to the trees like we talked about and tracking some game."

Kaen laughed as he turned to point at the deer carcass Pammon had left them an hour ago on the edge of their property. "He says he is hungry and wants another deer of his own."

A groan escaped Hess as he glanced at the carcass. "People in town have already complained about how hard it is to find any game out here. Some believe there must be a beast eating everything. How many miles does he go to find something now?"

Kaen pulled the quiver off his hip and held the bow in the other hand. "I honestly have no idea, but he has been better about hunting closer to the mountainside an hour to the southeast of us."

Hess grunted and motioned to the dead deer. "Let's get this thing cleaned so the meat doesn't go bad, and we can talk about next week."

"You are sure I am ready? I mean, I'm barely seventeen."

Hess nodded as he dressed out the deer. "It is time. You are good enough to pass the test and need to start working on your adventure rank. It will take us almost a week to get to Ebonmount, and you will need two days to do the test. After that, you will get your token, and once you have that, I will help you with your first few quests."

Hess stopped talking as he cut off the haunches and started working on the backstrap. For a man with such large hands, he handled a knife with the most delicate skill.

"Besides, I am not going to send you out into the world alone. Your father would never forgive me."

Kaen groaned. That comment always felt like a cheap shot when Hess did not want him arguing about why he was doing something. "You really think I will pass?"

Hess set the perfectly cut backstraps on the table and stretched his back. He pointed the knife he was holding at Kaen and smiled.

"You are far more skilled than those who attempt this test. I know you are stronger than most, and your speed and quickness make it difficult to hit you even when I try with a rock. Your dragon has given you a gift that would take most men years to achieve. It will only grow stronger as he grows. Besides, you cannot keep him hidden forever."

Hess drove the knife into the cutting board, moved to a pot of water, and washed his hands for a moment. Kaen could see from his expression that Hess was frustrated about something.

"Six months. Maybe a year," Hess said before he sighed. "That is all you will have before someone finds out about Pammon. Once they do, everything for you will change. You will be put into a position that you cannot escape. Do you remember the rumors that started a few weeks ago? Everyone else in town seems to."

Kaen pulled out a chair from the table, turned it around, and sat down and leaned his chest against it.

"Do you really think the last Dragon Rider in our kingdom is that hurt?"

Hess finished shaking his hands dry and shrugged. "Dragon fighting is bad business. That black dragon and his rider, Stioks, are rumored to have been injured, but Elies was said to have been hurt pretty badly. His dragon was rumored to have barely made it back to their keep."

Hess visibly shuddered and tried to play it off with a smile. "How both of them recover will determine your path. Your life will become complicated when word reaches them that you and Pammon are bonded."

Hess grunted and turned to face the fire. He started pounding his hands together in frustration.

"I know you are trying to help. Tell me what I need to do," Kaen said.

Hess suddenly laughed and then let out another sigh. He turned around and looked back at Kaen and gave a weak smile. "I cannot tell you what to do anymore. All I can do is help you as you pick the path before you. Everything from this point on will be your choice. You and Pammon will have to figure out what you two want—"

"I don't know what I want," Kaen interrupted. "I know I want to be an adventurer, but why must I choose to be a Dragon Rider?"

Hess roared in laughter for what must have been a good twenty seconds. When he finally stopped, he wiped a tear from his eye and shook his finger at Kaen.

"Choose to be a Dragon Rider? Why must you choose to be one? Because you have a dragon! How do you expect to survive if you are not on your dragon? Do you not yet realize that there will be a host of people who will want you dead? A bonded dragon that loses its human is much easier to kill. The simplest way for those seeking to harvest Pammon's scales and organs is to kill you," Hess repeated his previous warning. "The safest path for both of you is with you on his back. In another month or two, you will need to be riding him like a horse. This will help him build the strength he will need to fly with you."

Kaen started to open his mouth to protest but found himself unable to reply. His chest felt tight. He did not want Pammon to die, and he knew Pammon felt the same way about him. "I just don't want to be forced down that path. I want to be like my dad. Able to choose the path he wanted."

Hess walked over and pulled his chair out from under the table. He moved it next to where Kaen was sitting and leaned back in his chair.

"Your dad never went down the path he wanted. He took the path he felt was right. He did what was needed to help others and to protect and provide for you."

Kaen looked at Hess's eyes and saw that rare soft look in them. He knew Hess was telling the truth.

"I guess that means I must become a Dragon Rider," Kaen said with a slight sigh. "That is what my dad would have done, right?"

Hess nodded and smiled. "Your dad would have given up everything but you for a dragon to call his own. He had been enthralled when he met the first dragon we ever encountered. He was like a kid getting their first frozen treat during a snowfall."

"How many dragons had you two met?"

"Only two. One was by chance, and the other was on a quest, but now is not the time to discuss that. We need to take care of this deer and prepare for next week. So, get the salt and help me get this curing."

Kaen chuckled and nodded. He knew Hess was done talking about old times and fetched the salt from the storage closet. It was going to be a long night getting this deer processed.

"I can't believe you are leaving next week and heading to Ebonmount," Patrick stated as he chunked the broken rocks he was holding into the cart next to him. "It's not fair, I tell you. We were supposed to go as a team."

Cale saw the look of pain on Kaen's face and stepped in to help. "Patrick, you and I both know we were never going to leave this place. You and I don't have a lifestone. We can't become an adventurer like Kaen."

As the last rock fell from Patrick's arms into the cart, he turned and frowned at Cale. "I know. It's just not fair."

Patrick sighed and looked at Kaen, giving a weak smile. "Just remember us when you are some famous adventurer. Perhaps when you reach a high rank, you can come back and visit us. Maybe when you are iron rank or higher."

Kaen set his pickaxe down, walked over to where Patrick was, and held out his hand. "I promise I will return as soon as possible."

Patrick smiled, grabbed Kaen's hand, and shook it.

Before Patrick could let go, Kaen gripped it tighter and made another promise. "I'll bring both of you lifestones. Even if it takes years, I'll bring one for each of you. Then you can use them or give them to your children."

Patrick stood there, shocked at the words Kaen had just spoken. Cale also was silent as he knew Kaen never broke a promise.

"You would do that? For us?" Patrick asked.

Kaen put his free hand on Patrick's shoulder and smiled. "For my only two friends, I would do anything to help you achieve your dreams."

Patrick nodded and then started to do one of the silly dances he'd done when they were young. "You hear that, Cale?" Patrick asked as a smile flashed across his face. "We are going to have our own lifestone!"

Cale nodded and smiled as Kaen turned and looked at him. "You know you don't have to do that, right?"

Kaen moved over to Cale and grabbed him in a headlock, easily overpowering him with the strength he now possessed. "I know I don't have to do anything, but I will make you take it when I bring it."

Cale laughed and tried to fight Kaen, but it was no use. He knew he could not break out of the hold Kaen had him in. "Well, don't break my neck, or it won't matter if you bring me a lifestone."

Kaen released him and laughed. "None of this will matter if we don't finish this work. With Hess and me gone, I know whoever they put in charge here will require a lot more work from the two of you. So you better actually start working for once before everyone finds out neither of you knows how to swing a pickaxe."

Both boys laughed and returned to work. They wore smiles as they attacked the rocks with fervor. Only Kaen had to pretend to smile. He hoped he could make that promise happen sooner rather than later. He would do whatever was required to make it happen.

They continued working, enjoying laughter and the retelling of old stories from their forest adventures as young teens.

Suddenly Pammon called out:

I found a cave! A cave with a funny smell!

Kaen was shocked at the sudden message. Pammon usually only called out to him when he knew he was done at the quarry.

What kind of cave and where?

It is far south. A few hours at least by foot, maybe even more along the mountain. It smelled foul, and I could hear creatures inside the cave when I landed nearby.

The rules, Pammon! You know the rules! Hess told you to stay away from buildings and people. Did they see you?

These are not people. They are something else.

Kaen froze. Something other than people?

Come home fast. Come to the farm. I will find Hess and talk to him.

9

Preparing for Adventure

"I'm not happy with Pammon," Hess stated, glaring at Kaen. "He should know better than to explore a cave. You need to train him better!"

"Why is this my fault?" Kaen demanded as he walked next to Hess. "I am not with him when he hunts; he is doing what you told him to do. He is hunting far away from town. Do you know of any caves that far south?"

Hess huffed and walked faster toward their farm. He knew of caves and what could live in them. If what Pammon had said was true, it would ruin their whole week. "Just make sure he is at the farm when we get there. Tomorrow is going to be a hard day."

Kaen lengthened his stride and easily stayed next to Hess. Years of living with Hess had taught him how to read his body language. Hess was upset and concerned. There was no point trying to talk with him right now. It wouldn't be until later that Hess would settle down enough to talk again.

It smelled worse than you say my crap smells! It was dirty, and trash and bones were outside the cave!

Kaen repeated what Pammon had told him and chuckled at the smell description. Pammon's crap had gotten much more pungent as he ate more and more animals.

Hess nodded, reached out, and scratched the large ridges on Pammon's head. Pammon trilled, as always, and seemed to smile as Hess worked those spots he loved to have scratched.

"You can lead us there tomorrow morning, Pammon," Hess said in a cheerful voice. He then turned to Kaen. "We are going to do something I would prefer not to do until much later in your adventuring career, but I have no choice, if what Pammon is describing is this close to our town."

"What type of creature are they?"

Hess sighed and shrugged. "I hope it's goblins. I pray tomorrow that all we find are goblins."

Kaen's eyes went wide with excitement. Pammon started to get excited, also. He could feel Kaen's excitement at the possibility of fighting goblins tomorrow.

"And if it's not goblins?" Kaen asked, his voice higher than usual due to his excitement.

"Again, I will say, I pray it is goblins, Kaen. If it is worse, we may have to run back to town and explain how we found a danger worse than goblins."

Hess held up his hand and stopped Kaen from asking another question. "Both of you. Get some rest. Pammon, go sleep in the woods at your place. Tomorrow is going to be a test worse than what you will experience in Ebonmount." With that said, Hess turned and walked back to the house's back door and went inside.

Did I mess up?

Kaen shook his head and scratched Pammon's neck. "You did nothing wrong. I think by finding that cave, you actually may have saved the town or the quarry from possible danger."

Pammon smiled at the praise and put his nose against Kaen's forehead.

I'll sleep then. Thank you for the scratches. That spot has itched all day, and I could not get it as good as you can.

Kaen laughed and gave a hard and long scratching session as Pammon trilled in delight. After a minute, he stopped and patted Pammon's neck. "Get some sleep. Tomorrow, we have our first adventure."

Pammon nodded and took a few steps away before he leaped into the air. His wings beat rapidly, quickly launching him into the evening sky. His bronze scales glowed in the light of the setting sun. It almost looked like a bronze ball of light taking to the sky and cresting over the tops of the trees until he disappeared from sight.

After he lost sight of Pammon, Kaen sighed and turned to join Hess inside.

"Wake up," Hess called out as he banged his fist on the door to Kaen's room. "We need to get ready and go so we have as much time as possible."

Kaen sat up and squinted. The sun was not even up, but he could see Hess standing in his doorway. There was a little light from the main room, yet Kaen believed he must be dreaming, because he saw Hess dressed completely in armor with two massive hammers crossed behind his back.

"Are you really wearing armor and weapons, or am I still asleep?" Kaen asked as he let out a yawn. "You don't own any weapons or armor."

Hess grunted and banged on the door again. "Get dressed. Pants, boots, and a shirt. I'll have some stuff for you once you are dressed and at the table."

Hess turned and left the room, and Kaen shook himself awake. Realizing what was happening, he jumped out of bed and grabbed his clothes to prepare for today's adventure.

Pammon, wake up! We are getting ready. Start making your way here.

A moment passed, and Kaen realized that Pammon was barely awake. It felt like Pammon had just yawned. Kaen chuckled at the way they could feel and sense each other.

Kaen slapped his cheeks to wake himself up a little more.

Pammon! Wake up!

I'm awake, Pammon groaned through the connection. **I heard you the first time. I just was not ready to reply yet.**

Well, we don't have time to wait. Hess is ready to go, and soon, I will be too.

What about food? I'm hungry.

Kaen chuckled as he started lacing his boots up. Pammon was always hungry.

I'll ask Hess, but for now, just come here.

Fine. Pammon replied with a hint of displeasure coming through the link they shared. **Tell him I will be there in just a few minutes, and tell him I am hungry.**

Kaen nodded and got his last boot finished. He threw his shirt on and tucked it in as he started to walk out of the room. As soon as he got to the doorway, he saw Hess leaning against the table and what was draped over the chair he usually sat in. Kaen froze. "Where did that all come from?"

Kaen was staring at the leather tunic draped over the chair and a bow much nicer than the one he used every day.

Hess smiled and motioned to the items on the chair. "Something from your father. Something I promised myself I would one day give you. Today is the day I keep that promise."

"These are my dad's?" Kaen almost whispered. "His actual equipment?"

Hess chuckled and shook his head. "He had these made a long time ago for you. The tunic might be a little too tight, but that is because he had not expected you to have a dragon to help fill you out. The bow was something he had crafted for you after watching you smile the first time you shot a bow. He seemed to know somehow that you would use it."

Hess picked up the leather tunic and held it out toward Kaen. "Come here. Let me help you put this on."

Kaen did not remember moving toward Hess or lifting his arms so that Hess could slip the tunic onto him. All he could think of was that his father had purchased items for him. His father had done all this before he died. As if he somehow knew he would not be here to put these on him.

As the leather tunic hung on his arms and Hess moved behind him to pull it around him, Kaen could feel strength entering him. He felt stronger and faster.

"Is this magical?" Kaen mumbled as he ran his hands across the leather stitching on the front of the armor that was being tightened along his back.

Hess grunted as he threaded the leather strips through the holes and pulled on them to tighten the tunic. "It is but wait until we are finished getting you fully outfitted before you check your stats. These were to be a gift for you the day you passed your adventurer's test. I think you will need them today."

"How did he know what I would need?" Kaen asked, almost in a trance. All this felt too much like a dream to him.

"He always knew what you would be," Hess replied, cinching up the chest piece. He paused and sighed. "He knew you would pursue this path and that you would be a hunter. Your smile when he took you into the woods, and when he saw you shot your bow, told him all he needed to know."

Hess came back around Kaen and tapped his armor. "You honor him well by wearing this. Now, hold out your arms."

Kaen held both arms out and stood in awe as Hess picked up two forest-green leather vambraces off the chair. Each had a 'K' initialed on the outside of them. Hess carefully put them on his forearms and showed Kaen how to tighten them. "Can you feel something with these on?"

Kaen nodded. The shock of all this had still not worn off yet. He could feel some kind of energy flowing through his body. He was unsure what bonuses they gave him but could tell they were magical.

Hess smiled and turned and picked up the bow. He held it out in one hand and offered it to Kaen.

Kaen stared at the bow in awe. He had never seen a bow made of wood as dark as this one before. Small, delicate carvings were on the top and bottom of it—trees with animals that seemed to dance around them. A grooved place for the hand had a leather lining the grip he did not recognize. It seemed like it was perfectly grooved for a left hand. The bowstring appeared almost white. Not like a muddy or dirty white but one that reminded Kaen of fresh snow that had yet to be trampled on.

"Take it. This is his final gift. When Hoste showed this to me, and I first held it in my hand, I knew he had paid more than he would admit. This bow will last you a lifetime, if you care for it."

Hess nudged the bow closer to Kaen's hands.

Kaen felt his fingers trembling as he first touched the bow's wood. It felt like it called to him. Like, somehow, it knew him. A shiver of something ran through his fingers as they brushed against the polished wood, magic racing through his body.

"It feels like it is calling to me. Like it is a part of me."

Hess nodded and let go of the bow as Kaen gripped it in his left hand. "Do you remember your father ever cutting you and taking some blood?"

Kaen stared at the bow and tried to think back. It had been years since he had thought about a time that long ago. A time with his dad.

"Stop fighting me, and let me see your finger, son," Hoste grumbled as he wrestled with Kaen's hand. "I promise it won't hurt that much and will be worth it."

Kaen was only six years old, and the thought of letting his dad use a knife on his finger was not something he wanted to let him do.

"It is going to hurt!" wailed Kaen. "Why do you have to cut me?!"

Hoste smiled and gently increased his grip on Kaen's hand, not allowing it to move anymore. He could easily overpower his son, but he wanted him to trust him. "I want to make you something special. A gift most would dream of, but you will need to let me collect a little of your blood. That way, the gift will only work for you."

Hoste smiled at Kaen as he fidgeted and fought against him.

Finally, Kaen stopped and moaned. A few tears were welling up in his eyes already. "Do you promise? Will it be worth it?"

Hoste set the knife on the table and reached over and wiped the tears from Kaen's eyes. "Son, listen to me. In life, there will be many times that pain will come. You can fight against it and still suffer from it, or you can accept it and become stronger by enduring it. The gift I have planned for you will be like no other. I cannot do it unless you are willing to give me your blood. Do you want this gift?"

Kaen touched his lips with his other hand. His fingers were trembling. He trusted his dad and knew he would never hurt him unless there was a good reason. Kaen risked a glance at his mother, who was off to the side smiling. He saw her nodding and motioned to his dad.

"Ok. I'll let you have my blood for whatever you need," Kaen announced as bravely as he could.

Hoste smiled and ruffled Kaen's hair on his head before reaching over and picking the knife up again.

"A wise choice!" Hoste proclaimed with a wink and a smile. "One day, you won't remember the pain of this, but you will never forget what you acquired because of this small moment."

Kaen tried not to cry out as he bit his lip. He watched the sharp knife slice the top of his thumb and saw the blood drip into a small jar his father had somehow produced from nowhere.

His dad smiled as the bottle slowly filled. "A true adventurer already," Hoste said with a grin.

* * *

Kaen stood there in shock. He had forgotten that moment. Eleven years had passed, and he had never thought about when his dad had done that.

Holding the bow close to his face where he could examine it, Kaen knew his father had been right all those years ago.

He would never forget what he had acquired from his father.

10

What Lives in a Cave

Full Status Check
Kaen Marshell - Adolescent
Age - 17
HP - 231/231 (10%)
MP - 0/0 (10%)
STR - 18 + 3(10%)
CON - 18 + 3(10%)
DEX - 19 + 10(10%)
INT - 12 + 1(10%)
WIS - 11 + 1 (10%)
Blessings:
Dragonbound - 10% current bonus to all stats
Hunters Tunic - + 3 to Str / Con / Dex
Blessed Vambrace - + 1 to Dex / Int
Blessed Vambrace - + 1 to Dex / Wis
Bonded Bow of Archer - + 5 to dex + 3 to archery *Locked*

Kaen's mouth hung open as he stared at the small screen displaying his stats. He had looked at them often during the past three months. Each week he wanted to see how much he was improving from all the training Hess had put him through. It all seemed worthless when compared to what these pieces of equipment his father had left him offered.

"I take it you were not expecting such a boost?" Hess asked with a chuckle. "Your father spent a lot of his money over the years and traded heavily to acquire those things. The tunic alone could buy a large estate inside Ebonmount."

Kaen slowly nodded and closed his mouth for a second. "This bow. I had no idea items could be this powerful."

Hess roared and nodded. "Can you do me a favor and tell me what exactly the bow gives? It will only bestow its enchantment on you. It is bonded to you alone."

Kaen glanced at Hess; his eyes were as wide as an apple. "Are you serious? Like the bow won't work for anyone but me?"

Hess shook his head and chuckled. "The bow is just a bow to anyone else. A well-crafted and balanced one. The magical effects only work for you, though."

Kaen gulped and nodded. Only he would ever get the real benefit of the bow.

"It gives me five for dexterity and three for my archery skill. It also says *Locked* on it."

A low whistle came from Hess. His eyes went wide, and he shook his head before he started to laugh. "That bastard. He lied to me about where that rune had gone."

"What rune?" Kaen asked. "And is my dad the bastard you are talking about?"

Hess nodded. He pulled a ring off his finger and held it out to Kaen. Kaen stared at it. He had seen the silver ring on Hess's finger for years and thought nothing about it.

Hess's eyes narrowed, and his voice changed. It was deep, and the tone he used when he was serious. "If I ever die and you are near me, take this ring. Do not let anyone else take it. You need to promise me this!"

"Why would you die? You are, like, the strongest person I know."

Hess shook his head and moved the ring closer to Kaen's face. "Promise me!" he demanded. "This ring is more powerful than most will ever come to own in a lifetime of adventuring. Your father let me use three runes and more money than I should have ever spent on it. I will not tell you how powerful it is, but know it surpasses everything you own and then some."

Kaen swallowed the saliva that had suddenly appeared in his mouth. If that ring was that powerful, how had Hess acquired it? What had he and his father done during their adventures?

"I promise. But you better not die on me!" Kaen proclaimed louder than he had expected.

"I will do everything possible to avoid it," Hess joked. "I would prefer to stay in the land of the living as long as I can."

Hess deftly slipped the ring back on his finger and handed Kaen the quiver of arrows that were leaning behind the chair. "Now we need to go. Pammon is outside."

Kaen recoiled a little in shock.

Are you outside the house, Pammon?

Yes! I have been here for a minute! We need to go so I can hunt. I am hungry!

Kaen chuckled and looked at Hess, who was walking toward the back door. How had that man known Pammon had been outside?

Pammon led them in the direction of the cave he had found. They had been walking for an hour, and the sun came over the mountains to the east, casting a warm, gentle light through the forest. Shadows were everywhere, and the mist from the ground hovered a few feet from the forest floor. Birds were singing and squawking, and squirrels were chittering at them for invading their territory.

This way!

Kaen kept them following the direction Pammon was flying. He could sense him and where he was. Pammon had taken a slight detour when he'd spotted a deer that was lying on the forest floor, sleeping from a night of foraging. After receiving permission to kill it, Pammon was in a better mood after eating.

How much farther till we are there?

With how slow you walk, it will be at least another two or three hours, Pammon replied with a slight chuckle.

Pammon was frustrated that he could not yet carry Kaen on his back and fly. They had tried riding together on the ground like a horse, but Kaen weighed too much, and Pammon waddled as he tried to move across the ground. Neither one wanted to think about waiting another three to six months before they could fly together for the first time.

As they walked, Kaen had been occasionally asking questions. "So, if these are goblins, how will we fight them?"

Hess darted between the overgrown shrubs and foliage of the forest. This back part of the woods was untouched for the most part, leading to an overgrown mess of greenery.

"If it is goblins, we will see if they are awake. If they are sleeping, we will enter the cave and try to kill them in their sleep. We will try to flush them out if they are still awake."

Hess scowled when he stepped over a bush and in some dung from a random animal. "Neither option is a good option. We do not know how deep that cave is or how many there are inside. While they are not strong individually, if there is a large group of them, they can overwhelm a person quickly. They are smarter than some give them credit. A pack of goblins with a leader is a very dangerous thing."

Kaen nodded as he listened to Hess talk about battle tactics and more. In the last hour, Hess had shared tips on how to support a melee partner as a ranged person. He had not realized the number of factors one had to deal with when fighting.

"So, if you block their line of sight of me, I cannot shoot them?"

Hess nodded and raised a finger as he made a point. "It works both ways. Since I am so large, I will block your view of them just as easily as I block theirs of you. If they are small enough, like a goblin would be, then their ranged or caster can attack me while you still cannot attack them. Learning to work with your ally is important. Knowing what they will do in a situation is paramount to the success of your fight."

Hess continued sharing his wisdom on the need for short commands so that a party or group could know who to attack or how to shift in a fight. Kaen's head was reeling from all the information he was trying to absorb as they hurried through the woods to get to where Pammon was leading them.

After about an hour of traveling, they stopped for a quick break. Hess handed out some dried jerky and pulled a water skin from his carrying pack. Pammon took the opportunity to hunt for another deer, as the first one was too small to be considered a *real* meal.

"How far did Dad and you travel during your adventuring days?" Kaen asked as he gnawed on a bite of the venison Hess had dried out.

Hess sat there trying to finish chewing the jerky he had taken a bite of and was working on swallowing it. After a quick drink of water, he stared at the sky momentarily before speaking.

"Your father and I saw three of the four major kingdoms. You know there are more than four, but they are across waters, and most people never get to visit them unless they use a boat for trade. Even then, sailing across the water would be a long and sometimes dangerous trip."

Kaen wiped his fingers along his pants, waiting for Hess to continue.

After a few moments, Hess let out a sigh and shrugged. "Most of the travels to the other kingdoms came from us signing on to protect a caravan or someone who felt they needed it. While sometimes those quests from the adventurers' guild seemed beneath us, they prepared us for some of our harder quests. Finding yourself surrounded and outnumbered three to one by bandits will help you not lose your cool in the heat of battle. You learn to trust your partners."

"How many other people did you and Dad quest with?" Kaen asked.

Hess snorted and shook his head. "So many questions," he said with a sigh. "I probably should have told you more about all this years ago, but I knew if I did, you would be chomping at the bit to leave sooner for Ebonmount."

Kaen laughed and nodded as he took another bite. "So how muny did yoo travel with?" he asked with a full mouth.

"Dozens over the years. Some for a few months," Hess replied, then paused for a moment. "Only one other person stayed with us longer than that."

Hess stopped talking and was again staring off at the sky. Kaen looked up at the sky to see if there was something Hess was looking for but realized, then, that Hess was lost in thought.

"Who was it?"

Hess groaned and shook his almost finished piece of jerky at Kaen. "Maybe I'll answer that question when we are in Ebonmount. For now, we need to get back to moving. I want to be home before dark if we can. We do not want to stay in the woods tonight."

Kaen started to ask another question but saw Hess was putting everything back in his pack. For now, Hess was done talking about that topic.

After another hour, they finally arrived near where Pammon had been directing them. The mountains had sprung up around them, forming an impassable barrier at the edge of the woods. Large rocks, solid granite, and more, kept the trees from growing on the side of the mountain.

Kaen was trying to figure out why there were no quarries out here. With such a large quantity of granite, surely someone would have invested the time and money to build a road and start harvesting it.

Hess had set his pack down, fished out a few small items, and put them in his pouch around his waist. He started crouching and slowly walking along the tree line and the mountainside. He was slow and deliberate as he walked, making sure not to make much noise as he moved.

Kaen followed in Hess's footsteps and tried to mimic the large man who was able to move so silently. His size did not matter as he bypassed twigs that would snap and echo off the rocky wall. He avoided the rocks that would shift and possibly rattle against another rock, causing a clacking noise.

They crept along the edge of the two wilderness areas for a good ten minutes, staying hidden in the trees but making good time along the barren ground of the mountainside.

[Sneak Skill Increased]

Kaen smiled as he saw the sudden burst of text in front of his vision. He was hoping he might see his skill improve. It had been ages since it had gone up.

Hess suddenly stopped and held up a hand for Kaen to stop.

Kaen controlled his breathing even though he felt like his heart suddenly wanted to explode out of his chest.

Hess motioned for Kaen to sneak up next to him.

Kaen carefully placed his steps as he moved directly behind Hess and slightly off to the side.

Hess pulled down the bush that was in front of Kaen a few inches and pointed toward the mountainside.

Looking through the small opening, Kaen saw the cave about fifty yards away. He saw some movement near the cave's opening. Bones and something else were being tossed from the mouth of the cave. Another minute passed, and then another set of bones flew through the air, landing with bones clacking against stones.

Not a few breaths later, a small green creature stepped out from the cave to pick up a bone that had not gone far.

A goblin!

11

Learning to Fight

Kaen realized he had forgotten to breathe for a moment and tried to take a breath of air very quietly. His heart was banging against the walls of his chest, and he could feel his fingers tingling.

A goblin!

It was not very tall and did not look very threatening at all. It wore a small, ratty shirt that hung to its knees and had a rusted and bent sword in what Kaen assumed must be its belt. He could see blood on its hands and arms. There was dried blood across its mouth, and streaks ran along one of its cheeks, where it had probably wiped its face with its bloody arm or hand. His ears were pointy, and one even had what looked like a piercing in it. Kaen could not think of how to describe its skin color other than a puke green. Something similar to what one might throw up after eating rotten lettuce or some other vegetable.

Hess never moved. He was like a stone, sitting there on the balls of his feet. Kaen was doing his best to imitate him. Years of hunting together had taught him how to hold still as he waited for the prey to turn away from him so he could take a shot.

Not long after the goblin had picked up the bone that looked like a rib of some sort, it made a weird noise and moved back into the comfort of its cave.

Hess let go of the brush slowly, then quietly leaned toward Kaen's ear and whispered. "You have a choice to make. We can return to town and tell them we found a cave of goblins and gather a party to come and help fight them."

Hess paused and watched Kaen's face for a reaction. "Or we can try and clear the cave ourselves. I have no idea how many are inside, but there must be at least ten or twelve based on the number of bones outside the cave."

Kaen nodded and felt his throat go dry. What should they do?

Pammon, have you seen any other goblins as you have been flying around here?

I have not. I have stayed out of sight as I was instructed. I can scout the area if you want, but doing so would mean I would be visible and possibly alarm any creatures out here.

Pammon was right. Kaen was impressed at how fast he had learned to hunt and hide his presence. His ability to talk and communicate had improved greatly once Kaen had learned how to speak to Pammon via his mind.

"Do you want Pammon to scout the area? He says doing so might alert any possible creatures in the area, though."

Hess chewed his lip for a moment. After a few seconds, he shook his head. "If he is spotted, we will have no choice but to fight. Otherwise, they may move, and then we would have completely lost the element of surprise."

Stay out of sight. I'll tell you our plan in a moment.

Kaen tried to decide what they should do as he felt Pammon nod his head in understanding. He did not want to go home empty-handed. He was wearing all this gear his father had gotten for him to fight things like this. Not killing them left a bad taste in his mouth.

"Let's try and take them out ourselves," Kaen whispered.

Hess nodded. He had known that would likely be Kaen's answer. "Listen, there is no trying here. We have to defeat them all, or we will have a bigger problem on our hands. If any get away, they will flee and be harder to track down. Even with Pammon's help."

Kaen nodded, pulled his bow off his back, and readied an arrow. "I understand. Tell me what you want Pammon and me to do."

"Tell him to land as quietly as possible on the other side of the cave. Try to stay out of sight as much as possible. I will approach from the other side. You, however, will be the bait."

"The bait?!" Kaen asked louder than he had meant to. "Why am I the bait?"

Hess shook his head and narrowed his eyes at Kaen. "You need to trust me and just obey. This is not my first time dealing with goblins. It is your first time. If you cannot do as I command without asking questions, we will turn around and bring back people from town. Do I make myself clear?"

Kaen nodded and sighed. He knew he had acted poorly. The memory of not trusting his father when he had required blood, returned to his mind. Kaen knew Hess was doing what he thought would work best.

Hess grunted quietly, stood up just a bit, and pointed to the small clearing at the edge of the woods. "Go over there where the bones and remains are. Do not have your bow drawn, but be ready to use it if I shout or you feel you must. When you see me wave at you, you will make some noise. Only do that when I am ready and in position. Try to look weak but do not run. See how many might come out at you. You must trust that Pammon and I will protect you."

Kaen took a deep breath and let it out. It would not be easy if ten goblins rushed him, but he would trust Hess.

"Good. Go get in position and tell Pammon what to do."

Kaen was crouched at the edge of the tree line. He could barely believe that Pammon had somehow managed to land quietly. He had been working on it, Pammon proudly declared.

Hess was almost in position on the other side of the cave. In each hand were his massive hammers. Kaen could not imagine a goblin getting struck by one of those and living to tell anyone about it. As Hess crept closer to the cave entrance, he heard a noise from inside the cave.

That was a woman screaming! Pammon shouted in his brain.

Kaen winced and nodded. It did sound like a woman screaming.

Hess suddenly stood up and started moving his hammers in the air. It was time for Kaen to announce his presence.

Kaen walked out of the tree line and moved closer to the pile of bones. He held his bow in his left hand but did not pull an arrow out of his quiver.

The smell was awful but not as bad as when Pammon relieved himself.

As he moved closer to the pile, he saw the skull of some creature. He was not sure what it was, but he was thankful it was not human. He kicked it, and it clattered across the rocks. He took another step, bent, and lifted up a bone that looked like it had been in the sun for a good week at least. A few ants were running along the bone, working on eating whatever they felt was worth collecting for their colony.

Kaen heard a sound from the cave, and his head jerked up. He tossed the bone off to the side, listening to it clatter against the rocky ground.

The cave was so dark he could barely see anything inside it. The sun provided a little light, but it was a black hole of nothingness after about ten feet. Two goblins came slowly out of the cave, each holding a sword in their hand. Both were chattering and glancing around the area where Kaen was standing. He guessed they were looking to see if he was alone.

Kaen noticed they were hesitating. He knew he needed to do something to draw them out. Slowly he backed up and then faked that he tripped and landed on his butt. He saw the goblins smile and assumed the sound coming from them was a laugh. He held his empty right hand out toward them as he started to stand up.

If they get close to you, I will kill them! announced Pammon.

Stay, wait till I tell you to help!

Pammon was grumbling, and Kaen could feel it through their connection.

Kaen stood, acting as if he was frozen in fear and unable to move. He glanced around the mountains and the woods, looking as if he was trying to decide where to go.

The two goblins came out of the cave and were now directly in the sunlight. Both held up their hands to shade their eyes. It appeared they did not enjoy the sun at all.

As they approached, two more goblins came out from the cave. The one closest to Hess had a piece of wood in his hand that looked like a poor shield and leather wrapped around his chest. The small sword he carried looked to be in better condition than what the other two had. *He must be a higher rank than the other three.*

The one in armor with the shield grunted and said something, and the three other goblins started approaching Kaen, spreading out, trying to cut off any chance he might have to escape. They were only about twenty yards at the most from him.

Kaen glanced at the three of them and then waited to see what Hess would do. He could feel Pammon being anxious and barely staying away. The closer the goblins got to him, the more it felt like Pammon would attack.

Kaen's eyes tracked Hess moving up to the edge of the cave.

The goblin at the edge of the cave saw that Kaen was not looking at the three goblins approaching him and moved to the mouth of the cave to see what Kaen might be looking at. As he got to the opening and turned, Hess charged him.

A shriek escaped his mouth, and the other three goblins turned to see what had caused him to cry out.

Hess was faster than Kaen realized. In just a few bounding steps, he had closed the distance, and, with a swing of his hammer, crushed the shield the goblin had held up to try and block Hess's attack. The power of that strike split the wood in half and snapped the goblin's arm. Hess's second hammer fell with just as much power and crushed the leader's head in one blow. Its skull exploded like a melon being smashed by a rock.

Kaen did not wait. He stood up, set an arrow on the string, and let it fly, catching the goblin on his left in the chest. It cried out in pain as the arrow flew clean through its body. Kaen could hardly believe the power from the bow.

He quickly took another arrow, let it loose at the middle goblin, and pierced its neck. It clutched the hole the arrow had created for a moment, before falling to the ground.

[Archery Skill Increased]

Kaen smiled. He was now at twenty-one with his archery skill!

The third goblin froze, and a few seconds later, its head was missing as Pammon bore down on it in a flash. All those months of practice killing rabbits had taught him how to spring upon prey instantly.

Pammon spat out the goblin's head as its body fell to the ground. The weapon slipped from its hand, making a metallic cling against the rocks.

The cave suddenly erupted with screeching.

"We need torches now!" Hess shouted, pointing at Pammon. "Get some branches and have him light them on fire!"

Kaen nodded, slung his bow over his back, and ran to the forest to grab some branches.

Pammon had turned and was watching the mouth of the cave. Suddenly, Pammon leapt in front of Hess right as two arrows flew out of the cave toward him.

The rock-tipped arrows bounced off his hard scales, and Pammon let out a loud roar that echoed through the cave.

Hess jumped back to move around the side of the cave. He had been lucky Pammon could see inside the darkness, or both of those arrows would have struck him.

Pammon stood at the entrance of the cave, growling. He swayed his tail in the air. He moved slightly whenever Kaen moved, always keeping himself between the opening of the cave and Kaen.

There are two with bows. They ran deep into the cave. I can hear more, but I do not want to go in there without you!

Thank you for saving Hess!

Kaen felt Pammon's feelings toward Hess through their bond. He liked Hess, even if Hess made him sleep in the woods away from Kaen. Pammon knew Kaen was safe as long as Hess was around.

Kaen ran toward Hess, carrying about seven good-sized branches that would work as a torch.

"You sure we want to go in there? Pammon says he can see in the dark!"

Hess's eyes went wide, and then he nodded. "We do not have a choice. There is a woman in there, and we must act fast, or they will kill her!"

Kaen understood. They would have to enter the cave and trust Pammon to keep them safe.

12

Cave Fighting 101

Breathe on these.

Kaen held two branches out toward the front of Pammon's mouth. He took a moment, and then a small, tight stream of fire hit the top of the sticks, causing them to burst into flames.

Pammon stopped the stream of fire after the branches were lit. He could only produce around ten seconds of flame before needing an hour or so to recover completely.

Kaen handed a torch to Hess, who traded with him for a hammer.

"Think of the goblins as a rock, striking them like rocks you want to mine. You will naturally know what to do if you think of it like that. Aim for their bodies also."

Kaen nodded and shifted his hand around on the hammer's handle. This thing was three feet long! Its massive head on the end reminded him of something a blacksmith might use to pound metal. With his increased strength, he could carry it and swing it easily, but Kaen knew most people would struggle to be able to use it as he or Hess could.

Ready?

Yes! Stay behind me. I will protect you two and call out as I see them.

Pammon led the way as they entered the cave. The stench from inside was far worse than the pile of bones outside. There was a layer of filth and a slick film on the stone cave floor. When Kaen lowered his torch to the ground, he realized the cave floor was covered in shit! The goblins apparently crapped wherever they wanted!

"Ignore it and focus on what is ahead!" Hess snapped at him as the light of the outside faded behind them. "Forget the stuff at your feet and tell me the moment Pammon sees something."

Kaen nodded even though Hess was not looking at him. Their torches were sending shadows all around the cave. They were not the greatest lights, and he hoped the two branches he had stuck in the back of his belt would not be needed.

A few minutes passed as they walked deeper into the cave. The sound of goblins echoed off the walls all around them.

Two ahead! Pammon called out suddenly.

"Two goblins ahead!" Kaen said.

Hess grunted and threw the torch as far as he could.

As it flew end over end through the tunnel, its light dimmed from the air rushing against the flame. It almost died before it clattered to the ground, and the flame leapt along the pitch-filled wood. Hess saw the two goblins who were not much further past it, squinting at them from the torchlight. Each held a bow and shouted and pointed arrows at them.

Get them! Kaen ordered.

Pammon leapt forward through the cave. Kaen could not see the goblins because Pammon blocked his view, but Hess could.

"Careful! Do not rush ahead!" Hess shouted, but it was too late. Pammon was already past the torch and upon the two goblins.

The goblins screamed, and both pulled back their bow and let go of the arrows.

Hess sprinted toward Pammon, but everything was happening so fast, Kaen felt he could not even react. Suddenly, the Pammon's roar echoed through the cave.

Metal arrows! I'm hurt!

"Crap!" shouted Kaen the second he heard Pammon's cry.

Pammon cried out in pain as one arrow embedded itself in his right shoulder. Another arrow missed completely, flying over Pammon's head into the cave behind him.

Pammon stumbled for a moment but stayed true to his course. When he was just a few steps from both goblins, he spouted a flame from his mouth and moved his head from right to left, igniting both goblins on fire.

Their screams reverberated through the cave. The smell of burning flesh momentarily replaced the foul stench of rot and waste.

Kaen was running toward where Pammon was struggling to walk on his injured shoulder.

"Don't rush off like that!" Hess hissed as he made it to the burning goblin bodies that lay crumpled on the floor. "Let me know if more come, but I must get that arrow out!"

Hess moved in front of Pammon and dropped to his knee. Kaen arrived shortly after and saw Hess preparing to pull the arrow out. "This is going to hurt bad! Do not move!" he said.

Pammon grunted and kept staring ahead down the tunnel.

Hess put one hand on the spot where the arrow was embedded, and the other gripped the shaft as close to the body as he could. "On three!"

"One!"

"Two!"

Pammon roared when Hess yanked the arrow out on two.

He said on three! He lied!

Kaen wanted to laugh, but he was too worried about Pammon. Hess had done that to him —more times than Kaen wanted to remember—when he'd had something stuck in him. Hess had even ripped a massive splinter out on the first count of one once.

He did that so you would not move. Now, stay still for a moment!

Do not yell at me! You told me to get them!

Kaen realized that Pammon was right. He had ordered Pammon to attack. This was his fault.

Sorry. I should have let Hess give that order. I am sorry you got hurt.

Kaen set the torch on the ground near where Hess was working.

Hess had pulled some stuff out of his pouch and spit into it to make a paste. "This will hurt a little, but you will be ok in time. Please do not rush off for now unless *I* tell you to."

Pammon nodded and then turned and glared at Kaen.

"It's my fault he did that. I told him to get them," Kaen admitted as Hess put the paste on Pammon's injury.

"I figured," Hess mumbled as he worked. "I said that out loud so both of you would know better. Now get your torch and move behind him again."

The three of them moved back into their original position. Pammon was walking with a slight limp. Kaen could feel that Pammon was trying not to limp, even though he could feel the pain somehow through their bond.

How bad does it hurt?

Bad enough. I am just glad it did not go through my wing.

That statement smacked Kaen in the chest like a mule kicking someone. Had Pammon been shot through the wing, he could not imagine how long it might take to heal an injury like that. If it even could be healed.

I will be fine. Whatever Hess used has numbed the pain some, and I can feel it healing. I think he used something special on me.

Kaen could only imagine what Hess might have used. He was still not certain where Hess had pulled all of this equipment from. Was there a secret part of the house he was not aware of?

A few more minutes passed, and they heard noises up ahead. The cave was turning to the right, and Pammon had informed him that he could not see anything yet, since the cave had turned like that.

"Cave turns. Pammon cannot see anything about thirty yards ahead where the bend is."

Hess grunted. "Be careful at the turn. Pammon, try to hug the opposite wall, and we will trade positions, so I'm on that side."

Pammon moved to the left side of the cave, and Hess moved to the right side. The cave wall would not trap Hess if something came out.

"Slowly," Hess whispered. "Protect yourself as you look."

Pammon slowly arched his head and glanced around the bend.

The cave goes on for about thirty yards, and I see a large open area. A woman appears to be tied up in the middle of the space. I can smell them. There are more in there. I can hear them too. I think there are at least three more hiding inside.

"Pammon says there is a large cave area inside. A woman is tied up in the middle, and he thinks at least three goblins are in there."

Hess let out a sigh. "Give me the hammer back, and then light the other two torches. We need to light all four and throw them in there. It will blind them for just a moment and help us to see."

Hess took the hammer from where Kaen had set it down. Kaen saw the look on Hess's face. He was concerned.

"How dangerous is this?"

Hess snorted. "If that woman were not in there, I would have probably said we need to leave and deal with the problem later. Right now, we have no choice. We could die here if things are bad enough."

Kaen felt the worry coming from Pammon.

"How much more fire does Pammon have?" Hess asked as he helped light the other torches. "We don't want to waste it when we already have a fire."

I have a little over six seconds.

"Six seconds. Maybe just a little more."

Hess nodded and kept holding the sticks together, turning them to get them to burn better. "Save it if you can, Pammon. We get the woman, and we leave. I'll deal with the rumors she might tell."

Kaen had not even thought about that. If they did manage to rescue this woman, she would see Pammon. She could tell everyone that he had a dragon! How would they keep him a secret, then?

Hess saw the worry on Kaen's face. "Do not worry about what she might see or say. If she lives, no one will believe anything she says after what they have done to her. I pray her mind is not so destroyed that it won't matter if we save her."

Hess finished lighting the last two torches and handed them to Kaen.

"Now, Pammon, lead the way. Tell us when we are close enough to throw the torches inside. Once you see them, tell Kaen which side they are on. Everyone ready?"

Pammon grunted, and Kaen nodded. Hess gripped both hammers and motioned for Pammon to lead.

Throw them! I can hear them, but I still cannot see them. I think two are off to the left, but I also think there are more than two on the right.

"He cannot see the goblins, but he thinks there are two on the left and maybe even more on the right. I'm throwing the torches now!"

Kaen had been holding two torches in each hand. Dropping one from his right, he reared back and threw it into the cavern Pammon had said was ahead. As soon as he let it go, he grabbed one from his left hand and repeated the throw, aiming a little more for the right side of the room.

Shrieks and growls erupted from the room as the torches landed on the rocky ground.

The woman Pammon had described was naked, lying on the floor and not moving.

"Throw the third!" Hess ordered Kaen. "Pammon, start to move up. I will cover the right!"

Kaen tossed the last torch, trying to get it a little farther into the room.

From what he could see, Stalagmites and stalactites were connected to each other. There were plenty of hiding spots for the goblins. They also had no idea how much farther the cave went. The room was only maybe twenty-feet tall. From what he saw, they could fit their whole house in there.

Kaen took his bow from his back, bent down, and grabbed his dropped torch. He would toss it when the time was right and then try to help support Pammon and Hess like they had talked about in the woods.

When they entered the cavern's opening, four goblins wearing leather armor and carrying shields and swords rushed them.

The worst part was the monster that came from behind them.

13

Adventuring is Ugly

"ORC!" Hess shouted as he swung at the two goblins rushing at him.

The orc was easily seven feet tall and seemed to match Hess's size and shape.

Kaen almost tripped when he saw the creature coming at them wearing a hodgepodge of leather and metal armor scraps. He carried two long curved swords that reflected the light of the torches in the room.

"Shoot him!" Hess shouted as he took out one of the goblins who had gotten close to him by blocking its attack with his hammer and crushing its chest in with a solid hit.

Kaen dropped the torch and yanked an arrow from the quiver. He kept fumbling as he tried to put the arrow on the string. His fingers were trembling.

Pammon roared and swiped his claws at the goblins, who suddenly stopped charging. Seeing a dragon standing on its back legs and swiping at them was not what they had expected. Even if they had been warned, actually seeing a bronze dragon glowing in the light of the torches was enough to give them pause. A dragon, the size of a horse, was all it took to cause one of them to run off into the cave, fleeing for its life.

The orc shouted something at it as it ran, but the goblin ignored him as it fled. Pammon took the opportunity, pounced on the lone goblin before him, and crushed it under the weight of its attack. He pinned its shield and sword arm under its two front feet and bit the head off his victim.

"SHOOT IT!" Hess shouted again as he blocked the other goblin's attack while kicking it in the chest. The goblin fell back and struggled to get up.

The orc let out a roar of his own and charged Hess, swinging both blades at him in rapid succession. Hess used his hammers and blocked the swords. It appeared as if they might be equal in power.

Kaen took a deep breath and let it out. He slipped the arrow's nock over the string and focused on the orc. This thing was half a head taller than Hess and took a wild swing at his mentor.

When Hess moved to the left to dodge the strike, it felt like time slowed as Kaen's lifestone suddenly pulsed. His body felt alive as it throbbed with power, and Kaen somehow knew when to let his fingers release the string. The arrow leaped from the bow. Even in the darkness of the cave, Kaen knew where it would impact. The arrow sped toward the orc, who was facing Hess, ignoring Kaen completely. All of that ended the moment his arrow embedded itself in the orc's left eye.

A short howl escaped the orc's mouth as its head and body spasmed before it jerked and then finally stood still. Hess wasted no time and swung both hammers at the orc, pinching its neck between the two massive heads of his weapons, causing its head to pop off.

The goblin on the ground trying to stand up was cut down when Pammon swiped at it with his claw and ripped its chest open.

Kaen stood there trying to breathe, realizing everything had happened so fast, and the fight was now over.

[Archery Skill Increased]

Kaen tried to figure out what to do. Hess was looking around the cavern.

"Pammon, go track down that goblin that ran away! Tell Kaen if you see any more!"

His dragon took off, running into the darkness of the tunnel. Kaen wanted to shout at him to stay, but he knew he had to trust Hess.

"What about me?" Kaen asked, running up to where Hess was.

"Protect me while I check on this woman," Hess said. Hess moved to the woman on the ground. He put his hand on her neck.

Kaen came to stand beside Hess, glancing around the room. Kaen was trying to keep watch in every direction, but his eyes were drawn to the carnage on the stone floor under him. Blood was everywhere, still running from the wounds Hess and Pammon inflicted on the goblins and orc.

Kaen heard a sigh and turned to see Hess shaking his head. "She is dead. They crushed her windpipe. We will take her back to camp after we clear the cave. Please ask Pammon what he has found."

Kaen knew Pammon had killed the goblin he had chased. He had felt the excitement of the hunt and the kill.

Have you found any more goblins or anything else?

I have found nothing else out here. The cave ends on this side.

"The cave ends where he is, and he killed the one that ran away," Kaen relayed as Hess walked over to the goblins and started cutting their ears off.

"Tell him to bring the body back here. We need to collect a trophy, if he did not eat the head."

Did you eat the head off again?

I did. Was I not supposed to?

Kaen chuckled and shook his head. He had no idea they would need the heads, so he could not be upset that Pammon had killed them that way.

You are fine. Hess says we should keep the heads to prove we killed goblins. Just come back.

On my way. How is the woman?

Kaen paused. He did not want to say that she was dead. The dread of that filled his heart.

She is dead, isn't she? I can feel the sadness in your heart from it.

A lump in Kaen's throat formed. He was glad that Pammon had not made him say those words. She was dead. They had been too slow.

"What were they doing with her?" Kaen asked, even though he was certain he already knew.

"You know what they were doing. She was just a toy until they were hungry enough to eat her," Hess replied with a growl.

Kaen's eyes widened as he looked down on the woman's corpse. He knew what the goblins and orc had done to her. He could not imagine how often she had been subjected to such horrible things.

"Once Pammon gets here, I need you to put away your bow and help collect the ears and that head. Get some of those blankets I see over there and wrap all this stuff in it. You will carry it outside while I carry the woman. We need to check this cave for clues."

Kaen felt the bile in his stomach rising as he thought about cutting off their ears and collecting them in those nasty blankets. He did not have much time to stand there and contemplate it before Pammon returned, dragging the headless corpse of the goblin he had killed behind him.

"Nice work, Pammon," Hess said, scratching Pammon's head. "Protect us while we loot these guys."

Pammon trilled and started flicking his head from side to side as he watched in the cave.

"Get a move on, Kaen. These torches won't last forever, and I don't want to be here without light."

Kaen nodded and put his bow up. He moved to a dead goblin and pulled out his knife. As he tugged on the ear, he was grossed out by the dirt and grime he felt on his fingers. Slicing the ear off with his knife felt like cutting through tough leather. He had never done anything like this before.

"This feels weird," Kaen mumbled as he reached for the second ear. "Why does their skin feel like this?"

Hess laughed, finished cutting the ears off two other goblins, and tossed the ears at Kaen's feet. "You will find there are far worse things you will touch and taste as you adventure. All of the quests you think are famous and amazing have an element of filth or horror. Just wait till you have to harvest eyeballs from a Crudanat. Nothing I could say to try and describe them to you right now would come close. They, however, are very powerful when it comes to alchemy."

Kaen stared at Hess in the dying torchlight and wondered if he was making that all up. Surely, nobody would need any eyeballs! He then remembered how many times Hess had already told him that people would kill to have the organs and bones of a dragon.

"Hopefully, that time is a long way away for me," Kaen said with a shudder. "You really want me to use that blanket over there?"

Hess nodded, and Kaen sighed, walked over, and grabbed a small corner of the blanket. It smelled almost as bad as the piles of crap Pammon created. The only difference was he was getting used to that smell. These were pungent and foul. When he shook the blanket, maggots, rotten flesh, and a skull with a man's face, half eaten, fell out of it.

Kaen dry heaved when some of it landed on his leg.

Pammon and Hess turned and watched as Kaen stood there choking and gagging.

"It will get worse. Much worse," Hess informed him as he collected the weapons he felt were worth keeping. "Just remember you wanted this life. This is what your dad and I never talked about. No one wants to hear stories of when nasty stuff sprays into your mouth. Leave the skull; no one wants to see that."

Kaen gave a few more gags at the thought of any of this in his mouth, before he finally stopped. Was this really what he would expect to experience as he quested? Perhaps being a Dragon Rider would not be so bad if he could avoid some of this.

After a few moments, he regained his composure and pulled the blanket to the area where the ears and weapons were collected. He spread the blanket out as best he could and tossed the ears on the edge. He then picked up the orc's head. Half of the arrow was still sticking out from where he had shot it in the eye. Kaen smiled as he remembered getting another point in archery for that shot. He could remember every detail of that one. It felt perfect as he let that arrow go.

"Stop staring at that like you are going to kiss it!" Hess shouted. "One torch is out, and the other three are fading fast! We need to hurry."

Kaen nodded and got to work getting everything on that blanket.

The only thing left for him to do was roll the blanket up and carry it. His stomach churned the whole way.

* * *

When they finally left the cave, the last torch had barely any life. The flame was hot as it was close to Hess's hand from burning so low. He had the woman across his shoulder and was upset that they had nothing to cover her up with.

Outside the cave, the sun was well overhead, and the heat of the middle of the day struck Kaen. He had not realized how much cooler the cave had been.

"Drink and eat real quick," Hess ordered, handing Kaen a water flask and some meat. "Make sure to wipe your hands off on your pants before you touch the meat, though."

Kaen splashed a little of the water onto his hands and then wiped them on his backside. He sniffed his hands before finally taking the meat and eating a few bites.

"Pammon, fly over us and make sure we are safe. I don't want to be tracked by anything as we move back to town. It will be a long trip home as we carry all of this. And before you say it, I know you are probably hungry. If you see something close on our way back, quickly kill and eat it."

Pammon let out a small thrum and moved around happily on his feet.

"Hey, his wound is healed!" Kaen said, suddenly noticing it.

"I'd hope so. The herbs I used cost a fair amount, but I knew he would heal fast with them."

"Do dragons heal faster than us?"

Hess nodded and chuckled. "You will heal faster than anyone else would generally heal. You will share in the healing that Pammon has. I only know of a few perks that being bonded to a dragon brings."

Kaen chewed his jerky and tried to think about everything he had already learned. He did not get tired like he used to when he ran. He could go almost twice as long before he had to rest. His sight was better when it came to hunting, and more. Not counting the health increase in his body and how much stronger and faster he was, he felt like he was sharing part of Pammon's wisdom and intelligence.

"Oh my gosh! I hadn't thought about that yet!"

Hess glanced up at him and waited for Kaen to finish whatever he was thinking.

Kaen smiled and turned to Hess. "I never asked Pammon what his stats are yet!"

14

A Victor's Return

Pammon
Young Dragon
HP - 1000/1000
MP - 250/250
STR - 35
CON - 35
DEX - 40
WIS - 10
INT - 15

"Wow, that is insane! Those stats are hard to believe since he is only three or four months old."

Hess nodded at Kaen and then shrugged. "I'm not sure what the stats of an adult dragon are, but I would venture he is nowhere near the power he will one day have when he gets older."

Kaen shook his head in awe at the thought of that.

Pammon, do you remember your stats when you were newly hatched?

I do not worry about those things like you do. I do not need to constantly check how strong or fast I am. I just know I am stronger.

Kaen understood that thought. Pammon had always told him he knew when he was finally strong enough to fly. He knew when he could finally make fire. He occasionally practiced it to show that he could use it longer, but Pammon did not practice his skills for the most part. They just happened naturally.

"Enough daydreaming," Hess said, interrupting Kaen's thoughts. "Give me my skin back and pick up that blanket. This is going to take an extra hour before we get back. We should make it back with an hour or two of light left, but I do not want to be in the dark out here."

Kaen sighed and nodded. He reached into his small pack, pulled out a cloth, and tied it around his face. It might not help a lot with the smell of the goblin and orc parts, but he would take anything he could as the blanket would be next to his face.

He hefted the blanket onto his shoulder. He held back the desire to gag again and was glad the cloth covered his mouth, for the moment. His eyes watered, but he blinked out the tears that came from the smell.

Hess had wrapped the woman's body carefully in a small blanket he had in his pack. He always carried one in case they needed it for the night or for another reason. With the woman over his shoulder, they set off toward town.

"Hess, is adventuring always this bad?" Kaen asked after they traveled the first hour in silence.

Shifting the woman on his shoulder, Hess sighed and bobbed his head. "You will find that adventuring can be the grandest thing and also learn that death is always possible. There is no guarantee that things will go the way anyone plans, and one small thing can lead to disaster for you, your team, or the people you might be defending," Hess replied as he walked. "Sometimes a party loses a member, and that pain is unbearable. So when this happens, we must honor them as best they can. This woman died, yet we will give her the dignity she deserves even though we do not know who she is. If you ever lose someone, make sure they are remembered for what they sacrificed so you and the others could live."

After that, there was no need to talk, turning the remaining three-hour trip into a long and quiet one.

"Mother of goblin nuts," Mayor Storven muttered when Kaen and Hess arrived at his house and laid both blankets at his feet.

A crowd had followed the two into town. Pammon had stayed back at his shack once they had gotten close to town. As they walked through the dirt roads into town, people saw them carrying the items and realized that something was up. As more noticed that they were both wearing armor and weapons, it took no time before the entire town was beside them and asking questions.

"You two really killed ten goblins and an orc?!" the mayor asked again.

Storven was staring at the ears they had cut off the goblin's heads. He knew Hess would not make up a number, even if he hadn't had ten full sets of ears. He believed every word Hess spoke because he was one of the few men in town who understood how powerful Hess was.

"We did not find any more goblins or orcs in the cave," Hess stated. His voice was sorrowful as he pointed at the woman wrapped in the blanket. "I am afraid we were too late to save her. Though I am not sure she would have wanted to be saved if I am correct in believing how she was tortured before they killed her."

"Tortured," Storven murmured as he squeezed his cane tight. "I cannot imagine her mind would have been able to come back from that."

Storven poked at the orc's head with his cane. He stared at the arrow fragment sticking out from its eye. "I guess you are the one who will claim the honor of killing the orc, Kaen?"

Kaen glanced at Storven and then at Hess, who was nodding. "I'm not sure what that entails, sir, but I guess I do."

Storven chuckled and nodded. "I know you are not an official adventurer yet, but since you are headed to Ebonmount to take the test, I will send a letter with you. After you pass the test and turn in that letter, it will help them to determine your starting rank."

Storven paused and glanced at the blanket and everything they had brought back. In his house—with its dark wood panels, a stone fireplace that ran to the ceiling, fancy couches, and a bookshelf *filled* with books—the dirty blanket and other bloody items looked very out of place.

"Son, if I am being honest, and Hess can correct me if I'm wrong, I cannot imagine they will start you at wood. I doubt they will even consider putting you as a copper rank if you do well on your test." Storven poked at the orc's skull once more. "This alone would take you to copper, but combined with the rest, and you two bringing back the corpse of the woman, they may even start you at bronze."

Kaen felt his heart beating fast. Bronze rank! He had not imagined getting to a bronze rank for at least half a year or more. He glanced at Hess, who smiled and shrugged.

"Storven is right. You did help me with this. The orc and that shot will carry a lot of weight, as they make a decision next week."

Kaen nodded and swallowed. He suddenly felt like he could use some water to drink. He took a deep breath and realized he needed a bath and clean clothes. He stank!

Storven gave a small whistle, and a woman appeared a moment later in a long maid's outfit. She looked to be in her twenties, Kaen thought as she came in, not recognizing her since this was his first time in the mayor's house. He saw her face go white at seeing the items on the floor, but she said nothing and simply bowed.

"Ella, please fetch me three small glasses of the good stuff I enjoy after a celebration."

The woman bowed again before dashing off the way she had come.

"Storven, you do not have to do that," Hess said with a wink, "but I will not turn down a glass at all."

Storven laughed and bobbed his head. “I did not doubt that you would. Come, the two of you, let’s go outside on the porch and inform the townspeople who are waiting for news of what you two have done.”

Kaen felt weird as Storven ushered him and Hess out the front door, as he joked and laughed. He had only dreamed of something like this happening. He had never really expected it to happen.

“Citizens of Minoosh, allow me to present two men you know well. Hess and Kaen!”

Applause and cheers came from a few in the crowd. Kaen could see Patrick and Cale near the middle, cheering and hollering until some adults around them told them to be quiet. People had lit torches and placed them around the courtyard. The sun was almost gone, and lights from the torches and a few small fires lit the courtyard of the mayor’s place with an eerie glow.

“You saw them approaching town earlier, outfitted in armor and weapons and carrying two packages. Allow me to end all of the rumors and set things straight.”

The crowd hushed, and everyone leaned forward to hear what Storven would say.

Storven smiled and paused. He knew how to work a crowd. These people needed a good story.

“These two men stumbled upon a trail the other week, and as you all know, Hess is an experienced adventurer. Most of you probably do not know that he is a gold-ranked one!”

The crowd erupted in cheers and applause. None of them knew that Hess was that high of an adventurer. Hess smiled and gave a slight bow toward the people cheering for him.

Storven let them cheer for a few moments before raising his hand and quieting them down. “Today, these two men found a cave and investigated it. Ten goblins and an orc were torturing a poor young woman in that cave.”

Gasps and murmurs ran through the crowd. None of them wanted to believe that there were goblins or an orc this close to their home.

“Do not worry! Hess and Kaen entered the cave and defeated those evil creatures but sadly could not reach the woman in time to save her.”

A few cheers started to rise above the crowd until the mayor announced the woman had died. People shifted uneasily, not sure how to respond now.

“We should still cheer them for their heroic deed and saving us from such a possible fate! We should especially cheer for young Kaen, who single-handedly killed the orc with an arrow through its eyes!”

With that news, the crowd erupted, and Cale and Patrick were the loudest two in the crowd. Cheering and whistling, they went on far longer than anyone else.

With his hands in the air again, Storven silenced the crowd and smiled. "These two shall leave in a few days to head to Ebonmount, where our very own Kaen will take the adventurers' test and earn his token! So tomorrow, we will celebrate these two and their heroic actions and send them off with a reminder of how much they mean to us!"

The crowd broke out in cheers again. Most cheered not because they were losing Kaen and Hess but because they would get a day off and enjoy a night of food and drink.

As the people celebrated, Ella arrived behind Storven with three small silver cups on a platter. She tapped Storven on the shoulder, and he turned and smiled.

He took a cup in each hand and gave it to Hess and Kaen. After retrieving his cup from the tray, he turned and faced the crowd again. When they saw Storven holding a glass high, they all quieted down.

"In this cup is a very rare brew. Few people in town have sampled this fine vintage over the years. It has always been a reward for something great. Tonight, Hess and Kaen will enjoy this small taste."

Storven leaned forward and winked at the crowd. "In honor of what they have done, tomorrow, all men and women over the age to be married shall get a small taste to celebrate Kaen's killing of the orc! Make sure to thank him properly tomorrow!"

The roof and the porch shook on the mayor's house. All the gathered men and women shouted so loud, that Kaen almost thought he would go deaf. He watched grown men and women hugging each other and cheering. He could see Patrick and Cale groaning and probably cursing at their inability to enjoy a taste of the drink.

"Drink up," Storven shouted over the noise as he tapped the lip of his cup to Hess's and Kaen's cups.

Hess and Storven swallowed the drink in one go and smiled as they felt it go down.

Kaen looked at the glass and saw people in the crowd watching him. He prayed that he would not spit it out like he had the alcohol Hess had given him the other night.

He brought the small cup to his lips, tilted his head back, and let all the liquid pour into the back of his throat. He expected a burn, a nasty taste, something vile like he had the other night. Instead, he was shocked as the liquid ran down his throat.

It was sweet and smooth. It left a warm sensation that seemed to travel across every inch of his tongue and throat. As it reached his stomach, the sensation spread quickly through his body. He felt light and warm all over.

Kaen turned to Hess and smiled. His face felt a little different than usual. Like his lips and cheeks did not want to work right.

Storven saw how Kaen was looking and started laughing. He quickly snagged the cup from Kaen's hand and motioned for him to sit on a chair behind him on the porch.

"Sit, boy, sit!" Storven ordered. "You should do that before your legs give out on you!"

Kaen fell back into the chair and realized his legs *were* about to give out on him. "Whaz dat drienk?" Kaen asked, his speech already slurring.

Hess and Storven roared with laughter.

"Hess, you have failed that boy," Storven declared as he shook from laughter. "You should have prepared him for what awaits him out there in the world!"

Hess nodded as he walked over to Kaen.

Kaen tried to look up at Hess, but his left eyelid was not working.

"Let's get you home, son," Hess said, picking Kaen up and slinging him over his shoulder.

"Iey cunnz wulkz," Kaen mumbled before he passed out.

15

Life Changing Plans

Kaen, wake up!

Groaning, Kaen felt his head and moaned. "I'm up, I'm up!" Kaen groaned as he tried to sit up but failed.

I know you are awake! Answer me!

"Hess, I told you I am awake. Stop shouting!"

Lying in his bed, he realized his head was pounding. What had he drunk last night?

Please don't make me come to the house and tear down your door!

Another groan escaped his mouth as Kaen realized Hess was not calling out to him.

I'm awake! Please stop shouting, Pammon, you are killing me!

What happened to you? I have been trying to call out to you for hours!

Opening his eyes as little as possible, Kaen saw that the light from outside was streaming in through the windows. It was late in the morning. He placed a hand on his chest, his fingers feeling his bare skin. Had Hess undressed him?

I drank something last night. It was alcohol, and I think it made me pass out.

Why would you drink that, then? That is not smart!

Kaen squinted and winced. When Pammon had shouted like that, it was not pleasant.

Please stop shouting. I know you are upset, and I am sorry. I am ok. How are you?

There was a momentary pause, and Kaen felt relief flowing through his bond with Pammon.

I am fine. I have been scouting the area near the cave just to make sure nothing came out again. I have seen nothing all morning. I will return near to you after I get something to eat.

Kaen almost chastised Pammon for scouting the cave but realized he was not in the position to get onto anyone for making a poor choice.

It took him a few minutes to feel like he could sit on his bed without the world spinning. Glancing around the room, he saw his clothes folded up on the floor at the end of the bed. He still could not find his armor or bow from yesterday.

Slowly and painfully, Kaen managed to get dressed. Putting on his shirt and pants was not terrible, but his boots took much longer than he expected. His mind was cloudy, and when he looked somewhere, it seemed his eyes took a moment to catch up with where he was looking.

He tsked and ran his tongue over his teeth; the taste of whatever was in his mouth was awful. From this moment, Kaen knew he was done drinking for a while. He realized how weak he was to alcohol and how anyone could have easily robbed or killed him last night had Hess not been there.

Kaen opened his door and wondered if it was always that loud when it swung open. Hess was sitting outside in his chair and smiling at Kaen.

"I was beginning to wonder if I would need to drag you out back and toss you in the well. How is your head?"

Kaen grimaced and nodded slowly. "I'm not sure who makes it hurt more. You talking now or when Pammon was shouting at me."

Hess chuckled behind his hand to muffle the noise. "Come sit. I have a drink for you that will help some. You need to eat, also. Tonight will be a long evening filled with noise, food, and drink."

Kaen staggered over to his chair and sat down. "I do not think I will be drinking tonight," Kaen muttered as he reached for the cup on the table. "I really want to know what Storven gave me last night, so I can avoid it for the rest of my life."

Hess erupted in laughter and tried to stop but could not, even when he saw Kaen's reaction to the noise. "There are many names that drink goes by," Hess said softly after he stopped laughing. "Dragon's Breath is probably one of its most well-known names, but others have called it Dwarf Piss or Elf's Milk. In the end, all that matters is that you know when drinking it, you best have a high tolerance to alcohol, or it will take you down very quickly."

Kaen nodded and lifted the cup to his mouth. As he prepared to drink it, he got a whiff of the cup's contents and felt his face turn green. "What is this?!" he said gasping, louder than he had expected, causing him to hold his head with his free hand. "It smells worse than that goblin cave."

Hess nodded and shrugged. "That is a rare combination of plants and herbs your father introduced me to long ago. It tastes worse than anything I have ever known, but it will absorb the alcohol in your body faster than you can imagine. You will dance around in less than an hour and act like your normal self."

Kaen stared at Hess and realized he was not giving the usual tell he had when he lied. With a groan, he opened his mouth and sucked down the drink as fast as possible while tipping his head back.

Gagging but swallowing the thick liquid, Kaen thought he would never finish it. As soon as he put the cup down, Hess produced another cup and motioned for him to drink it.

"More?" Kaen asked with a raspy voice. His tongue almost felt numb momentarily, and his throat tingled.

"It is water. You need to drink a lot of it. Every few minutes, you should drink a cup."

Kaen nodded and took the cup and guzzled down the water. It reactivated the taste of that horrible first cup again, causing him to gag a few more times as he finished it.

Hess had sat there snickering at him until he finished. Once Kaen had drunk it, Hess jumped up, grabbed Kaen by the arm, and pulled him to his feet. "Good. Now comes the worst part: we need to hurry outside."

Kaen was about to object until the moment his stomach suddenly clenched. He then realized it was his entire midsection. As he stood in shock from the clenching of his entire core, Hess drove him toward the back door, quickly opened it, and pushed him outside.

Kaen staggered a few steps till he stood at the edge of the porch.

Soon, Kaen was wondering what he had done to deserve the next ten minutes of his life. All he could remember was eating a few pieces of jerky yesterday. Yet somehow, he managed to throw up almost a whole bucket's worth of vile green gunk. Over and over, his stomach emptied itself. Each time, another mouthful of this never-ending stream of vomit appeared. His whole body ached, and his hair matted to his head from the sweat pouring out of every pore in his body. Hess was leaning against the back of the house the entire time, watching as Kaen thought he would surely die from bringing up his innards.

When the vomiting finally stopped as suddenly as it had started, Kaen felt a hand on his shoulder, and Hess handed him an uncorked waterskin. "Drink it and tell me how you feel."

"What the hell do you mean how I feel?!" Kaen shouted as he snatched the waterskin from Hess. "I feel like I just threw up everything I've eaten since last week! Why would you do that? My clothes are soaked, my stomach is sore, and my head is—"

Kaen momentarily paused the tirade he was launching at Hess when he realized his head did not hurt. Other than the sweat and the sore stomach from throwing up, he felt perfectly fine. Hess grinned like a fool as Kaen figured out what had happened.

"Holy crap! My head feels fine, and so do I! How did that happen?"

Hess laughed and pointed to the waterskin. "Drink that water, and do not worry. You are done throwing up. You will need plenty of water and to bathe and change. Before you do that, I recommend a trip to the outhouse just in case you need to purge from the other end. After you do all that, we will talk and prepare for tonight and tomorrow."

Kaen started to ask something, but Hess was already turning to go back inside. He lifted the waterskin to his mouth and drank and felt the cool water running down his throat. The awful taste was almost gone, but it still lingered. Had that been magic of some sort?

Standing there, Kaen drank heavily from the waterskin till he suddenly felt the pang of his bowels calling to him. As he shouted in surprise and took off, running toward the outhouse, Kaen heard laughter from inside the house. Hess obviously knew what would come next and thought it was humorous.

A while later, Kaen and Hess sat at the table as Kaen devoured a large plate of food Hess had set out for him.

"You will be fine, but remember, if you decide to drink tonight, sip it slowly and be careful. Two times now, you have experienced the dangers of alcohol, and I hope you learned your lesson last night."

Kaen nodded as he chewed on some venison and tried to wash it down with water. He was famished after the vomiting and bathroom episodes.

"I have your gear in my room with mine. Under my bed, you will find a false floor you can easily move. I'll show you the two spots in the floor to pull from simultaneously. We will leave our equipment there where it is safe."

The news of a secret hiding place excited Kaen. He could only imagine what other things Hess must have hidden down there.

"Tonight, you will need to say goodbye to your friends," Hess informed Kaen as he held up one finger. "After you do that, you must tell those two girls you have been flirting with that no matter what they offer you tonight, you are leaving tomorrow."

"What would they offer?" Kaen asked with a boyish grin. "I mean, according to the mayor, we are the only thing that stood between this town and its sure destruction."

Hess rolled his eyes and shook his head. "I know you have spent many hours with both of those girls over the last year, but I would caution you not to do anything stupid. You are about to embark on a long journey, and as the son of an adventurer, you know firsthand how difficult of a life it can be for a young child."

Kaen almost choked on the bread he was chewing as Hess said those words. Not many words would have caused him to reject the offers either girl might give him tonight, but Hess's words did. A twinge of guilt and hurt lodged in his throat as that dry piece of bread made its way down to his stomach. He would not do that to a child. He had lived that life and would not force someone else to endure that kind of loss if he could help it.

"Second," Hess said holding up another finger after seeing that his first point had struck home, "we will be leaving at first light tomorrow. We will dress for travel, and you must make sure Pammon is ready to go. I will instruct you on the path that he will take so we can avoid any eyes seeing him. Any question on that one?"

Kaen shook his head before he took a drink of water.

"Finally," Hess said holding up a third finger and grimacing. "As of tomorrow, this place will no longer be our home. I know you have made promises to your friends, and I will do what I can to help you keep them, but you cannot call this place home any longer. Once word of you having a dragon reaches far and wide, you would endanger these people we call friends by calling this place home. Do you understand?"

Kaen nodded and gently set his cup down on the table. He knew why Hess had said this, but the truth of it hit harder than he had expected. "Thank you," Kaen said, reaching a hand across the table toward Hess.

Hess looked at Kaen quizzically and shook his hand. "For what?"

"For keeping your promise to my dad and me."

Kaen looked on in shock as he saw Hess nod and a few tears roll down his cheek.

At that moment, Kaen was ready for tomorrow and the first few steps that would lead him from this town and toward the one place he had dreamed of for years.

16

A Threat to All

Kaen was packing a few things up in his room since he had time before he and Hess would head to town to prepare for tonight. A few men had stopped by earlier, and Hess had given them all the extra meat they had. Since they were leaving tomorrow, they would only take as much as they could in their packs. Anything else would have to be hunted.

Kaen felt sadness and excitement as he gazed around his small room, looking for things he needed to take. This had been his home for as long as he could remember. The years he had allowed himself to remember. The bed was not huge, and he had outgrown it in the last year, yet Hess had made sure since the day he had come to live here that he had a room of his own. Glancing at the bed made him remember he had not checked beneath it yet.

Looking under his bed for lost items, Kaen saw all the dust and cobwebs that had moved in and started reproducing at an alarming rate. It was good that Hess had not found this mess, or Kaen would not have heard the end of it.

Something reflecting under his bed caught his eye, and he crawled underneath it, wondering what it was. He had just grabbed the item, when he felt a sense of angst through his bond with Pammon before the dragon shouted.

Kaen! We have trouble!

Kaen backed out from under the bed, cursing when he smacked his head against the wood planks that kept his old mattress from falling through to the floor.

What is it? What's wrong?

Goblins and orcs are slowly moving toward the town! They are probably two or three hours away, but they found your trail from yesterday and are following it. Kaen, there are thirty goblins and three orcs!

Cursing under his breath, Kaen rose to his feet, rubbed the spot on his head that had hit the planks, and turned toward the kitchen. Glancing down, he saw a small button in his hand that he did not remember losing. Not a prize worth the bump he felt on his head.

"HESS! WE HAVE TROUBLE!" Kaen bellowed as he ran out into the main room.

Looking around, he saw Hess was not there. Kaen quickly ran out the front door and started to shout at Hess when he noticed one of the women from the bar was with Hess near the property line, and they were talking very close to each other.

"Hess! I need you now!"

Hess turned and groaned. The young woman looked frustrated as well. Kaen wished he could remember her name, but he did not know any of the women from the bar. He never went in there.

Kaen tapped his head with a finger and motioned toward the woods as Hess glared at him. Realizing what Kaen was trying to tell him from across the yard, Hess whispered something that made her laugh. She nodded and waved goodbye to Kaen and then started to leave.

Hess jogged over and saw the look on Kaen's face. "I'm scared to ask. What is it?"

"Orcs and goblins are following our trail," Kaen whispered as he watched the woman walk away. "Pammon says at least thirty goblins and three orcs are due here in a few hours. What are we going to do?"

Hess immediately ran past Kaen toward the house. "Follow me!" was all Hess shouted as he ran through the front door.

Kaen was right on his heels when Hess ran into his room. Kaen had not been here in ages but now remembered Hess's room was three times the size of Kaen's.

"Grab that end and help me lift the bed. I can do it myself, but we can do it faster together."

Kaen grabbed one corner as Hess grabbed the massive front end of the bed. Even though it was solid wood from the trees he had harvested from the forest long ago, they lifted it easily with Hess's strength and the strength Kaen now had. Both men worked silently as they moved the bed across the room. Years of moving stuff together made it so they could know which way the other would go by how they leaned.

After they set down the bed a few feet from the wall, Hess moved to the middle of the floor and pointed at two spots. Kaen realized there was not a single bit of dust or dirt under Hess's bed.

"Here and here," Hess said touching the knots in the wood of two small boards with his fingers. "Push simultaneously and watch."

Hess pressed both boards, and a click could barely be heard before a board section lifted from the floor. Kaen was momentarily mesmerized, realizing the secret he had been unaware of in Hess's house. Hess picked the section up and stood it against the wall. Hidden in the floor were stone stairs leading underneath the house.

"When did you do this?" Kaen gasped as he watched Hess descend the steps into the darkness.

"Long ago now hurry up!"

Kaen scrambled to follow Hess and had only made it five steps in before he saw that he had stopped moving. Hess tapped on a weird glass thing five times, and suddenly, it burst with light.

"A mid-level light orb," Hess informed Kaen. "They last for decades if one uses them every day. This one will last forever with how little I use it."

Kaen tried not to look shocked as Hess continued down the steps with the orb in his hand. All this time, Hess had been holding out on him! There was no telling what was down this staircase.

Twelve steps later, Kaen found himself in a room that almost matched the size of Hess's bedroom. Large rocks lined the wall, and support beams braced the ceiling above. There was even a small rock ceiling that Kaen guessed was used to keep noise and light from spilling into the house.

All along the wall were wooden chests and crates, pouches and bags, barrels, and other things he did not recognize.

Hess moved to a leather backpack, grabbed it, and tossed it to Kaen. "Get those on now! We can discuss this later, if we survive, but we must be prepared for the attack. Tell Pammon to keep you updated on their movement but to stay out of sight!"

Kaen relayed the information while he opened the backpack. In it he found the equipment his father had left him. He put the vambraces on, fumbling with them and using his teeth to tighten them. After he put the leather piece on, he realized he needed help to tighten it. "A little help?"

Hess grunted and nodded. He had already put on some chain pants and a chain vest. Far heavier and stronger armor than the leather stuff he had worn when they had gone to the cave.

Hess moved quickly, not as gentle as he had been the last time he helped Kaen dress. This time, he yanked on the leather cords and pulled the chest piece tight. He wasted no time, ensuring it was snug and tied off in the back.

"Your bow is in that corner in that barrel. Take it and the green quiver in there. Find a yellow quiver and put the arrows from it in that one," Hess stated, moving to a chest and pulling out a chain head covering. "Those arrows are higher quality ones and will fly truer."

Kaen went to the barrel Hess had pointed to, popped off the lid, and stood there in awe. He could feel something special coming from the barrel. There was no moisture or anything. It was as if the entire contents were dry and protected somehow. *Magic!* Burn Hess for hiding all of this from him.

He took his bow out, braced it, and felt the white string go tight as he secured it to both ends. He could feel it calling out to him. Finding the green quiver, he pulled it out and started to grab an arrow from the yellow quiver he saw. The moment his fingers touched the first arrow, he could tell the difference. The shaft was perfectly straight, and the feathers were in pristine condition and placement. As he pulled the arrow out all the way, he saw the four-sided tip of it was heavy but not too heavy. The whole arrow felt balanced and ready to kill.

"Stop gawking and load that quiver!"

Kaen nodded and quickly put as many arrows as he could into the green quiver without overfilling it. Soon, it was almost full. *Twenty-five of these arrows . . .* How much would these cost? Kaen wondered.

"Ready," Kaen stated as he put the lid back on and affixed the quiver onto his back.

"Almost done here. Now grab a small pouch holder from the chest two over from where you are now."

Kaen looked and saw the plain wooden chest Hess must be talking about. Opening it, he found pouches and small boxes and more. He took a pouch out, shut it, and turned to see Hess holding two small potions out to him.

"These will heal you if you need them," Hess informed him as he held them out. "Only drink them if you are truly injured. They cost more than I want to tell you, but they will save your life. Do you understand?"

Kaen nodded and carefully took the two glass vials, slipped them into his pouch, and then tied the pouch around his waist. They were brown, and even though they were glass, they felt surprisingly tough.

"Let's go. We do not have any time to waste!"

Kaen went up the stairs, Hess close behind him. The orb's light suddenly stopped glowing. Kaen turned to see Hess returning it to where he had taken it from. Once they returned to the bedroom, Hess lowered the floor and pushed on the same two spots again; another clicking noise sounded.

"Let's move the bed, and then we need to run to town. What is the time on those goblins and orcs?"

How far away is that group?

Kaen could feel Pammon thinking. It was weird that each day, it was as if he was experiencing Pammon's thoughts and desires as his own. The excitement was almost overpowering sometimes when Pammon was hunting.

Maybe an hour and a half. Two hours tops! They are moving faster now!

"They are only an hour and a half away. Pammon says they are moving faster."

Hess cursed as he and Kaen put the bed back in place. "We need to go now!"

Running toward town was not a problem, even at the speed Hess was setting. His legs felt amazing, and his lungs barely had to work to keep up with the physical demands of his body. Whenever they passed a farm or saw someone, Hess shouted that an attack was coming.

People stood momentarily frozen until Hess yelled at them again to grab any weapon they had, get their children, and join the rest of the people in town.

Soon, the entire town was leaving food and decorations wherever they were and gathering inside the center of town, holding pitchforks, clubs, hammers, scythes, and other assortments of tools. Even Patrick and Cale were there holding axes.

"LISTEN TO ME!" Hess bellowed over the clamor of calls by the people wanting to know what to do. "In an hour or thereafter, we will be set upon by thirty goblins and a few orcs! We do not have time to act like fools! We need a plan, and I need you all to listen to what I say!"

"But we are not adventurers like you and Kaen," Peter, the town's baker, cried out. "We do not know how to fight!"

Hess growled, shook his head, and pointed at Peter. "That is a lie! You have had your fair share of fights with people over the years, and you know it. You are not trained, but we do not have time to argue this. Everyone will have a weapon of some sort, and we must protect the town and the children."

Hess paused and glared across the crowd. "Anyone who desires not to fight, can flee north of the town, but know you will never be allowed back here again. You will be branded a coward and traitor, not a Minoosh resident. So, who wants to flee now?"

"You cannot make that order!" Peter shouted over the crowd, which was murmuring amongst themselves. "You are not the mayor!"

Storven strode forward and spoke up. He had been belting his sword to his hip and still had a few pieces of armor to put on. "Hess might not be the mayor, but I am. I will back his decision. Flee this town, and you forfeit everything of value you own. You may only leave with what is on your back when you go!"

Peter started to talk again but shut his mouth. He realized he was backed into a corner, and everyone in the crowd had moved away from him as much as possible. He stood alone at that moment, and he suddenly realized it.

"Now then, all of you know our safety lies with following Hess's plan, so, no matter what he says, his word is final. Do I make myself clear?"

No one spoke after Storven's last two statements. Death was not something any of them wanted, but if the town survived and they chose not to help in its survival, they would lose everything. That fate somehow seemed worse.

Hess moved closer to the crowd of people.

"Now listen, this will be difficult, but I know we can win."

17

Battle in Minoosh Part 1

Kaen lay against the roof, waiting to give the signal.

How far are they?

They are outside the town. They stopped checking the farms because of the noise coming from the people at the center. They should be entering the streets soon on those two sides.

Kaen grunted. Hess's plan seemed crazy, but he understood why it needed to happen this way. They couldn't allow any of the goblins or orcs to live, or they might return with more. Splitting up was a higher risk but needed to be done since Pammon informed them of the goblin's movements. The orcs and goblins had stopped a few miles from the farmlands and scouted. Hess said they would wait closer to dark before they attacked. Even if they did attack early, the town would be ready for it.

Kaen's mind wandered as he nocked the message arrow Hess had given him. He was so close to having a natural twenty in his archery skill. He knew once someone had reached a level of twenty, their skill improved drastically. Hess had told him years ago that the few who managed to hit thirty or forty were considered gods and could do things many would never imagine possible. Kaen wasn't sure what those skill levels provided, but he was excited to learn.

He shot the prepared arrow, its shaft covered in red paint, and embedded it in a post near a group of men. When they saw the arrow's color, the four men dashed off to relay the news to the men waiting all over the town. The attack was starting.

Music was playing, and the sounds of forced laughter and noise echoed from the town center. Lights had been lit, while women, children, and a few men pretended to enjoy themselves. Hess had ensured that everyone else who would take a role in this ambush on the goblins and orcs was hidden inside the buildings and waiting for the signal to attack.

Glancing up at the sky where the sun was almost down, Kaen wished they had more torches burning. If it got much darker, it would be harder to see.

They are slowly coming into the town. Each orc is taking ten goblins with them. You are in the middle of two groups.

Kaen watched the sky. Even with his eyesight, he could not see Pammon. He knew where Pammon was but was too far to see him. Perhaps, if he were fully grown, he could spot him then, but since he was only a youngling, he was just a speck in the sky.

Kaen glanced at the other archers on other roofs near him. There were five of them with bows. Hess had informed him most of the men were a decent shot, but none of them would come close to Kaen's skill. They would protect the women and children from behind while Kaen took out as many as he could.

A dog started barking off to the south, and suddenly a yelp sounded before it was cut off. Anger filled Kaen's chest because he knew these creatures would do that and worse to anyone they could get their claws into. He would not let anyone get hurt if he could help it.

They have left the first row of houses. Some went in, but the orcs called them out. It looks like three goblins are moving in to scout where all of the townspeople are. The others are staying behind. You should see a scout soon on your left and right.

Kaen kept his back against the roof. He was ahead of all the others by a row of houses. Beneath him, Patrick and a group of men were hiding inside the house. Cale and even more men were a few houses to his left. He knew Hess and a few other groups were spread a few streets past Cale. The thought of fighting in the city streets and the normal people of town being attacked by a group like this was hard to handle. Seeing Pammon getting hurt back at the cave had made him fearful for the rest of the town.

To your right behind the building across from you, you should see the scout soon. He is almost near you. I cannot see the other one who was near you. I think he entered a house, or he is under a porch.

Kaen sighed quietly and rose to his knee. His hands shook as his worry and fear for his friends and town overwhelmed him.

Relax, I'm here! We can do this!

Taking a deep breath, Kaen felt the confidence of Pammon through their bond, and his hands became steady. He held the bow ready to draw as he waited to see the goblin that Pammon had warned him about. Seconds ticked by slowly, and then he saw the goblin peering out around the corner of the house. It was holding a sword and shield and wore armor on its chest. Kaen knew this meant it was smarter than the other goblins he had faced outside the cave. This was one to be careful with.

The goblin saw the lights from the few streets ahead and heard the crowd's noise. The smell of meat cooking filled the air. Hess had ensured they cooked a lot of meat to help cover the scent of people hiding and waiting in the houses. Kaen could see the goblin's eyes darting across the streets before it slinked toward the next row of houses.

As the goblin moved, Kaen pulled back on the bow and saw the tip line up with where he wanted it to go. Thirty yards would have seemed difficult with his old bow, but this one easily could hit seventy. He needed to be precise.

His eyes and skill took over his hand and his breathing. He held his breath, and as the goblin slowly moved forward, the arrow's tip was where it needed to be. He let the string go.

The string made no noise that anyone, but him could hear. The arrow blew through the goblin's throat, causing it to crumple into a heap on the street. The arrow buried itself into the ground on the other side of the goblin.

Good shot! On your left, two houses down, a goblin just went under a porch! It should move again soon, but it is faster than the one you just shot.

Kaen put another arrow on the string and twisted on his foot and knee to look toward the house Pammon had mentioned. He could feel where Pammon's gaze was focused. They were both hunting the same goblin.

The goblin suddenly dashed toward the next house across the street, running with its shield and sword.

The arrow was off just a hair and struck the goblin's shoulder and not his chest as Kaen had hoped. The goblin fell to the ground with a clatter as his sword and shield fell from his hand, and he started to scream.

Kaen had already pulled another arrow out. Wasting no time, he let it go, catching the goblin in the head and dropping it as it tried to shout a warning.

Please let the music and laughter have drowned that out, Kaen thought. He glanced around to see if there was any other movement, but he saw none from either goblin.

Are the other groups moving?

No, but the last scout is on the move still. It will reach a point where it will soon see the people in the center of town near Hess's location.

Quickly, Kaen pounded on the roof with his foot three times. Patrick came outside to the street and glanced at Kaen.

"Two goblins are dead. We need to move them now," Kaen ordered as quietly as he could. He pointed toward the goblin scouts he had taken out.

Patrick nodded and went inside, and four men soon ran out in pairs of two, each pair headed to gather the goblin's corpse.

Loud screaming could be heard from the northern part of town.

It looks like the goblin saw someone. They have killed it, but the orc and the goblins on that side are now starting to come into town. It looks like the other two groups are moving as well! They will be on you all in a minute!

Keep me updated!

Joy and happiness flooded through their link. Pammon was glad to know Kaen thought so highly of him.

Kaen tapped the roof two times, paused for two seconds, and then tapped it two more times, signaling to the men inside that the goblins and orcs were coming.

Kaen took a deep breath and then let it out slowly. Things were going to get ugly in the next minute, and he knew that people would possibly die. He could almost feel his dad with him at that moment. Wearing the armor and holding the bow his father had left for him seemed to calm his nerves.

The right side, maybe twenty seconds out, are four between the building closest to you. Three more on the other side of that building. The orc and the last two are moving slower and have not picked a path yet.

Kaen wished he could tell Patrick and the men inside where the goblins would appear, but he would have to do what he could to help with the horde that was about to crash upon them.

The odds were not good, even with almost fifty men scattered around the town. Goblins were skilled fighters, and these men were not. Kaen remembered the first time he had to fight and how he had frozen. Freezing here would mean injury or death.

Movement came from where he had shot the first goblin scout. One of the goblins ran into the street and tugged on the arrow Kaen had used to kill the first scout. The men had either missed it or forgotten to pull it!

The goblin called to his two friends, and one of them stepped out to look at the arrow.

Kaen knew it was now or never and drew back the bow and let it fly. He could now see the spot he wanted to hit, as if it was ten yards closer. Kaen felt that while their necks were neither large nor wide, he could somehow reach out and touch them with his hand.

I can do this! All that practice paid off, Kaen thought as he let the arrow go. The bow was gifting him with a major bonus to his stats.

The second goblin was knocked to his side and fell as the arrow shredded his spinal cord. The shot had been off just a hair, but it had actually worked better that way.

Kaen again wasted no time pulling and letting go of a second arrow as the first goblin stood, momentarily confused at what had happened. His lifestone pulsed, and he felt it somehow take over his next shot. This time, the arrow struck true and ripped through the goblin's leather chest piece and went straight through its heart and into the ground behind it. The goblin jumped up a few inches before falling dead.

A heart shot!

[Archery Skill Increased]

Kaen wanted to celebrate but knew he did not have time for it. The arrow he was drawing now felt smoother and faster. He knew he had hit twenty naturally, and he could feel the power of the lifestone and his skill, allowing him to see better and farther. He could feel the wind across his cheek and hair and knew how much it would impact his next shot.

The third goblin in that group started screaming, and the group hidden by the edge of his building made a loud shouting noise.

They are coming toward your building!

Kaen popped up and moved quickly to the edge of the building and risked a glance. He saw a goblin with a bow aimed in his direction and whipped his head back as an arrow flew by, missing him by just a few inches.

"Goblin shite!"

Kaen looked again and saw the goblin reaching for another arrow.

Smiling, Kaen released the arrow he had ready and watched as it ripped through the goblin's left shoulder, pinning him to the side of the wooden building.

It shrieked and yelled as it found itself stuck to the building and unable to move.

Another arrow found its mark in its chest, pinning it solidly to the wall and ending its struggles.

Underneath him, Kaen heard screaming and shouting. The goblins found themselves being attacked by the townspeople who had hidden in the building. None of them were gifted warriors, but the blacksmith was with them, and he was hefting a huge two-handed hammer.

Kaen could not see what was taking place on the porch beneath him.

Your left! Quickly!

Spinning on his feet, Kaen dashed across the roof and saw the pack of nine goblins moving with the orc behind them. The men had come out earlier than they should have, giving up ground as they were pressed from the front.

Two sprinting goblins were seconds away from attacking someone falling to the ground.

Kaen cried out when he saw it was Cale.

18

Battle in Minoosh Part 2

Cale lay on the ground, moving slowly as if dazed. His axe lay on the ground just past his reach. There was not enough time to shoot one goblin and then the other. For a brief moment, Kaen realized he could not save his friend. His hands shook again uncontrollably, knowing his friend would die and there was nothing he could do about it. He felt frozen in place. Suddenly, his lifestone roared to life, surging in his chest in a way it had never done before.

[Archery Skill Twinshot - Available]

Kaen let his hands move on their own as he grabbed two arrows and felt his hands knock both. His lifestone and his body were in unity. Knowledge and power surged and flowed through him as he lifted the bow to his face and saw the angles, knowing they would strike true.

The string rushed forward, and the arrows loosed at their targets.

Both goblins had been running at Cale as he held up his hands, preparing to be butchered by their swords. Just two steps before their swords would slice his arms off and most likely kill him in the next second, an arrow struck each goblin in the head, sending both tumbling to the left and away from Cale.

Kaen almost cheered, but he saw Cale was still frozen on the ground. More goblins would be on him in a moment.

"MOVE, CALE!" Kaen shouted as he drew another arrow and struck a goblin in the leg, causing it to pitch forward and fall to the ground. The man who had been fighting it wasted no time, bashing the goblin in the head with a club before looking around to see who he could help.

Cale crawled backward on the ground a few feet before he stood and turned to see Kaen on the roof. Kaen could see him smiling through the tears on his face.

Cale had just started to wave when an arrow struck his shoulder and knocked him to the ground. Unable to groan, let alone do anything to help Cale, Kaen knew he had to find out who had done this to Cale.

Kaen turned and saw a goblin archer. He could barely see him, as the roof was blocking his sight. Taking a quick breath, Kaen moved over the ridge of the roof and let an arrow go as he slid down along the side of the roof.

The arrow struck the archer in the shoulder, causing it to tumble and fall backward. The force of the shot allowed it to move behind a building, preventing Kaen from finishing it off.

To your right! The orc and his two are coming!

Kaen had forgotten about Pammon but could now feel where the three creatures would appear. He could sense them moving on the other side of the building as Pammon tracked them from high above.

Kaen moved back to the other side of the roof to protect him from any archer he might not be aware of and to hopefully give him an element of surprise. The sounds of battle raged underneath and to the north of him.

Two goblins who were different from the others, came striding from behind a house. One carried a staff and looked to be in a robe. The other had some weird bone wand or something. Kaen knew these were not the usual goblins he had seen, so he tried to activate the skill he had used a few moments ago.

[Archery Skill Twinshot - unavailable - 120-second cooldown - 83 seconds remaining]

Had so little time passed since the first time he'd used it? Time felt like it was zooming by, but he now realized it was not.

Which one should I aim for?

The one on the left carries bones for a weapon. That cannot be good.

Kaen nodded as he drew an arrow and aimed at the one on the left. He wanted to aim for the orc decked out in chain armor and a helmet. Its shield was also massive, and in its other hand, the orc was carrying what could only be described as a huge meat cleaver.

Kaen's shot struck true, and the goblin carrying the bone thing in his hand stumbled as the arrow tore through its gut.

The orc roared, looked in Kaen's direction, and saw him on the roof. He moved and blocked Kaen with his shield and body. The other goblin ran behind him, and Kaen wondered why the orc was standing there, not moving, just keeping his eyes on Kaen and holding his shield the way he was.

The one with the staff is healing the other one! I told you to attack the wrong one!

The panic of that decision filled Kaen's mind as he considered his options. He did not know how long it took to heal an injury like that, but he also knew he could not get past the orc's defenses while it was aware of him.

"PATRICK! How goes it below?!" he shouted as he moved out of view and to the edge of the room.

"The three goblins are dead, and one of the men is pretty badly injured!" Patrick shouted from underneath. "What should we do?"

Kaen thought momentarily and knew one goblin was still missing from the original group. Staying here was not safe, especially with that orc approaching.

"Move to help the group on the left. We need to defeat them before we get pinched! I'll deal with the healer!"

Kaen heard the gasps from underneath as the men shuffled and moved to get to the group to the left of them.

Kaen jumped down from the roof and rolled once before standing and looking around the street. He saw the blood from the fight that had happened on the porch of the house he had been on top of. Three goblin bodies were smashed and hacked to bits by the men and the everyday tools they knew how to use.

"Go now!" Kaen ordered the men as he ran to the house across the street.

Slinging his bow over his back, he leaped up, grabbed the ledge of a nearby roof, and easily swung himself up and onto it. It was still hard to believe how high he could leap and how easily he could lift things that had once been difficult. He was thankful every day for something else about his bonding with Pammon.

Hurry! Two goblins are pressing toward your friend.

Kaen stood up, pulled his bow off his back, and turned to see two goblins about seven yards from Cale and about two yards from another man from town.

[Archery Skill Twinshot - unavailable - 120-second cooldown - 13 seconds remaining]

Kaen winced and pulled out a single arrow and let it fly. It pierced through the armpit of the closest goblin and knocked it to the ground. As he pulled another arrow and aimed, the other goblin leapt for the man on the ground, who was not moving. Kaen aimed and watched as the arrow struck the goblin in the hip. It bounced off his hip bone and caused the goblin to scream in pain as it fell, pitching forward and skewing the townsman with its sword.

Wincing, Kaen saw the sword pierce the man and saw him shudder for a moment before going still.

Behind you!

Rolling along the roof, Kaen felt something hot slam into the roof where he had been standing a moment earlier. The roof caught on fire as Kaen rolled over the peak and onto the other side of the roof. He could still feel the heat of whatever had come toward him.

The magic-user sent fire after you! Your roof is on fire; you need to move!

There was no time to move to a different roof, and Kaen knew it. He had to use this moment to strike and strike fast.

Watch the two goblins near the orc. Tell me when he is not in my way!

Kaen moved back a little from the roof's peak and prepared himself for the moment Pammon informed him the massive orc was not protecting the two goblins. He could feel that twin-shot was ready and did not want to waste it on normal goblins. He had to take out these two simultaneously, or else he might never get another chance.

It felt like an eternity as he waited for Pammon to tell him to move. The sounds of battle near where Patrick and Cale were getting louder.

How much longer till I can attack them? The longer I wait, the more people who might die!

If you are that worried, I can join the battle. Otherwise, trust me. It will be in a moment. They are going to pass by you soon.

Kaen stayed perfectly still when Pammon told him that. He could feel the three of them walking past him as his dragon surveyed them from the sky.

Now!

Kaen popped up. His lifestone was surging with power like never before. In all his life, it had never acted like this before. It took over again as he stood above the peak in the roof. The orc held his shield before him and scanned the street as the two goblins walked slowly behind him. Kaen watched in horror as the goblin with the bone wand thrust out his hand to blast Henry, the miller's son, with a gout of hungry flame. The flame covered Henry's body in an instant; he was already dead. But he didn't know that. He screamed and writhed on the ground while his comrades could do nothing but watch helplessly. Patrick and the men froze momentarily as they watched Henry die, before they turned, running away in fear.

Both arrows leapt from the bow, and each struck the goblins in the temple, causing them both to crumble to the ground.

The orc heard the noise and turned and saw Kaen aiming his bow at him.

"KILL THE ORC!" Kaen shouted at the men who had started to flee. "I will draw his focus!"

Patrick and two other men stopped running and turned around. They saw Kaen walking along the top of the roof, holding his bow and the orc holding his shield over most of his body toward Kaen.

Patrick motioned to the two men, who nodded and charged the orc. Patrick and another man had an axe, and the third man had a pitchfork. As the three ran up behind the orc, Kaen feinted as if he was going to shoot. The orc lifted his shield to block most of his face.

The man with the pitchfork dashed forward and speared the orc's right hamstring where no mail covered its massive leg. A roar erupted from its mouth as it stumbled forward from the injury. The other man drew close and swung his axe at the same leg, but the orc blocked it with his cleaver, unaware that Patrick was launching an attack on his other leg.

All those hours lifting rocks and swinging a pickaxe had caused Patrick to be strong enough for this moment, even if he did not have a lifestone. Patrick swung that axe and struck the backside of the orc's left knee; the axe sliced all the way through it.

The orc bellowed in pain and fell to the ground, and as it fell, its shield slid to the side.

"Perfect," Kaen whispered. His lifestone was pulsing again as he let the arrow go. Its eyes closed in pain, the orc never saw the arrow coming and stumbled to the ground. The arrow flew through his closed eyelid and lodged itself in its skull, causing the orc to jerk and then fall down dead.

[Archery Skill Increased]

Kaen moved over the ridge of the roof and looked down at the battle taking place before him.

Patrick and the other two men cheered Kaen as they looked at the orc dead on the ground. They glanced up at Kaen and saw him point behind them.

"It's not over! Let's do it again!"

The men nodded and turned and found that where Cale was, the battle was not going in their favor.

"Get Cale out of here!" Kaen ordered as he leaped off the roof and dashed to the one closest to the battle. He needed to get right over them and use the height to his advantage.

Careful, the orc there has a bow!

Kaen cursed as he saw one of the other men from town get struck down by an arrow fired from where the orc must be. The arrow looked like a small spear compared to the arrows he used.

"I'll cover you!" Kaen was scrambling on the road, letting Pammon lead him to a roof across the street.

Two goblins under you on the left, and two more have moved off to the north toward Hess. His team has almost defeated all of them. Just one goblin and one orc left.

Kaen grabbed his bow, nocked an arrow, and reached out to Pammon.

Tell me when it is safe to shoot.

Ten seconds passed before Pammon spoke.

Now, take a shot at the orc. He is occupied, waiting for his goblins to move.

Rising over the ridge, Kaen saw the orc and let the string go, watching as the arrow sped toward it. As it flew at the orc, Kaen realized that the orc had launched its own arrow at him when he'd popped up. He tried to dodge but could not and felt the pain of a massive arrow pierce his lung and knock him back.

The arrow was the only thing that prevented him from rolling off the roof, hurting him even worse when it slammed into the roof and forced itself through his back.

I'm going to die.

19

Battle in Minoosh Part 3

Kaen! I'm coming!

Blood dripped down the arrow's shaft , and Kaen felt himself choking on blood. His whole body shivered when he tried to sit up and take pressure off the arrow that was sticking through his chest and back.

No! If you come, we will both die!

Kaen tried to think. He needed to do something. He then remembered the potions in his pouch. He reached for the pouch with trembling fingers. As he grabbed a potion and pulled it from the pouch, pain shot through his body from moving his arm. His shaking fingers fumbled the potion, and he watched it roll down and then off the roof.

Groaning, Kaen realized he had to do something fast, or he would die, and Pammon would die also.

Kaen took out his hunting knife. His whole body shook as he glanced over his right shoulder and saw the one-inch-thick shaft sticking out his back. The head of the arrow was huge, and he knew what he must do.

With his left hand, he started hacking at the shaft.

Lights. Bright lights flooded his eyes when he hit the shaft with his knife. The force of it banging in his body throbbed all over.

I will come! Let me help!

Kaen could feel Pammon and the fear and angst in his mind.

No! It is too dangerous if you come! The people would attack you as well!

Pammon was frantic, and Kaen could feel it. There was a deep fear in his mind. Suddenly Pammon's feelings changed completely, a peace coming over him.

I will give you my strength, but I must land. Use it to do what you must.

Kaen wanted to ask what that meant, but right after Pammon said those things, Kaen felt power and energy flowing through him. Even with the pain he was experiencing and the blood he was coughing up, Kaen felt alive.

He gripped the hilt of his knife and hacked at the shaft again.

It hurt just as bad, but he was now able to overcome the pain. He was able to endure it.

The shaft snapped, and Kaen gave a sigh of relief. He could sense Pammon falling fast toward the ground. He was not sure if he was falling from the loss of the life force Pammon was sharing with him or if it was a controlled fall.

With the tip of the arrow cut off, Kaen dropped his knife, grabbed the shaft, and started pulling it out through his chest.

A cough rose as he pulled on that shaft, wracking him with pain.

I am enough. Be strong!

Kaen nodded. He felt the strength Pammon was giving, surge again. It would be enough.

With a roar and a grunt, Kaen grabbed the arrow's shaft and yanked it free. Blood spurt from his chest and ran down his back, between his leather jerkin and his body.

Wasting no time, he reached into the pouch and pulled out the last potion Hess had given him. He broke the seal on top, put the drink to his lips, and let the liquid pour into his mouth. The taste was like warm dirt or some other earthy taste. The moment it ran down his throat and hit his stomach, he started to shudder.

He could feel the hole and torn skin of his body begin to close. He wanted to shout and scream from the pain, but for some reason, no words would come from his mouth. Instead, he screamed in silence. He screamed in his mind.

You are safe!

Pammon was on the ground in the woods outside of town to the west. He was hurting. Kaen could feel it.

Pammon! Are you ok? How are you hurt?

I'm not sure. It is not an injury but from giving you my life force. I just knew that you needed my strength. I did not know what it would do.

There, kneeling on that roof, Kaen felt the spot where the arrow had punctured his chest. It was completely closed and healed, and he felt amazing. Kaen wondered how he could ever repay Pammon for what he had done for him.

You're welcome.

But I never said thank you. How did you know?

A peal of laughter came across the bond.

You forget I can read you. I can feel what you are feeling and know what is in your mind. I know you would do the same for me.

Pammon was right. If Kaen could give his life for Pammon, he would, in a heartbeat.

Now go finish that orc! He was wounded too.

Bounding to his feet, Kaen grabbed his bow and reached back for an arrow. The quiver was almost empty.

Five. Five arrows left.

He had no idea how many more were alive, but he knew Hess would soon be here to help. There was no time to waste, and he needed to help save his town.

Peering over the peak of the house, Kaen saw the orc kneeling on the ground. His right arm was across his body, and his right hand was near his artery. The arrow had missed the middle of his throat but had pierced his neck and cut the artery. Blood was spurting slowly out of his fingers and under his hand.

Kaen let go of the arrow and struck the orc in the same spot, pinning his hand to his neck. A roar erupted from him, and the orc struggled to stand but failed, landing face first in the dirt. Kaen was not sure how much blood it had lost, but as it kneeled on its left hand in the dirt, Kaen shot another arrow, striking the orc in the spinal cord. It fell to the ground, and the arrow that had barely been sticking out of its neck was thrust forward, tearing the flesh and skin open. Blood gushed from its neck as it lay in the street.

Is this what it is going to be like? Kaen wondered as he moved to the left of the roof. *So much death, and I have not even gotten my adventurer token yet.*

Leaning over the roof's edge, Kaen saw the last two goblins, who were both wounded. They saw that their leader had been taken out, and they were facing the two men who had helped Patrick with the orc and another man from Cale's party. They looked unsure if they could win and were slowly backing up.

Three arrows left. Using them meant those three men would be safe for now. Not using them might mean they could still get injured or killed.

There was no hesitation once Kaen realized he could save two more people so easily. Each goblin fell from the arrow he shot at them, and he saw the group of men collectively sigh before cheering and thanking him. Kaen nodded, moved to the roof's edge, and dropped off it.

He needed to check on Cale, who Patrick had dragged to the side of the street. He could hear the groaning and knew the arrow was most likely still in him.

"How is he?" Kaen asked after he'd arrived and stood behind Patrick.

Patrick turned to Kaen, and Kaen saw the concern that covered Patrick's face.

"It's bad, Kaen. His whole shoulder is destroyed."

Kaen bent down and saw that Cale was a pale white color. He had lost a lot of blood, and Patrick had been correct in his concern. The arrow's shaft had blown through the socket and destroyed it completely. Blood was seeping out past the wooden shaft, and Cale was shivering from the blood loss.

"I'm so . . . sorry, Kaen . . . I . . . I tried," Cale said, his teeth rattling from the cold he was feeling.

"Don't give up yet!" Kaen ordered Cale as he tapped his friend's leg. "I'll be right back!"

Kaen sprinted over to the house that he had been on.

"Please do not be broken," Kaen thought as he looked for the glass potion that had dropped and rolled off the roof. The sun had gone down now, and it was dark, the only light coming from torches, but his eyes seemed not to be as affected as the others around him were. Glancing through the dirt, dust, and a few weeds along the house, he saw a small reflection in the green and brown weeds.

Moving to it and bending down, he saw the vial had indeed busted open, and over half of the liquid was gone. Carefully, Kaen picked up the vial and carried the remaining liquid back to where Cale was, praying there would still be enough to help his friend survive his injury.

When he got back, he set the broken vial on the ground a few feet away and motioned for Patrick to help. "Hold him, I'm going to cut the tip off, and we are going pull this arrow out. Once I do that, I'll have to pour what is left of this drink into his mouth. I'm not sure if it will save him, but we have no other option."

Patrick nodded, and Kaen saw the brief look of hope on his friend's face.

"Cale! Look at me, Cale!" Kaen shouted as he watched his friend's eyes start to close.

Cale was struggling to focus on him. "I am going to save you, but I need you to stay with me! Now brace yourself!"

Patrick moved behind Cale and helped support his back by bracing Cale's body with his knee and arm. Kaen thought cutting the feather side off and pulling through the back would be best. "Here it comes!"

Kaen held his knife and grasped the end of the arrow shaft in his hand. He focused with his mind on one point as he swung his knife down on the shaft and cut it cleanly in half with only a little jerk from the contact and force.

Cale groaned and whined as the force of the arrow getting hit rocked his shoulder joint.

Kaen grabbed the vial and lifted it to Cale, who was mumbling.

"Drink this! After you drink this, I will pull the arrow out, but you cannot waste a drop!"

Holding Cale's head back, Kaen poured the remaining liquid from the vial into his friend's mouth and watched as he swallowed it. The second he saw Cale's throat force the liquid down, Kaen let his head go and pulled the arrow through his shoulder and back.

Cale opened his mouth to scream, but no words came from his mouth. Moments passed, Cale screamed silently for a bit, and Kaen saw Cale's shoulder moving under the skin. The hole was closing slowly, but it was closing.

"Watch him and keep him safe!" Kaen told Patrick as he stood up and turned back to face the fight that had been around them just a few minutes ago.

He saw the men standing behind him a few yards, glancing around, keeping an eye out for any other goblins who might still come.

"A few goblins are still missing. You three watch these two and keep them safe while I try to find the two I know were part of this group."

The men nodded and shifted closer to Patrick and Cale, holding their axes and pitchfork out in different directions.

Kaen ran toward the two goblins he had killed last and bent down. They smelled as awful as he had remembered from the cave. He pulled one arrow from one of them and found it was unusable; the feathers were rubbed wrong from passing through its body and scraping against bones and armor. The other goblin had an arrow that would still work, hopefully, as no real damage was done to it.

He felt better with two arrows now in his quiver as he climbed onto the roof across from the building on which he had defeated the orc and these two goblins.

Pammon, how are you feeling now?

Pammon snickered through the link.

I am still weak, but I am fine. I think I feel this way because I am still young. I believe when I am older, it will not impact me as much as it did this time.

Swinging himself onto the roof, Kaen nodded, wondering about that. There was still so much about a dragon and this bond that he did not know or understand. As much as he did not want to be known as a Dragon Rider right now, he realized how much he and Pammon could learn if they met with one and learned from them.

Putting those thoughts out of his head for a moment, Kaen scouted the streets, trying to find movement. He could see nothing, even with his vision. The noise he heard from the north sounded more like men celebrating than fighting. He wished Pammon was able to fly; he had not really appreciated until now how helpful it was for him to be able to tell Kaen where their enemies were.

Glancing at the house to the left of him, Kaen saw that he could manage the distance and dashed forward and jumped over the six-foot gap between buildings. A few tiles broke free from the roof as he landed, and he skidded as he got his feet and balance under control.

Where are these last two goblins? Kaen wondered as he looked from all sides of the house. Could they have fled?

Kneeling on the edge of the roof, Kaen looked intently at the ground below him.

His eyes saw what he was looking for.

Tracks!

20

Battle in Minoosh Part 4

[Tracking Skill Increased]

A smirk crossed Kaen's face when he saw that notification. He could now see the small indention of their steps on the dirt without having to search as hard.

From the looks of the tracks, the goblins had gone north and were moving between buildings. There was no way he could leap to the next house across the street, and Kaen knew he would have to give up the tactical advantage and safety of the roof if he was going to find these two goblins.

Without hesitating, Kaen dropped from the roof and landed silently on the dirt street. Nocking an arrow on the bow, he followed the tracks in the dirt and did his best to watch for any movement of his prey.

Dark shadows covered the houses as he hugged buildings and listened for noise around him. These goblins must have been smarter; they had not run into the battle like the others. Had the orc sent them to assist elsewhere, or had they run off on their own?

The goblins had now moved two streets over and up. They would soon be where Hess and his group had been.

Kaen glanced down and saw that the tracks split up at the next street.

Crap, which one to follow? Kaen wondered. One had gone toward the edge of the town. There was only one more row of houses left in the village behind this one, before it turned into farms and woods.

He could feel the rough wood siding of the house against his shoulder as he pressed against it, trying to stay in the shadows while he considered his options. Glancing at the roof above him, Kaen tried to decide if it was worth going on the roof in the hopes of seeing something. It would take a little while, but every second spent doing nothing meant the two goblins were most likely moving closer to their end goal.

Time was ticking, and Kaen chose to track the one moving toward Hess and his group. It would be best if he could meet up with Hess; this goblin presented the best opportunity for that.

Dashing across the small gap between houses, Kaen followed the trail and suddenly realized he was at crazy Mrs. Kelsteer's house. He saw the tracks go across her section of the street and groaned. The woman had brought in pea gravel and covered her yard and street section, claiming it made it prettier and helped keep the mud down in the rainy season.

What it did now was create a crunching noise every time someone walked on it. Kaen glanced at the goblin's trail and saw it went across her yard. Taking a quick breath, he double-checked the arrow on his string and slowly walked in the goblin tracks. Doing so minimized the sound his steps made on those stupid little stones. Halfway across the twenty-yard section of gravel, he saw movement up ahead at the next house.

Kaen prepared to draw his bow and focused on the spot where he had seen movement. The goblin kept popping out around the corner of the house before retreating behind the edge.

What the hell is the goblin looking at?

Something was itching in the back of his mind.

Crunch.

Kaen spun around and saw a goblin coming at him, a rusted dagger in each hand. Apparently, the goblins realized they were being followed and had turned the tables on him. He was now the prey!

It would not be a full draw of the bow, as the goblin was only five yards away now, quickly covering the distance between them.

Releasing the string sent the arrow into the goblin's lungs, but the goblin's momentum was too much, and it crashed into Kaen. They tumbled, skidding along the ground in the pea gravel. The goblin howled in pain. It had dropped one dagger and was trying to stick the other into Kaen's face.

His bow was the only thing keeping the dagger away. Kaen used the wood to press the goblin away as it snapped at him with its teeth and attempted to stab him. Kaen grabbed the arrow's shaft that was embedded in the goblin's chest and started moving it around and twisting it. The goblin screeched in pain and thrashed around. The moment it sat up to get a better position to drive its dagger down at Kaen, it made a mistake it was unaware of.

Kaen yanked the arrow's shaft from the goblin's chest and plunged it up through its throat and into its jaw. The goblin went slack on the arrow, and Kaen kicked the goblin to the side, starting to sit up when he heard the familiar sound of the pea gravel crunching behind him.

The other goblin was running at him from behind, and there was no way he would be untangled from the goblin he'd just killed and prepared for that charge in time.

His lifestone and his archery skill called out to him. He had one arrow left. His body shook, knowing life and death would be decided here.

Giving into the lifestone and the power of it, Kaen let it and the skill take over. He remembered trying to shoot from different positions as Hess had trained him all these past months. Standing, kneeling, running, jumping, and lying down.

He leaned back, and his right hand drew the arrow from his quiver as his back touched the ground. The arrow's bloody shaft fell perfectly into his fingers, and the arrow's nock seemed to place itself against the string. His right arm drew back on the string with a power that came from every part of his body, as his left arm pressed the bow over his head. He looked at the goblin who was just four steps away from him.

Kaen could see the shock in the goblin's eyes as it came at him with a sword raised above his head. A smile flashed across Kaen's face as he let the string go, and he watched the arrow impact the goblin's eye, jerking its body back and off the ground. It was flung off its feet, and then thudded into the gravel.

Kaen lay there, gasping for air. His body hurt, but he felt his lifestone pulsing in his chest. He had never felt it act like that before today. Hess had mentioned years ago that a lifestone had power most would never unlock until they were on the very edge of death. Had this been what he was talking about?

With no time to waste, Kaen freed himself from the two goblins beside him and checked both arrows. Neither was salvageable. With a sigh, Kaen put his bow on his back and picked up the goblin's sword. He was not proficient with it, but he had trained with a wooden one several times against Hess. It was better than nothing.

I cannot wait for the day I can ride on your back as you fly. City battles on the street with no one defending an archer are not good.

I cannot wait either. Then, we will not have to hide my presence. Soon, I will be strong enough for small flights together.

A smile broke across Kaen's face as he ran toward the part of town Hess should be in. He moved quickly, sticking to the shadows. Being out there alone when the sun was down was not the best plan for an archer with no arrows.

The townspeople were cheering despite losing four men who had defended the town. Thanks to Hess and his healing herbs, four more who had gotten hurt were on the mend. One would have a limp for a long time, and the other three would recover with some rest.

Hess had checked out Cale and broken the bad news to him. His shoulder would never work right again. The potion had done enough to close the wound and remove any infection, but his bones had fused together. The joint was gone, and there would be no way to fix it.

"I'm sorry, son," Hess consoled Cale as he watched the young boy struggle with the news. "The truth is, had Kaen not given you the little bit of potion he had, you would not be alive. That might not seem like much now, but hold on to what you mean to him and the others. Find joy in life."

Hess motioned to the families mourning the loss of their husbands and fathers. "There are far worse things than losing one's arm."

Cale gazed at the family of the man he had fought alongside. The man had a farm on the north side of town. For whatever reason, he could not remember his name right now, but the man had saved him twice in that first skirmish that broke out on the street.

"I'll try to remember that," Cale replied and sighed as he glanced up at Kaen. "Thank you for doing what you did."

Kaen nodded and smiled at Cale. It broke his heart knowing his friend would be disabled like that. He would ask Hess when they were alone if there was any way to help fix that. If he could find the money to pay for it, he would.

The planned town celebration now struggled to find the joy they had initially expected. Thirty goblins and three orcs had been killed, numbers that would bring the town fame and prosperity. The fact that only four people had died was a major cause for celebration. They had spread out all the men and teen boys around the town, with the majority of experienced men staying with Hess and Kaen. The townsfolk had been amazed at how Hess's strategy had preempted the orcs' advances, and nobody could understand how he appeared to know the enemy's every movement.

The truth that Kaen and Hess had a dragon in the sky, relaying information about how the enemy traveled, was not something the town was privy to. Kaen struggled to accept all the honor and praise people gave him. He had defeated two orcs on his own and had over sixteen solo goblin kills.

No one would let him give credit to Patrick and the two men who had attacked the armor-covered orc. Patrick had commented to multiple people that it was Kaen who had held the orc's attention and allowed them to attack it from behind, and that had Kaen not been there, they would have all been butchered.

Hess tried to cheer Kaen up as the people came by and gave their thanks. "Smile and be gracious. Being an adventurer means we sometimes put aside how we feel and celebrate the victory because these people need us to. They would be dead if it were not for you and me, and they know it. Yes, losing the men of this town hurt, but we will not forget them. Storven has already told me he is going to build a small monument in this town for them and us. Every time a townsperson passes it, they will be reminded of the sacrifice. He will also receive aid from the adventurers' guild to help the families who lost someone. It will help them for years to come."

Kaen listened to Hess, smiled as people came by and shook his hand or bowed slightly to him. He saw Mrs. Kelsteer behind a few of them, making her way toward him. The words Hess had spoken to him the other day echoed in his mind.

"Mrs. Kelsteer!" Kaen cried out even though she was about four people back.

The woman's face brightened in the light of all the torches surrounding their area. "I am so grateful for the pea gravel you have in front of your house! Had it not been for those tiny rocks, I would surely have died! Thank you for saving me!" Kaen proclaimed loudly as he gave a small bow toward her.

Mrs. Kelsteer grinned from ear to ear, and some people around her patted her on the back and thanked her for helping keep Kaen alive.

Hess chuckled and leaned toward Kaen. "You learn quick," Hess whispered. "She will become a hero for what you just said."

Kaen nodded and smiled while he fought back the tears that, for some reason, wanted to flow. He did not feel like a hero, but he was glad someone else could enjoy that title for a while.

21

Leaving Home

Are you ok? I can feel how sad you are.

A tear escaped, and Kaen quickly wiped it away as Hess walked on the road leading north out of town and toward Ebonmount. Saying goodbye to Cale and Patrick had been harder than he had expected. They had been his friends for most of his life, and he would be gone for at least a year or two.

He knew Cale had tried to put up a good front, but he could see the hurt behind his eyes. Being crippled like that left him with a hurt that would take a long time to heal. Sure, the mayor proclaimed him a warrior who fought through the pain and gave up so much for the town and its people. The truth of battles and fights Hess had tried to warn and teach him about etched itself on his raw heart.

Just because a town survived did not mean carrying the scars from the battle was easier to wear. Four men had died, their families were suffering, and it would be another few days before they were buried. Other men would limp for the rest of their lives or swing an axe or pickaxe slower because of the wounds they received. Cale would never have the life he had before. Every day, he would be unable to use his arm, and now all he had known had been ripped away.

He would have to find a way through it or become trapped in despair and depression. Either seeking alcohol to numb and blur the pain of life or end it in some horrible fashion. None of those options were easy.

I'm fine, just sad, is all. You know how much the town means to me. I cannot tell you again how thankful I am for you. How you guided me during that battle allowed me to accomplish what I did.

Kaen paused a moment as he spoke to Pammon, who was flying a few miles off to the west of them.

You are the greatest thing in my life now, and I cannot wait to see what this world offers the two of us! Imagine all the places we will travel and the things we will uncover! Maybe we can visit the great oceans!

Pammon bubbled with excitement and joy as Kaen spoke those words. His happiness infected Kaen's mind, and soon, they were in a good mood.

They had not talked much for the first hour after they had left. Hess was dealing with a few things that had transpired with the mayor. A second letter was stored in a pouch meant for the adventurers' guild.

An attack like that on their village had not happened in over a generation. If orcs and goblins were moving again, a group of adventurers would need to come and handle the potential infestation. If anything, the guild would have to send a scouting party to determine what was happening.

"I want you to know you impressed me last night," Hess said.

Missing a step, Kaen glanced at Hess, walking casually ahead. "Thanks?"

On the dirt road that would take a good week to reach Ebonmount, Hess broke out in laughter that echoed off the trees along the side of the road. He stopped and turned and shook his head at Kaen. "Get up here and walk next to me, boy! Stop walking behind me like a dog who lost its favorite stick."

Hess motioned with his hands for Kaen to move beside him and waited until he was by his side to start walking again. "I am serious. I am thinking about what you told me and the other men from town have said. You and Pammon worked together in a way I could not have imagined or even prepared for."

Hess waved his hands in big circles and smiled as he glanced at Kaen.

"I do not think you realized how huge of a deal this is. I am a gold token-carrying adventurer," Hess pointed out as he pulled the necklace he had not worn until this morning from under his shirt. "Look at this! I have been around and seen many amazing and unbelievable events in my time, but what you did last night is right there at the top of all of them. Even your father would have been overwhelmed to know what you pulled off."

Kaen found himself smiling and his chest was light. Between the words of praise that Hess was gushing upon him and how Pammon felt, life could not get any better.

"And you have an archery skill of twenty-one! Do you know how long it takes new adventurers to acquire a number that high? Most will not reach that for years unless they come from a rich family who has trained them from childbirth."

Hess's huge hand slapped Kaen across the shoulder, knocking him forward a little. "AND you have not even taken the test yet!"

That blasted test! Kaen knew he had to wait for the test. It would provide everything he had hoped for.

Hess mumbled to himself as he almost seemed to skip down the road, lost in his happy thoughts. Kaen thought that for a man of Hess's size and stature, it felt weird for Kaen to see him acting like a school-age boy who'd just gotten his first kiss.

"They may not make you take the test!" Hess suddenly blurted out a minute later.

"What do you mean I wouldn't have to take the test? Everyone has to take the test, I thought?"

Hess shook his head and stopped in the middle of the road. He turned to face Kaen and leaned into his personal space. "No, they don't! Some adventurers have done things like you did this week. Sometimes, the guild master will make an exception. Kaen, it might just happen, and if that does . . . " Hess started walking forward again, a low whistle coming from his lips.

Jogging a few steps to catch up with Hess, Kaen chuckled. "Are you ok? You are more excited about this than I am, I think."

Nodding, Hess smiled and let out a chuckle. "Kaen, I have been waiting almost as long as you have. I have waited for you to become the man I know you can be. Your father entrusted his greatest treasure to me, and I swore an oath after he passed that I would do everything I could to help you succeed and be someone who could carry on the Marshell name and do it justice."

Hess stopped walking again and put his hand out to stop Kaen.

"Listen, Kaen. You will be in the spotlight when we walk into the guild hall and they hear what you have done. Even if you have to take the test, you will pass it with flying colors. I expect you could easily get a perfect score if you give it your all. You need to do your best and secure yourself as a breakout adventurer. The higher you rank, the easier it will be for you to get the quests we need you to take."

"What do you mean *we need me to take*?"

Hess let out a sigh. "I cannot help you if you are wood or copper rank. It would look like I was carrying you or that we were lying about what had happened in the village. Everyone will know that the cave did not threaten my life."

"No threat?!" Kaen exclaimed. "You acted like it was a huge risk!"

Hess shrugged and then gave a slight wink. "Kaen, I could have gone into that cave if I needed to and killed all those creatures easily. I only pretended they were a threat because you needed to believe they were. You had to learn small tactics and risks," Hess explained. "Like when you made a foolish decision and sent Pammon ahead, and he got injured because of it. Had I known the woman was in there beforehand, I might have run in and tried to save her. Once I heard her scream, I knew it was too late. They would not risk letting her be saved."

Kaen stood there stunned. Words failed him as he tried to comprehend what Hess had just said. "So there was no risk at all?"

Hess chuckled and shook his head. "There was no risk for me. You were only in danger if you did not obey."

Kicking the dirt with his foot, Kaen wondered what else Hess was not telling him. "Could you see in the darkness of the cave?"

Hess grimaced before he gave a small grin. "When you went off for torches, I equipped an item that would let me see as Pammon did. I was thankful Pammon blocked those two arrows for me, but they would not have done anything unless they had struck my face."

Blowing a raspberry, Kaen shook his head in disgust. He felt slightly betrayed but understood why Hess had done what he did. "So, is that why people might not believe I accomplished these things?" asked Kaen.

"Even with Storven's two letters and recommendation, many people would struggle to believe that you killed three orcs and twenty goblins this last week," Hess stated. "They won't question my word or shouldn't, but some might wonder how much assistance I gave. You needed to learn not to freeze in that cave. That gave you the battle experience that helped you accomplish what you did in town."

Hess held out his token and pointed to it. "This means a lot. Traveling with me, questing with me, and having me by your side can be both good and bad. At some point, you will have to quest with others, but for a little while, you can do it with me. These rare moments will be a foundation of tricks and strategies that the adventurers of your rank will lack. Some of the advice I have shared with you would mean the difference between life and death, depending on the situation."

"Take a breath and slow down," Kaen said, interrupting Hess. "Why are you suddenly saying we can't stay together?"

Shaking the golden token, Hess frowned, took a deep breath, and let it out. "Duty. I am bound by the oath I took when I got my token. I was given a reprieve because I took a long quest. The guild master knows what I agreed to do for your father and you."

Kaen's eyes went wide, and he realized what Hess was saying. "I have been a quest for you?"

Hess shook his head no for a second, then stopped and nodded yes.

"Yes and no. The only way I could keep my adventurer rank and not lose it was to tell the guild master what I would do for your father. That I was going to raise another adventurer. That one day I would return with you and that you would pass the test. After all that, I would rejoin the role and answer the quests they require of me."

Hess put a hand on Kaen's shoulder and squeezed it. "All those times your dad would return home for a month and then disappear for some time was because of his duty for the token he carried."

Memories flooded into Kaen's mind. Things he had long forgotten. He had forgotten all those months his father would be gone. His mother would tell him stories about the adventures his father was on. Letters would come and remind his mother and him that his dad loved them and was thinking of them.

A light went off in Kaen's brain. "My dad's duty was higher because he was a platinum adventurer?"

Hess nodded.

"I knew one day you would ask the real question. The most important question. Duty to the guild is hard to balance with life. He was a great man who loved you more than life itself and felt the best way he could show that love was by protecting the kingdom you lived in."

Hess let go of Kaen, moved a little, and pretended to swing a sword in a mock battle. "He was an amazing swordsman. I had seen some masters of the sword, but your father was beyond them all."

Pretending to fire arrows and then switching up like he was holding a spear, Hess moved through motions, acting like a bard telling a story of an epic battle.

"To watch him fight with any weapon was impossible to follow for all but the strongest. He was quick, strong, and steadfast. His plans were as amazing as his mind was sharp, and he could read people and monsters in a moment."

Hess rushed back to Kaen and smiled. "He was close to being a Mithril token adventurer in another year or two."

Suddenly, just as fast as Hess had been excited, the joy left him, and he looked pained. Hess stood up, stretched his back, and motioned for Kaen to follow him.

"What are you not telling me?" Kaen demanded. "You have never told me about the quest that got him killed!"

Hess nodded and stared off down the road. "You're right. I have not, and I cannot yet. We have talked about this before."

Kaen ran a few steps ahead and stopped before Hess. "Tell me now! We are headed to the guild hall. Surely you can now!"

Hess stopped and looked at Kaen and shook his head. "The guild master has sworn me to secrecy. There is an item that . . . " Hess shuddered as he paused. "You must get the story from him or attain a gold rank. I am no longer bound when you achieve the rank I have now."

Kaen started to object, but Hess shook his head and crossed his arms.

"We can argue on this road all day and for the next week, or we can get back to traveling to Ebonmount so that you can find out sooner rather than later."

Kaen growled and shook his fist at Hess. "That isn't fair! I had not thought about that until you brought it up right now! You owe me!"

Hess nodded and walked around Kaen. "I do. One day, I will make sure you know what happened. The day you find out will change the whole course of your life."

Kaen watched as Hess slowly walked past him. He looked down and saw a rock on the ground, picked it up, and tossed it in the woods.

Pammon, when the time comes, I am going to need your help. I need to reach the gold rank fast!

Through their link, Kaen knew that Pammon was confused. He had explained the ranks to him many times.

I will do anything I can to help you reach that goal. You have my word.

22

A Whole New World

Six days on the road with a man who would not share the truth about how his father had died had made Kaen very grouchy. By the time they could see Ebonmount in the distance, they had not talked much, and their times around the fire at night were not much more than grunts.

Hess had left Kaen alone, figuring he would outgrow his anger and hurt and eventually realize he could not break an agreement like his. He wanted to tell Kaen so much, but his oath prevented it. Even though he wanted to tell Kaen, his lifestone would not allow him to.

Kaen and Pammon had spent each night curled up next to each other. They had moved miles into the woods and found a place where they could be together. Pammon always brought a deer or boar for them to butcher and eat. Whatever they did not cook, he gladly finished for them.

Kaen seemed content only when he wedged himself against Pammon's scales and slept.

The city's massive walls came into view as they reached the forest's edge. The once thick and often overgrown wall of trees turned into a well-managed and trimmed farming area. Farms started appearing on the outskirts of the area cleared of trees. Guards patrolled the roads, and the rare cart they had seen the first few days of travel turned into a steady stream of carts headed along the well-traveled dirt road.

Houses were rare at first, and then more and more brick houses appeared across the land until small groups of homes and buildings clustered together became common.

The fields were full of workers and kids who laughed and played when they were not helping with the work.

All of this, which stood on a scale grander than anything Kaen had ever seen, meant nothing when compared to the actual city of Ebonmount.

When the walls came into view, Kaen stopped and stared at the city as the sun illuminated the towers and walls. The wind blew across the field, making his brown hair move and twist, almost seeming to push him toward the city whose name came from the mountains themselves.

Ebonmount had been the name for as long as anyone could remember. Thousands of years ago, a massive battle occurred here, and the mountain was split down the middle on the north side. What had once been a valley trapped within a bowl of rock was now a place of trade due to the amount of metal in the mountains and the trees and fertile farmland inside it. Only dragons or other flying creatures had made it over the high mountains and lived here with the animals that ran free. The stories that had been passed down about dragons living there seemed plausible to Kaen since he knew there was a reason the land was so fertile. All that dragon crap would have made the soil fertile beyond belief.

When the mountains had been split, dwarves had first moved there and started work, commissioned by the human kings of old. They cut into the mountainside and crafted roads and houses built directly on the side of the mountain. A huge solid stone wall was cut from the mountain's base in one section. A solid, fifty-foot high and forty-foot-thick wall ran from the mountain's base, enclosing the city they had built behind it for over four miles. The only opening was the main gate in the middle of the wall. It provided a yet-to-be-beaten barrier for any army that had once dreamed of taking the place for themselves.

No war had been fought there in over five hundred years, and the city had become a place of economic growth and prosperity. It served as a major hub for the kingdom's adventurers' guild. There was always a need that could only be met by the gifted men and women of the guild .

On a dirt road surrounded by fields, workers, caravans, and Hess, Kaen saw for the first time the place he would now call home .

"It's . . . How do they . . . " Kaen fumbled for words for a few moments and turned when he heard Hess chuckling.

"It's ok. I was unable to fathom what I saw the first time I arrived. It was actually harder on me because I came through the mountain pass. I had thought the pass was impressive until I saw the city walls."

Kaen nodded and shook his head in disbelief. "How far away are we?"

Hess moved closer to Kaen and pointed to a group of buildings outside the wall that were nothing more than specks in the distance. "We are a good two hours from there. Even walking on a road, it will take a while before we reach a place to stay and eat. Tomorrow, we will enter the actual wall and arrive at the guild."

"We aren't going in today?"

Hess shook his head. "I need to see if someone still owns a place in the outer city. If they do, it will be better in the city's outer ring than inside. The cost of living inside the walls will have increased since I was here many years ago. While I am not poor, I would find myself having to join other parties and leave you alone if we stay inside the city walls for any length of time."

Money. It was not something Kaen had thought about or considered the need for. Hess had bartered or paid for everything they owned. Kaen had a pouch of silver coins, but he had no clue how much food and a place to live cost out here.

Turning, he saw how far away the forest was and realized staying out there and returning to the city would not be an option. "How long will I be away from Pammon," Kaen asked, leaning closer to Hess.

"I told you to make sure you said goodbye this morning," Hess answered with a sigh. "It may be a week before you can see him again. The rank you get and the quests we can take will determine how soon we can all be together once more. For now, talk with him the way you two do, remind him to stay safe and out of sight, and focus on what will happen tomorrow."

Hess started walking a little faster, and Kaen became frustrated again. He had not been paying much attention this morning when Hess instructed him to make sure they said goodbye. He had not considered how long it might take to see Pammon again. Knowing they would be apart that long, a piece of him already felt like it was missing.

Pammon . . . I just found out I may not be able to see you for about a week. I am sorry I did not realize it would be so long. Will you be ok?

I should be fine. You may not be, because you are still upset with Hess. Stop pouting and be the man you claim to be. We will do much harder things than not see each other for a week. I will be content to hunt and eat till my belly almost bursts. Do not worry about me.

Kaen started to reply and stopped. Damn, his dragon knew where to hit him. He was upset with Hess, but Pammon was right. He was not acting like the man he said he wanted to be.

Thank you, Pammon. I needed that reminder.

Pammon was laughing, and Kaen knew it.

I will always tell you when you act like a fool. You put up with me when I was hardheaded and acted like an eggling.

Kaen burst out laughing, and a few people on the road near them turned to see what he was laughing about. He had not realized he had stopped walking, and Hess was now a good thirty yards ahead of him.

You were hard headed. Thank you for reminding me of that.

Kaen ran down the road, reached Hess, and punched him on his arm.

Hess turned and saw Kaen smiling at him.

"Sorry, I have been acting like an eggling."

Hess squinted and then broke out in laughter, drawing the attention of those around them as Kaen had a moment ago. "I do not think I could have said that better. Glad to see your *friend* has helped you see the truth of that."

Kaen laughed and nodded. "Sometimes we all act like one, don't we?"

Grabbing Kaen in a headlock, Hess ran his knuckles against Kaen's head before letting him go. "Yes. Yes, we do."

Kaen had been awestruck at how many houses and shops were packed against each other in the outer part of Ebonmount. They had not yet reached the main section, but the roads had gone from hard and dirt-packed to stone roads three carts wide. Each stone was perfectly flat, and all the corners and edges were flush against each other. The roads ran straight and square, forming a perfectly laid out city section.

"Magic," Hess said with a chuckle. "They use magic to make the stones and keep them from wearing down. Most stones would break down quickly, but these will last years before they need to be replaced. There is a team that keeps the roads clean and in shape."

Hess pointed to a cart with a horse and three men working it. Whenever a horse or another animal defecated on the road, the men would run out, collect it, and throw it into the back of the cart. Kaen had not paid attention to the other, similar-looking carts until now. There was one every few blocks .

"Sewers," Hess said pointing to the grates that were inset occasionally along the stone roads. "They take water and waste and run it to a special location way off to the east of the city. Some who are gifted with magic help to remove the bad stuff from the water and find a use for it again."

Everywhere they went, Hess pointed out different aspects of the city. He told him what each of the signs meant and answered every question he could that Kaen asked.

Kaen had no idea that there were so many different shops that all sold the same thing. They had passed multiple weapon shops, countless bakeries, healing and potion shops, churches, temples, bars, inns, and more. It was staggering to think there were this many businesses that somehow functioned and stayed open.

"What are those?" Kaen asked, pointing down a street at some large signs outside of a warehouse-looking building.

"Those are training schools," Hess answered. "Those who can afford it and need extra training with weapon skills can find a few scattered around here. Most of those who visit them are individuals with lifestones that are trying to get good enough to pass the adventurer's test. Sometimes those who pass the test still come here for some one-on-one training with the master of the school, if they have enough money."

Hess paused, glanced at the street corner before them, and then turned right. "Sorry, I was trying to make sure I remembered the way. Anyways, when one is an adventurer, mastering one's skill is the difference between life and death. You should know that better than anyone. You know the difference between having archery at nineteen and twenty."

Kaen nodded as he walked next to Hess. He wondered if one of those schools could help him improve. The real question would be if the price was worth it.

Miles of wandering through the town finally ended when Hess stopped at a corner, wrung his hands, and made a weird face.

"Why are we stopping?" Kaen asked as he looked around. "You lost?"

Hess shook his head and sighed. "No. Up there is where we are headed."

Kaen looked to where Hess started to point and saw a sign for an inn.

"The Fluffy Ingot?"

23

The Fluffy Ingot

"That is an interesting name," Kaen declared with a heavy dose of sarcasm. "Why would someone call an inn a name like that?"

Kaen thought he saw Hess's cheeks turn red.

"Are you embarrassed or anxious about going in there?"

Hess shook his head and groaned. "It is a long story, but I need to just go in and face the possible crap storm that might be inside."

Smirking, Kaen started to walk toward the door and motioned for Hess to join him.

The building had the standard stone exterior of all the town's buildings. Hess had informed Kaen earlier that morning that all houses in this area were built from stones provided by the town. With so many people living this close to each other generations ago, the city wanted to reduce the risk of a fire taking out the town and the population. The downside of these bricks is that no paint would stick to them. Now the town was a sea of homes and businesses using signs and people outside to showcase their small differences.

The only real thing that told someone the building was an inn was the noise coming from inside through the open door and the huge wooden sign that featured a golden ingot that seemed to expand and shrink a little. The words even sparkled regardless of where the sun was shining.

Hess quickly stepped in front of Kaen when they got to the open doors. Laughter and music could be heard, and the smell of something amazing cooking wafted from inside.

Kaen's stomach growled. It had been a while since they had eaten this morning. He was ready to enjoy whatever might be inside.

As they walked past the bright gold-colored wooden doors that were pushed inward, Kaen saw the room was fairly bright. There were small light globes like the one Hess had hidden away in the floor of his room. People were sitting in booths around the walls and along tables, laughing and talking as over half a dozen women in outfits that were a little tight on their *fluffier* bodies, brought out food.

"The women here are a little larger the women at than the inn back at home," Kaen whispered to Hess.

Hess grunted and headed for an empty booth along a wall.

A bard was playing a flute and tapping his feet to the quick melody. A large stone bar ran the entire length of the back wall. Casks and bottles of liquid stood behind it, and two dwarf men could barely be seen above the bar anytime they moved.

Hess took the seat facing the main door, allowing Kaen to sit and watch the rest of the inn.

Elves, humans, dwarves, and some other short race with long noses were laughing and getting along. Card games took place, and the air of excitement and fun filled the room.

"Those dwarven men are awfully short," Kaen stated as he pointed at the bar. "Why do they keep popping up and down as they move along the bar?"

Hess glanced over his shoulder and chuckled. He turned back and shook his head at Kaen. "First, there is only one dwarf man there. The other is a woman."

Kaen looked over again and started to speak, but Hess did not wait for him to talk. "Yes, they both have beards. The difference might seem hard to tell at first but notice how the one on the right has curves where a man does not."

Kaen leaned over, squinted, and saw that when the dwarf appeared above the bar while giving drinks, indeed, *she* did have curves the other one did not. "Wow . . . I had not noticed that."

Hess nodded and motioned to a waitress who was looking at them. "They *pop up* because they are standing on blocks at the bar. When they go to get drinks, they move around behind the bar."

Nodding, Kaen realized that should have been easy to figure out on his own.

"What can I get for you, fine gentlemen," a red-haired waitress called out as she deftly wove her way between two chairs that led to their booth.

Kaen grinned like a fool at the woman. She was easily thirty but looked prettier than any woman from back home.

"My friend and I will take a serving of today's special as well as something to drink. Give him some milk or water, and I'll take whatever ale the house is serving today."

The woman nodded and bent down to wink at Kaen. As she did, her extra helping of bosom almost fell out of her top that seemed much tighter than it should be on a woman with curves like her.

"What would you prefer? Milk or water?" she asked with a wink.

He could feel the color rising in his cheeks as he tried to keep his gaze up at her green eyes.

"Wa . . . water, please!"

She giggled and then winked at Kaen before she sauntered off to the area near the bar.

"Oh, they are going to have a field day with you," Hess teased. "They like giving young ones like yourself a little extra attention. It will worsen once they find out you are testing tomorrow."

Kaen coughed, trying to clear his throat.

"We did not have women like that in our town."

Hess shook his head and sighed. "No, Kaen, we did not. Nothing like a woman with a full figure and some meat on her bones. I don't mind the skinny ones, but I was always afraid I might snap one in half."

"How would you do that?" Kaen asked as he watched their server talking at the bar.

Hess suddenly choked and held out his hand. "Uhmm . . . We have had *that* talk, right?"

Laughing, Kaen nodded. "We did, but if I remember correctly, you used the cows as an example. Not the best illustration for a young boy, mind you."

Hess bit his lip and grinned a second later. "I'd like to say I did that on purpose, but I had no idea how to explain how that stuff works to one I'm supposed to raise."

"You did fine, and anything else I was missing was taught to me by Cale and Patrick."

"That is not the place to learn anything good, son." Hess howled in laughter as he spoke. "Those two could barely swing a pickaxe, let alone have any idea how to care for a woman."

Shrugging, Kaen motioned to their server, who was returning.

"One water and one tankard of ale for my favorite patrons of the day," their server said, her face twitching as if she was trying not to laugh as she put down two giant wooden tankards on the table.

"Excuse me, ma'am, but I realized I never found out your name," Kaen stated as he leaned toward the woman. "I always like to know the name of a beautiful woman when I meet one."

The woman broke out in a fit of laughter and leaned backward with her hands on her hips. Her whole body shook, giving quite the show to those interested in one.

"My, my, my. What has this man across from you been teaching you?" she said with a wink. "My name is Beatrice, but I must say you are a bit young for me. Perhaps when you grow some hair on your chest in a few years, you can try that line again."

Kaen could feel his cheeks burning up. He had not expected her to say anything like that at all. The girls in town had always gotten embarrassed and blushed when he had spoken like that. Were all the women here like Beatrice?

"He will need to rest tonight and the next few days," Hess interrupted as he moved his drink closer. "Kaen will be taking the first day of the adventurer's test tomorrow. No point in wearing the boy out so he can barely stand."

Beatrice giggled and her eyes went wide with excitement. "A soon-to-be adventurer?" she asked, her voice increasing a few octaves as she leaned against the table toward Kaen. "Do you think you will pass the test on your first try?"

Hess smiled as he watched the woman prepare to pounce on Kaen. "He should pass it easily if they make him take it at all. Last week, he killed twenty goblins and three orcs all on his own."

At Hess's words, Beatrice spun on her heel to look at him. As she turned, she saw that Hess had pulled out his gold adventurer token and let it hang against his shirt.

"You aren't lying, are you?" she said, gasping at the token on his chest.

Hess shook his head and smiled. "Ask Kaen if I am telling the truth."

Beatrice turned and smiled, leaning so close to Kaen that he could feel the heat from her breath as she spoke.

"Is he really telling the truth, Kaen? I can call you Kaen, can't I?" Beatrice asked as she supported her chest with an arm against the table. "You managed to kill all those awful and horrible creatures on your own?"

Kaen coughed, grabbed his cup, and took a drink. His eyes never left hers lest she think he was a letch. "I did, ma'am. I used my bow and the training he taught me. I did have a little help with one of the orcs, though."

Beatrice leaned her head back and laughed so loud that the patrons in the room nearby hushed to turn and see what could bring such a reaction from one of the serving women.

"Brave, strong, and modest. Not many men would offer to share the fame of killing an orc, especially if they are not an adventurer yet. Come stand by me for a moment while I share your success and the news of what you will be attempting tomorrow," Beatrice said.

She grabbed Kaen's left arm and yanked him from his spot, not giving him a choice. Kaen could hear Hess chuckling and barely caught a wink from him as Beatrice dragged him behind her toward the bar. As they made their way closer to it, the room got exceedingly quiet because everyone knew something worth sharing was about to be proclaimed.

Beatrice held up her hand as she walked, waving it around in a circle multiple times. Once they reached the bar, she took a deep breath.

"PATRONS OF THE FLUFFY INGOT, MAY I HAVE YOUR ATTENTION!"

Kaen whipped his head around and saw the female dwarf had almost magically appeared on top of the bar and was shouting to everyone in the inn. Now that he knew what to look for, he could definitely tell it was the female dwarf.

"Beatrice has something she wants to share with you all!"

The female dwarf nodded, and Beatrice beamed as she put her arm around Kaen's shoulders. He was by no means short, standing just a hair under six feet, but she was a few inches taller than he was.

"I have a special friend with me! This young man is Kaen and he will take the adventurer's test tomorrow!"

The entire inn clapped, and men, women, and servers cheered loudly. Many called out his name as a chant! Soon, a loud banging of cups echoed through the entire inn for almost half a minute. As the people chanted and cheered, Beatrice pulled Kaen's head close, and he felt his face brushing up against the exposed skin of her chest. As much as he wanted to pull away, he felt it would be rude to, so he let her hold his head as she bobbed up and down.

Beatrice waved her hands, and suddenly, a sharp shout came out from the bar. "Oi! Hush it so she can talk!" cried the female bartender.

Laughter broke out, and everyone quieted down quickly.

"Now it gets even better, let me tell you, fine citizens of Ebonmount! Wait till I tell you what he has already accomplished!"

24

Kaen's Future and Hess's Past

"That's not possible!" someone shouted.

"That has to be a lie!" another yelled.

Boos came across the room, yet Beatrice never flinched an inch. She held Kaen's head and gently stroked his hair with her other hand.

She held her hand up again, and the bartender quieted everyone down again.

"You might not believe this young man or me, but would you believe the gold-token-carrying adventurer he travels with?!" Beatrice shouted as she pointed to where Hess was at.

Chairs creaked and scraped across the floors as everyone turned to look at Hess.

"He is a gold adventurer," someone shouted as they pointed at Hess.

"Could he be telling the truth?" another asked.

"That seems impossible! Three orcs!" still another said.

Murmuring and conversations were scattered across the room.

"Enough with your whining and complaining!" Beatrice shouted above the noise. "Now for the real fun! Tomorrow, young Kaen will take the test. In two days, we will determine if he is telling the truth and what rank he will be. So in a few minutes, Eltina will take down your wagers and bets at the bar. Bet on if you think he will pass. Bet on what rank you think he will end up with. Bet on how many women he sleeps with before then!"

With that last comment, a roar of laughter and feet banging on the floors echoed across the room. The inn's patrons were laughing and cheering. Some stood up and walked over to congratulate Kaen with a handshake or a slap on the back.

"I need you to come with me for a moment," Beatrice whispered as she tugged Kaen toward the bar.

* * *

"Kaen, was it?"

The bartender, Eltina, snapped her fingers a few times above her head and broke Kaen from the dazed look he had on his face.

"Sorry, what did you ask?" Kaen replied as he stared at the dwarf.

"I'd say my eyes were up here, boy, but really they aren't," the bartender joked as she stroked her beard and gazed up at Kaen.

Kaen took in the female dwarf and tried not to stare as she stroked her blond beard that connected to her blond hair via two amazing sideburns. It was difficult to think of her as a *her*, with a beard like that.

"Now, Kaen, I need you to tell me the truth," Eltina said as she pointed a stubby finger at him. "Did you really kill twenty goblins and three orcs?"

Kaen smiled and nodded. "I did. It was actually more than twenty, but not being specific would be easier for us, Hess, my gold adventurer friend, says. The three orcs were killed across two days."

Eltina's eyes went wide, and she grabbed a chair and stood on top of it, bobbing and weaving as she tried to get a glance at Hess.

Her eyes almost seemed to pop out of her head when she recognized him, and she smashed her fist into her hand. "Mother goat lovin', goblin humpin', no good bastard of an orc bitch!"

The words coming from Eltina's mouth and her temperament gave Kaen and Beatrice a bit of concern as they backed away from the filthy-mouthed dwarf.

Eltina raised her fingers to her mouth and let out an ear-piercing whistle that silenced everyone in the inn. "HESS BRUMLIN, GET YOUR SORRY EXCUSE FOR A DAMN ADVENTURER OVER TO THIS BAR NOW!"

The entire inn turned and looked at Hess, who adjusted his shirt and casually walked across the silent inn toward the bar as if he were taking a casual stroll through the woods. He took his time and smiled and nodded at each patron as he passed them. No one made a sound, except for the occasional chair scraping across the floor to move from Hess's path.

"Hello, Eltina. It has been a while, hasn't it?" Hess asked with a smile and a playful wink.

"Hello?! HELLO?! Who the hell do you think you are, coming in here after seven years without a single letter or anything?! You must have balls of iron and shite for brains to think that Sulenda isn't going to hang you upside down and strip the skin from your sorry hide!"

Patrons closer to Eltina slowly backed away while a few patrons started to move closer to the exit.

"Eltina!" Beatrice hissed. "You are scaring all the customers away. No matter what that man has done, Sulenda may do the same to you, if you chase anyone off!"

Eltina turned and looked at Beatrice and then grunted. "FREE DRINKS FOR ALL! COURTESTY OF ADVENTURER HESS!" Eltina suddenly shouted with a smile that magically replaced her sour scowl.

Silence hung for a few seconds, and then a roar of shouting and cheering replaced the awkward silence that had gripped the entire room.

Eltina hopped off the chair and strode up to Hess, glaring up at him. "You and your lackey need to come with me! No more food or drink till Sulenda says you can have some."

Poking Hess in the stomach with as much force as she could muster, Eltina growled and yanked on her beard. "And you *will* be paying for all those drinks, or I will get it from you another way!"

Kaen stood in awe as he watched Hess laugh and nod. Clearly, he was not worried about the fury of this dwarf or this *Sulenda* woman she had mentioned a few times.

"Beatrice!" Eltina snapped, turning on her stubby feet. "Since you are so fond of that young one, get him back to the office and start working on odds for the rank he will possibly be."

Grunting, Eltina motioned with her finger at Hess. "He will know what you need to know. For now, I must serve all the alcohol this giant idiot is paying for."

Eltina moved back behind the bar, and when she popped up above it, she was again all smiles and laughter. Her mood that could have curdled milk a second ago had now been replaced with something so sweet, bees might carry her off to their hive.

"What the heck was that?" Kaen asked, turning on Hess the moment Beatrice shut the door to the office they had entered.

Hess ignored Kaen and started inspecting the office. On the wall was a massive map of the kingdom, printed on some old paper and attached to a huge frame. It took up most of the wall on one side of the room.

Shelves with rolled-up packs of papers, books with more dust on them than the ground outside, and random odds and ends were stuffed everywhere. It looked like no one had touched most of the stuff scattered across the room in ages. Two wooden chairs were near a spotless desk. Compared to the rest of the room, the desk did not seem to belong. On it, stacks of paper were neatly bound together in tight bundles. A small quill and ink set was next to a stack of blank paper. There was no dust on the desk, and a tiny light globe sat on it, turned off but ready to be used.

"She hasn't changed a bit," Hess said with a sigh.

Kaen noticed a chalkboard on the back of the door with multiple rows and columns with names and numbers written all over.

"That right there is where the real money is made," Hess stated pointing at the chalkboard as he went to stand next to it. "Looks like these are the real odds and points one should know if they are betting on anything."

Beatrice coughed and motioned for Hess and Kaen to sit in the chairs. She moved to the desk, slowly pulled out the thick, well-padded chair, and carefully sat in it.

"She lets you sit in it?" Hess asked, smiling at her.

"Miss Sulenda will not mind since I will be doing the inn's work," she stated, but the way she shifted in the chair did not convey she believed that statement herself.

"It's your funeral," Hess joked, leaning back in the chair. "Pull out paper and pen, and let's get this done."

Beatrice nodded, took out a sheet of paper, and fetched a pen from the drawer. "The magicians who created these tools got rich. The pens held the ink inside and would allow anyone to write with ease. When the ink ran dry, a simple spell could be cast, and the pens would refill from an ink jar. No more messy drips everywhere or having to fetch quality quills. I wish I would've invested in them," she told Hess.

Beatrice drew columns and rows on the sheet and then started writing out three ranks. When she was finished, she smiled at him. "Tell me what rank you think he will be in two days."

Beatrice had gone outside with a new sheet of paper with different odds written on it. She had copied the original sheet onto the chalkboard on the back of the door.

Kaen had sat there the entire time, almost silent, unless one of them asked him a question. People were going to bet on what rank he would start! When Hess mentioned he might not even be made to take the test or score a perfect score, Beatrice had brightened up and adjusted her top more times than Kaen thought a woman would need to in a lifetime.

"So why are we here?" Kaen asked as the door shut. "Obviously, you and this Sulenda woman do not get along."

"We might not get along, but you will help me return to her good graces."

Hess stood and moved to the map. He ran his finger along a few roads and counted some things in his head.

"How will I help you get back in her good graces?" Kaen asked, joining Hess next to the map.

Hess finished whatever he was calculating as he ran his finger along a few roads outside the gap of Ebonmount. "We will earn a percentage of whatever money they make on the bets people put on you. Every inn on this side of town will hear about you and what you have *supposedly* done, and Sulenda will bankroll the wagers."

Hess paused and turned and pointed at the chalkboard. "This town has seen more gold won and lost on adventurers' tests and placements than some kings will see in a lifetime. You, Kaen, may break the record when your results are decided."

Kaen stood there, totally confused. Why would anyone risk money guessing how someone would do on this test? Until Pammon came into his life, he would not have bet on himself to pass the test.

25

Letter from Dad

Kaen stood silently for a few minutes while Hess returned to study the map. He could not fully grasp everything he had seen and heard since they had entered the town that day. It was as if a whole new world had been revealed to him.

"Hess, why won't you tell me who this Sulenda woman is to you?"

Sighing, Hess turned and ruffled Kaen's hair. "You remember that adventurer I said your father and I had traveled with longer than anyone else?"

Kaen nodded. "She is the one?"

Hess nodded and picked his teeth with his pinky. "She was the *one*. She was the one in more ways than I would care to admit."

Hess moved to the chair he had sat on earlier and spun it around, then sat on it, leaning his chest against it.

"There was a time I might have married that woman, but things happened, and it did not work out how I think both of us had expected it to. Now I live with a hole in my heart, and I may have one in my back when she sees me."

Kaen put his hand on Hess's shoulder and squeezed. "No one is putting a hole in your back until I get my token."

Hess chuckled and rubbed his face with his hand. "You are your father's son, Kaen. That is exactly what he would have said."

Kaen sat down and leaned back in the chair. "I guess until she gets here, we wait?"

Hess nodded and then rested his forehead on his hands. "Nothing to do but wait."

Kaen had never seen a door explode before, but when Sulenda kicked the door to her office open, he had, for a moment, believed he just had. He did not scream like a child, because of the explosions he had witnessed over the years at the quarry.

"You are a foolish bastard to come here," a woman who was as tall as Hess screamed as she tried to shut the door that had come off one of its hinges. "Who the hell do you think you are coming in here and acting like you can buy your forgiveness with this adventurer you found and are telling stories about!"

Hess never lifted his head. "Sulenda, it is good to see you too. I see you haven't changed."

Kaen scooted his chair some as the woman stormed toward Hess. She was the first woman Kaen had ever seen who looked like they could go toe-to-toe with him. Kaen wondered who would win that fight based on how she was acting.

"You better look up at me, or I will kick that chair out from under you!"

Hess leaned back and stood up. Every move he made was slow and deliberate. It looked like he was dealing with a timid animal, and he made sure that he made no sudden movements. He lifted the chair from between his legs and carefully set it down near Kaen. He then turned and faced Sulenda, staring directly into her blue eyes.

"You look as beautiful as the last time I saw you."

Sulenda opened her mouth and shut it in frustration. Her jaw was working, but no words were coming out. Her hands were trembling as she made two fists and unclenched them.

"You would dare say those words to me?" Sulenda growled, taking a step back.

Hess slowly took a step toward Sulenda and nodded. "You know I have never lied to you. Why would I start now?"

Color rose in Sulenda's cheeks, and she grunted, turned, and rushed past Hess toward the safety of her desk. "Sit! We need to talk!" she ordered.

Kaen sat wide-eyed watching Hess slowly retrieve his chair, turn it around, and straddle it.

"You still sit like a thief who has their horse unhitched for a quick getaway," Sulenda said, groaning as she pulled out her chair and sat in it. "Now, tell me what you must speak about, and be quick. I have a betting nightmare on my hands because of you!"

Hess nodded and motioned toward Kaen. "Kaen meet Sulenda. Sulenda meet Kaen. Sulenda this is Hoste's son."

The color in Sulenda's face drained like a bucket of water that suddenly lost its bottom. All the color she had was gone, white like snow. "Ho . . . Hoste's son?" she asked with a tremor in her voice. "It can't be."

She had not paid much attention to Kaen since she had entered. Her frustration and anger with Hess had blinded her to him. Looking at him now, she saw just how much he looked like his father.

Hess nodded and smirked. "This is why. For so many questions and reasons, he is why we are here today."

"I'm sorry," Kaen interrupted, "but why do you two keep talking about me and my dad like this?"

Sulenda turned to Hess and gasped. "You haven't told him?!"

"Why would I tell him? Until this afternoon, it was none of his business. Now that we are here, it is his business!"

Kaen leaped to his feet, slammed his fist on the desk, and glared at both of them. "One of you better tell me what the hell you are talking about before I get pissed!"

Sulenda looked at Kaen, shook her head, and then nodded at Hess. "Tell him. He deserves to know."

Hess nodded. "Sit, Kaen. It is a long story; it is time you knew."

Kaen's face was red and hot, but he sat down. He needed to know what these two were keeping from him.

"When your father took the job that killed him, Sulenda and I were on a break from the adventurers' guild. She took over this inn and wanted me to join her. To do this, she had to quit the adventurers' guild," Hess informed him. He nodded at Sulenda. "Show him."

Sulenda grunted and pulled on a chain that was hanging between her massive breasts. Kaen had not noticed them yet, but now he realized why all the serving women looked similar. Sulenda only hired women who shared her large physique.

At the end of the chain was a gold adventurer's token cut in half. A hole was punched in it near the top.

"To no longer be bound to the guild, I had to quit. There was no way around it. I was willing to quit the guild because I thought he was going to join me."

Kaen saw the hurt in Sulenda's eyes when she said those words and tucked the token back between her breasts.

"I was going to. I had one job left, and then I had planned on leaving the guild and starting a life with just the two of us," Hess said.

Hess was smiling, and Kaen realized that Hess could have been happy here.

"Why didn't you?" Kaen asked. "Why didn't you stay here?"

Tears formed in Hess's eyes. Kaen saw tears in Sulenda's eyes too.

"It was because . . . " Hess choked and struggled to speak. "It was because your father did not return from his mission."

"What does that have to do with you not quitting the guild?" Kaen implored, lost on what they still had not told him.

Hess took a deep breath and held it for a moment before letting it out. "I returned from my quest to find out what happened, and there was a letter for me from your father. He knew the risk of the mission, but he also knew the need for it. He knew he might not return, yet he accepted it for the kingdom's safety."

Hess pulled a letter from inside his tunic. It was faded and worn. He handed it to Kaen with trembling hands.

"Read it."

My Ugly Should Be Brother,

If you are reading this, it means I failed and died. Do not cry for me. We have spent most of our lives side-by-side, and we both know the risks of what we do. I knew the risk of what I was doing, and you know why I took it.

I need you to keep the promise you made. Raise Kaen for me. Raise my son as if he is your own. Help him to be a man that I know he can be. Teach him to be honorable and to work hard. I know he will emulate you and the great heart you have. When the time comes, give him the gifts I made for him. You and I know he will one day be an adventurer like us.

Find somewhere away from Ebonmount and raise him to see the common man. I have left a fortune to draw from for his future. I cannot give you any gift greater than my son. You know he is more important than life itself. You know this is why I took this risk.

Hoste

Someday, when the time comes, give Kaen this letter.

Son,

If you are reading this, then Hess has done what I asked. I am sorry you have to hear from me this way. There are so many things I wish I could have said, and had spent more time together, but the world did not allow it. Things happened faster than I had believed, and I had to risk everything. For that, I am sorry.

I know that you are an amazing man! I know you will be an adventurer they will tell stories of. Never forget that family and friends are more important than anything else.

Surround yourself with them and remember why you do what you do. Remember why you choose to become an adventurer. It is so they can live. It is so they can love. I will watch from the sky as you make a mark on this world because I know it will be great!

Be a man worthy of others to emulate!

I love you, son.

Dad

Tears ran down Kaen's face like a downpour during the springtime. He tried to hold the paper out from him to prevent the tears from smudging the words. At some point, Hess had put his hand on Kaen's shoulder and gotten down on a knee near him.

Are you ok? Why are you so sad?

Kaen tried to smile but could not. His heart was crushed knowing his dad took a quest that would most likely get him killed. Yet he was overwhelmed by the joy of reading words from his dad. These were actual words from his dad to him. He was also hurting because of what he knew this letter had cost Hess. He was so grateful he had Pammon.

I am fine. My heart is just confused. I got a letter from my dad, who told me he loved me. It hurts but also makes me happy.

Pammon's emotions ran weird, hard for Kaen to understand for a moment before he spoke.

I remember when my mom told me goodbye. I knew she would never return. I knew she did what she did so I could live and find you. I know how you feel.

Kaen sat up in shock.

Your mom said goodbye when she left you at the quarry?

Her last words were: *Someone will find you and help you. Grow strong!* I have done that with you. Maybe our parents both knew we would meet. Maybe fate did this. All I know is I am happier than I could ever imagine.

Kaen smiled and wiped the tears from his eyes.

As am I. I am happier than I can imagine because of you. Thank you, Pammon.

"Is this why you took care of me?" Kaen whispered. "You gave up a life with Sulenda for me?"

Hess nodded. Words were stuck in his chest, and he could not even think of what to say.

"You don't have to say anything," Kaen said, wiping the last tears from his eyes and handing the letter back to Hess. "I am the one who should say thank you. Thank you for loving me and my father and doing what you did. You sacrificed everything for me. You sacrificed love."

Kaen turned and saw Sulenda staring at him. "I am sorry you lost Hess all those years ago because of me. Perhaps I can help him regain your trust, and you will find that he still cares about you."

Sulenda closed her eyes and chuckled quietly. A single tear from each eye rolled down her cheek. "You are just like him," Sulenda muttered in disbelief. "I owe him, and that debt is extended to you."

Kaen lifted Hess's hand from his shoulder and stood up. "After I pass the test, you two are free from any obligation to my dad and me. You two will be free to see if there is still love between you."

They all sat there for a moment, teary-eyed and quiet. Kaen felt something in his chest. His lifestone was gently pulsing. It led him to look at the chalkboard on the door, and an idea floated through his mind.

Kaen walked toward the door that was barely hanging on by the hinges and pointed to his name on the chalkboard.

"Let's stop crying. I need to get out there and help you earn money."

26

Never Stand on a Dwarf's Bar

Kaen walked out of the office and back into the main section of the inn. The weight of so many things churned in his stomach as he strode up to the bar where Eltina and her male counterpart were slinging drinks and laughing with patrons.

His lifestone felt weird. It wasn't overpowering him, yet it was leading him to do something. Wanting him to be different than he would normally even begin to think of being.

Taking a big breath, Kaen stepped onto a chair close to the bar, put two fingers from each hand into his mouth, and blew a long, loud whistle.

The bar quieted quickly as every eye turned to see who had called for their attention.

"Fine men and women of Ebonmount, may I ask you all one simple question?!" Kaen shouted. They all turned and leaned toward him, eager to hear what he might say.

"Now, I really want your answer before I ask the real question. How many of you got to enjoy a free drink paid for by my friend Hess, the gold token adventurer who trained me?!"

Cheers broke out, and people held up cups as they laughed and smiled. Most of the inn patrons seemed lucky enough to have scored a free drink.

Kaen raised his hands and encouraged them as they celebrated. He finally held his hands up for silence, and the room quieted down. Kaen glanced at Eltina, who was looking at him, wondering what he was doing. He had seen her turn and look at Hess and Sulenda, who had moved to stand outside the office door when the first cheers had erupted. It was obvious to her that Hess and Sulenda had no clue what Kaen was doing.

"Now I know that many of you might doubt the stories going around about me and how I have slayed three orcs and over twenty goblins." Kaen paused as a few jeers were heard across the room, but the majority of the people were waiting for Kaen's real purpose in calling for their attention.

Before he could speak again, Kaen felt his lifestone gently pulse. It was a different kind of pulse than what he usually felt. It had nothing to do with combat, but instead, it was as if it was guiding him somehow.

"While I am not gifted in the art of storytelling, allow me to tell you how these feats took place, and then you can decide for yourselves if I am telling the truth."

Kaen jumped onto the table next to him and started regaling the patrons with his and Hess's first encounter with the cave, ten goblins, and the orc.

Kaen held the rapt attention of everyone in the bar with his storytelling, moving between the patrons and acting out his words as he described how things took place. He rolled across the floor, sprung to his feet, and used his invisible bow to slay goblins by the dozens. People cheered and laughed when he pretended to take a hard pretzel stick and stab a dwarf in the eye as if he had shot it, before holding it high and cheering for himself.

When he got to the part of the story where the orc shot him with the arrow, he suddenly stripped off his shirt and pointed to the marks on his chest and back. The crowd leaned in and gasped when they saw the scar.

When he reenacted the final battle for his life between the two goblins who had tried to ambush him, Kaen climbed onto the bar and lay on his back to mimic how he had shot his bow and killed the last goblin.

Kaen then stood on the bar, quickly flexed—having never put his shirt back on—and smiled. "And that, my friends, is how I killed three orcs and twenty goblins! Now, what do you say?!"

There is always that moment of silence after a good story has been told. Everyone is sad to know it is over but wants to cheer because of how it ended. Here, that silence hung for just a few seconds, and then the patrons leaped to their feet and cheered. Men and women approached the bar, offered their hands, and shook Kaen's as he smiled and laughed. Suddenly he felt his heart and the lifestone surge again for a moment.

[Story Telling Skill Acquired]
[Story Telling Skill Increased x8]

Kaen was stunned, even as people kept rushing up to him. He had not acquired a new skill in what had felt like ages. This was not one he had intended or even thought about trying for. Had his story been that good, or was it something else?

After a minute of people streaming by, he felt Eltina tugging on his pants leg.

"Sell some alcohol or get off my bar, you shirtless fool," she said with a mischievous grin.

Kaen winked at her and nodded. Whistling again, he gathered everyone else's attention in the inn. "For my last act of tonight, I have one small treat left! Everyone who places a wager on which rank I will be and gets it wrong," Kaen paused as he could feel everyone waiting for what came next. "I will personally pay for their drink at my celebration here in the greatest inn in all of Ebonmount!"

Cheers broke out, and cups thumped the tables.

"He seems sure of himself." Sulenda had to shout into Hess's ear over the noise.

"That's because he takes after his father," Hess replied with a laugh.

Sulenda laughed and elbowed Hess in his ribs. "He better score well if he hopes to pay for all their drinks."

Hess elbowed Sulenda back, not nearly as hard as she had him. "If what I believe might happen does, this boy will earn you more money in the next few days than you have had in a long time."

Sulenda nodded and smirked. She believed Hess was right. The son of Hoste appeared to be just as big as his father had been. She prayed that he would succeed where Hoste had not. Knowing that he was already making a name for himself, as his father had, was intimidating because she would have to ensure they kept who his father was a secret, or the bets would be drastically skewed. She already wondered if the odds were against her.

Eltina climbed up on the bar next to Kaen, grabbed his hand, and raised it. She motioned to her counterpart, who started ringing a bell on the side of the bar. Everyone in the bar began shouting and cheering louder.

"Why are they cheering so loud?" Kaen shouted at Eltina, who was smiling at him.

"It's because you just bought everyone in the bar a round tonight!"

Kaen's eyes went wide. He looked at Eltina, who was smiling and stroking her beard with her other hand.

"I told you to get off the bar or sell drinks! The first rule is, if you stand on my bar, you buy a round!"

"Do I want to know the second rule?" Kaen asked with a groan.

"Get off my bar, or you'll find out!" Eltina replied, getting down from the bar herself.

Kaen shook his head and jumped down to the floor. He was immediately on the receiving end of countless backslaps and thanks for the free drink. The sting of the slaps was bad enough, but knowing he had probably spent most of his money tonight hurt even more.

* * *

The night had flown by, and soon Kaen and Hess were in a room upstairs at the top of the inn.

"You still look a bit sore about what Eltina did to you," teased Hess, lying in his bed. "Most inns and bars will let it slide if you get on top of a chair or a table, but you better have a damn good reason if you actually climb on the bar. Otherwise, it will cost you more than just your money."

Kaen sighed and nodded as he lay on his bed. His brain was running in twenty different directions. What would happen tomorrow consumed his mind, but he was also thinking about the letter from his dad. The fact that Hess had held onto it for so long and not shown it to Kaen, burned him. On the other hand, he knew why Hess had waited. He now realized, there was so much about this world he didn't know. The idea, that all these years he'd understood everything the world could offer, burst like a soap bubble on the wooden floor.

Turning to his side, he smiled at Hess and grunted.

"You got something to say?" Hess asked as he opened one eye.

"I gained a skill tonight," Kaen stated nonchalantly.

"Hairy dwarf balls, Kaen! You got a what?" Hess roared as he rolled off his bed and jumped to his feet. "What did you get and when?"

Kaen grinned. "When I finished telling the story of how we fought the orcs and goblins, the moment they cheered, my lifestone pulsed, and I got the notice."

"What skill?" Hess asked, groaning.

"Story Telling. It gave me level eight from the start. I'm not sure how good the skill is, though."

Hess shook his head and sat back down on his bed.

"You know every skill is important. It might seem like a wasted skill to you, but those who master it can walk into any room or even into the king's court and find themselves able to bend a crowd to their will," Hess explained. "Some of the greatest bards had mastered this skill and could change the direction of a kingdom's war plans. They could shift opinions and change minds without people realizing it was being done. A true silver tongue was a dangerous enemy if you did not know who they were."

Kaen lay on his side wondering about that skill. He had no stat increase or anything else besides the skill. Maybe Hess was right.

"Anything else you need to tell me or perhaps ask for a loan from the amount of alcohol you paid for tonight?"

Kaen groaned and then laughed as the night's memories flashed through his mind. "You and I know I easily increased our take on all this betting from that stunt. I am sure both purchases will be well covered by what people will spend on this silly betting thing you all do."

Hess nodded as he massaged his quad with his hand. He had not yet told Kaen how much they could earn or that he now believed that after all the funds were collected from this event, he could easily find them a place inside the walls of Ebonmount. Of course, that would mean leaving here and upsetting Sulenda. Sure, he could tell her it was because of Kaen and his desire to be inside the walls and closer for quests, but she would know that wasn't true.

"Kaen, I need to ask you a question."

"The way you say that sounds bad."

Hess chuckled and nodded. "You are smarter than I give you credit for. I am going to ask a hard question, and I need an honest answer. Not one with misdirection, just tell me the truth. Will you free me from the bond I have with you?"

Kaen turned on the bed till he faced Hess and then sat on the edge. He felt his bare feet on the wooden floors. The floors had been rubbed smooth from being cleaned and from countless guests walking over them. He looked around the room and stared at the picture in the middle of the room. It appeared to be an image of Beatrice. He wasn't sure if she had made sure it was hung there for him or any guest that stayed in this room.

"You avoiding the question?" Hess asked, watching Kaen look everywhere but at him.

Kaen sighed and looked at Hess. The man he saw across from him was hard to figure out. Part of Kaen saw Hess as a father figure. Part of Hess was a boss who worked Kaen, not because he wanted to take advantage of his strength or lifestone, but because he wanted him to grow strong. The other part Kaen saw was a man who was tired. Somehow Hess was real at this moment and exposed. There was a weakness in him that Kaen had never noticed until now.

"You still love her?"

Hess winced at the question. Without thinking, he touched his chest where his heart and gold token were. "I thought I was the one asking the questions," Hess joked.

"Your answer won't change mine. I just want to know if you can be honest with yourself and me."

Hess closed his eyes and faced the ceiling.

He sat for what felt like hours, not saying a word in the quietness of their room. Earlier, Kaen had asked how it was so quiet this close to the inn, and Hess had told him magical sound spells dampened the noise once they entered the room.

Finally, Hess opened his eyes and smiled at Kaen.

"Part of me still loves her just as much as I did all those years ago. The other part of me is scared we have changed so much over the years, we are in love with who the other person was back then and would not be in love with the person we are now. Does that make sense?"

Kaen nodded. There was a truth he needed to share now, or it might not get shared at all.

"I understand that completely. Sometimes if I am honest, you have felt like a father to me. I know I never would call you that to your face, but tonight, I can tell you the truth. You filled a hole in my heart I could never imagine being filled. With Pammon in my life now, I have felt joy again. It has been far too long since I have felt that."

"Joy is hard to come across. Cherish it," Hess said. He smiled, leaned back, and crossed his arms. "Now, what is your answer to my question?"

Kaen grimaced and sucked wind in through his teeth. "I guess all I can say is after I pass the adventurer's test, I will have to keep you bound to me. A gold token slave is hard to—"

"WHAT?!" Hess erupted and bounded out of his bed. "How dare you call me a sla—"

He stopped shouting when he saw Kaen laughing.

"Boy, I am about to beat you like I should have all those years ago!" Hess growled, then took a deep breath, letting the redness fade from his face.

Kaen fell over on the side of the bed and laughed. He laughed so hard, he started crying. "Oh . . . oh . . . Hess . . . You believed me . . . " Kaen couldn't talk, he was laughing so hard.

Hess flopped down on his bed and sighed. "I swear you wear me out in a different way every day, Kaen."

Kaen nodded and wiped the tears from his eyes as he sat up. "No worry, Hess. Soon, you will no longer be bound to me. You will be free. You have my word on this."

Hess smiled and tossed his pillow across the room at Kaen's face. Kaen reached up and easily caught it, and the second he pulled it down, preventing it from hitting his face, his eyes went wide at the sight of Hess towering over him. Hess had crossed the room in the blink of an eye.

Hess bent over and started tickling Kaen in a way he hadn't in years. Kaen tried to fight back as he laughed, upset that his ribs were that ticklish.

"Someday, boy, you will become a man, but tonight I'll pay you back for that joke!" Hess roared as he tickled Kaen for a good minute.

After all the horseplay was done, and they both lay in their individual beds and turned off the light globe, Hess was about to fall asleep.

"Hess, you awake?"

Grunting, Hess acknowledged that he was.

"I know I never said this, but thank you," Kaen called out across the darkness in the room. "Thank you for raising me. Thank you for loving me. I . . . I want you to know I love you."

Hess froze. His heart leaped in a way it had never before.

Ever so silently, Hess whispered, "I love you too, Kaen."

27

One Road Leads to the Guild Hall

The light came on before the sun was up.

Kaen was not sure if he had slept much at all. He was excited about this morning more than he realized.

You need to calm yourself. You are making me anxious due to how fast your heart is beating.

Kaen laughed.

Sorry, Pammon, I am just so nervous and excited about today. It has been the only thing I have dreamed about for so long. How have you been?

Bored. You know I miss your scratches and when you are close. I understand my need to stay away, but it is not easy. I have to stay farther away and closer to the mountains. There are more people and adventurers out in these woods than back home. I am easily a day away from you.

Are there that many people out in the woods?

There are groups of four to twelve sometimes out here. They are often gathering stuff in the woods closer to the town. I fly high so they cannot see me when I scout. I am getting bigger, though. I must fly every day as long as possible so you can ride with me.

Well, I will do my best and let you know once I know what rank I get!

You know I do not care what rank you are. I care that you are safe and that we grow stronger together. If you need my strength, ask, and I shall give it.

Thank you, Pammon, but I hope I do not need that kind of help today.

Breakfast had been half a chicken, four soft rolls, milk, and a few pieces of fresh fruit. Beatrice was the one to serve him, and she was a little tamer this morning. Kaen was unsure if she had acted as she had yesterday for show or if she had been told who he was and not to push herself upon him.

"Good luck today," Beatrice said as she cleaned off his table. "We all cannot wait to hear how things go!"

"Thank you," Kaen replied, finishing the last bit of the milk in his glass. It was extremely cold, even though it was not the time of year when most people could get milk this cold. He knew it must mean magic of some kind was responsible.

As he stood up, he saw Hess coming from Sulenda's office, and he was smiling. He made his way through the few patrons who were up early and eating. Most acknowledged him with a slight bow or waved hand. Then, Kaen noticed no one besides Beatrice had really talked to him this morning.

"Why are they not talking to me," Kaen asked when Hess was next to him.

"People believe it is bad luck to wish you a good day or even acknowledge you on the first day of your testing. Most will be better tomorrow, but there are strange beliefs about the adventurer's test."

"Do you believe in this thing?"

Hess laughed and shook his head as he pulled his gold token out of his shirt and let it hang outside of it. "If I did, I would not be talking to you," Hess joked. "I believe you are either ready for the test or not. Someone wishing you good luck or ignoring you, I don't believe will help. I actually believe the opposite. It puts some people in a bad state of mind and makes the test harder. Perhaps it was done to help weed out the chaff that is not ready."

Hess adjusted the backpack he was wearing and motioned to Kaen's bow. "Put it on your back, and let's go. It is a good walk, and I want to be at the gate first thing."

Kaen reached down and felt the power of the bow flow through him. It was not just the magic it infused him with that made him enjoy carrying it, it was also that his dad had made it for him.

The sun was starting to rise on the other side of the mountains, and the sky took on an amazing orange color in the clouds. As they walked north out of the inn, Kaen instinctively turned and looked in the direction he knew Pammon was. He could sense him hunting already. A week without seeing him seemed impossible to imagine, but Kaen was thankful that he knew Pammon longed for him also.

The streets were empty compared to when they had entered town yesterday. Wagons filled with goods needing to be transported moved slowly and steadily. People were setting out signs and preparing the outside of their shops. With fewer people on the street and the sidewalks, Kaen marveled at how much work people did to attract customers.

They passed one shop that had rugs for sale, and though it seemed a bad decision, the sidewalk outside their shop was covered by six different rugs. Each rug was of a different thickness and material. One felt like he was walking on wool, and another felt like he was squishing something wet.

"What is up with these rugs?" Kaen asked after they passed the shop and the man who had been watching Hess as he walked by. When an adventurer of Hess's level passed, and people saw his token, they all believed he could easily buy anything in their shop. "Why would people want something that feels like those?"

Hess chuckled and motioned backward with his head, never slowing his stride.

"There are many reasons why someone would want rugs like those. You might never know how amazing that soft rug feels on your bare feet. Once you do, you will gladly consider purchasing one. After a long day on the road or working a standing job, that brief moment brings a relief that is hard to describe."

"Well, what about the squishy one?"

"Good for jobs that require you to stand behind a counter or a desk. It will help relieve the stress in your legs and joints. There are actually some armors that feature something like that. Useful against blunt weapons."

Kaen glanced back at the shop and shook his head in disbelief. "How long will it be before I know everything like you do," Kaen joked.

"Trust me, Kaen, if you are smart and obey my wisdom, before you know it, you will surpass me in knowing the world. Your *special* friend and you will see things I can only dream of."

Kaen walked in silence next to Hess and thought about those words. Would Pammon one day be big enough to carry Hess and Kaen both through the sky? He could only imagine what Pammon saw as he soared above Ebonmount.

A good hour passed, and they were almost to the gate as the sun broke over the mountain's surface. The sunlight gleaming off the top of the stone keeps and walls made Kaen cover his eyes as he tried to gaze at them.

"You will go blind staring, so stop," Hess ordered as he put his hand on Kaen's head and lowered it. "You will need your vision for today's exam, so do not glance up at the sun unless absolutely necessary. Also, close your mouth and stop acting like a country fool who has never seen a woman with all her teeth."

Kaen laughed but still checked to make sure his mouth was indeed closed. He could not help the staring.

Coaches with elaborate woodwork and gold and silver would occasionally roll past them from the gates. Teams of horses that appeared in perfect health and size worked in harmony as a man or woman wearing clothes better than any he had ever worn kept the team moving, all while calling out at those who might get in their way.

Occasionally, a curtain would not cover the carriage windows, and he could see a man or a woman dressed in ornate clothes and with perfect hair or makeup. Hess had told him that many nobles, other rich merchants, and more lived inside the walls of Ebonmount. They played dangerous games to get adventurers to work for them and help their causes. Knowing the right ones to align with was a problem too many adventurers failed to appreciate. They became bonded, like Hess was to Kaen, and were unable to break that bond without terrible consequences.

Soon, they passed through the gate that Kaen swore was wider than three of their houses side-by-side. As they approached it, a guard came toward them, checking the flow of early-morning traffic. When he noticed the token on Hess's chest, he nodded in acknowledgment and moved back to his post.

"That's it?" Kaen whispered as they walked. "He didn't check anything else!"

Hess chuckled and nodded. "They might stop a wood or copper adventurer if they really wanted to, but one with a gold rank can come and go as they please unless the city has declared a special state of emergency."

Before Kaen could ask another question, Hess shushed him and pointed up ahead. "Now, pay attention to where we go. You will be tested on directions, and the city differs from the forest. Figure out landmarks, shops, and other things that will help you find your way. Be certain the thing you use to help you remember cannot be moved around like a sale cart or something else."

Kaen grunted as he tried to pay attention to where Hess was leading him. He was conflicted, wanting to stare at the huge buildings that beckoned him to come inside. Massive signs and decorations were everywhere, tempting those new to the city, like himself, to come and spend their hard-earned money inside. Men and women who were dressed in clean, pressed outfits harkened to him and Hess to come to see their wares or try their food and drink.

His senses were being assaulted. The sounds of music, people calling out for him, the smell of something amazing cooking, and even the smell of a forest after a rainstorm, found its way to his nose. Signs sometimes changed colors or shimmered in the light. One had an image that featured people actually dancing.

Kaen put his hand to his temple and groaned.

"We are barely two streets in, and I can barely focus on what you want me to do!" Kaen protested as he put his hands over his face. "Everywhere I look, I see something I want to stare at in amazement. That shop back there has the best-smelling bread I have ever smelled in my life! The woman over there would make Beatrice look ugly, and it feels like my heart wants me to go and see what she is selling! It feels like I'm going to go insane. It's like my mind is waging war against my senses!"

Hess nodded and stopped. He turned around and faced Kaen. "Close your eyes and pinch your nose, and just listen to the sound of my voice."

Kaen felt like a fool, but he trusted Hess and did just that. He stood in the street and closed his eyes and pinched his nose. He could still hear the people calling out and offering services and things to buy, yet he was straining to hear Hess's voice.

Kaen cocked his head, struggling to hear Hess. He knew Hess was talking, but it felt weird. He wanted to open his eyes, but he knew Hess would get upset at him for doing so until he was told to.

"Kaen, focus on me. Focus on my voice."

There! Hess's voice could barely be heard over all the noise around him. It sounded like Hess was a field away. It was so faint. He strained his ears and started to ignore all the other things calling for his attention.

"Kaen, listen to me. Listen only to me. When you can hear me clearly, nod your head."

The voice was stronger, but it was still muddled. Still being drowned out like someone shouting into the wind.

Kaen forced himself to breathe slowly and calm down. He focused on what he wanted to hear more than anything else. Hess. The man who raised him.

His heart and lifestone surged again. They beat together like they always had in situations like this.

[Charm Resistance Skill Acquired]
[Charm Resistance Skill Increased x5]
[Wisdom increased by 1]

"When you can hear me clearly, nod your head."

Kaen started nodding his head furiously. He was smiling from ear to ear.

Hess was training him, and he had not realized it.

28

Inside the Guild Hall

As they walked through the rest of the city, Kaen was smiling like he had just danced with the prettiest girl in all of the town. He saw the people and heard them and could still smell everything, but now it was not as overpowering as it had been.

"You're telling me they can use magic to lure people like that?" Kaen asked as they walked. "Doesn't that seem wrong?"

Hess shrugged, never missing a step. "I know why they do it. If you cannot learn to resist the temptation of the first few streets, you will find the adventurer is not ready for the test. Anyone who enters those streets at this time of day is either already impervious to those charms or being tested. You remember how the guard did not stop us?"

Kaen did. He had commented on it.

"He knows I don't need to be told to take a different street. Anyone else coming in during this time of day is like you or works in the outer city. They will direct all other people down a different street until the second hour after sunrise. Only those like me or you are allowed on this street, and that is why we must be here in the morning."

"So what happens if someone like me showed up in the afternoon at the gates?"

Hess turned his head and winked at Kaen. "They would tell you to come back tomorrow at this time. You would not be allowed in the city unless you had money to stay inside. If you have money for that, then you would already have that skill. Those families ensure their children are prepared for that part of the test."

"I want to ask how you can be certain," Kaen argued. "What if someone was to make it through somehow?"

"They would fail the test. I doubt anyone will be here today where you could see that, but during part of the test, you would be lured out of the testing grounds, if you do not have that skill with at least a two in it. Again, all of this has been designed to help make sure adventurers are ready for actual adventuring."

Hess pointed at a man who stood guard at the end of the street they were approaching. The man bowed, smiled at Hess, and then tipped his head toward Kaen.

"He is there to verify you made it through on your own. Not because I am pulling you or carrying you. It would look very bad if I did that, but some have tried it before," Hess said with a sigh. "Thousands of adventurers died over the years devising a system to ensure recruits were ready for this life. Just having a lifestone doesn't make one an adventurer. Many people use them for business, crafting, and more."

"So why is my starting skill so much higher?"

"I believe it is a combination of your *friend* and the experience you've already had with the orcs and goblins. You have a connection that helps your mind, and you have already experienced moments in battle where one can freeze and fail. The five you have right now will possibly take many others a year or more to gain. As you fight stronger foes, yours will slowly increase."

A light globe went off in Kaen's head. "That's why there are different tiered adventures and quests! To make sure that what one faces isn't something that will overpower them from the start!"

"Exactly," Hess agreed, picking up his pace. "We need to hurry. We aren't late, but we aren't early either. I want to be there sooner than later."

Kaen started walking faster and heard Hess laugh as he passed him a bit before slowing down. "Do I still need to focus on remembering the way we are coming?"

"No, that was part of the training. It would be good to remember, as you will travel this path a lot, but it is a straight shot to the guild. That is why most of these shops now feature weapons, armor, healing potions, and other adventuring things. You can sell stuff for a good price at most of these shops, if you have the haggling skill. If not, then you should see what the guild offers."

"Should I work on getting the haggling skill?" asked Kaen.

Hess shrugged. "I have it but can't say it was worth all the time and effort. These shopkeepers are well-skilled and willing to help you, but they also don't like giving up too much. Better to try it outside of town where people might be more inclined to buy something because you tell them a story how you got the item."

Kaen nodded, realizing that his storytelling skill might serve him even better if he did manage to pick up the haggling skill.

"Enough daydreaming. The guild is just two blocks ahead."

Kaen glanced down the road and saw a massive building looming at the end of the street. He could make out a huge water fountain out front and saw people talking and hanging out next to it.

Just a few blocks more till he would be inside the building of his dreams.

"Hess Brumlin!" a short, squat man with white hair called out as he came from one of the rooms to the side of the questing desk.

Hess approached the man, and Kaen stood mesmerized to actually be inside the building.

They had just entered through the doorway. Kaen was trying to take in the main room. Huge trophies of orcs, goblins, animals he had never seen before, and more littered the walls and the floors along the walls. A massive rug ran the length of the entire fifty-foot-long room up to a dark wood counter where a few people he guessed were adventurers talked with the guild employees behind the counter. One man had two small rapier-like swords and was covered in some light leather armor like Kaen's. His head was shaved, except for a patch at the back that turned into a long braid running down to the middle of his back. He couldn't make out what the man was saying to the employees, but it seemed he was unhappy with how the conversation was going.

A pair of women wearing plate armor, each carrying a massive weapon almost as tall as them, were leaning against the counter while an employee counted out a stack of coins. Both women stood about six feet tall and had black skin. Their plate armor had runes running all over the front and sides that he could see. Each of them had a gold token that stood out against their silver armor.

"Kaen!"

Kaen jumped and realized he had not been paying attention.

Hess shook his head and smiled as he waited for Kaen to acknowledge him. "Forgive me, Herb, but it seems my young friend Kaen is still awestruck by his dream finally coming true."

The man Hess was talking to chuckled. "It happened to all of us our first time, I would believe. We never want to rush that first moment of making it to the guild before all the hard stuff starts."

The man waddled over to Kaen and extended his hand. "Pleasure to meet you, Kaen. Any friend of Hess's is one I feel sorry for," he joked.

Kaen laughed and shook the man's hand. "Thank you. Sorry, I just can't believe I'm finally here. It is like a dream."

Herb nodded and motioned to Hess and Kaen to follow him. "I wondered if you were going to make it today. I have heard the news," Herb said, leaning in close and whispering. "Some of us know who Kaen is, and we *might* have bet on the higher end. Of course, none of us have a role in the final decision, so no worries about things not being legit."

Hess laughed and shook his head as he leaned over and rubbed Herb's white hair, messing it up horribly.

"Well, I won't tell Sulenda. I'm sure she will cause an uproar if she felt it was. Can't have a dishonest woman believing someone else is ruining her income."

Herb chuckled and reached up to fix his hair. The way he did it without seeming to be bothered, told Kaen it was not the first time Hess had done that.

"Why all this betting? I mean doesn't it seem a bit too much? Are things really that boring around here?" asked Kaen.

Hess and Herb both chuckled.

"A generation or two ago, the betting thing really took off," explained Herb as they walked through the building. "It was originally just between adventurers betting on new test takers. Word got out after a few years, and soon others in the city wanted in on the action."

Herb glanced around and made sure no one was looking. "A *different* group of individuals ran the betting for a generation, and there were some bad moments. The last ten years were much better, and once Sulenda took over, her reputation as an honest adventurer and her skill with odds had her taking the whole operation over. Some recruits don't draw much betting, but I see you changing that this time around."

Soon, they were in a side room with massive wooden stairs running along the wall to the second floor.

"If you two will follow me, Fiola is waiting upstairs for the two of you."

Hess groaned and glanced down at Herb, who he saw was trying not to laugh out loud.

"Tell me she isn't still the guild master!"

Herb nodded with glee. "She spent the night here to make sure you didn't slip in before she arrived. She has been waiting all night, once word of your arrival reached our ears."

Another groan escaped Hess. He glanced at Kaen and licked his lips. "I can't say this will go as smoothly as I hoped, Kaen. I have no doubt she will make things difficult for you, but I know you will be fine."

Kaen glanced at the two men who were staring at him with weird looks on their faces. "Why do I feel like I'm missing out on something I should know?"

Herb motioned toward Hess with his head and raised his eyebrows.

Hess saw that motion, reached over, and messed up Herb's hair again as he turned and started up the stairs.

"Let's go and get this mess taken care of. Better to clean the stables out the first day than to have to smell it all week while you cry about the mess."

Kaen glanced back at Herb, who was fixing his hair again, and motioned to Hess.

"Not my place, boy, but your father and Hess had a way of upsetting people who sit behind a desk. Some often wondered if they both had a skill in that, with how easy it came."

Not knowing if he should groan or laugh, Kaen started up the stairs after Hess.

As they walked up the stairs, Kaen realized the wooden rails had gold etched in them. Not like some thin line occasionally, but a solid gold line at least an inch wide running the whole way up the rail. The wood was something he had never seen. The detailed work of the wooden panels next to him was finer than anything he had ever witnessed before. Battle scenes were carved in some. Others featured a forest or what he believed was what one called an ocean. One featured a dragon and a man on its back, flying through the clouds. He almost stopped to stare at that one, but he knew he needed to keep up with Hess.

When they reached the top of the stairs, Hess led him along a broad hallway across a beautiful green rug that covered the entire floor. Every step seemed to want to make him feel relaxed and at ease. Huge metal armored decorations stood inset inside the walls, each one holding a single sword at the ready. They looked prepared to jump out and defend at a moment's notice.

Kaen could hear Hess grumbling as they walked. What could Hess and his father have done to make Hess act this way? A few dozen feet led to a small room on their left, and a young elf woman sat behind the desk. Her outfit was a solid olive green pressed suit; she was smiling, looking at them the moment they stepped around the corner.

"Adventurer Hess Brumlin, it is a pleasure to meet you finally," the woman said with a smile. She motioned to the door behind her. "Please go in. The Guild Master is waiting to see you!"

29

Choices To Make

The woman had motioned to two massive doors that were a good twelve feet tall. Gold and silver outlined the door in a pattern of trees, birds, and other small animals. The door appeared to be made from the same wood as the rails. Kaen could see small runes running the entire length from the bottom to the top. He could only imagine what kinds of wards and spells might be enchanting it.

Hess gave a slight bow and motioned for Kaen to follow him. They stood outside the door for a few seconds before Hess put both hands on the doors and pushed them open simultaneously.

Even though Kaen knew Hess had used a lot of force, they only opened a few feet each, creating a narrow path for both of them.

Stepping into the room behind the door was like being transported to a library. The walls were fifteen feet tall, and books lined huge shelves around the room. A glass dome sat at the top of the room, allowing the morning sun inside. Light globes hung along the walls, giving off just enough light to keep the entire room looking like it was bathed in sunlight. A massive desk sat at the back of the room where the rounded half-circle section came together, covered in books, papers, and more, but in the middle were two couches, green and etched with gold tread. The one on the left held a woman who appeared to be maybe forty, but Kaen knew she was much older than that, if she was an elf.

Her beautiful blond hair was tied down her back in a single braid with gems and other adornments. Her outfit was composed of flowing silk-like material that he had seen only once in his life. It seemed to breathe as she breathed. Her skin was white like snow but in a way that screamed life, not frigidness. Her face, however, screamed cold steel, ready to be plunged into someone. Her blue eyes gazed at Hess with a look of anger and frustration. Her elegant fingers tapped together as her hands rested, clasped together on her knees.

"Hess," the woman said, in a voice that sounded soothing and terrifying simultaneously. "It has been far too long. Please sit across from me and have your charge join you."

Hess sighed and then gave a bow. "Guild Master Fiola, it has been far too long. Thank you for personally taking the time to see me and Kaen this morning."

Hess sat on the couch and motioned for Kaen to join him. Kaen gave a slight bow before sitting down next to Hess.

Hess scooted all the way back and leaned against the plush fabric. His massive frame allowed him to sit against the far edge of the couch and still keep his feet on the floor, making him look at ease and relaxed. Kaen, however, could not reach the floor if he sat all the way back, so he stuck near the edge, lest he look like a child with his feet dangling off the ground.

"Hess," Fiola tsked.

"Fiola," Hess replied with a smile.

"Are you trying to goad me on the day your charge is supposed to test, or are you still as pleasant as a thorn in one's backside?"

Hess smiled and shrugged. "I am the same man I have always been, except a little softer now that I have cared for my charge. Today is not about me or the problems you and I might have. It is about Kaen Marshell and his testing. Perhaps we can call a truce for his sake."

As if Hess had somehow managed to land a strike on an unguarded foe, the rough exterior of Fiola gave way to a soft smile for the first time since Kaen had entered the room.

"For his sake, I will forgo our problems and deal with them later," she replied as she glared at Hess one last time before turning her attention to Kaen, smiling.

"Welcome, Kaen. I have been waiting for this day. I must say you look so much like your father. It is uncanny."

"Thank you, Guild Master Fiola," Kaen answered with a slight head nod.

Fiola nodded and leaned forward a little. "Now I have heard of some exploits you have already accomplished. As rousing as the story I heard you shared with some people at the inn where you are staying do you have anything to prove what you say is true besides your word and his?"

Kaen almost said something he knew he should not. This woman was doubting Hess's word, and that upset him more than he thought it would.

"I do. I have a few letters from our town's mayor and most of the ears or heads of the ones we defeated," Kaen said.

"Most?" Fiola inquired, raising an eyebrow.

"Sometimes heads get destroyed, and I did not know I would need the ears until after we had defeated the goblins. Only after we found out the woman was dead, did Hess inform me we would need the trophies."

Fiola nodded as she tapped her fingers on her knee. He could see she was considering everything he had said.

"Very well. Turn the trophies in at the counter. I will take the letters, if you please."

Kaen nodded, reached into his small pouch, and pulled both letters out. Hess had given them to him earlier that morning when he'd told Kaen he would have to present the letters himself.

He watched as Fiola broke the seals and read each letter twice. Her fingers followed the lines, and occasionally, she would tap a word or two on a page and glance up at Kaen. She never glanced in Hess's direction.

"So, a slayer of three orcs and twenty-plus goblins. That is an impressive feat for a tokened adventurer, to say the least," she declared, pausing momentarily to finally glance at Hess, who was had not moved. "I am torn about how your testing should go after such a feat by one like yourself."

"I'm sorry, ma'am. What do you mean when you say *one like yourself*?"

Fiola smiled and nodded. "You know who your father was and what rank he held?"

Kaen nodded slowly as he watched her, wondering what she was getting at.

"The son of an almost mithril adventurer has some mighty large shoes to fill. Do you not think?"

Kaen frowned and shook his head. "I am not here to fill his shoes. I am here to do what I have dreamed of since I was a child. To be an adventurer who would help keep this land safe and accomplish something great. I never thought I would live in my father's shadow until you said something."

Hess let a small snort out, and Kaen glanced at him but his expression was blank again.

Fiola glanced at Kaen and then at Hess. Her eyes seemed to shimmer with fury. "Did you coach him to say those things?" Fiola asked as she glared at Hess.

Hess leaned forward, and his face became hard and almost ugly. "I would not sully his name by doing such a thing. To even ask that proves a point I made almost eight years ago."

Fiola flinched backward as if Hess had struck her with his hand along her face. She sat quietly for a moment, trembling. Her whole body seemed to shake, but with what, Kaen was not sure.

No one said a word, and Kaen did his best to sit still like a statue as the two adults stared at each other.

Finally, Fiola moved forward, put her hand to her forehead, and bowed it. "I must ask forgiveness from both of you. I was wrong to accuse Hess of coaching you on how to respond, and I was wrong for doubting the sincerity your pursuit of this path. For that, I will make amends the only way I can."

Fiola stood up from the couch, moved to the desk, and set down the papers Kaen had given her. She moved a few things, found a small silver box, and opened it, then pulled some items from it. After closing it, she moved back to the couch and leaned forward at the edge of her seat.

"Kaen, based on your achievements before coming here, I could normally offer you two choices." Fiola held up bronze and iron adventurer tokens. Kaen gazed them both, trying to calm his hands and not shake.

"I can offer you the bronze token right now," Fiola declared as she held the bronze one closer to him. "You can leave today with it in hand and start your journey here today as our newest recruit. No need to take the test. No need to prove yourself, since your deeds have already done that. Just reach out and take it right now, and we are done here today."

Fiola held the token just a few feet from Kaen. He had wanted to be an adventurer his whole life, and here it was. Starting as a bronze was more than he had dreamed of. Now, though, he knew that was not enough. He wanted more. He had earned more. He had trained all those hours and worked so hard, cleaning, hunting, practicing, and even breaking those rocks to be able to be strong enough for this moment.

"What is your second option?" Kaen asked.

Fiola smiled and pulled the bronze token back. As she did, she extended the iron token toward him.

"You will take the test, and I expect you to pass it easily. Simply pass, and I will start you as an iron-ranked adventurer. An impossible task, except for the truly mighty and amazing men and women of our guild. Those who have done this have often risen to the rank of gold or platinum with ease," she stated, smiling. "Pass the test with a perfect score, and I will start you halfway to silver. With a perfect score and the trophies you have brought to prove your feats, I am within my power to start you there. Your name would be known throughout this land and other lands as one of renown. Undoubtedly, many would try to woo you to join their team or squads to help take down higher-ranked quests."

Kaen could feel his mouth going dry and wet all at the same time. His heart was beating faster, and he was trying to breathe normally and slow his heart down. There, right in front of him, was a token he had not even considered he would earn for years. Years!

Hess had said he would be able to get a perfect score. Why would he not take this? What else could she offer him that was better?

"What is your third offer?" Kaen asked with a slight tremble in his voice.

Fiola laughed and nodded, and as she pulled her hand back, she extended the other. Nothing was in it, but a moment later, a silver token on a chain fell a few inches from her fist.

Hess sat up and glanced at Fiola and at Kaen. He knew that for one to start as silver was almost impossible. A guild master would have to have some very good reasons for a thing such as this to take place.

"This seems too good to be true," Kaen said with a wary look at Fiola and the silver token.

Fiola laughed and nodded her head.

"Oh, Kaen, it is far worse than you can imagine!"

30

Trapping the Trapper

"You want him to do what?!" Hess shouted as he jumped off the couch. "You can't be serious!"

Fiola focused on Kaen and ignored Hess, who was acting like an upset child looking for attention.

"Let me get this straight," Kaen said, tapping his finger against his chin. "If I attempt this more difficult test and pass, just pass, and I share my stats with you, you will let me start at silver. If I fail the test or lie about my stats, I start as an iron with no points toward silver."

"Correct!" Fiola answered with a smile. "Think of the renown you would gain from starting as a silver! Even if you fail, you would still be an iron, and people would know you attempted the impossible!"

Kaen saw the perk of both of those things. Starting as a silver would provide him with so many opportunities and wealth that starting as an iron would take forever to acquire. It would allow Hess to be free of his oath without any worries.

His biggest concern was not being ready for the next level. Being silver meant that he would be expected to take on silver quests. He thought about his lack of experience and training in actual quests. He did not want to risk himself, or Pammon, on things they were unprepared for. He also had no idea what this test might involve.

As he considered those things, one last thought came to mind, and he knew it would be the one that made the decision for him. Right before he started to speak, he felt his lifestone pulse. It was different than all the other times. Usually, it guided his hands, but now it wanted to guide his mind and words.

"How long do I have to decide? Can I come back tomorrow morning and tell you my answer?"

Fiola smiled at Kaen and then smiled a little more as she turned her gaze to Hess, who was trying not to yell.

"I will give you till tomorrow morning," Fiola answered.

"No matter what I choose, I have a few other requirements," Kaen stated as he stood up and moved around the couch.

"Requirements? From me?" Fiola scoffed. "Do you forget who I am?"

Kaen stood behind the couch, leaning against it with his arms. His lifestone was throbbing, as it had been for the last few minutes since she had revealed the third option. He had to stand and lean over because the lifestone felt like it would rip itself out of his chest.

"I have not, but I also realized a few things as I think about all this. If you want me to possibly pick option three, which I think is what you really desire, you will agree to them, or I won't even consider it. Either way, I'll walk out of here iron ranked."

Fiola almost growled at the way Kaen was speaking to her. It was as if his father was standing behind him, coaching him how to speak.

"And what if I removed all those options and made you start as a wood?"

Kaen laughed and shrugged. His lifestone told him to be brave. To trust what it told him to say. "I would start as a wood, but only after I told everyone about the three options you offered, how you defamed my father's name and, how, with no proof, you accused a gold token adventurer of breaking the rules."

Fiola rose to her feet, and that white, ivory skin on her face turned red. She opened her mouth, pointed one of those elegant fingers at Kaen, and froze. She saw him smiling at her. She knew that smile. She also knew she had just been trapped in her own snare. She had let her frustration and anger with Hess blind her to what she was doing to herself. The walls she had intended to put around this boy now enclosed her, and he held the key to her livelihood.

She knew if those words were spoken and the guild heard them, an inquiry would be started, and she would lose her position. She was crossing thin ice by even offering that third option. Her own pettiness had caused her to do such a thing. She was furious, but that also meant she was not thinking right.

It took every ounce of her strength to lower her finger and close her mouth as she walked around the couch. When she was behind the couch, she mimicked Kaen's stance and used her arms to lean against it. A controlled breath returned her face to its normal ivory color.

"What are your two requirements?" she asked as meekly as she could force herself to.

Kaen smiled and nodded. His lifestone had a beat of its own right now.

Hess was sitting as quietly as a mouse, not moving, as he had no clue what game Kaen was playing.

"First, I want whichever option I choose, to start the day after tomorrow. I'll give my answer and then have one day to prepare for it. Everyone knows a good night's sleep is important, and I'll probably be tossing and turning all night trying to decide which one to choose."

Fiola scrunched an eyebrow at Kaen. That request was not a terrible one at all. "I accept. And the second?"

His lifestone moved him. It emboldened him. He felt the power of the situation and knew he needed to portray the strength he had. Kaen straightened and appeared a little taller as he crossed his arms.

"I will only share my stats if I pass the more difficult test," Kaen declared. "If I fail it, my stats remain a secret, and I get to use my equipment during the test as well."

Fiola tapped her fingers loudly against the couch. Kaen was outmaneuvering her more than he could know. She had anticipated knowing his stats beforehand and had planned to strip him down to everything except standard clothes and a bow. She wanted to see if his stats were like his father's. There had been rumors about how Hoste had grown so powerful, but no one really knew. Some said it was because he always worked passionately and gave everything he had. Others thought it was magical equipment. She knew the truth about who Kaen was and what he had. If she told Kaen no, she would have no chance to learn how high his stats were until another time came, and the way Kaen was controlling her now, she was not certain when, if ever, that time would come.

"And if I say no?" Fiola asked, trying to control her tone.

"Then I say today or tomorrow, I can attempt the normal test, and we can let you get back to your usual duties."

Kaen stood there as if he was watching grass grow and did not have a care in the world, even though he felt his heart and his lifestone thumping so hard, they would burst in his chest. Something was happening, but he was not sure what. He somehow knew he had the upper hand in this whole conversation. The whole *telling everyone* what Fiola had told him was more of a bluff; he did not want to think about how many different ways that could go wrong. He just knew if he could pull this off, everything would work out for Hess.

Fiola fidgeted first. Her options were limited, and her plan had backfired. She had not anticipated Kaen realizing he held all the power and that she could never achieve what she had hoped for. Worse for her was that Hess was getting a front-row seat to it all.

"I will accept," Fiola said, "as long as we agree none of our conversations is ever mentioned in public, regardless of the outcome."

Kaen nodded and moved to stand near Fiola and held his hand out to her.

Fiola eyed Kaen up and down. This teen boy had just bested her, and she knew it. Even worse, she knew Kaen had realized he had bested her.

They shook hands, and Kaen smiled.

[Haggling Skill Acquired]
[Haggling Skill Increased x9]
[Intelligence increased by 2]

“Thank you for giving me this opportunity,” Kaen declared as he let go of her hand and gave a deep bow, putting his hand to his heart.

The bow was not an actual show of respect but a way to allow him to put his hand on his heart to try to calm it down. He held the bow a few seconds and then rose, noticing Fiola’s weird glance at him.

“If there is nothing else you need from the two of us, would it be ok if we departed? I need to get back to our room and consider the best course for myself and how I can help the guild the most.”

Fiola smiled and shook her head. “I believe you may be worse than Hoste,” she muttered, motioning with her hand for Kaen to go. “Remember our agreement, and I expect you to be here at the same time tomorrow with your decision.”

Kaen nodded and motioned for Hess to come.

Hess glanced back and forth between Fiola and Kaen and quickly got to his feet, giving a slight bow as he made his way to the door.

“Hairy dwarf balls, Kaen! What in a dragon’s turd were you thinking?” Hess hissed as they walked down the stairs. “Do you realize what you just did?”

Kaen tried to laugh as he led Hess down the stairs. His heart was pounding even though his lifestone had stopped pulsing. He reached out and could feel that Pammon was happy and content also. Soaring across the sky to the southeast somewhere. He knew Pammon could feel how Kaen felt too.

“We will talk outside where it will be safer. I’ll explain everything in a moment, but first, we need to turn those ears and heads in at the counter.”

Hess grunted and followed Kaen down the stairs. *Blast Hoste,* he thought. That man must have known who his son might turn into. In mere moments after coming into this place, Kaen seemed like a different person.

The men and women behind the counter were excited to see what Kaen presented, and other adventurers came over to hear what the commotion was. Many were amazed that an untested person had accomplished these things, and none wanted to argue how improbable it could be with a gold adventurer by his side.

“Hess!”

Kaen and Hess turned and saw Herb appearing from a door behind the counter.

“I heard from Fiola that Kaen would be turning in his trophies! I wanted to see the orc he shot through the eye in the cave,” he proclaimed louder than he needed to.

The others around them started murmuring.

"He shot an orc in a cave and somehow struck him in the eye!"

"Look at the bow! It must be magical!"

"Could a kid really do that? I am not sure I could even do that!"

Chuckling, Hess acknowledged Herb and waved him over. He knew what Herb and Fiola were doing. Word would spread quickly about Kaen, and no matter what decision he made, the others would be hard-pressed to complain about it.

"This is the one he shot in the eye," Hess declared loudly, "and this one is the one he shot in the neck after firing two arrows at once and killing his warlock and shaman. The other is the one he killed while getting shot in the chest by its bow."

Some of the adventurers came up and congratulated Kaen and asked to hear his story. Not wanting to miss an opportunity, Kaen shared what he had shared at the inn last night but found better ways to pause at the right moment and when to increase or lower his voice.

When he finished the story, all those gathered in the hall cheered and laughed, impressed with his feat and ability to tell it so well.

[Story Telling Skill Increased]

"When will you take the test?" one of the bronze adventurers asked.

Kaen smiled and shrugged. "Guild Master Fiola wanted to look over some things, and she asked me to return tomorrow to discuss that. So tomorrow, I expect to know how things will go. Maybe I will take a test, and maybe I won't!" Kaen exclaimed.

"Won't take the test?! Is that even possible?"

A gold token adventurer who was standing next to Hess chuckled. "It is rare, but it is possible if this boy is telling the truth."

Kaen grinned and looked around the room. "I plan on taking a test if I can. I hear there are people all over town betting on how my testing goes and at which rank I will end up. I don't want to disappoint anyone for sure!"

Adventurers around Kaen started murmuring, and there was discussion about which rank he might end up at.

"If you will excuse me, all I need to do is head back to the Fluffy Ingot and rest up for tomorrow! Feel free to stop by if you want, and you can share your stories with me," Kaen said as he motioned for Hess to go.

Hess chuckled, patted the gold token adventurer next to him, and started to leave. "Looks like my charge has summoned me," he stated with a smile.

Laughter followed and some well wishes for tomorrow also.

Kaen was grinning from ear to ear, as he knew his plan appeared to be working out the way he had hoped it would.

31

The Reason to Bet It All

"You are killing me, Kaen," Hess grumbled as they walked down the same street on which they had arrived in the main city. "Why are you waiting to tell me what you thought when you did that to Fiola?!"

Kaen glanced around the street and shook his head. "Until we are in our room with Sulenda, and I am not sure that no one is following or listening," Kaen whispered as he smiled at Hess, "I will wait. Just know something just came to me, and I went with it."

Hess groaned but gave up trying to get Kaen to talk. He was actually impressed that Kaen had considered that someone might be spying on them.

The trip back had gone quickly, as Kaen set a fast pace. He had gotten confused several times about which direction to go, but Hess was more than willing to help him figure out where he had turned wrong.

When they entered the inn, Beatrice saw them and cheered. "So, Kaen, what is the news? We are dying to hear!"

Kaen and Hess noticed there were more people in the inn than either had expected. Kaen had not yet learned how much betting and interest in his placement there was. It was far beyond anything the town had seen in years.

"I wish I had an answer, but after meeting with Guild Master Fiola and her learning of my deeds and accomplishments, she has decided to think about it and let me know tomorrow what I will do," Kaen answered loudly.

A groan echoed across the inn from the people waiting for an update and perhaps considering how they might want to bet.

"Fear not though, Miss. Beatrice," Kaen continued loudly as he walked toward the bar, "I have no plans on anything lower than bronze."

Gasps were heard across the inn, and a few people cursed, obviously ones who had bet on a lower rank for him.

When he arrived at the bar, he winked at Eltina. "Is Sulenda in? We need to talk to her."

"She is in the office. I'll check and see if she is ready for you," she informed Kaen and jumped down from her box behind the bar.

"No worries. She said she wanted to see me first thing when I got back," Kaen declared as he walked past her. He motioned for Hess to follow him.

"Who the hell do you think you are?" Sulenda shouted as Kaen entered her office without knocking. "I don't know what game you think you are playing or what Hess has told you to do, but you best not think I will tolerate you disrespecting me in my own place just because I got sentimental last night."

Kaen nodded and let out a slight chuckle. Even when faced with her threat, his laughter caught Sulenda off guard. His lifestone was raging at the moment, and it was filling him with power and ideas he had never considered. He felt like a new person, and it was intoxicating and amazing at the same time.

"Hess, go sit in the chair so the three of us can talk. I have a plan to set the two of you up for life," Kaen announced, ignoring Sulenda and her reaction.

Hess's head shook in disbelief at how Kaen was behaving. He shut the door behind him and glanced at Sulenda. He saw the rage in her eyes and the curiosity about what Kaen was doing.

"I'm sorry, Sulenda," Hess said as he moved to a chair. "I have no idea what the boy is talking about, but you should have seen him back Fiola into a corner in a way I have not seen anyone do in a long time."

Sulenda's eyebrows rose as she looked at Kaen, who was still standing and smiling as if he had just won a competition against the best in the world.

Sulenda shifted the glass on her desk, having yet to take a drink since Kaen had started telling her what had happened. He had made her swear to secrecy on her lifestone. She had only done it after Hess had told her to.

Knowing Kaen could attempt a high-level quest by himself and skip all the other ranks seemed tempting, but there was a lot of risk with that. She knew far too well how badly things often went for solo adventurers.

"So what option will you choose?" she asked as she stared at her glass.

Kaen smiled, leaned forward in the chair, and pointed at both her and Hess. "You two get to decide," he teased. "As I listened to her talk, I knew she must have a reason for that third option. I realized that she wanted to see my stats. There has to be something really important about it because no one, and we all know *no one*, ever asks for that. That means her reason must have something to do with my Dad."

Hess glanced at Sulenda and nodded. He had realized the same thing but could not interfere in their discussion.

"Your dad never shared his stats with me," Hess informed Kaen, "but I knew he was much more powerful than I ever was. I was not sure if it was all the items he owned or what, but he could defeat everyone of his rank outside of a few mages with exceptional control spells."

Kaen nodded and tapped his chest. "Do lifestones work differently for each race? Are there perks for noble families?"

Hess leaned back in his chair and shrugged. "I wouldn't know. That is outside of my knowledge. There have been lots of rumors over the years. You would need to find someone high up in a king's court or in the guild who might have any actual information about such things."

Sulenda stopped playing with her glass and looked at Hess. "Children of adventurers are often stronger, though," she mumbled. "The longer the line of adventurers, it is rumored, the stronger they can become. Nobles and the line of the king are often stronger."

"There haven't been that many traceable lines of adventurers in hundreds of years," Hess argued. "Most die out, and very few ever marry another adventurer." When those words came out of his mouth, he knew he had made a mistake.

Sulenda growled and leaned back in her chair. "No. No, they do not," she declared with an air of anger.

Hess sighed and shook his head. "That isn't what I meant," Hess groaned.

"What you mean and what you said doesn't matter," snapped Sulenda. "It is the truth."

Kaen sighed. "Would you two please stop fighting for a moment? You cannot change the past, but you can hopefully help us all enjoy the future."

Sulenda stared at Kaen. Her eyes finally softened, and she nodded. "Why do you ask these questions, Kaen? You know who your mother was, even if she died earlier in your childhood. I do not believe she was an adventurer."

Kaen looked at Hess, and Hess saw the question in his eyes.

"You and I both know that she wasn't," Hess stated.

Kaen nodded and smiled. Even though there was a look of hurt in his eyes, he knew he had to move on. "I know, but I'll forget this line of questions for another day. For now, we must focus on tomorrow and what we need to decide."

Kaen walked over to the desk and picked up a piece of paper from the neat stack on the corner of the desk. "Can I borrow a pen?"

Sulenda opened her drawer, pulled one out, and handed it to Kaen.

Kaen smiled and started drawing columns and rows like the ones on the chalkboard. "Ok, now pay attention because I think we can use Fiola's desire to know my stats to set us all up for a long time."

Kaen pointed to the column he had made and the ranks he had written down. "We all know I won't be wood, copper, or even bronze. So everyone who bet on those will lose their money. That means we can focus on how many bet on iron."

As Kaen wrote these things, his lifestone started to fade. The power it gave him and the direction it wanted him to go was almost gone.

Kaen stared at Sulenda. She realized that Hess and Kaen were both looking at her now.

Mumbling to herself, she pulled a small box from a drawer in her desk. It looked plain but had no opening. She took the quill from her desk, pricked her finger, and put the now bloody finger on the edge of the box. Suddenly, the side of the box closest to her popped out, and she pulled a small piece of paper from it.

"That is pretty cool," Kaen mumbled in adoration.

Sulenda nodded and smiled. "Always protect the secret, you must."

She read the paper a few times, and Kaen saw the smile grow as her eyes moved down it.

"Right now, only a handful of people have bet on iron. Less than maybe 3 percent," Sulenda stated as she ticked the fingers on her other hand, doing math in her head. "We stand to make a fair amount of money off the current bets, knowing that none of them will win now."

Kaen laughed and pointed to the silver square. "If we wait until tomorrow and we announce that I choose to attempt the harder test, everyone who has lost would know it. They would then have another chance to bet on what rank they think I will become! If you two were honest and you had to choose between me being iron rank or silver rank, which one would you bet on?"

Hess groaned and rubbed his chin, while Sulenda smiled. She spoke first. "Iron. I would never bet on silver because it is impossible. Even knowing what I know now about you, I would still bet iron. I cannot begin to believe you or anyone else can pass a test worthy of starting at silver rank."

Kaen nodded and looked at Hess, who was still struggling with his decision.

"Blast you, boy!" Hess lamented. "I want to say silver, but she is right! I would not wager on you getting silver, and I'm your bloody trainer."

Kaen laughed and waved both of them off. "What if I could guarantee that I became silver?"

"That isn't possible," Hess argued. "No one knows what the test will be. We both remember what it takes to be silver, and it is not easy at all."

Kaen shrugged and never let his grin leave his face. "You are forgetting something, though. One of the finer details of my agreement with Fiola. I can take the test with any gear I want. So what if we help me out a little by outfitting me with a few more items?"

"That's cheating!" Sulenda practically shouted as she stood from her seat and smacked her desk. "You would cheat for your adventurer rank?"

Kaen scoffed and held Sulenda's glare. "What makes it cheating? Why should I get to take a special test when others are not allowed to? Why should I have an opportunity no one else gets? Just because of who my dad was? Or just because of the goblins and orcs I killed?"

Sulenda started to speak but held her tongue. She knew Kaen was right about that. She was already upset that he was being allowed to even try for a silver rank from the start. She had worked hard and long to earn hers, and this young boy now had the chance to bypass years of all that work without the toil.

"Even if we gave you gear that helped you, how can I be certain it is worth the risk? I already stand to make a large sum of money off your current bets. I could call it quits and walk away. After what you said earlier, I am sure there will be even more betting tonight."

Kaen nodded and smiled. "What if I share just one of my stats and skills with you?"

Hess scraped his chair back and gasped. "Kaen, think about what you are saying!"

Kaen held up his hand toward Hess and kept his eyes on Sulenda. "I am. I am saying I trust Sulenda more with the knowledge of who I am and what I am capable of than the woman who is our guild master. I trust her because my father and you both trusted her. As such, I believe she has earned this from me."

Sulenda's knees felt weak, and she staggered briefly, thankful for the desk to lean against. *Kaen trusted her that much?* There was no one she trusted enough to share her stats with. Not even one of her employees she had known all these years.

"Why? Why would you risk that?"

"I already told you. My dad trusted you, and my dad's request of Hess cost you greatly. If we do this right, I can at least help ensure you are financially stable for a long time."

Kaen turned and smiled at Hess. "I can also help ensure that Hess is compensated for raising me. What either of you do with the money you make from all of this is up to you. I want to repay both of you for what you have done."

Sulenda reached back, finally found her chair, plopped into it, and stared at Hess in disbelief. "He is just like his father," she whispered.

Hess groaned and nodded.

"And I have had to live with him for all these years."

32

Items Are an Adventurer's Best Friend

Kaen smiled as he watched Sulenda and Hess sitting in their chairs in shock.

"A twenty-nine in dexterity," Hess groaned.

"And a twenty-one naturally in archery," Sulenda added in the same tone, struggling to believe one so young could be that strong.

"Don't forget the equipment adds a lot of dexterity," Kaen reminded them, smiling. "I only have a twenty-one in dexterity without any equipment."

Sulenda chuckled and let out a sigh she had been holding in. "'Only' he says . . . 'only.' How much would we have paid for a twenty-one at his age?"

"I would have gladly paid a king's ransom for that number for years," Hess joked. "He acts like that is normal."

Sulenda rubbed her face and her forehead with her hand. "I can only begin to imagine what Fiola will think if she learns of your stats. I pray she would not do anything to keep you for herself."

"Forget Fiola!" Kaen exclaimed. "Focus on what I asked for. Will you help me with items to make sure I can pass this test?"

Sulenda sat back in her chair and ran her tongue along her teeth. Kaen knew he was putting her in a hard position.

"You do realize that once we choose which thing to pick, we get a whole day to promote it, right?" Kaen reminded her. "When we leave her office and tell all the adventurers in the guild hall that I am attempting a special mission for silver rank, they will not be able to contain themselves. I am sure some will be upset, as you were, Sulenda, but they will go back wherever they stay and talk about it. Word will spread, and something like this will be like a wildfire. You will have a day to get ahead of it. We can determine if I want to succeed or fail based on how the profit lands."

"What?!" Hess cried out. "You would throw your own test to make money?"

Sulenda groaned loudly, leaned forward, and gently banged her head against her wooden desk. "He is just like you, Hoste," she said over and over again as she hit her head against her desk.

"What does it matter?" Kaen asked, waving his hands in the air. "If I succeed and we lose money, everything I have done is pointless. It only matters if we make enough money to make this worthwhile. If I pass, which I intend to, then all that matters is if we get paid. If it is better for me to fail, then you seem to forget that I will still be an iron adventurer."

Hess grunted then chuckled before scooting his chair up and mimicking Sulenda's head banging. "It does help a little, doesn't it," he joked.

"Just enough to keep doing it," Sulenda replied.

After all the complaints and debating, they finally came up with some numbers that would work for the betting. Sulenda put things in motion, and they prepared for tomorrow. Extra scripts were written and sent to all the inns and betting areas in town. Odds were adjusted slightly, not enough to gain notice that they knew Kaen would at least be iron. Many would feel it was the house adjusting numbers based on bets already placed to hedge their current ones. Something that happened often enough.

The rest of the day was spent seeking out items that might help him in the coming days without anyone knowing who the items would be for. Constitution and dexterity items were the focus, and any others that might give bonuses to archery were on their list. Finding archery skills would be difficult, though, as only bows typically had those, and everything would be expensive.

Evening time led to the Fluffy Ingot being packed to the limit. People from all over town, inside and outside the walls, had come to glimpse Kaen as he sat in a booth Sulenda had reserved for him.

Kaen had been told that people would be coming in to size him up before heading to the bar to place a bet, and that others would come and want to meet him or speak to him. Everyone was hoping for some clue on how good he might be and where their money was best spent.

Dwarves, humans, elves, and even a few taxabi came through. Kaen had never met one of the cat people before but was enthralled by their fur and tails.

Some of the adventurers they had previously met at the guild stopped by and joined him for a bit.

"Do you really think you have a chance to make bronze?" asked a bronze adventurer everyone called Chubbs.

Chubbs was the same height as Kaen, but he weighed at least two times as much. His studded armor, shield, and sword spoke volumes that he was a tank-class warrior designed to soak up damage. Kaen wondered if he was saving up for metal armor, as the studded armor would not protect against most attacks.

"I plan on doing my best; if I'm lucky, maybe I can make bronze for sure!" Kaen declared with a smile.

Chubbs ate it up and nodded as he tossed back his second drink since he had entered. "I knew it! I told Twin Dragon that you could do it!"

One of the adventurers who had come in with Chubbs groaned. He had twin short swords on his back with a dragon head on each handle. Kaen knew that he was likely some ranger or DPS warrior class, as he only wore leather armor.

"For the love of all, please stop calling me that. My name for the hundredth time is Earnest."

Kaen laughed, and Chubbs joined in as well. "Would you consider joining us if you make bronze rank?" Chubbs asked as he checked his empty glass again before setting it down on the table.

"He isn't going to join us," Earnest chimed in as Chubbs waved for one of the servers to come refill his drink. "You don't understand, there is no way he will be bronze. I'm betting on iron."

Kaen smiled and shrugged as Earnest watched for a reaction from Kaen. "I'm just excited to see what tomorrow brings from the guild master," Kaen told them as a few other people approached their table. "I just hope I can get some sleep with all the people coming in tonight. I never dreamed that anyone would cheer for someone trying for the adventurer test."

"It was not this exciting for me," Earnest said, pushing Chubbs to get up from the spot in the booth. "I also did not kill goblins and orcs before I came."

Earnest laughed when Chubbs fell out of the booth and landed with a thud on the wooden floor. "No more drinking!"

Chubbs stood up, swayed a little, and smiled. "Perhaps I should pass on the third drink," Chubbs said with a sigh. "Good luck tomorrow, Kaen! I'm betting on you to succeed no matter what!"

Kaen shook his head as Chubbs and Earnest shuffled off across the room. He would have gladly partied with them if he had not been in this situation. They seemed like a really fun group, and if they found a healer, it would be a solid party for handling tougher quests and assignments.

The night wore on, and before Kaen knew it, Hess came over and led him away from all the patrons who had drunk more than they should have.

"You need to get some sleep, and we need to talk," Hess informed him.

As Kaen headed toward the stairs on the other side of the inn leading to their room, he waved and laughed at those who cheered for him.

"Goodnight to all of you, and thank you for supporting me!" Kaen shouted as he walked away. "Tomorrow, I look forward to discovering how my adventuring life will begin!"

Cups banged against tables, and alcohol sloshed on people and the floor. Everyone cheered and wished him a good night's rest.

"What has gotten into you?" Hess growled as they walked up the stairs. "You have been acting totally different than you did back in town!"

Kaen laughed and pushed against Hess's back, forcing him up the stairs faster.

"It's because I can somehow now see how this all works. It is like I somehow know this is exactly where I belong. Something inside me is different!" exclaimed Kaen as he ran up the stairs. "It's like my whole life was built for this moment, and the second I stepped into the guild hall, I felt at home."

Hess continued to grumble as they walked up the stairs, and the noise down below faded thanks to the magic runes that limited noise. "I still think you are holding something back from me. You used to never do that."

Kaen frowned, though Hess could not see it. He had not told him everything yet, and he needed to, and he knew it. "Once we are inside, I'll tell you everything," Kaen promised.

Hess sat on his bed, looking at Kaen, who was shifting a little under the gaze Hess would occasionally give him while waiting for information.

"So I gained the haggling skill while I bargained with Fiola," Kaen admitted.

"What? How?"

Hess rubbed his thumb against his palm as he listened to Kaen talk. In all his years of adventuring, he had rarely had moments like the one Kaen was describing now. He remembered Hoste talking about the very thing Kaen was describing. He was now beginning to wonder if there was something that impacted how fast Kaen was growing because of who his father had been.

Kaen shrugged and tapped his chest. "Lately, it is like my lifestone has been guiding me to do things. To say things. In those moments when I let it take over, I achieve skill growth, gain new skills, or easily succeed when I attempt something. It is like I can see where to shoot without actually looking," Kaen said as he stared at the ceiling. "It sometimes seems as if I can feel it coming. Like a breeze blowing from a direction, you smell a meal being cooked and know that if you go the way the wind is coming from, you will find yourself somewhere with food."

Kaen's eyes lit up when he saw the pouch Hess was holding. He had known he needed more items to help with whatever Fiola would throw at him.

"We will come back to that later," Hess told Kaen as he reached into his vest and pulled out a small pouch. "I have some items we need to look at and discuss."

Hess got up and grabbed a small wooden table from the corner where a bowl rested. It was big enough for what he needed, and he moved it between their beds. He then pulled out four rings and held them up one at a time between his fat fingers before setting them down on the table.

Kaen gazed at the four rings. One had green leaves wrapped around a silver band. Another sparkled as if it were almost glass, and it had a yellow shine to it. The blood-red one seemed almost to radiate on the rough wooden table. The last one was just a golden ring, simple and plain, with nothing special-looking about it.

Hess then pulled a necklace out and let it hang from his fingers. It had a silver pendant with a gold eagle affixed to one side of it. The chain looked dull and rough compared to the bright and shiny pendant.

A laugh escaped Hess's lips as he watched Kaen's eyes move from piece to piece. "I guess you are wondering what each of these do?"

Kaen giggled. An actual giggle escaped from his lips. "You are torturing me on purpose," Kaen accused Hess.

Hess leaned back and roared loudly as the necklace in his hand swung. "Yes, yes I am!"

33

Magical Jewelry Confirmed

Hess handed the necklace to Kaen and smiled as Kaen rubbed his thumb along the ridges of the eagle. It had been made by someone with a decent talent in jewelry making and had a lot of detail not often found on a magical item. It had taken a few favors to get one of the merchants he knew from years past to let him borrow the necklace for this test. He did not want to tell Sulenda that he might have also had to tell the merchant not to bet on anything until tomorrow.

"That pendant will give you a bonus of two dexterity points and one point in your archery skill," Hess informed Kaen as he watched him put it around his neck. "Do not lose it! It is borrowed, and we would lose a large amount of gold if something happened to it. Do you understand?"

Kaen nodded and grinned. He could feel the magic of it as the pendant touched his skin under his shirt. "What's next," Kaen asked with a laugh.

Hess shook his head and picked up the silver ring with the green engraving all over it. In his massive fingers, it looked so small.

"This will be yours to keep. I will take it out of your cut from all the betting, but it was not as expensive as it could have been. It will only add one point of dexterity to you, but I think we would both agree that every point counts."

Hess flicked the ring off his finger with his thumb, sending it flipping through the air toward Kaen, who easily snatched it with one hand.

"How many new adventurers start with magical gear," Kaen asked as he slipped the ring on his finger and felt it shrink so that it was snug.

"Unless they are from a rich family, acquired something from a benefactor, or stole it, very few. You are being gifted far beyond what most new adventurers would. Adding to the fact that you have a *partner* who gives you an even bigger increase, you are well beyond the stats most silver token adventurers have."

Hess paused for a moment and looked outside the window at the night sky. "How is Pammon doing anyways?"

Kaen smiled and pointed southeast. "He is sleeping right now, that way. He has been traveling most of the time, gaining strength so that I can ride with him when we finally get together."

Hess sighed, and Kaen could not imagine why. "You ok?"

Hess nodded. "It still boggles my mind that you have a friend like Pammon, Kaen. Thinking about what we talked about earlier and your lifestone and what is happening, I can only imagine how strong you might become. That scares me because it also means you will pose a threat to many different people."

Not waiting for a response from Kaen, Hess picked up the glass ring and held it out to Kaen. "This ring is a gift from Sulenda. She used to wear it long ago," he said, then paused. "It was a gift to her, and I am surprised she still had it after all this time."

Kaen took it from Hess's hand and held it toward the light globe. He could see right through it. It looked like glass but felt as strong as steel between his fingers. "Did you give this to her?"

Hess nodded. "A long time ago," Hess mumbled. The look on his face showed the pain he felt upon seeing that ring. "There were some promises with that ring, and I was not able to keep them back then."

Kaen held the ring, wondering if he should wear it or not.

"Put it on. She wants you to have it. I'm unsure why she showed it to me, but I know Sulenda expects me to remember it and its promise. The ring will give you two dexterity points. For a ring, that is actually a lot. Most people only have rings that give one stat point."

The glass felt cool as Kaen slid it over his finger. It expanded past his knuckle and then tightened on his finger. Gazing at his right hand now, his pointer finger and his ring finger both looked weird to him with jewelry on them.

"I feel so weird with these on," Kaen said, chuckling. "I never imagined wearing rings."

Hess shrugged. "I have seen adventurers with one on each finger. They spent a lot of money trying to help fill in those gaps and weak points. Depending on what you are fighting, one quickly realizes the need to be careful not to let a stat fall too far behind, or it might hurt you later."

Pointing at the red ring, Hess shuddered and bit his lip. "Pick up that ring and put it on."

Kaen cocked an eye at Hess but reached out and picked up the ring which seemed to almost glow when his fingers got near it. Sitting back with the ring, Kaen noticed Hess staring intently at him. "What is it?"

"Put it on, but let me see it as you do," Hess instructed Kaen.

Kaen was unsure why, but Hess watched the ring as he slid it on his ring finger on his left hand. It glowed as he slid it over his finger, and then the ring suddenly *bit* down on his finger, and a little bit of blood ran from where the ring had attached itself to him.

"Mother clucker!" Kaen shouted as he flapped his hand in the air. "Why did it do that?"

"I'm sorry, I was not sure if it would do that or not."

"Do what?" Kaen asked, gasping. He felt a warm sensation running from his finger all through his body. "What is up with this ring?"

"It was one of your fathers, Kaen. I fetched it this morning from the guild vault. I have access to it; it was the only item I felt safe taking."

Kaen jumped off the bed and forgot about the ring and the blood that ran down his finger and onto the floor. "My dad has a vault?!"

Hess nodded and pulled out a folded piece of paper. "This permits me to enter the vault and remove items occasionally. Once you become an adventurer, you can access the vault, but only after the gold rank. None of the items in there are for anyone below that rank. That ring was a gamble."

Kaen stood, glancing at the paper and watching Hess, who was watching the ring on Kaen's finger.

"What could have happened with this ring?" Kaen demanded. "Could it have killed me?"

"No, and sit down and relax. I'll tell you more, but stop acting like that. You want to do the impossible, and I am willing to help you, but you must learn to trust my judgment."

"You just said you weren't sure it would work!" Kaen yelled, holding up his hand. Blood had stopped flowing, but it was still all over his finger and near the ring. "What could have happened?"

"It might have bit your finger off, and I would have had to reattach it with a high-level potion I have on me," Hess stated as if something like that was an everyday occurrence.

"Lost my finger? Like it would have eaten my finger or just cut it off?" Kaen was going crazy, waving his hands around in the air, and occasionally, a drop of blood would fly somewhere across the room.

Hess stood up and grabbed Kaen's shoulders with both hands. He was shocked at how much more effort it took to hold him in place for a moment.

"Look at me and snap out of it!" Hess barked as he looked down at Kaen. "You are fine, and it was your decision to take on this blasted path, so shut up, sit down, and act like an adventurer and not some kid who is playing at it!"

Kaen stood there, held in place by Hess, and glared at him. He was angry that Hess had taken this risk, but he was more upset that he was still learning about all these things about his father. It was not fair that Hess knew so much more about his dad and would not share those details.

"Fine, but do not keep secrets about my dad again!" Kaen yelled, jerking himself free from Hess's grip and flopping onto the bed. "I have spent all these years not knowing these things about my dad, and you just casually mention he has a vault of his old adventuring gear and that you can access it whenever you want!"

Hess sighed and nodded. "Be angry with me, I don't care," Hess said, pointing a fat finger at him. "The way you are acting right now is why I do not share everything with you. You are growing stronger and will quickly pass me, but you are still immature and act like a fool when it comes to your dad! Stop being stupid and use your head!"

Kaen's mouth opened, and then he closed it. He wanted to shout and scream, but he knew Hess was right. Every year when something happened and his dad was mentioned, he got angry. He was pissed right now, but he knew he needed to calm down.

He took a deep breath, let it out, and repeated it again. "Tell me what the ring gives me," Kaen said with a humph as he took another deep breath.

"It will add four to your constitution. It is a ring that is selective. To take it off will not be easy, but after a while, it will let go on its own. You will know when it happens because it will start to loosen. When it does, you must decide if you will keep it on or take it off."

"How long does it usually take for it to loosen?"

Hess shrug and shook his head. "I have no clue. I just remembered what Hoste told me."

Kaen picked up the last ring on the small table. He held the gold ring between his fingers and extended it toward Hess. "This going to do anything bad to me?"

Scoffing, Hess shook his head. "It will add two to your dexterity and one to your constitution," Hess told him as he tried to smile. "It was to be your gift from me once you passed your adventurer's test, but I decided you needed it now."

Kaen's heart dropped into his stomach. He suddenly felt like a heel as he held the ring between his fingers. "I'm . . . " Kaen stuttered. "I'm sorry I acted like a fool. Thank you for the gift."

Hess waved off Kaen's attempt at an apology. "I don't fault you, Kaen. This isn't easy, and I know it. It will only get harder, and I fear the next few days will be like nothing we have had to endure before. Please try to remember that I am here to help you and have no ulterior motives like so many others will."

Kaen slid the gold ring onto his pointing finger and smiled as he felt the magic rushing into his body. "Thank you, Hess. It means a lot to know you have had this for me."

Hess stood up and held out his hand to Kaen. "No worries. Now shake my hand like a man and stop pouting like a child," he declared as he winked at Kaen.

Kaen grasped Hess's hand and smiled. "Want to know my stats now?" Kaen teased.

Pulling his hand free, Hess smiled, returned to his bed, and sat down. "Only if you want to share and *only* if you want to make me jealous."

34

Small Lessons in Adventuring

Simple Status Check
Kaen Marshell - Adolescent
Age - 17
HP - 286/286
MP - 0/0
STR - 22
CON - 26
DEX - 36
INT - 16
WIS - 14

Hess let out the long whistle he only gave when he was actually impressed by something.

"I doubt there are many silvers, if any, who have the kind of stats you do. You are in a world to yourself and may find your path lonely until the world finds out about Pammon."

Kaen shrugged and thought about those numbers. He would have reached out and talked to Pammon about them, but he knew that Pammon did not care and was sleeping. He doubted Pammon would want to be woken up for that.

"I'm a little concerned about the test Fiola will give me," Kaen admitted, "but I also know she wants to know my stats and may sacrifice her desire to see me fail for a glimpse at them."

Hess nodded, grabbed the wooden table and walked over to the corner where it had come from, returning it to its spot. "We need to get sleep. I have no clue what tomorrow will bring, but we need to be up early. Showing up late will cause Fiola to be even worse than usual."

Laughing, Kaen started to undress. He could only begin to imagine how bad that woman could be if she held all the cards.

Kaen almost jumped out of bed when the light globe woke them in the morning. He had tossed and turned for a bit last night but eventually fell fast asleep. He had focused on Pammon and his heart, and the gentle lulling of the dragon's calm and steady beat had allowed him to settle down and relax.

"Time to get ready," Kaen announced, squinting against the light as it grew brighter in their room.

Hess mumbled and groaned as he rolled over and pulled his pillow off his head. "I don't want to get up," he moaned.

Kaen tossed his pillow at Hess and then grabbed his boot. "If you don't get up, I'll throw my boot at you," he threatened playfully.

Hess rolled over and smiled. "Not any fun when the boot is on the other foot, is it?" Hess teased. "How many mornings did I have to toss a boot at you to get you out of bed?"

Kaen smiled and dropped his boot, then reached for his pants on the end of the bed. "More than I want to remember."

Breakfast passed quickly as they inhaled their food and left earlier than they had the previous day. The streets were almost barren in the gray morning, with the only light coming from the poles, which held greater light stones every fifty feet. People were getting ready for the day, but most looked unexcited to be out that early.

Kaen noticed that Hess had his gold token on his shirt again, announcing his presence to anyone who might try to interact with them. This early, no one did, as most shop owners had yet to put their signs or sidewalk decorations out.

Kaen chuckled as the guards at the gate motioned for them to head straight ahead to the guild hall. The sun was still hidden behind the peaks of the mountains to the east, but it was sending its orange and red rays across the sky, creating a picture most painters wished they could come close to capturing.

"It feels weird," Kaen said as they walked past all the shops. He sensed the magic of the shops and streets calling to him but knew they were not anything more than a fly buzzing near one's ear. "Do you even notice them anymore?" Kaen asked as he pointed at the people already on the street calling for him and Hess to come and visit them.

"Not unless I am just completely exhausted," Hess admitted. "These streets aren't anything special compared to other quarters with real deals and sales. Some cities will make this street look tame. There will be wild beasts for sale, people hawking magical gear and putting on demonstrations, all within arm's length. It will be crowded and filled with people seeking to take advantage of someone not paying attention. Some will have partners to help make an uneducated or uninformed buyer spend more, an attractive man or woman to weaken one's resolve."

Hess stopped and pointed at the woman beckoning for them to come. She smiled at them, but she could tell neither Hess nor Kaen would come to her.

"There will be women and men who will find a mark and work them for days, weeks, and even longer sometimes. All with the intent of that one moment when they fleece them of everything of value," Hess stated as he held out his hand to Kaen. "Missing something?"

Kaen looked at Hess's hand and saw when Hess turned his palm up that his money pouch was now in it. "When did you . . . How did you?"

Hess laughed and tossed the pouch back to Kaen. "When I turned you by pointing at the woman, you were distracted. I simply used the skills I knew and have refined over the years to take an opportunity to show you why you must always be on your guard."

Kaen retied his money pouch to his belt and then, opening his jerkin a little, stuffed the pouch inside. "Better?"

Hess shrugged and winked. "Not against someone skilled in lifting one's pockets, but good enough against me."

Groaning, Kaen grumbled as they started back toward the guild hall.

"Don't worry too much on this side of the wall. Here, people will help you, as the guards are very protective of the adventurers. Outside the wall is another story. One of the reasons I wear my token outside is so that would-be thieves of opportunity will know better than to risk it. Wood and copper adventurers are better off keeping their token hidden, as most have yet to learn how to protect themselves from the skilled thieves."

"When did you learn to protect yourself from them?"

Hess coughed at that question and shrugged. "Most left me alone because of my size. Only a few risked it, and only one ever succeeded. Those who failed were a warning to the others. Many cities are very loose when it comes to justice involving an adventurer and a criminal. You can often play judge, jury, and executioner if you are willing to stand before the guild hall if the city finds you were in the wrong."

Kaen almost stopped walking when he thought of killing someone like that. It would have to be a serious crime for him to do that.

Kaen gazed ahead and saw the sun cascading on the stonework outside the guild hall. They were here a lot earlier today than they had been yesterday. Just a day ago, he had walked inside, filled with awe and wonder, and now he felt that he belonged, ready to claim the status he had spent the last few years preparing for.

"Just remember not to push Fiola too hard on anything beyond what you agreed upon yesterday," Hess warned. "She has had a day to think about what went wrong with her first encounter with you, and I have no doubt she will be prepared for you today."

Hess was right, and Kaen knew it. He had spent some time thinking about how things could go wrong today.

Through his bond with Pammon, he felt a sudden rush of joy and excitement.

You seem in a good mood, Pammon. Did something happen?

YES! I found a green stag and managed to take it down. He fought back instead of running away like all the deer try to. He got a few scrapes on me as I did not use my fire, but nothing you should worry about.

Nice! I have heard about them but have never seen one. How big is it?

It was as tall as I am now, and his horns are as tall as you!

Kaen stopped walking and tapped Hess on the arm. "Do you know of a green stag as tall as Pammon?" Kaen whispered. "He just killed one."

Hess gasped, his eyes widening as he glanced around them at the few people on the street. "Are the horns still intact?"

Kaen held up his hand to pause Hess for a moment.

Did you eat the horns? Hess wants to know.

I have not. I'm still enjoying this beast. I doubt I will fly much today after eating all of this. It is at least six times more meat than a usual deer!

"He says he has not done anything to them yet. I'm assuming you want them?"

Hess nodded and tapped his fingers together under his chin. "Make sure he hides them somewhere away from other animals. Squirrels, hogs, and all sorts of other creatures will gladly eat those. They have a magical aspect to them and are desired by crafters."

Hess says to hide them somewhere other animals can't find them. Trees won't work because squirrels will start to chew on them. Maybe bury them in the mountainside?

I will find somewhere to hide them. Do you know when we can see each other again? I feel a little weaker in some way since it has been so long without contact. I know that the longer it goes, the harder it gets.

Kaen understood that. A part of him felt like it was missing, as if a piece of his soul was gone from not being near Pammon. It must be a part of their bond that neither of them or even Hess knew about.

I don't, but I will tell you as soon as I know. I will find out what I must do for my adventurer's token in a little while, so hopefully, it will not be much longer.

Pammon's sigh of sadness came through their bond, and Kaen did his best to try and send some form of a mental hug through the bond. Not seeing Pammon and getting a chance to scratch him and be in his presence was tiring. Like a part of his heart was being ripped off.

"Pammon will hide them," Kaen said, sighing. "The time away from each other is starting to affect both of us."

Hess raised an eyebrow and slowly nodded in understanding. "I had no idea that might happen," Hess muttered, looking at Kaen. As Kaen described what he was feeling, Hess was trying to see if he could notice anything off. "I am sorry I do not know more about how that all works, but perhaps it will be ok in a week."

Kaen nodded and motioned at the guild hall. "We can worry about it later. For now, I need to focus on what is right before us."

Hess laughed loudly, and it echoed off the walls of the street. "Where was this kind of commitment and dedication when I gave you rocks to split at the quarry?"

Kaen shrugged as moved toward the guild hall. "Perhaps you just were a terrible boss," he teased.

"I probably was. The real test will be tomorrow when we discover if I was just as bad of a trainer."

Kaen groaned at the joke and smiled.

Today was going to be a bad enough test. He could feel it in his lifestone.

35

A Quest For Kaen

"You are trying to take advantage of our initial agreement," Fiola stated as she held her teacup away from her lips. "You have clearly outfitted yourself to have a better chance at succeeding tomorrow."

Kaen shrugged as he set his cup of tea on the small plate it had been brought on. The tea was incredibly smooth, far nicer than any he had ever experienced before. It left a clean and refreshing feeling in his mouth while making his mind feel energetic.

"I assume you still *want* me to succeed tomorrow, right?" Kaen asked, leaning back in his chair. "I am simply trying my best to ensure we both get what we want."

Fiola darted her eyes over her cup at Hess and saw him holding his tiny cup between his massive fingers. She wasn't sure if Hess was making a mockery of her by holding his pinky up like she was as she drank hers. Hess continued avoiding eye contact, staring off at the rows of books on the shelves behind her.

"You are not the same boy who walked into this hall a day ago," Fiola said, running her pointer finger along the rim of her cup. "Something has changed inside you, and you are right that we both want you to succeed."

Fiola set her cup on her saucer and stood up, smoothing out her long green dress as she moved toward her desk. "Since I will allow you to wear the other items you appear to have acquired, the only thing left to do is discuss what your test will involve."

Digging around on her desk, Fiola pulled out a folder from a small stack in the middle. She opened the folder and glanced inside, glad her back was turned and neither of them could see the smirk on her face. Regaining her composure as she turned around, she moved back to the green couches and set the folder down before Kaen on the small table.

"Open it," she commanded him.

Kaen picked up the folder and slowly turned the cover. His eyes went wide, and his mouth opened when he saw the only piece of paper inside it.

"You cannot be serious!" Hess exclaimed, when he saw what was inside. "An iron group quest?! That one calls easily for a party of four people!"

Kaen ignored Hess as he looked at the paper and felt it between his fingers. The writing was impeccable, and he could almost feel it raised against the paper. An iron group quest just for him, tasked with clearing a camp that was last rumored to be the home of five orcs two days north of town through the pass in the mountains.

"Do you want him to die?! Who else will be going with him?" Hess continued to berate Fiola with questions as she ignored him, watching only Kaen's face.

"I accept," Kaen announced, leaving the quest sheet inside the open folder and setting it on the table. "We leave tomorrow morning, I assume?"

Hess began shouting again, but Fiola's glare turned on him and shut him off.

"He will be sent with two observers. Both will be silver ranked and tasked with only observing, unless Kaen calls out for assistance or is struck down and they deem help is needed," Fiola informed them both. "*Only* those three will be going on this quest. They will take an enchanted cart and hurry to where the camp was found. Once he either completes the quest or fails it, they will return."

Fiola flipped the quest sheet over. Kaen had not realized there was a map on the back of it. It was the first time he had ever seen one.

"This shows the distance and route of the trip. The cart will take a little less than two days to arrive there. Proof of completion will be the orcs' heads and the observers' word that no aid was rendered."

A pen magically appeared in Fiola's hand, and she extended it to Kaen. "All it requires now is your signature. Once signed, you must be here tomorrow morning, equipped and ready for the trip. The guild will provide all food and water, as this is an official test."

"How? How did you get this approved?" Hess asked as he grabbed Kaen's wrist and kept him from taking the pen. "You know how dangerous an orc can be. Five orcs in the woods where they live and hunt?! That is foolish!"

Kaen recoiled when he heard Fiola's tone. "Adventurer Brumlin, I have been gracious in allowing you to speak freely, but if you question my ability to make a decision like this again, I will make sure you are not permitted to sign for or accompany anyone on a quest for half a year," Fiola growled, glaring at Hess. "Do I make myself clear?"

Hess's whole face was red. A vein that Kaen had only seen a few times in his life throbbed in Hess's forehead as he glared at Fiola. He knew she had the power to make that happen, and breaking her order would cost him his token at the least. If that happened, he would not be able to help Kaen at all in the future.

With a grunt, Hess let go of Kaen's wrist and crossed his arms over his chest as he leaned back on the couch. "Forgive me, *Guild Master Fiola,* for taking too much liberty with my words."

Fiola simply nodded and turned back to Kaen, ignoring the pouting oversized man. She wiggled the pen in her left hand as she flipped the paper over and motioned to the line on the bottom. "Sign it, and I can get everything that will be required taken care of."

When he glanced at Hess, Kaen saw the fear in the man's eyes but knew that this was possible. Fiola did not know about Pammon, and he was going to use his dragon to help with this mission. It was not breaking the rules of the contract in his mind.

Kaen took the pen from Fiola's outstretched hand and sat back down on the edge of the couch. He pulled the folder toward himself and began signing his name. As he signed, he felt his lifestone throbbing in his chest. He paused halfway through signing his name, but nothing happened, so he finished his signature.

Looking down, he saw *Kaen Marshell* etched across the bottom of the page, and the ink seemed to glow for a second.

"The contract is signed. You are free to go and share the news with everyone you wish," Fiola announced in a cheerful voice as she quickly grabbed the folder and pulled the paper from beneath Kaen's left hand. "I am sure that Sulenda and the others will be excited to hear about this news and how it will provide another opportunity for people to bet on your success."

Kaen looked up, stunned. As much as he tried to hide his shock, he saw the slight smile on the edge of Fiola's lips when she saw his face.

She knew!

As if she could read his mind, Fiola leaned her head back, and a throaty, feminine laugh escaped her lips and echoed in the room. After she stopped laughing, she winked at Kaen.

"I will admit I was confused about why you were very specific about the details of how this would take place. I had a few people follow you, and when they heard of your antics at the Fluffy Ingot, I knew what you were up to. I almost thought Hess would have put you up to all of it, but I know him well enough to realize he is not this smart or willing to risk you like that."

Fiola paused and tapped the closed folder she held in one hand against the palm of her other. "That tells me you are smarter than most might realize, smarter than I realized. Somehow, you have gamed the system in such a short time. If you can pull this off, before you know it you may become just as great as your father was."

She turned, walked to her desk, and set the folder on top. Then she smiled and looked back over her shoulder. "I hope you do succeed, for all of our sakes. Now go and get a good night's rest. You are going to need it."

* * *

Standing at the top of the stairs that led down from the second floor and Fiola's office, Kaen and Hess were surprised to see over twenty adventurers standing at the base of the stairs.

"What did Fiola say?" Herb called out from the front of the crowd. "We are dying to know what is going to happen!"

Murmurs of agreement echoed out over the crowd. Hess elbowed Kaen. "It is your show. You might as well break the news," he whispered.

Kaen took a deep breath and smiled as he started down the stairs. Everyone's eyes following him, and he kept smiling until he was about eight steps above everyone and could see them all. "I have a special test!" Kaen shouted, a grin plastered over his face.

"What?"

"Impossible!"

"What does that mean? Special test?"

Kaen saw that the last question had come from Chubbs. He extended his hand, palms toward the group of adventurers who were trying to understand what his words meant, and got them to quiet down.

"Tomorrow morning, I will leave on a two-day journey with two observers, both silver-ranked."

Kaen paused and watched as a few in the crowd glanced at one another. Three silver token adventurers were present, but, based on their expressions, none of them knew if they would be part of this test.

"I will be taking on an iron group quest alone!" Kaen announced loudly. "I will have to slay five orcs in a camp two days from here without any assistance from my observers. If I succeed, I will be a silver rank. If I fail, I am not sure what rank I will be."

Kaen tried to feign a little bit of sadness as he said that last part. He knew precisely what rank he would be.

The adventurers clamored together, some complaining about the danger of the test. Others could not believe that Kaen might have the ability to earn a silver rank from the start. That was unheard of.

A moment later, Herb left the group, moved up the stairs, and shook Kaen's hand. "I am sure you will be fine," Herb stated loudly. "I cannot imagine you failing this quest at all!"

The noise behind Herb quieted down. Everyone knew he was gifted in reading people's strengths. If he had this much faith in Kaen, maybe they should as well.

Hess descended the stairs and stood next to Kaen. "We need to get back to the Fluffy Ingot for a bit of planning and some rest, but if you all want, feel free to stop by tonight, and I'll buy each of you a round!"

A cheer rose from the adventurers. Most of them did not need to worry about purchasing their own drinks, but having Hess offer it to them meant something special. Over the last day, rumors and stories of Hess had started springing up all over town. Knowing a gold token had trained Kaen only affirmed why this young man might be so amazing.

After a while, Kaen and Hess managed to work their way out of the crowd at the guild hall and got back on the road to the inn. Neither one said a word the entire time they were inside the gates.

"We need to talk," Hess whispered once they finally reached outside the gates. "I already know what you are planning."

Kaen smiled and nodded. He couldn't wait to tell Pammon about their quest.

36

The Golden Goose

I will fly to the edge of the mountains north of you today! Any chance you can escape into the woods when you travel?

I do not know, but I will let you know if I can! Soon we can see each other again!

Pammon was excited, and Kaen felt it as a constant wave of joy radiated through their connection. He was smiling and almost started whistling as he walked with Hess through the outer part of Ebonmount.

"You seem rather happy," Hess whispered, glancing around them. "I take it you have some good news about your friend?"

Kaen nodded and quickly spun in a circle. "We can talk about it back in our room tonight," he replied cheerfully. "For now, we need to ensure Sulenda has the latest information, and we can get the news out around town."

Hess chuckled and shook his head in amazement. "You almost seem more concerned with this whole wagering thing than the quest you are supposed to head out on tomorrow!"

"I am not distracted! I just need to make sure that you and Sulenda are compensated for what you both lost because of me."

Hess grabbed Kaen by the shoulder and spun him around. "Listen, Kaen, I need you to pay close attention to the next few things I say. You do not owe me anything."

Kaen started to talk, and Hess held up his massive finger and silenced him. "I would not trade the last six-plus years of my life. Other than having Hoste alive and watching him raise you, nothing compares to our time together. I have watched you grow and become a man I am proud to say I had a small role in creating. So stop worrying about me and making up for what you feel I *lost* by raising you. Do what you want tomorrow and every day after because it is the life you and your *friend* want."

Hess smiled and pulled Kaen in and hugged him. It had been almost five years since he could remember sharing an embrace like this with Kaen. He felt Kaen slowly put his arms around him and squeeze.

"Ogre nuts!" Hess exclaimed. "When did you get so strong?"

Kaen let go as Hess broke the embrace, and they both laughed. "Soon, I will be able to break out of that embrace of yours," Kaen joked.

"Probably sooner than you think," Hess stated as he turned and motioned with his head for Kaen to follow. "Let's get back to the inn and take care of that business you have in mind. I also need to take care of a few things while everyone in town shows up tonight to wish you luck."

Groaning, Kaen nodded and walked a little faster to catch up with Hess.

"Don't whine about all this. You asked for it," Hess reminded him. "No matter what happens in the next few months, you will be a celebrity. You need to learn to deal with it."

Being a celebrity did not bother Kaen, it was the lack of getting to see Pammon that was going to frustrate him the most. If he was expected to group with other adventurers on quests, he could not have Pammon's help for a while.

Ignoring the truth of what the next few months might bring, Kaen focused on the moment. The plan that he had started appeared to be coming along nicely. He just needed to make it to the morning.

When they turned the last corner of a street that would bring them to the Fluffy Ingot, Hess and Kaen stopped when they saw a line of people stretching down the sidewalk and around the corner at the door.

Two massive women stood at the door, keeping people in line and preventing them from pushing to get inside.

"What the heck is going on there?" Kaen asked Hess.

"Ungghh," Hess moaned as he grabbed Kaen and led him back the way they had come. "We need to move to the back entrance, or things will get ugly if everyone sees you."

"That was all for me?" Kaen called out as Hess dragged him backward.

Hess nodded, not caring if Kaen saw him acknowledge that question. "Sulenda is either going to kill us or kiss us," Hess muttered, picking up his pace.

"Why would she be mad?" Kaen asked as he jogged to catch up with Hess. "We are bringing in a ton of business!"

Hess dodged a few people on the sidewalk and motioned for Kaen to keep up. "The amount of money that will change hands is hard to imagine. Many people will want their piece of this pie, and hopefully, no one gets stupid and tries to take someone else's slice."

"What does pie have to do with this?" Kaen called out as he dodged someone who barely missed running into Hess.

"Just wait! We will talk later!"

Hess kept moving faster, and Kaen finally decided just to stay in his shadow and let Hess do all the work of dodging people or making them dodge him.

Kaen and Hess had to double back around a block to find the alley entrance between all the buildings, eventually leading them to the Fluffy Ingot loading door. A pair of guards were at the dock. Thankfully, there was no line of people trying to get in back there.

"Is it really that bad?" Hess asked as he walked up to the two female guards and flashed a grin.

A tall, dark-haired woman who looked like she had seen a few fights, based on her broken nose and the sword hanging from her hip, acknowledged their approach. Her expression did not change from someone who lived in a constant state of being pissed at the world.

"News broke this morning that your *wonder boy* somehow has a chance at a silver token, and the people are clamoring to make bets," the woman informed them as she opened the door behind her. "Sulenda has held off all bets until she can confirm details with you two, so get your arses in there!"

Hess nodded and danced by the woman and slipped through the open door. Kaen smiled and winked at the woman, who simply grunted and rolled her eyes at him.

The loading area was filled with boxes and casks, and a few people moving them around. Light globes provided enough light to work by, but it was not as bright as Kaen would have preferred. The room smelled like a few casks had busted open at some point, and it gave the room a cherry wood scent.

"This way," Hess stated as he danced around a few boxes and waved at one of the workers who glanced at them. "We need to hurry! Time is money."

"Were you two out there picking flowers and daydreaming?" Sulenda asked when Hess opened the door to her office, and they both walked through. "Have you seen the line outside? Perhaps the room full of runners waiting for an update?"

"It's good to see you too," Kaen joked.

Sulenda glared at Kaen and then let out a sigh. "I need details to ensure everything works in our favor. I already know what level you might end up at, but I need to know the specifics to make the numbers work better in our favor."

Hess gave a quick rundown of the quest, and Sulenda sat wide-eyed and in shock at hearing Kaen would be attempting an iron group quest on his own. "Five orcs . . . that seems a bit dangerous."

"Dangerous means better odds, right?" Kaen asked.

Sulenda grimaced and nodded. She glanced down at her paper and started writing quickly. "Five orcs gives a lot of betting opportunities. We can run odds on how many you will kill, if you will need assistance," Sulenda's voice faded off a moment before she added, "or if you will die."

"If I die?!" exclaimed Kaen. "Why would we have that as an option?"

Hess chuckled, and Sulenda looked up at Kaen and winked. "You might be surprised how many people may bet that way."

Kaen groaned and leaned back in his chair.

After looking over it once more, Sulenda handed her paper to Hess, who quickly glanced at it.

"Change the odds on these last two here, and I think you will be set," Hess said.

Sulenda took the paper and scratched out the odds she had set for killing the fourth and fifth orc. Tapping her pen against her head, she did some quick math and wrote down her final sets. "You two sit still while I go run this out to the bar," Sulenda said, rising from her chair and heading toward the door. "We have a few more things to discuss."

After Sulenda left, Kaen leaned toward Hess and poked him. "Do I want to know the odds she put on me dying?"

Hess chuckled and banged his fist against his chest when he started to cough. "With the odds she put on you dying, I might almost risk a little money just in case," teased Hess.

Kaen smiled and gave Hess the middle finger. When he turned to look at Hess, Kaen spotted the map on the wall behind them and went over to it. He saw where the pass was and remembered the map on the back of the quest sheet. Using his finger, he traced the road to the spot where the orcs should be.

Pammon, can you do me a favor and focus on where I am right now?

A few seconds passed, and Kaen could feel Pammon gazing across the land from where he was flying over, looking at him. Kaen placed one finger on Ebonmount and another southeast of him.

"He is here," Kaen whispered.

The chair Hess was sitting on scraped as he stood and moved to stand by Kaen. "You can tell that how?"

"He is focused on me, and it's not that I can see this far or what he sees, but I just know where he is and where I am now. I can feel the distance somehow." Kaen shrugged and tapped his two fingers on the map.

"He is moving north up to this edge of the mountains," Kaen explained as he dragged his right finger from where Pammon was now to where he would be. "Tomorrow, I will head to about here, and he will start scouting where we will end up. I should know exactly where they are by the time I arrive."

"That is . . . " Hess paused for a moment as he studied the map and what Kaen had told him. "Impossible? Amazing? I am lost on how to describe it. This is one of the reasons you and Pammon will be unstoppable."

"Who is Pammon?" Sulenda asked suddenly, the door closing behind her.

Kaen jumped, but Hess never flinched. "Pammon is the name of his bow," Hess replied, keeping his eyes on the spot where Kaen's fingers were. "The silly boy felt it needed a name."

Sulenda huffed and blew a raspberry at them. "Why do men feel the need to name their weapons? At least he didn't give it a girl's name, did he?"

Kaen laughed, but it came off a little weird. "Does it matter if it is a girl's name?" he asked.

Sulenda plopped down into her chair, leaned back, and put her feet on her desk.

"It does not, but I would not tell people you named it. People are already worked up about you. Telling them you named your bow would not be advised at the moment."

Kaen nodded and moved to his seat. "So, how did the news of my test and quest go out there?"

Sulenda closed her eyes and smiled. "Kaen, you are going to be the golden goose for me. You know the only bad thing about being a golden goose?"

Tapping his chin, Kaen recalled the old story about a golden goose that laid golden eggs. "Everyone wants one?"

Sulenda's smile grew wider, and she chuckled and opened her eyes. "While that is true, the real problem with being the golden goose is at some point, the owner of the goose killed it to see if he could figure out how to get more gold for himself by learning the goose's secret," she explained, removing her feet from the desk and leaning against it with her arms. "The goose's owner lost all the money he could have made because he got greedy and killed the goose. We need not be too greedy, or something bad might happen to you, and then none of us will get what we really want."

Kaen swallowed the lump in his throat.

He was certain she was warning him about greed, but he was not sure whose greed.

37

Getting Carried Away

Yesterday's excitement in the Fluffy Ingot had nothing on tonight's. The inn was packed to the walls, and guards only let more patrons in as others left. Kaen had heard at one point that the estimated time to be let in was at least a half hour.

Drinks flowed, and almost fifty adventurers were inside the inn, drinking and celebrating, all on Hess's tab. Kaen was seated in the *booth of honor,* as Hess called it. Located across the entire inn and near the bar, it had enough room for six people to sit comfortably, but now it housed ten adventurers packed in so tight, they were almost sitting on each other's laps.

"Kaen, I may not have enough money for a room if you fail me," Chubbs stated as he picked up his empty cup again and tried to find another drop to enjoy. "I'll have to come and collect those free drinks after you get back!"

Kaen laughed, as did a few of the new adventurers packed in. The one closest to him was a silver token, an elven rogue who felt the need to press right against him.

"So how should we all bet," Amra whispered in his ear as her hand somehow found its way onto his leg. "We are all wondering how you think this test will go."

Kaen gulped, his face red as her fingers squeezed his thigh. Never in his village life had girls or women been this forward. He was thankful Hess had removed all his jewelry, except the blood ring and money, before they left the office, and had locked it up in Sulenda's safe.

Kaen had not noticed that Amra's other hand was now draped around his shoulder and twisting his brown hair in her finger. She could have taken everything he owned, and he would have never noticed.

"I plan on succeeding," Kaen said with a slightly higher pitch than he had meant to. "I just hope I can somehow reach iron!"

Everyone at the table laughed, as they all saw the effect Amra was having on Kaen.

"Leave the boy alone," a male dwarf iron token adventurer called out. "Can't ya see that boy doesn't know how to handle a woman like you? He's practically as red as an elf after a day topless at the lake!"

Kaen chuckled, and the others banged their hands and cups on the table and laughed. He could still feel the heat in his cheeks.

Amra smiled and turned, and then she pulled her green braid over her shoulder and started running it along Kaen's arm. "We all remember what it was like when we tested. How many made us squirm? Why not have a little fun with this one?" Amra inquired as she ran the tip of her braid up to Kaen's shoulder. "Besides, he looks like he could easily handle a few of us. I'm sure he could make this fun for all of us, if he wanted."

Chubbs laughed, as did the dwarven adventurer whose name Kaen could not, for some reason, remember right now.

Kaen could feel his heart beating quickly because of Amra and her actions. He also realized that his lifestone was beating just as fast. He took a breath and let his mind and his lifestone guide him. He felt like there was something he was supposed to say or do.

"Perhaps we could make a private wager on how this quest might go," Kaen stated, emboldened by his lifestone and how it throbbed within his chest. "Something that might be fun no matter who wins."

As Amra started to reply, Kaen felt a hand on his collar, and then he was suddenly lifted free from the snare of Amra's grasp. He found himself standing next to a smiling Hess.

"Sorry to ruin this moment," Hess said, "but I need to go over something with Kaen before he prepares for a good night's sleep and an early morning!"

Groans and moans erupted from the booth, and the frustrated look on Amra's face was evident.

"I promise you he will be back soon, and you can all continue the right of passage with him," Hess stated, dragging Kaen away.

"But I wasn't done," Kaen argued, trying to stop Hess from turning him around and leading him to the stairs.

"You are done," Hess whispered, embracing Kaen from the side. "I am saving you before you do something you shouldn't."

Groaning, Kaen glanced over at his shoulder and saw Amra looking at him. It was evident she was not happy with Hess by the scowl on her face.

* * *

"What were you thinking?" Hess said from his bed, watching Kaen pout on his own bed. "Do you know what that woman might have done to you?"

Kaen blew a raspberry and shook his head. "I was hoping to learn what she might do, but the truth is, I was letting my lifestone lead me before you yanked me from my seat."

Hess leaned forward and peered at Kaen. Hess looked confused, but the way he stared at him caught Kaen off guard.

"Your lifestone doesn't do that, does it?" asked Kaen.

Hess shook his head. "Mine has only helped me in great times of life and death. It has never done the things you say yours has helped you with," Hess replied as he reached into his leather vest and pulled out a pouch. "I have a few people looking into what you say a lifestone can do, but I doubt I will hear anything back for at least a month since they are trying to be discrete."

Hess tossed the pouch to Kaen, who, barely looking, caught it in one hand.

"The lifestone has been really weird lately," Kaen admitted, bouncing the pouch in his hand. "Ever since Pammon, it has been more active."

Kaen sat up, looked at Hess, and saw they were both thinking the same thing.

"Pammon!" they both exclaimed at the same time.

"You think it could be that simple?" Kaen asked.

Hess shrugged, rocking on the bed while rubbing his chin. "I have nothing to go off. We can ask later when you meet someone in the same position as you, but until then, I guess we should expect it to happen more."

Kaen nodded and opened the pouch, revealing his rings and pendant. "What should I do if it happens again with Amra?" Kaen asked with a grin as he dumped his jewelry into his hand.

Hess groaned louder than usual and then chuckled. "I guess if your lifestone is leading you to do something, then I will have to trust it, and you, to do what you must. I have never heard of anything like this in all my years of adventuring," Hess warned Kaen. "Do not share this information with anyone but me. Not even Sulenda."

Kaen nodded and slipped the pendant over his neck before setting the empty pouch on the night table beside him. "It seems you have been shopping," Kaen said, pointing to the big pack on the floor at the end of Hess's bed. "That for you or me?"

Ignoring the question, Hess kicked off his shoes and tapped the light globe four times with two fingers.

"We will talk in the morning, but now you must sleep, even though it is still not late. Tomorrow will be a long day, and you will need your rest." Hess pulled the thin blanket over him and then glanced at Kaen, who was still sitting on the bed watching him. "You need me to repeat those instructions?"

Sighing, Kaen shook his head and started taking his boots off. "I feel like we are still back at your place in Minoosh, with how you are still bossing me around."

Hess chuckled and closed his eyes. "Pass this test, get your rank, and I'll try to remember you don't need me to tell you how to wipe your arse anymore."

"You never taught me how to wipe my arse," Kaen declared and picked up the empty pouch and threw it at Hess.

Hess kept chuckling, ignoring Kaen's comeback and the weak throw he'd attempted with the pouch, and then rolled over on his bed. "Get some sleep. You might be surprised how hard it is to come," Hess muttered.

"You're not even going to turn the light off, are you?" Kaen asked as he watched Hess's massive chest and shoulders slowly rise under his blanket.

Groaning, Kaen got up from his bed and went and held his finger on the globe till it turned off. He moved back to his bed and almost cursed when he caught his toe on his boot.

Stupid Hess!

Climbing into his bed, Kaen tried to relax and slow his breathing. Hess was right that sleep did not come as quickly as he had hoped. His mind was racing with thoughts about tomorrow and getting to see Pammon, hopefully.

Battle plans and ideas on how things might go versus five orcs had his heart pounding. He could sense that Pammon was asleep and knew that he might wake Pammon up if he could not get his heart under control. Pammon was now north of the town and somewhere in the mountain range.

It only took about an hour for Kaen to finally fall into a fitful sleep that ended sooner than he had wished.

"I'm up!" Kaen mumbled as the light globe flooded the room. Hess had set it to wake them up earlier than it had yesterday. If it wasn't for his lifestone and the connection to Pammon, Kaen believed he would be too exhausted to even move.

About time you woke up, Pammon declared with a hint of sarcasm.

It is too early to be that excited. How long have you been up?

I have been up for a little bit. I finished a small snack I kept from last night and am now flying over the mountainside. It is so tall, one almost has to fly into the clouds to get over some peaks. A little snow was on a few sections, always in the shade.

Is it cold up there where you are?

When Pammon laughed at the question, Kaen wondered what he had said that was funny.

I do not feel cold or heat like you. I would imagine you might feel the cold, and the wind would make you want to have some extra padding. I think in another month we can probably try flying together.

Kaen's heart leaped when Pammon told him that. Flying!

Well, I will just be traveling by cart today and will reach out to you when I know more about where we are stopping. Are you going to stay closer to me after you cross the mountain?

I will stay as close as I can. Let me know when you think you will be stopping, and I will try to find a place we can meet in the area.

Smiling, Kaen rolled out of bed and noticed Hess was watching him.

"Talking with Pammon?"

Nodding, Kaen moved to the edge of his bed and started digging through his pack for a new pair of foot coverings. The pair from the other day felt stiff enough to stand on their own.

"I may need some warmer clothes and a cloak in a month. It could be pretty cold how I intend to travel."

Clearing his throat, Hess stood up and waited for Kaen to turn around. "I can see how that might be important, but I would caution against rushing things too fast. Low and slow. Like riding a horse. You learn to simply sit on the horse before jumping on one and letting it gallop away."

Kaen laughed at that illustration and realized Hess was right. He would have gladly jumped on Pammon and gone to the sky without trying to learn how to just sit on his back.

"You're right," Kaen said pulling on his foot coverings. "I am a fool and need you to help keep me from jumping onto something I could fall to my death from."

Grabbing the large package at the end of the bed, Hess chuckled and plopped it down on his bed. "And that, Kaen, is why I went ahead and took care of a few things for you."

Hess started pulling out different kinds of arrows wrapped together and bound in a few strings, an extra quiver, a knife, and other things he might need for the journey. As Hess laid all the goods he had procured during the day on his bed, Kaen finished putting his boots on and walked over to look at everything.

"That seems much more than I should need for just five orcs."

Hess cocked his head and grunted at Kaen, elbowing him in the arm. "You would go out with only five arrows and one pair of undergarments for this?"

"Well, no," Kaen stuttered, "I mean, it seems like more than I would need for a quest like the one I have. I mean, this is enough for a whole party of archers!"

Hess turned to face Kaen while pointing to the stuff on his bed. "Rule number one of a quest: *always* bring more than you think you might need! Never take just the minimum unless the quest requires it! Always store a backup bow, just in case, with more arrows than you might need. I always have an extra weapon or three because you never know what will happen on the road. Do you understand?"

Kaen glanced again at the goods strewn across Hess's bed and back at Hess, who gave him the stink eye. "I mean yeah, but . . . " Kaen trailed off as Hess's nostrils flared. "Thank you. Thank you for helping me be prepared for this."

Hess huffed, pulled the pack he had just unloaded off the bed, and handed it to Kaen.

"Rule number two: pack your own crap!"

Kaen rolled his eyes and groaned as Hess moved to the end of his bed to finish getting himself ready.

"Hurry up and make sure you don't break those arrows! I don't want to tell you how much that cost! You still need to get your armor on, and we have to hurry if we want to make it to the guild house on time."

With one last sigh, Kaen started packing the stuff into the leather pack Hess had given him. It wasn't the first time Hess had ever made him do this, but he sensed this time was different. In a few hours, he would not have Hess by his side.

38

Leaving Ebonmount

Kaen had been surprised to see almost a dozen adventurers at the guild hall waiting to see him off. Fiola was waiting, as was Herb, and they had been talking quietly together about something when he and Hess had arrived.

The cart that they would be taking was a new thing for him. It looked like a standard cart with a brown tarp over the top in a horseshoe fashion, yet no horses were required. This one had some magical crystal inside it that would allow it to travel for up to eight hours straight before it would need a full eight hours of rest before it could go again. Hess had started sharing more details about it, but Kaen had stopped him, interested in meeting the people who were going to be traveling with him.

"I knew you would arrive early as usual," Herb called out as Hess and Kaen approached the fountain. "I know you are never one for being late to anything!"

Hess chuckled and went to talk with Herb while Kaen walked over to the cart and saw the two people he assumed would be traveling with him.

"You two are my guides?" Kaen asked. He stared at the man in a green robe holding a staff with a yellow gem at the top and a woman dressed in chainmail with a shield on her back and a sword on her hip.

"I am Aubri," the female warrior chuckled and then pointed at the male in the robes. "That guy with the dirty red hair is Luca. He is our mage."

"Nice to meet you, Luca!" Kaen exclaimed, extending his hand toward the man.

Luca gazed at Kaen with a look one might give a younger sibling they were annoyed with. He appeared to be in his thirties, but it was hard to tell since the lifestone slowed down the aging process for many people.

With a sigh, Luca finally nodded in acknowledgment and motioned to the cart with his hand. "Put your gear in there. We leave as soon as Fiola says we can.

I want to be up front: I am not excited about a babysitting mission or knowing you are being given a chance to gain the same rank I hold with just one quest. It's not right, but I will abide by the contract."

Kaen smirked and nodded. "Sorry if I'm putting you out. It was her idea, so I'm just taking the chance she has given me. Wouldn't you have attempted a quest like this if given a chance?"

Aubri laughed, put her arm around Kaen, and led him to the cart. "Ignore Luca," she stated, "most of us do. He comes from a well-off family and felt it wasn't fair that he was never offered a chance like you are getting."

Kaen glanced back at Luca, who had turned and was already ignoring him.

This is going to be a fun trip . . .

"I can see you are already flustered," Aubri said with a giggle. "I'll do my best to cheer you up and make the trip enjoyable. Some of us were not given a silver spoon or a leg up on everyone else. I, as are all those gathered here this morning, am excited to hear of what you have done and what you might accomplish!"

Kaen smiled, and as they arrived at the cart, Aubri pulled back the back flap and showed him the inside. There were benches with cushions in there, as well as multiple barrels of supplies.

"Just throw your pack in there, and we will get everything situated once we leave. For now, we must get with Fiola and endure the *send-off*."

Aubri flashed a wink and a grin at Kaen, and he found himself already looking forward to the trip because of her. He turned, watched as she walked away, and realized he had no clue how old she was. Her hair was brown like his and cut short, probably done that way for practical reasons when wearing a helmet or fighting. Her brown eyes were soft, and she had a great smile.

"Stop admiring her backside," Hess whispered, sneaking up on Kaen. "You need to focus!"

Kaen groaned and put his pack into the back of the wagon. "I was just trying to get to know who I would be spending the next few days with," Kaen answered with mock innocence. "She was the one who put her arm around me first."

Hess chuckled, leaned in close, and handed Kaen a small hip pack while they were behind the wagon. "There are three in there. Please try not to break or need them if you can help it. I only have a few of those left."

Kaen opened the pouch just a little and saw that they were the same potions he had been given back in Minoosh. "Thank you," Kaen whispered, strapping the pouch around his waist. "I'll try not to break any this time."

"Or need," Hess repeated. "Try not to need any either."

Kaen chuckled and shrugged. "I can't promise that, but I'll try. Now let's go see what Fiola wants."

"To talk and make herself feel better about all this," Hess declared as they walked to where the small group of adventurers were gathered.

* * *

Thirty minutes later, Kaen was finally leaving. Hess had been right. That woman had talked for over twenty minutes. Most of what she had said was about herself, what she saw for the future, and other stuff he had ignored after the first few minutes.

"Is she always that long-winded," Kaen asked when he turned to Aubri, who was driving the cart with a magical set of reins attached to a wooden piece near the front seats.

"Oh my gosh," Aubri replied as she burst out laughing. "She loves to hear her own voice, I believe."

"Stop that, you two!" Luca exclaimed from inside the wagon. "She is our guild master, and we should not discuss her like that. It is only because of her kindness and actions that you are even allowed on this quest."

Kaen and Aubri both groaned at the same time. When they realized they had done that, they burst into laughter. Kaen spent the next few hours talking and listening to Aubri share stories of the adventures she had gone on.

We should be near this spot, Kaen directed his thoughts toward Pammon as he pointed at the map on his lap.

Fiola had permitted him to take a copy of the quest map so that he could learn the lay of the land for future quests. It was more so that Pammon could know where he was planning on being.

I do not know why you are telling me this. You know I am above you in the clouds. I can see you just fine.

I just wanted to make sure you know more of an exact location so you can fly ahead and scout out a spot where we might be able to meet up tonight.

I will see if I can find the location you are focused on. I still need to find myself something to eat.

Kaen laughed, and Aubri looked at him with a questionable look. "Care to share what is so funny?"

"All this," Kaen lied, motioning with his hands toward the road and the trees around them. "My whole life, I have been waiting to become an adventurer, and here I am, on the road, a beautiful woman by my side and a cranky mage in the back of the cart."

Aubri laughed, and suddenly, she started snorting as she laughed. She looked embarrassed when she realized she was snorting in front of Kaen.

"Why are you upset?" Kaen asked, smiling at her. "I think that's a cute laugh."

Her cheeks went crimson red, and she yanked a little hard on the reins, causing the cart to weave hard to the right for a moment as she regained her composure.

"What the heck are you two doing up there?!" Luca yelled from the back of the wagon. "Do I need to take over up front so we don't get killed?

"You are going to get yourself and me in trouble," she whispered when she got the cart back on the road. "Your mentor, Hess, told me if anything happened between us while on this trip, he would make my life one I would regret."

Rolling his eyes, Kaen shook his head in disbelief.

Gosh, damnit Hess!

"I'm sure he didn't mean that," Kaen pleaded as he glanced back into the cart. There, staring at him, was Luca with that same annoyed look he'd had the first time. "Is he going to snitch on us?"

Aubri's snorting started again as she laughed and nodded that Luca would most definitely rat them out.

Sighing, Kaen shifted slightly away from Aubri and crossed his arms over his chest.

"Don't pout too much," she teased Kaen. "He didn't say anything about after the quest."

A coughing fit came over Kaen, and he laughed once he caught his breath and saw the way Aubri raised her eyebrows playfully at him.

"I swear you two are acting like kids up there!" Luca shouted. "Keep your eyes on the road and stop worrying about getting into each other's pants!"

Kaen and Aubri laughed as Luca continued grumbling from the back of the wagon.

They had passed more travelers than Kaen had expected, both in the pass and along the road through the woods. One band of guards had even ridden past them, patrolling the area closest to the pass to ensure safety for those who traveled. Kaen had been impressed with the smoothness of the road and learned that there were actual crews that came out and managed the roads from time to time.

"Safe and fast roads are important for the safety and well-being of the kingdom!" Luca had repeated multiple times.

There had been small caravans of goods and other merchants that had passed by. Most had at least two or three guards or adventurers with them. It reminded Kaen of what Hess had said about him and his dad doing quests that involved guarding people.

"We have about thirty minutes left on the crystal," Luca called out from where he sat in the back of the cart. "Need to make sure we are close to the spot Fiola picked out."

"Fiola picked a spot for us?" Kaen asked, glancing over his shoulder at Luca. "Why would she do that?"

Luca shrugged and motioned to the map. "She knew how far our cart could go and wanted to ensure our *special* adventurer would be safe. From the spot she picked, it is only about four hours to where we will need to set out on foot to find that orc camp. This gives us plenty of room not to have to worry about being close enough to them."

That seemed to make sense to Kaen, and he felt he should appreciate that Fiola was doing her best to keep him alive. Even if he knew it was because she had some hidden desire and secret for wanting to know his stats.

We are close to where we are going to stop for the night. I know you are near us. Does that mean you found a spot for us to meet?

I have, but it may be a bit of a walk from your camp. I'll be off to the east, where a small clearing is. I can catch an animal if you want to take it back to camp.

Kaen thought about that for a moment. It seemed like a good idea except for having to explain why it died by claws or teeth.

Maybe next time. I will tell them I am going to go out scouting and hunting to practice for tomorrow, though.

Ok! Just hurry and get here! I cannot wait for a good scratching session!

Kaen chuckled and played off the reason for laughing to Aubri. "Who knew the guild master could be so kind? I would have almost imagined she would make me hunt for my own food."

"Food is all taken care of!" Aubri quipped as she motioned with her head toward Luca. "Luca isn't a bad cook and will manage everything once we arrive. You need to relax and enjoy yourself."

"Actually . . . I want to get off into the woods, work on my tracking and sneaking skills, and maybe see if I can find something small to shoot. I want to prepare a little for tomorrow since I have been sitting all day today."

Aubri nodded in understanding and shrugged. "It is up to you. I can have Luca wait about an hour after we get settled for dinner to be ready. Think that would be enough time?"

"That would be perfect!"

39

Reunited

The moment the cart stopped at the clearing near the side of the road that Fiola had picked, Kaen grabbed a full quiver and his bow and took off through the woods, laughing.

"For wanting to practice being stealthy, he does not appear very good at it," Luca remarked, pointing at the barrel he wanted Aubri to unload.

Aubri nodded and leaned over the cart's edge and undid the rope holding the barrel to the side of the cart. "From what I hear, he isn't even eighteen yet. So I cannot imagine he is acting any different than I would expect."

"And you appear more than willing to climb into his blanket tonight with him," Luca declared from where he stood in the cart looking down at Aubri.

Blushing, Aubri gave a small shrug and finished undoing the rope. "I'm not saying he isn't easy on the eyes. That brown hair, eyes, and body do not look like a kid his age. And to think he is that powerful at seventeen!"

Aubri shook as a shiver of excitement passed through her and then laughed when she saw the look that Luca was giving her. "I'm just saying, from a woman's perspective, he sounds like a fun friend! Now, stop getting your staff all knotted up. I ain't going to do anything with him. I know better than that, but it doesn't mean I can't have some fun, does it?"

"Pfftt . . . So it's better to lead that boy on? You seem to forget you are almost old enough to be his mother," declared Luca. "You going to tell him how old you are?"

Aubri grabbed the barrel and lifted it easily off the cart and then set it on the ground near her feet. Even though it weighed at least one hundred pounds, she lifted it like it was nothing. "I don't think any of us need to comment on my age again," Aubri said with an edge to her voice. "Doing so might not bode well for those individuals."

Rolling his eyes, Luca turned around and retrieved a small wooden box near him. "I'm not that dumb to do such a thing. Besides, I need to start preparing stuff for dinner in an hour. Apparently, no one asked me if I was hungry and wanted to wait that long."

Aubri picked up the barrel again and walked with it toward the part of the clearing they would cook in. "That's why I like you, Luca," Aubri declared sarcastically. "All those brains. Most men aren't smart enough to know they shouldn't talk about a woman's age unless they want to get smacked across their head."

I'm almost to you! Kaen shouted through his connection with Pammon. *I can feel you are close!*

Pammon sent just as much joy and excitement through the bond as Kaen felt.

I can smell you and that woman you were sitting next to on your cart!

Kaen laughed as he ran toward where he knew Pammon awaited him. He dodged trees, rocks, and bushes, totally not caring that he was scaring off all animals that might be nearby. He only had one thing on his mind: seeing Pammon again.

As the last hundred yards loomed between them, Kaen could see a small clearing opening up before him and took off with a burst of speed and energy. It was as if his body knew he was returning to Pammon and filled him with something he had been lacking all these days.

The last three trees that blocked his view flew past him as he sprinted through the woods. Kaen slowed and shook his head in awe.

Oh my gosh, you have grown!

Pammon trilled, and it echoed through the fifty-yard-wide clearing. The bronze dragon jumped and frolicked like a lamb as he rushed toward where Kaen was exiting through the trees.

"You're so much bigger!" Kaen declared as Pammon rushed at him, slowing down just before bowling him over. "You are at least two feet taller and have gotten thicker too!"

Stop talking and scratch my head. It itches!

Kaen laughed and nodded and reached up as Pammon lowered his head to where Kaen could get his hands around it. Kaen first embraced his dragon, slowly stroking each side of Pammon's neck, and received a gentle trill and thrum from his massive body.

I have missed you. It feels weird to say this, but it is like a piece of my soul was gone when you were away all those days.

"I know," Kaen whispered. "Now, lie down so I can give you that scratch you want!"

Pammon trumpeted loudly and dropped to the dirt carefully so as not to crush him. Kaen moved over, sat against Pammon's body, and let him bend his neck so that his muzzle was facing Kaen.

Laughing, Kaen began scratching all the scales, grooves, and ridges from the tip of Pammon's muzzle up to his ears and horns, which had also grown.

Pammon's soft trill remained steady as Kaen worked his fingers along his head. It was evident from how he had curled his lips back and smiled at Kaen that he was enjoying this just as much as Kaen was.

You know just all the spots that I needed to be scratched!

Kaen laughed and kept working the ridges along the top of Pammon's skull, and then started working his neck. Pammon lifted his head and provided a better scratching opportunity for Kaen. Five minutes later, he stopped scratching and shook his hands as Pammon let out a long breath of air that sounded like a sigh.

"I need to let these rest a moment, but I can give it another go before I have to leave."

Stop talking about leaving already!

Kaen laughed and nodded. "Fine, I'll stop talking about it. Now stand up, and let me see how much you have grown!"

Kaen untangled himself from Pammon and backed up as Pammon rose on his haunches to his full height. Pammon raised his head high and pretended to stare off toward the sky so he could look majestic as Kaen walked around him.

"How much have you been eating?" Kaen asked in amazement. "There is no way you should be this big already!"

I think it had something to do with that massive green deer I ate. I felt different after I ate all of him.

"You ate all of him?!"

Pammon chortled as he nodded his massive head.

In two days! He was so massive! After that, I started to get bigger, it felt like. Perhaps eating different animals or special ones helps me grow.

Kaen gazed at Pammon and smiled when he finished circling him. "You think I could try climbing on your back, and you just walk around this area for a bit?"

I was going to say we should try! I feel strong enough now!

Laughing, Kaen moved to stand by Pammon as he lowered his head and neck and went down on his front claw.

Be gentle with my wings and watch the ridges. There should be a spot that might work for you to sit.

Putting his hand on Pammon's neck, Kaen tried figuring out how to get up onto him. There were a few spots he could grab and pull, but he did not want to risk injuring Pammon, especially with tomorrow being so important.

After a few attempts, Kaen got both hands on two ridges on Pammon's neck and jumped as he leaned against them. Things went great until his weight shifted, and he fell over the top of Pammon's neck, holding on upside down for dear life.

Kaen gasped. "Lie down!" he said as he stared at the dirt four feet from his face.

Pammon lowered himself, and Kaen let go with one hand and managed a soft landing in the dirt.

The thrumming of Pammon laughing caused Kaen to chuckle as he stood up. "I guess it was asking too much for that to work perfectly the first time."

I thought you had it until you didn't!

Kaen grinned and shook his head. "Let's go again. I won't jump as high this time!"

Four minutes later, about seven failed attempts had led to their first successful venture of Kaen getting onto Pammon's back. Kaen had to readjust a few times as some ridges poked in spots he did not want them to. With a little help from Pammon leaning forward and letting gravity do its job, he was finally seated and ready for Pammon to stand.

All those times Kaen had ridden a horse had not really prepared him for the power he felt between his legs. The moment Pammon stood up, lifted his head, and started walking around the clearing, every step Pammon took reverberated through Kaen's thighs, and he could tell that there was a mountain of power in his body. Kaen had to hold onto the ridge of Pammon's neck as they moved. He wished he had a rope or harness of some kind to make this easier and safer, as Hess had mentioned.

Want to try holding on while I move faster?

Kaen laughed loudly and patted Pammon's neck. "Go for it!" he shouted.

Pammon picked up speed as he ran circles around the clearing. Kaen had to lean close to Pammon's neck because his strides were started to buck Kaen slightly. There were moments he felt he would launch right off Pammon's back.

Slow down some! I think I'm going to need a break!

Pammon grunted and started to slow down, obviously not impressed with how easily Kaen had quit.

I was going to ask if you wanted me to try flying with you, but I guess you aren't ready.

Kaen laughed and thumped Pammon on the neck as they came to a stop. "There is no way we can try flying today! I could barely stay on you now. Besides, I can tell you are joking about flying."

Pammon thrummed as he laughed, causing his whole body to convulse and shake, sending Kaen almost over to the side as he tried to hold on with both hands around the dragon's neck.

That is cheating if you can sense that I was joking! I had not realized you could feel that coming through our bond.

Kaen laughed and slowly released his death grip around Pammon's neck. Sliding off was much easier than getting on.

"I'll need to ask Hess how we can find a harness of some kind. Neither of us wants me falling off while we are airborne with no way to hold on."

I would catch you before you hit the ground.

"I have no doubt you would try," Kaen stated, patting Pammon's neck. "I would not want to put you in a situation where both of our lives depended on that. There is no rush, and tomorrow is what is important."

A big blast of air rushed out of Pammon's snout as he huffed.

I am a dragon. You are my rider. Everything inside me longs for that to happen. Perhaps I can find another animal to eat to help speed my growth so that it can happen soon.

Kaen nodded, moved to the front of Pammon, and started rubbing under his chin. He smiled when the trilling sound he had missed over the past few days echoed through the grove, and he felt the skin under Pammon's mouth vibrate.

"You know what I am about to say," Kaen whispered, leaning his head forward and letting it rest against the top of Pammon's snout.

I know. Just scratch that spot one more time before you go. Tomorrow, I will hunt early and start scouting to ensure you return in one piece!

Frantically working his fingers between and along Pammon's scales, Kaen laughed as Pammon let a small amount of drool drip from his mouth onto the ground.

"That is nasty!" Kaen exclaimed as he moved back from the saliva.

Pammon laughed and shook his head, spraying the slobber in all directions.

Sorry, just that spot you hit relaxed my jaw, and I couldn't stop it!

Kaen laughed as he wiped off the small amount of slobber that had landed against his leg and patted Pammon's snout gently. "Tomorrow, we finish this quest, and soon, we will have more time for moments like this!"

Rest well! You best not fail, or I will not be happy!

Laughing, Kaen walked backward to the trees, keeping his eyes on his friend, who watched him just as intently.

When the tree line blocked his view, Kaen started jogging back to camp. A few tears were in his eyes. That feeling that he was leaving something important behind him returned. Pammon had been right.

It felt like he was leaving a part of his soul behind as he jogged back to Aubri and Luca.

40

Arrived

Luca had prepared salted pork fried in a pan and covered with some herbs he had been carrying. The smell of it hit Kaen while he was still almost a quarter of a mile away. It made him smile as he realized how hungry he was, and it gave him something to think about besides the pain in his chest from leaving Pammon.

"This is amazing!" Kaen declared as he finished his third helping of pork and vegetables. "You could open a restaurant, and I would gladly visit and pay for a meal like this!"

Luca flashed the only real smile he had given Kaen since meeting him. "I enjoy cooking. It was something my grandmother and I used to do when I was a kid. She taught me to find ways to express myself when I cooked. It was not easy being different from the others in our town."

Kaen nodded as he used a piece of bread to collect the pork's salt and crust from the bowl's bottom. "I used to cook all the time also. After my dad died, I . . . " Kaen paused and realized he had started sharing more information than he had planned to, as he was lost in his meal.

He glanced up from his bowl and saw that Aubri had a sympathetic look on her face. Even Luca seemed to be listening to Kaen.

"I mean . . . I cooked for the man who raised me. You all know Hess. He might be a gifted adventurer, but his cooking was horrible, to say the least," joked Kaen.

They chuckled and nodded, and no one else felt the need to add anything to that conversation.

Kaen and Aubri cleaned the dishes while Luca cleared away the food and other ingredients he had used.

"Sun will be down in a few hours, yet I think we should get into the cart and get a good night's rest," Aubri stated as she added a few logs to her fire contraption.

"Does that actually work?" Kaen asked, pointing at her log-adding set up for the fire.

Nodding, Aubri pointed to the metal stakes she had driven into the ground at the fire's edge and the logs she had stacked on top of each other against the stakes.

"The log at the bottom will slowly burn, and when it has burned enough, it will fall apart and into the fire. The logs will roll down and catch on this top piece, preventing them from falling into the fire. Sometimes they don't roll off, and the fire will lift the stakes and light all of the logs, but usually, it doesn't," she informed Kaen with a smile. "I have been practicing this for years, and I think I finally got it working how I want."

Kaen inspected it a little more and tried to commit to memory what he could of the design. It would be an asset for sure at some point in his adventuring career.

"We need to take turns tonight on who stays up?" Kaen asked.

Luca chuckled and shook his head. "The cart has a warning system built in. It is a rare guild cart and not one we would usually get to travel in, but Fiola thought we should have it. An anti-animal ward keeps most of them away from us, and if anyone approaches within a hundred yards, we will hear a noise and wake up."

Kaen's eyes widened as he looked at the cart with a new appreciation of what was possible to make with magic. There was so much he could not wait to explore and learn.

Luca had woken them up and started a quick breakfast of dried meat, fruit, and bread and then pulled out a container of milk that was still cold. One of the barrels had a rune on it that would last for a few days but would keep everything at a certain temperature. Kaen wished he had been able to enjoy one of those back at Hess's old house.

They had loaded up their supplies, put out the fire that had lasted all night, and still had two logs waiting to roll into the fire, as they set off along the road. The sun was just beginning to send its rays over the tops of the trees.

Luca and Aubri were not chatting at all. They both believed at a time like this, Kaen should be preparing his mind for the task ahead.

Sitting by himself in the back of the wagon, Kaen had put on his gear and was going over each of the arrows he had brought along. He had picked out twenty-five arrows from the ones Hess had bought him. While all of them were high-quality arrows, he found a few with details that made them slightly imperfect.

He could feel his lifestone guiding his hand as he thought about picking the best ones. Each of the feathers was perfectly straight and aligned as they should be. Two arrows were removed as potentials because the weight of the tips was just enough to alter the arrow's flight. Small things he doubted he would have noticed back in Minoosh.

Pammon had been flying the area the camp was believed to be in and had located it already. It was a good hour into the woods from where they would stop. The trees were dense around the spot the orcs were staying, and Pammon pointed out that they were a half day from a few small villages that appeared to the east and north of the orcs.

Do you see all five of them?

No. Only three are visible to me. They have some tent-like structures, but the camp is a mess. The clearing they are in appears to have been widened. It is as big as the one we were in yesterday. Just know that the side you will come up on and the north side of their clearing has thick, massive trees.

Kaen grunted as he closed his eyes and imagined what Pammon was looking at. He couldn't see it, but it felt like he might be able to one day. For now, he could sense how the camp was laid out. The thick trees would offer him cover but also limit his ability to shoot once they got into the woods.

I have a few hours till you arrive, so I will scout and see if I can find the other two. Be safe!

Thank you, Pammon.

Kaen paused a moment and smiled to himself.

Thank you for yesterday also. I think I needed to see you as much as you needed me to scratch those spots.

Pammon's laughter as he flew across the sky washed over Kaen like a fresh rain shower. He knew that Pammon enjoyed the comment even if he did not reply.

"We're here," Aubri shouted as they moved the cart over to the side of the road.

Kaen went toward the back of the cart and looked down the road. They had passed a few small carts that morning, and he wondered if they had traveled all night or stopped somewhere to rest as they had. Judging by how the animals barely moved, Kaen believed it was the former.

Once Aubri managed to get the cart off the main road, they all piled out of it, and Luca went around it, tying the covering to the wooden part of the cart and sealing it up.

"Before you ask, the cart is warded. Most people traveling on this road won't be able to overcome the ward that prevents someone from opening the sides, and if someone attempted to cut their way through, they would not like the traps they would encounter." Kaen nodded, appreciating all the knowledge Luca was sharing with him.

"Any idea which way we need to go?" Aubri asked Luca.

"I have an idea," Kaen replied before Luca could. "I studied the maps of this area and the one on the quest. Combined with that knowledge and my skill in tracking, I would like to try to find the orcs on my own."

"It's your quest," Luca answered. "We are here to support you. Any last questions before we let you lead us into the woods?"

Kaen paused momentarily as he looked at Aubri, who had taken up a position behind Luca.

"How close do you need to be? Stealth is important for what I want to do, not that I think you two aren't stealthy, but . . . "

Luca nodded and motioned to Aubri with his head. "We will stay behind you. One hundred yards would be enough?"

Kaen grinned and nodded. "That would be perfect. Now, I don't plan on calling for help, but is there anything specific you want me to yell if I need it?"

Aubri laughed, and when she saw Luca turn and look at her, she stopped. "Just yell '*help,*' or do you have some safe word you prefer to use instead?"

Kaen scratched his chin and pondered what word might be better than *help*. If orcs were smart, they should know that word and realize he was calling his allies. "Let's do the word *bacon* instead."

Luca shook his head and rolled his eyes at the choice of bacon, but Kaen could see that he appreciated the logic behind the decision.

"Ok. From this moment on, you are on your own. Lead on, testee Kaen Marshell."

Grinning, Kaen nodded and gave his gear one last check. His bow was ready across his back. His armor was tight and in place. The arrows and quiver hung on his back, and the pouch of potions was easily accessible by either hand.

Everything was as it needed to be for this.

I'm heading in.

I'll head that way soon. Scouting to the east still. No sign of the other two yet.

Walking through the woods could be a fun thing. With his bow in his left hand, Kaen made his way through the overgrown area of the forest, leaving small marks on trees to help Luca and Aubri follow him. He was not attempting to hide his path, and he doubted he needed to leave marks for the two silver token adventurers behind him, but it was always better to have something just in case.

He weaved and moved a little to make it look as if he was not taking a straight line to where he was going. Pammon had that clearing in his vision, and

Kaen could find it blindfolded. The trees were thick here, and the light from the sun was not very much, even with it being up for a few hours now.

Birds sang and chirped, and the small forest animals sought food. A non-poisonous snake he recognized had crossed his path earlier, and he had let it slither away before continuing. Its presence reminded Kaen that these woods differed from his own, and he had no idea what might be out here.

"Be smart about this," Kaen muttered as he moved around bushes that might have a snake or some other creature hiding in them.

I'm about two hundred yards from where you say they are. Any update on the missing orcs?

No. One orc in camp came out of its sleeping area and is eating something from a pile in the center of the camp. It looks like a pile of animals and possibly a human or something. It is by itself right now.

Kaen's heart started to beat faster as he felt the anticipation of everything beginning. So much was riding on this moment, and he needed to succeed. Pammon needed him to succeed. Suddenly, he felt his heart rate spike as he thought about how much money was riding on his success in this. Hess and Sulenda would be well cared for if he pulled this off.

Focus your thoughts! Pammon shouted through their connection. **Your heart is racing like a rabbit who I am hunting! You need to calm down.**

Kaen stopped moving and took a few breaths. Pammon was right. He took four more long breaths and let them out. His heart slowed down, and he began making his way through the trees again. As he wove around the tight-packed trees, Kaen paused for a moment.

Can you see me at all?

No. I told you the trees are too thick. I know where you are, but the forest where you are and running along the north side of the clearing is impossible to see through.

Kaen wondered how long he could hide in the tree line if it were this thick. If one of them from the camp reached the tree line, he would be in trouble. He would have to leave it and stand in the middle of the camp, giving up the trees' protection.

Well, let me know if anything changes. As you know, I'm getting closer.

41

Quest Battle Part 1

The one is still eating in the middle of the camp, east of you. The other two I have yet to see. What do you want to do?

Nocking the arrow, Kaen hid behind two trees deep in the darkness the forest provided. He had a clear shot, but it was a long shot, easily forty-five yards to the orc from where he stood.

Do you think the other two will notice if I take this shot and kill him?

Kaen sensed Pammon as he thought about that question.

I cannot hear him now nor know how heavily an orc sleeps. When I sleep at night, I am aware of everything around me as I merely doze. If you kill him and he makes no sound, I expect them not to be alerted.

Pammon paused, and Kaen could feel the pause over their connection.

What are you leaving out, Pammon?

The last time I told you to shoot the goblin with the bones, you did, and it was the wrong choice. I don't want to be responsible for you making the wrong choice again.

Kaen understood that. He felt guilty when the goblin shot Pammon because he told him to charge in the cave.

Don't forget I messed up, and you got shot in the cave because of me. You forgave me, and I never felt you needed to ask for forgiveness from me. We are partners, and I trust you with my life.

As do I.

Kaen sent a hug, or as best as he could imagine sending one through the connection, and felt Pammon return something similar to him being nestled up against his chest.

Ok, I'll take the shot. Let me know if anyone moves.

Just remember there is one hidden from your sight north of this one. The other, you should be able to see if it comes out of its tent.

Kaen nodded and took a deep breath, then slowly let it out. He focused on the orc, his lifestone gently pulsed, and Kaen smiled to himself as his eyes drifted to the hollow of the orc's skull. The creature was facing north, his jaw working as he ripped a large chunk of raw meat from an animal bone. Kaen let his lifestone pulse harder and harder for a few more breaths until he knew it would take over if he let go.

His arms rose on their own as he drew the bow back to full power. A slight breeze rippled the grass in the clearing just past the trees, circling slightly to the north. The tip of the arrow lifted slightly to the south. As the orc lifted the meat once more toward its mouth, Kaen's fingers slipped from the bowstring, and the arrow flew through the darkness of the forest around him out into the opening in the clearing. It flashed across the open ground and pierced the orc's temple, knocking it clean off his haunches and to the ground. The only sound was a gentle thud as the massive creature fell on its side.

Great shot! I could feel it when you let go of the string. None of the others have moved yet. How do you want to proceed?

Kaen's fingers trembled, and his lifestone had calmed down. He had hoped for a skill increase but was glad to have made the shot.

I'm afraid I need to find a way to draw one out without setting off an alarm. I would prefer not to leave the trees if I have to. Any ideas?

Kaen waited as he felt Pammon circling high above him. He knew he couldn't see Pammon as high as he was, and it still blew his mind that Pammon could see so clearly from that kind of height.

I could swoop down and smash off a treetop and drop nearby. It would create some noise, but I would also need to get back into the sky, which would take some time and limit my vision.

Mulling that over, Kaen slowly crept closer to the camp through the trees. The smell hit him about ten yards later, and the stench of filth and rotting flesh sparked memories of the cave with the goblins. He had not liked going in blind in that cave, and knowing he was in a similar situation here was not pleasant.

How long would it take you to fly down here and do that?

From this height, probably four minutes tops. I could come faster, but I didn't want to risk that kind of speed unless I had to.

Let's do it. Be safe, and let me know before you break off the tree. Which side will you do that on?

Pammon chuckled as he started his dive. Kaen realized what Pammon was going to say before he even did.

You hadn't picked a side to break the tree off at yet, had you?

Cheater! You did it again . . . no I had not. Which side do you think would be best?

Do the east side. I can see the tent to the east. I prefer to draw them that way.

East it is!

Kaen knelt on his knee and foot, shifting silently and quietly as he stayed pressed against a tree, watching and listening. The orc he had killed had no weapon on him that Kaen had seen. Perhaps they were not worried about adventurers, and the other two might come out dressed in nothing but filthy clothes like the other one had.

Kaen tracked Pammon, knowing he was getting close. He tried seeing if he could spot him, but the trees were too thick and blocked his vision overhead. He could barely make out the tops of the trees and a small piece of sky across the grove. The sun was lighting up the area more now.

I am about to strike the tree! Be ready!

A few seconds later, a loud crack echoed through the forest off to the east, and a host of birds and other animals cried out. Kaen could hear the ruckus of the birds and knew a group of them had taken flight by how their sound echoed at the top of the trees and forest.

So many birds! Dropping the treetop!

A moment later, a loud echoing of wood hitting wood and the sound of whatever Pammon had snapped off thumped through branches and ended with a loud bang against the ground. Kaen knew the sound had echoed for a good distance and hoped it would not draw Luca and Aubri to investigate.

I'm climbing back into the sky. I have no vision for now, but soon! Be safe!

Kaen watched the camp surge to life. Grunting and calling from both tents burst forth as the two orcs in the camp moved out of their tents. Kaen could not yet see the orc to the north, but he could hear him. The one to the east was holding a club and a shield as it stood up from the opening of its dwelling and quickly turned to face the east of the camp.

That orc was a good forty yards away and, thankfully, had not noticed its friend lying on its side in the middle of the camp. It was holding up its shield and peering toward the trees, and Kaen could hear it sniffing the wind.

A roar broke out from the north, and Kaen saw the orc that had been hidden dashing toward the orc in the middle of the camp. It held a massive two-handed axe in one hand, or at least it would have been a two-handed axe for Kaen. It appeared to be nothing more than a normal axe for this hulking brute in clothes that barely covered its manhood.

As it ran toward its fallen ally, Kaen drew his bow.

He tried to take a breath and slow his heart and called for his lifestone to help. Nothing came, and he realized he would be all on his own for this moment. The other orc turned around to see what his partner was roaring about.

Time was passing, and Kaen knew his element of surprise from his location would quickly be gone.

The massive orc was facing away from him. None of the shots he could take would be great unless he managed to hit a vital spot. Options were limited, and Kaen decided critical mass was better than possibly missing a headshot.

Kaen focused on the orc's massive back. He knew roughly where its heart might be, possibly protected by the huge spinal cord that seemed overly bony. A lung shot or heart shot would have to do.

Drawing back the string, Kaen took a breath and held it. He knew the wind had not changed, and he aimed where he knew the orc would be the moment it stood up. Right before he let the string go, the orc suddenly whipped around and turned to face Kaen's direction, his nostrils flaring in the clearing.

The wind! The gosh damn wind!

Kaen adjusted his aim quickly, letting the arrow go. It flew from his hiding spot and managed to pierce the left chest of the beast, causing him to flail in agony as he roared.

I need eyes on me and these guys now, Pammon!

Twenty seconds or so, I'm swinging around and coming in lower than I want to!

Cursing under his breath, Kaen pulled another arrow out as the orc staggered to his feet. It grabbed the arrow and yanked it from its chest, taking with it a chunk of flesh, as the barbs had dug into its lungs. It tried to roar again but coughed, blood spewing from its massive mouth.

Wasting no time, Kaen sent another arrow after the orc and immediately moved around the trees to the southeast. The roar that came again told him that it had struck the leg he had aimed at.

Pammon!

I'm hurrying. Give me a few more seconds!

Moving with another arrow ready to fire, Kaen tried to peer through the trees, looking for movement or one of the orcs possibly coming at him. He could hear the sounds of the orcs in the camp; one was groaning in pain, and the other was shouting loudly.

I think he is calling for his friends! What do you see?

Nothing through the trees! Three more seconds!

Kaen kept moving and saw a glimpse of the one orc from the east with the shield and club. It was near his friend, and glancing around the tree line, trying to locate him. Since he had moved, the orc had yet to find him and was holding his shield toward the direction he had last been.

Just the two. One is down on his knee, and the other is looking for you! I hear noise from the north, but I cannot see anything! I need to climb higher and will lose vision for a few moments!

Grumbling to himself, Kaen had no choice but to engage the third orc while it was distracted. If more orcs were coming from the north, he had a brief window before things would go arse up.

Stopping next to a tree, Kaen found a tight shooting lane that kept him in the shadows and only gave him a small window to fire through. It actually helped him focus, as it blurred away all the other things and outlined the orc he was aiming at.

The orc kept turning and looking to the east. It shifted with the same movements each time as it glanced north and south, trying to find where he might be. There was just a brief moment when its four-foot-tall shield would not cover its midsection.

Drawing the bow to full power, Kaen held his breath and waited for the orc when it would turn to look north for just a moment. He knew that brief moment would come, and he would have to aim for its stomach. Not a shot a hunter ever wanted to take when hunting, but Kaen knew this animal he was stalking now did not deserve the same treatment he usually gave.

The moment came, and the orc glanced to the north, twisting his shoulders and hips just enough. The moment he did, Kaen let the arrow fly and watched as it streaked toward the orc. The soft belly of the orc did nothing to stop the arrow's flight as it tore through his side and disappeared into its belly.

The creature howled in pain, dropping its shield and club as it reached for its sides. As it turned and grabbed its midsection, Kaen saw the arrow sticking a few inches out of the other side of its obliques. That was not the kind of death anyone would want. The creature roared in pain as it pulled the arrow out from the side it had penetrated completely, causing blood and dark bile to gush from its wound.

Almost back! I hear noise, and lots of it coming from the north! Be ready!

Kaen was already moving to the east, as Pammon called out to him. He needed to prepare for whatever might come.

42

Quest Battle Part 2

Kaen moved as quickly as he could while staying quiet in the darkness of the woods. While Pammon could not provide vision, he had to move a little closer to the edge of the clearing as he could not risk missing out on what might come into it. The truth of how much height mattered for his ability to help here was something he hated learning the hard way. Perhaps they should have practiced this more, but he had never considered how flying and looking from above worked.

Kaen pulled an arrow and watched as the two orcs attempted to wrap bandages around their wounds. The first one he had shot was barely moving now, leaning on the handle of the axe it had once easily carried. Each breath was causing blood to escape from its chest where it had pulled the arrow out. Blood was foaming and running down its mouth. Kaen knew from all the animals he had hunted that this orc would be dead in moments.

The other orc was still in the fight, even as wounded as it was. A gut shot was horrible, but he knew that many creatures could live for hours after one. Wanting to take another shot at the orc while it was not defending itself was an option, but Kaen could hear shouting and loud noises coming from the north.

I hear something coming, and I can see trees shifting; its friends must be hitting trees as they run. They will be on you in less than thirty seconds if I gauge their speed right!

Kaen dropped the arrow he was holding and grabbed a punching tip from his quiver. Thirty seconds was a lifetime in a moment like this. He took a deep breath, drew his bow, and aimed for the orc's back. 'Smart shot placement,' Hess had drilled into him all those months ago. It was far better to make a shot that would be a solid hit versus taking a shot one might miss completely.

The arrow zipped across the clearing and blew through the back of the orc and out of its chest. The creature stumbled forward and dropped to a knee, bellowing in pain as it let go of the cloth it had been using to wrap around its waist.

Ignoring the arrow on the ground, Kaen pulled another arrow out, another barbed one, and nocked it, waiting to see what was coming.

Can you see anything yet?

No, but they are closer! Maybe fifteen seconds max! They are running faster now! Be ready!

Are you going to be here to give me vision when they arrive?

I will be five seconds or so later. I will circle around from where I am, but my vision will be limited to just the clearing! Wait for me!

The orc he had shot was struggling to stand. Perhaps he had gotten a better shot than he had hoped for when that arrow burst through its chest. With those two injuries, it could not fight at all.

Crashing sounds and roaring were coming from the trees across the clearing. The orc he had shot called out faintly, and its friends, hidden by the trees, answered back with a roar that echoed through the forest around Kaen.

Two massive orcs, larger than the three he had been facing, burst through trees and knocked over a sapling that was on the edge of the clearing. They were wearing full leather armor, carrying a sword in each hand. Kaen realized both swords must be at least four feet long, yet each carried them like they were wooden training sticks. Both of these monsters stood at least eight feet tall, and their skin was dark. A crashing sound was still coming behind them, and Kaen realized there were more than five orcs. There had to be a sixth, at least!

Do you need to run?! There is another, and it is louder than the other two! I had not heard it over them!

Kaen took a deep breath. He had time. He had to have time. This was the moment he had been training for all those years. He took another breath, grabbed another arrow, and put it on the string.

Both orcs were advancing slowly toward their companions, who were down on the ground and struggling to stand.

Slow breaths.

Let it out slowly.

Focus.

Kaen willed his lifestone to hear him. To answer his call. It pulsed softly.

Kaen breathed again and knew the skill he wanted to use. He needed it to guide his shot. Time seemed to slow down, and this time, his lifestone answered with a surge. It seemed to know what he needed.

What he wanted.

It chose to answer his call.

[Archery Skill Twinshot - Activated]

Kaen's arms and body did what they had just done not long ago. The bow was pulled back and moved to where it needed to be. His body rotated and turned slightly, flattening the bow sideways. The tips of the arrows shifted slightly when his fingers separated the shafts just enough so that they would strike where they needed to.

In mere seconds, the bowstring snapped forward, and two arrows raced across the empty space in the forest, signaling death for two creatures that had no idea what was coming at them.

A gurgle sounded from both orcs at the same time. Each of them dropped both swords in unison as they grabbed at their necks, where an arrow had pierced their windpipe. Kaen stood, holding his bow in shock at what had just happened.

[Archery Skill Increased]

Each orc gasped for air, taking a few steps forward and stumbling to their knees.

The crashing behind them grew closer.

Kaen, you should run! This thing is massive!

Snapping out of the fog that he had been in as he witnessed the death of two orcs far stronger than any of the others he had faced, Kaen knew what he needed to do.

Dropping his bow briefly, he cupped both hands to his mouth and shouted. "BACON! BACON! BACON!"

Grabbing his bow again, he started moving back to the west in the direction Luca and Aubri would be.

Let me know when it comes out! I'm calling the others!

You do not have time! I can see it now. It's less than forty yards and coming fast!

Ignoring Pammon's warning, Kaen sprinted toward where he expected to find his observers. He tried to remain as quiet as possible but knew he was making noise. Nothing he made would compare to the sound of trees breaking and crashing as he ran toward the others.

"BACON!" he shouted once more as he ran toward where they should be.

A loud crashing sound came as a tree fell to the ground.

Kaen didn't risk a glance lest he trip and fall or smack into a tree. Whatever had been coming to the clearing had arrived.

Kaen heard Aubri before he saw her. She came bursting through the forest with her shield and sword out, rushing past trees in the direction she believed him to be.

He waved his hands, and she noticed him and turned to intercept him, with Luca in tow only a few yards behind.

"Five orcs are dead, but there is one larger than all of them!" Kaen explained quickly as Aubri and he stopped running and almost crashed into each other. "I killed five! Two were at least eight feet tall, and a sixth one just arrived in their clearing. I don't know how big it is, but it has to be massive from the sound it made!"

Aubri took all of Kaen's information in and glanced back at Luca, who had just arrived.

"He fulfilled the quest, but there appears to be a Master orc!"

Luca's eyes went wide, and he glanced at Kaen. "You saw it?"

Kaen shook his head. "I killed five orcs and ran as soon as the final two died. It had just arrived in the clearing when I made it back to my original trail. I do not know what it could be, but it is larger than the last two I killed, and they were easily eight feet tall!"

Aubri and Luca peered behind Kaen and listened to the noise coming from the clearing a good fifty yards off. The roaring and thundering of steps were loud enough to reach this deep into the forest.

Kaen, it is at least twelve feet tall! It has a huge mace taller than you and a shield easily as large as Hess!

"If I ventured a guess, it must be close to twelve feet tall from the sound it made compared to the sounds of the smaller ones," Kaen lied, relaying the information from Pammon. "Will we kill it?"

Aubri grimaced, and Kaen could tell she was not certain this was a fight for them.

"It is too dangerous to leave it, and you know it," Luca stated, reading Aubri's body language.

"If it's as big as Kaen says it is, we may be vastly outclassed," Aubri argued. "You and I both know that is an advanced silver party quest of six. There are only two of us, and we have no healer!"

Luca sighed and nodded. He moved up a few feet and put his hand on Aubri's shoulder, and she spun around to face him. "We both know we cannot leave that creature here without at least verifying what it is. We will use a triangle formation and let the forest help us. Can you tank it while we attack it?"

Aubri shuddered, and Kaen realized she was shaking because she was actually afraid.

"If it's too dangerous, should we not just flee?" Kaen asked, interrupting them. "I would prefer to be safe, if we can."

Luca shook his head and motioned toward the clearing and the noise coming from it. "It will have our scent soon enough and will track us down. If it overtakes us in the forest, we will be at a disadvantage. We need to press the attack while we can."

"I will try," Aubri suddenly blurted out, but it was so quiet Kaen almost missed hearing her at first. "I cannot promise I can hold him off long, and I may die, yet I will do what I swore an oath to."

Aubri stood upright and rolled her shoulders a few times. "What's the plan, Luca?" she asked, her voice sounding braver by the second.

Luca nodded and pointed at Kaen. "We need to move now. Lead us to the edge. You will go to the other side of the clearing. Aubri will stay with me until she has to engage. I will use the few enhancement spells I have on her and then do what I can damage-wise to the beast. You need to help weaken it or find a way to end its life."

Kaen nodded and checked his arrows. Only five more puncture arrows were left, and the other twelve were barbed.

"We need to move out before it leaves the clearing," Luca declared as he moved toward it.

The sounds in the clearing quieted down as they stopped near the edge of the opening.

Luca and Aubri froze when they saw the orc rampaging through the camp, sniffing the arrows and the air.

Kaen glanced at the grass near the clearing and was thankful to see it blowing southward. "We must go before the wind shifts again, and he gets our scent. It is searching for me," Kaen whispered, motioning toward the beast.

Kaen could not imagine how strong this creature must be for the two silver adventurers to freeze like that. Pammon had been right. This thing was easily twelve feet tall. It seemed taller than most roofs and houses back home. With its armor on, it was as wide as a cart at its shoulders. Massive chain mail covered every inch of it, that he could see. Kaen had no idea how they would manage to harm this beast, even if they got past the range it had with that club.

Luca nodded, and for a second, Kaen saw a slight green glow from his hands, and then Aubri's entire body glowed the same color for a moment. Luca repeated this process a few times, and each time, Aubri mirrored the color of his hands.

"Go!" Luca instructed both of them.

Kaen nodded and took off quietly, running to the east through the woods while Aubri shook her head from side to side a few times and loosed her shoulders once more.

We are about to engage this thing. Let me know if you see any openings, Pammon.

Kaen felt worry oozing through their connection.

I am not sure this is a good decision, but I am here. I will give you my strength if needed.

Kaen prayed it would not be needed this time.

43

Quest Battle Part 3

Aubri shouted as she entered the clearing, drawing the orc's attention. It dropped an arrow it was holding and grabbed the club next to it. Aubri was immensely intimidated at the sight of the orc standing upright holding its shield and easily moving a club most would consider a decent-sized log.

The orc glanced around the opening, aware that just because a warrior was approaching with a shield and sword in hand didn't mean others weren't nearby. It snarled, and in a guttural voice said to Aubri, "A treat for me. Where is the one who killed my men?"

Aubri froze mid-stride. She glanced back toward Luca, and the orc followed her eyes.

"In there?" it growled. "I will take my time and enjoy this!"

The orc kicked the body of one of his slain orcs at Aubri, sending it flying through the air so fast, she barely had time to raise her shield as it slammed into her.

The force of the orc pushed her back several feet, and it split in half and erupted in gore. Blood, guts, and bone covered her shield and armor, blinding her as the orc dashed across the opening toward her.

"Aubri, step A!" Luca shouted as a fireball erupted from where he was in the forest. Without seeming surprised the orc blocked it with his shield as it ran through the fire that billowed over him.

Without hesitation, Aubri darted to the east, holding her shield in the direction she knew the orc would be coming from.

The orc swung its massive club, changing the direction of its original swing as Aubri darted to its right. It caught her shield and sent her flying through the sky like a rock hit by a stick. The orc planted its foot, halting its momentum, and turned to follow Aubri as she skidded along the clearing, rolling a few times before quickly jumping to her feet.

Kaen kept moving to the east and saw an orange glow momentarily flash around Aubri's body. He had no idea what it was, but he took it as a bad sign the way its light had flickered out.

The orc covered the distance between it and Aubri at an alarming rate, holding his shield like a charging bull.

Vines suddenly sprung up from the ground at its feet and tried to wrap up the running orc. He tripped and missed a few steps, getting his shield caught on the ground as he pitched forward.

Aubri wasted no time in counterattacking, moving to his exposed left side, becoming a blur as she ran.

Kaen aimed his arrow at the orc, holding the shot and waiting to see if a weak point would reveal itself.

Aubri slashed her sword at the orc's side as she ran past him. She planted her feet, and had started to swing at its hip again, when the orc's shield arm came from nowhere and smashed into her shield. Kaen grimaced as Aubri flew backward from the blow.

The only spot Kaen could find to aim at that wasn't covered by armor was the orc's hand holding onto his club for support.

The arrow struck true and buried itself into its hand and the wood, pinning it against the handle.

The orc searched in the direction Kaen was in the woods. An awful snarl crossed his face as his eyes looked into the darkness of the forest for Kaen.

"Come and play, archer boy," the orc taunted as he flexed his hand and snapped the arrow shaft before pulling his massive hand from the arrow that had skewered his hand.

The orc suddenly groaned and shook as lightning arced across its body and armor.

Kaen moved east again and saw that Luca was standing at the edge of the clearing, holding his hands out, lightning streaking across the field in a never-ending arc. Smoke rose from the creature, but it stood up, leaning against its shield and club, ripping the roots that held its feet in place.

After taking the blow across her shield, Aubri was still down on the ground, almost ten yards from where she had landed.

Kaen drew another arrow, choosing a piercing one this time, and tried to reposition to find a better shot as the orc stood to its full height.

Your friend is down! You need to run!

Kaen could feel the fear in Pammon's heart. Kaen was really afraid for the first time in his life but knew running was not an option. The orc would kill him if it ran him down. Running away and abandoning these two was not how he would start his adventuring story!

We fight! I will not abandon them just like I would not leave you!

Kaen ignored the frustration he felt from Pammon and watched as the orc turned and faced Luca. The orc fought through the pain and the burning of the steady stream of lightning that had been going on for a good ten seconds.

Luca was fading fast. He lowered one hand to use as support against his knee as he fell to the ground. Less lightning leaped from him now. Only one hand sent a stream of magic at the orc.

With the creature's back to him, Kaen released an arrow to its blind side and watched it barely pierce the armor that was starting to glow on the inside from the lightning burning it. Even at full draw, it had only pierced the orc by maybe four inches.

The orc took another step, fighting a battle of wills with the mage who was sending everything he had at it. Four arrows lined the creature's back, but they did not stop its slow progression toward the mage. It was only twenty-five yards from Luca, who was at his limits. Lightning only flew from his fingers every few seconds. The stream was gone, and just remnants of Luca's last bits of magic sparked out.

Unexpectedly, the orc tossed his club at Luca.

Kaen watched in horror as the club fell short but bounced on the ground and smashed into Luca, knocking him aside and causing him to slam into a tree. Kaen could hear the thud and crash of Luca's body against the wood.

Heavy breathing came from the orc as it slowly turned to face Kaen, who was standing near the far edge of the clearing. Its face was burnt and bleeding, but it was still smiling as it readjusted its shield and used it as a crutch as it walked toward Kaen.

"Boy, I will suck the marrow from your bones," it gasped as it moved toward him. "Save me the trouble, and do not fight back. I will make it quick and painless if you do."

Kaen recovered from his stupor and began firing arrows at the orc. It used its shield to block the arrows coming at its head, and the barbed arrows did nothing against its leg armor.

It laughed as it walked. "You choose a slow death then."

Kaen held the arrow he had knocked, fully drawn in his bow. It was a barbed arrow. He only had one piercing arrow left and needed to save it for the shot he knew would matter. As he watched the orc stagger toward him, he felt something.

I'm here! Be ready!

Kaen let the arrow go, aiming for the orc's face. He watched as it lifted its shield, blocking its vision. Kaen had played this game before. The orc believed he was all alone.

Pammon's sudden strike from the sky echoed loudly enough to hurt Kaen's ears.

Sweeping in from behind, Pammon used both back claws to attack.

The orc's weight and size were too much for Pammon to lift it into the air and carry it away, but his talons pierced through the orc's shoulder blades and into his collarbone. It lifted him off the ground. The orc's arms were wide from surprise and shock. Its shield fell to the side.

Kaen's lifestone exploded with force the moment Pammon struck. His hand moved to the quiver, drew an arrow, put it into position, and drew it back. The tip of the arrow moved, tracking the orc's movement as Pammon carried it across the top of the clearing for a few feet. The moment its arc reached its peak, and that brief moment of weightlessness was achieved before it would start its journey back to the ground, Kaen's fingers let the string go, and the arrow flew at the orc's head, piercing its right eye and burying a few inches into its skull.

The orc roared in pain as Pammon's grip slipped, his claws giving under the weight and dropping the orc to the ground, causing it to slam face first into the dirt.

Pammon flapped his wings and continued to soar upward, circling to avoid the trees around him.

Groans and growls came from the beast as it tried to roll on the ground. It was struggling to stand up, but its upper body was destroyed. In that single attack, Pammon had broken its shoulders and collarbone. Its arms failed to work even as it pushed with its legs, trying to rise.

Kaen ran up close and pulled out the last arrow with a piercing tip.

The orc had lost its helm. Its head was exposed. The Masur turned to face Kaen, trying to look at him even though his left eye was buried in the dirt. "I'll kill you," it growled as blood seeped from all the wounds it had suffered.

Kaen nodded and let the arrow go, piercing the beast's temple and pinning it to the ground.

The moment the arrow struck, Kaen ran to where Aubri was on the ground, unmoving.

As he ran, he felt pain coming through his link. Pammon was hurt!

Are you ok? How are you hurt?

My legs are injured from the impact. I may have broken a part of my back claw. I will be fine for now. Save your friends if you can! I will scout and make sure no more are coming.

Thank you, Pammon! You saved me!

I will always risk everything for you, Kaen. You know that just as I know you will for me.

Kaen wanted to smile, but as he arrived at Aubri's body, he could not bring himself to.

Her arm was twisted backward where the shield had been broken and lodged into her arm. Blood was seeping from a multitude of wounds. He put his hand against her neck like Hess had taught him. Her pulse was faint.

He opened his pouch, pulled out a potion, and broke the seal. Carefully, he lifted Aubri's head and started pouring the drink into her mouth. She started to choke and Kaen closed her mouth, covering it with his hand to keep the liquid inside, and pinched her nose. She struggled a moment, and he saw her swallow the liquid. Her mouth opened again, and he poured the rest down her throat.

Aubri's eyelids sprang open, her eyes bulged, and her mouth stretched as wide as possible. He could see the pain in her eyes as she screamed. Bones started to pop and crack. Kaen pulled the broken shield from her arm and watched her skin close, healing from the potion.

Twenty seconds later, Aubri closed her mouth and looked at Kaen. "Luca?" she gasped when she was finally able to speak.

Kaen gently set her head down and ran to where Luca had been hit. He slowed down when he saw Luca's body broken in two, wrapped around the tree's base like a rope.

He's dead. I'm sorry that he died.

Kaen nodded, and a few tears rolled down his cheeks. Luca had never been one he could imagine spending a night with at an inn, laughing and drinking and sharing stories or jokes with. Luca would have been more of an amazing mentor and instructor due to his mind and calm demeanor. Even when faced with this impossible challenge, he had not backed down.

Kaen jumped when he felt a hand on his shoulder. Turning his head, he saw Aubri moving beside him, tears in her eyes.

The air was heavy, and what should have seemed like a moment worth celebrating, surviving a colossal battle, was instead somber and hard, knowing Luca had given everything to buy the time Kaen and Aubri needed.

"He fought this thing on his knees, even when he had no more magic left," Kaen whispered as he turned his eyes back on Luca's broken body. "He couldn't dodge the attack because he was willing to risk everything for us."

The sound of sobs filled his left ear. Turning, Kaen saw Aubri openly weeping. Her armor was caked with her own blood and covered in dirt and grime from the beating she had received. Her face was a mess from dried blood and fresh tears.

Kaen took her in his arms and held her close, letting her cry on his shoulder for a while. Aubri clung to him, her chest heaving, and she required the strength Kaen offered via his body and arms to remain standing. When no more tears were left to cry, Aubri gave Kaen a hug.

He watched a grown woman wiping her cheeks with her hands, leaving a blood streak across her tear washed face.

"Thank you," Aubri whispered. "I have not cried like that in years."

Kaen nodded and motioned to a spot on the ground where a decent-sized rock was. "Grab a seat and relax for a moment. I'll claim the heads, and then we can care for Luca and his possessions. He deserves a burial worthy of the feat he accomplished."

As Aubri moved toward the rock, Kaen glanced around the clearing and at the carnage around him. Death was everywhere, and he now realized what Hess had meant when he had warned that adventuring was not pretty or glamorous like the bards sing about.

With that last thought, he retrieved one of the swords from the orcs. Their own weapon would serve as justice when he removed their heads.

44

The Trip Home

I cannot imagine what I would do without you. Even now, I know that I would be unable to continue without your strength.

Kaen was handling the cart. Aubri sat silently next to him on the front bench, her head on his shoulder. The three hours since they had traveled with the heads of the orcs and Luca's body had been in almost complete silence.

Aubri had not complained when he offered to take over and let her recover after everything she had suffered. She had not paid attention to any of the dead orcs, which made things easier on Kaen. No one would see the wounds that Pammon had inflicted upon the massive orc. Kaen had cut off its armor and hacked off its shoulders, in case anyone attempted to investigate the scene. No use leaving evidence that might point to Pammon.

How is your injury?

I am fine now. My haunches and claws are still sore, but I have recovered. As you know, I ate a deer, which seemed to help. I might have eaten the orcs, but you are probably correct; someone will come and investigate the scene. I would rather not leave tracks for them.

Did you know you could attack like that? We had never practiced that before.

Pammon chuckled through their connection.

I have killed many deer with an attack like that. Often, I would scoop them up and finish them in the air if they were still alive. I had to learn to control my speed as I snapped a few in half from hitting them too hard, wasting a lot of meat.

I'm just glad you didn't crash when you hit that monster of an orc! I cannot imagine how heavy it was.

A chuckle drifted through the bond. Kaen knew Pammon was overhead now, high above them, watching out for him.

I am glad also. I am sure he will be easy to lift off the ground in time, but that day is a long time away. Possibly years.

The thought of years being required for Pammon to grow that big boggled Kaen's mind. Pammon had already grown larger and faster than he could have imagined. Hess had mentioned the size of a full-grown dragon, and it seemed impossible to believe six months ago that Pammon might ever reach that size. Now, that growth potential seemed only a time problem.

Lost in his thoughts, Kaen found himself drifting toward the edge of the road, and a few bumps from rocks and divots jolted him from his mind and caused Aubri to sit up.

"We are almost to the camp spot. I can cook dinner," she stated.

"I don't mind cooking and setting things up," Kaen replied. "Or, if you prefer, we can just eat some dried jerky and fruit and enjoy a fire."

Aubri nodded and leaned her head back on Kaen's shoulder. "Maybe just a simple meal today would be best. I should be fine in the morning."

Kaen nodded and patted Aubri's knee while making sure to stay on the road.

They slept in the cart that night, and she asked if she could sleep next to him. She nestled up against Kaen's side and put her head on his chest. She was asleep in less than a minute, and all Kaen could think about was how hot it was with her next to him like that!

Aubri appeared to be her usual cheerful self when they woke up the next morning.

She was wearing the leather armor she had stored in a backpack with just a sword on her hip.

"Let's just eat the dried food again and get on the road, if that is ok with you."

Already prepared for that potential, Kaen pulled out the jerky and fruit pack Hess had somehow known he would need. "I will have to thank Hess for this. He is the one who told me I would need it."

Aubri laughed, took the pouch Kaen offered, and pulled out a strip of meat. "Hess is a great mentor. He knows that many times you may not have the time or feel the need to stop for hours and cook."

Hearing Aubri laugh made Kaen relax. He had no idea how one handled losing a friend like this. It was hard enough on him when Cale was injured in Minoosh during the orc and goblin attack. Knowing his friend was alive was a blessing, but he also felt the pain of his friend forever being crippled.

I need to fly to the east and let you be. I do not want to risk flying over the pass in the mountains. I am not certain if there is anyone watching the sky from there.

Thank you for watching over us, Pammon. I will let you know as soon as I find out how things go.

Kaen smiled at Aubri, who was still talking. For the last hour, she had been talking non-stop after she had made him tell her his whole life. She had gone crazy for a while when she learned he was Hoste's son. The thought that Hoste's son had saved her seemed more special than when he had just been 'Kaen.' Now she felt the need to share about her life as they were only an hour or so from the pass.

"So, for my forty-seventh birthday, my youngest sister bought me the sword I carry. I have enjoyed using it for the last five years."

Kaen snapped out of the fog he had been in and jerked to the side. "You're fifty-two years old?!" he exclaimed. "You don't look like you are out of your twenties!"

Aubri grimaced but still blushed when she realized she had shared something she had not intended to share. "Ahh . . . can we forget I just mentioned how old I am? I did not realize I was rambling on like that!"

Kaen laughed, shook his head, and opened his mouth to speak.

"I swear if you say I'm old enough to be your mother, I will beat you within an inch of your life," Aubri threatened her eyebrows furling as she scowled.

Kaen laughed and shook his head. "I was just going to say how this all makes sense now! Hess does not look as old as I think he is, and most adventurers seem younger than I would expect a silver or gold token adventurer to be! How much does the lifestone affect aging?"

Aubri laughed and shook her head, her scowl fading. "Once you hit about twenty-five, it slows down how fast you age. Most adventurers can live sixty-plus years without looking past thirty-five, if they have not suffered too many injuries in battle. I am afraid even with the potion you gave me, I will age a bit in the next year after the injuries I received yesterday."

The moment Aubri spoke about the fight with the orc, her attitude shifted for a few seconds, and she glanced back into the cart where Luca's body was wrapped in a special cloth that greatly slowed the aging of a corpse. They had set it outside the cart last night when they slept; its presence had been too much for her.

"Well, I doubt you will lose any of the beauty you obviously possess," Kaen teased as he attempted to bring her back from the depression she was shifting toward. "In fact, if I happened to see you in a bar and didn't know you, I would absolutely walk over and use my best lines on you."

Aubri saw the smile on Kaen's face and frowned. "Do you flirt with every pretty face you see?"

Holding up his hand and shaking his head, Kaen winced. "Sorry, I was just trying to lighten the mood."

Aubri shook her head and rolled her eyes. "For now, we need to focus on the report we will have to give once we are back. Most of it will fall to you. Make sure you tell the truth, because if they doubt anything, they might use other methods to test what you reported."

He had heard of those methods from Hess. If deemed worth it, there were crystals they could use to force the truth from individuals, though it was frowned upon unless there was a valid reason.

Kaen nodded and pretended to listen to Aubri as he thought about what he would say. Luca would get all the credit for the giant orc. He still did not know what it was classified as, and even Aubri seemed hesitant now to say what it would be finally labeled as. He would say he got lucky with a shot after Luca gave his life, burning it with lightning and finishing it with his final arrow. The more honor he gave Luca, the less they would push.

The guards had seen them as they approached the pass, and once word was conveyed about the success of the mission and the loss of Luca, riders were dispatched on some of the fastest horses Kaen had ever seen. The sentries had cheered for a moment and then gone silent in honor when they learned the fate of Luca. Everyone seemed to appreciate that Kaen was somber and did not mind when they acted as such.

As Aubri led the cart through the gates, adventurers and others from the town had already lined up along part of the road and were cheering for Kaen. It appeared that Fiola had not released the full truth of what had transpired on the quest.

It felt like a hero's welcome, and Aubri smiled and waved as the people cheered for them. "Keep smiling and waving," Aubri whispered as they reached the halfway point of the merchant's alley. "These people do not yet need to know the cost of this success. In time, they will find out, and they will pay honor to Luca."

Nodding, Kaen kept waving and smiling. His heart was torn. One side of him wanted to rejoice in what he had achieved with Pammon. The other side of him was still struggling with the truth of how brutal an adventurer's life would be.

Up ahead, Kaen could see the crowd of people standing in a line that ran from both sides of the street up to the fountain and in front of the guild hall. "How many are here?"

Glancing at those behind her and those up ahead, Aubri shook her head and silently counted.

"Total, I would say, at least four hundred since we entered the gate. Probably almost one hundred adventurers are gathered here today to celebrate you and what you have done."

Aubri smiled at Kaen and gave a playful wink. She then cupped Kaen's cheek in her hand and stroked her thumb against it. She slowly moved her hand to the back of his neck and pulled his head toward her.

Closing his eyes, Kaen quickly licked his lips and puckered them up.

When her lips brushed his forehead, his eyes popped open, and he saw Aubri chuckling.

"Oh, Kaen, Kaen, Kaen. You are going to make some girl a lucky woman. Thank you for saving me, but you are thirty years too young for me. I will never forget what you did for Luca and me."

She let go of his neck, and Kaen sat back and tried to hide his embarrassment with a laugh.

"Can't blame a guy for trying, can you?"

Aubri shook her head and laughed. "No. No, I can't."

45

The Rank Earned

"Welcome home, adventurer!"

Fiola shouted those words, and it somehow seemed louder and carried across the yard and the area of the fountain. The people who had gathered had closed the wall around him and the wagon, leaving only a small opening to the guild hall doors where Fiola stood on the steps.

Hess stood a few steps below her, smiling and nodding at him.

"We have heard the report that you managed to slay the five orcs all on your own!" Fiola projected loudly to the crowds. "You slew three tier-one orcs and two who are classified as tier-two orcs!"

When Fiola paused her proclamation, a few people murmured at her statement before the crowd erupted into cheers and applause. Five tier-one orcs would be a difficult feat for a standard iron team, but for an unranked testee to do this was an unbelievable event.

After a few moments, Fiola held up her hands, and the crowd quieted to hear what else she might say. "It appears that our scouting report for this quest failed to gather enough information, and there was also a tier-three orc at the camp!"

People glanced around at Fiola and at Kaen, who stood at the base of the steps, looking at her, unmoving or flinching at the words she spoke. Hess raised his eyebrows even though the rest of him did not move. It appeared no one else but Fiola knew the truth about the sixth orc.

"Kaen completed his quest as the sixth one arrived. He sought out his observers, who assessed that he had accomplished the quest. Even though the beast they faced was far beyond the one a group such as theirs should ever attempt, they each knew the risks of letting a beast like that roam free." Fiola paused again, taking a few breaths and watching the crowds. People waited to hear what she would say next.

When Fiola nodded, a man moved to the back of the wagon and pulled out the large barrel that contained the six heads. He carried it to the steps and placed it next to Fiola's feet before retreating.

Fiola twirled her fingers, and a dagger appeared in them. She smiled, placed the dagger in the top of the barrel, and popped the lid off. "This is the result of what they faced!"

After speaking those words, Fiola picked up the barrel and dumped the contents. Six orc heads rolled down the steps and came to rest at Kaen's feet. When the crowd saw the orc head twice the size of the three smaller ones with a broken arrow sticking out from its eye and temple, their cheers shook the courtyard.

Hess clapped his hands in amazement as he stared at the head and then at Kaen, who nodded and gave a small smile.

Aubri suddenly appeared next to him, lifted Kaen's hand, and shook it in victory. She turned him around and made sure he smiled and cheered for each person who was there to celebrate this victory.

For almost a full minute, whistles, feet stomping, hands clapping, shouts and yelling went on without end. The moment Fiola held up her hands, the crowd went deathly silent, the eerie silence resting upon the group standing there in awe.

"Testee Kaen Marshell, is there anything you wish to say to those who have come to celebrate your great feat today before I pronounce the rank that shall be bestowed upon you?"

Kaen glanced at Aubri, who was by his side. She shook her head slightly, but he could still see the pain in her eyes.

Kaen moved between the orc heads until he reached the largest one, grabbed its matted top knot, and carried it up a few steps with him. When he was just two steps below Fiola, he bowed and turned to face the crowd.

His heart was beating fast, and even more, was the lifestone that knew what he must do, what he had to do if he would accept whatever token was given to him.

From the time Kaen started telling the story of what happened when they engaged the orc whose head he held, to when he finished it, the crowd did not make a sound.

"This trophy," Kaen shouted as he held the orc's head high for all to see, "shall serve as a reminder of the commitment to that which we swear as adventurers. Luca gave everything he had, even to the point of being unable to stand or move, so that Aubri and I could live. He knew the cost and gladly paid it so that we who call ourselves adventurers might fight another day to protect the kingdom and its people we swear to protect! So join me in honoring Luca and his sacrifice! Shout with me his name so that his spirit can hear we honor him!"

Everything changed in the next breath.

His lifestone surged as the crowd took a breath as one.

[Story Telling Skill Increased x3]

"Luca! Luca! Luca!"

The noise as the crowd chanted Luca's name repeatedly, washed over Kaen and reverberated off the stone walls and street. Kaen moved the orc's head with the rise and fall of each syllable. Kaen saw Aubri below him, tears flowing from her eyes as she shouted Luca's name with the crowd. Time seemed to stretch on, and finally, the shouting died down as Fiola moved down two steps, put one hand on Kaen's shoulder, and held the other up for the crowd's attention.

A few more calls of "Luca" sounded before the area went quiet again.

"This young man has demonstrated not only his courage, skill, ability, and commitment to this hall, but he has also done something even greater than all of that." Fiola wore on her face the first smile Kaen believed was heartfelt. "Kaen reminded us that we must never forget those we lose and why we attempt these tasks. Kaen understands the life of an adventurer. He understands the call."

Fiola motioned to Herb, who had been standing off in the crowd to her left. Herb descended the steps and held up a small, plain-looking wooden box toward Fiola. She opened it up and smiled.

"Today, we honor this young man by granting him a silver token! Three cheers for Kaen!"

Pandemonium broke out through the crowd as people started cheering. None could remember the last time an adventurer had ever started at that rank. None could doubt that Kaen was not deserving of such a rank after the feats he had accomplished.

As Fiola turned Kaen around, slipped the token on its chain over his neck, and connected it in the back, she leaned forward and whispered in his ear. "Congratulations, Kaen. I cannot wait to speak in private."

Kaen smiled and nodded as he waved to the crowd.

Somehow, the chain around his neck with his token suddenly felt more like a noose placed there by a hangman.

Kaen sipped his tea and watched Fiola sitting on the other couch in her office, smiling at him like he was a piece of meat to purchase in a market.

"You know it might just be easier to get this over with," Fiola declared as she leaned back against her couch. "You got what you wanted, and now I believe we have a deal to complete."

Kaen nodded and sat his cup on its little plate. He glanced at Fiola and wondered if she wore the black pantsuit outfit on purpose. The color seemed disheartening to him, as if an executioner had led him here.

"I won't ask why you want it, but I am curious about why me," Kaen said, slowly fondling his silver token. "I know you have a reason, and I have realized it somehow has to do with my dad. I don't know the exact reasons, but I believe in time, I may understand. Do you wish to share anything with me before I do?"

Fiola smirked and shook her head. "I have risked much for what I feel is a fair price in return for what I gave you. Rumor has already spread that the king may invite you to his palace soon to see this rising star in the guild. My fellow guild masters and the council cannot deny you earned what you wear around your neck. Who knew this quest would take the turn it did."

Kaen felt his lifestone surge with Fiola's last sentence. His mind and his stone called out to him, and he stared at her, his face blank. Had she known there were more than just a few standard orcs? Was there any chance at all she knew of the tier-three orc?

Kaen suppressed the fire he felt building up in his chest and resisted the urge to press further. Something about this seemed wrong now. It left a bad taste in his mouth, but until he could speak privately with Hess, there was nothing he could say or do about it.

"Very well, I will honor my part of the bargain."

Simple Status Check
Kaen Marshell - Adolescent
Age - 17
HP - 242/242
MP - 0/0
STR - 19
CON - 19
DEX - 21
INT - 15
WIS - 13

Fiola's eyes betrayed her as they dilated with excitement. The rest of her body was rigid like a statue. Her breathing never changed as Kaen informed her of each stat. Many great gamblers had mastered the art of giving no physical tell, but *the eyes are a pathway to the soul*, Hess had said to him many times.

"That is impressive," Fiola declared, finally venturing to speak. "I cannot imagine all of the things Hess must have made you do to achieve stats as high as that."

Kaen nodded and shrugged.

"I broke a lot of rocks, ran a lot of miles, and dodged an assortment of projectiles for many years. Sleep was a privilege I earned. Food was also a part of my training," Kaen lied. "I think any young man or woman who gets a chance to live how I did and be trained by a man like Hess could have stats similar to mine."

Fiola narrowed her eyes as she tried to read Kaen. She could tell he was telling the truth but felt he was leaving something out. "And you swear those are your stats, and you are not lying about them?"

Kaen stood and put his hand over his lifestone. "I swear the numbers I just shared are my actual ones."

Fiola smiled and stood. She smoothed out her black pants and then extended her hand over the table that separated them. "It has been a pleasure getting to know you, Kaen Marshell."

Kaen nodded and shook Fiola's hand then gave a slight bow.

"I cannot wait till next time," Fiola stated with a wink. "Be safe out there and do your best as you protect our kingdom."

Kaen nodded and exited the room. As the massive double doors shut behind him, he swore he heard a cackle from Fiola just before the doors sealed the room and the runes that blocked sound engaged.

Staring at him from across the room was Hess.

Kaen smiled and walked toward him. He had so much to say.

46

A Promise Kept

Hess embraced Kaen, lifting him off the ground, almost cracking a rib when he shook him like a rag doll.

"I'm so proud of you!" Hess exclaimed, jostling Kaen around.

"Great, but can you let me breathe . . . " Kaen said, gasping as his face turning red.

Laughing, Hess quickly dropped him and slapped Kaen on his back. Kaen coughed a few times to get air back.

"I cannot wait to hear how things went, but first, you must deal with the people downstairs and outside!"

Kaen took a deep breath and nodded at Hess as he let it out. He could see the gleam in Hess's eyes, and the smile Hess wore was one of the biggest Kaen had ever witnessed from him. There was no doubt Hess was proud of him.

"How bad is it downstairs?"

Chuckling, Hess winked as he gave a shrug. "There are probably still over a hundred adventurers wanting to congratulate you and shake your hand. I don't think any could deny you earned your rank after hearing what you pulled off or after that speech you gave honoring Luca," Hess declared, his eyes almost turning misty as he remembered the words Kaen had spoken. "Between those two things, I doubt you will have trouble finding a place to call home or a girlfriend or two for a while."

Kaen laughed and motioned down the hallway to the stairs. "I guess I shouldn't keep my audience waiting," Kaen joked and walked down the hall.

He could hear people talking and a consistent hum of noise coming from the end of the hallway.

Hess ran ahead and held his hand up to slow Kaen's advance. "Give me one moment," Hess whispered, pointing to the end of the hall before the stairs. "Let me tell them you are coming!"

Kaen smiled as Hess ran ahead.

When Hess got to the stairs, the noise below stopped. Kaen moved to the edge of the hall, just out of sight of anyone below who might be looking up for him.

"Friends and fellow adventurers!" Hess boomed out from the top of the stairs. "Allow me to introduce the boy whose diaper I changed and whose arse I wiped! Kaen, our newest silver token adventurer!"

Laughter and cheers broke out as Kaen waited against the wall.

"You never wiped my arse!" Kaen exclaimed when Hess reached over and yanked him from his hiding spot.

The crowd erupted in cheers and shouting that echoed off the walls and almost caused the building to shake.

Kaen glanced down the stairs in awe. The room was packed, filled with adventurers from wood all the way up to a female platinum adventurer he saw standing closest to the stairs. Men and women of all races and classes cheered for him. For him! It felt like a dream he would never want to wake up from. Time seemed lost as he stood there, taking in the moment.

"You need to say something or move downstairs," Hess whispered in his ear.

Kaen smiled and nodded as he lifted his hands, silencing the crowd. "I am honored that all of you would do this for me," Kaen declared as he gazed upon the smiles on everyone's faces. "I am thankful that Hess did not injure me all those times he nursed me on his tit!"

The crowd erupted in laughter.

"I know, I know," Kaen joked over the noise. "Had he breastfed me, I would no doubt be bigger, but alas, he did not!"

People continued to laugh, and when Kaen turned and glanced back at Hess, he saw that Hess had joined in on the laughing.

"Now, let me say just a few more things before I return to the Fluffy Ingot and purchase a few thousand drinks!"

The laughter died down, and everyone leaned forward, anticipating Kaen's words.

"I am grateful to the guild for letting me undertake such a quest and to Aubri and Luca for escorting me. What happened to Luca pains me, but it also reminded me of the cost each of us is willing to pay. It is a price I know too well."

Kaen grabbed the chain his token was attached to, lifting it off the leather outfit he had not had a chance to remove yet. He held it up for everyone to see. "My father wore a token once. His was different than mine. He gave his life on a quest, and Hess . . . " Kaen turned and grabbed Hess's arm, pulling him forward.

"What are you doing?" Hess gasped as Kaen pulled him to the front of the stairs.

"Doing what I promised to do," Kaen whispered with a wink. "This man, Hess Brumlin, took on the greatest quest for my dad. He forsook love and his own greatness and raised me when my father, Hoste Marshell, died over seven years ago."

A gasp and murmurs came from those gathered below who knew of Hoste and his accomplishments.

"Tonight, I release Hess from the duty he bound himself to when he took on the quest of raising me," Kaen smiled as he spoke those words. "Tonight, he is more than just a mentor, a father figure, and a friend. Tonight, I honor Hess for completing a quest harder than most of us will ever attempt! I would be nothing, unable to have accomplished what I did if it was not for him. So help me in congratulating Hess on the completion of his quest!"

Kaen gently pushed Hess down the top step, his hand on the center of Hess's back.

Hess tried to protest a little, but Kaen had him moving down the stairs before he knew it.

The adventurers started to clap quietly and then cheered loudly when they absorbed what Kaen had just said. They realized the sacrifice and dedication it must have taken Hess to raise a boy for seven years, and for Kaen to succeed as he had was a testament to Hess's skill as an adventurer.

Herb stood at the bottom of the stairs, clapping louder than the others, smiling as Hess reached the bottom. He gripped one of Hess's hands in both of his and pumped his arms quickly.

"Amazing work, Adventurer Hess!" Herb exclaimed. "Perhaps this will be enough points to move you to the next token!"

Hess stood in shock as people came up and clapped him on the back, cheering for him. He smiled and nodded, shaking hands and waving at people who shouted their praise.

As people congratulated Hess, the platinum token adventurer who had been standing at the base of the stairs made her way up to where Kaen was.

Kaen saw her coming and smiled. Her hair and the robes she wore were the same onyx color. It made her token stand out against the dark material. She smiled and looked at Kaen intently with her green eyes.

"You do your father proud," the woman said with a slight bow. "I only met him a few times when I was a silver token, but you look just like him."

Kaen returned her bow and smiled. "I'm not sure if that is a compliment," Kaen joked. "Sorry, I am not sure who you are, even if you are a platinum token. I am new to all this."

"I'm sorry, I am Selmah and obviously bad with manners," Selmah said with a small laugh. "I just wanted to say I look forward to one day questing with you. It is obvious from how you handle yourself and how you know just what to say, that you are bound for great things."

Kaen chuckled and pointed at Hess, who was near him. "I actually had promised him I would release him of his quest once I passed. I figured it was the least I could do at this moment. Nowhere else would people really appreciate what he gave up for me and my dad."

Selmah smiled and nodded. She had been impressed with Kaen's words and actions earlier in the day. He had now taken all the focus off himself and put it onto Hess. She was unsure if Kaen realized how much easier it would make things on himself while allowing Hess, someone used to the spotlight, to deal with all the commotion.

"As you might have noticed," Selmah declared as she swept her hand at the room, "they appreciate it immensely."

Kaen laughed. Hess was facing him, beaming ear to ear.

"Come on, Kaen!" Hess shouted above the noise. "We need to work our way through this crowd and get to Sulenda before I get in trouble for being late with you!"

Selmah waved at Kaen as he moved down to join Hess, working their way through the crowd of adventurers toward the door.

Walking to the Fluffy Ingot felt like leading a parade for Kaen and Hess. Hess had declared free drinks to all if they could escape the guild hall and arrive at the Inn sometime before tomorrow. The crowd parted, and everyone streamed out behind the two of them.

Adventurers took turns coming up alongside them, asking questions, and giving their well wishes for what they had accomplished. Kaen and Hess would be able to start actively looking at new quests, and Kaen had already received multiple invitations to join different parties that would *love* to have someone of his caliber on their squad.

Hess had prepared Kaen for these requests days ago. Kaen responded to each of them, informing them he would need time to figure things out, quest with Hess, and learn a few more skills before he chose his own path. Most nodded in understanding, even if they knew he would be an almost impossible party member to get.

Local townspeople shouted and waved as the throng entered the outer city and along the streets. They narrowed into a column of adventurers that looked more like they were about to go off to war instead of a group intent on drinking copious amounts of alcohol till many of them would pass out.

Children and adults alike pointed and waved as word spread through the city that Kaen, the newest silver token adventurer who had slain six orcs *by himself*, was coming.

Even though it was still hours from dinnertime and the sun was not ready to hide behind the mountains, people stopped their work, choosing to come to cheer for Kaen.

"What the heck is all this?" Kaen asked Hess as he shook his head in awe and waved at those who kept calling out his name.

"Sulenda sent me a note earlier," Hess tried to whisper as he leaned in toward Kaen. "Basically, the majority of the city bet on your quest."

Kaen snapped his head toward Hess, and a look of shock came over his face. He gasped.

"The entire city?"

Hess nodded and chuckled. "Son, you will need a cart when Sulenda gives you your cut," Hess joked. "Rumor has it even the king and many nobles put large bets on you yesterday. I don't know the exact number, but I know most of them guessed wrong."

Hess put an arm around Kaen and kept him moving forward even as Kaen slowed down, leading to a traffic jam behind them.

"You and I are going to have to discuss some very important things regarding money and how to protect it and spend it," Hess informed Kaen as they picked up their pace. "We will deal with specifics later, but for now, just know that you will not *need* to earn money unless you become an idiot and try to buy an estate."

Shaking his head in disbelief, Kaen continued waving at the people lining the sidewalks for him.

When they were a block from the Fluffy Ingot, Kaen suddenly whirled on Hess and walked backward, beaming at his mentor.

"Lifestones! I need two!" Kaen exclaimed louder than he should have, but the sounds of the cheers drowned him out.

Hess nodded and smiled. "Already taken care of," Hess stated as he spun Kaen around. "They will be there in a few days, escorted by adventurers from the guild."

Kaen started to skip a little bit as he walked next to Hess.

What has you so happy?

It looks like my promises have been kept, and everything is working out better than I could have hoped! Soon, it will be the two of us adventuring together!

I cannot wait! Try not to be stupid and drink tonight. I hate it when you do. Ask Hess to help keep you out of trouble, Pammon warned Kaen.

Laughing, Kaen leaned in toward Hess. "Someone reminded me I must keep from drinking tonight and ask you for help."

Hess roared with laughter, grabbed Kaen in a side headlock, and rubbed his knuckles against Kaen's hair. "I make no promises tonight!"

47

A Party to Remember Part 1

Kaen turned the corner and gasped when he saw the entrance to the Fluffy Ingot. The spectacle he witnessed on the street and sidewalk informed him that tonight would be like nothing he had ever experienced.

Outside the inn and its gold-colored wood doors were street performers acting out *Kaen* slaying multiple orcs with a bow. People were blocking the street, watching the skit unfold.

Kaen laughed when he saw it and pointed it out to Hess, who nodded and smiled. The actors who dressed up as orcs were standing on some device that made them taller and wore costumes that added girth.

When the crowd of adventurers started streaming around the corner toward the inn, the people on the street became ecstatic and began chanting Kaen's name. Young children ran over, laughing and shouting as they approached, trying to touch or shake his hand. Kaen laughed and shook every hand he could, as Hess ushered him toward the inn's entrance.

Women and men shouted congratulations, and many called out how much they looked forward to the drink he owed them.

Kaen smiled and waved, wondering exactly how many drinks he would have to pay for. All those who bet on him and lost did not seem a big deal until Hess informed him that most of the city had placed a wager on him at some point.

It took almost ten minutes for them to make their way through the throng of people.

Kaen stopped and bowed before the actor who was playing him, surprised to learn it was an elf woman. He tossed a silver coin in her tip box, and she bowed. Moments later, as the other adventurers passed, silver coins cascaded into her box from the stream of higher-ranked adventurers. Smiles and cheers broke out from all the actors, who received more coins at that moment than they had in a month.

The two female guards he had seen earlier in the week stood outside the golden doors and opened them inward, bowing slightly as Kaen entered the inn.

Had Hess not pushed Kaen gently on the back, Kaen would have frozen in the inn's doorway.

The entire layout of the inn was changed inside. A massive table ran along the north part of the inn. Huge plates of food, from smoked boar to chicken, beef, and other meats, were piled high, ready to be dug into. Delicate cuts of venison and quail sat nearby, able to be easily picked up and eaten in one bite. Pieces of fruit had been cut and molded into different animal shapes, frozen desserts that seemed to beckon you to ignore the heavy meats and enjoy the cold, sweet taste they offered.

"Keep moving," Hess whispered as Kaen tried to take it all in.

Ten massive barrels of ale were scattered around the room, each with a person standing with empty mugs nearby, all offered freely to anyone who came up to them. Kaen had known they would have some slightly watered-down ale offered for free, but seeing this much had him wondering how many people Sulenda expected to come through tonight. The adventurers who were following him would easily take up most of the space.

A small band of lutes, drums, and other instruments played a fast-paced song. A few people were already dancing in an area near the bar, laughing and twirling to the music.

"Over here!" Sulenda shouted.

Kaen's eyes followed the sound of her voice, and both he and Hess suddenly stopped moving.

Standing near a long table on a platform near the bar was Sulenda, wearing a dress that fit her like a glove. The curves she often hid behind her pants and blouse were no longer a secret. She made the women who worked for her look like undeveloped teenage girls in comparison.

Kaen glanced at Hess and saw the way his eyes took her in. Hess's mouth was slightly open as he stood in awe of the beauty of the woman he had once loved and pledged his heart to. Seeing her there with her hair done up, makeup applied perfectly, and a smile that seemed intent on competing with the sun's glow, Hess was the one who needed a hand to get moving again.

"Go tell her she looks amazing," Kaen whispered as he pushed Hess toward Sulenda. They dodged the tables and patrons already seated and enjoying the celebration that had yet to truly begin.

Hess strode up to Sulenda and bowed. "You look . . . stunning," Hess finally declared, and Sulenda's face turned a slight shade of red.

"Thank you," Sulenda replied, her smile widening. She motioned to a large chair in the middle of the table on the platform. "Kaen, if you would do us the honor of taking your seat, I can kick off this evening properly!"

Glancing around him, Kaen saw the room quickly filling up with the same men and women who had been in the guild house, all of them watching him and waiting.

He nodded, jumped onto the platform, moved around the small wooden square table, and sat in the large, almost throne-like chair Sulenda had procured for him.

Once he was seated, the people who had made it into the inn started clapping and cheering. With a helping hand from Hess, Sulenda moved onto the stage next to Kaen and smiled, looking over the crowd of people gathered in her place.

She motioned for them to move forward, and as they did, the flow from outside continued to stream in. It took a few more minutes before one of the guards outside came in and waved a hand, motioning that they had stopped the line of people entering the inn.

Eltina had been watching from the top of the bar, and when she saw Sulenda nod at her, she grabbed the rope on the bell and gave it three solid rings. As the bell's tone pealed across the inn, every eye focused on Sulenda and Kaen.

"I'd like to welcome all of you to the third annual shite show!" Sulenda joked loudly.

The room broke out into applause and laughter, most having understood the depth of the joke she had just made.

"I tease, but welcome to our celebration of Kaen Marshell and his earning of an adventurer token!" she shouted over the noise.

Cheers and applause thundered inside the room. Everyone was excited to celebrate such an impossible feat.

"I know what has happened this week has been the talk of the town! A young man, the son of Hoste Marshell, trained by Hess Brumlin, single-handedly defeated five orcs with nothing but a bow and his mind!"

As the people cheered and whistled, Kaen felt a twinge of guilt in his heart. Pammon deserved credit for his accomplishments, but it would be a while before he could share the honor Pammon deserved with others.

Sulenda waited for the noise to quiet some before continuing. "Now I know many of you are unhappy with Kaen and his feat! The only thing that has kept him in your good graces was his promise to purchase everyone a drink that bet on and lost!"

Laughter echoed through the room as her joke struck true.

"Tonight, all the casks around the room are free for as long as you can stand! Courtesy of the guest of honor's coin purse!"

Cheers rang out, and a few people started moving toward the casks, eager to partake in the free liquor provided from Kaen's purse.

"Now, as we begin tonight, I want to say one thing before we all pay honor to this young man!"

Sulenda leaned forward toward the crowd. A more serious expression had replaced the smiling one she had been wearing. As she leaned forward, her dress caught the attention of many, her breasts appearing ready to fall from the heavens, barely held back by a small piece of lace.

"Tonight, we celebrate more than just a new adventurer. Tonight, we celebrate more than just a new token. Tonight, we celebrate something our kingdom has not seen in its entire history. No testee has ever started out as a silver in our kingdom before! It has happened less than five times in the history of the entire adventurer's guild. Tonight, we celebrate an adventure that may soon rise above all of us, protecting the innocent and helping this kingdom to grow!"

The room exploded in cheering, whistles, and clapping a few seconds after Sulenda ended her rousing speech. Each adventurer acknowledged the real truth of what they were witnessing.

One who may someday be called a *hero* sat before them.

Hess bent down as the crowd started to disperse to grab drinks and whispered in Kaen's ear. "Remember, drink slowly. Sulenda has some special alcohol for you that is very watered down. Even with it being that way, you are not used to its effects, and I don't want to have to put you to bed long before this celebration has started."

Kaen nodded and laughed as he listened to Hess and watched people wave and congratulate him. "How long do I have to sit up here in this chair?" Kaen asked with a groan. "I'd prefer to be down there with the rest of them, eating and dancing and celebrating with them."

Hess grabbed the chair Kaen was sitting on and pulled it out from under Kaen, laughing when Kaen barely caught himself from falling backward.

"It's your party! Go celebrate it how you want!"

Chuckling, Kaen turned and smiled at Hess. He gave him a quick hug before breaking the embrace.

"Thanks, *Dad*," Kaen declared, emphasizing the last word. "I'll try to behave tonight!"

Hess stood there a little shocked but smiled as Kaen turned and walked to the platform's edge and jumped off, then headed into the crowd of men and women excited to have him in their midst.

As Hess watched Kaen talking and laughing with everyone around him, he felt a twinge in his heart. He knew Hoste would be so proud of his son, and hearing Kaen say that word, *dad*, even in jest, filled a hole he had not admitted was in his heart. He had done everything he could to raise that boy and make sure he could be the man his father would want him to be.

A hand touched the back of his leg, and Hess turned to find Sulenda standing on the ground at the base of the platform, smiling at him.

Hess jumped down and stared at her, shaking his head. "I'm at a loss for words to describe how amazing you look," Hess whispered in her ear over the noise.

His breath felt hot on her neck as he spoke in her ear.

Sulenda had worn this dress when she'd heard the news of Hess's freedom. She had been frantic, trading the outfit she initially had on for this one, upsetting Eltina that Hess could still make her act like this. After all those years, she had finally admitted to herself that she still wanted to be with Hess.

"Is it true what I heard Kaen said at the guild hall? Did he really free you from your quest and bond to him?" Sulenda asked.

Hess nodded and grinned but also appeared conflicted with the admission of that news.

When Hess had heard Kaen speak those words on the steps, freeing him from his oath, all he could think about was Sulenda. He knew he would still have to help Kaen grow, but now he would risk everything and let her know how he felt.

"What are you going to do with your freedom?" Sulenda asked, a slight waiver in her voice.

Hess held out his hand and waited for her to put hers in his. "If you are willing and still want to, I would enjoy nothing more than trying to find out if what we once felt for each other is still here. I managed to raise one kid and have him turn out ok. Perhaps it might not be too late to try again if I could find someone willing to love a fool like me."

A single tear fell from Sulenda's eye, threatening to ruin her makeup.

Hess reached out and cupped her cheek, using his thumb to wipe the tear away and save her from a makeup emergency.

"Perhaps I could find a way to love a fool of a man like you," Sulenda responded as she grasped Hess's neck and pulled him to her, kissing him on the lips. Hess found his arms around Sulenda and on her neck, returning the kiss he had longed for a lifetime ago.

The clanging of the bell on the bar broke their embrace, and they turned to see Eltina standing on the bar, shaking her head at the two of them, rolling her eyes.

Eltina turned to the patrons in the inn and smiled. "Free shots for everyone! Courtesy of adventurer Hess for finding his testicles after all these years!"

Cheers and laughter broke out as the crowd turned and focused on Hess and Sulenda, who were still locked in each other's arms.

They both laughed, and Hess gave a small shrug before pulling Sulenda in close again and giving her a kiss, letting the sounds of cheering and whistling wash over them.

48

A Party to Remember Part 2

"So tell me your plans," Gertrude asked. "Are you really going to try and find a group to quest with or try to keep doing quests alone?"

Kaen glanced around at the pack of adventurers who had been firing off questions at him for the last twenty minutes. Gertrude was a silver token warrior, and she was more forward than the others around him. Perhaps it was the dwarf side of her that made her this way, but regardless he appreciated her direct approach.

Glancing at her as she twirled her finger through her well-oiled and braided brown beard, Kaen smiled and winked. "My first plan is to complete a few more quests with Hess and learn some of the basics I know I lack. While everyone seems to think I know a lot about fighting, the truth is I realize I need to learn how to quest with others." Kaen glanced at the others and saw them smiling and listening. "After that, I would love to join a party that would help me learn the ropes."

Kaen leaned closer to Gertrude and whispered loudly enough for those around to hear. "The truth is, I need to learn a lot of things. Growing up in a small town has not given me much experience."

Gertrude suddenly yanked hard on a braid, and her cheeks went flush. She moved her head back in shock as she let what he'd said sink in. She stared at Kaen with a hard look, uncertain what he was trying to say.

The other adventurers were snickering and laughing, and she glanced at them before shaking her head and smiling.

"I've heard rumors about your tongue, boy," Gertrude stated as she went back to stroking her beard. "I'll have you know, dwarven women do not enjoy being led on or teased."

Kaen's face turned red, and Gertrude grinned with satisfaction, knowing she had gotten the upper hand.

Gertrude laughed and slapped Kaen on the arm, impressed to find that he did not flinch or move, considering the effort she had put into the slap. She knew he could be a fun friend indeed.

"Stop hogging the boy," a voice called out from behind Gertrude.

Turning around, Gertrude saw Amra slinking over to stand next to Kaen. "He already promised me just the other day that we would make a bet that would benefit both of us. I am still waiting to collect on that."

Kaen suddenly felt like a deer, or some other animal trapped between two predators, both fighting over who would get to devour it.

"Uhm . . . ladies," Kaen said with a slight squeak in his voice as he cleared his throat. "I need to let you two sort this out and see what that group over there might need."

Freeing himself from Amra, Kaen quickly moved to find another group of adventurers who were waiting nearby to talk and engage with him.

A few hours later into the night, the music became the main attraction.

Lines were formed on both sides, and the band started to play a fast-paced song. The men and women lined up on different sides, finding a partner and moving to the music. The song, often called the Parade of Mates, was played in most towns and inns. People who were married were not allowed to dance to it. Every thirty seconds, the partners would shift down the line and dance with a new friend, doing their best to impress them with their grace and quick feet.

The steps were not overly difficult, but some had improved on them, adding kicks, twists, and even flips for those well-versed in the arts of dancing or blessed with exceptional dexterity.

Kaen had not enjoyed a lot of practice when it came to dancing, as in Minoosh, festivals only happened once a year, and he had yet to reach the age where he was permitted to dance to this song on the main dance floor. Any practice he had gotten was off to the side with his friends and the girls in town, preparing for when they could officially participate.

With his dexterity being what it was, he found the moves far easier than they had been a year ago. His feet moved exceptionally fast, and the rhythm felt much easier to follow. As the song continued, with each partner he danced with, he experimented more, watching the moves of those who were showing off and mimicking most of them with success.

Applause and cheers came from the crowd around them as the onlookers encouraged them to attempt higher degrees of difficulty as they danced.

Three minutes into the song, everything changed when he found himself dancing with a partner who took his breath away from the moment she stood across from him; an iron token adventurer with a smile that made his heart skip a beat and green eyes which reminded him of a day in the forest, left him breathless. They danced and twirled, kicking and spinning as if somehow connected in perfect unison, and when the moment came to switch, neither Kaen nor his dancing partner broke away as they were supposed to.

They ignored the call to change, instead drawing closer to each other.

Kaen was smiling and laughing over the music. When he saw his dance partner smiling back at him, his heart began to pound in a familiar way, and Kaen realized what was about to happen. His lifestone joined in with a surge of power. Letting his lifestone take over, Kaen reached out and grasped her hand and side, starting a harder move usually only done by men who had spent years practicing it.

With the speed he felt flowing through his body and the realization that his lifestone was now directing his steps, Kaen took over the movements of his new friend. He twirled on his feet as he drew her close, creating the point they would both pivot on. She let herself go, and he felt her body become light as her eyes widened and her smile grew.

Faster and faster, they spun. The room and the people around them were a blur. The music had picked up its tempo, and Kaen felt like he was watching his body as a spectator, unsure how he moved so quickly or so easily placed the next step.

Bounding and leaping, he glided through openings of other pairs on the dance floor, twirling this mystery woman like a top, watching her flow like an extension of his own body.

A part of the song he had only heard a few times in his whole life began, and Kaen knew somehow what was supposed to come next. His lifestone roared inside of him, and the fear he had felt for the briefest of moments faded as he gave himself over to it.

The song's tempo sped up again, and the beats of the music marked the movement for each step he now took. The others on the floor had backed away, though Kaen had not realized it. All he could see was the smile on the girl's face and those eyes that gazed back at him.

A twist here, a leap there, two bodies moving as one. Her legs spun around him, and he leaned back, balancing her length and his mass.

Louder laughter erupted from Kaen's mouth, yet he was unaware of it.

Four more beats. He knew what was coming.

Using their momentum, he pulled her close and flung her out again, twirling her like a top attached to his hand.

Three more beats.

Pulling hard on her hand, he drew her back, spinning her toward him, bending his knees, and preparing for what came next.

Two more beats.

He swept her into his arms and then spun her around his waist, around his back, and to the front of him again in a matter of a heartbeat. He prepared for the last part of this all. He smiled at her as she was bent slightly over his knee. He could see in her eyes that she knew what was coming next and was somehow ready for it.

Kaen launched her into the air as the last beat began to play.

Like an angel, she flew up, spinning around and around, her hair whipping from the force and her dress fanning wide, giving any letch out there a view of things she had most definitely not meant to show tonight.

Kaen felt it all as she tumbled through the air as the song was about to end. His body was alive. His lifestone made him feel like he could do anything.

The moment she came down toward him, Kaen reached up and caught her, absorbing the energy of her fall into his arms and legs, ending the dance with her bent over his knee and his face just six inches from hers.

The final beat struck, and every instrument went silent.

[Dancing Skill Acquired]
[Dancing Skill Increased x13]

For a few moments, the room hung in silence. His lifestone went quiet, and his chest pounded from the exertion. He breathed deeply and could smell the flowery scent coming off his dance partner.

The moment was perfect for Kaen. His heart had connected with someone in a way he had never known was possible during this dance. An urge to keep her close to him and breathe her scent overpowered him.

The room roared to life as people rushed forward to compliment them.

Kaen stood her up, and she swooned momentarily as she caught her breath and smiled at him. "I'm sorry you never gave me your name," Kaen exclaimed as people started getting between the two of them.

"I know!" she shouted back over the throng that was congratulating her as well. "Perhaps later, I might just share it with you."

She winked at Kaen and allowed herself to be taken away by a group of female adventurers wanting to talk to her about what she had just experienced.

Kaen groaned and smiled as he saw her wink and wave, moving to the other side of the dance floor, leaving him caught by the throng of people.

"Did you teach him that?" Sulenda asked.

Hess shook his head. He and Sulenda had watched the whole thing as they stood close to the band. He had an idea how Kaen had pulled it off, but the very thought of it almost scared him. If Kaen could do that without any training, what else could that boy learn to do?

"He was always light on his feet, but maybe he had someone teaching him things I was unaware of back home."

Sulenda huffed and drew close to Hess, finding comfort in his arm around her. "Should I ask him to dance with me like that?"

Hess turned and winked at her and shook his head. "That poor boy wouldn't know how to handle a woman like you," he said with a mischievous grin.

Rolling her eyes, Sulenda bumped him with her hip, causing him to move sideways and bang into a random person.

"Sorry, sir," Hess quickly blurted out when he saw he had caused the man's drink to spill all over him. "Allow me to get another one!"

The bronze adventurer waved him off and smiled. "It's okee, Mr. Heeasss. Itzz prubly mah fuault," he replied with such a slur one might have wondered if he was speaking a foreign language.

Nodding and smiling, Hess turned back to Sulenda, who was laughing and moving toward the bar.

"Blast that woman," Hess cursed under his breath as he took off after her.

49

A Party to Remember Part 3

Grumbling, Kaen fished a gold coin from his pocket. Over the last few hours, he had not seen the woman he had danced with earlier in the evening, and he was trying to find entertainment in other ways. The gold coin was his only one, but Hess had told him he would be rich. He figured it was worth seeing this trick once as everyone who had seen it swore by it.

He was sitting at a table with a pair of bronze adventurers who had gathered a large crowd over the evening. The female, Samantha, appeared to be some warrior or paladin, as her armor had a cross on the chest piece. Wearing chain armor in an inn at night seemed crazy to Kaen, but he knew adventurers were a weird bunch.

The interesting thing about Samantha was that she supposedly had some skill in taming and training animals. Her partner, Jay, was a massively built ranger with a huge sword on his back, wrapped in cloth. When he had leaned across the table to shake Kaen's hand, Kaen noticed the blade was black when the cloth had come unwound for a moment.

Samantha's pet crab was on the table. Apparently, the crab, Baltha, would collect a coin from someone in its pinchers, but only if it was gold. Kaen had tried to lure it across the table with a bronze and silver coin, but it sat there, playing with the single gold coin it already had in its claws. Next to it was a small coin pouch in which it had already deposited a few coins, courtesy of some of the higher token adventurers who could afford the show.

"Just hold it out?" Kaen asked as he rubbed the coin between his fingers under the table.

Samantha nodded and pointed at the crab. "The second he sees it, just keep your fingers on the edge so you don't lose any skin," she stated with a grin.

Shaking his head in disbelief that he was about to spend a gold coin on this, Kaen slowly lifted the coin above the wooden edge of the table.

As if the crab had some uncanny sense, it stopped playing with the coin it held in its claws, and its eyestalks both rotated to look across the table at the golden metal slowly creeping up.

It turned and opened its small pouch, tossed in the current coin it had been playing with, and pulled a monocle from it.

Kaen laughed when the crab affixed it to a small dimple on its shell. He wasn't sure if the dimple had always been there or if it had been earned from wearing the monocle.

The crab skittered quickly across the table to where Kaen sat then stopped and glanced at Kaen.

He would have sworn the crab narrowed its eye stalks at him for a moment before it motioned to the gold coin between his fingers with its claw.

Kaen smiled, nodded, and held the coin out toward the crab.

It gave a slight bow and moved the few inches it needed to pluck it from Kaen's fingers. The moment it snatched the coin from Kaen's fingers, the crab started to do a little side-to-side dance and lifted both claws in the air, showing off its latest trophy.

A few seconds later, it lifted the coin before its monocle and peered at it intensely. It flipped the coin over, checking the other side before nodding satisfactorily. Glancing back up once more at Kaen, it gave a slight bow and skittered across the table to its coin pouch.

Once there, it carefully set the coin down on the table, glancing around to make sure no one would try and take it before it quickly removed its monocle, returning it to the pouch. When the monocle was secured, the crab motioned to Samantha with its claws.

Samantha reached into a pouch and pulled out a lemon then set it down on the table near the crab.

Moving around the lemon, Baltha pushed it toward Kaen with its claws, stopping right before him. The crab then started tapping the lemon with one claw while pointing at Kaen with his other.

Kaen looked at Samantha. "Does he want me to take it?"

"You paid for it. It's yours," Samantha informed him with a smile. "He believes you should get something for your purchase."

Shaking his head and laughing, Kaen picked it up. "Thank you, Baltha."

The crab nodded and raced back across the table, picking the coin back up and playing with it just as it had its last one.

Kaen laughed harder, and Jay and Samantha joined in with him. All those standing by the table who had seen this occur clapped and laughed.

"You trained that thing?" Kaen asked as he stared in disbelief. "A skill that could train an animal to do something like that would be powerful."

"Trained?" Jay scoffed. "No, she didn't train it to do that. We were camped near a small pond, and in the middle of the night, we woke up to the sound of coins clinking together. Turning on a light orb revealed this guy trying to take my money!"

Samantha laughed and nodded. "Thankfully, he wasn't too hard to deal with," Samantha admitted. "I had some leftover pie, and after a few crumbs, he was content to stay with me and count my, I mean, *his* gold coins. Where he got the monocle from, though, I have no idea."

"Sometimes I think Baltha believes he's a damn banker or merchant or something. Imagine that, a merchant crab," Jay said with a wink. "Anytime we try to spend money, he always wants in on the action."

Kaen laughed and shook his head. He hated giving up a gold coin, knowing it was more money than he had ever owned until this week, but that had indeed been worth the lift in his spirit.

The night drew to a close with only a few hours till the sun would start to crest over the mountains, signaling the start of a new day.

Patrons were asleep in booths, and a few had been left alone, sleeping along a wall. Kaen's eyes were heavy, as he had stayed up and thanked everyone who had come and congratulated him on earning his token. Hess had told him he could go to bed hours ago, yet he had stayed up, hoping his dance partner would show herself to him again.

Now, with the light of the new day not far away, he stumbled upstairs to his room and gently opened the door. He had taken his boots off outside the door, trying to be quiet and not wake up Hess.

Lying in his bed, about to pass out from exhaustion, he realized his room was absent of noise.

Groaning, he moved out of bed and felt along the table between the two beds for the light stone. When his fingers found it, he gently touched it, and a low light appeared.

Hess's bed was empty and a smile crossed his face as he shook his head and turned off the light stone. "Good luck," Kaen whispered to an empty room as he lay his head on the pillow and passed out.

I know you are awake, Pammon called out. **I can feel your heart beating differently and sense your thoughts. What has you so distraught?**

With the afternoon light streaming through the window, Kaen sat up in bed. Pammon was right; he had been up for an hour and could not get that woman out of his mind.

Just someone I met last night at the party. I don't know what it was about her, but she . . . she made me smile and feel different from the other girls I have talked to or flirted with.

A groan came through the connection, and Kaen laughed as he sensed where Pammon was flying.

You are too young to worry about that stuff right now. In a hundred years, you will be able to consider a relationship.

Choking on hearing those words, Kaen shook his head.

A hundred years? That's an awful long time to be alone!

You are not alone. You have me!

Pammon was frustrated, and Kaen knew it.

It's not the same for us. For me. I feel complete with you, but last night was weird.

I will feel that pull as you do, but it will not be for a long time. Dragons don't search for a possible mate till they are usually at least a century old. I'm not sure how I know that, but I do.

Mulling over what Pammon was saying, Kaen started pulling out new clothes to wear. He glanced down and realized he still had on his leather jerkin and vambraces. He had never taken them off, as there had been no time.

As he undid the knots of his armor, he was assaulted by his body odor and decided it would be pertinent to wash up before beginning a new day.

I am not sure what the next step will be. Now that I am silver, I must do some quests with and without others. Thankfully, Hess can come with me for a few, and we can find a way to connect.

A grumble and pouting session trickled through from Pammon.

Don't wait too long to get where we can see each other. I have scratches that need you!

Laughing, Kaen nodded and sent a hug through the connection.

He was clean and fresh, having bathed himself and wiped down his armor as best as he could. It was still a little damp but nothing bad compared to some of the wet clothes he had worn before.

When he arrived downstairs, he paused at the last step that led up to the rooms.

The entire area was spotless. The tables and chairs were back in their places, and nothing reflected that there had been a party last night.

Glancing at the bar, he saw Eltina leaning over it, working on some papers. There were a few other servers slowly milling about. He waved at one and motioned for something to eat, and the woman ran off. He couldn't remember her name but knew it began with a G . . .

He walked to the bar, grabbed a stool, and plopped himself in Eltina's face. "How are things this morning?" Kaen asked as he leaned upon the bar with his arms.

Eltina glanced up, shook her head at Kaen, and frowned. "Bar business isn't something I discuss. Talk to Sulenda if you want to talk about that."

Kaen laughed, leaned forward, and grinned at her. "What about the betting business? Can you share details on that?"

Without even looking up from her paperwork, Eltina shook her head and tried to ignore Kaen.

"That doesn't seem fair at all," Kaen complained. "Surely you can tell me something about how it all turned out or how much I might have earned."

Setting her pen down, Eltina took a breath and then let it out slowly before smiling in a way that seemed almost threatening.

"Listen, Kaen, I like you, I really do. I appreciate what you did for Sulenda and the rest of us. She told me a little bit about how all of this was your plan. I also know you freed Hess from his obligation to you, which has the two of them shacking up like rabbits. Now I have to run a bar, manage the betting, deal with all of the other bookies who do not want to turn in their numbers like they are supposed to, and prepare for tonight, which will probably be a packed house again."

Eltina motioned to the back of the bar. Kaen looked behind her and saw that most of the shelves were empty, and only one cask was left.

"I have runners around town, trying to secure more alcohol because it seems your horde of adventurers can drink a lot more liquor than the average person. I still have to find more food for tonight and get our storeroom restocked," she informed him with a sigh. "So while part of me would love to talk with you and listen to how wonderful life is as the new play toy of the city, I must instead turn my attention to these papers and get back to my job of *running the bar!*" Eltina emphasized the last part as she waved her hands around in the air.

"I'll let you be," Kaen stated as he slowly eased off the stool and moved toward a table.

Eltina, still face first in her paperwork, didn't even acknowledge his last statement and mumbled something under her breath.

"Sir Kaen!" a voice exclaimed behind him.

Kaen turned and saw one of the serving woman approaching him with a plate of food. It looked like meat leftover from last night with a few fresh rolls and a glass of milk.

"Thank you . . . "

"It's Ginny," the woman stated with a laugh.

"Sorry, I . . . "

Ginny smiled and placed his food and drink on the table. "Don't be! I wouldn't expect you to remember my name after everything that has happened over the last few days. I do want to compliment you on your dancing last night, though! It has been the talk of all of us women. Very few men have ever moved as gracefully as you did last night."

Smiling, Kaen gave a slight bow from his seat. "I'm just glad I didn't trip over my feet or hers!"

Ginny laughed and shook her head. "You and your dance partner were amazing! Do you know who she is?"

Kaen perked up. "I don't. Do you, by chance, or anyone else?"

Ginny's face scrunched up and she shook her head. "None of us servers had ever seen her before, but I'm sure you could ask at the guild hall, and they would tell you!"

"That is a great idea! Thank you, Ginny!"

She nodded and moved off so he could start eating. Kaen took a bite of meat and washed it with milk, wondering about asking who the woman at the guild hall was.

"I wonder if that's considered stalking," Kaen mumbled to himself between bites.

50

Leveling Up

Enjoying another glass of cold milk, Kaen considered what he should do for the day. It was half over, and while the walk to the guild hall wasn't a long one, he wanted to do something that would take his mind off the mystery girl for a moment.

As he watched the servers prepare for that night, a thought entered his head when his gaze swept the area where the dancing had taken place the previous night.

Skill Check
Tracking 9
Cooking 8
Mining 13
Archery 25
Brawling 7
1-H Sword 4
Sneak 8
Story Telling 12
Charm Resist 8
Haggle 9
Dancing 13

He was excited about his archery skill but realized that the higher it rose, the slower the growth and skill rank would be. Even with his lifestone helping him with shots, it had not increased the way he had originally thought it would. Kaen focused on how he had so easily acquired the last four points in archery. Each time, it had something to do with his lifestone calling out to him.

If he could *make* his lifestone more active, he could find a way to learn many more skills and perhaps master them all.

Contemplating those things made him think about his dad and how *his* lifestone might have worked. Had his dad found a way to make his do this? Was it only something he could do because of Pammon? A groan escaped Kaen's throat when he remembered Hess had mentioned it might be a month before someone would have any helpful news about all this.

Standing up from his chair, Kaen smiled and stretched. "I'll be back!" Kaen announced to the inn, and besides a few of the servers waving at him, it appeared no one else cared.

Laughing to himself, he moved toward the front door. Time to try something out.

"Quit dropping your shoulder, and use your hips when you swing!"

Kaen nodded and attacked the master who was in charge of training at this school. When he had walked in, someone had recognized him and summoned Master Bren. Bren was more than happy to personally train him in skills with one-handed weapons and shields.

The last two hours had been a flurry of different weapons, all with a shield. All were wooden training weapons, but getting hit with one still left a mark, even with the padded helm and other armor he wore.

Not once in the two hours he'd been training, had his lifestone activated. No matter what he tried, he could not get it to react. Focusing on something, trying to be angry, letting himself get hit a few times, or even his usual breathing trick didn't help. He was frustrated even though he had managed to gain five different skills because they were not as high he expected them to be.

"Enough!" Bren shouted as he backed away from Kaen. "Where is your mind at? You seem to be all over the place with your focus."

Kaen nodded and lowered the wooden club and shield he was using. "I'm overthinking this," Kaen admitted. "I guess I had some wild hair that learning and mastering these skills would be easy."

Bren shook his head, chuckling as he watched Kaen slowly smile. "Kaen, how old do you think I am?"

It was Kaen's turn to laugh. "If you were a woman, I would say twenty-nine, but since you aren't, I will say you must be at least fifty."

Bren leaned back and roared in the private room they were sparring in. "You are close. I am sixty-eight. Do you know how long it took me to master each of these weapons I am trying to teach you?"

"A lifetime . . . "

Bren nodded and moved to a bench along the side of the room, setting down the shield and club. "Join me a minute, and let me share a little wisdom from a guy who knows a thing or two."

Kaen went to the bench, set his gear down next to Bren's, and grabbed the water skin he had filled earlier.

"I am an old gold adventurer," Bren informed Kaen. "I don't wear the token anymore because it no longer matters what I once was. What matters now is what I can do for people and how I can help them be smart when they are questing. I have known too many adventurers who have died because they were unprepared or over their heads."

Kaen nodded, well aware of both of those circumstances.

"What are the skill levels for each of the ones you gained today?" Bren asked.

Weapon Skill Check
Archery 25
1H Sword 5
1H Mace 3
1H Axe 3
1H Club 3
1H Shield 6

Kaen shared with Bren the ones he had just learned, choosing not to disclose just how high his archery was.

Bren smiled. "Those are great starting points for one afternoon with an old guy like me," Bren joked. "Don't be ashamed of where they sit right now. I am more impressed that a man with your talent with a bow is smart enough to pursue other weapons. If your bow breaks, then what? If a sword shatters, then what? You are thinking like the silver adventurer you are."

Kaen smiled at that praise. He had done this for all the wrong reasons, but he realized Bren was right. He had a lot of ground to make up that he had missed by not questing for years like most silvers.

"Do you know how many skills most people would earn with me after sparring for an hour or two?"

"The way you ask that, I'm guessing not many."

Brin chuckled. "Hess did a great job training you, Kaen. I knew him, not as a friend, but I know of his skill with hammers and other weapons. He has a sharp mind, also. Keep learning from him as long as you can."

Kaen took a drink from the skin, relishing in the water as it ran down his throat. He offered it to Bren, who took it and drank, as well.

"How many more sessions do you think it would take me to get a ten in each skill?"

Bren handed back the water skin and then stretched out on the bench, putting his hands behind his head as he thought.

"I think your sword will take you another two or three days of four hours a day to hit ten. From practicing with Hess, you're already proficient compared to the rest of your skills. The shield will likely be the first to hit ten because you use it with every weapon here. The rest will probably take five or more days to reach ten."

Doing the math in his head, Kaen realized it would take two or more months to get all of them to ten, if he could spend two days a week practicing with them here.

Chuckling, Bren looked at Kaen and saw him doing the math. "You focused on the wrong thing, though. Ask yourself, is it better to train all of them to ten or focus on one and try to get that to twenty?"

Eyes going wide, Kaen realized Bren was right. "A level-ten skill isn't going to do much against silver-ranked quests, is it?" Kaen asked, realizing what Bren was getting at.

"Exactly," Bren declared, leaping off the bench as a twenty-year-old might. He started doing a mock air battle. "When you face a silver-ranked monster, you need to be at least above a twenty. Their defense skill and armor will require much more if you want to land a shot on them."

Turning to Kaen, Bren pretended to shoot a bow. "When you fought those orcs, were they easier to kill than a goblin?"

"Goblins were far easier," Kaen answered with a laugh.

"And the tier-three one you faced, how did it fare against your arrows?"

Kaen recalled what had happened. "The same arrow that seemed to puncture or pierce the tier ones and twos easily, barely did anything. All the shots I fired only went about four inches into the tier-three orc."

Returning to a relaxed standing position, Bren crossed his arms and nodded. "Exactly. That orc was a class three silver monster. I know that one of your observers died, but Kaen, listen to me when I say that the fact the three of you managed to kill it is a testament to Luca, Aubri, and you. We both know what would have happened had it just been one of you."

Kaen's throat felt dry as he recalled how Pammon had repeatedly asked him to run away and leave the others. Even Pammon could tell how outclassed they had been against that creature.

"It was all Luca," Kaen whispered.

Bren shrugged and shook his head. "You all played a role. You all gave him the room to do what he did. He chose to fight to the end," Bren stated as his voice intensified. "He knew he had to run or fight, and he chose to fight, knowing he would die. He did what he did because he believed in what you will become!"

Kaen struggled with what Bren was saying. It made no sense that Luca would die for him.

"Why would he die for me? I wasn't even ranked yet!"

Bren moved to where Kaen sat on the bench and squatted so he could look up at his face. "Luca may one day have become a gold token. He was smart and decently powerful. Many thought he was an ass because he saw things differently," Bren declared, smiling. "He was intelligent enough to know that you three stood no chance. Most others would have run for the cart. Some would have told you to split up because they knew the orc would have followed your scent. He didn't. He knew at that moment what you had done. You single-handedly defeated five orcs, which was a feat he could have never done, not even at that moment."

This was too much for Kaen to absorb. For most of the trip, he had thought Luca hadn't liked him. Hearing that Luca believed Kaen would be greater than Luca could have been and that Luca had sacrificed himself so that Kaen could live, hit Kaen hard in his chest.

"What if I can't?" Kaen mumbled.

"If you can't, what?" Bren asked.

"What if I can't be what he thinks I can become?"

Bren stood and grabbed his shield and club. "Then the only person who can determine how great you will become is you. Will you honor Luca's death and sacrifice by giving everything you have, working to be the greatest adventurer you can be, or will you slack off and do only the minimum amount of work, enjoying moments you experienced yesterday?"

Looking up at Bren, who was standing with his shield and club in his hands, ready for Kaen to decide, Kaen knew what he needed to do.

Four hours later, Kaen smiled as he dropped his shield and crashed onto the bench.

Bren sat beside him, breathing heavily and laughing between those deep breaths. "I take back what I said earlier," Bren said between gasps.

"Take back what?" Kaen asked between his labored breaths.

Bren wiped the sweat pouring down his forehead and smiled. "You can easily get a skill to twenty in a month if you train that hard every time."

Kaen grinned. Deep inside, he knew he had to. The sacrifice Luca made so that he could live was not something he could squander.

51

Starting a Fire

On his return to the inn, Kaen felt bad for the people approaching him on the street. Many had wanted to congratulate him on his quest and the token he earned, but once they got within smelling distance, they quickly found a reason to leave.

Kaen lifted an arm and took a whiff and realized immediately just how bad he smelled. Six hours of training had left him smelling like a pile of his dragon's crap. Well, maybe not that bad, but pretty close.

The sun was almost down over the western wall of the mountains, and as he walked through town, Kaen thought about Pammon and where he was.

Are you lying down for the night? Seems a bit early.

All I can do is fly and hunt for now. My focus has been on training my attacks from the air and finding more food so I can get big enough to carry you. Any luck with finding a harness?

Kaen groaned. He had forgotten to ask Hess about that once they'd returned. There had not been a chance with the celebration at the inn and Hess sleeping elsewhere last night.

I haven't, but I'll make sure to talk to Hess about that tonight if I can find him.

Is Hess missing?

He is making use of his freedom from me and has rekindled a flame with his old friend. They spent the night together and are together right now.

Kaen sensed a grumble or something that felt like Pammon was not excited about that news.

He is still going to help train and quest with you, right?

He will. He just needed some time to figure a few things out. Remember, he gave up almost eight years to raise me. I cannot fault him for that.

When he felt Pammon huff through their connection, Kaen laughed out loud as he walked along the street. Maybe Pammon thought Hess was old enough to look for a mate.

I'll be fine. You focus on your training, and I'll keep focusing on mine. If there is no quest this week, I will ride out to the woods, and we will meet somewhere.

I'll hold you to that! Pammon declared as joy and happiness flooded through their bond.

As he walked, Kaen saw a pair of children coming toward him, laughing and giggling.

"Hey, Mr. Kaen! Congratu . . . oh my gosh, you stink!" cried out the taller of the two.

His friend on the right nodded, and they both grabbed their noses.

"Is it that bad?" Kaen asked, chuckling and pretending to smell his armpits.

The boys nodded and grinned. "Did you fall in something and then roll in it?" asked the smaller of the two boys. "My mom always accuses me of that when I come home smelling!"

Kaen shook his head. "I just finished training with Master Bren for six hours straight. I'm trying to get better at more skills."

Both boys' eyes went wide at the news.

"Six hours straight!"

The taller one turned to the shorter one and poked him in the chest. "We need to start training that hard so we can be like Mr. Kaen!"

The other nodded and grinned. "Think we can be like you someday?"

That question caused Kaen's lifestone to surge. Kaen was pissed. All day, he had tried to get it to do this. It was throbbing differently this time. That question the smaller child had asked *moved* him. Raw emotion and pain from the loss of Luca and his conversation with Bren overwhelmed him. He could feel what his lifestone wanted him to say. What it wanted him to do.

Kaen bent down, and both boys struggled between wanting to move closer to hear what Kaen was going to say and moving back because the smell was so bad.

"What's your name, boys?"

"I'm Frederick, sir; he is Phillip!" replied the taller one.

"Good names," Kaen said, smiling and pulling two silver coins from his pouch. "I'll make you a deal. You two tell your moms and dads that I will pay for you to train at Master Bren's place, if they let you. If they say yes, you must train as hard as possible and do what Master Bren says."

The boys stood in shock. Kaen could see their minds trying to understand what he had just told them. "How old are you both?"

Frederick puffed out his chest and dropped his hands to his side, standing as tall as possible.

"I'm nine, sir!"

"I'm eight!" chimed in Phillip right after.

Smiling, Kaen handed a coin to each boy. Each grabbed a coin and smiled as they held it close to their eyes, inspecting their newfound wealth.

"Remember, you could spend that on candy or some toy, but it will be gone, and you won't have anything left. But if you do what I said and I find out in two years that you continue to train hard, I'll buy each of you a lifestone!"

The boys almost dropped their silver coins and took a tentative step toward Kaen.

"You would do that, sir?" Phillip asked as tears welled in his eyes.

"You wouldn't make a promise like that and back out?" Frederick blurted out.

Kaen shook his head and stood. "I'll go to the guild hall this week and draw up a quest sheet for both of you and drop it off at Master Bren's or your houses. If you keep up with your end of the bargain, the guild house will know what I have promised and complete the quest. You have my word on it!"

Both boys had tears running down their faces even though they had smiles as big as a quarter of a watermelon. Kaen could see that they both knew such a thing would never have been possible in their life, yet now, with this chance, they could become something most kids would only dream of.

Kaen ruffled their hair as he walked past the two, then turned and winked. "Remember what I said. Talk to your parents, go see Master Bren, and work harder than you have in your life, and you both can become an adventurer like me!"

The boys nodded, and when Kaen was five about five steps down the street, he felt two small bodies suddenly wrap around his legs.

Glancing down, he saw each boy had embraced one leg and was smiling, ignoring the dampness of his sweaty clothes.

"We will never forget this, Mr. Kaen!" Phillip shouted as he let go and motioned to Frederick to go. "We need to go tell our moms!"

Kaen turned and watched as they sprinted down the sidewalk and around a corner, laughing and smiling. His heart felt full, knowing he was doing all he could to honor Luca.

"Upstairs! Now!"

Eltina was pointing at the stairs at the back of the inn and watching the crowd in the room move away from Kaen as he weaved through them.

"What in the world did you fall into?" asked Hess as Kaen passed him and Sulenda when he neared the stairs.

"Training for six hours," Kaen replied. He knew he smelled but had no other way to get to his room than the front door.

Nodding in understanding, Hess grimaced and watched Kaen as he walked by.

"Perhaps I should get him a tub to soak in," Sulenda called out as Kaen's odor assaulted her nose. "I'm not sure a simple cloth and small jug will handle that mess."

Laughing, Kaen moved quickly and embraced Hess in a hug. The large man attempted to dodge Kaen's sudden attack. He failed to dodge it and held his hands up in the air as Kaen squeezed him and rubbed his face all over Hess's shirt.

"Boy, I would thump you if it wouldn't mean me putting my arms around you," howled Hess. He was trying not to laugh, but he knew Kaen had probably planned that attack the moment he had seen him.

Laughing, Kaen broke the embrace and quickly dodged away before feinting an attempt to hug Sulenda.

"Don't even think about it," she said.

Kaen shook his head and held his hands up when he saw a glare that could freeze milk coming from Sulenda's blue eyes.

As Kaen ran up the stairs and disappeared from sight, Hess let out a chuckle. "Seems he did learn a thing or two from me after all," he muttered.

"He learned that from you?"

Hess nodded and grinned like a fool. "I cannot tell you how many times I hugged that boy after a hard day of work at the quarry and made him smell my pits."

Sulenda pretended to gag and then chuckled. "Do that to me once, and I will make sure it's the last time you ever attempt that," she informed him.

"I'd never do that to you, my dear," Hess replied, coming in for a hug.

She put her hand on Hess's chest and pushed him away. "You need to go change," she said, with a smile. "You smell like the backside of Kaen."

Having used a few jugs of water and multiple rags, Kaen finally felt he could stand in most people's presence without causing them to pass out.

He had gone through his backpack and realized he did not have multiple changes of clothes, and he needed to remedy that in the coming days. Arriving at the bottom of the stairs, Kaen noticed that Hess had on a different shirt and chuckled, knowing he was the cause.

The inn was packed tonight, nowhere near as busy as last night's celebration, but they were still almost two-thirds full.

People saw him as he came around the stair landing, and some cheered or raised their cups in honor of him. Or they were raising their cups to appreciate the drinks he still had to buy for most of the town.

Hess was motioning to join him over at a table near the office door, and Kaen made his way to it, shaking a few hands of those who stood up as he walked by.

"New shirt?" he asked, once he'd reached Hess.

Hess groaned and nodded. "I was an ass for all the times I did that to you, wasn't I?"

Kaen smiled and pulled out a chair and sat down. "I think I remember a few too many times of you doing that with no shirt on. I almost did that, but I wasn't sure if Eltina would make me buy the entire bar a drink for such a maneuver, and I don't want to know how many more drinks I still owe."

Sulenda snickered and winked. "Between your bar tab and how well we did on the betting, I can probably retire to a nice estate off to the east."

"Any chance we could go over the numbers now? I made a promise to two boys, and I want to know what I can do with the money I have."

Hess furrowed his eyebrows at Kaen and leaned across the table. "Should I ask?"

Shrugging, Kaen motioned to Beatrice, who was a few tables over.

"Kaen!" Beatrice exclaimed, coming over and wrapping her arms around his head, letting him enjoy the warmth of her chest against the side of his face. "It has been far too long, and Miss Sulenda said I cannot give you hugs like this anymore without your consent."

Sulenda rolled her eyes and shook her head at Beatrice. "That is entirely not what I said. I stated you needed to restrain yourself and not take advantage of the boy. We both know he might not survive such an encounter, and it would not be fair to the kingdom to take out one of its newest adventurers."

Hess almost snorted ale out of his nose, having taken a drink when Sulenda had started speaking. Coughing and gagging, he wiped his face as tears filled his eyes.

"Kaen, you know I'm here if you ever need *anything*," Beatrice answered as she let his head free from her embrace. "Now, what can I get for you? Milk?"

Kaen nodded and when he heard Hess snicker, said, "It has done me good so far. Why mess with a good thing?"

Laughing, Beatrice nodded and moved off to the bar. Kaen watched her and shook his head. Her movements reminded him of the girl he danced with last night, and suddenly, the frustration of still not knowing who she was, hit him.

Turning back, he saw Hess and Sulenda watching him.

"You two ok?"

They smiled and nodded.

"I'm just wondering when the boy I knew became a man," teased Hess.

Kaen laughed again, surprised to find he was still so happy. All those years in Minoosh hadn't been bad, but he had always been on edge and angry. Once Pammon came into his life, everything changed.

Now, sitting in the inn with Hess and Sulenda, he was ready to start his adventurer's career. All he could think about was how great things were.

"Once she returns with my milk, I want to go into the office and know how I stand on the money side. I got things I need to do."

52

How Rich Am I?

Kaen sat his mug of milk on Sulenda's desk, but after her eyes narrowed at him, he picked it up and set it on the ground near him.

A small smile flashed across her face, and Kaen remembered what Hess had said about Sulenda's desk. The rest of the room be damned with its dust, dirty shelves, and overgrown piles of paperwork, but that woman's desk was off-limits.

"Now tell me why you need money?" asked Hess.

Kaen glanced at Hess and realized that he was looking at him differently. He had asked for money back in Minoosh to spend in town occasionally, but this was different, like grown-up talk.

"You both know what Luca did for me, right?"

Hess and Sulenda exchanged a look. It was uncanny how they both seemed to cock their head the same way when they looked at him.

"Be specific, Kaen. What are you getting at?" inquired Hess.

Kaen shared what Master Bren had told him about what Luca had done, and they nodded that they also believed that to be true.

A sigh escaped Hess's lips as he leaned back in his chair, lacing his fingers behind his head. "Well, I'm glad you figured that out. How are you handling the pressure of all that?"

"I'm doing ok with it," Kaen admitted. "It was hard to hear, but if I am going to achieve what Luca felt I could, I need to do more than just adventure and quest. I need to build something greater than myself. That is why I need to find out how much money I have and use it right."

"This has to do with the boys you mentioned?" Sulenda asked.

Kaen nodded and informed them about the promise he had made them. When he finished talking, he noticed Hess smiling and nodding.

"Boy, you never cease to make me proud or amaze me," he declared as he leaned forward and slapped his hand on Kaen's knee. "That is something your father would have done."

A sense of pride flooded Kaen's heart, knowing that what he had felt was the proper thing to do had indeed been right.

"I can help with the guild request," Hess continued, shaking his head in disbelief at Kaen's maturity. "I can probably get you a discount on the lifestones since you are attaching them to a *quest* for these two boys and the prospect of two new adventurers in nine or ten years."

Kaen nodded and looked at Sulenda. "So, how much money do I earn?"

A groan came from her throat as she opened her desk and pulled out that same small wooden box he had seen her use before. She once again pricked her finger with the quill, and after placing her bloody thumb on the top of the box, a small drawer popped out.

As she took the paper out, she shifted in her seat and gazed at Kaen. "I need to say something before I give you actual numbers. I need you to understand a few things about what took place this last week in town and how you will need some help managing the funds."

Kaen glanced at Hess and saw Hess smiling at him. "Do you know how much it is already?"

Chuckling, Hess nodded and shrugged. "One day, you will learn the need for pillow talk, and nothing is better than talking about how amazing the person next to you is or how rich you just made them."

Sulenda shook her head and groaned again. "Please don't fill that boy with nonsense. You and I both know you fell asleep afterward."

Kaen burst into laughter as Hess turned red and held his hands in protest at her statement.

"Just tell the boy what we discussed," Hess declared as he sat back in his chair.

She winked at Hess, then returned her attention to Kaen. "Hess told me, you know, that almost four-fifths of the entire population who could place a wager did. I am sure he did not mention that many side bets took place outside of the places I am responsible for. The truth is, more than 90 percent of the people who bet *lost*. Usually, that would end in a blood bath, but because of your early statement of buying alcohol for all those who lost, combined with what you actually managed to pull off, and," Sulenda paused and took breath, "how you spoke about Luca and gave him the honor that most would never do, the city cannot help but love you and somehow not care that they lost their shirts!"

Sulenda chuckled and grabbed a piece of paper from the always neat stack she pulled from. She took a pen from her desk and started writing a few numbers on the new sheet. "The king, his house, the other nobles, and most of the merchants are what drove this number as high as it is," Sulenda said as she drew columns on the page. "I heard you gave away a gold coin last night to some crab. Is that true?"

Kaen grimaced and nodded but realized Sulenda had never looked up from her paper.

"I did," Kaen admitted.

Sulenda grunted. "You know how much a gold coin is worth, right?"

The tone that Sulenda used obviously meant that she did not believe he did.

Kaen sighed and shrugged. "I know one hundred silver coins is worth one gold coin. When I worked at the quarry, I earned seven copper coins daily," Kaen paused and looked at Hess. "I should have gotten more, but it is what it is."

Hess chuckled and shrugged at the comment directed at him.

Sulenda sighed then looked up from her writing and focused on Kaen.

"So tell me, how many days did you need to work to earn a silver coin?"

Using his fingers, Kaen started to count.

"Roughly fourteen days, Kaen," she interjected, not waiting on him to do the math. "How many days would it take for you to earn a gold coin?"

"One thousand and four hundred days," Kaen answered weakly. He knew what she was pointing out to him.

Nodding, Sulenda returned to her paperwork and started drawing a few more columns and rows. "So you gave away what is basically a large chunk of what someone might make after years of working, to watch a crab dance around with it. Seem like it was still worth it?"

"I thought it was, but now I realize it was not a good use of the coin."

Grunting in approval, Sulenda went on. "Your choice to help those two boys is a cause worthy of a gold coin. Your decision to watch a crab dance and give you a lemon was not. Even if you were like most men and chose to spend coin on a woman's company, not that I expect you to have to do that for a while, very few men, even nobles, would spend a gold coin on that one experience."

She raised her head just enough to glare at Kaen and momentarily held his eyes with hers.

"Do you understand what I am saying?"

Kaen nodded and fidgeted in his seat. "I do. Thank you for the lesson."

Sulenda squinted at Kaen, trying to decide if Kaen was being serious or sarcastic. Eventually, she gave up worrying about it and returned to the paper before her.

"Back to what I said, the real money came from the nobles and merchants. A wager placed by the king was a gift to you."

"A gift?"

"He placed a bet that you would be a wood-rank. He did this after you set out on the road with Luca and Aubri. He knew he would lose and that I would know it and tell you about it. He bet ten gold, countless years' worth of work, knowing it would be lost."

Sulenda sat back in her chair and stretched her neck before leaning on her desk with both arms. She tapped her pen against the desk and grimaced.

"Hess told you the king wants to meet you?"

Kaen nodded.

"You need to meet with him. It is a courtesy for what he did. Of that, ten gold, eight of it goes straight to you. He paid a fair price for when he wants to meet with you."

A lump in Kaen's throat started to grow. Meeting with the king? He knew he would need to find much better clothing if that was going to happen.

"The king wasn't the only one who made bets like this. A few other nobles also did, but Hess will help you deal with those. I'm here if he needs help, but this is your total for now."

Sulenda folded the paper she had been writing on and slid it across the desk to Kaen. When he reached to pick it up, her hand held it firmly on the desk, and she leveled a serious gaze at him.

"Do not," she emphasized, "share that number with anyone outside this room. You will also learn to carry a small amount of money, but you will not keep more than one or two coins on you at a time. Golden goose or not, remember the lesson in the story. People sometimes think killing the goose is the best way to get richer."

After speaking, she let go of the paper, and Kaen pulled it from the desk and held it in his hands. He could see Hess and Sulenda watching and waiting for his reaction to the number she had written on it.

He opened the paper and scanned all the numbers and columns. His eyes quickly found a number circled in ink. "SEVEN COPPERS?!" he shouted.

Hess and Sulenda started laughing uncontrollably.

Kaen stood up, shook the paper at both of them and then flung it on the desk. Huffing and puffing, he groaned as the other two laughed so hard, they began crying.

"Seven coppers is your normal day's wages, right?" teased Sulenda as she leaned back in her chair.

"Perhaps he does deserve a raise," Hess chimed in.

Kaen growled and sat back down on his chair. He knew it was funny but had been expecting a real number. He took a deep breath, let it out, and then repeated the process.

What has you so worked up? Pammon suddenly asked through their bond. **You woke me up with whatever that was.** Kaen sighed and shook his head.

Hess and Sulenda played a joke on me and told me I only earned seven coppers for my help with all the betting.

Pammon began to laugh through their connection. No, it was more than laughter. It was a hardier and heavier than he had ever experienced; a special form of amusement coming through their bond.

Are you laughing about this?

Yes! That number isn't worthy of being part of a horde I one day hope to call my own. I wouldn't get up and move to lie down on seven coppers.

Kaen groaned and realized even his dragon was having a laugh at his expense.

Turning to Hess, Kaen tapped his head where he always did when mentioning Pammon. "It seems everyone thinks this is pretty funny. I seem to recall you all forgetting that I worked more than one day. It was at least five days, so that number should be at least thirty-five copper."

Sulenda nodded and wiped a tear from her eye, opening her desk drawer and pulling out a small coin pouch. "Would you like that all now or just a little bit of it," she teased.

"Just a few coins, if you please, ma'am," Kaen joked back. "I wouldn't want to carry too much around town, risking a dagger in my back over my fortune."

Not missing a blink, Sulenda undid the pouch and slid two copper coins toward Kaen.

"As you wish!"

Kaen groaned and picked them up with a smile. "Now, any chance I can find out how much I really made?"

Hess nodded, pulled a piece of paper from his pocket, and handed it to Kaen.

"You bastard!" Kaen called out. "You had that this whole time? What then was all the time we spent watching Sulenda writing numbers on a paper?"

Hess winked as he handed Kaen the paper. "That, my son, was for the both of us. We needed a good laugh!"

53

Money Well Spent

Kaen was a bit apprehensive as he took the paper from Hess. Part of him wanted to open it, but he feared they might play with him again.

"This is the real number?"

Hess nodded, and from the expression on his face, Kaen knew that Hess was not messing around this time.

Taking a deep breath, Kaen unfolded the paper and then sat in shock as he read the number multiple times. "This can't be right! Can it?"

Sulenda chuckled and motioned for Kaen to hand her the paper.

Kaen handed it to her, and Sulenda quickly glanced at it and smiled. "Looks right to me."

"How is that possible? Based on percentages and what I learned from Hess, there is no way that number is feasible! The amount of money everyone would have wagered would create a massive debt that this kingdom would suffer from."

Hess chuckled and motioned to Sulenda. "You want to tell him, or do you want me?"

Fidgeting in her chair, Sulenda glanced at Kaen and scratched her chin. "You tell him. He knows you better, and I think it will mean more."

Hess smiled and winked at her and then turned his attention to Kaen. "Focus on me, son."

When "Son" hit Kaen's ears, it felt raw and painful. He knew Hess only used that word in rare moments, and for him to use it now meant something.

"That number includes a large portion of Sulenda's and my share. We both decided that even with your best intentions and your desire to *take care of us*," Hess stated as he held up his hands in air quotes, "we will be fine with less, and you have already shown us we were right because of what I think you are planning on doing with your money."

"But why?" gasped Kaen. "I owe you both a lifetime together."

"You don't owe me shite, Kaen!" Hess exclaimed louder than he had intended, slapping his hand against his knee. "You have earned everything you have ever gotten and worked harder than I could have ever imagined. Your tenacity will have driven you to be the man you are now. I cannot imagine you would have turned out any different if your father himself had raised and trained you."

Kaen was in shock. That was more praise from Hess than he had ever received in his life with him. The last sentence stung and warmed his heart at the same time.

"Listen to me, Kaen. What you just did with those two boys proves that Sulenda and I are right. It proves that Luca was right. You are going to need money, and you are going to need friends. Powerful friends like the king and some of the nobles. If you use the skills you have now, that stupid, fantastic smile of yours, and the kindness of your heart, you will form a group of people who will gladly help you make that dream happen!"

Kaen glanced at Hess and then at Sulenda. They were smiling, and both seemed content with what they had done.

"What do you think I will try and accomplish with this money?"

Crossing his arms, Hess leaned back in his chair and smiled. "It seems to me that you might be starting a school or academy to train the next generation of adventurers."

A school? Kaen had not considered an official one, but he had already considered asking Master Bren if he would take on more kids in the area and train them. Was a school even possible? How would he manage that if he was out questing and adventuring? Would he have time with Pammon if he was involved with it?

"I mean, I had considered something small with Master Bren," Kaen stated as he stood up and moved to the map on the wall across the room. "I wanted to give more kids a chance to be what I had dreamed of." Putting his finger on the map where Minoosh was, he turned and faced Hess.

"You sent those two lifestones to our town for Cale and Patrick. I guess I just felt if they could have had that chance earlier in life, perhaps Cale wouldn't be hurt like he is now."

Hess grunted and nodded. "Don't worry about Cale. I got some people working on that."

"You got—"

Hess held up his hand and stopped Kaen. "I said don't worry about it right now. Keep talking about the other stuff."

A weight was suddenly lifted from Kaen's shoulders, and a knot that had been in his stomach since the day he found out Cale would be unable to use his arm, was gone. If Hess was working on it like he said he was, then there must be hope. He would hold onto that right now.

"What about quests and everything else and training to be an adventurer?" Kaen asked as he returned to his chair and sat down. "I still need to learn how to quest properly, work with a team, and more."

"You do," Sulenda interrupted. "Hess will be there to help. I know he is free from the bond he owed, but now he can help because he wants to. Because we both want him to help."

Kaen also saw how Sulenda was smiling at Hess and how he returned that affection.

"I will help you in the ways that I can. I will be the one who gets things moving for this *school,* as Hess calls it. You will need a contact in town, and I will also be able to help make solid candidate choices at first. Trust me, news of what you did already reached my ears while you were upstairs getting cleaned up."

"Everything you are doing is impossible to believe," Hess said when Sulenda stopped talking. "News has spread about how you just promised to train two boys from poorer families and pay for it until they could earn a lifestone! Fire couldn't spread that fast in a dry field on a windy day! You have given hope to people who had none. Who grind out each day, doing whatever they can to survive."

Hess stood up waved his hands in the air. "Kaen, you trained for six hours after a night spent celebrating your token! SIX HOURS!" Hess was worked up, and though he wasn't shouting, it felt like it, as his voice echoed in the small room. It was a good thing the walls were warded against noise.

"The townspeople, the adventurers, are in awe that you went training to learn skills you did not know! Others have commented that they might need to work a little harder after seeing what you are doing."

Hess turned on his heels and moved to Kaen and touched his shoulder. "Son, I mean . . . "

"It's ok," Kaen replied. "You can call me that."

Hess nodded and choked up. Fighting back the tears that felt like they would burst from an emotional dam he had kept up for so long. Hess took a breath and let it slowly out, then regained his composure and looked Kaen in the eye.

"You are going to be great because of who you are. Not because of who your dad was. Because of who you are," Hess declared as he gently thumped Kaen in the chest. "You will do wondrous things and not just because of Pammon."

Sulenda groaned loudly when she heard that name. "I know it's a special bow, but come on, you two . . . really? Must we talk about the bow as if it's a living creature?"

Hess and Kaen burst out laughing, and Hess stood up and moved to his chair.

"I'll try not to talk about my bow too much," Kaen replied, wiping a few tears that had somehow appeared in his eyes.

Sulenda nodded and crossed her arms as she leaned back in her chair. "Now, about the money. Let's get past all this emotional stuff, or we will never get to the important stuff," she stated with a wink. "The money is in the bank and already under your name. Only you, Hess, or I have access to it."

Kaen whistled. "You trust Hess with that kind of money?"

Sulenda chuckled and nodded. "I trust him with my heart again. If I can trust him with that, I can trust him with a small sum of gold."

Hess winked and blew a kiss at Sulenda.

Kaen shook his head in disgust. What had happened to the man he had known all his life? Acting like a fool in love.

"One hundred and six gold coins," Kaen had repeated that number a few more times after they had gotten back down to business. "I'm unsure how to even comprehend a number like this."

"Imagine going to work for almost four hundred years," teased Sulenda. "That is how long it would take."

"And most of it came from the king and nobles?"

Both Hess and Sulenda nodded as Kaen shifted in his chair.

"I guess I do owe them all a visit."

Hess roared with laughter. "You're going to have to buy a few outfits and possibly hire someone to escort you," Hess informed Kaen. "Again, Sulenda will help with that side of things. We need to finalize a few small details and get to the adventurers' guild tomorrow morning."

"What is so pressing there?"

Hess stood and stretched then let out a yawn. "We need to get you a quest. I want to see what is available, and you need to see how the system works. Because of where you are starting, you missed out on the normal training they give new recruits. This is going to be a bumpy ride."

A yawn escaped Kaen's mouth after he saw Hess yawn, and then he started to chuckle when he noticed Sulenda yawning as well.

"I guess we all had a long night yesterday, and I think I'm still expected to be back in the inn to congratulate everyone I'm buying a drink for."

Sulenda nodded and stood. "I'm going to say something, and I want you to listen and think about what I say later." She moved around the desk, stopping before Kaen and putting a hand on his shoulder.

"I knew your dad just like I know Hess. He was an amazing man; the boy I saw here the first day is not the man I see before me today. You will be greater than him, if you keep on the path you are on now."

She tapped Kaen's chest where his heart and lifestone were. "Keep following this. If you do, I will follow you like I followed your father."

Hess grabbed Kaen and Sulenda, each in an arm, and drew them to his chest.

Sulenda hesitated and then wrapped her arms around Kaen and Hess, laying her head on Hess's shoulder.

A few seconds later, Kaen embraced them both. As he did, he realized he was sobbing, tears running down his cheeks. This embrace reminded him of the last time his mother and father had hugged him at the same time, well over ten years ago.

For a few minutes, they all stood there, lives intertwined and baring their souls and need for connection. No one was in a hurry to end the moment.

54

Making Plans for The Future

The world felt brighter as Kaen shook hands and conversed with people in the inn that night. Between the moment in the office with Sulenda and Hess and feeling Pammon through their connection, his heart was full.

"Thank you for what you did for those two boys!" a man exclaimed.

Kaen nodded and shook the man's hand. He was older and looked like he might not normally visit an inn.

"I still can't believe people have heard about what I told them," Kaen replied, shaking his head. "That only happened a few hours ago."

The old man slapped Kaen on the shoulder as he waved around his mug of ale. "My boy, the whole town is on fire! What I wouldn't give to be in your shoes!"

Other men who were standing around listening all nodded in agreement.

"Master Kaen, Freddie is right. You are giving us hope we have not had in ages! We'll be keeping an eye on you!"

The men around him all cheered, and Freddie squeezed his shoulder.

"Be safe out there! We can't lose you!"

Kaen waved and smiled as he moved away from the group and to a booth to take a breather and let it all in. Hess had warned him, but the last hour of all these people and what they said about him felt impossible to achieve. Had he bitten off too much?

"This seat taken?"

Kaen glanced up and saw that Gertrude had appeared near his booth. She was wearing leather armor, twisting her beard in one hand and holding her drink in the other.

"Got room for a lesser adventurer?" she teased.

Kaen motioned to the bench across from him. "I doubt you are lesser than me. How have you been, Gertrude?"

Gertrude slid over on the bench until she was halfway in the booth. She sat her drink down on the table and leaned against the wooden back, stroking her beard braids and smiling.

"I appreciate that you think that about me. It is a testament to your character that everyone is talking about. Do you intentionally plan ahead trying to make your name greater, or are you just stumbling like a fool into greatness?"

Milk almost gushed out of Kaen's nose as he choked on her comment. Drinking while listening to Gertrude might not be the best idea. "Am I an idiot or a genius?' he asked between coughs. "Is that what you are asking?"

Gertrude leaned her head back and laughed, banging on the table with her free hand.

"You aren't a fool, and we both know it. You also do things and say things that prove you aren't a genius. That is why I am here. I'm back to let you know I'm serious about questing with you, if it's something you want."

She leaned forward and tapped the table with her pudgy finger. "I know you are still green; our group is ok with that. I also know you will get some good experience with Hess, but we are willing to help show you how a team works. To make you better," Gertrude paused, smiling, "and I have no doubt you will also help us rise through the ranks."

Kaen nodded. "I appreciate your honesty and willingness to say what others won't. Too often, I feel people are just blowing smoke up my arse."

Gertrude nodded as she downed her ale, wiping the foam off her beard with the back of her hand. "You aren't worthless. You have a lot of skills. You just lack a few advanced techniques. I see your potential, but best of all, I realize you are willing to work hard to improve. That is why I am telling you to join our squad. There are going to be many other squads who will ask you to join. Many will blow smoke up your arse, as you said," Gertrude winked as she said that last statement. "I'll always tell you to get your head out of your arse, and I'll kick your backside if you shoot me in the rear with an arrow."

Kaen felt in awe at what Gertrude had said. He needed people like her who were willing to tell him the truth and not pull punches. "Tell you what, I'll join your squad once Hess says I can. How does that sound?"

She leaned over the table and extended her hand. "Shake on it?"

Kaen grabbed her hand, both pumping their hands fast a few times before letting go and sitting back.

"Now that's settled, you still on the market, or did that pretty young thing sweep you off your feet?"

Kaen closed his eyes and groaned. "I had put that all out of my mind until you mentioned her. I still don't know her name, and anyone I have asked has not told me her name either."

Gertrude smiled and began twisting a beard braid around her finger. "So is that you wanting to forget her, or you having forgotten her?" she asked in a playful voice and with a wink. "I can help in either of those situations, with the forgetting."

Waving his hands in surrender, Kaen chuckled. "I haven't forgotten her and don't want to yet. I need to find someone who can tell me who she is," Kaen answered. "Besides, I'm not sure fooling around with a potential squad mate is the best idea right now. I wouldn't want to be mad at you and miss on purpose."

She roared with laughter and tugged on her braid as she narrowed her eyes at Kaen. "There is that genius side of you again," she teased. "Just enough to lead me on but not make me hate you for doing it."

With a sigh, Gertrude let go of the braid she appeared on the edge of yanking off. Her smile turned a bit mischievous, if that was possible to believe, through her beard as she bit her top lip.

"I guess I will tell the rest of the party that you will join us soon. Just ask the guild hall to message me when you are ready." She scooted out of the booth and stood at the table's edge, adjusting her armor as she stood. "If you ever need me for anything else, you can also check in at the guild, and someone will make sure I get the message."

She winked as she strode away, shaking her head at him.

Kaen sat there wondering if he had momentarily dodged an arrow. He had forgotten about the mystery woman, and now his mind was focused on her. When he closed his eyes, he could almost smell her again, like flowers in a field during springtime.

He glanced around the room and saw that the crowd looked content, and in that moment, no one was seeking him out. Most were engaged in conversations with their tablemates or drinking alone, trying to forget the problems on their minds.

Kaen slid out of the booth and quickly headed to his room. A good night's sleep was exactly what he needed.

His breakfast was almost all gone when Hess descended the stairs and sat in a chair at his table.

"I was beginning to wonder if I was going to have to come and wake you," Kaen said.

Hess grunted and motioned to the only serving woman up at that time. "Hot tea, make it strong, and get me a sandwich to go, please."

The woman moved toward the kitchen door, not missing a beat that Hess was a bit gruffer than usual.

"You ok? Why are you so cranky?"

Hess looked around the room and leaned close to Kaen after making sure no one was listening in. "She snores. Like a boar or a bear. I had forgotten that about her."

Kaen laughed, and Hess's eyes shot daggers at him, causing Kaen to muffle the laughter and shrug. "She snores worse than you?"

"I don't—" Hess stopped speaking, and a small smile broke out over his face. "That isn't true, and we both know it. Yes, she snores louder than me. I need a little more time to adjust to her snoring. I have not gotten much sleep the last two nights."

"Sounds like your own choosing," Kaen teased as he motioned at the serving woman returning with Hess's food. "I won't tell Selunda what you said about her snoring, but we need to get a move on. My friend is upset I have not visited him in a while."

Hess nodded and stood as the woman returned with his food wrapped in a cloth.

"Thank you, Stacey. Sorry, I was a bit gruff earlier."

The server laughed and waved Hess off. "I've endured far worse, and we are all grateful that you have made Miss Sulenda smile again. If enduring what you call *gruff* is the worst we have to experience, I'll take it daily."

Hess chuckled as he took his food and motioned to the door. "Let's go, boy. We got a busy day ahead of us."

Being up before most of the town was better for Kaen. He preferred not having to shake hands or wave at every person who saw him. It would almost make him consider finding a new place to stay, as the attention felt undeserved. He struggled to believe he had yet earned the renown people said he had.

What has you troubled this morning already?

Just a lot on my mind. Trying to figure out things and how to be worthy of what people say I am. Hess and I are headed to the guild hall to get a quest to see you. It appears you have already found some food.

The early dragon gets the stag.

Groaning out loud, Hess turned to Kaen and nodded in understanding when Kaen tapped his temple.

What does the early stag get?

Pammon did not answer for a moment and then a chuckle came through the bond.

He gets to be in my stomach. It really doesn't matter at this point. I am hunting in the woods to the east near the lake out here. I can easily see through the trees, and taking down one that is awake or asleep is exceedingly boring. I have started chasing them some, working on my ability to track them down as they run.

A tinge of frustration washed over Kaen.

I just want to be near you. I don't know how to say it any way other than that. It's a longing that aches the more time you are away. Our time together last week helped, but I think we need to be near each other for a while to fix this ache.

I understand that. Soon, we will figure this out, even if I have to buy some land closer to the forests.

Don't make promises you won't keep. I think this is why the Dragon Riders lived with their dragons. The bond is that important.

Maybe Hess can help with that. I'll talk to him and let you know. Enjoy your hunting.

You too.

I'm not hunting. What are you talking about?

That is a lie, and you know it. You are hunting a different prey. The woman from the other night. I can feel your thoughts, remember?

Hess elbowed Kaen when he laughed so loud, people turned to see what was so funny.

"Keep it down," Hess declared as he pretended to laugh with Kaen.

Nodding, Kaen took a few breaths and stopped laughing as they walked.

Perhaps the early Kaen gets the girl!

Dwarf balls, I hope not. I don't want the competition for your time!

He couldn't help himself and burst out laughing again, dodging the elbow he knew was coming from Hess.

"I'll tell you in a minute," Kaen explained through laughter.

"I'm not sure I want to know," answered Hess. "You two are still too young."

55

First Quests for Everyone

"These are the three quests the two of you are authorized to take right now," Mandy, the clerk, stated as she placed the three silver quest sheets on the counter. "The first one is a cave with a fire ant problem, rumored to be a hive. Usually, I would recommend a group, but with Adventurer Hess with you, it shouldn't be a problem. The second one is a group of bandits a few days from here. They have set up camp somewhere in the woods along the northern wall of the mountains. They move around a lot, so none of the groups who have taken this quest yet has had any luck. When they strike, they usually don't kill, but it has happened, and they have acquired a lot of goods. Rumor is there are at least ten of them."

"And the third?" Kaen asked.

Mandy smiled and pushed the last paper toward him. "I doubt you would want to take this quest, but in the mines here in the mountains, a swarm of goblins, hobgoblins, and orcs has invaded a shaft. They have been contained, but no one knows their true numbers. Some say it is up to fifty, while others say maybe only twenty-five."

Glancing at Hess and then at Mandy, Kaen raised his eyebrows. "Why would you say that?"

"Do you really want to be known as a one-trick pony? Someone who can only kill goblins and orcs? Some might enjoy that title, but I doubt you want that to be your reputation."

Kaen tisked and nodded. That was not something he wanted to be known as. The third quest really didn't work anyway since there was no way Pammon could get into the mines.

A cave was not something he really wanted to experience again anytime soon. Though he doubted the ants would pose much of a problem to Pammon, he would prefer the open area where Pammon's eyes could be their real chance at success.

"We'll take the bandit quest!"

Mandy smiled and presented a pen to Kaen. "If you would, just sign right there, and it will be all yours until you complete it or forfeit it."

Kaen nodded and signed his name, watching in awe again as the page shimmered once he had signed it.

"Very good. I will get you a map like the one on the back of the quest sheet to take with you. I also heard you need to put in a special question?"

Mandy winked and had already pulled out a sheet of paper with words written on it.

"You already know?" Kaen gasped in shock.

A throaty laugh escaped Mandy's mouth as she put the paper on the counter before Kaen.

"As I am sure you have been told, word of your promise and action has spread through the city. Two boys being promised a lifestone by our newest token adventurer is not something to be taken lightly."

"And will the guild help with the cost?" Hess asked, leaning on the counter with his massive arms. "They used to help with costs on lifestones if the reason was honorable."

Mandy let out a sigh and drummed her fingers on the counter. The look on her face told both Kaen and Hess what she was about to say was not the answer they had hoped for.

"The guild cannot help with that right now. I can ask Guild Master Fiola if she is willing to assist with the cost, if you want. You might need to pursue other benefactors who I believe would be willing to assist you in lowering your costs."

Hess grunted. He knew exactly what Mandy was alluding to.

"We'll cover the cost. That will have to come down the road," Kaen answered before Hess could say something. "Besides, I have a little time before I have to purchase them, right?"

Mandy nodded and smiled. "Sign here, and I will get you copies for the boys to sign."

Mandy returned a few minutes after he had signed the documents with two exact copies, both with his signature on the *Sponsor* line.

"How do you do that?"

"Do what?"

"Make an exact copy of the paper with my signature?" asked Kaen. "If I didn't know better, I would think I had signed it myself."

She smiled and winked at Kaen. "Some things aren't knowledge I can share, but you are smart. I'm sure you'll figure it out."

Hess chuckled and motioned for Kaen to drop it. "You aren't the first to ask them that question," Hess informed Kaen. "There used to be a bounty for that knowledge, but the guild crushed it fast because of possible financial implications if it got out."

Nodding, Mandy cleared the spot where she was standing. "If you gentlemen are done, I need to help the next person in line," she stated, motioning to the five people patiently waiting for a turn.

"Sorry," Kaen blurted out when he turned and saw everyone looking at him.

"It's ok!" exclaimed the short gnome wearing a set of robes who was first in line. "We were all new like you were once."

"What do you mean once?" asked the female elf behind him. "You got your token like two months ago!"

The others in line laughed, and the gnome turned and spat on the ground near the elf's feet.

"You got yours the day before me because I had to wait on the mage tester! Don't act like you have been an adventurer longer than me!"

"You just admitted I have—"

"If you two want to keep this up, you can take it outside!" Mandy declared, rebuking them loudly in the hall before everyone. "This will be reflected in your advancement if you continue."

Both adventurers turned and saw the look they were receiving from Mandy, and each cowered a little from it.

"Time to make our escape," Hess whispered as he pushed Kaen past the crowd of adventurers gathering to see what the commotion was.

Outside, the sun was barely above the eastern mountains, spreading its light over the city. Kaen had seen the view many times before, but somehow it felt different. Knowing he had his first official quest made this morning special. It was the dawn of a new day in his life. Soon, he would rise through the ranks, and one day, he would announce his relationship with Pammon. He would announce that he was a Dragon Rider.

"What the hell are you doing?" Hess asked as he stood off to the side, looking at Kaen.

Kaen glanced around. He had not realized he had stopped in the middle of the street and was staring at the city and hadn't noticed the cart that had stopped a few feet away from him because he was blocking the road.

"Uh . . . sorry, sir," Kaen blurted out as he moved to the side of the street.

As the driver got his horses going again, and the cart rumbled passed an embarrassed Kaen, Hess still stood there wondering what had happened. "What is going on with you? Is everything ok, or were you thinking too much?" Hess was tapping his temple.

"No, it wasn't that," Kaen said, chuckling. "I was just lost in the moment of today."

Kaen opened his pouch and pulled out the copy of the quest Mandy had given him. Holding it out for Hess to look at, he smiled. "This is my first quest! My actual first quest!" Kaen beamed. "Everything I dreamed about starts today!"

Kaen moved closer to Hess and leaned in close. "How long till I can tell the kingdom about my friend? It might sound weird, but we are hurting from not seeing each other regularly. It hurts," Kaen declared as he tapped his chest, "right here. The only way we don't feel it is when we are close. Close enough to touch."

Hess rubbed his thumb along his chin and nodded. "I wish I had known. I would have ensured the two of you could see each other."

Kaen shrugged. "I didn't realize how bad it was at the time. You know why I took this quest, right?"

Hess smiled, then nodded and put his hand on Kaen's shoulder. "If you had picked either of the other two, I would have smacked you across the head," Hess growled playfully. "It's obvious you are thinking and not just listening to your heart. You're going to use him to find the crew no one else can, right?"

Grinning like a weasel caught in a chicken house, Kaen nodded. "Just doing what you taught me. The best part is once we are outside of the pass, we can find somewhere to meet up with him. I would also rather not hurry to finish this quest or at least take a day or two longer, if you don't mind. We both feel the need to spend time with each other."

Squeezing Kaen's shoulder, Hess grinned at him. "I'll gladly take a few extra days in the woods with you two over the snoring I'm getting right now at the inn," Hess joked.

Kaen smiled, letting Frederick's dad, Dave, shake his hand for the hundredth time.

"We will never forget this!" Dave exclaimed again. "You do not know what it means to us!"

"I may not know exactly what it means, but I know how important hope is," Kaen replied as he freed his hand again. "All I can give is hope. Your son has to do the hard work."

Kaen smiled at Frederick, who was sitting at the table, listening intently to his mother read the contract Kaen had given them. Kaen bent down at the table's edge when Frederick's mother, Gemma, finished reading it and poked Frederick's arm.

"Here," Kaen said, offering him a pen. "All you have to do is sign your name however you want, and I will take it to the guild. After that, the rest falls on you."

Without hesitation, Frederick grabbed the pen and quickly signed his name, grinning the entire time.

"Did Phillip already sign his?"

Kaen nodded and pulled out the folded contract Phillip had signed earlier, showing Frederick that both of them now had quests.

"Thank you again, Sir Kaen," Frederick declared as he stood up and saluted.

Chuckling, Kaen reached over and ruffled the boy's hair before reaching for the contract on the table, folding it with the other boy's contract, and sticking it in his pouch.

"I made a promise, and so did you. Work hard like Master Bren told me you two have been. It may seem like it takes forever, and you will get discouraged, but don't give up!" Kaen proclaimed enthusiastically. "I need more adventurers like you two. One day, I plan on getting to bet what rank you and Phillip will be when you take your test!"

Dave groaned when Kaen said that last part, and his wife, Gemma, shook her head at her husband.

"Yes, we are well aware of betting on those," she said with a little displeasure in her voice.

Laughing, Kaen nodded and put a pouch on the table. "That is to help pay for Frederick's equipment and clothes he will need, as well as a little extra food. With the amount of training he will be doing, he needs to make sure to eat a lot, especially once he gets his lifestone."

Dave and Gemma started to object, and Kaen cut them off with a raised hand. "I promised both boys I would cover their training. This is part of it. I fully intend to see them succeed."

Glancing down at Frederick, he rested a hand on the boy's shoulder. "If your parents ever have to come and find me because you are slacking in your training, either with school or with Master Bren, you will not like it if I have to come and visit. Do you understand?"

Smacking his lips, which seemed awfully dry at the moment, Frederick nodded.

"I promise I won't fail you!"

"Good! Now, I have one last treat for you before my mentor and I head out on my *first* quest tomorrow."

Hess deposited a leather bag he had been holding over his back onto the table.

Frederick and his parents glanced at the bag, wondering what could be inside.

"Consider this repayment for losing your bet on me and my congratulations on Frederick's first quest. May you three enjoy a great evening as a family tonight!"

Gemma started to cry openly as she smiled, reached out, and brought Frederick to her side, hugging him tightly. His father was just as shocked and seemed unable to find words, even though his mouth was open.

"If you will excuse us," Hess interjected, "we need to get moving if we are going to get all of the supplies we need for tomorrow."

Without waiting, Hess and Kaen bowed, and Kaen waved at Frederick, who could not escape his mother's grasp.

"Goodbye, Sir Kaen! I'll make you proud! I promise!"

Kaen let Hess push him out the door, content not to let the family see the tears in his eyes, just like the ones he had when he'd left Phillip's house.

"I'm proud of you, Kaen. Prouder than you will ever know."

Kaen nodded, not turning to risk a glance at Hess. His heart was bursting with raw emotion, and he knew if he spoke now, he would not be able to stop the tears that were already leaking down his face.

56

The Itch That Needs Scratching

Calm down, Pammon, please. You are killing me right now!

The amount of excitement and anticipation coming from Pammon was overwhelming. It was actually making Kaen jittery. Since mentioning the quest yesterday and their getting to see each other once they were outside the pass, Pammon had been impossible to settle down.

I am calm!

Kaen chuckled and winked at Hess, who knew what Kaen was doing. They were halfway through the pass, riding two horses and pulling the pack horse behind them. Sulenda had seemed ok until this morning when they headed off, requiring a few extra kisses from Hess and a promise he would not come back dead.

She had not deemed Kaen's joke on how Hess would bring himself back if he were dead funny, threatening him with a beating if he let Hess injure himself.

Eventually, they had managed to ride off from the inn, both ready for what awaited them a few days from now.

You say you are calm, but I know you just as well as you know me. Your heart is racing, and you are flying around in circles. Go do something useful and scout out the area for a place to camp and meet later.

Pammon grumbled through the bond, frustrated that Kaen did not seem as excited as he should be.

"Any idea when they grow out of the *kid* stage?" Kaen asked after checking none of the other travelers were close to them.

"I'm still waiting on you to grow out of that stage," Hess joked as he gave his horse a gentle pat on the neck. "Some days, you act like a man, and others you act like a kid. I'm just glad lately it's been more adult days than the latter."

About to open his mouth and ask what actions Hess considered *kid* ones, Kaen paused and thought through his actions over the last week. The memory of giving a gold coin away to a crab popped into his head first, making him close his mouth before enduring that conversation again.

"Well, I'm sorry for all the frustration I put you through. I swear it's like that with my friend sometimes as well. He can be so serious and focused, and other times he acts like a dog who has been shown a bone. Excited about it and forgetting everything else."

Hess tipped his head back and laughed loudly, the sound echoing off the pass's stone walls. The walls were cut as if a god from heaven had come down with a sword and taken one single swipe, creating a smooth, polished finish and a straight shot through the mountainside. The dwarves who had been hired had carved out drains which carried the runoff from rain and water that came from the top of the mountain. The same stone path had been laid here as on the streets, providing safe and smooth travel.

"Remember, he isn't even a year old yet. Keep that dog and bone illustration in your head. None of us, not even him, knows where the *knowledge* he has comes from. It has to be something they are born with, possibly passed down through birth," Hess explained. "He is still young, he is still needy, he is still bonding. Remember how you, Patrick, and Cale felt and acted once you started working at the quarry. You three lamented how it wasn't fair you couldn't see each other except on the weekends. When the weekends came, you three spent every waking hour together. Now, you all would occasionally hang out for a few hours on the weekend, content from the time you spend every day breaking rocks together."

"Pfft." Kaen blew a raspberry at Hess, then let out a long sigh as he shook his head.

"Parenting isn't easy, is it?" This time, the echo of Hess's laughter extended farther down the pass. His face was bright red from how hard he was laughing. By the way it moved between steps, the giant horse he was riding on did not appear to appreciate how much Hess was bouncing in the saddle.

"OH, my boy," Hess cried out as he took a few breaths and wiped tears from his eyes, "you are in for a world of hurt if you ever do have a child. Your friend is way better behaved than kids are, and this is nothing more than a stage any creature goes through. When they have a relationship with someone, they want to be with that person. Just like a dog or cat will sleep in the bed of its *person*, your friend wants the same thing. Closeness and a connection."

Hess stopped speaking and adjusted in his saddle before returning his attention to Kaen.

"You two are connected in a way that seems impossible. You told me how he lost his mother, hidden away for some reason. You lost your parents. You feel each other's pain from that, strengthening your bond. All he has left is you, so he will guard you with every part of his being."

Riding his horse in silence, Kaen realized how right Hess was. He had not appreciated the bond he and Pammon had and, no doubt, had hurt Pammon's feelings by his words.

Found a spot yet? I can't wait to see you tonight and get all those spots you need to be scratched!

Joy leaped through their bond, and Kaen now had no doubt that Hess was right.

I have so many spots that need a good scratching! I am almost near a location that might work!

Well, I can't wait! See you soon!

As a constant stream of contentment and joy washed over him, Kaen smiled, grateful for Pammon and Hess. Two things he hoped he never took for granted.

"This blasted brush is way worse than I ever remembered," cursed Hess as he led his horse behind him through the woods.

His horse was easily three feet taller and a lot wider than the horse Kaen had. Of course, most horses would have died having to carry a man Hess's size.

"You actually remember being in these woods?"

"Mother . . . dwarf . . . half-elf . . . goblin piss."

Kaen turned around, trying to figure out why Hess was cursing so much. When he glanced behind his horse, he found that Hess had somehow found a stink bell.

"Oh man, that smells already," Kaen announced as the horses started trying to get away from Hess and the smell that was emanating from his foot.

"There were none of these damn things in the woods when I was here! I didn't see it because of this damn horse fighting me about coming through here!"

Kaen froze and looked around the part of the woods they were in. Sure enough, there were a few other stink bells along the ground and near the base of the trees. Their green pods blended with the mature foliage and plants they were traveling through. The horses and their sensitive noses had known they were walking toward and through them, causing them to resist where they were being led.

"This stuff smells worse than goblin piss!" bellowed Hess as he let his horse start backing up on its own, trusting it to put its feet where it needed to. "We need to get out of this unless we want to stink for a week!"

Kaen's horse had not been acting as badly as Hess's horse had, until the moment Hess popped one of the bells, named after the shape of the pod after it was busted open. Now Kaen's horse was struggling against the reins in Kaen's hand.

"Shhhh . . . it's ok," he said, reaching out and gently patting the horse's nose.

Kaen released the reins, and the horse quickly moved through the patch they were standing in, dodging the little plants with amazing finesse.

Chuckling to himself, Kaen followed the path the horse had taken and soon cleared the area and the trouble it presented.

When Hess reached them, Kaen saw that the vein on his forehead throbbing. It was so active it almost appeared to be dancing.

"This boot will stink for days," Hess huffed as he held his horse, who was fighting being close to him.

"It's my fault. I was in such a hurry to get to Pammon, I didn't watch where we were going. I'll make sure to be more attentive."

A grunt came from Hess, yet he said nothing more, and Kaen didn't press it. It would be a while before Hess calmed down.

You are so close I can feel it! I can also smell Hess like you said I would . . .

It took a lot of effort for Kaen not to laugh at that announcement. He knew Pammon was close. Hess was keeping the horses tied up a quarter of a mile away from the clearing Pammon had found. In the woods, there were two small open areas not far from one another. From the road, it took a little over an hour of trudging through the woods to reach them.

When Kaen got his horse tied off, he sprinted toward Pammon.

Hess had told him he would bring dinner, knowing Kaen would spend the night with his dragon.

"I know it feels weird when I say this, but it is like I can feel the scratches through our bond," Kaen declared as he slowly scratched between Pammon's scales on his neck. "It's like when you feel it, I somehow feel it. Is this the way it is supposed to be?"

Pammon snorted and bent his neck to look at Kaen's face. Huffing in Kaen's face, Pammon quickly licked from ear to ear across his head, leaving a trail of slobber dripping down his face.

"Ung, that's nasty!" Kaen shouted, wiping his face with his arm and spitting out the saliva that had gotten into his mouth.

Nope, I didn't feel that at all. Pammon started a low thrum that Kaen recognized as his laugh.

"That was so disgusting. Why would you do that?"

No matter how much Kaen wanted to be angry with Pammon, he believed it was funny even though he was on the bad end of that trade.

I have no idea how all this works. I somehow know fragments of some things and have no idea about others. Perhaps when you can ride on me, and we search out another Dragon Rider, they will tell us.

Removing the last of Pammon's spit from his face, Kaen stood up and reached around Pammon's neck, pretending to wrestle with him. "If I could hold on, I would let you fly me now, but Hess said he will work on a harness. You can ask him tonight if you want."

I will. Like being away from you, I need to fly with you on my back. It's one of those things I know . . . or just feel.

"Soon, that will happen. For now, I am just content to be here with you."

With Kaen holding onto his neck, Pammon jerked up off the ground, lifting Kaen easily and dangling him from his neck. Pammon shook his neck a little, letting his low thrum reverberate through his body as he tried to playfully toss Kaen off. After several small attempts and no luck, Pammon stood on his haunches, lifting Kaen a good seven feet off the ground.

"Pammon!" Kaen shouted as he glanced down. "What are you doing!"

I won't drop you. Just hold on. I know you are strong enough to.

"Wait, what are . . . "

Pammon started waddling backward. His low thrum was so loud, Kaen could feel his chest vibrating from it.

This is good practice in case you fall, right?

Realizing Pammon was messing with him, Kaen lifted his leg, got a foothold on Pammon's shoulder, and slowly shifted himself till he was behind Pammon's neck, ready for what he somehow knew Pammon would do.

When Kaen's feet were set perfectly on the ridge of Pammon's shoulder, and he had a solid grip around his neck, Pammon dropped to all fours and began picking up speed as he moved around the clearing. Kaen somehow knew where to slide his legs and feet as Pammon began moving. At that moment, he found the perfect spot on Pammon's neck. The other day, he had struggled to sit comfortably, but now he found a groove made just for him.

This moment was different.

The connection they both felt at that very moment as Pammon ran around the small clearing, made their hearts pound faster.

It's happening!

As if Pammon had willed it, his lifestone surged, and it seemed to flood both of them through the connection they shared. They both knew what to do next.

It's time! Hold on!

57

First Flight

Leaping into the air, Pammon beat his wings, creating the lift needed to clear the treetops with the added weight of Kaen. Over and over, his wings moved air, launching him upward as Kaen's legs gripped his neck. He could feel Kaen's arms wrapped around his neck and how tight his hands were clasped together.

Open your eyes, you fool!

Kaen realized he had squeezed his eyes shut. He opened them, and his breath was lost in the moment of what he saw.

The sun was setting to the west, turning the sky into an artwork of oranges and reds. The wind rushed by him, and the forest below turned into something mysterious and dark; the shadows from up high gave it an evil look.

Kaen shouted, and Pammon laughed.

I didn't hear what you said. The wind swept it away.

I could do this forever!

That is my hope. Now, hold on as I turn around.

Kaen's lifestone was still surging, and as Pammon adjusted his wings and the angle of his body, he gave himself over to it. His hips shifted to lean against the turn, keeping him upright and less likely to fall off. His shoulders and arms adjusted their position, keeping him right where he needed to be.

As Pammon banked to the right, Kaen gazed at the forest stretching to the horizon. The number of trees seemed impossible to believe; the maps he had seen did no justice to his current view.

This is amazing! Everything looks so . . .

Magical?

Yes! Like something from a tale I heard sung by a bard as a kid. Not even the stories my dad shared with me compare to this!

Is your lifestone doing something right now? I feel a direction from inside you to me. Do you feel it?

It is going crazy and acting differently. I can feel it flowing between us. When it happens, I let myself go and let it take over. That is how I am able to stay balanced so easily, and all this seems possible. Until that moment before you took off, I had no idea where to sit or how to hold. Now it seems like second nature.

Neither spoke for a bit as Pammon glided a good quarter mile above the trees. The view made everything seem so small, and even the clearing they had flown out of was barely visible from the sky.

Joy, connection, belonging, peace, contentment, and many other emotions flowed between them both.

Kaen wondered, if this was how a bond between a Dragon Rider and their dragon was, why were there so few dragons now? What had been so bad to cause them to all but disappear?

We need to land . . .

Is something wrong?

I have a hunch there will be when we return. Hess is in the clearing, and it appears he is not happy.

Kaen leaned to the side a little and stared at the ground where he could see the break in the trees under them.

Can you see him that clearly?

Pammon's body pulsed, and the thrum of his laughter vibrated against Kaen's backside.

I can count the hairs on his head even when I am much higher. I won't mention to you or him the few gray ones he has growing.

Kaen rubbed Pammon's neck with his right hand and gripped a scale.

Let's go down and deal with it.

Pammon started their descent, taking his time and relishing the moment they still got to experience. As they banked and approached the clearing, Kaen saw Hess looking up at them and shaking a fist. He didn't need Pammon's ability to see far to know Hess was unhappy with him.

As they approached the ground, a last surge of Kaen's lifestone roared into Pammon, and he adjusted his wings, slowing down quickly, angling his body and landing at a different angle than usual. The movement kept Kaen in his spot, allowing him to reach the ground without any issues.

[Dragon Riding Skill Acquired]
[Dragon Riding Skill Increased x10]

What was that?

Kaen couldn't help but laugh when he was informed of the skill gained by his lifestone. Even with Hess shouting at the two of them as he dashed across the opening, Kaen was amazed at how all this had occurred.

I got a skill for dragon riding just now. My lifestone actually gave me a ten, which is a huge starting point!

I could feel a change in you and me when it happened.

Did you gain a skill? I mean, do dragons gain skills?

I do not . . . .

"WHAT IN THE HOLY MOTHER OF HAIRY DWARF BALLS DO THE TWO OF YOU THINK YOU WERE DOING?!

Hess's shouting had cut off Pammon's message, and Kaen noticed the vein in Hess's forehead appeared to have a long-lost brother with it at the moment.

"Hess, it's ok, we—"

"IT WAS NOT OK! IT WAS FOOLISH!"

Hess stopped a few feet from Pammon's snout and gazed furiously at the two of them.

"Get off him right now and come down here!" he shouted, pointing his finger at the ground.

"Hess, listen!"

"No, you listen! You could have died! Then what? Just because you felt you couldn't wait and needed to try it out?! Everything I have done! Everything this world has offered you! You would throw it away?"

Pammon huffed and moved his head to block Hess from Kaen's sight.

I am getting angry. I will not let him talk to you like that.

Let me handle it. He is hurt and upset and worried. He is only acting like you did when I drank that alcohol, remember?

The frustration and anger that had been seething from Pammon and their bond decreased a little. Not a ton, but enough to let Kaen know he understood Hess's side a little better.

Swinging a leg over Pammon's neck, Kaen slid down and landed easily on both feet. He tapped Pammon on the neck and pushed his head out of the way so he could get to Hess.

"Hess, listen—"

Kaen was cut off as Hess bear-hugged him, squeezing him so tight it made breathing almost impossible.

"You fool," Hess declared as tears flowed down his cheeks. "I was afraid, you idiot! Afraid you would get hurt or worse!"

Grunting through the pain, Kaen put his arms around Hess as best he could and patted his back. "I know. I'm sorry. We had not meant to do that, but my lifestone made Pammon do it."

Hess pushed Kaen back and scrunched his face. "Your lifestone did what?!"

Kaen took a deep breath, recovering the air he had lost from that hug and explained exactly what had happened.

After Kaen stopped talking, Hess mulled things over, staring at the ground and walking around in small circles with his hands behind his back.

Do all people do that when they are thinking?

No, but what I just told Hess is something he has never heard of or knows about. We are dealing with things no one but a Dragon Rider would have any idea of. He is trying to weigh everything he knows about lifestones and what I just said. He has also told me many times that mine is different from his, and he isn't sure if it's because of you or something else.

Pammon blew a breath of air at Kaen's face and then poked him on the shoulder with his snout.

It has to be because of me. We both know I'm special like that.

Kaen laughed out loud, and Hess turned to see why he was laughing.

"Dragon conversations?"

Nodding, Kaen motioned to Pammon. "He says all this with my lifestone is because of him. Because he is *special.*"

Pammon started laughing himself, causing Hess to shake his head and roll his eyes at the two of them.

"This makes it *really* hard for me to be upset at that stunt you two just pulled," Hess finally stated, waving his hands in the air. "You know how I feel about it, but if your lifestone *made* the two of you do that and you gained a skill like you said you did, then I was wrong. So please forgive me."

"You don't have to ask for forgiveness. You were worried because you care about me."

Sighing, Hess nodded, walked up to Pammon, and held his hand out toward him. Pammon moved his head and let Hess scratch the scales, then trilled in delight.

"I'm sorry too, Pammon," Hess said, smiling at the sound of the trilling. "I know you would never endanger Kaen like that. We both know you are the smarter of the two."

Pammon laughed, and Kaen playfully slapped him on the neck.

Tell Hess I forgive him, and he is right. I am smarter.

"Pammon says he forgives you, even if you are wrong and says I am smarter."

Pammon's wing came forward, catching Kaen on the back and sending him to the ground. Hess and Pammon laughed as Kaen stood up with a grin on his face.

"Ok, maybe he didn't say that last part."

"I had no doubts about that," Hess replied with a wink.

Kaen and Hess ate dinner, leaning against Pammon's body as he encircled them both. The fire they had built a short distance away, cast a warm light on the three of them as they relaxed in the darkness of the night, looking up at the sky and the shining stars. A half-moon was out, lending just enough light to see the tree line.

"You have grown," Hess admitted between bites. "I will admit I am shocked at how fast it has happened. How much are you eating now?"

Four to five deer a day, at least now.

Seriously?!

I would gladly eat a cow, but I doubt I could get away with that without causing problems near the city. It isn't too bad, though. There are a few areas with plenty of deer, and I move around so I don't wipe them out.

"He says four to five deer a day but wishes to eat a cow or two. He just doesn't want to cause problems in the city or the farms."

Hess nodded and smiled as he chewed his apple. "That proves to you why he is smarter than you," Hess declared, enjoying the vibration of Pammon's laughter as he leaned against him. "On that note, I think it is time for me to head back to the horses. I know you two will stay here tonight, so I expect Kaen to be sent back to me in the morning."

Hess motioned to Kaen to stay seated as he stood up. He moved over to Pammon, gave his neck a good scratch session, and then patted him. "Take care of Kaen for me like I know you will. I know you two are perfect for each other."

I'm not sure how to take what he just said.

Kaen roared in laughter, and Pammon bopped him on his head with his snout.

"He isn't sure how to take that last comment, but I do."

Hess smiled as he walked in the direction of the horses. He pulled a lightstone from his pouch, turned it on, and walked through the darkness toward the trees.

"Remember, be up at first light!" he called out as he walked away.

Kaen watched Hess walk away, enchanted by the glow of his lightstone as it moved through the trees, until it disappeared completely.

You know he still smells.

A snort escaped Kaen, and he nodded. "I didn't feel like mentioning that to him after what we had put him through."

He was hurt because he cares for you deeply. I know you say he isn't your father, but I imagine this is how one would act.

A twinge of hurt pierced Kaen's heart so badly, he unconsciously put his hand on his chest and rubbed it.

I'm sorry if that upset you. I was just telling you what I have noticed since the day you found me.

"I know," Kaen replied quietly. "He is like a father to me. It feels like I betray my real dad if I call him that though. I know it doesn't make sense and shouldn't, but it does. It's like . . . if I give him that title, I wonder if I am erasing what my dad means to me?"

Wrapping around Kaen a little tighter, Pammon extended a wing to cover him up some.

I do not think so. Just because he is not made from you does not mean he cannot love you. You have told me many times about what he has done and how he has trained, cared for, and shaped you. I believe that your father picked him not just because he was his friend but because he knew Hess would love you as his own son.

The wind in Kaen's lungs seemed to have been pulled out, and it took a second before he could take a breath. He knew Pammon was right. All those years he had resisted a name or a title because of what it meant; he had ignored how much it must mean to Hess.

"I'm glad you're smarter than me," Kaen joked, trying to lighten the mood. "I am also glad you aren't afraid to tell me what I need to hear. I'll think about it and see if I can let myself call him that."

Go to sleep. I'm tired, and I know you are too. We can talk tomorrow. For now, I just want to enjoy the connection I have missed.

Using his hand, Kaen hooked Pammon's snout and moved his face before his. "I love you, Pammon. I'm unsure how to describe the love or what it is, but I am thankful your mother hid you where she did."

Pammon put his forehead against Kaen's and trilled.

I love you as well.

58

Honest Feelings

Did you tell him yet?

No, let me set the mood. I don't want to just drop something like that on him.

Fine, but I think he will be really excited when you do.

Later. I promise. For now, just let me know if you see anything. I really wish I could fly with you and help, but we both know I wouldn't see anything.

And the fact you would need heavier clothes up here. Hess told you that, remember?

Kaen grumbled to himself and focused on where he and Hess were going on the road. It had split to the east yesterday, leaving the path north he had gone on his first quest. The woods here were just as overgrown, making it easy to see the occasional trail something or someone had cut into them. Hess mentioned that people entered these woods for different reasons. Sometimes quests for gathering alchemy supplies and other times for ones like what they were doing now.

After two hours of little conversation and constant updates from Pammon, Kaen slowed his horse and fell into position next to Hess. "So there's something I wanted to tell you."

Hess cocked his head and raised an eyebrow. "That sounds ominous."

Chuckling, Kaen shrugged. "I know last night I had you pretty worried, and I understand why," Kaen stated as he stared down the road. "I want you to know I know why you acted how you did."

Holding his reins loosely, Kaen turned his head and smiled at Hess. "Pammon and I talked for a bit last night; he is smarter than me. He wanted me to tell you something, and I figure now is the best time."

"You're dancing around this like you did with the girl on the floor the other night. Just spit it out already," Hess declared with a frustrated tone.

"I need you to build or help me build a harness or some sort of rein system for Pammon. I don't want any accidents while I fly, and I don't want you to be worried about something bad happening to me. Pammon also told me that once we have something like that working, he would be honored if you would let him take you flying one day."

Hess jerked in his saddle in surprise. The frustrated look on his face was gone, replaced by complete shock. "Pammon says he wants to fly with me?" Hess asked in disbelief.

Kaen nodded and smiled. "He says you're family," Kaen answered with a wink. "Distant family, but still family. This is his way of saying thank you for letting me bond with him, caring for both of us, and loving me."

"I mean, it's my job to care for both of you and to . . . " Hess froze for a moment as he saw the smile on Kaen's face.

"I know you love me," Kaen admitted. "I love you too. We have occasionally spoken about it, but I realized I have never told you the one thing I should have. I was wrong for those times I yelled at you and reminded you that I'm not your son and you are not my dad. I was wrong. You have been the greatest father I could imagine these past years. You loved, disciplined, forgave, and taught me to be the man I am trying to be. Pammon was right when he said my dad didn't just pick you because you were his friend. He picked you because he knew your heart. He chose you out of everyone else because he knew you would love me like a father."

Kaen wiped a tear that had formed in his eye and blinked a little wider to hold off the others trying to form. He smiled when he saw Hess struggling with the same thing.

"I would be honored for you to tell people I am your son. I look forward to telling others that I love you as my father."

Hess's horse just kept plodding along as Hess gazed at Kaen, no longer able to hold back the tears. He smiled and moved his horse over enough that he could reach over and pat Kaen on the shoulder.

"I cannot tell you how much that means to me. Would you do me a favor?"

Kaen nodded and smiled. "Anything."

Hess sniffed the mucus that was in his nose back up and smiled. "Tell Pammon I have been waiting for him to let me fly with him."

A brief pause followed as what Hess had just said registered in Kaen's brain. He scowled and grunted at Hess, seeing the grin on Hess's face. "You're a bastard, you know that!" he declared with a huff.

Roaring with laughter, Hess nodded and shrugged. "What does that make you then, son? A son of a bastard?"

Kaen let out a giant breath and gave Hess the middle finger before chuckling. "This is why I can't be serious with you," complained Kaen.

"I know, but we both know if I didn't joke with you about this right now, I would be blubbering like a baby."

Sighing, Kaen nodded. He would have been too.

I think I found something, but there are maybe two camps. I have been scouting this area for a while, and there is a camp closer to the road and a camp deeper in the forest. The one near the road has tents, and the other has an actual house, a building of some sort, and a lot of carts and animals. It appears they have cut down trees and even built some walls around part of it.

After Kaen relayed that information to Hess, they looked at the map and where Kaen pointed to. "It's close enough. We could be near it by nightfall, but I would rather find a place to sleep and approach in the morning," Hess informed Kaen. "Ask Pammon to see if there are any clearings near the camps he found."

Hess wants to know if there are any other clearings near the camps you found.

There are plenty. There are smaller ones within a mile or two of the one with buildings. The others are a few miles away. From up here, I would guess perhaps they move around those clearings.

"Pammon believes they are rotating between the clearings he has found but have a camp way back in the forest with structures they built."

Hess grunted and readjusted himself on his saddle. Kaen could tell he was not excited about that news.

"Ask him how many people he thinks there are, but don't spend much time on that right now. Something feels real off about what he is describing, and I believe we may be in over our heads."

"What do you mean?"

"Consider what the guild quest said. There might be around ten bandits out here. How long would it take to build what you said Pammon described? How many people would it take to clear out a section, build a wall, and construct those buildings? This feels like how your orc quest went. Not enough information or incorrect information."

They rode for a few more minutes in silence. Kaen struggled to understand what Hess was hinting at, but he wondered if his test information was wrong.

"If what you say is true, are you implying that someone within the guild is giving out wrong information or incomplete information? Or are you implying someone might be intentionally doing either of those?"

"I cannot answer those questions yet," explained Hess. "Until we actually figure out what we are dealing with and how bad this is, I am left wondering how many adventurers before us died trying to complete this quest. That scares me because that also means the bandits are skilled."

I can feel something is wrong. What is it that has you so worried?

Kaen focused on his heart and took a few breaths, working on calming himself down.

Hess wants to know how many people there are in those two camps, if possible. He said not to spend too much time finding out, though. Once you get a quick glance, come back to us and stay above us.

This request makes me worry, but I will do what Hess wants.

Pammon was worried, and Kaen could sense that it was more than his usual amount.

The good news is we get another night together, and after we finish this quest, we will spend an extra day or two just getting to spend time together. If things feel right, Hess, as agreed, won't freak out about us flying again. So, let's focus on our quest and look forward to enjoying our time together.

Pammon's worry was replaced quickly with the thoughts of them flying together, and Kaen smiled at knowing Pammon was feeling better.

Don't think I am unaware of what you just did. I completely expect you to spend more than five minutes in the air next time.

I cannot wait for that either!

Hess was poking the fire he had started, still having not spoken for a few minutes as he considered the information Pammon had told Kaen earlier.

I am having trouble understanding why Hess is so upset. I know it is not directed at us.

The guild told us there were maybe ten bandits, and you told us there appears to be closer to twenty. That number is a lot higher, and based on the facts Hess knows about this quest, it means they must have a solid group that isn't stupid. I think he is trying to decide if we should return to town and get more people. The problem is, if we report that many people, they will want to know how we found out and why we did nothing. We still need to wait a few days, as it would take days for someone to scout that out safely.

And you cannot just say 'because my dragon told me.'

Kaen chuckled and shook his head. Pammon thrummed, laughing at his own joke.

"I guess I should ask what is so funny, as I could use a change in my temperament," Hess declared without looking at the two of them.

Kaen glanced at Hess again, watching him sit on the rock he had moved for a seat near the fire. He had resisted the invitation to sit against Pammon, feeling instead he would think better alone for a few.

"Pammon said we could just tell the guild that we got all our information from him."

Hess chuckled for a few seconds before sighing and tossing the stick he had been holding into the fire. "I wish we could do that, Pammon. It would make things a lot easier for just a moment, but I also know it would make life impossible for Kaen and you as well."

Hess turned around as he spoke and joined them, scratching Pammon's scales as he walked into the small area Pammon called his *scratching circle*.

Trills rose as Hess scratched him for a few, a smile appearing quickly as Hess let the worry he had slip away and enjoyed the moment.

"Pammon, I have said it many times. Kaen needs to get more experience under his belt and understand how all this *adventurer* stuff works before you two have to deal with the dragon-riding side of things. Once you two are announced, everything will change."

Hess slid down against Pammon and dropped his butt to the ground in the clearing. "If you want to start that school we discussed, you must have things in place before Pammon, as that would change everything. This means meeting with the king and other nobles as well."

"Are you saying if I waited to attempt that until after I announced Pammon and me, people wouldn't help?"

Sucking air in through his teeth, Hess shook his head. "Oh, I have no doubts many would be even more interested in helping out, which is the cause for my concern. You want to have people who are willing to help before that news because then you know they are helping for better reasons than simply earning the *favor* of you and Pammon. Remember, there hasn't been a new Dragon Rider in two or three generations. Most dragons have disappeared or been hunted down."

Pammon shifted at that news. He never understood why people would hunt him.

"As always, my focus is on getting you two as prepared as possible so that both of you are stronger. The stronger you two are, the more people will think before they consider doing something stupid."

Kaen gently rubbed the scales at the top of Pammon's snout. He could feel Pammon's breath against his legs, since Pammon had his head on the ground beside him.

"I know. You had asked what we were laughing about, so I told you. Now tell me the plan for tomorrow."

59

First Quest Part 1

With Pammon's help, Kaen's guidance, and a lot of patience from Hess, they managed to draw what Pammon had seen from the sky.

The main camp with the buildings appeared to have over ten people living and working there. Pammon had mentioned he was unsure how many more might be in the buildings but counted what he could see. The other small camp closer to the road had eight people.

A steady stream of merchants and other people had traveled along the main road as they had made their way out here. Merchants had hired more guards, and people were traveling in larger groups. Hess had commented the previous day that people understood the risks and were doing what they could to make them less of an opportunity to be attacked.

They had set out as the sun had begun to climb into the sky. Kaen's horse had been timid this morning when he'd approached. Hess had stated they could *smell* or *sense* Pammon's presence on him. That is why he had kept them in the woods outside the clearing.

They were only about thirty minutes away from the clearing with the small camp. Pammon was giving Kaen updates every so often.

"This feels just like a quest with your father," Hess grunted as they moved through the woods. "Doing something, my gut tells me we shouldn't, praying it all works out."

Kaen wanted to chuckle, but he wasn't sure if he was supposed to. "It always worked out, though. Right?"

Hess just shrugged and kept moving through the brush. He was almost impossible to hear, even wearing a full set of chain armor as he moved through the forest. He had his shield out and only one hammer right now. Kaen had been surprised to see him pack it on his horse but understood a good shield might be useful if he had to draw the attention of everyone.

"*Worked out* is a weird way of describing things. If you mean stuff always went elf tits up, then yes, everything always worked out."

"I'm sorry, I never understood that phrase," Kaen interrupted. "What does *elf tits up* mean?"

Hess's body started to shake, and Kaen realized as he followed him that he was laughing quietly.

"Oh," Hess answered with a sigh. "I guess you wouldn't know about that yet. It is because female elves' tits always stay perky and point out. No one knows how or why, but it has been that way for thousands of years."

Kaen felt his eyes going wide, and he smiled. "Should I—"

"No," Hess declared, interrupting him. "For now, focus on the task at hand. Worry about breasts another time."

How do things look from up there? Any changes?

Only five people at the camp that I can see. They are doing small chores, and one more might be leaving soon as it appears they are packing things into a backpack. The other three left early this morning for the road.

Hess had believed they were sending scouting parties out on the road, most likely riding in each direction to see if there were any soft targets and to prepare for it. His concern was that there would be teams of scouts traveling days in each direction, which meant there were more than the number of bandits Pammon had counted. There had to be a brilliant person leading all of this.

How far away are we?

With how slow you walk, it will be days . . . or a little longer. You are about as far from Hess's farm was to Minoosh.

A twinge of homesickness hit him, but Kaen still chuckled. He knew they were easily within twenty minutes. Pammon had started figuring out better ways to describe how far they were from something by using distances he knew well.

"We are about as far from the bandit's camp as we would be from your farm to Minoosh."

Coughing for a few seconds, Hess turned, looked at Kaen, and rolled his eyes. "He is killing me with that one."

Kaen smiled. "Stealth mode time, I guess?"

"Yeah. From here, no more talking, and stay behind me. Remember the calls if I use one."

Moving through a forest while trying to be quiet was not difficult when Hess set the path to follow. Kaen had asked Hess how high his stealth had been years ago, and he'd just replied with a *high enough*. It seemed impossible that he could move so quietly and smoothly in that armor of his.

You are right on the edge of the opening, and there are only four at the camp, as you will soon see.

Kaen tsked quietly two times, causing Hess to pause his movements and glance back at him.

Holding up four fingers, he motioned to the direction they were headed. Hess nodded and started moving toward the clearing.

The trees here were a different type of hardwood than the ones where he had fought the orcs. They were wide around the base with a bark that one could easily pull off. These trees had been here for hundreds of years, according to Hess. A problem was the ten to twenty-foot gaps between the trees. It allowed for moving through them quickly but provided a limited hiding area. The needles they dropped carpeted the forest floor, making it easier to sneak around quietly in the woods.

Less than twenty yards later, Kaen could see a few tents, all in rows and laid out in order. No one was visible yet, but he could tell where they were from Pammon's watchful eye.

Leading them to a tree closer to the edge of the clearing, Hess motioned for Kaen to keep low and pull out his bow.

Crouching, they made their way to the base of the tree and scouted the clearing.

Three men and a woman were managing chores in the middle of the camp. A good twenty-yard ring of clear space was between the first tent and the tree line. They had obviously prepared to be ready for anyone who came near them.

On the north side of the camp, two men were swinging axes, chopping wood, and tossing them into a pile. Both were topless, and Kaen could see they were accustomed to hard work, their upper bodies tanned and rippling with muscles from manual labor. They were laughing and joking as they cut log after log.

A woman was working on something at a table in the middle of the camp while the last person was not far away, chopping and preparing food for a pot near him.

"Pammon still hasn't seen the ones who left, has he?" Hess asked softly.

Kaen shook his head. "He can scout the road or the other camp if you want, but then we won't have any vision here."

Hess nodded, frustrated by the knowledge that the guild was completely wrong about how many were involved. If they left and returned, they could bring enough help, but the fact that someone might be robbed or killed in that time left a bad taste in his mouth.

"Can you take out those two in the center of camp? That would leave us with the other two to the north," Hess said.

"And Pammon? Want him to come down and be close?"

"Not yet. The vision is more important. Worst case, we make a getaway, and he covers us. He is our secret weapon if things go south."

Kaen nodded, pulled two arrows out, and nocked them to the string of his bow. He sighed knowing what was about to take place. Hess had spent half an hour talking about what it meant to take a human life. "It will be a tough shot, but I am confident I can hit them both."

"Can you kill them both at the same time?"

Kaen gazed over the distance between him and the two in the center of camp. The breeze here was steady to the east. It was not blowing that hard, but the distance was slightly over fifty yards. He was at the range where body mass was more important than a risky head or neck shot.

"I'll do what I can, but it's going to be tough to promise. I'm using two piercing arrows to make sure wherever I hit bleeds."

Hess nodded and shifted his shield and mace. "When you're ready. I'll shout to let you know whether we rush or stay low and go slow."

It's starting.

Kaen took a few deep breaths, trying to get his lifestone to assist him. After the third breath and no reaction from his lifestone, he knew he was on his own. One day, he would figure out how to activate it.

Hess inched forward, using his shield to provide cover as Kaen stepped out from behind the tree, his bow raised and the two arrows pointed toward the middle of the camp.

Kaen knew he wouldn't have a lot of time to stand there, holding the bow drawn. Even with Hess providing a little cover with the shield, if someone paid much attention to that side of the clearing, he had nowhere to hide.

The woman was standing sideways, providing a smaller target than the man currently lost in his butchering of something, his back providing a massive target.

With his breath held, Kaen focused on both of them, feeling the skill he was about to use, directing his aim and adjusting for the wind.

Both arrows moved the second his fingers left the string, each traveling quickly across the open space. There was an arch in his shot because of the distance. As both arrows quickly fell, Hess was already moving, and Kaen had pulled out another arrow.

The first arrow hit the woman in her arm, ripping through it and into her side. She let out a scream, and Kaen knew it had pierced the bone in her arm when he saw how it deflected and came out of her side.

The second arrow was a better shot, piercing the man's spinal column halfway up his back, causing him to fall down immediately as it ran through his body.

The woman's scream alerted the two men who were chopping wood, and they turned, trying to see why their member was crying out.

Hess had maneuvered and was rushing the camp, using the tent to block their view of him as he ran, bent over slightly.

They are grabbing weapons! One has a shield and sword, and the other has a bow like you!

Never missing a step, Kaen ran behind Hess, knowing he needed to stay behind him for now.

"Turtle!" Kaen called out, informing Hess of his plan.

Hess had gone over so many things with him about today and the need for small words that both knew and could react to.

They had cleared the open ground and were now among the tents and other small furniture pieces these bandits had set up for lounging on. Hess was making his way to the woman who appeared to be struggling to stand up. As he crashed through their outer ring of things, the woman turned, shocked, and saw Hess closing the distance quickly. He was only seconds away from reaching her.

Her right hand, which had been clutching her left shoulder, started to radiate fire. She snarled at him as she turned sideways and prepared to unleash her attack upon him.

Hess chuckled the moment the woman began to turn, hefting his weapon at her, watching as her eyes went wide and her face lost its unpleasant look.

His massive mace caught her right in her chest, knocking her back and causing the spell she had begun to cast to launch off in the direction of the tents.

Hess wasted no movement after throwing his weapon, reaching his hand to his back during his next stride, and freeing his other weapon.

Kaen followed Hess, having seen him toss his mace but not seeing it hit.

"Eleven and one!" shouted Hess as he knocked over a table and sent papers and other things flying.

The sound of an arrow striking Hess's shield rang out as he pulled it up enough to block what was coming.

Dashing to his left, Kaen saw the archer pivoting to their left, grabbing an arrow and preparing to shoot again.

Kaen lifted his bow and let it fly the moment he had a clear shot between the tents and Hess.

It flashed across the space, and Kaen almost tripped when he saw the man suddenly twist his body and dodge the arrow mere moments before it would have struck him on the side.

"Focus one!" Hess called out, seeing what the man had done, preparing for the man with the sword who was seconds away from him.

Kaen quickly moved back behind Hess and positioned himself on his other side. His mouth went dry, realizing someone had just dodged an arrow he knew he could not.

How tough can these guys be?

60

First Quest Part 2

The clash of sword and shield versus mace and shield was one that left much to be desired.

The man charged Hess, moving into a series of swings designed to easily cut and disarm an opponent. He had started to move to Hess's right side until he saw Kaen pointing an arrow in his direction, then he quickly fixed the error of his step. Being left-handed gave him no shield on the side Kaen was on.

No one ever wanted to give an archer a free shot at them, just like he had been trying to do with Hess and his partner.

When Hess swung his mace, and the man lifted his sword to block the blow, the strength discrepancy between the two of them became extremely evident. Hess's weapon shattered the man's sword in half, continuing to the man's shoulder and chest, driving him to the ground and popping him like a pimple. His cry of pain and agony lasted only a moment before his entire left side was flattened completely.

The archer is turning to run!

Keep your eyes on him so I can track him!

Hess lifted his shield, blocking the arrow the man had fired as he began to run. "Get him!" Hess shouted, maneuvering around the camp items blocking his path.

Leaping onto the table the woman had been working at, Kaen tracked the man and saw he was faster than anyone he had seen run before. If men like this were doing evil, the world would be in a bad spot, and countless people would suffer. It angered Kaen, knowing one would do this.

As if his lifestone had waited all this time for him to ask for its help, the rage he felt at these bandits, and something else he could not figure out yet, caused it to react with a power he had not felt before.

It consumed him, and without thought, it took his body over.

Arrow after arrow suddenly disappeared from his bow. Before Kaen had realized it, five arrows were gone, each on a different path, with a different angle, yet all were closing in on the man simultaneously.

It was as if the man had a sixth sense, dodging quickly to the right as an arrow was about to hit him, only to be struck by one in his right shoulder, and then stumbling and taking a second arrow to his leg. As he crashed to the ground, the fourth arrow found his other leg, and when he could finally cry out in pain and skidded across the ground, the fifth and final arrow pierced his back.

[Archery Skill Increased]

The man lay still. Kaen breathed a sigh of relief when no more noise or movement came from him after a few seconds. A few seconds after he relaxed, he fell down on the table. His body felt weak and tired.

That was amazing! How did you do that?!

The bond told him that Pammon was overjoyed.

It wasn't me. It was my lifestone. I didn't even know that was possible.

It was incredible. I could barely keep up with how fast you moved! Relax a minute. I need to go scout!

Hess slowed down his charge and snapped back around to look at Kaen in shock. "Are you level thirty already?" he gasped as he glanced around the clearing, ensuring no one else was coming.

Kaen shook his head and saw he was sitting in the blood the woman had left on the table. He took a moment and, after a few breaths, felt his body return to normal. Sliding off the table, he saw Hess making his way to check the bodies near them.

"It . . . it was my lifestone. It took my body over," Kaen muttered as he tried to think about what happened. "Usually, I surrender to it. This time, it never waited on me. Instead, it took control of me."

Hess grunted, and after confirming that the woman and the man Kaen had first shot were dead, he secured his second mace and retrieved his first one, cleaning it off on the woman's clothes.

"That's impossible," Hess stated as he finished wiping off his weapon before attaching it to his hip. "That was the level thirty skill for archery. You shouldn't have access to that yet!"

"I did get a point in archery after it, so now I am twenty-six."

Hess let out a sigh and shook his head. "You ok? You have a weird look on your face."

Kaen sighed and pointed at the bodies on the ground. "I tried to tell myself they were bad. It wasn't easy to think of them the way I think of goblins or orcs.

They are still people. Bad, thieving, and sometimes killing, but still people. Once they attacked, I knew your life and mine were in danger. I put that thought in my mind, but after it was over and I found myself sitting in that woman's blood, it hit me. Does it get easier? Is it bad if it does?"

Hess came closer to Kaen and put his hand on his shoulder. He squeezed it like he had done countless times. "It never gets *easier,* but you can deal with it," Hess answered softer than usual. "Death is not something we want to think about. Killing a person is not glamorous. This is another one of the ugly sides of adventuring. Everything you are experiencing is normal, and anytime I can help with these problems, I will."

Kaen put his hand on Hess's, gave it a tap, and smiled. "I'm good now. It bothered me some, but I focused on the bad they were doing, and it helped me push through that concern. I also think that might be what made my lifestone act like that."

Giving one more shoulder squeeze, Hess moved back and finished securing a few last items he had. "Let's not worry about this right now, if you believe you are ok. Help me collect these papers, then let's see what we can find on these bandits. Pammon is scouting, right?"

Kaen nodded. "As soon as they were dead, he took off as you instructed."

"Good. That scream might have been heard."

Stacks of papers were collected and secured in a small pouch on the table when Kaen returned from looting the bodies.

"That guy had a lot of jewelry," Kaen stated as he dropped a pouch on the table. "Did you see him dodge my arrow? How could he do that?"

Hess picked up the pouch Kaen had put down and hooked it to his belt. "You break his bow?"

Kaen nodded that he had.

"Good. We don't have time to deal with their equipment, and I would venture his bow was magical."

"How did you know there would be a black spot on his chest?"

Folding his arms across his chest, Hess grunted. "He had a lifestone. When a person with one dies, it dissolves and leaves a black mark on their chest. It is how we know when we are dealing with people who are dangerous."

"Should I ask about the other three?"

"The female owned one also. I had no doubt once I saw her casting magic. Only elves can cast magic without a lifestone, and even then, they are limited in power," explained Hess. "The one you killed was just an average person, like the man with the sword."

Kaen grabbed the documents and put them in between his armor and his chest. "How common is this? I thought lifestones were rare?"

Hess nodded and glanced around the clearing once more. "Eight years ago, they were. The amount of magic and ingredients required to make one, limited them to only the richest or those able to earn them via other methods. If these many bandits have them, then business must be really good for them, or they are finding a different source."

Kaen started to ask another question, but Hess held up his hand, cutting him off.

"We need to move. I want to check out their main camp and see what we can learn about them. Get Pammon to focus on the main camp."

Kaen closed his mouth and nodded. He had another dozen questions, at least, he needed answers for.

We are going to head to the other camp. Hess wants you to focus on that area. Has anything happened since our fight?

No. I have been bored flying circles while I watch you two loot bodies and the people in their camp move boxes out of the building and into wagons.

Are they moving boxes into wagons?

Yes. Right now, at least six people have been moving boxes for the last hour into three wagons. I did not realize that was important, or I would have mentioned it.

You are fine! Great work, and keep me updated if something changes.

"We need to go!" Kaen exclaimed as he pointed in the direction the other camp was in. "Pammon says they are loading three wagons with boxes. They must be planning on moving out soon!"

Hess grinned and nodded. "Remind me to give Pammon a few extra scratches tonight," Hess blurted out as he started jogging toward the other camp. "This is exactly what we need right now!"

Slow down. You two are almost on top of the western wall. No one is keeping a watch right now. Two people occasionally come out of the house and talk to another person who disappears inside the building for a while. The same six people are still moving boxes, but they are almost done.

Are there any other people in camp right now besides those?

Not moving, but I know there were more the other day. Perhaps they are sleeping or hunting?

You are probably right, as always. Hess told me to remind you we may need help if we end up fighting. Remember to be safe and hit hard if you have to come.

"Pammon says they are all either in the house, building, or moving boxes. A few are missing, but he isn't sure if they are hunting or sleeping."

Hess nodded and slowed down. Pammon was supposed to tell them when they were close, so now the tough decisions were about to take place.

* * *

Ten minutes later, they were staring at the wall that had been erected around the western side. It appeared to run around the whole camp, even though they knew it did not. Massive ten-foot sections of trees were cut and buried in the dirt, lashed together with solid technique.

The same twenty yards of clearing were here as well. Whoever was in charge of this operation was meticulous.

"Do you want to go around the wall to the south and see if we can find a way in?" Kaen asked.

Hess motioned for Kaen to follow him a little deeper into the woods. "Let's scout and see what it looks like first. This setup scares me, and I am close to deciding we need to go back to Ebonmount."

Skirting through the trees, they found the edge of the wall that ran a good seventy-plus yards along the southwestern side. It suddenly stopped, and there was about a fifty-yard gap between it and the south end of camp.

"That seems weird," Kaen stated as he motioned to the opening. "The trees back here are not any less dense, and it doesn't look like anyone has actually moved around back here."

Hess nodded and pointed to a spot of dirt that was just a tad higher than the rest of the forest ground. "I'd bet money that is a trap," Hess grumbled. "The person who is in charge is dangerous. That is evident."

As they made it through the woods and near the west side wall, they could hear shouting and horses being moved inside.

Are they hitching horses up to the cart?

They just started. I was about to tell you once I knew they were doing that.

"They are doing what it sounds like. He says they are preparing the carts now."

"We need to move now, then!" Hess exclaimed and motioned to the woods up north. "Have Pammon keep an eye out for them. We need to find the trail and set up an ambush."

We are going to look for their path through the woods. Do you have any idea where it is?

Kaen sensed Pammon as he glided near the clouds and felt his gaze sweeping over the woods. After a few moments, his gaze returned to an area northeast of them.

I think it is where I am looking now. The trees are split enough that carts might go through there.

You are amazing, Pammon! Let me know if things change!

"I think I know where their trail is," Kaen declared as he tapped his temple. "Let's move!"

* * *

Dashing through the forest, Kaen found the area Pammon occasionally kept looking at, directing him to it as if a beacon fire was going.

As they drew near where Pammon had led them, Hess slowed Kaen, checking for potential traps. When none were found, Hess slowly exited a small clearing that weaved between the trees. Bending down, he glanced at the ground and shook his head in shock once he started moving some of the needles from the trees.

"Magic . . . it has to be magic," he muttered under his breath.

"What did you say?"

"It has to be magic. That is how they hide their tracks," Hess explained, motioning for Kaen to come closer. "Look at this here. A scout would have never found these if Pammon had not led us here by noticing the path through the trees."

Kaen bent down and saw what Hess was pointing to. Small ruts for a wagon were in the ground, almost completely gone. The way the needles from the tree had fallen had almost hidden them completely.

"So you think there is another magic-user in this group?"

Hess nodded and slowly put the needles back where they had been. "We need to move and decide what we will do and fast."

"What if we—"

You need to hide! They are climbing onto the wagons and appear to be moving out! Pammon shouted through their connection.

"We need to move! They are coming!"

61

First Quest Part 3

They are just a few minutes away from you two. The three carts are spread out, but two people are on each cart. The rest of the people have stayed back in the camp.

"They will be here soon, three carts, two people in each. Pammon says another may be leaving the camp soon."

Hess nodded as he checked the few lone bushes he had moved along the path. He knew it would be a mess fighting in these woods, and not knowing who these people were or what skills they possessed or if they had lifestones, made planning an attack difficult.

"Odds are the first wagon and the last will have the strongest people. There will be at least one or two ranged people, and I must trust you with handling them. As you engage the last, I will spring the trap on the first cart. Run if you need to, and call Pammon if you must. This will not be an easy fight, I am afraid," Hess said.

Kaen grunted and saw the look of concern on Hess's face. Why were they still doing this quest if he felt it was this dangerous?

Hess started to move ahead from the spot he had created for Kaen. Two shooting lanes between trees only forty-five yards from the trail they would follow, gave him a few good options. The bushes Hess had moved gave him a little more cover when he took that first shot. None of the bandits should be worried about an attack here, but that did not mean they could expect things to go as planned.

Just as the sounds of horses and carts echoed through the woods, Pammon started to call out.

The carts are almost upon you, and someone has left the camp on a

horse in the direction of the clearing where you killed all those people. They should reach it very quickly.

"Orc tits," Kaen muttered to himself. This plan was going to get screwed quickly.

Be ready to help us. I'm not sure how these woods are going to treat you if I need you.

I told you I have been practicing chasing food. I will be fine in these trees once I am in them. I will begin my descent.

The first cart came into view through the trees, and Kaen could make out the two men sitting on the front bench, lazily chatting as one handled the reins. Neither appeared to be paying any attention to the woods as they moved a cart stacked high with crates and a tarp over it between the trees.

How many people have they robbed? Kaen was flustered to see what looked like a seven or eight-foot-tall stack of stolen goods running the length of a twelve-foot-long cart.

As they got close enough that he could make out details like their hair color and the leather armor they were wearing, the second cart started appearing through the trees. Kaen glanced at the second group and then turned his attention back to the first set. They were well-developed men, and he now saw the shield and sword on the cart of the man closest to him. According to Hess, he was the one with the reins, which most likely meant the other man had a bow or some range attack.

A new voice joined the din of their traveling, and Kaen could now see the second set of bandits as they came into view. One was a female wearing leather armor and holding the reins, and the other was some guy in normal clothes, talking up a storm at his riding partner. It appeared she was not interested in the conversation, as her eyes never seemed to move from the trail ahead of them.

When they got closer, Kaen realized neither of them had a weapon showing, which might have seemed weird if not for Hess's earlier explanation that often the weakest might end up in the middle. That did not mean it was true, but there was a chance of it.

As the two carts rolled by, Kaen realized something was wrong with Hess's plan. The carts were too far apart. If he sprung the trap he had planned, the third cart would not be in range, and the group would not be bunched up as they had hoped.

This is not looking good, Pammon. How far away are you?

It will be at least a minute. I will come down faster. The one who left for the other camp will be there about when I get to you. I won't be able to see them in a few moments.

Hess was right . . . this plan is about to go elf tits up . . .

Confusion over the statement reverberated through the bond.

I don't understand what that means . . . but I also don't think I need to. Stay safe. I will protect you both if it goes badly.

Cursing to himself, Kaen pulled two arrows out, knowing what he needed to do.

Please . . . please work. I can't let Hess or Pammon get hurt.

Taking two deep breaths, Kaen willed his lifestone to help him. This shot had to work. The second cart would be out of position, and if it did not work, things would definitely go *tits up*.

Slowly rising to his feet, lifting the bow in the air, and preparing to release his shot, his lifestone pulsed gently. Not a raging torrent it had earlier but just a small faint trickle of acknowledgment. It was as if it knew how important this shot was and why it was important.

Kaen grinned as he moved his bow slightly to the right, before turning it a hair to the left, the tips up just a fraction of space. All those things happened because he felt his lifestone telling him, or maybe showing him, how to make the shot he needed.

The arrows flew between the trees. Death was in the air the moment his fingers gently slid from the white bowstring. He wanted to watch the arrows fly but knew he needed to prepare for his next targets, who were slowly coming up the trail.

As he pulled an arrow from his quiver, the sound in the woods from the man who had not stopped talking abruptly ended. No screams or shouts had come from either of them.

[Archery Skill Increased]

"Thank you," Kaen whispered as he took another small breath. There was so much he didn't understand about lifestones, but he hoped to know why his acted differently than Hess's or everyone else's in time.

Looking at the second cart, Kaen saw the damage he had caused. The man and the woman were dead, arrows protruding from their skulls. The woman had not even dropped the reins, keeping the horses following the trail and the other cart.

Ten seconds later, shouting and screaming horses rang out through the woods from the first cart.

Kaen glanced at the second cart, seeing it starting to diverge as the horses came up on the first cart that had stopped.

The people from the third cart started yelling, and Kaen heard a whip cracking, sparking a neigh from the horses at the end of the strike.

Hess is moving toward the cart he stopped from the side. It does not appear they have seen him yet!

There was no time to worry about Hess. Hess could handle two men on his own. Kaen had to deal with the next two.

The third cart coming quickly down the road. One man was standing holding a bow with an arrow ready to fire, scanning the woods and trying to see what the commotion was.

"Finn! Bruce! What in blazes is going on!" the man with the bow shouted as they rumbled down the path. "Trinity! Someone!"

They were still too far for a clean shot, but Kaen knew they would be in range in just a few seconds. The second cart was almost at a stop now as the horses were running up against the backside of the cart.

"Something's wrong!" the man with the bow declared loud enough for Kaen to hear over the noises of fighting now breaking out from the first cart. "I'm getting Mel!"

The bowman jumped off the cart on the far side, disappearing from Kaen's view.

Pammon one is running back to the camp to get help! Can you get him?

Glee . . . it had to be glee flooded through their bond.

Finally, something for me to do! Pammon declared as Kaen sensed him diving faster toward the trees.

"That poor guy," Kaen whispered to the tree he was leaning against. "I don't envy him."

The last cart kept coming, and Kaen could clearly make out the driver, who was holding the reins in both hands as the horses thundered down the trail. He appeared to be cursing to himself, as his lips were moving, but no sound was coming out.

With the man distracted, Kaen released an arrow, aiming for his chest. It flew true, but as Kaen watched it, waiting for it to pierce the man's chest, it suddenly ricocheted in a different direction a few feet before striking the man.

The driver yanked on the reins, his head snapping in Kaen's direction.

"Shite!" Kaen cursed out loud as he reached for another arrow, realizing he had been an idiot for standing still and watching. He moved behind the tree and tried to create distance from the driver of the cart.

Kaen heard the horses whinny from their reins being jerked, and a few seconds after he had disappeared behind the tree, massive chunks of it exploded on the other side, flying in different directions, causing the tree to crack and pop.

Shards exploded from the tree. The distance he had taken from it protected him from most of the wooden pieces that flew out, but a few still struck him, cutting his face and neck as he raised his arm, trying to block them.

I need help, Pammon!

Kaen stumbled as he ran toward another tree a few yards behind, realizing how bad of a position he was in. That man had not been cursing. He had been casting some shield spell, waiting to discover where any possible attackers might be. This was much worse than fighting the goblins or orcs had been. These people were smart!

Another explosion rocked the tree again, and the sound of it cracking and falling made Kaen glance back, thankful to see it was going to fall away from him and toward the south.

I am almost on the one running. I can't change direction! Give me a minute, and I will be there!

Gulping, Kaen used his shoulder to wipe the blood flowing from his forehead as he ran. He hoped he had a minute, as this guy was way stronger than he had imagined possible.

Dodging behind the tree he had been aiming for, Kaen kept moving, not being stupid enough to stay behind it lest the caster blew it up like the first.

He tried to run while glancing behind him, looking to see if the man was gaining on him or flanking him. His vision was muddled from blood and sweat that poured down his forehead. *How bad did I get cut?*

When he glanced back, he saw the man moving to the north. The man held up his hands, and Kaen dove to the south, using the tree as a shield. The ground he had been standing on erupted a second later from whatever attack the mage was using, tossing up dirt, needles, and hidden rocks and roots. A two-foot hole was smoldering on the ground when Kaen rolled to his feet.

Turning to prepare a shot, he saw his arrow had broken from the move he had just made.

Another explosion rocketed the ground on his left, leaving another gaping wound in the earth and pelting him with more rocks and dirt. The caster had attacked that side, perhaps hoping Kaen would have run without pausing.

A sense of success and excitement came from Pammon.

I'm on my way!

Kaen knew he had just taken out the runner, but he could also feel where Pammon was, and it seemed so far away at the moment. His chest was pounding as he drew an arrow.

Slowly he backed up, keeping the tree between him and that caster. He had not seen the man in those last few seconds, and Kaen wondered what he could be doing. Was he approaching? Waiting to see where Kaen might pop out from and attack?

The man's spells seemed to be instant, and it bothered Kaen that he had not done any research on how magic worked. It was hard to know how many spells a person could cast; this man seemed as strong as Luca.

Luca . . .

That name caused an eruption of emotions to explode within Kaen. Luca had died for him because Luca believed that he would be great. Dying here would mean Luca's sacrifice had been in vain, and Kaen would not allow that.

His lifestone began to pulse harder and stronger within his chest. A connection with Luca he had not known existed.

Kaen's eyes ignored the blood that was blurring his vision. No longer did the pain he had been ignoring even register. He planted his feet, holding the bow steady.

He was done running.

62

First Quest Part 4

Time felt like it was barely moving as Kaen held the bow fully drawn. Doing so was not something most could hold for very long, but his body didn't feel tired or weak at this moment. It was powerful, and he waited like an animal ready to pounce upon its prey.

I'm coming! Hold on!

Pammon's frantic voice didn't faze him. Time was on his side, and death was in his hands. The moment he saw the opportunity to strike, it would fly from him, destroying what it must.

An eruption exploded closer to the tree in the ground. A few seconds later, another explosion happened on the other side, a few feet past the first.

He's trying to scare me.

The mage didn't know where Kaen was, and he was hoping to flush him out. What could that man be experiencing as he waited for Kaen to move? Was he scared?

I am looking right at where the man will be. He is focused on me, but he is a magic-user. If I see him, I will shoot.

I can feel the power flowing through you right now . . . your lifestone?

Kaen wanted to reply, but he felt his lifestone flickering. How many seconds had it been? Was there a limit to how long it could stay like this?

Shaking his head slightly, Kaen focused on what had started all this.

Remember Luca and his sacrifice. He died so that I can stop men like these!

Power surged again through him as his lifestone seemed renewed. The key to what drove him was right here, and he knew it. Kaen just needed to figure out the name for it.

I see him!

Kaen saw him or felt him, somehow, through Pammon's eyes. He was a good twenty yards behind the tree, watching where he knew Kaen must be but occasionally checking to the north near the wagons. He was distracted, as the sound of fighting had died off.

He was backing up! Slowly, the man tried to move back, realizing he might be in a bad position.

I have him! Pammon declared as Kaen felt him weaving near the branches that were thirty or forty feet in the air. He could see Pammon maneuvering between the trees, coming in from behind the man, unaware of the impending doom.

A horse whined and snorted in fear as it spotted a dragon flying over them.

Kaen could sense and see the man turn toward Pammon, raising his hand and preparing to unleash magic.

Moving like lightning, Kaen leaped to the right, releasing the arrow when the tree no longer blocked his vision and sending the arrow into the man's back. The man jerked forward. His arms shot outward as Kaen's arrow poked through his chest, nicking the mage's heart.

Two balls of lightning flew from his hands, having been intended for Pammon, striking the trees on both sides of him. Large branches plummeted toward the forest floor, blown off the trees they were once a part of.

Pammon growled as he swooped down on the man, landing on him with his back claws and massive body, driving him into the ground, splattering the earth and Pammon's scales with blood.

Kaen ran toward Pammon, looking around through the trees and ensuring no one else was coming. "Are you ok?!" Kaen shouted as he watched Pammon bite off the man's head and swallow it with a growl.

I am fine, thanks to you. I am a fool for flying over the horses. I had not thought about them noticing me and alerting him to my presence. Had you not shot him, I am afraid he would have injured me. How did you know when to attack?

Reaching Pammon and checking on him, Kaen started to speak and then realized what he was about to say. "I saw through your eyes . . . I mean, I actually saw through your eyes," Kaen explained, shaking his head in disbelief. "I could see him facing me, backing up. I saw him turn around when the horses went crazy. I . . . I didn't know that was even possible."

Pammon snorted and licked his muzzle with his long tongue and shook his head.

That sounds like something we should be able to do. We will figure it out later. For now, how is Hess?

"Crap!" Kaen cursed as he drew another arrow and dashed toward the first cart. When he got close, he saw Hess sitting on the ground, tying a cloth around his massive calf, his chain mail pulled up to his knee. Kaen could see blood seeping through the cloth.

"Are you ok?!" Kaen called out as he ran to Hess.

"One minute, let me finish tying this stupid bandage," Hess muttered, cinching tight the white cloth. "Stupid archer got me with a dual shot. I'll be fine. It's merely a flesh wound."

Kaen shook his head in shock and heard the thrum of Pammon's laughter behind him. The horses started panicking as Pammon approached where the two of them were.

Perhaps I should back off and go scout? It appears everything is ok for now, and I need to find the man who was on the horse.

You are a genius! I had forgotten about him. I owe you a lot of scratches tonight after we finish with this mess.

I will hold you to that, Pammon replied, his excitement and joy of a battle won exuding from him.

Kaen watched as his dragon turned and moved away a bit before leaping off the ground, rising quickly in the air. While it was a tight fit, Pammon had really learned how to fly proficiently in the narrow collection of trunks and branches. Kaen realized he was holding his breath as Pammon dodged past the trunks and then disappeared behind the branches, sending a few small ones crashing to the ground as he knocked them off.

He turned to Hess and saw his mentor sliding his chainmail back over his calf. "You going to drink a potion?"

Hess sighed and shook his head. "Those are not for things like this. A few herbs like I used on Pammon, and I'll be fine in a while. The potions are for life-and-death situations. Trust me, I've been injured far worse."

Kaen glanced around the area and saw the two dead bodies. Just as the first man with a shield and sword, this man had his chest caved in. His shield was splintered beyond all recognition. The horses were still acting skittish from the rope Hess had pulled across the road that had blocked them, tangling their legs. Kaen went to the horses and did what he could to calm them down. He noticed the archer's body and quickly turned his head from the destruction he saw.

Kaen gagged a moment and then caught himself.

"I should have warned you about that," Hess stated as he carefully stood up and tested his injured leg. "I might have gone a little overboard on him after he injured me."

Kaen nodded and swallowed the stuff that had begun to rise up from his stomach. "That's . . . "

"Gruesome? Horrific? Awful?"

Kaen nodded.

"You will see far worse, and one day, you will cause damage worse than this," Hess replied, his face twinging as he put more weight on his right foot. "Each of these men was a trained fighter, and something tells me all of them had a lifestone."

Hess motioned to the man he had crushed beneath his hammer. "He used a skill one only gets at level twenty with the sword. It surprised me, actually. Someone has gathered men and women that feel like an iron or silver party."

Hess grunted as he took a few steps and waved off Kaen when he started toward him. "I'll be fine. We need to loot these bodies and see what we can find. Any update on the rider?"

Kaen chuckled and shrugged. "He just took off, as you saw. You and Pammon both remembered that guy, while he had slipped my mind."

Tapping his head with his hand, Hess nodded. "Pammon is smarter than you. He knows the danger of someone like that. You must learn not to let small details like that escape your thoughts, or they may be what gets you or someone else killed."

It hurt, knowing Hess was right. He kept focusing on everything else, and the big picture seemed to escape him too often.

Found the rider yet?

Pammon huffed through their connection.

I just got airborne. It takes time to climb. I have not seen him yet, but I will let you know when I find him.

"No update on the rider. Pammon is still gaining height in the sky."

Hess nodded as he began to rip off the armor from the sword person he had crushed. "Go check out the other four . . . god damn, four . . . " Hess paused and glanced back at Kaen with a smile. "You are like your father more than you know. He always defeated the most people or creatures we fought."

Kaen's heart felt Hess's words crush him and lift him all at the same time. He wasn't doing these things to be praised or compared to his father, but hearing Hess say them and knowing why he did, meant the world to him.

"Stop standing there like a fool and loot those bodies, and let me know when you find out something from Pammon!"

Kaen smiled and shot Hess the middle finger, moving toward the mage he and Pammon had killed. He could hear Hess chuckling as he jogged away.

Kaen's pouch was bursting with a few gems, silver coins, and a lot of jewelry when he finished looting the two on the second cart. He understood why Hess had told him not to worry about trying to grab weapons or armor, but as each of the bodies had a black mark on their chest, surely more of their equipment could be worth something.

I finally found the rider! I had lost him, as he had gone west and south toward the main camp. I cannot stop him before he gets there. He is less than a minute from reaching his friends!

Don't try and stop him. Be safe, and just let me know what you see. I'll get Hess and see what he wants to do.

"This is a bad . . . " Hess declared, trailing off as he looked at the carts and horses. "We need to cut the horses free and send them off. There is still almost half a day of light, and we are in their territory. Even with Pammon, we are at a disadvantage."

"Do you want to take a horse and ride off on it?"

Hess shook his head and motioned to his calf. "It is doing better. The herbs are helping, but I cannot run for long without it ripping open and leaving blood everywhere. Riding a horse sounds great, but they have no saddle, and I would prefer not to trust my life in the woods on a random horse unless I have to."

"So what are you thinking?" Kaen asked, frustration evident in his voice and body language.

Hess pointed at the horses. "I'll tell you in a few, but for now, cut the horses loose, help me get them moving away, and then I will share my idea."

63

Pammon's Fight

They are still holed up in their fort. They have moved two carts to the front entrance of the wall, and the three missing people are out there now. They appear to be in a hurry and are setting up wood for fires tonight.

"Gosh damnit, Hess," Kaen complained. "You were right. How did you know they would hole up like that?"

Grinning like a fool, Hess put his hand on Kaen's shoulder. "Remember, I did this for decades. People all act a certain way based on the information they have. The camp is wiped out, each of the bodies looted, and the papers we took are troubling. I assume the rider found our trail somehow, so they are good at tracking and probably found both trails around their base and up north. That means they assume we have found or ambushed the caravan like we did."

Hess took a deep breath and pointed in the direction of the base.

"They think they know how many of us there are, but they can't be sure. I was an idiot and should have made you cut up that archer at the camp. It would have removed any chance of the person perhaps recognizing the skill you used." Hess paused again and shook his head in disbelief that Kaen had managed that feat again. "Now they know there are powerful people out here, and if he did recognize the skill, they believe you have a thirty in your archery, which would make anyone cautious before moving into the woods."

Hess pointed at the map he had drawn in the dirt of the fort. "Tonight is going to be when we will end this. They will be on guard, but we have Pammon, the Joker, in our deck. They cannot begin to fathom a dragon or the destruction he can really bring."

"You know Pammon is excited about this," Kaen said with a slight groan. "He has been waiting to prove how good he is."

Hess chuckled and nodded.

"Tonight, you will learn just how deadly a dragon, even a young one, can be."

Waiting had been torture for Kaen. Depending on Pammon to keep them updated on the camp's movements while they set up a few distractions outside, had been hard. They had managed to loot the last body from the carts. The body had been mangled, and Pammon had torn it apart.

Hess had him create a couple of bonfires to light once the time to attack began.

With it having been dark for two hours, Kaen poked Hess, waking him up from his slumber. "It's time."

Hess stretched and nodded then grabbed his equipment beside him. "No change yet?"

"None. They still have two guards at each opening in the wall, and the fires are burning brightly around the camp."

Using his shield, Hess stood up, testing his right leg before putting all his weight on it. "Everyone wants to be a big guy like me until they discover how hard it is to move when your ankle or leg is injured. All that weight hurts more."

"I'll go get the fires started. Anything else you want before I go?" Kaen asked.

"Be smart. Do what I told you; do not engage unless you have to. Remember our advantage and get back to me once they are going."

Kaen grinned, even though he knew Hess couldn't see it on his face in the dark. The clouds covered the moon, turning the forest into almost complete darkness.

"I'll be back."

Three of the guys are now at the north wall, and the people who were in the house are moving around the opening. Just one guard left on the south side.

Kaen chuckled as he started to light the third bonfire. Keeping one eye closed as he struck the flint and steel together, he watched the sparks ignite the pile of tinder. A few tiny breaths got it going, and it roared into a blaze, ready to take over the wood he had stacked upright.

I don't want to tell Hess how right he was. Keeping one eye closed while staring at the fire helps me not lose my night sight. I can actually still see as I run through the woods.

Just be careful. I can't see you from this height.

Kaen dashed through the forest back to where Hess was.

Four fires were burning. Hess had lit one but had made Kaen light the one farthest from where they would actually be. They were scattered all over the northwest to northeast side of the base, casting dancing lights through the woods. Even though the fires were over a hundred yards from the base, their warm light could be seen from a reasonable distance.

Once Hess has me give the signal, go ahead and take out the south guard.

Glee and excitement surged through the bond, and Kaen knew Pammon was smiling at what was about to happen.

"Start it!"

Kaen nodded and began loosing arrows at the people in the fort. They were well out of his range, but he wasn't actually trying to hit anyone, just draw their attention.

After the second arrow reached the fort, the men inside started shouting. Their reaction unleashed a foe they were not prepared for.

Pammon smiled as he watched the men rushing to the walls, holding up shields as they glanced out into the forest, trying to see where the attack was coming from.

Swooping down, he saw his prey. The man stood on a raised platform, having turned his attention to the north side of town before quickly turning back south, trying to see if anyone would come from that direction.

Tucking his wings, Pammon fell silently from the treetops, increasing his speed and angling for the man's backside. A bestial urge inside him drove him forward, and he knew he was following a natural instinct.

Reaching the height and speed he needed, Pammon flared his wings and spread his back talons on his feet, preparing for the contact that was seconds from happening. All those hours he had spent in the forests and in the fields practicing on his meals made this seem like second nature now.

The man cried out, the tiniest sound, as talons pierced his back on both sides of his spine. Pammon's front talon pierced the man's chest as he rotated his wings slightly, rising quickly into the sky. A few flaps carried him over the wall and trees into darkness.

Pammon glanced down at the man who was dead, his head hanging limply to the side. Part of him wanted to bite his head off, but now was not the time for it. He had more prey to deal with.

He saw the tree he wanted and flew to it, impaling the man on top of it as he flew past, beginning his climb and turning to repeat the process.

They are looking for their man from the south side. One of the men from the north wall and one of the men from the middle of their camp have moved to the south wall.

You can do this!

Pammon felt the surge in his chest. He'd had this feeling before.

Is your lifestone pulsing?

Pammon felt Kaen chuckle.

It is. How did you know? Can you feel it again?

I can. I can feel the power coming through it and into me.

Use it then. My life is yours to have.

Pammon had to resist the urge to roar. He could feel the power of Kaen pouring into him through their bond. The world seemed to move slower as he flew. As if he was faster now.

The two men climbed up the towers on both sides of the opening to the south, glancing in all directions around them. The only light they had were the ones behind them on the ground and the ones they had set up in the clearing between the wall opening.

These fools blind themselves with these torches and lights.

Pammon gauged the distance and calculated the weight of the men and the speed he would need to do what he wanted. Speed and power were critical here. He had never attempted to kill two creatures in one attack. The orc taught him the importance of not taking on too much without practice.

He finished his circle, diving again, coming from the east. There was more room for him to gain the height he would need on the west side. As the tree line ended, he barely missed clipping a few branches by a dragon scale, tucking his wings again for another attack.

His first target was a woman, and he believed she was a caster of some kind due to the staff she held and the robe she wore. Her red hair, cascading down her back, seemed alive in the light of the fire. She was glancing over the wall but not looking up at the sky, unaware of his approach.

Ten yards before he struck, Pammon saw her look up in horror as he dove at her. Her head turned in slow motion as she tried to lift her staff, but she was too slow. Pammon wondered how she had noticed him. Perhaps the light of the fires that were now glowing brighter, had reflected off his bronze and copper scales, creating a sight for her to see.

As she lifted her staff, Pammon's right back claw knocked it from her hand. He pierced her heart with a talon through her chest, shattering a shimmer of magical energy around her body. She was so light, he would have thought he had missed her if it wasn't for the magical barrier he broke through.

Angling his body to the left, he streaked across the opening between the two platforms, slightly missing his mark but taking the head off the man on the platform who had yet to hear him coming. The man crumpled to the platform and then rolled off onto the ground with a thud as Pammon took off into the dark night of the sky.

Two more are down. Just three left!

You are amazing! Hess and I are still outside, trying to draw their attention. Tell me when you need our help!

Joy filled Pammon's heart. When Kaen cheered for or encouraged him, it made him feel fulfilled. Those moments when they were not together hurt. His skin itched, and he could not figure out why. Like a part of him was missing.

Getting to show Kaen and Hess how far he had come meant something to him tonight. The fire that was always in his belly was roaring, wanting to be set free. He needed them to know that he was no longer an eggling but that he was powerful and could do his part and be more than just a scout.

Be ready for the fire arrows when I call for it. I am going to end this in a moment.

He had already deposited the woman on a tree for later. Hess and Kaen both wanted to check these bodies for loot, and putting them on top of a tree was the easiest way for him to gather them when this was over.

Gazing at the clearing, he saw panic taking over among the last three people inside. One of them jumped on a horse and started riding toward the north exit. The one in the middle, wearing a robe and weaving their hands in the air, sent some sort of magical attack that struck the horse and the man, knocking them over like a leaf in the wind.

With only two left and the one on the front of the wall, Pammon decided it was time to announce his presence and made his move.

Launch the arrows now. I am ending this!

Pammon came from the south, preparing to engage the person who had just struck down one of their own. He could see the person, their silver hair gleaming in the light of the fires, pointing at the person on the wall near the gate. He had no doubt the man was threatening his last companion.

Two arrows on fire came from the tree line where he had seen Kaen appear. They arched up into the sky, flying over the wall and landing a few yards past it. Nothing was in danger of burning, but now both men were focused on them.

One more arrow streaked through the sky as Pammon came over the southern wall. The fire inside him roared to life, yearning to be loosed. It felt like ages since he had used it. He would not risk injury to himself or Kaen. The one who must be the leader would learn the true power of who he was.

Of what he was.

Pammon's mouth opened, and the fire burst from his core, racing up his throat and out through his open maw.

His speed slowed as he hung in the air for a moment before needing to beat his wings. The flame raced across the ground and streaked toward the man in the robes. The man turned as the fire reached his feet, sending heat hot enough to melt metal through his clothes and his skin.

He screamed in pain, his eyes wide, mouth open as Pammon's stream of death engulfed the man, roasting him alive in seconds.

The scream may have stopped, but the shell of the man stood as if frozen in place. Snapping his jaws shut, Pammon turned and saw the man on the wall, shaking like a branch in a windstorm. If the smell of burning flesh had not filled Pammon's snout, he would have smelled the urine running down the man's legs, as the last defender could not react or move.

Pammon flew toward the wall and landed on the ground a few feet from the tower the man was standing on. Petrified with fear.

Rising to his haunches, Pammon stood, tall enough to stare into the man's eyes, his shield being held before him, trembling with every breath the man tried to take.

Pammon put his mouth a few feet from the man, gazing at him, and roared, sending flecks of spit and burning embers onto the man, who could still not move.

Having declared his presence, Pammon slammed his front claws together on both sides of the man, causing him to pop like a stink bell, showering the wall and Pammon's scales with blood and flesh.

Finished with the last man, Pammon took a few steps back and gazed at the destruction around him, the fire that was burning in the dirt from his flames.

I am Pammon, and I will no longer sit idly by.

He lifted his head upward, noticing the clouds separating just a sliver where the moon could shine through.

He roared once more before releasing the last of his dragon fire straight into the night sky, illuminating the trees around him with the light of his power.

When he finished, he lowered his head and shook off the few stray pieces of hot embers from his snout.

They are all dead. It is safe to enter.

64

Grave News

Kaen surveyed the damage and destruction Pammon had done, all on his own.

"I'm not sure what to think or even say," he blurted out. "Six people gone, having had no real chance."

"And he isn't even a year old yet," Hess answered as Pammon watched them talk. "When he gets older, he won't even need the distractions you and I provided."

The thrum of Pammon's laughter reverberated as he lounged on the ground as if he had no care in the world.

Beside him were the two bodies he had retrieved from the treetops; the rest he had not touched since landing.

You are not afraid of me, yet I sense angst from you. What is it?

Kaen moved to where Pammon was and put his hand on his snout.

I know you are not the only dragon, and I guess part of me wonders how we will fight them if it ever comes to that. They are all older and larger, meaning the destruction they can bring will be greater than what you did today. I don't want to risk you like that.

Pammon leaned his head forward and gave a gentle head butt against Kaen's body.

No one will threaten you or me. We will find our own path and strength. I have no doubt about it.

Chuckling, Kaen pressed against Pammon's head, pretending to wrestle with him. "One day, we will go where we want when we want. I cannot wait for that moment."

Neither can I.

Hess moved through the camp to the spot where a few flickers of flame burned in the dirt from Pammon's dragon fire. The heat was so hot it cracked the earth, forming the same crust-like surface they had found the day Pammon had come into their lives. *Seven months ago, was it?*

Hess left the spot and checked the building he knew must have housed the person in charge. If anything had survived Pammon's fire, they could wait till morning to try and retrieve it.

"Kaen!" Hess called out as he walked away.

"I'm on it!" Kaen called out, rolling his eyes playfully at Pammon. "Time to see what I can find on these bandits."

Pointing at the horse lying near the wall, Kaen moved toward the two bodies near him. "You should go eat that horse. I can tell you are hungry."

Without waiting for Kaen to say anything else, Pammon quickly got up and returned to the horse, ripping off huge bites and swallowing most of them without chewing.

Ignoring what his dragon was doing, Kaen turned to the task at hand. Being an adventurer meant looting corpses like a grave robber, hoping to find something of value.

Morning came quickly, and even though it had not been the most comfortable choice, Kaen had again slept outside with Pammon. Nestled up against his body, the beat of his heart and the warmth he provided had quickly put Kaen to sleep.

"I hate leaving all those goods because there must still be a few bandits left, but I think I found more than I had hoped for," Hess declared as he cinched the rope that held the saddle bags and an assortment of small chests on one of the horses. "I only read some of the papers, but we must get out of here and report back in. Other bandits may return, yet I doubt they will stay here long if they do. With no horses or food and everyone dead and rotting, some might not risk even checking if anything is left."

Kaen nodded and finished raking up the dirt Pammon had broken up with his claws. Hess had told them they needed to hide the dirt so that no one could determine a dragon had been there.

One black ring with a green gemstone had managed to survive Pammon's fire, and Hess had tucked it away into his pouch.

"Seems like a waste not taking stuff with us, but then again, I don't want to be sitting on a cart for days, trying to get all this stuff back." Hess laughed and nodded as he turned and gazed again around the base the bandits had built. "I wished I could have questioned one of them, but I am glad I did not have to play executioner also."

Kaen wiped the sweat from his brow after tossing the rake to the side. "All we need to do now is go find our horses and return home, victors, once again," Kaen declared as he flexed his arms playfully. "If we keep this up, Fiola will probably get mad."

Hess burst out into a roaring laugh. "Is it that obvious I dislike that woman?"

"I would say most people can read your dislike for her as easily as they can read how badly you want to sleep with Sulenda," Kaen teased.

Hess snorted and shook his head at Kaen. "One day, I will make sure to remind you of how easily we can all read you," Hess fired back, pointing a finger at Kaen. "I'll just make sure to do it when others are present."

Laughing, Kaen gave Hess the finger again and moved to grab the other horse they were taking back with them.

"One day, that finger might get cut off, then what would you do?"

"Use the other hand," answered Kaen as he lifted both middle fingers at Hess.

It had been years since Hess had given Kaen both fingers at once, yet he felt it was time to remedy that.

They laughed as they stood there for a few seconds, waving both hands in the air with only their middle fingers showing.

"Come on, old man, I need to get you back before you hurt yourself more and Sulenda keeps her promise."

Hess grinned and nodded. "I'm sure I won't hear the end of it."

The two days back to Ebonmount had been uneventful. The three of them took their time, not overworking the horses, and Pammon was always scouting, seeing if anyone on the road was someone he recognized. As tempting as it was for Hess to stay and try to catch some of the bandits who would return from scouting for new targets, their work was done, and he needed to get home and recover.

Pammon and Kaen were more than content with the pace Hess had set, enjoying more time together than they had since leaving Minoosh.

Only four hours of sun were left when they finally arrived back at the guild hall.

News had beat them back to the guild house, and Mandy and Herb were waiting outside on the steps for them when they arrived. Both had grim looks on their faces.

"That appears to be quite a bit of stuff on those two horses," Herb called out when they got within hearing range. "Do I even want to know?"

Hess grinned and shook his head. "Your intel on the quest was completely off," Hess replied as he gazed around the courtyard. There were fewer adventurers out than he had expected, and those around did not seem in good moods. "What has happened?"

Holding up a hand, Herb cut him off and motioned to the building with his head.

"What happened?" Kaen asked quietly, leaning closer to Hess as they rode up to the front of the hall.

"Nothing good, Kaen. Nothing good."

Two more clerks came out with a few extra helpers, and when they finally arrived at the steps, the clerks took the two horses laden with boxes and saddlebags and led them around the building to be unloaded.

"I am glad you two have returned," Herb said as Hess and Kaen climbed off their horses and handed the reins to Mandy. "It has been a hard week, but we must talk inside."

Kaen grabbed his bow and supplies while Hess left his on the horse.

"You don't trust them?" Hess asked, furrowing his eyebrows.

"After what just happened and how people are acting, I feel better with it on my back," Kaen replied.

Hess paused and nodded, returning to the saddle and removing one of his maces. "I guess you are right," Hess mumbled, watching Herb and Mandy and noticing they were still upset.

"I will ask for forgiveness later," Mandy suddenly blurted out as they walked up the stairs.

Hess glanced at Mandy and saw tears on her cheek. Something was definitely wrong.

The moment the doors closed in the room Herb had led them into, Hess spun on his heel and confronted him.

"Tell me what is going on? Why all this cloak-and-dagger stuff?"

Herb held up his hand again, drawing a frustrated breath from Hess. Then Herb put his other hand on the door and activated a rune on it, causing the walls to shimmer momentarily.

"We can talk safely now," Herb said with a sigh as he moved to a chair. "Sit, none of this will be good news or delivered fast."

"Twenty-three adventurers dead," Kaen whispered, still trying to wrap his head around the news. "In just the last five days? I talked to some of the ones you mentioned just last week."

Herb nodded and slowly straightened his papers on the table before him. "I have never seen in all my years of doing this, such a bad misrepresentation of quests given to adventurers. There is no excuse for this. Someone had to intentionally do this."

Hess sat, his fingers laced together and his chin on his hands as he leaned against the table. He had not spoken for a few minutes.

"Hearing how dangerous your quest was, I am thankful you two survived. It is a testament to both of you to have defeated this many," Herb said.

Kaen gave a weak smile as Herb praised them. They were alive and had succeeded only because of Pammon. A shudder flowed through Kaen as he admitted to himself what would have most likely happened if it had just been the two of them.

"When are their funerals?" Kaen inquired. "I need to get something to honor Chubbs and Amra."

Herb flipped through a few pages and then ran his fingers along one and grimaced. "Chubbs's was two days ago, and Amra's will be tomorrow. We have not had this level of loss in a long time. Never since I have been here."

A twinge of sadness hit Kaen as he thought of those times he and Chubbs had laughed together at the inn. The young man was full of life and joy. He wanted to be a great adventurer and help protect the kingdom and its people.

I am sorry for the pain you are feeling. I know it is heavy on your heart.

We might have been in those numbers if not for you, Pammon. I can't believe all this happened in five days! We need to figure out what to do.

I am here and will always be here to help you with anything you need. Just tell me what to do, and I will do it.

Kaen took one of those deep breaths people do when they know they need to refocus. He held it for a bit and finally let it out when his lungs began to burn.

Thank you. More than words can say, I know you feel how much you mean to me. For now, fly and enjoy it so I can feel it through you. It always lifts me when I feel you flying across the sky.

I will touch the clouds for you and imagine you are up here with me.

A smile crept across Kaen's face. "What can we do to help?" Kaen asked, watching Hess, who was staring at him.

"I'm not sure how to answer that right now," Herb replied. "We are investigating things inside the guild. Fiola is holed up in her office, and the council has contacted her and said they are sending out an investigator. She is beside herself with that knowledge, and the entire staff suffers under it. She has not left her office the last two days, and the wear on her is obvious."

Herb snapped his fingers at Hess. "You could talk to her? See if you could help?"

Snorting, Hess shook his head. "Seriously? Would you ask me to help her? After everything you know she did before I left?" Hess shouted as he slammed a hand against the table. "This is her doing! She let it happen under her watch, and by a dwarf's beard, I have no problem letting her take the blame and fall for it!"

Herb's chair scraped as he stood up and pounded the table with his fists.

"Stop being an ass, Hess Brumlin! Be the hero you swore you would be!" shouted Herb. "This isn't about your dispute with Fiola. This is about other adventures who are dying because someone is doing something underhanded! In the last year, we have lost more than in the years before. Something is happening, and we need help! I need help!"

Hess glared at Herb, who was giving him the same look back. Kaen watched the two grown men get red in the face, seeing whose vein in their forehead would burst first.

"I will help," Kaen answered as he stood up from his chair. "I promised myself and the guild to do whatever I can to protect anyone who needs it. Right now, it appears Fiola needs it."

Herb turned, focusing on Kaen, his frustration visibly vanishing as he saw the expression on Kaen's face. "Thank you for your help, Kaen Marshell."

Nodding, Kaen moved around the table until he stood by the door. "Hess, you going to come with me or sit there, whining like a calf who misses its mother's teat?"

A grunt came from Hess as he glared across the table at Kaen. "You don't know what you are asking me to do."

"You're right," Kaen replied. "Because I don't care. Now get off your fat ass and act like the man who raised me all these years. Do what Herb said, and be an adventurer worthy of the token around your neck."

Kaen opened the door, never taking his gaze off Hess. "With or without you, I will do what I know is right." Done talking, he left the room, shutting the door behind him.

"He's just like his damn father," Hess cursed, pounding the table with both fists.

Herb nodded and remained silent for a moment.

"What?" Hess erupted in frustration as Herb continued to stare at him.

"I'm just waiting to see how long you pout for before you decide to follow Kaen, just like you followed his dad when you knew that Hoste was right," replied Herb with a slight grin.

"Hairy, goat-loving, orc-humping bastard of a goblin!" Hess shouted as he stood up, knocking his chair over. He pointed his massive finger at Herb and shook it frantically. "If you weren't my friend, I would pop you in the face."

Herb laughed and shrugged. "If popping me in the face is what it takes for you to do the right thing, then come and do it," he replied, putting both hands behind his back. "Otherwise, stop wasting time complaining about something you know is right, and go do it."

Herb smiled and shook his head after the door slammed behind him with enough force that it almost cracked the frame.

"Hoste, your son is just like you," he muttered in the empty room. "May the spirits be gentle with Hess for having to suffer through the two of you."

65

Someone on the Inside

"That was faster than I expected," Kaen said drolly, as Hess climbed the stairs to join him at the top. "I had wondered if you might make me wait longer."

"Let's get this over with," Hess grumbled, pouting about the course of action they'd chosen. "I am going to do what I did the last two times and sit quietly while you two talk."

Kaen shrugged and began moving toward Fiola's office area, letting Hess stomp behind him like an angry child.

"Are you sure you want to go in?" the woman behind the desk asked. "Guild Master Fiola has not been the kindest to those who have entered."

Kaen nodded. He could hear the trembling in the woman's voice. She was not the same woman who had been there the last two times Kaen had been there.

"I guess I will have to depend upon my adventuring skills to dodge anything Miss Fiola throws at me," joked Kaen as he moved to the door. "I'd say if you hear screaming, send help, but we both know sound doesn't come through these things."

The woman smiled, the first real look of something other than anxiety Kaen had seen since he'd arrived. She nodded and motioned for them to enter.

"Lissandra, I told you not to disturb me," hissed Fiola from where she sat at her desk, not bothering to look up from the paperwork she was reading.

Shock hit Kaen as he took the first steps into the room. Papers were everywhere, scattered across the couches, table, floor, and everywhere else there was a flat surface. Fiola's hair was a mess, her braid long gone, and an odor of some kind hung in the air.

"Guild Master Fiola, I am here to lend you any help I can," Kaen announced as he dodged the paper strewn across the floor. "From the looks of it, you could use some help."

When Kaen spoke, Fiola's head snapped up, and he saw the bags under her eyes, highlighting her bloodshot eyes. Her normally ivory-white skin almost looked gray, and exhaustion was written all over her face.

"What are you . . . " Fiola's angry tone faded she and took a deep breath. "Why have you come, adventurer Kaen?"

"Rumor has it that twenty-three adventurers have died since we left on our quest. We almost joined them. It appears the information about quests has been wrong lately, and you have not found out how this has happened."

Kaen smiled slightly as he spoke, gliding through the room to her desk. Standing before it and gazing down at Fiola, he gently tapped the desk with his finger. "I am here to lend aid, as is adventurer Hess. We know more lives are at stake, and something must be done soon."

"Herb," Fiola grumbled, her voice growly and curt. She leaned back in her chair and tried to fix the unruly hair around her face. "I must deal with that breach of guild hall details later."

"That *breach* cares about the lives of the adventurers just as much as you," Hess informed her from across the room. "He knows you need help, and apparently, we are the only two he can trust right now when you cannot trust anyone else. So instead of complaining about him, why not accept the best help he can give and get on with solving this mess!"

Fiola grimaced and glared at Hess. A few seconds later, she sighed, her shoulders sagging as the tension left them. "You are right. I have no one I can trust, and with you two being new and sent on a quest that was beyond what you should have handled alone, I must trust Herb's assessment of you both."

Glancing around the room again, Kaen shook his head in disbelief. "What is all this?" he asked, motioning with his hands at the papers.

"Every quest we have offered in the last year. Each with a report of success or failure and if anyone was killed due to bad information."

After rubbing her eyes, Fiola glanced at the teacup on her desk and saw it was empty. She sighed and motioned to a large stack on her desk to the right. "These are all quests where someone has died in the last year."

"That many!" gasped Hess. "There must be—"

"Yes, over a hundred," Fiola interrupted. "Most originally believed that deaths happened from mistakes or the adventurer not being as far advanced as they should have been. We often felt the report was a little off in the ones where a group returned stating what they had faced had been more than expected. Usually, it has been the lower ranked quests, but these last few days, everything went wrong."

Fiola grabbed a stack of dog-eared papers. "The last week had a massive number of quests that were offered where entire groups were killed. Some experienced serious injuries but made it out alive. All of those had one thing in common. The number of monsters, creatures, or adversaries they would face was completely off."

Fiola gave a weak smile and locked eyes with Hess. "I am being honest when I say I am glad you and Kaen returned safely. Losing both of you would have been a massive blow to all of us."

Hess opened his mouth but ended up closing it. The snarky comment he was going to make never left his lips. He knew Fiola would have been blamed for both deaths, and losing Kaen would have ended her career.

"What is the common theme?" he asked as he approached the desk to join Kaen. His body language had relaxed from one prepared to fight to one who needed to solve a problem.

"I don't know," she answered with a sigh. "I have read all these reports multiple times. I have checked the scouting reports thoroughly. Some, so many different scouts signed off on them, which makes it impossible to find the source of the problem."

Rubbing her forehead with a hand, Fiola could barely be heard when she whispered, "For two days, I have done nothing but look, and I have no answer that shows how this happened."

"I am assuming no more quests are being given?"

Lowering her hand, Fiola looked up at Kaen and nodded. "We cannot, in good faith, give anymore. I would be asking people to risk their lives, more than usual, to set out on a task I cannot guarantee was correct."

She grabbed another stack of papers and held it out to Kaen. "These six quests all have people currently on them. One of them was one you were offered. I sent Selmah, our highest token, in after a six-man team checking the number of orcs, goblins, and hobgoblins in the mine. If there are more than fifty in there," Fiola paused and shuddered. "They could all die."

Quickly flipping through the pages, Kaen found the quest she was talking about. Yanking the sheet out, he glanced at the bottom of it, and his heart sank.

Gertrude signed up for this one.

"How long ago did they set out?!"

"Three days ago," Fiola said, grimacing. "I only sent Selmah yesterday. If anyone could save them, it would be her."

"Against that many? One person?"

Kaen stopped firing questions off at Fiola, who winced at each one, when he felt Hess's hand on his shoulder.

"Selmah is unlike anything you can imagine," Hess interrupted. "If the little bit I know about her is true, she could easily walk into that mine and clear it all on her own."

Glancing at Hess, Kaen saw that he was confident in his assessment of the woman.

Just how powerful is she?

Closing his eyes momentarily, Kaen took a deep breath and let it out slowly. "Sorry for that. She and I had talked about grouping, and I . . . "

"I understand. I feel that way for everyone under my charge. Even Hess," Fiola added with a slight wink.

Hess grunted and then shook his head and chuckled. "Perhaps we need to move on from the past for the future?"

Fiola's eyes began to well up as she saw Hess's face and realized he was not jabbing at her.

"Perhaps the exhaustion is getting to me, but I would like that. I need to do something first before that can happen, though."

Hess's eyebrows scrunched as he watched Fiola stand from her chair.

"I owe you an apology." Her voice trembled as she bowed her head slightly. "I may have . . . no, I have done things wrong in the past, and I acknowledge my temper did not help."

Raising her head, Fiola gave the best smile she could muster. "Hess Brumlin, would you forgive me for being a fool-headed, absent-minded, angry, and pissed-off elven woman who did you and others wrong just to advance myself?"

Hess's eyebrows had shot up during the declaration and apology. He knew Fiola well enough to know it had been difficult for her to say.

"I accept your apology," Hess replied, "but I cannot promise I will behave myself all the time and hold my tongue when I probably should. I can be just as stubborn, even though I am not an elven woman."

Fiola chuckled and nodded as a single tear slipped from her eye. Wiping it off, she straightened out her completely crumpled dress and stood tall again. "Now, with that settled, Kaen, what do you want to know? I could use a fresh set of eyes on all this."

"Tell me how all quests begin," Kaen said.

The three of them had been sitting on the couches for a few hours discussing everything known about the quest process. Only the two stacks of papers from the previous year and the current quests they were trying to get updates on remained.

Kaen was tapping his chin as he leaned back on the couch, watching Hess and Fiola drink their tea and glance at a quest sheet that had already been looked at dozens of times.

His mind itched, and his heart knew they needed to find the missing clue. It just felt like they were looking at something wrong.

Kaen stood up and scratched his back as he stretched. As he did, his hand brushed the pouch still on his hip from their quest. He and Hess had not yet had a chance to change or drop off the loot they had procured from the corpses.

His left hand felt the other pouch on his hip when he bent sideways to stretch again. He had the map and quest information in there.

Kaen's lifestone pulsed hard, almost doubling him over as it sent a bolt of energy to his brain. He squinted from the surge, and both Hess and Fiola noticed his movement.

"You ok, Kaen? Pull something?" Hess asked.

Standing straight up, Kaen reached into his pouch and pulled out the papers he had inside: the map and a copy of the quest sheet he had requested from Mandy. He had wanted to have a copy since it was his first official quest. She had been kind enough to go and bring him a copy to keep.

"Goblin shite!" Kaen muttered as he moved to the table and started digging through the papers, looking through the quest sheets on it.

"Kaen, what is it?" Hess gasped as he noticed the fervor Kaen was searching with.

"I think I know how it's being done!"

66

Finding the Mole

"How? How is it being done?" asked Fiola as she leaned forward to see what he was looking for.

"I need the quest sheet for our quest! Where is it?"

All three began digging. Hess held it up when he found it.

"Let me see it a moment," Kaen declared as he took his hand and swept a clear area on the table, sending paperwork onto the floor.

"I hope you're right," grumbled Fiola as she watched the papers spill everywhere.

Kaen snatched the quest sheet from Hess and then placed the copy he had and the original Hess had, side-by-side.

"What is the difference between these two?" Kaen asked.

Hess moved to Fiona's side as Kaen turned the quest sheets around on the table so they could both see them.

After a minute of comparing the sheets, they shrugged and looked at Kaen with absent expressions.

"Nothing, they are the same," Hess said.

"I agree with Hess," answered Fiola. "They should always be an exact match. That is how the process works."

Kaen nodded and tapped one of the sheets where his signature was. "Hess, you remember what I asked Mandy the day I saw her return with the quest I made for both the boys?"

After a few seconds, Hess nodded. "You wanted to know how it was made, and I mentioned there had once been a bounty on learning the process."

Kaen grinned like he had just eaten a whole pie by himself. "And why was that bounty stopped?"

"Because of the potential financial problems that could . . . wait. Are you saying someone has figured it out?"

Kaen shook his head and tapped the page again.

"Fiola, once this is signed, is there any way to change the document?"

"Absolutely not! That is why the magic in the paper shimmers, so all know it is bound."

"What about before it is signed? Could someone make a new quest sheet with different information? Would it be possible to do that?"

Fiola's eyes went wide as that possibility hit her. "No one would do that, though! It would have to be someone in the guild house, and we are all sworn to assist the guild. Our lifestones bind us to that!"

Kaen laughed, and then he began to howl at some joke in his mind that neither knew about. "Really? You are telling me that you have never done anything the guild would not approve of because your *lifestone* prevents you?"

Fiola opened and closed her mouth but words failed to emerge as Hess chuckled.

"Hairy dwarf balls, Kaen!" Hess exclaimed. "I hate when you do that."

Hearing Hess curse and chuckle, Fiola realized Kaen was right. She could get away with actions some of the higher-ups on the council would disapprove of, if she believed hard enough that it was better in the long run. A groan slipped out of her.

"Are you telling me that someone within our guild house is changing numbers on our reports and quest sheets because they believe their actions are better in the long run for the kingdom?"

"It is the only possible answer. You said it yourself: All the scouting reports match the numbers on the sheet. All the sheets match up with the quest forms."

Kaen tapped both sheets where his name was. "If there is no way to change this exact copy once the magic has set in, then the only way to accomplish this is before the magic prevents change. That means someone is modifying the report, copying it, and using it for the basis of everything else!"

Kaen dropped back onto the couch and stared at Fiola. "How many people have the ability to do this?"

Staring at the sheets before her, Fiola began to count who could do such a thing. "Ten people *could* do this," she answered as she shook her head at the thought. "Herb is one, but I believe we could rule him out. Three of my clerks, Mandy included, have access, but it would be hard for them to be in that room for the time needed without a reason. They also would never be alone in there."

"That leaves six people," Kaen interjected as Fiola paused momentarily.

"It does," she said as she nodded, tapping her fingers against her knee. "We have guards in place to prevent abuse from happening, but I guess it's possible they aren't really paying attention to what the others in the room with them are doing."

"Goblin Shite!" Fiola shouted.

Kaen and Hess watched in shock as Fiola jumped up from the couch, ran to the door, and opened it.

"Lissandra! Get Herb in here now!"

"I guess it could be possible," Herb declared as he listened to Kaen explain what he thought was happening. "There are three teams of two who handle that task. How are you planning on finding out if any of them are doing it."

"That's where Fiola comes in," Kaen answered as he motioned to her to begin.

Fiola sighed, obviously not excited about saying the next part. "We will have to make them use the crystal and verify that what they say is true."

"You can't be serious!" exclaimed Herb. "The consequences of making them do that may cost you your job, even if you find out one of them is guilty of such an offense!"

"I know!" shouted Fiola, banging her hand on the table. "My options are limited. My position doesn't matter right now. Saving the adventurers who are out there and finding out who is behind this does more! How quickly can we get all six of them here to begin testing?"

"A couple of hours? Two are asleep right now, and the other four are working in the report room. How do you plan on doing this?"

"As quietly as possible," Hess answered. "You need to get someone to fetch the two who are sleeping and set up a room where we can have all six at once. Tell them that you and Fiola must share some insight you gained and that you want to stop rumors. If one of them is doing what Kaen believes they are, we don't want to tip them off."

"Then we will turn to the task of taking them one at a time to the crystal and making them answer questions. If they decline when told what is happening, I will offer them two choices, neither of which is good."

Herb stared at Fiola. Her face was like stone, and he saw the determination in her eyes. "I will get started then," he said as he stood up from the couch. "Anything else?"

"Send a message to Sulenda for me?" Hess asked.

Nodding, Herb smiled. "I would be happy to, my friend."

Blowing a burst of air from her mouth, Fiola stood up and pointed at the door. "Since we have a plan, you two must head downstairs and hang out for a while. I need to shower and change clothes before all this happens. I am afraid I smell almost as bad as Hess does. It's like he stepped in something."

Kaen laughed as Hess groaned.

"You told me the smell was gone!"

Kaen shrugged and grinned. "I couldn't smell it anymore because I am used to it."

Fiola watched as the three men left her office.

That boy . . . he really is just like his father.

"That is kind of intimidating," Kaen declared as he walked around the crystal ball on top of an ornate wooden stand.

Someone had done fantastic work sculpting a wooden base for a crystal ball as big as a grown chicken. "I can feel it radiating power even from over here."

Kaen was moving around a circular twelve-foot room with six lightstones that lit the room like an early sunrise. Dark wood panels covered the walls of the windowless fifteen-foot tall room, and the only entrance was the door they had come in.

"It is even worse if you ever have to use it," Hess replied as he leaned against the wall and used one of his knives to clean his fingernail. "The way it feels when you answer questions is a bit discerning. Like your mind and lifestone are being ripped from you."

Grimacing, Kaen moved a few more feet from the crystal.

"How did you figure it out?" Hess asked. "Was it like everything else you *magically* do?"

Moving to stand against the wall by Hess, Kaen nodded. "My lifestone took the knowledge I knew and put it together so that it made sense," whispered Kaen. "I remembered the line of questions I had asked and what you and Mandy had told me. Suddenly, all the dots connected in an instant. It overwhelmed me when it happened."

Hess stopped moving his knife and glanced over at Kaen. "I still have no information from the people I asked to help about *that*." He tapped his knife point against his chest where his lifestone was. "I hope someone can shed some light on how all this is happening."

"When we get back to Sulenda, I'll share something I figured out."

Groaning, Hess flipped his dagger into the air and caught it after a few flips, then tucked it back into its sheath.

"I just want you to know that you are way more trouble than your dad ever was," he said, elbowing Kaen. "I wouldn't trade anything in the world for you."

Shifting slightly, Kaen leaned against Hess's massive arm and bumped it.

"Me either, *Dad*."

As the two of them joked, the door suddenly opened. A woman entered, Herb and Fiola behind her.

"This is unheard of!" argued the woman. "You know I will file a complaint!"

Fiola nodded, and Herb stood by, writing down everything the woman said.

"Herb has a letter already drafted for you to sign. You can do that now or after," Fiola declared, staring down the woman. "You have two choices. Put your hand on this orb and answer the questions I ask truthfully, all of which pertain only to your duties and the incident we are currently investigating, or refuse and be locked in a cell and under guard until the guild inquisitor arrives and *makes* you answer the same questions I will ask now."

The woman swallowed hard, looking around and seeing that no one else seemed to have a problem with what Fiona was telling her to do.

"And those two?"

"Adventurers who will testify to what is seen and heard," answered Herb. "No doubt you recognize Kaen, our newest adventurer, and Hess, a gold token adventurer. Both are highly thought of, and we trust them as men of their word."

Hess gave a slight bow and smiled as the woman looked at him.

"Well, if you insist," she finally replied curtly. "Let's get this over with."

"Three down and three to go," Herb said with a groan. "We are halfway from breaking most rules we promise to adhere to."

"And yet," Fiola replied, "we can do so because we believe that our actions are for the good of the guild! Someone must believe they are doing this because it is for the guild's betterment in the long run."

"It is true," Herb said as he pondered that realization. "I, at first, was hesitant, and it was difficult to overcome, but now it feels much easier to do after you explained it that way."

Nodding as if she had been right all along, Fiola motioned to his list. "Grab the next one. I'm tired and want to end this sooner than later."

67

The One Behind It

"There is no way by the spirits I will touch that thing!" shouted Alzama. "You know you cannot make me do that even under the threat of an inquisitor."

Hess sighed and nodded at Fiola, who had glanced at him. This young clerk was adamant about not using the crystal. The other three had gladly used it once given their two options.

"I understand," Fiola replied with a frown. "Well, just so you know, your side will be recorded as it has been for everyone before you. Let me introduce to you Adventurers Kaen and Hess."

The woman glanced at both of them as they began to move toward her, extending their hands as if to shake hers.

"It is an honor to meet you, Sir Kaen!" the woman exclaimed as she rushed to shake his hand.

When she shook Kaen's hand, Hess moved beside her and quickly grabbed her other arm. "Forgive me, Miss, but the guild master has given us instructions, and we must obey."

"What?!" she hissed as Kaen and Hess easily lifted the woman by her arms and carried her toward the ball. "Put me down right now! You cannot do this!"

She began to thrash and kick, but both men were far stronger than she was, and her petty attempts at kicking them did nothing.

"Now." Fiola ordered.

Kaen and Hess simultaneously placed Alzama's hands against the crystal. Even though they were in fists, her fingers popped open the moment she touched the crystal, and her whole hand slid, palms open, embracing the round shape.

Groans and moans came from the woman's mouth as Kaen and Hess set her on her feet and backed away from her.

"Please don't!" she cried, tears streaming down her face. "You don't understand!"

Fiola winced as those words struck her ears. She closed her eyes momentarily and let out a breath of air. "Alzama, did you change the scouting reports or modify anything about them to make quests not match their true danger?"

Alzama's body thrashed and shook, but she was unable to free herself from the orb. It flashed red, causing her to scream a horrible banshee wail.

"Answer truthfully and end the pain!" shouted Fiola. "Stop fighting against telling the truth!"

Even though she only lasted about fifteen seconds, Kaen would have believed it had been a whole hour. The woman's cry was one of the most soul-wrenching screams he had ever heard.

"YESSSSSSS!" she finally uttered, the ball turning clear again as she took in huge breaths, her chest throbbing from the pain she had endured.

"Noted," whispered Herb, wincing from what he was watching.

"I do not know what to ask next," Fiola confessed, in shock. "I would never have suspected her of this."

Hess nodded. He understood the predicament she was in.

"What am I missing? Why not ask her why or who?" Kaen asked.

"It doesn't work that way. Only yes or no questions work. You cannot get names from a person unless you know the exact name to ask. The inquisitors have other methods to dig deeper than this. Now, what do we ask? We have found our culprit." Hess said.

"Have we? It's simple," Kaen argued. "Does anyone else in the guild hall work with you?"

Alzama did not reply or move when Kaen asked that question.

"Is anyone else in the guild hall helping you change those numbers?" asked Fiola.

The woman's body jerked again, and the orb took on a slight red tint, not as dark as the first time.

"It only works for the guild master's questions," Hess whispered.

The woman fought, but not as hard or for as long before she shook her head. "No! No! It is just me here working on this!"

"There it is!" Kaen yelled as his lifestone sent a jolt of thought to his brain. "Ask her for each kingdom!"

Fiola glanced at Kaen and chuckled while the woman moaned and pleaded for Fiola not to.

"You are too good at this," she admitted. "I would hate to be on the receiving end of your questioning," Fiola said to Kaen before turning to Alzama. "Did anyone specifically in this kingdom, the one the king who sits on the throne in Ebonmount, help you with this task of changing numbers and quests."

The orb flashed bright red again, and the woman howled in pain. Her tears were like rivers flowing down her body, and Kaen was afraid the woman might pop out a shoulder joint from how she thrashed.

"NO!" the woman cried out.

"At least she was smart enough not to say anything else," Kaen whispered to Hess.

"What about the Kingdom of Pensworth?" Fiola asked.

Again, Alzama thrashed and fought against the same bright red orb until she cried out no.

"What about the Kingdom of Roccnari?"

A lighter shade of red still convinced Alzama to tell the truth and shout no.

Fiola paused and thought for a moment. "Did anyone from the Kingdom of Luthaelia help you change the numbers and quests?"

The orb turned blood red the second Fiola mentioned the kingdom's name.

Without pause, Hess plugged his ears and shouted to Kaen to do the same. Kaen lifted his fingers to his ears, and in the short time his ears were unprotected, he felt the pain of the noise coming from Alzama.

The first time she had howled, he had been overwhelmed, but it paled compared to now. Kaen remembered what Hess had said about one's lifestone being ripped from one's body. The woman looked possessed. Unable to move from her spot, she pulled and tugged as if her hands were joined to the blood-red crystal ball for eternity.

Even with his fingers in his ears, Kaen could hear her screaming. As she thrashed her head, he saw that blood had replaced the clear tears streaming from her eyes, leaving rivers of red down her face.

He glanced at Fiola, who winced from the screams but refused to plug her ears. Herb had one finger in one ear, and the other was forced to endure Alzama's suffering as the orb forced her to tell the truth.

They all grimaced in pain from what they were seeing and hearing.

Alzama would take a breath, gasping for air, and then drain her lungs again with her screams.

Kaen had lost count of how many times she had done that. Finally, after easily a dozen times, she must have said something, because the crystal became clear again, and her screaming stopped.

"Noted, dear spirits, I have written it down," Herb told Fiola as he watched her cover her mouth with a hand in shock.

Kaen and Hess removed their fingers from their ears and heard no sounds from Alzama. Blood was on the white tile of the room and on the wooden stand, yet somehow, none was on the orb.

Fiola nodded to both of them as they gazed at her.

"What does that mean?" Kaen asked.

"Look at her," Hess said, pointing at Alzama. "She is dead, still bound by the orb's magic until Fiola lets her free."

Kaen moved a few steps closer to the woman and saw that she was not breathing, and her chest was not moving. Her body was rigid, and the only blood drops that fell from her face were ones squeezed out moments ago.

"She died?"

"The magic of the orb took the answer the only way that remained. It pulled the answer from her soul, killing her," Hess whispered. "All she had to do was be honest, and she would have lived."

Fear and horror over something as powerful as the crystal made Kaen step back from it. If he was forced to use this and they asked about Pammon, could he fight it? Would he die to hide him?

"You have the answers you need, Fiola," Hess called out as he tapped Kaen on the back. "The boy and I have been here far too long, and we need to get some sleep. You and Herb should let the other two go, as they are innocent, unless you expect another kingdom to be involved."

Fiola shook her head. "I doubt there is anyone else involved but that kingdom."

"What is so bad about Luthaelia?" Kaen asked.

"That is where Stioks rules, Kaen. That is where a man as evil as anything I know lives," Fiola replied.

The walk back to the inn was unpleasant. It was dark, and the moon was well into the sky. They had turned down the offer of a horse, both content to walk back and give thought about what had transpired.

"You ok? You seem pretty upset," Kaen said.

Hess nodded and tried to play it off with a smile. "There are things afoot that I do not know about because I have been gone too long," Hess admitted. "Stioks is a horrible creature who preys on the weak and takes liberty with his power. Many would try to stop him, but it would take a nation or a Dragon Rider to give him pause. Even Elies was injured badly the last time they fought. Neither has made a move again, but many fear Stioks will attempt it when he feels he has the strength to. He almost won, from what my sources say."

Walking along the roads through town, with just the light orbs to provide enough light to keep from tripping, Kaen wondered about the two dragons fighting each other. Stioks and his dragon were much larger and way more powerful than he and Pammon were. The thought of Stioks and his dragon attacking Pammon sent shivers down his spine.

"Don't worry about it," Hess said as he watched Kaen reacting to that news. "For now, we worry about what we can do. We rest up, help where we can, and fight the battles before us."

Hess put an arm around Kaen and pulled him in close. "I'm amazed at you and what you did tonight. Hell, I'm amazed at what you did this past week! You are the reason we found Alzama, and you are the reason we discovered who was helping her!"

Kaen nodded but felt overwhelmed by all that was going on. He had just begun his adventuring career, and it felt like the whole kingdom, no, the whole world was about to explode in war or worse.

"I just wanted to be an adventurer," Kaen whispered. "I wanted to do good and help others. Right now, I'm wondering if any of that matters. What if a war breaks out? All I can think about is taking my friends and running away to keep them safe! Does that make me a coward?"

Stopping, Hess spun Kaen around and looked him in the eye. "No, it does not! If that day ever comes and you must choose life or death, run. Run as fast and as far as you can until you are strong enough to come back and overcome! You dying right now will hurt this kingdom and its people far more than a wasted life on the battlefield. Every life has value, but some lives mean more because of what they can become."

Hess paused and then tapped Kaen's chest. "Luca knew that."

Closing his eyes and shaking his head, Kaen's breath struggled to fill his lungs. "That is a lot of pressure to have on one person."

"Is it?" Hess demanded to know. "Is that really so difficult? What about having to raise a boy to be a man? A man he and the boy's father knew and know has great potential? The fear of screwing up and not doing justice by the promise one made."

Hess popped Kaen on the head and waited for him to look up at him. "Do you think Pammon doesn't carry that weight?" he asked quietly. "That he doesn't lose sleep when you are about to go on a quest? He worries what will happen to you when you fight. How do you think he felt when you faced down that mage in the forest? Or how he worried when you faced those orcs, knowing you could not win."

He cut off Kaen's reply with his hand. "Listen, we all carry weight. How you carry it is what determines the kind of character and person you are. So act in a way that brings honor to your commitment. Like you did tonight."

Standing there on the street, feeling the coldness of the night seep into his body, Kaen nodded.

"For now, let's get back to the inn and rest. Tomorrow, we need to accomplish a few things if you will be the man you want to be."

68

Lifestone Unlocked

"Stop!" Bren shouted as Kaen sent one of his students to the floor with a swing of his club.

Disengaging from his training partner, Kaen smiled as another notification popped up.

[1 Handed Club Skill Increased]

It was the tenth one he had received in the four hours he had been training that day.

"Everyone out except for Kaen!"

Kaen glanced at the room as the four other students he had been sparring with exited the training area. He was one skill increase from a twenty in shield use. For the last four hours, he had channeled his need for justice. Every thought was about those who were being injured or hurt. His lifestone would respond in spurts, sometimes letting him gain two points quickly and other times not responding.

He had learned to take a minute, relax, breathe, and then start the same process.

Remember Luca.

Remember Chubbs.

The power he had been calling upon began to hum again gently. His lifestone was already answering his intent.

Lost in his thoughts, Kaen did not see Bren's swing until the last moment. Actually, he had not seen Bren's attack, but his lifestone reacted, shield rising on its own, knees bending to absorb the blow, his club swinging at Bren's legs.

Bren blocked Kaen's attack and lunged forward, using his shield as a battering ram.

Kaen's lifestone drove his legs out and into the shield, meeting the incoming charge head on.

Both men struck each other with their all, the cracking of their shields and pieces exploding around them as their forces collided with everything they had.

[1 Handed Shield Skill Increased]
[1 Handed Shield Skill Waiting To Be Chosen]

Kaen's eyes widened at the notification, distracted to the point where Bren's club came forward, smacking into his chest and knocking the wind out of him.

"You ok?" Bren called out as Kaen bent over, holding his chest and trying to suck in some air.

"Yes," Kaen responded after a few seconds in a squeaky voice. "You got me good. I was distracted."

"I noticed. Why the sudden change? All day, you have improved your skill with the shield and club. I am surprised you managed to stop both of my first two attacks. Is that why you got distracted?"

Kaen took a few more shallow breaths until he could breathe normally and shook his head.

"I will tell you, but I need your word it stays here."

Bren's eyebrows bunched up as he considered what Kaen could tell him that would require such secrecy. "I would offer my word on that. You need not ask for that ever again, especially after you sent those two boys the other day," Bren replied with a smile. "Their presence and fervor to learn has made all my students work harder."

A smile flashed across Kaen's face as he could only imagine what those two must look like, learning to use a weapon and a sword. "I would normally ask Hess this next question, but since we are here, I want your opinion. How does one choose which skill to pick at level twenty for shields?"

Bren had been picking a few wood shards off his training armor and froze, eyes locked on Kaen. "Are you *asking* me that for later, or are you *telling* me you just hit twenty in shields?" Bren asked in a very slow and steady tone.

"I'm telling you."

Bren's mouth opened wide in shock, and he shook his head, trying to grasp what Kaen had just told him. "You haven't been training except when you are here?"

"Just when I am here with you," Kaen replied with a boyish grin. "I know you have questions, but all I can tell you is that I have a twenty in my shield skill, and I got a notification to pick a skill. I did not get that with archery when I hit twenty."

Bren motioned to the bench against the wall as he walked toward it. "Forget the mess. We can clean that up later. For now, I'll resist the hundred questions or more I have and how impossible what you are telling me is, but let's sit down and figure out your options."

As they moved to the bench, Kaen wondered what he could mean by options. How many different skills were there?

"Ok, focus on asking shield skill choices," Bren instructed him, "and then tell me what it says.

Shield Skill Choices
[Shield Bash]
[Shield Charge]

"I just have two: shield bash and shield charge."

Bren bobbed his head and rubbed his eyes as he thought about those choices. "I'm glad you did not get stuck with shield toss. Nothing worse than removing your only defense by tossing it at someone," Bren stated with a slight chuckle. "If you were a true melee warrior, I would say the charge skill would be the best choice, but since you are not, shield bash is the one I would pick. It can stun someone, knock them down, or even kill them, depending on your strength, which I know is close to twenty also."

"How do you know that?" Kaen asked in shock.

"When we collided, you did not budge, and I know my strength and how much I had put into it. I had an idea and wanted to see if I was right," answered Bren as he winked at Kaen. "Remember, some of us are older and wiser and can tell things by what we see."

That made sense, and as Kaen was going to ask another question, a different one entered his mind. "How strong would someone have to be to break another person's weapon and still crush their chest into their back?"

Bren reeled back as he saw Kaen mischievously smiling at him. "That is an oddly specific question," Bren stated. "I am assuming you have seen this happen?"

"Maybe," Kaen replied with a shrug, his grin increasing. "I'm just saying, based on your knowledge, what would that take?"

"I mean . . . " Bren started to reply and then paused as he rubbed his chin and gazed at the floor. "So many things to consider . . . quality of the sword broken, angle and size of the attack, the direction of swing, elevation—"

"Just a simple number with it being a well-made sword and standing toe-to-toe," Kaen interrupted.

Sighing, Bren rubbed his head a few times with his hand. "For a person to do that, it would have to be in the forties. A creature who is bigger, like an orc or an ogre, has more mass and size, so they could possibly do it with lesser strength, but typically, it would need to be at least a forty to shatter a weapon and still have the momentum needed afterward. Should I ask why?"

Kaen shook his head and winked. "As you said, it pays to know what someone might have stat-wise. I just wondered how strong they must be."

Chuckling, Bren grabbed a waterskin and held it out for Kaen. "I know who you are talking about, but you are also probably forgetting he was fully equipped. That means his base stats are unknown. I would imagine a man of his size and strength still needs some help to hit the number he has. It's like you," Bren explained as he motioned to the ring on Kaen's finger. "I only see one ring on you now, and you appear to have no other items besides it. This tells me you either wear it in memory of something or because it gives you stats you don't want to give up."

Fingering the red band he wore, Kaen just nodded. He couldn't take off the ring if he wanted to, but he wasn't sure he would, even if that was possible. It had been his father's, and that meant something to him, even if he thought it was going to cut his finger off at the beginning.

"Back to business, go ahead and select your skill. Just think of the one you want."

With a single thought of the skill he wanted, a new notification passed through his mind.

[Shield Bash Acquired]

"Huh . . . that was easy," Kaen muttered. "I'm glad I didn't accidentally choose the other. Any way to learn both skills or change them out?"

"I wish it were possible, but no one has ever been recorded being able to do that," Bren answered. "You mentioned your archery skill was chosen for you when you hit twenty. Were you in the middle of a fight?"

Kaen nodded and explained what had happened in Minoosh and how the skill had just presented itself.

Nodding, Bren tapped his chest where his lifestone was. "That isn't uncommon. In the heat of battle, when those moments mean life and death, a person may acquire a skill if they hit the threshold based on the need. Some also never get a choice. No one really knows how it works anymore."

Thumping the bench they were sitting on, Bren sighed. "I want to know how you managed to get a twenty already in shield use. I guess you might say I also want to know what your club skill is as well."

"Do you?" Kaen asked, grinning at Bren.

"No . . . I probably don't, but tell me anyway."

"I am only at a seventeen right now."

"Hairy dwarf balls!" exclaimed Bren. "That's impossible! Do you know how you are managing to do this?"

"I don't, but my lifestone has been vibrating and pounding for the last four hours as I have been practicing. During that time—"

"Four hours!?" Bren yelled as he jumped up from his seat. "Don't move!" He ran off to the doorway the other men had left through and started yelling for people to come quickly.

"What is it?" Kaen asked, suddenly nervous as Bren ran back to him and put his hand on Kaen's forehead.

"You should be dead or unconscious!" shouted Bren. "No one's body or lifestone should be able to handle that kind of stress!"

Rubbing his chest and thinking about how he felt, Kaen could feel fatigue in his bones and muscles, yet he wasn't sure if it was anything different than a normal day of training.

"I'm fine," Kaen protested, trying to stand up, yet unable to because Bren pushed him back down. "I mean, I am tired, but I am fine."

Bren shook his head and kept his hand on Kaen's shoulder and his butt planted on the bench.

"You come to me for training and agreed to do whatever I say. You will not move until the men get you and help you return to the inn."

Kaen started to protest, but the look on Bren's face made him stop.

"You will eat, drink, and go to sleep. I will also talk to Hess. You cannot allow this to happen again."

Bren leaned forward and whispered in Kaen's ear as men started streaming into the room. "In the old days, thousands of years ago, some men did what you proclaim to have done. Those men's hearts and lifestone exploded in their chests from constantly doing what you have told me you just did."

When Bren moved away from his face, Kaen saw the fear in Bren's eyes and realized he had possibly made a horrible mistake.

"Maybe some food and sleep would be good," Kaen acknowledged as men brought a chair with wheels into the room.

69

Partners in Plans

Kaen had felt like a spectacle as people watched Master Bren pushing him down the street in that *wheelchair,* as he called it. It did not ride well along the sidewalks, and everyone who saw and recognized him felt the need to come up and ensure he was ok. Having an army of people accompany them to the inn only would have created more of a fuss, so they made the journey without them.

They all had been relieved to hear that Bren wanted him to rest after another long training session to prevent injury or burnout after having just returned from a quest the day before.

As he let Bren push him back to the inn, Kaen had a thought enter his head.

Pammon, are you ok?

I am fine, why do you ask?

Kaen could tell Pammon was not flying but was instead up in the mountains to the east, probably basking in the sun.

You are usually flying unless you find food. Why are you sitting still?

I ate well, and finding a pack of boars helped reduce the required time. I am a little tired today.

Wincing, Kaen wondered at the thought running through his head.

When did you get tired?

It's been a few hours, but I felt drained, so I decided to relax and let the sun recharge me. Why do you ask?

I'm not sure if it was me and what my lifestone was doing. I think I unlocked how to make it respond, so I trained with it for four hours. The instructor told me that days long ago, men did similar things, but their hearts and lifestones exploded from doing so. I am afraid I may have caused you to be weak or tired by doing what I did.

A wave of something that felt like confusion or disbelief hit Kaen. When Pammon struggled with an emotion that wasn't joy, anger, or something simple, Kaen had a harder time understanding it.

I could feel your lifestone, but I knew you were focused and not in danger. I think I . . .

About ten seconds passed, and Kaen was about to ask Pammon why he had stopped.

I know I can feel it more now. Before we flew, I had a harder time knowing your lifestone was doing something. Now, it is like we are connected more. I am sure this is something we would know if we had one who could train us. Perhaps one day, we can find out more.

Should I be worried about the drain it might have on you when I use my lifestone?

A huge wave of laughter covered Kaen in his mind, and he found himself smiling from it.

I would not want to call myself a dragon if I were in danger because of what you did today. It was nothing that I could not have dealt with easily. I simply choose to enjoy a warm day with a full stomach. You do not need to worry about hurting me. I'm not weak like you two-legged people.

Pammon was laughing again, and it helped more than Kaen realized. The pit that had been growing in his stomach was starting to dissolve.

Well, thank you for telling me that. I'm glad to know someone isn't overconfident in their abilities.

A sudden jolt of the chair and a quick stop caused Kaen to realize that Bren had reached the street the inn was on. Parked out before the inn was an ornate coach with four horses and a small crowd of people standing around it.

"I'll be a giant's uncle," Bren murmured as he tapped Kaen's shoulder. "You need to stand up and walk from here."

Kaen climbed out of the chair and stretched before pointing at the cart. "I'm assuming you know who that is?"

"That is Lord Hurem," Bren stated as he pointed at the emblem on the front of the coach. "See those two snakes intertwined? They represent his family's crest, as they have been part of a medicine line for generations. Most of the healing potions one sees that are worth buying in this town come from their production facility."

Kaen tried to remember names Sulenda had mentioned earlier about lords and all those who wanted to meet him; Hurem did ring a bell, yet he could not remember why.

"I guess that means I'll have to go inside, even if I smell like a sweaty goblin?" joked Kaen.

"Odds are they are here to see you," Bren admitted, glancing around the street. "Most of their kind would never come here unless they had a significant reason to. By the looks of the people watching, you are that reason."

Glancing at the people on the street, Kaen finally noticed all of them had turned to watch him and Bren as they moved toward the inn and the coach. Most smiled and waved, but they gave them a wide berth so their path would not be blocked.

"I wish I had a different pair of clothes," Kaen stated as he glanced at what Bren was wearing. "Perhaps we both might wish for something other than this training armor."

Shaking his head, Bren smiled. "Better to show that you are constantly working on improving than lounging around all day inside an inn, if you ask me. Then again, no nobles are coming to visit me at my place."

Kaen nodded and smiled as they made their way to the door. There was no telling what to expect inside.

"Lord Hurem, allow me to introduce to you Adventurer Kaen."

Kaen gave a slight bow as he approached the table Hess, Sulenda, and the man he now knew was Lord Hurem were sitting at.

The man's back had been to him, but when he turned around and saw Kaen, a wave of shock hit him. The man looked maybe forty, if he was lucky, and his clothes were finer than the ones Kaen had tried on this morning. A fine gold chain ran across from each vest button, keeping the vest in place over his fit figure. The man's salt and pepper hair was cut short and spiked a little at the front, not the way he had imagined a Lord at all. His face had one small scar on it near his ear, but other than that, his skin looked perfect.

"Pleasure to meet you, Lord Hurem."

The man smiled and held out a hand toward Kaen. "Do me the pleasure of skipping the normal pageantry and welcome and join us at the table for a drink."

Grasping the man's hand, Kaen felt strength in his handshake. There was no doubt the man had a lifestone or that he was stronger than a normal man his age might appear.

"Lord Hurem, the man with me is Master Bren, who has been training me in the art of one-handed weapons and shields. Is there room at the table for him as well?"

Without delay, Lord Hurem extended his hand to Bren, who gave a firm handshake. "I would be honored to have the man working hard to keep you safe by training you join us. Nothing we discuss today isn't anything I plan on keeping quiet."

Sulenda snapped her fingers, and the server, Stacy, quickly brought another chair to the table while Eltina brought over a glass of milk and a small cup of alcohol for Bren.

"Sulenda tells me that you are interested in starting an academy or something like a school in the town. I reached out to a few of my friends in town, and we would be honored if you might allow us to help you in such a noble adventure."

Sitting there, doing his best to keep his mouth from hanging open, Kaen slowly drank his milk while glancing over the top of his mug at Hess and Sulenda. They were both smiling and nodding, but neither was helping in the conversation.

"I am interested in that," Kaen finally replied after putting his drink down. "I feel it is the least I can do as I originally intended for it to honor Luca and his sacrifice, but it is now helping to replace the large number of adventurers we have lost recently."

Lord Hurem frowned and nodded, rotating his glass cup between his fingers. "Nasty business, for sure. I heard the culprit had been found. If no women were present, I would spit for how disgusted I feel about this situation."

"Feel free to spit if you think it merits it," Sulenda proclaimed, and she leaned over and spat on the ground.

"While I am glad they were discovered, I wish we could have interrogated them correctly," Hess added.

Each of the men around the table mimicked Sulenda's action and spat on the room floor before sitting straight in their chairs again.

Kaen realized the room was almost empty when he sat back up. Sulenda had cleared out the inn, keeping most of the town outside, which now explained the crowd of people he had first seen by the carriage.

"Bad business to know a nation was behind this. We are considering slowing down our shipments of potions to them, even knowing how it might impact others," Lord Hurem declared, looking at Hess and Kaen. "I know I have the two of you to thank for finding that group disrupting trade in that direction. This is one of the many reasons I am here today to support your endeavor." He undid one of the chains on his vest, pulled out a piece of folded paper, and slid it across the wooden table to Kaen.

"This is a signed letter of promise that the bank will accept to help with what you are planning on doing, Kaen. I have also talked with a few people I know who have land that might be usable for such a place. I can have someone show you the grounds or let Sulenda act in your stead."

Picking up the letter, Kaen felt his face go white. There on the paper were eight signatures, all committing five gold each to the purchase of land, building supplies, and more for an academy to be started by him.

"I . . . I . . . "

No one said anything as Kaen sat stammering and glancing from the paper to Lord Hurem. "This was just an idea a week ago," Kaen finally declared as he held the paper out toward Hess and Sulenda. "How has it already gotten this far?"

"I was busy while you and Hess were off having fun and questing," answered Sulenda. "I told you I would pick the nobles to meet with. Things just got sped up a little bit after what you two squashed and after the news of this past week. The men and women on that paper are committed to what you want to do because they all see the importance of it now."

"You bringing Master Bren here was just a sign that this was meant to be," interrupted Lord Hurem. "I have heard great things about his training and the two boys who are currently under his tutelage. We do not doubt this place will be a success and a launching pad for the next generation of adventurers."

Kaen glanced at the others sitting around him, seeing all of their faces, each covered with a smile and eyes sparkling in excitement at what he would do.

"Kaen, I would be honored to help in any way I can and to recommend other instructors for the academy," Bren said as he put a hand on Kaen's shoulder. "Your name will carry a weight right now that no one else will. You will draw boys and girls across the kingdom who are willing to commit to something great."

"I don't know what to say," Kaen finally replied as he bobbed his head, still in shock at what had happened so quickly.

"Don't say anything," Hess declared as he tapped the table with his fist. "Drink your milk and smile. We will do what needs to be done."

Grinning, Kaen rolled his eyes but lifted his glass and took a long drink from his mug. "Actually, I do need to do something. I could really use a bath and some clean clothes. I know I stink."

Everyone laughed and nodded, rising from their seats.

"Lord Hurem, I promise to do the best I can for the school and will find some way to repay you for the aid." Kaen extended his hand toward Lord Hurem and waited for him to shake it.

Lord Hurem shook his head at Kaen while looking at Hess. "He doesn't know, does he?"

Sighing, Hess shook his head. "Remember what I said about not making promises or binding yourselves to lords and nobility?" Hess asked as he crossed his hands across his chest. "You are about to do that."

Kaen lowered his hand and, confused, looked at both men. "What do you mean?"

"You told me you would find a way to repay me. Worse is that you used the word *promise* during that. Had I wanted, I could have tried to use my lifestone and forced a bond across us. What I would have required to repay me could be years of service or something else. You must be careful what you pledge or promise to a noble."

Shock hit Kaen when he considered what that meant, and when he realized a bond like that might force him to use Pammon for something, he almost turned green from being sick. "I didn't know," he whispered.

"I assumed as much," Lord Hurem admitted as he clasped his hands behind his back. "I am not a man to abuse one like yourself, but there are many who would, especially as you grow in power. The only advantage you have is, the stronger you become, the harder it will be for one to invoke that kind of bond on you. So choose your words carefully when you promise someone something and shake on it, if they are of a noble line. Most do not possess the skill to force a bond, and the few that do are careful not to be accused of abusing it too often for fear of the king."

Standing there, lost in thoughts of what all he still did not know, Kaen nodded. "Thank you again, Lord Hurem, for your kindness. I shall do my best to remember it."

Slowly extending his hand toward him, Kaen smiled when Lord Hurem reached out and clasped his hand and shook it.

"Much better!" he replied, smiling at Kaen.

70

Dancing Again

The past day had been a whirlwind of activity. Four different properties had been visited, and Hess, Sulenda, Bren, and Kaen had selected one with ten acres of space on the outside of town. Better still, it was about two hours from the inn by foot, the land was owned by one of the signers of the promise letter.

Once the land had been chosen, they had gone to the central bank within Ebonmount, signing documents for what seemed like hours.

Kaen had been amazed at how much of the paperwork had already been drawn up. Sulenda had a list of numbers, expected costs, foremen she had in mind, estimated time for the build to be complete, and more. Barring a major rainstorm during that time, she expected at least a third of the academy to be finished within six months. That included a section of dorms for students and workers who would manage the children living on the property. Kitchens, laundry stations, and more would be ready for use from the day they opened the doors.

A small section of the training grounds would be completed, and classrooms and other buildings would be finished within another six months.

Sulenda would handle all the applications and begin the process of vetting and preparing for employees and students. Eltina was not excited about the added duties she would have to undertake at the inn. Still, she had begrudgingly admitted the difference she had seen in Sulenda since Hess had returned.

The city was abuzz with the news of an academy being constructed by Kaen. Hess had now required him to ride a horse as people were flocking to him, bringing their children, hoping they might be chosen.

Hess had handled everyone who came forward and approached him, letting them know Kaen had no part in the selection process and that there would be information coming out soon. He had also made it clear that anyone who continued to pester Kaen about anything academy related would be cut off from it.

That news spread just as fast, and soon, Hess and Kaen could ride their horses through town unmolested.

"Can we go get a quest?" Kaen asked as he watched Hess chew the pheasant that was tonight's dinner. "I need to take care of some things."

Nodding, Hess swallowed his bite and washed it down with a few big gulps of the ale Eltina had procured for him. "I figured we would need to do that soon. Tomorrow morning, why don't you go and pick us one, and I will prepare the horses and supplies for it."

"Don't forget the quest after this, I'll go with Gertrude and her team. I need to get some practice with them, like we talked about."

"I won't forget," Hess replied as he tore off a piece of his bread and rubbed it around on his plate, letting it soak in the juices and sauce from the bird. "I also need to pick up something for this quest. Something for our friend."

Kaen smiled, knowing that the harness was ready to pick up. It would take some modification to ensure that it worked properly, but with the straps and buckles on it, Hess believed it would stay in place once tightened down.

"I know someone who is excited about that."

Chuckling, Hess rolled his eyes. "I know two someones who are excited about it."

As they chatted, Kaen lounged in his chair, watching people drinking and eating in the inn. The city had calmed down, but business here was always strong. There was another adventurer who was supposed to be testing, and the city was betting on her, even though she was not expected to be anything but a wood-rank adventurer.

Sulenda had surprised him with the number of options people could place on their bets, from how well they would do on the test. Each percentage carried a different betting odd.

Sitting there, letting his mind wander, Kaen suddenly felt a hand on his shoulder and heard his name called out.

"Trouble you for another dance?"

He had not noticed Hess's reaction when the woman had walked up behind him, but that voice and that smell struck Kaen like a bolt of lightning.

He leaped to his feet, spun around, and saw the young woman he had danced with the night of the celebration. Her long black hair was over one shoulder in a braid, and she wore a green dress that accented her eyes and hugged her form like he wished he could.

"I . . . I . . . I still don't know your name," he said in shock, struggling to get the words he wanted out of his mouth.

"You don't?" she replied with a mischievous grin. "I wonder why that is."

Stifling a cough, Kaen calmed himself and bowed slightly as he backed up. "I believe it is because you ran off after we danced."

"I would never have run off. That wouldn't be very ladylike. I think your adoring fans and followers carried you off while I had to walk home, all by myself."

He could see her smiling innocently and felt the heat in his cheeks as he tried to appear calm and cool, but his heart ignored that request. "Well, perhaps you could share your name with me now?"

She smiled, and her white teeth looked like a perfect row of pearls, adding to the beauty she already possessed.

"Well, Sir Kaen, my name is Ava. Ava Hurem."

A sudden coughing fit erupted behind him, and Kaen turned to see Hess choking on his ale. It was running down his face and out both nostrils as he tried to suck in air.

"That is a beautiful name for a beau . . . " Kaen froze and saw her smile get a little larger as his brain processed the name she had just shared with him. "Hurem? As in Lord Hurem's daughter?"

"I do believe some people call him that. I just call him father. I heard you met the other day, and he spoke highly of you. Was it a good visit?"

The room almost seemed to spin, and Kaen leaned over and put his hand on the chair back to support himself.

Lord Hurem's daughter had been the one he had danced with? The old man had not mentioned any of this to him when they met!

Suddenly, the knowledge of that meeting, the Lord not making an oath bind him, hit his chest like an ogre had with a club.

"Can we sit down a moment," Kaen mumbled as he pulled out the chair he held onto.

"I'd be delighted!"

Hess had managed to clean himself up, yet his face had not lost the red tint from all the choking he had done. Sulenda had joined them, and now they sat smiling at each other, and very few words were being spoken.

"Kaen, I do believe you wanted to know her name, and now you do," Sulenda declared, breaking the long silence.

"I did. I did want to know your name, Ava," Kaen answered, still trying to figure out how to act. "I'm just not sure how to go from here."

"What is there to worry about Kaen?" Ava asked. "My father knows I am here, and he is certainly ok with me spending a little time with you and getting to know you. You are considered to be all the news in every part of the city. Rumor has it you are to meet the king in a week."

Kaen nodded. The original plan had changed when the guild hall informed the king of an entourage of higher-ups from the guild council arriving. Kingdom duties were to be put before a meeting with an adventurer. Now, he could go and take a quest and spend some time with Pammon.

"I believe that is still the plan, unless someone informs me otherwise. I am planning on heading out tomorrow on a quest," Kaen informed her, not realizing he was rambling on as he stared at her. "I would enjoy spending time with you once I got back if you wanted."

Laughing, Ava batted her eyelashes at him. "Are you telling me you are done with me for the night?"

Waving his hands in the air and shaking his head, Kaen laughed. "No, I just seem to have forgotten how to talk. You have been on my mind since that night, and seeing you here has me seeing stars."

Ava blushed just a little bit, and Hess let out a small groan before Sulenda kicked him under the table.

"Well, I am glad to know I have that effect on you. I would still enjoy a dance tonight if you were willing," she stated as she motioned to the area where a man was sitting and playing a song on a lute.

"I'd be delighted to," Kaen said, sliding back in his chair and helping Ava from hers.

As Kaen and Ava moved to where their first dance had taken place, Hess grunted. "This might not be a good thing."

Sulenda nodded in agreement as she watched the two of them laugh and begin to dance. "All sorts of odds are going off in my head right now. I'm not sure I want to bet on them either."

An hour later, Kaen and Ava waved goodbye to those who had joined them on the dance floor and moved to a booth to chat.

Their hair was matted and sweaty, yet neither cared as they crashed into their seats, waiting for one of the servers to come and get their order.

"I had not expected to dance for that long," Kaen said, laughing. "Once everyone joined in, it would be wrong just to quit!"

"That was the most fun I have had in over a week," Ava replied as she adjusted her dress and fixed her braid that had come undone a little. "If parties at my parents or other nobles were that much fun, I would actually want to attend them."

Beatrice showed up with two cups of water and some bread, giving a wink to Kaen as she set the drinks and food on the table. "What can I get the two of you to eat or drink? Surely, you both must be famished after all that dancing!"

"You know what I want," Kaen answered quickly, motioning to Ava.

"I'll have what he is having," Ava replied.

"You sure?" Kaen asked as he grinned and winked at Ava.

Laughing, she nodded. "It can't be that strong, can it?"

Beatrice chuckled and shook her head. "Two Adventurer Kaen specials coming right up!"

"They named a drink after you?" Ava asked with a questioning look on her face. "Doesn't that seem a bit overboard?"

Kaen gave a playful shrug and motioned around the room with his hand. "I didn't name it after me. It is more of a joke since I never drink anything else."

"Two Adventurer Kaen's! Enjoy!"

Ava laughed when she saw the tankard of milk sitting in front of her and Kaen. "Milk?!"

Kaen nodded and took a few long drinks before setting his mug back on the table and wiping his mouth with his arm. "Only the best!" he quipped.

Beatrice laughed as she left to help someone else in the room.

"Give it a try if you think you can handle it," Kaen said.

Rolling her eyes, Ava grabbed her drink and took a few swallows before setting it down on the table in the mock achievement of managing such a feat. "It does taste pretty good," she admitted.

Snickering, Kaen tapped his lip and winked at Ava. "Got something right here. I didn't know you were part dwarf."

With her face turning slightly red, Ava reached up, felt the milk mustache on her face, and groaned as she wiped it off with her hand. "I'll get you back for that comment," she replied playfully.

"I can't wait."

Lying in his bed, staring at the ceiling, Kaen found himself smiling from ear to ear. He and Ava had talked for hours, and she had promised to try and find another chance to visit.

Knowing her name and learning so much about her felt different than the usual women he had flirted with.

"Pammon is going to kill me," he muttered aloud in his empty room as he closed his eyes, knowing he would dream about Ava all night.

"I swear if that man brushes my privates again, I am going to punch him in the face," Kaen declared with a growl as Ava kept laughing.

"I believe my father had mentioned that it does happen occasionally when they measure you for a new outfit like this," she answered, her face red from laughing for so long. "Besides, Kaen, you cannot wear your current clothes when you see the king."

"I know," Kaen replied as he rolled his eyes. "I just don't want to know how much this will cost. The fabric alone is nicer than anything I can imagine one wearing."

"To impress and deal with the people you need to occasionally meet, you must look enough like them to fit in. Your manners will take more time to teach, but all we can do for now is fix the outside. The inside will come later."

Kaen blew a raspberry at Ava and glanced back in the mirror the tailor had set up. He didn't recognize himself in this outfit. The black pants fit rather snug but not so tight he couldn't run or jump if needed. The copper vest went amazingly well with the white shirt he was wearing. He was not sure about all the jackets he had tried on already.

"You do look rather charming," admitted Ava as she took a sip of the tea Cedric, the tailor, had brought her. "In fact, that would be a perfect outfit to wear to one of my father's balls."

"Why did we have to do this right after breakfast? I had plans."

"And what were these plans?" Ava asked as she motioned to the return of the tailor. "I thought part of the plans was spending time with me."

Kaen groaned and then smiled. "I wanted to go see Master Bren. I needed to test something."

She peered at him over the edge of her cup and nodded. "I'm not sure if I should be offended or impressed. Most would relax, yet you continue pressing yourself to get better. An impressive trait, to say the least."

"I just want to be the best I can," he replied with a smile. "After all, I'm just a backwoods commoner about to meet the king!"

Kaen laughed, until the older man pulled out a measuring tape again.

"Sir," Ava called out as she moved quickly to get between the tailor and Kaen. "Perhaps we could forgo any measurements. *Master Kaen* has a few other things to attend to today."

"I understand," he answered with a bow. "I can have the first outfit ready by tomorrow evening. The others will take me a week, unless you also want to pay the rush rate on those."

"A week will be fine," Kaen declared, moving to Ava's side.

Cedric bowed and then motioned Kaen to the changing area where the clothes he had been wearing when he first arrived were waiting.

"If you will excuse me, Lady Hurem, I must change from my kingly clothes to my play clothes," Kaen stated as he gave a bow and a wink.

Shaking her head, Ava rolled her eyes, but still smiled. "I'll be here, waiting to see this transformation."

Darting across the floor, Kaen laughed again as he pulled the curtain behind him. With the curtain closed, he took two quick breaths. His heart had been racing the whole time.

Who knew a date with Ava to watch him pick out clothes would make him feel like this?

71

Learning Things We Don't Know

We will be scouting the southwest mountains about four days from here. Do you want to start heading that way?

I will, but let me finish with the boar I am eating. I need to clear out a few more if I can. It appears these piggies have been breeding with no one hunting them. I have managed to kill about thirty or more in the last few days.

Is it that infested? We always killed them when we saw them back near Minoosh. They always tore up the land.

I have probably seen well over a hundred, and they are getting closer to the farms and properties to the east. You should tell Hess what I have seen, and let him figure out what should be done.

Ok, but I can't wait to see you tonight. I have something to tell you later.

After sending that thought, Kaen felt the wave of wonder and interest flowing through the bond.

You cannot tell me now?

I would prefer to see your reaction when I tell you. Nothing bad. I promise.

Pammon grumbled but stopped after a few seconds. His frustration at being told to wait was evident.

You better not have done something stupid.

Kaen laughed.

He was only a few blocks from the inn and knew Hess would be ready to go.

None of the quests were any that he wanted to do, and most everything being offered right now were guaranteed weaker ones, as the guild wanted to verify that no one was walking into a trap again. Mandy had looked worn out, and he could only imagine the hours they were working as they prepared for the coming visit of the higher-ups.

* * *

"This seems like a waste of time," Hess said with a grunt as he finished reading over the quest details. "Are things that bad that they are just giving us simple scouting reports?"

"I couldn't take the other three they offered, as all of them were cave related or too close to people. Rumor has it there has been an increase in goblin, hobgoblins, and orc activity like never before. You remember what we found at Minoosh."

Hess nodded as he handed back the quest sheet to Kaen. "You are right. I guess something feels strange, though, for this to be the last quest we do before you join the others. I had hoped for something better."

Kaen rolled his eyes and saw Hess grin. "On a side note, did you ever get the jewelry we brought back identified?"

Hess nodded before walking to where his horse was hitched. "Let's talk about that on the road. I must go before Sulenda asks me for more thoughts on your project. I believe she wants me to retire and work for you."

Kaen laughed as he thought about that. "Work for me, huh? I might be able to afford that. Seven coppers a day?"

Settling himself in his saddle, Hess grunted and spat on the ground. "I don't know if I would get out of bed for seven coppers," he answered with a frown. "I would probably need at least a silver a day, if I knew I had to deal with kids again."

They sat on their mounts, staring at each other and thinking about Hess's words. A few seconds later, they started laughing and got their horses moving.

"Was I that bad?"

"No, son, you were not. I would gladly do it again."

Kaen smiled and moved his horse next to Hess.

"Thanks, Dad."

The farms were almost out of sight as they reached the tree line. They had a few hours before they would have to take the split in the road; otherwise, they would find themselves back in Minoosh, and Hess knew it was not time to return yet.

"Can we talk about the loot now?" Kaen begged again, having already asked twice before they reached where they were now.

"Fine," Hess groaned as he glanced around, ensuring no one was near them. The last cart they had seen had been a good fifteen minutes ago, and the path ahead was empty.

"The truth is most of the items we found were nothing great. Most of the rings were a plus-one for strength or intelligence. The ring that survived Pammon's flame is still being identified. The man who does this for adventurers has said it is one of the highest he has seen in years and is hoping to have it finished in a week or two."

"It's that powerful?" interrupted Kaen as he leaned closer to Hess, intently listening.

Pushing Kaen back onto his horse, Hess nodded and grunted. "Don't fall off your horse, or I'll never let you ride Pammon," warned Hess. "I don't think he would appreciate that at all."

Settling back in his saddle, Kaen started to give Hess the finger and stopped, lowering his hand back to his reins, and then sighed. "Fine, forgive me if I'm a bit excited to learn about the loot from my first quest. It's not like it's a dream I have had for years."

"I know," Hess answered with a chuckle. "If you would stop interrupting me, I could tell you the rest. The necklace from the mage you fought in the woods is a magic-user's dream. It adds three to wisdom and intelligence. It will sell nicely, as neither of us needs something like that. There were two rings with two dexterity and one ring with two constitutions. Both of those will be returned to us when we make it back from this quest."

Kaen sat there, fidgeting in his saddle, waiting to ensure Hess was done before speaking. "That's it? No kick butt rings or necklaces?" Kaen asked with a groan. "I thought there would be stuff better than what I got when I did my quest!"

"We discussed this the night I gave you that equipment for that quest. You are lucky the man let me buy that pendant you still wear!" exclaimed Hess. "A plus-one ring is a good ring for most adventurers. The items we won't use will fetch a good price, and that necklace will probably bring in ten to fifteen gold! That's over fifty years to earn enough gold for one necklace! Most adventurers never get that kind of money to toss around until they hit the platinum rank. I myself would struggle to purchase that item if it wasn't for the years of adventuring I spent or the money I left in the bank to earn interest."

Kaen let out a sigh, and he closed his eyes for a moment. "I just thought they would have better loot since they were so strong."

"Hairy dwarf balls, Kaen! How often do I have to remind you that adventuring isn't like you hear in the stories? There aren't magical swords everywhere or rings that add one hundred strength! Most people you will adventure with would be excited for a ring that gives them one stat!"

A long moan left Hess's lips after he finished the smackdown he had just delivered.

"I'm not trying to be mean, but if you go walking into a group and expect stuff to show up like this, your fellow adventurers are going to be a disappointment," Hess explained after he caught his breath. "Unless you fight people as we did, which could have easily taken out an unprepared party, finding any magical items is rare until one hits a gold or higher rank. The stuff you see trickles down or comes from people crafting and selling them."

"You never explained how magical crafting works!" Kaen interjected when Hess paused. "I have no idea how most of this stuff works because you wouldn't share it when we lived in Minoosh, and there isn't some book I can just read to know it all!"

Kaen jerked on his horse's reins a little harder than he wanted, causing it to almost come to a full stop.

Hess tugged gently on his horse and slowed it down. "I know . . . I know it is my fault, and I keep forgetting that you haven't gotten a clue as to how most of it works because you were able to skip so many ranks."

"Well, why not tell me how it works now? We got like six hours, at least, before we get somewhere we can stay with Pammon at."

Rubbing his face with his massive hand, Hess sighed and nodded. "Ok . . . let's talk about magical item crafting first . . . "

Hess took a drink from the waterskin on his horse. His throat felt tired after talking for about four hours. He had tried to impart as much knowledge about how items were made, how magic worked for casters, the farming of resources and ingredients, and more. It reminded him that they still needed to get those antlers from the massive buck Pammon had killed, if an animal had not consumed them.

"I had not realized it took so much power for a ring to be enchanted with just a plus-one stat," Kaen said out loud as he thought about all the stuff Hess had just said. "Three weeks or more from a person silver rank or higher, just pouring energy into it?"

Hess nodded as he wiped his mouth, offering the water to Kaen, who waved it off.

"Years, son . . . Years if someone wants a plus three. Whoever owned that necklace before the man you killed took it, invested a lot of time and money for it. No doubt it has an owner who still wants it back."

"And you said Luca was strong enough to cast how many spells before going dry? Fifteen to twenty? Is that why his lightning spells seemed to fizzle and barely send anything at the end?"

Hess nodded as he hooked his drink back onto his horse. "For him to have enchanted Aubri and still be able to do what he did, his energy pool must have been pretty big. Imagine it like Pammon and how he slowly grows in how long he can use his fire. He is almost to what, fifteen seconds?"

Kaen nodded. It might be more now, but he had not asked in a while. Pammon rarely spent time testing it since he always just *knew* how long it lasted.

"You still believe he would have beat me in a fight?"

Hess nodded and gave a slight shrug. "Toe-to-toe in an arena without a doubt. He would have finished you easily, just like your dad would have struggled against someone like Selmah. Mages have a lot of power, if they keep you at a distance. Once that distance is erased, they can fall quickly, or if an archer shoots them before they know they are there."

Muddling all that information over, Kaen was beginning to grasp how magic worked, and knowing that he could try to learn some was exciting. Hess had told him that most magic users spent years developing the ability to cast spells but that with the way his lifestone seemed to work, he would succeed faster than the rest.

Pammon was waiting at the edge of the mountains and the woods, lying down near the trees to stay out of sight if someone or something came out there. They were going to follow the tree line for a few days, as getting to the place they needed to scout was not accessible any other way besides trudging through overgrown woods.

"He is excited," Hess said with a chuckle. "You tell him about the girl yet? What is her name again?"

Rolling his eyes, Kaen shook his head. "I wanted to tell him in person and have the harness with me when I did it."

"Using your brain. I like it. You two planning on flying tonight?"

The mischievous grin that Kaen had worn for most of his teen years flashed across his face.

"Did you really need to ask? You and I know the only way I won't have to listen to him whine tonight is if we go flying."

Hess nodded and started to undo the bag that held the harness he had constructed for them. "You take it and get with him. I'll manage the horses so they don't get spooked by his presence again."

Kaen nodded and caught the bag after Hess tossed it to him. "I guess this means you will take care of dinner also?"

"Of course, we both know my cooking is the best."

Groaning, Kaen slipped off his horse and brought his reins to Hess. "Yes . . . We both know that to be a lie."

Hess watched as Kaen took off, running toward Pammon, swinging the bag as he ran. Knowing this was their last quest together for a while, he understood it was more than that. It was time for Kaen to grow up and be on his own. The pain of that realization hit him, and he felt his chest tighten up.

"Hoste, if you're watching, I've done what I can. Keep an eye on him for both of us, if you would."

72

Everyone Flies

Neither one had spoken a word for the last fifteen minutes as they glided a mile above the tree line. Kaen had only commented once about how cold it had gotten, but he did not want to complain as he gazed at the world beneath him.

Trees looked like ants, small paths and streams carved through them, turning a mush of green into a maze of some sort.

The mountain stretched higher still, seeming to go on forever, making Kaen understand why no one had entered this *bowl* of mountains till an opening had been cut into it. Even with the sun setting to the west, he could see far across it, a picture better than any painting he could ever imagine.

The harness was working perfectly. The leather wrapped around each of his wrists, keeping him secure. A few gusts of wind had initially scared him, but Pammon reacted perfectly, and with the harness, Kaen did not fear falling.

I cannot believe you get to see all of this every day. It is amazing.

Pammon thrummed underneath him.

If you think this is amazing, wait till we are in the clouds. Then you will know what true beauty is. Not some dark-haired, green-eyed, iron token adventurer woman.

Pammon's displeasure was still there, but Kaen ignored it, letting the moment blow away all the negativity.

How about you fly higher if you promise not to act like an eggling and pout over not getting to eat the chicken you want?

Snorting, Pammon shook his snout, launching snot out that hit Kaen in the face.

I would rather not talk about that chicken. I have considered flying back and finishing it off for how it spoke to me.

Kaen laughed, even as he wiped the goo from his face with his shoulder. Nothing would ruin this moment right now.

Higher and stop complaining. I want to enjoy this.

Pammon didn't hesitate, angling his body upward and flapping his giant wings, sending them soaring into the sky. Soon, they were halfway up the mountains, making Kaen wonder just how tall they were.

Pammon glided by the mountains, staying near the rocky edge as he rode along their updraft, easily handling the twisting winds that occasionally struck. His long hours of practice over the past month had paid off.

Look over there where I am watching. A herd of deer.

Kaen focused on where he knew Pammon was looking. He couldn't see the pack for a moment, until they moved a bit, their brown hides slowly moving across a small field of greenery.

I would go and eat one or two if you were not here, but I am not sure I could do that with you on me right now. Perhaps one day.

Nodding even though he knew Pammon could not see it, Kaen looked forward to when they could hunt from Pammon's back. He could even shoot from Pammon's back with a saddle and a few ropes. That thought made him realize what he was missing out on.

I have an idea. Do you think you could fly with Hess at all tomorrow? Even if it was for a little bit?

Let me think about that. He is much larger than you, but with his harness, and maybe if you tied him down, I could manage for a few minutes.

Smiling to himself, Kaen knew that if he could get Hess up here for just a little bit, his plan for tomorrow would definitely work.

"You want me to do what?" Hess asked, a bit of concern in his voice.

"Fly with Pammon tomorrow. Use the harness, as it works perfectly! I'll even tie you to him with a rope if you feel you need it!"

Glancing at Pammon, who Hess swore was smiling, he shook his head in disbelief. "I know we talked about me flying, but does he really think he can carry me?"

Pammon moved his snout before Hess and nodded it up and down.

Please tell him I can answer those questions for myself.

Busting out in laughter, Kaen took a moment before he could relay that message. "Pammon says he can answer yes and no questions. No need to rely upon me to play middleman."

Reaching out, Hess scratched Pammon's nose ridge and smiled. "Sorry, old habits, Pammon," he said as he shook his head at what he was getting into. "If you believe you can carry me, then I would be honored and excited to fly with you."

Hess's voice had changed. Kaen could tell he was no longer afraid but looking forward to what tomorrow might bring.

"Alright then. Tomorrow, you will go up with him for a few, and I will watch the horses and be the one who stays down here worrying."

After Hess returned to the horses to turn in for the night, Kaen checked on the fire and saw that the log technique he had picked up from Aubri was working well. All night, the fire stayed going, never needing someone to wake up and add to it.

Are you going to tell me your actual plan for why you want Hess to fly with me?

Without turning around to face Pammon, Kaen smiled. He knew that the bond betrayed him when they were this close.

I will see if I can ride you, and we'll fly to the area we are supposed to scout. If we can, you could easily be where we need to be by afternoon tomorrow. That would allow me to gather the necessary intel and give us a few more days together. A few more days to fly.

Pammon thrummed, and joy flooded over him. Kaen turned and saw a twinkle in Pammon's eyes.

You may be smarter than I give you credit for. Perhaps we can borrow the rope Hess will need, and you could try shooting if we have time.

Kaen jogged to where Pammon was and leaped at him, grabbing his snout with both hands, trying to wrestle his face to the ground.

Pammon growled playfully, and when Kaen was unprepared, nut-racked him with the tip of his snout.

Kaen let go, falling backward, coughing and choking, trying to catch his breath.

Why!?

Pammon thrummed loudly, shaking his head as he looked up at the sky, his whole body vibrating from laughing so hard.

You and Hess do that all the time to each other. I thought it was something you did when playing.

Groaning, Kaen held his privates as he staggered forward and leaned against Pammon's neck.

Yes, but we have mastered the art of hitting with just enough pressure to make it ache, not to make me wonder if I will ever have children!

The trees started to echo with Pammon thrumming as his body shook. It was obvious to Kaen just how funny he thought this was.

Well, even though I did not intend to do that, perhaps it is a good idea. Tiny ones like you might not be the best thing.

Kaen slapped Pammon's neck, knowing it didn't hurt. Still, doing it to let out some of the frustration.

Perhaps I should return the favor to you.

The thrumming stopped immediately, and Pammon put his snout in Kaen's face.

There are some things worse than death. I would not advise it.

Kaen started laughing, ignoring the pain, knowing Pammon was dead serious.

"Don't forget to open your eyes!" Kaen shouted as Pammon leaped into the air.

It had taken two ropes and a bit of adjustment on how the ropes crossed Pammon's body to make Hess feel comfortable. He still looked more nervous than any other time Kaen could remember.

Be gentle with him.

I won't drop him, I promise!

Thinking he would lose his breakfast, Hess forced his eyes to stay open as Kaen shouted at him to do so. The ground disappeared quickly as Pammon launched them off the ground and into the air.

Soon, the treetops were at his shoulder level, quickly falling underneath him as Pammon rose higher and higher. His heart missed a few beats as he saw over the tops of the trees. He had seen many forests from different mountainsides, but glancing down, he saw no stone underneath his feet. Just a less-than-a-year-old dragon carrying him toward the clouds.

A few deep breaths later, Hess roared in excitement as Pammon continued climbing, letting him see the sunlight streaming over them from the east across the forest. The whole valley was below him, and if pressed, he would struggle to say what was more beautiful, this sight or Sulenda.

As Pammon flattened and took Hess across the treetops, Hess could not believe how much he could really see. If he had his map out, he would compare what was on it to what he was seeing right now. It made him think about the map in Sulenda's office. It was drawn to scale, which meant it must have been created by people on dragons.

He shivered a little, some from the cold but also from knowing what he was doing. He was flying! A dream he'd had as a kid and was now fulfilling as a grown man.

Gently easing the hand on the reins, he realized he was gripping them like a man thinking he was going to die. Hess gently patted Pammon's neck. He would owe Pammon something for this. Perhaps a cow might be possible.

After a few more turns, he realized Pammon was slowly approaching the trees. They appeared less like ants or insects now, and more like plants, growing faster as his and Pammon's altitude dropped.

I guess I should not expect him to be able to carry my weight for so long.

Hess chuckled as he imagined how much more he weighed than Kaen. Perhaps he owed his horse a treat too.

Suddenly, Pammon surged ahead for a few beats of his wings as if energized or showing off, picking up speed for a moment before settling back down.

Laughing to himself, Hess wondered if Kaen had put him up to that, knowing he would clench the reins how he had just now.

As they approached where Kaen was waiting and waving, Hess smiled, realizing he finally understood a small part of what these two must feel. They were bonded, and Dragon Riders were supposed to *ride* their dragon. He had been a fool for not trusting and letting them do what they were meant to do.

The time is coming, and I think you know it, Kaen. Soon, you must announce that Pammon is your dragon.

As that thought slipped through his mind, Hess was grateful for the wind that carried the tears that had slipped from his eyes. His time teaching Kaen was at an end.

I have to land! He is sooo heavy! moaned Pammon. **I cannot keep this up, or I will not be able to fly with you today!**

Then land. He will understand, and I know he will appreciate that you let him fly with you. It means a lot to both of us.

Kaen could feel the struggle Pammon felt. It was as if he somehow knew how hard it was to carry Hess through the air. As he watched the two begin to descend, he closed his eyes and let the things Pammon felt flow through him.

He could feel Pammon's body struggle as it descended. Hess's weight and having to lift him as high as they had gone, had taken its toll. Pammon was right. He might be too tired to fly today with Kaen. Wishing he could help, Kaen felt his lifestone pulse; no, it was thrumming.

Vibrating.

Like a thread was tied to it and connected to Pammon, Kaen sensed it as he stood there, eyes closed, focusing on his dragon. Giving over to it, he felt his strength slip through the bond, flooding into Pammon.

What is that? gasped Pammon as the strength from Kaen surged through his body.

Kaen almost stumbled to the ground before catching himself and realizing what he had done. He had given Pammon endurance from his own body, just like when Pammon had kept him going during the battle of Minoosh.

I found out how to return the favor! I found out how to help you when you need it.

Kaen stood there, amazed at how it felt; it was as if his heart and Pammon's were connected.

I . . . thank you. I can tell the difference in our connection. I can tell you do too.

Kaen nodded, realizing he did. They were now bound even closer than before.

73

Aerial Scouting

Hess stood there, scratching Pammon's head while Kaen undid the ropes they had used to fasten his legs.

"I owe you for that, Pammon. I cannot tell you how amazing that was, but I will treasure that moment for a lifetime."

Pammon trilled as Hess scratched his scales, content to receive a few extra scratches.

Tell him I can try to do that again if he loses weight.

A coughing fit came over Kaen as he heard Pammon, requiring him to take a moment to compose himself.

"I'm guessing he made a joke?" Hess asked.

Kaen nodded as he moved from under Pammon, pulling the rope with him. "He said if you lose some weight, you could fly longer."

Hess roared in laughter and patted Pammon's neck gently. "I could probably stand to lose a few pounds, but I am sure you will be strong enough to carry me, the way you have been eating."

The thrum of Pammon's laughter reverberated, and Kaen joined in. "I'm just glad he hunted this morning, so I don't have to listen to him complaining about needing to eat all day. We are seriously going to have to figure something out with how much he is eating."

"I have a few ideas," Hess stated as he turned to face Kaen. "Now tell me about the plan you have in your head. It's written all over your face you are thinking about something."

"Am I that obvious?"

"I've raised you and learned your tells. I know this flying trip was part of the plan. I'm just not sure what that plan is exactly."

Kaen grinned and then shrugged as he dropped the rope he had been coiling up onto the ground. "You saw all of the forest and could see me while you were up in the sky, right?"

Hess nodded, narrowing his eyes at Kaen. He felt he knew where this was going to go.

"So if Pammon and I took off after he has rested from carrying you, he and I could scout part of the quest. Just like a real Dragon Rider would."

Hess nodded slowly and crossed his arms over his chest while he mulled over Kaen's plan. "You think you two could fly over there, scout it out from the sky, and then come back? Would you bring a weapon or would you just be scouting?"

Kaen bent down and started drawing in the dirt with his knife. "This is the mountain line, and over here is the forest. We cut out a good day or two of riding if we fly. We were never supposed to engage in anything unless we needed to. We are just checking on the goblin, hobgoblin, and orc movements. Once that is done, we would have two days to spend hanging out and practicing."

"Practicing what?" Hess asked as he realized the real reason for all of this was about to be given.

Flashing the grin he always gave when he wanted something, Kaen motioned to Pammon.

"I want to practice shooting from his back. If we strap my legs like we did yours, I should be able to stay seated and take a few shots on some targets or even deer if we can find some. I need to get some practice in while I can. After this quest ends, you know it will be harder for me to get time with Pammon, especially for things like this."

Hess saw Pammon and Kaen both looking at him. The stupid dragon almost looked like he was trying to make his eyes seem gentle, and they even appeared a little bigger, if that were possible. Hess knew this day would come, which was why he had the harness made. They would need to figure out how to make a saddle. Hiding the reason for creating a saddle for a dragon would be difficult.

"If we do this," Hess began, holding up three fingers. "First, you will not try to engage anything you find while scouting. This is a scouting mission, not a fighting one."

Kaen started to talk, and Hess cut him off. "Second! If Pammon feels he is tired at all, he will not risk you two. He will land somewhere safe and then only fly once he is certain he has fully recovered."

Pammon nodded, causing Hess to lose his serious expression and chuckle.

"Lastly, I want the two of you to remember you have a lifetime together. Do not do something stupid or rush into something. I want to watch the two of you grow old together."

Kaen smiled and darted forward, giving Hess a big hug. Returning the hug, Hess laughed when Pammon moved close and encircled them with his neck and body.

He is a soft one, even though he pretends to be mean.

That he is, Pammon, that he is.

The wind swept Kaen's laughter away as Pammon flew higher than he had the day before. It was a lot colder up here, but for some reason, the wind did not affect him as it should have. His eyes and body felt sharper, more in tune, if he had to describe it. Since he had shared a bit of his strength with Pammon, it was as if something had changed inside him. Pammon had already commented on how it felt more comfortable as they flew through the sky with him on his back.

It is like you weigh less, even though I know you do not.

One day, we will talk to a real Dragon Rider and learn about what we don't know. There has to be so much more that we are not aware of.

Well, the day you start breathing fire is the day I want a bow of my own.

Kaen scratched the scales near his hands and smiled. At that moment, everything was perfect.

For three hours, they had flown, the landscape below them moving like a current in a river. The trees, small towns, streams, and small lakes all disappeared as if they were constantly moving. The mountain bowl had been estimated to be well over a hundred miles wide, but flying on Pammon, it seemed like he could cover it in a day, if he wanted. All those days spent walking or on horseback were so slow compared to this. He wondered how far they could travel before running out of land.

How much of this have you flown over before?

Not much of this part. The cave we were in is off to the northeast. I am a lot faster now than I was then, and we could quickly get there if we wanted to try.

Can you hover for a moment again? I want to check the map, and I don't want it to fly off like the first time.

Pammon slowed down and beat his wings faster, keeping them from moving much. The first time Kaen had tried pulling the map out had been a disaster. The wind had snatched it from his hand, and it had taken him a few attempts to retrieve it midair. It had gotten him two points in his dragon riding skill, as Pammon had to maneuver, and Kaen had to reach out to get it.

Kaen glanced at the map and down at the shape of the forest and the mountain. To the south was their target, and they were only about ten minutes away from where they were supposed to scout.

Just a little farther ahead, where I am looking at, Kaen informed Pammon as he put his map back into his pouch.

He tapped Pammon's neck, and Pammon dropped from the sky a little, picking up speed and focusing on the area Kaen was looking at.

Kaen glanced at the mountains off to the west and saw that they were now three-fourths of the way up them. He saw where even the shrubs disappeared on the side of them, becoming nothing but rocky, dry areas. Seeing it all left him in awe at the sheer amount of rock surrounding this valley.

This isn't good. There are goblins, orcs, and hobgoblins down there. I can see around forty or more, cutting down trees and going in and out of a cave. Do you want me to take you lower?

No, I don't want to give them a chance to see us.

Kaen could barely make them out when Pammon had lowered their altitude a little, seeing the mass of creatures working and a huge tree falling near the edge of the mountains. What they were doing was a mystery, and why were there so many of them here? Hess had told him there had not been any real presence of these creatures inside the bowl for a long time.

Can you tell me how many of each you see or think there are?

Pammon grunted and kept flying circles overhead, slowly gaining altitude since Kaen did not want them to be spotted.

I can tell there are at least twenty goblins and four orcs, and I am not sure if the rest are hobgoblins or just goblins. There are some bigger ones, or maybe I should say more muscular ones, that are what you described as a hobgoblin. They don't look like the ones we killed in the cave. Three orcs are small, but one is bigger, just not as massive as the one I had to help kill.

Kaen grunted in frustration. If that was the number that Pammon could see, and there was a cave with this much activity outside, he wondered how many more might be out there.

Pammon suddenly turned the other way and drifted over the forest section a little more.

Wait, I see a few more. There are some in the trees deeper in the forest. It appears they are hunting for food.

Goblins?

No, those would have to be hobgoblins. Traveling in packs of two. I see two packs right now, but there might be more. The forest is decently thick down there.

Hearing that news left a pit in Kaen's stomach. Fifty-plus of those creatures was a problem the adventurers' guild would have to deal with quickly. Allowing them to continue growing out here would only spell trouble for everyone.

I'm glad you and I are scouting this out instead of Hess and me being on the ground. Things might have gotten bad had we stumbled upon that group.

Do you think I would let the two of you stumble upon a group that size? I am not blind.

No, you are not. I am just saying I wouldn't want to be that close to a group like that. Imagine if they found our scent and tracked us during the night. I would not want to wake up to a group like that coming at us, and yes, before you complain, I know you would detect them, even in your sleep.

Pammon vibrated with laughter, and Kaen knew he had dodged a comeback from him.

Are we ready to return?

Yes. Let's get back to Hess so we can fill him in on what we found and then let you hunt. I want to spend all day tomorrow practicing and getting better at this.

Hess poked the fire with his stick while mulling over the report.

"If what you said is true, there has to be at least a hundred or more in total," Hess finally said as he watched the fire burn. "Somewhere in that cave is a leader, possibly like the orc you and Pammon took down, directing them to do whatever it is they have planned. He would not send out more than a third of his minions unless he had a reason to."

"Why would they be cutting down trees? Are they building fires? I thought they hated light."

Hess shook his head and looked up at Kaen. "There are lots of reasons, and none of them are good. They could be building weapons, making fortifications, or worse, if they are smelting ore and forging metal weapons."

Kaen stared back at Hess in shock. "They do that?!"

Nodding, Hess went back to poking the fire with his stick. "They have, and days like those were bad ones in the history of battles and wars. An army of them, outfitted with armor and weapons like ours, is a terrible sign. I had hoped that when you mentioned what the orcs were carrying and wearing on your quest, I might be wrong, but it looks like I was not."

Tossing the stick into the fire, Hess sat up straight and folded his arms across his chest. "One day. All I can give you is one day," he said with a frustrated look. "I know you two want more to practice, but we need to report this news ASAP. I will deal with the fact that we return sooner than we should, but I already know how I will manage that. This news just can't come at a worse time."

Hess spat on the ground and grumbled something to himself.

"What are you not telling me?" Kaen asked, knowing how to read Hess by how he was acting.

Hess took a deep breath and let it out slowly. "Think, Kaen. What are the odds that someone from the Kingdom of Luthaelia just happens to send someone into our guild house to start killing off adventurers, all while what appears to be an army of orcs, goblins, and hobgoblins build up in our kingdom? The group outside the pass that you two took out could have done major damage if there were others they were supposed to join."

Hess stood up and kicked a rock, cursing to himself. "An army on both sides, adventurers dead, another kingdom making moves. All this spells for something bad to happen, and soon."

74

Bow Practice in Flight

Pammon had risen early and found himself a quick breakfast, promising that it would tide him over for a few hours, and that he and Kaen could get to work on the practice side of things.

Hess had collected some targets and set them up along the side of the clearing near the mountains while Kaen went through his arrows, picking out twenty-five he did not mind wasting out of the seventy-five he had brought.

With everyone prepared, Hess helped Kaen get tied in and settled. Hess also tied a small strip of rope to Kaen's bow, on the off chance he dropped it while flying. With everything ready to go, they were set up for the first pass through the area near the mountain.

I'll go slower this first time, so let me know if I need to slow down or speed up.

Understood, Kaen answered, focused on what he knew was going to be a long day.

Kaen watched as the targets sped toward him faster than he had expected. Flying above them by about thirty meters created a whole different shooting perspective. He wasn't sure how the drop would work or how Pammon's speed would impact the arrow.

As the first target came into view, Kaen lined up where he thought he would need to aim, using his legs to hold him tight against Pammon's back and let the arrow fly.

Were you actually aiming? teased Pammon as the arrow went twenty yards past the target and high up into the mountain area.

It is a lot harder than you might think! I had no idea how this would work at all.

Pammon's body thrummed as he continued flying toward the second target.

Kaen felt a little more comfortable and adjusted his aim much lower. The last one had taken a flight path he had not expected.

He let the string go and watched as the arrow flew above the target but only by about four meters this time.

That one looked much better. The third one is coming up quickly!

Kaen nodded to himself and drew the next arrow. He had to do this one quickly since Hess had felt there needed to be a challenge by having two targets closer.

Kaen could feel how he needed to focus and where his target would be. The arrow leaped from the bow and missed the third target by only a foot or two.

So close! You got the last two!

Smiling, Kaen drew the next arrow and prepared for the fourth target. They had flown hundreds of yards already, but he knew this day was a training opportunity he would not get again for a while.

Taking aim, he felt he finally understood how the altitude and speed impacted his shot. He took a breath, held it, and let it go.

Fantastic! I knew you could do it!

That is a lie, and we both know it! You were thinking I was going to miss again!

Pammon's body vibrated again from laughter, and Kaen was trying not to laugh himself as the arrow hit the outer section of the three-foot targets Hess had set up.

It wasn't a killing shot, but it would have hurt someone from the speed at which it hit.

The last one. I'll bet you can hit this. Say seven coppers?

Kaen tried to ignore the taunt from Pammon and focused. He knew it was possible now and felt he could do it in his mind and heart.

As he got within range, he knew the exact moment to let go of the string, and the arrow flew off and struck the target, missing the center circle Hess had drawn with charcoal by just a few inches.

That means I win seven coppers, teased Pammon again as he chuckled.

We never bet on if I would hit the black mark. Besides, we both know you wouldn't even get out of bed to collect seven coppers.

The second pass resulted in two more strikes on targets, and Kaen finally managed to strike the last target in the black section. He had hoped for a skill point, but it did not want to come.

Again!

The third pass went much better, with five strikes on target; two were in the black.

Again!

The fourth approach was almost perfect, missing the third target's black spot by just inches. He still managed to hit the other four in the black.

Last run before I have to restock! Let's go!

Kaen was zoned in on each target as they began their path again.

Pammon took the same path each time. Kaen knew when to shoot and where. The speed never changed, and he had figured out how to time the shots between strokes of Pammon's wings.

I believe in you! Show me what you can do!

Kaen let the arrow go as the first target appeared and watched it strike the black spot again.

The second target took its arrow to the center mark as well. Again, the third target also found its arrow right on the outer edge of the black mark.

Focus! You almost missed that one again!

Kaen grunted and breathed, as he had a quick break before the fourth target appeared. As it got in range, he let the arrow go, striking the black spot again and setting everything up for this last target in his run.

Breathing slowly, Kaen held the arrow against his finger, bow lifted in the air and fully drawn. He watched as the target came closer, knowing it was seconds away from when he should shoot.

He smiled as the arrow leaped from his bow, knowing the shot would hit. As they flew by, Pammon tilted his head back as he had for all the others.

[Archery Skill Increased]

You hit it right in the center! I knew you could do it!

Kaen grinned and rubbed Pammon's neck as his friend turned slowly in the air, getting ready to land so they could retrieve the arrows before trying again.

Best of all, I got a point in archery on that last one!

The wave of excitement from Pammon struck Kaen more than usual. It almost made him dizzy for a second, as it was more intense than before.

Are you ok? You felt like you went limp for a second.

I'm fine. It just felt overpowering when your emotions hit me just now. Much more than usual.

Pammon glanced back at Kaen and watched him momentarily as he flew over the trees.

I felt it, too, when you celebrated the point. I'm unsure why, but everything has been more intense since you gave me strength the other day.

Kaen nodded and motioned for Pammon to focus on the area they needed to land.

We'll figure it out. For now, we need to restock and do this again.

Hess came running up with the arrows he had retrieved from the targets and those that had survived his missed shots.

"Looks like you got it figured out!" he called out as he handed a stack of arrows to Kaen. "I had to replace some with your stash, as some broke. There are twenty-five there, and you need to try this again before we mix it up."

"Mix it up? Like how?"

Hess flashed a grin, and Kaen groaned, knowing it would get worse the longer they did this.

"Worry about that later. For now, focus on targets and take them down individually. When you run out of arrows this time, I'll change the course."

Groaning, Kaen took the stack from Hess and refilled his quiver. He could only imagine the stuff Hess would want him to do. "I guess I should mention I got a point from that last run?"

Hess's face lit up in excitement. "Nice! What does that put you at now?"

"A twenty-eight. I'm closing in on thirty and wondering what skill I might get."

Hess nodded and began to move backward, giving Pammon room to take off. "Worry about that later. For now, focus on hitting them all like that last run!" he shouted as he jogged backward.

Any bets on if he thinks you will hit thirty today?

I know both of us hope I do. Something tells me he wants us to be prepared for what he fears is coming.

Pammon grunted as he leaped from the ground and began to climb, preparing for another run.

"Twenty-four out of twenty-five bullseyes is pretty impressive," Hess informed Kaen, handing him another bundle of arrows. "Honestly, I thought you might have been perfect, until you missed that third shot again."

"It was the wind," groaned Kaen as he took the arrows from Hess. "Right after I fired it, the wind lifted it a bit higher.

"It happens," Hess answered, shrugging. "Pammon, I want you to start changing how far away you are from the first and last two targets. Be closer or farther away. Make it harder on Kaen and make him learn distances. Also, give me a minute to fix the course. Kaen, you must figure out how to do this next part."

"Figure out—"

"It's not the same if I tell you what to do versus finding out on your own. Figure it out."

He is right, Pammon informed Kaen as they watched Hess jog to the area where the targets were. **You won't have targets waiting for you to hit them**.

"I know, but something tells me Hess enjoys making me work this hard. He hasn't trained me like this since Minoosh, which means I know he is serious."

Let's fly for now. I want to feel the wind on my snout while he takes care of that. I will know when he is ready for us.

Pammon turned around and took off into the air, facing away from where Hess was. He didn't want to give Kaen any chance to see what Hess was doing.

And here I thought you were better than this, teased Pammon, as Kaen had missed all of the shots on the first run.

That bastard put the second and third targets next to each other. Not only did I miss both with my skill, but we must waste time for it to refresh.

Breathe, relax. I can feel your frustration. Let it go and focus. You can do this. He and I both know you can.

Grumbling, Kaen took a few deep breaths and let them out. He knew Pammon was right. Hess believed he could do it, but failing before them like this wasn't enjoyable.

The second pass went a little better, with two arrows on target. He had still missed the second and third targets, but only by a little bit on both. Lining up two arrows on two targets while flying was not as easy as he had initially thought.

The third pass got better with four arrows on target, even if none of them were a bullseye. The third target felt like the bane of his existence. It seemed not to want to be struck by an arrow.

The fourth and fifth pass were alike. Four on target, two in the black, the third target taunting him with its wooden body.

Let's take a break and then try again. You are too worked up.

We can't take a break. What if this was a real fight? I wouldn't be able to sit down and do nothing. I would have to keep fighting as long as possible. I just want to refill my arrows and do this again.

Pammon nodded as he flew, knowing Kaen was off in his head, fighting battles inside.

"You seem to have trouble with the third target. Why is that?"

From Pammon's back, Kaen spat on the ground, frustrated that Hess would bring that up. "The twin shot just isn't hitting it. I'm not sure why. I think it will line up, and yet it doesn't."

Hess nodded as he watched Kaen put the arrows in his quiver. He reached out a hand and scratched Pammon's neck as he thought about it for a moment. "Are you trying to activate your lifestone, or are you doing this on your own?"

"I'm doing this on my own," answered Kaen. "I can't depend on my lifestone for every situation, and I also don't want to be dependent on it, especially since Bren told me that overusing it could result in my heart or lifestone exploding.

"I don't think you have to worry about that," Hess answered, seeing the frustration on Kaen's face. "Pammon, slow down just a hair while Kaen tries to use his lifestone. Kaen, remember the lifestone is more than just how we get skills. What you say yours does and how it guides you will make it the greatest teacher. Let it show you how to shoot, how to aim. Let it be the instructor I can't be in this."

"What do you mean? You're teaching me now."

Hess shook his head as he patted Pammon's neck and began to back up. "I can't tell you what you are doing wrong, how you are turned wrong, or where the arrow is aimed at from down here. Pammon can't help you, either. This is between you and your lifestone. Let it guide you this time. See what it does. Bren told me you used it to get a twenty in one day of practicing. I know now that you and your dad are alike. Let it guide you like I know it guided him."

Hess took off jogging, not letting Kaen respond.

He's right, you know. I have felt your lifestone guiding you, and I know you can do this. Remember when it guided both of us the first time we flew? Let it do the same thing now.

Closing his eyes, Kaen tried to remember all the times his lifestone had shown him how to shoot, talk, or dance. It had taught him things he had never imagined. Perhaps Hess was right, and he was being foolish trying to do this on his own. Without Pammon, he would not have a need to practice this.

That is when it struck him. He was trying to be an adventurer, a hero by himself. He couldn't do this on his own. It had taken a life with Hess and all the hours he had put into guiding him. It would take a lifetime with Pammon if he would accomplish what he hoped to become.

Let's do this!

Pammon gave a bestial growl, surprising Kaen as he leaped into the air.

It's about time you stopped acting like an eggling!

75

Kaen's Real Purpose

Say when.

Letting himself go, Kaen focused on where he was and why he was doing this. Feeling Pammon's body beneath him, knowing all this was so he could protect others, *the real truth* pierced his heart, causing tears to stream from his eyes.

What is it? What is wrong?

Kaen wiped the tears from his face, yet they kept coming. The truth of why he had wanted to be an adventurer stung too deeply.

I finally know why I am really doing this. I finally figured out why this is so important to me.

Pammon continued to glide around the spot where they were, feeling what Kaen was feeling, his heart aching for him.

I'm here. I can sense it, but I don't know what it is. It is a loss . . .

Pammon's heart broke when he discovered the truth about Kaen. Before yesterday, he would not have been able to figure it out, but now, with their new connection, he was able to.

You're doing this so no one has to go through what you went through. Losing their dad . . . losing their family.

Sobbing, Kaen leaned against Pammon's neck, letting the tears fall onto his scales.

He had thought he had gotten over this, but at that moment, he felt the truth of it all hit. He knew precisely why he was doing this, why he needed to do this no matter the cost.

[Charm Resist Increased x3]

The skill increase smacked him in the chest as his lifestone pulsed briefly.

As soon as it hit, Kaen felt a peace overcome him. The realization that he had accepted the real reason for all of this.

What was that?!

My charm resist skill just went up three points! I think it is because I finally admitted to myself why I am doing this and committed to it no matter the cost. Maybe even more because I admitted to myself that I don't want someone else having to deal with the loss of a parent if I can help it.

So does this mean you are ready?

Kaen smiled, wiping away the last of his tears with his sleeve.

I've never been more ready in my life. Let's do this.

As Pammon turned to begin the path that would take them down the practice lane, Kaen opened himself to his lifestone. He was committed and knew this was more than just about his honor or pride. This was about *protecting others.* Protecting people from those who meant harm. More importantly, it was about *protecting families.*

His lifestone roared like an inferno inside his chest. It almost ached, feeling the true commitment of one bent on a single path for their life. Things might change in what Kaen did to follow this path, but the truth was, he would always be bound to this one task.

As they entered the training path, his lifestone cooled itself, burning like an ember that would not go out instead of a raging fire that would consume him.

I can feel it! It was so hot for a moment, I was worried something was wrong.

Kaen couldn't answer. His lifestone had acknowledged his need in this moment.

Kaen was just a participant, watching his body move smoothly, lining the arrow up and letting it go, striking the dead center of the black circle on the first target.

As the two targets approached, he felt both arrows between his fingers. He now knew how he had held them wrong all those other times. The angle seemed so minute, but it was why he could not hit the targets. At this range and speed, what he had done before was like purposely shooting to miss. His twin shot skill activated precisely when he needed it, both arrows speeding away, striking each target simultaneously, right in the middle.

Target four came up quickly, yet it felt like he was moving so slowly, watching his arms draw and load the arrow before sending it to the heart of the target.

Target five came into view, his lifestone began to radiate, and something strange came over him as he felt his body throb. The arrow was loaded, and he held it. Power filled him like never before. His lifestone roared into the fire it had before they entered the training area. He felt something flowing through him, unsure what it was.

Energy, pure energy, something he had not felt before.

The tip of the arrow began to glow, burning red.

Kaen watched and felt all this happen as the arrow disappeared from his bow. When it struck the target, it exploded in a fiery mess, throwing wood and fire all around for a good five-foot area near it.

What was that!? Pammon roared as he quickly slowed down, moving closer to the flames as Hess sprinted toward them.

[Exploding Shot Skill Acquired]
[Mana Use Acquired]
[Magic Skill Acquired]
[Magic Skill Increased x10]
[Archery Skill Increased x2]
[Archery Skill Waiting To Be Chosen]

"Magic? I can use magic?" Kaen mumbled to himself as Pammon began to land near the flames, trying to put out the brush that had started burning.

What?! I couldn't hear you.

Kaen glanced at the flaming mess around him, snapping out of his stupor.

Let's solve this first!

Kaen cut the rope around each of his legs, slid off the harness on one side, and began kicking dirt on the brush as Pammon used his body to extinguish the fire. The flames were put out in a matter of minutes, leaving just a tiny cloud of smoke drifting up and a burnt patch on the ground.

"Hairy dwarf balls, Kaen! What was that?"

As he started to talk, Kaen suddenly noticed the area around him going dark. With his adrenaline not pumping and his lifestone quiet, the impact of what he had just achieved hit his body. The last thing he saw as he crumpled to the ground was Pammon's head turned sideways, watching him pass out.

"Slowly, sit up slowly."

Kaen heard Hess, but his voice sounded weird. Almost concerned.

"I'm fine," Kaen answered as he sat up, realizing that Pammon was sending strength through their bond to him. "Pammon is helping me recover."

Hess glanced at Pammon, who was nodding.

"How did I get here? Did you carry me?"

Hess chuckled and nodded. "I'm glad you still haven't put on a lot of muscle," Hess teased as he handed a waterskin to Kaen. "It was better to get you here where I had some water and could lean you against something. Now tell me, son, what in the hell was all of that?"

Smiling, Kaen looked at Pammon and bowed his head a little. "You can stop now. I am fine, but thank you for your strength."

Are you sure? I do not mind, as we are close, and it is barely a fraction of what I can give.

Kaen chuckled. He couldn't believe Pammon had more to give. He felt like he had slept all night and had enjoyed a full breakfast. "I'm fine, really. I feel like I could go run for hours right now."

If you say so.

Kaen felt the link cut and the flow of strength end. A small bit of weakness hit for a moment, but after that, he knew there was no lasting impact of Pammon stopping the flow.

"I appreciate being left out of the conversation," Hess said as he glanced between Kaen and Pammon, "but I would really like to know what happened sooner rather than later."

Kaen nodded but held up his hand as he lifted the waterskin and took a long drink, relishing the fact that he knew Hess was dying, having to wait to learn what happened.

"I figured it out."

"Figured what out?" Hess asked, scrunching his eyebrows in confusion.

"I figured out why I wanted to be an adventurer. The real reason."

Kaen set the waterskin down and smiled at Hess. "This may sound wrong, but please do not take it that way. I have nothing but love for you and appreciate all you did for me. I was upset and angry after my dad died and you started to raise me. It felt unfair as I watched other kids get to enjoy their families, even the ones with family problems. That is when I committed myself to becoming an adventurer. So that no one else would lose what I lost."

Hess slowly nodded, the pain of what he heard written on his face. He didn't take what Kaen was saying as an attack on him, but a realization of what a boy who experienced what Kaen had experienced must have felt.

"And so you trained," Hess whispered quietly.

"Yes. You remember those first years. All I wanted to do was train. Night and day till I wore myself out. You had to put me to bed. I was so tired I couldn't stand. That is when you finally convinced me to work in the quarry, to *put some meat on my bones* as you said."

Hess chuckled and nodded. He had forgotten those years.

"Everything I did, all the times I wanted to be an adventurer, was for that reason. When I acknowledged it, really acknowledged it while I was on Pammon's back, my lifestone burned in a way I have never felt before. I thought for a moment it would burn me from the inside."

Glancing up at the sky, Kaen rubbed his chest where the lifestone was. "I felt like I was riding a small log on a raging river, carried along and forced to watch it go where it wanted. The lifestone was responsible for each of those shots. Every one of them was perfect. I got to see exactly how they should be held, where they should be aimed, and when to release."

Letting out a small sigh after taking a big breath, Kaen turned and looked at Hess once more. "That last shot was . . . it . . . Sorry, I'm finding it hard to explain," Kaen said with a grumble as he shrugged. "Power that I didn't know was inside me started pouring into the arrowhead. My lifestone raged again like a smith's furnace, and when it was ready, it streaked off, doing what you saw."

Kaen tapped his chest with his finger and then lifted both hands, holding up five fingers on one hand and one on the other.

"I got six notifications. One was for acquiring a skill called exploding shot. I am assuming that is what the fifth target got hit by. I was notified that I had gained mana use and the magic skill."

Kaen paused when he saw Hess open his mouth. After Hess sat there for a second, trying to catch flies in his open trap, he shut it and motioned for Kaen to continue.

"I also gained two points in archery and am now supposed to pick the skill for level thirty!" Kaen exclaimed.

"Hairy dwarf balls, Kaen!" Hess shouted as he jumped up from where he was sitting. He started moving around, waving his hands in the air, obviously dealing with the news Kaen had just hit him with.

"Do you understand . . . no, obviously you don't," Hess caught himself as he tried to speak. He was utterly flabbergasted. "No one outside your dad has ever reported acquiring what you just did. It seems impossible!"

"Well, it happened. I still haven't checked the skill choices yet."

Archery Skill Choices
[Multi-shot]
[Empowered Shot]

"My choices are multi-shot or empowered shot," Kaen informed Hess, ignoring how his mentor struggled with the news.

"I can't . . . I can't handle this . . . You have no idea, Kaen, what this means."

"The skill choices?"

Hess strode over to where Kaen was and kneeled before him. "No, you fool. If you live as long as a Dragon Rider should, you will be the strongest person in all the kingdoms. You two will be an unstoppable force with what you can apparently do, combined with what Pammon gives you. We just need to keep you alive to get there."

Kaen struggled to understand what Hess had just said, but Pammon started to thrum.

I told you we would be a force to reckon with.

I never intended to be one. I just want to keep you and everyone else safe.

"You two ignoring me?" Hess asked as he watched the two of them staring at each other.

"Sorry, we were talking. What did you say?"

"Choose multi-shot. After you do that, tell me your stats."

Kaen groaned. If Hess wanted to know his stats, it meant something important.

And that scared him.

76

Pammon's and Kaen's stats

"What do you mean you haven't checked your stats in a while?"

Kaen shrugged and then pointed at Pammon. "He told me to stop worrying about every increase I gained and to focus on training. Since then, I haven't paid much attention to anything but my skill points."

Hess grumbled and nodded as he heard Pammon begin to laugh.

You two and your silly concerns over whose is bigger.

Kaen snorted, caught off guard by Pammon's comment and how true it was.

Fine, I'll see what they are.

Full Status Check
Kaen Marshell - Adolescent
Age - 17
HP - 403/403 (15%)
MP - 173/173 (15%)
STR - 22 + 3(15%)
CON - 22 + 7(15%)
DEX - 24 + 14(15%)
WIS - 15 + 1(15%)
INT - 17 + 1 (15%)
Blessings:
Improved Dragonbond - 15% current bonus to all stats
Hunters Tunic - + 3 to Str / Con / Dex
Blessed Vambrace - + 1 to Dex / Int
Blessed Vambrace - + 1 to Dex / Wis
Bonded Bow of Archer - + 5 to Dex + 3 to Archery *Locked*
Blood Ring - +4 Con

Eagle Pendant - +2 Dex + 1 to Archery
Gold Band - +2 Dex + 1 Con

It took Kaen a moment as he saw the stats he had resisted looking at before he could share them with Hess.

Hess let out a low whistle and shook his head.

"Improved Dragonbond . . . I think I know how that happened. I learned to share my strength with Pammon, and everything changed once I did."

Hess held his hands up, indicating he had no idea. "Dragon stuff is again not my purview. Hopefully, we can find more information soon, but I would gladly take that boost, as would every other adventurer."

Kaen smiled while Pammon thrummed.

"Most people will never reach those numbers, especially not a silver," Hess informed him as he scratched a few things in the dirt. "Your strength and constitution are unbelievable for one your age. Perhaps all that rock breaking was worth it."

Kaen chuckled and nodded.

"Your dexterity is your greatest asset. Especially with the gear. Forty is a special number, as you know."

Kaen knew that twenty, forty, and the elusive sixty stat numbers were all significant milestones. "What happens at forty?" asked Kaen.

Grunting, Hess tapped his chest with his thumb. "You know what my strength is?" he replied with a grin.

"Bren said you are probably in the mid-thirties before factoring in items. So I would assume you are over forty fully equipped."

"Damn that Bren," Hess said, nodding. "Fully equipped, I sit at a forty-two or forty-five, depending on my gear. That is why I can break through most people's weapons or shields when I attack. Beyond just the strength it provides, that number comes with an overpower bonus. If I attack you and your strength is below that twenty threshold and your gear is not special, it will shatter. Even if you have a shield that is magically strong enough to resist being broken, the force of my attack will flatten you to the ground."

Ask him what would happen if he and I swung at each other and hit our weapons and my claw simultaneously.

Did you check your stats again?

A snort of air came from Pammon's snout as he grunted.

No, but I can.

Simple Status Check
Pammon
Young Dragon

HP - 2000/2000
MP - 400/400
STR - 40
CON - 40
DEX - 45
WIS - 20
INT - 25

"Elf tits," muttered Hess as he listened to Kaen rattling off Pammon's stats.

"So who would win? You or Pammon in a swing of the hammer and claw?"

Hess laughed as he motioned to Pammon with his head. "Size would win that fight. As big as I am, Pammon weighs so much more than I do. I can overcome some weight and size factors, but there comes a point when the size and weight difference can outplay the strength."

Hess stood and walked over to a log and grabbed it with both hands, easily lifting it, as it was only five or six feet long and a foot wide.

"Is this heavy? Yes. Can I easily lift it? Sure! What about if I swing it?" he asked as he demonstrated swinging the log in his hands. "I can imagine the ogre you saw that was twice my size could swing this in one hand. Even though we are close to strength levels, the force it can generate is different."

Hess tossed the log down and sat on it. "Your problem with the archer we fought in the woods was that his dexterity was closer to yours. He most likely had a skill that helped him dodge, and those two things make it hard for you to pin him down. Once you hit a forty on your agility, you seldom miss a standard shot on a creature or person under twenty."

"So how about a sixty?"

"That is a hard one to explain," replied Hess as he bent over and picked up two rocks. "This small rock would be you, and this rock that is four times bigger would be the person with a sixty. The exponential level gap is massive. Only Dragon Riders have ever hit these numbers, which is why I told you at the beginning, they can take out an entire army on their own."

Dropping both rocks on the ground, Hess chuckled. "Legends tell of a Dragon Rider who cut down thousands of men and women in a few hours. He waded into the field in full plate armor with a shield and a sword. Every swing of the sword cut people in half, and every time he slammed someone with his shield, it turned them into ground meat. The armies ran, killing their own general on the way out. A person with multiple sixties is like a god."

Someday, that will be you!

Kaen shook his head and laughed.

I doubt it. I'm not sure I want people to think of me like that.

Imagine all the families you could protect if we reach that!

A different wave of something hit Kaen as Pammon spoke. It wasn't an emotion but a sense of . . . purpose.

You are just as committed to my purpose of being an adventurer as I am.

We are one. You and I are bound till one of us dies. If you are that committed to this task, I shall help you with everything in me.

Kaen stood up and walked over to where Pammon was, and then grabbed his snout, pulling it close and scratching it with fervor. "Let's ensure that doesn't happen for a few hundred years."

Pammon snorted, blowing snot and air on Kaen, causing the three of them to laugh as Kaen began to wipe the snot off him and back onto Pammon's scales.

"I'll find a way to get you back for this," joked Kaen as he flung mucus in Hess's direction.

Hess rolled to avoid the incoming dragon slime and then stood up and pointed a thick finger at the two of them. "Play all you two want, but keep that stuff off me!" he growled. "I don't need any help going back and getting in trouble for how my clothes and armor smell."

Kaen began slowly moving to where Hess was, holding both hands out, preparing to fight with his snotty hands.

"Payback isn't fun, is it?" asked Kaen as he charged Hess.

"So we are going to stay here tonight? Won't the guild know we are back in town?"

Hess nodded, eating off the plate he held as they sat in Sulenda's office. "It will be ok. It's dark and late," he answered between bites of the boar they had been given. "Remember, we needed to lose some time so they don't wonder too much why we are back so early. Most would not have expected us for another day. This lets us show up because of the urgency of what we found."

Kaen nodded in understanding and turned back to his plate of food. It really was amazing how good Sulenda's cook could make stuff taste. So far, nothing he had eaten had been awful.

"Three more days . . . " Kaen said with a slight sigh.

"Yup. You and I need to go tomorrow and try on those outfits. Unless the king changes his plan, we will have a long day ahead of us."

Sulenda was tapping the desk with her pen. Obviously, she was anxious about what they had just told her.

"That report is going to cause a lot of problems. You know that, right?" she asked as she looked at Hess with worry all over her face. "They will probably send out multiple squads to try and handle what is out there."

Kaen folded the map he had marked up, since Sulenda was done looking at it and moved to the large map on her wall. Looking at it, he realized how much of it matched what he had seen while on Pammon. Some small streams and other things were missing, yet the scale looked well done. "How old is this map?"

"Excuse me?" Sulenda asked.

"How old is this map? Where did you get it?" Kaen asked as he tapped the area where they had done their scouting. "The lines here match up with what it was like. How does one get a map like this?"

"I don't know how old it is, but I know what it cost. It was from a noble house who lost their fortune, and I got it for a *steal*," she replied with a wink. "There are not many maps as nice as that one in the kingdom. I am sure you can only guess how that level of detail and exact scale was created."

Kaen nodded as he turned back to the map. "A Dragon Rider," he mumbled.

"Exactly. So that must be well over five hundred years old as no one has performed that service, that I know of, since Elies took up residence in our kingdom and in Roccnari. The elves have been generous to share him, knowing we would struggle to keep one for our own."

"Why is that?" Kaen asked without turning around. "Why is it hard to have one of our own?"

Sulenda glanced at Hess with a questioning look and saw him shrug. "Well, there haven't been any new ones in ages. The dragons that are left alive keep away from us and protect the rare egg that does hatch. Their lack of trust for us and our people's fear of them makes having a Dragon Rider hard to come by."

Kaen nodded as he ran his finger along the lines on the map, comparing points and distances.

"What if there was one? Would our king or the people welcome them?"

Sulenda started laughing and motioned to Hess for help with this line of questions. "What if? What if?" Sulenda asked as her voice got louder. "Get your head out of the clouds, Kaen. There hasn't been one and won't be one ever again."

Letting out the breath he had been holding in, hoping for Sulenda to say something more than that, Kaen turned and looked at her. She saw how his eyes held her, making her sit back in her chair, uncomfortable.

"What would you do, Sulenda, if Elies decided to stay here instead of in Roccnari? Would you support him? Would you demand that he leave?"

Hess covered his face, trying to hide the smile he was fighting behind his massive hand, and watched Sulenda squirm at the line of questions.

"I guess I would accept him," she finally replied, obviously flustered by Kaen's refusal to drop the question. "You keep forgetting that people fear what lies just a kingdom over. Stioks and his dragon threaten all who would not bow to his will. These mountains have kept us safe for generations, but to a dragon, they mean little. Eventually, he will come, and when he does, we better hope Elies is willing to help."

"Or another Dragon Rider," Kaen replied with a grin.

"Holy mother of dwarf balls!" Sulenda shouted as she stood up from her chair and pointed at Hess. "You deal with this shite! I can't handle this esoteric bull." She stormed toward the door and slammed it behind her when she left.

"That did not go as I had hoped," Kaen stated after the room returned to silence.

"Nor will it," Hess answered as he glanced at Kaen. "The kingdom is not ready for a Dragon Rider, but she is right. It needs to be."

"Does that mean we can tell them about Pammon?" Hope was evident in Kaen's voice.

Hess sighed and shook his head. "Let's see how the meeting with the king goes first. Do not worry. I am afraid we are running out of time to keep Pammon hidden."

77

Leadership is Cruel

Sitting on the couch, Kaen shifted a few times as he glanced at Hess, who never seemed to move.

Fiola was leaning into the corner of her couch, rubbing her eyes with her fingers just as she had been for the last minute after hearing the full details of their report.

"How did the meeting with the guild council members go?" Kaen asked, trying to end the silence.

Lowering her fingers a little, Fiola glared daggers at Kaen before shaking her head at him.

"Really? You went from bad news to asking about that? Do you know what those people mean to someone in my position?"

"Uh . . . I guess not," Kaen answered, glancing at Hess, who was slightly smiling but not responding to Fiola's comment. "I thought they might be excited you could locate the person responsible for everything."

She shifted forward on the couch, fixing her dress and leaning toward Kaen. "Oh, I did all that? I found the person responsible. I wish I had known that because all I thought I had was the dead body of someone who was used by a kingdom that the entire world is afraid of," she replied, ice coming from her voice. "I had nothing to give them but that horrible news. I had to admit that I used a technique completely against the rules and had to use the aid of my newest adventurer and his mentor. I also had to stand before the king and do my best to show that there were no other weak points within our hall. I'll ignore the fact that I am on a cliff's edge, and the slightest breeze might push me over it, ending the career I have worked on for centuries."

Kaen tried not to react when she mentioned how long she had been doing this. It let him know he had been right, that she was much older than he had assumed she was. "So where are they now?"

Fiola rubbed her eyes with her fingers and shook her head. "For now, let's forget about the council members and focus on what you can play a role in," replied Fiola as she regained her composure. "Hess has informed me that you will seek a position with a silver party you have already engaged with. How soon can your party leave to join two other groups and try to rid ourselves of this threat?"

"Three or four days. I have an audience with the king in two days. After that, I would expect I could depart the next day."

Laughter filled the room as Fiola suddenly let out a throaty laugh. "You say that like the king and you are best friends," she replied, trying to stop her laughter. "You have no idea what you are walking into. I have already had my hand forced to help you with the lifestones for this *academy* of yours that you are trying to build. Imagine my shock when I was questioned about it by the king and council members, and I had very little knowledge of how much you had already procured."

"That's not his fault," Hess interrupted. "Right before we left on our quest, Lord Hurem came and brought a document we had not expected. While we were doing the quest with the bandits, Sulenda had been working on all of this, so Kaen had no knowledge to share. When he came to the guild hall, you were busy, and thus, no information again could be given."

Fiola huffed and nodded. "Correct, but it put me in a bad position, and I do not like getting caught unaware like that," she stated. "As such, I am now on the hook for the lifestones. Depending on how successful your academy is, the guild will provide as many as we can at a *reduced* cost, and I believe some of your benefactors are willing to help cover the other part. Just know a limited amount is being produced right now. Certain ingredients required are not being brought in due to the recent events. Once we solve these problems, we can hopefully increase their production."

Kaen nodded and smiled. He hated that Fiola got trapped in service, but it was her fault for not wanting to help the first time they had asked. "Is there anything you want me to tell the king on your behalf?" Kaen asked as he grinned at her.

A groan escaped as Fiola closed her eyes and shook her head. "I am afraid I have let myself become too *friendly* with you and am going to have to work diligently to remedy that," she answered with a scowl. "I have work to do, and you, Kaen, need to get with your new party and set things in motion for a quick departure once the king is finished with you. I will expect the same results you have achieved with Hess, or I will be forced to rethink how much of a role you played in each of them."

"I understand, Guild Master Fiola. If you will allow me, I will leave you to the duties you have."

A slight flick of her fingers sent Kaen scurrying toward the door. As Hess rose, she held out a hand to stop him. "A moment of your time, Adventurer Hess, if you please."

Kaen paused at the door, looked back at Hess, and saw him motion for him to leave.

"He is a bit troublesome, is he not?"

Hess nodded, smiling at her. He had no idea why she would want to talk with him alone, but he did not care either. Soon, he would be done with all of this.

"I would ask the next few things we speak about be kept between the two of us. That means not sharing them with Kaen or Sulenda or anyone else."

Hess saw how she looked at him and still had no idea what she might say, so he nodded.

"Good," she replied with a small head bow. "I will most likely lose my position here unless something changes drastically. The blame still falls upon me as the head of this guild, and I would not expect it to be different had this happened to any of the other guild halls. I have already mentioned to the council that if I lose my position, Herb should be my replacement until they either vote for him to have the permanent position or he is replaced by one they elect."

It made sense, and Hess knew it. Herb was loyal and always defended Fiola, even when he knew she was wrong. He was loyal to the adventurer hall.

"So why tell me this? What is my role in all this?"

Fiola smiled a real smile, not one of the ones she often hid behind. "I have realized many of my past mistakes; one of them was fighting against you and Hoste on a few things I should not have. It was my mistake for allowing Hoste to pursue the quest that . . . " She gulped, as the words were too hard to say.

"The quest that took his life?" Hess finished for her.

Nodding, she sighed. "I have carried that weight for years, and seeing Kaen here, growing into what may be an adventurer just as great as his father, has brought it all back."

"Trust me when I say that Kaen will surpass Hoste in many things," Hess proclaimed, cutting Fiola off. "He will be the greatest adventurer this hall has seen in its life."

Fiola watched Hess as he spoke. She saw the passion and belief behind those words and his eyes. "I pray that is true," she whispered. "I need to tell you some things that cannot be shared yet but that will come to pass in the coming weeks. Things that will change the landscape of this bowl we live in and possibly for some great time."

Hess leaned forward, wondering what she was going to say.

"Remember, no one, I repeat, no one can hear of this for now. Do I have your word?"

"I cannot swear on my lifestone," Hess informed her, "but I will swear on my token. I will not bind myself again like I did eight years ago."

Watching him, she tapped her lip with her finger as she considered what he said. "That will work for now."

Fiola got up, moved to her desk, and pulled out a wooden box that was about three feet long and about six inches wide. She brought it back to the table they were sitting at and pulled out a small knife from seemingly nowhere, cut her finger, and ran the bloody edge along the entire length of one side. The lid popped open, and Hess chuckled.

"Women and their secrets," he muttered.

Nodding, Fiola pressed her two fingers together, and a small glow surrounded the tip of the bleeding finger, which was clean and injury-free when she pulled her other finger from it.

She bent over, pulled out the rolled piece of paper, and let it unfurl on the table before him.

It was a map of the southern part of the bowl with multiple *X*'s along the southern mountain area.

She picked up her pen off the table and put an *X* where they had just scouted.

"Is that what I think it is?" Hess gasped when he saw six other marks spread across the entire base of the mountains.

"It is," she nodded as she tapped the spot she just marked. "Each of these spots is reported to have the same number of creatures you two reported. That means there are most likely a thousand orcs, goblins, and hobgoblins out there, preparing for an attack of some sort. Something major will happen in the coming days, and we are not prepared for it."

"Have you told anyone yet?" Hess asked as he approached the map and started measuring the distances between the marks. "Can we get an army?"

Laughing briefly, she leaned back, closed her eyes, and shook her head. "I have only just confirmed it these last two days. No army can help. The king has not raised one in years. The kingdom is weak, and he and I know it. Every other kingdom knows it. He could easily defend Ebonmount for years with what he has now, but outside of the walls . . . "

"Everyone would die," Hess whispered.

"Yes."

Suddenly, Hess realized what was happening. "You're sending adventurers to their death!" he shouted.

Shaking her head, Fiona quickly leaned forward and tapped the mark she had just made. "No! I am asking adventurers to do what they committed to, just like I am about to ask you to do the same!"

Hess glared at her. He was pissed and wanted to grab her throat in his hands and strangle her, knowing he would most likely die in the process, but he didn't care.

"You are sending Kaen to die! Those three groups won't be able to handle that many!"

"I have faith, and I need you to have it also," she replied, her shoulders hunched over. "There are no other options. The longer we wait, the more they can prepare, and countless people will die once they invade. I need you to lead a group of adventures, skilled to match—"

"No! Send me with Kaen!"

Fiola watched Hess as he jumped to his feet and glared at her, his nostrils flaring in anger. "And do what? Tell him? Make him worry? What about his promise that this would be his first quest with that dwarven woman and her party? You would take away all of this?"

"Damn it, all!" Hess shouted as he slammed his fist on her small table, cracking it and almost sending his hand through it.

He glanced at it, realizing what he had done, not caring that his hand was bleeding. "You cannot do this! You don't understand how special that boy is! He needs to live!"

Hess dropped to a knee and held out both hands, blood dripping onto the table and map. "Please rethink this. Please let me go with him!"

Fiola's heart broke as she gazed down at Hess. The mountain of a man she had resented and tried to break so many times was here, defeated and ready to surrender, and she had not meant for this to happen. She felt shame for trying to make a man like him act like he was now.

"I wish I could, but I cannot. Hear me out if you would, and listen to my plan."

Fiola sat down and spent the next two hours laying out the last thing she expected to do as guild master.

Sitting on the stairs, Hess leaned his head against the wooden rail.

He was done crying, and he knew Fiola was right. As he rubbed his hands together, he saw where she had healed the cuts he had gotten from the table. She had not acted how he had expected at all.

Her plan was the best he had ever heard for something as significant as this. There were too many moving pieces, and things could quickly go wrong, but she was right. Each of the seven teams had to strike at the same time, and all seven of them needed to win.

Hoste, if you're listening to me, please keep Kaen safe. I cannot help him with what is coming.

After a few more minutes sitting on the stairs, he got up and descended them.

Three days . . . he had three days to plan and do everything he could to ensure victory.

78

Separation Problems

"Gertrude, that makes no sense," complained Rory, the healer for her party. "We are going on a three-squad mission. We need to let each squad handle their own crap. How are we going to train Golden Boy over there while working with others?"

"It's Silver Boy," Gertrude replied as she pointed at Kaen, "and you and I both know he could kick all of our asses. So stop worrying about him, and let's focus on what we need to collect before the mission."

Rory snorted at her and picked up his drink, diverting his eyes to his cup only.

"Anyone else want to speak up?" she asked, looking at the other group members sitting with Kaen at the table.

Brazuc, her cousin, laughed and shook his head. "If he's good enough for you, I'll stand next to him the entire time," he roared as he wiped his beard, drenched from the amount of ale he had already drank.

"Aila?" Gertrude asked as she glanced at their elven mage.

"You know me, I prefer having someone in the back with me raining down destruction," the elf woman answered with a laugh.

Kaen could see the advantage of standing behind everyone and casting spells.

"Then it's settled!" Gertrude exclaimed as she slammed her fist into the table. "Once *Silver Boy* finishes his fancy meeting with the king, we'll head out the next morning. I'll update the hall and let them know of our plans."

Kaen glanced around the table, and everyone seemed completely fine walking into a fight against a hundred-plus creatures.

"Is no one worried about what we are going to face?" asked Kaen. "I know you are all experienced, but you almost died on the last quest you took."

Each of their faces twisted differently, some upset and some with a bit of fear.

"That was different," Brazuc informed him. "We didn't have enough range damage. Aila couldn't handle that many by herself. With you and a stack of arrows, I don't see how they will be able to get close."

"What about the orcs? What if there is one of the tall ones?"

Waving Kaen's questions off, Gertrude tapped the table with her stubby finger. "Listen, Kaen. You have three full parties, all experienced and each with a solid grouping of classes. We could handle one of those guys on our own. Sure, it would hurt. Yes, Brazuc might die, but we are all ok with that."

Roaring with laughter, Brazuc nodded before taking another drink. "You just want the land I'm owed when I die. I'm afraid I'll disappoint you again!"

All the others except Rory laughed at some joke Kaen was not aware of yet.

Listening to them tell their stories or share private jokes felt weird. He was enjoying it but knew he couldn't get too close. Soon, he would leave all of them to join Pammon, limiting his ability to work with others.

"Why are you frowning?" asked Aila. "Your cat died or something?"

Kaen saw everyone looking at him and quickly put on a smile. "I just realized what I had been missing by not having a party like you. Don't get me wrong, Hess is pretty awesome, yet he snores loud, smells, and can't cook."

"You just described Gertrude," stated Brazuc, earning an elbow and a scowl from Gertrude as she began stroking her beard braids.

"Ignore him, he's an idiot."

They all laughed again, agreeing that she was right.

"What is wrong?" Sulenda asked as she watched in horror as Hess tore through some pouches he had brought from Minoosh. "You are scaring me!"

He turned and seeing the look on her face, tried to smile but knew he could not. "I need to make sure Kaen has everything he needs for this next mission of his!"

Sulenda approached Hess and grabbed his hand as he reached for another pouch. "Tell me! Tell me what I am missing!"

He hung his head and shook it. "I cannot tell you anything other than what his squad is going to face will be harder than they expect."

Sulenda caught him off guard as she grabbed his arm and pulled him in for a hug. "It's ok if he grows up. You can't always be there to watch him," she whispered and felt him squeeze her back.

He nodded, but no words came out. He couldn't bring himself to speak. Doing so would betray his promise. "Thank you," he replied, holding the embrace for as long as he could.

She nodded, letting herself enjoy the moment, believing Hess was finally letting go of his obligation to Kaen.

* * *

"You look distracted, Hess, what's up?"

Kaen had noticed it all during dinner; Hess had been quiet and not his usual talkative self.

Hess looked up from his mug of ale and smiled at Kaen. His heart ached to tell him the truth, but he knew he couldn't.

"Just preparing for the next stage in things," he lied. "You are going to be off on your own, forgetting about me, saving the world, while I'll be stuck in this place, probably cleaning dishes if I'm not careful."

"Well, thank the spirits. Sulenda is smart enough not to ask you to cook!" teased Kaen. "No one would come here to eat if she did that."

Hess chuckled and nodded. "I got something for you, one last gift as you go off on your own with your group." He pulled a small pouch from a pocket inside his vest and tossed it across the table, where Kaen snatched it midair.

Kaen's eyes lit up when he opened it. "Are these what I think they are?"

Hess nodded and smiled. "That should put you above forty. Make sure to wear all your gear on this next mission. No point in taking any chances."

Kaen nodded as he plucked the two rings out and slid them onto his fingers. "If I said it sometimes feels like I move faster than others, would that make sense?" Kaen asked as he flipped the pouch back to Hess. "Is it because of how I stack up against others?"

Nodding, Hess took the empty pouch and returned it to where he had taken it from. "When we fought in the woods, I was not too far behind you, but now you would easily dodge me unless I used a skill you weren't prepared for. If things keep progressing as they seem to be, I doubt anyone here could land a shot or blow on you when you have all your equipment on."

Kaen started to pick up a potato from his plate and stopped. "How close would you say you were before these, dexterity-wise?"

Hess shook his head and shrugged. "Just because I know your numbers doesn't mean I will share mine."

Groaning, Kaen picked up the potato and popped it into his mouth. He enjoyed these small ones, as the cook always had them cooked perfectly and seasoned to his taste.

"Gertrude's squad is different," Kaen blurted out as he watched Hess, waiting for a reaction. "She told me they had been together for a few years and only lost one person in all that time. A rogue, which is why she doesn't want another one in the group."

Hess just nodded, taking a drink and not responding.

Frustrated, Kaen tapped the table with his fork. "You sure you're ok? Something seems off. Was it what Fiola wanted to talk to you about?"

Hess closed his eyes and sighed. "Kaen, I need you to listen to what I'm going to say."

Opening his eyes, he leaned back and crossed his arms over his chest. "I have a quest, as do a lot of other people in a few days. I have a lot of things on my mind, and making sure you're prepared for this next step is my biggest concern," he declared as he began to scoot out of the booth. "So I am distracted. Worrying about you and the team I'm going to be leading. Enjoy your dinner, enjoy tomorrow, and be ready for the king in two days."

Kaen started to say something as Hess moved off after he finished speaking.

I can feel you are frustrated. What is going on?

Hess . . . he is just acting weird. I think he is taking the whole last quest together badly. I don't know.

Give him some space. I can tell he is still worried about you. I'm upset I can't see you for a week. Thinking about it drives my scales crazy already.

I know. I don't want to think about it either. After this quest, I'll come out to the woods, and we will hang out for a few days. Hess says soon enough, we will get to tell others about us and not have to hide it anymore.

I can't wait!

They both felt the feelings they had mixing through their bond. It was like missing an arm, not having the other nearby.

As Kaen sat there, chatting with the occasional adventurer who visited the inn and felt the need to engage him in conversation, a man dressed in fine servant clothes made a beeline to his booth.

"Sir Kaen?" the man asked as he bowed slightly.

"Just Kaen or Kaen Marshell, please," Kaen answered with an eye roll. "I prefer no fancy titles, as I don't think I am owed them."

The man nodded, and a slight smile of approval crossed his face. "I have a letter for you," he stated as he handed it to Kaen. "If you would, please read it and let me know your answer."

Kaen saw the smooth ivory envelope with a wax seal on it in the man's hand. He took it, feeling the exceptional quality of the paper. As he brought it to his face, he could smell something.

Smiling, he knew it was from Ava, even before he glanced at the seal and noticed the two intertwined snakes.

Kaen,

If you would like, my servant here will bring you to my carriage outside, and we could go for a ride for a few hours.

Ava

After reading the letter once, he read it again to ensure he understood it correctly. "She's outside?" Kaen whispered as he leaned toward the man.

He nodded yes, and his smile only showed now on one side.

"Would you like me to take you to her or tell her you are too busy?" he asked as he motioned around the inn, which was only a fourth full tonight.

"Take me to her!" he announced, almost leaping from his booth.

"Follow me," he said, turning immediately and leading Kaen to the inn's entrance.

Outside sat the same type of carriage Ava's father had arrived in. It was a slightly different color. A little more . . . feminine, he figured. A soft rose color. The twin snakes were embossed on the door, and small lightstones were on each corner of the cart, gently glowing in the evening light.

When the man opened the door, Kaen saw Ava sitting inside smiling, with a book on her lap, wearing a dress that was too formal compared to the standard tunic and pants he was wearing. Her hair was done, and she looked more radiant than he could remember.

"You going to stand out there with your mouth open trying to catch flies or join me?" Ava teased as she smiled at him.

Bounding into the carriage, Kaen almost ran into her from his excitement. He glanced around and saw two benches inside the cart and almost sat down on the one across from her till Ava moved over a little and tapped the spot next to her.

He nodded and sat beside her, not realizing that her servant had closed the door behind him. "What are you doing here?" he asked as he looked at her outfit. "You look like you are going to some ball or something."

Ava batted her long eyelashes and nodded. "There was a dinner and event at another lord's house, but I was bored and left. I have a few hours before I need to be home and thought I might ask you what you think of my dress."

Looking at her, he tried to keep his eyes from betraying his thoughts. The dress's neckline was low enough to show that Ava was a well-developed woman, and her skin was tanned everywhere it showed. With her hair done behind her and the ornaments in it, he could not believe he had ever managed to dance with her.

"I am afraid words would not do justice in describing you as anything but beautiful."

She chuckled and rolled her eyes. "That will do, I guess, only because I can tell you can't keep your eyes off me."

Kaen shrugged and glanced around the inside of the carriage. The two lightstones inside lit up the space they shared enough to notice the fine cloth on each seat and the gold and silver used as decorations on the walls and ceiling.

When his attention returned to her, he saw her tapping her book and waiting on him.

"What do you think?"

"Of you? I already answered that question," teased Kaen.

"The carriage, you fool. I can see you have never been around something like this before."

Nodding, Kaen pointed to the gold line that ran across the ceiling. "I'm a guy who grew up breaking rocks at a quarry. The idea of using gold as a decoration seems . . . well, it seems like something stupid. We would have spent that on food or other necessities."

Ava nodded, not put off by his honesty. "And yet you are meeting with the king in two days, and I feel you might need some help. My dad told me about your mishap and how you tried to promise him something. I want to help prevent such a thing from happening, if you are willing."

"I would appreciate that!" exclaimed Kaen as he stared at her green eyes. "What do you have in mind?"

"Tomorrow, you will come to my house and meet my mother while my dad is busy with business matters," Ava stated as she leaned closer to Kaen. "I must warn you she is extremely excited to meet you."

Kaen felt his face turning red, and his eyes were lost on Ava, who had stopped just a few inches from him.

"Uh . . . ok," he finally blurted out, his brain lost in the fog of hormones and things running through his mind.

Ava rolled her eyes and shook her head as she leaned back. "Kaen Marshell, what am I going to do with you?" she said with a mocking sigh. "Rumor has it you like to tease girls and lead them on, yet I don't get that from you right now."

She tapped her finger on her book again, watching him process what she had said.

"I'm sorry," he finally blurted out as he took a breath. "You caught me off guard. Showing up in a carriage, dressed like you are now, looking and smelling the way you do! I smell like a guy who has sat in a tavern for a few hours, and I look like it as well. My hair isn't done, my breath probably smells like potatoes and pheasant, and all I can think of is how amazing you look and how much I want to kiss you, but I don't want to because I'm afraid you'll think I smell or that my kiss tastes funny."

Holding his hands up in frustration, he grunted. "Does that make sense?" he asked as he watched her smile.

She nodded and put her book on the seat beside her. "Yes, it does," she answered quietly as she moved closer. "So stop talking and thinking and just kiss me already."

79

Hess and Pammon

"If I didn't know you were an adventurer, I might confuse you for one of them snooty nobles," teased Eltina as she gazed at Kaen.

He was sitting at the bar with Hess, reviewing a few pieces of paperwork for his academy, and waiting for the carriage to arrive that would take him to Ava's parents' residence.

"These old clothes?" Kaen joked as he hopped off the stool and spun around. "Why, I've had these things for a whole week. You know these must already be out of style by now."

Chuckling, Eltina bobbed her head as she stroked her beard. "I think you are finally growing up into the man Sulenda says you are," she replied. "I'm glad you haven't lost your sense of humor yet. Good luck today. You're going to need it."

Kaen started to ask what she meant, but Eltina had already hopped off her block and was moving to the other side of her domain.

"Is it going to be that bad?" Kaen asked, sitting down.

Hess grunted as he flipped through the stack of pages he was double-checking. "I can't give advice other than not to promise anything and to beware a woman like Lady Hurem. I doubt she will harm you, but I have no doubt that she is well aware of her daughter's affection toward you as well as her husband's opinion about you."

Looking up from the paper, Hess smiled awkwardly as he put his hand on Kaen's shoulder. "I can't help with this next part. Lords and Ladies do not often get along with me," Hess explained. "I am a little too forward and brash and don't give a hairy green goblin arse about them and their wants. I don't play games and have a history of telling people what I think, which is why Fiola and a few others have not always been my greatest allies."

"What about tomorrow? You are coming tomorrow, right?"

Snorting, Hess rolled his eyes and nodded. "Sulenda would not let me miss it. Knowing the outfit I must wear for that, I feel like a fool."

"That makes two of us," joked Kaen as he put his hand on Hess's shoulder. "At least we will be a pair of fools in the king's court."

Shaking Kaen a little, Hess grinned and gave a little push, almost knocking Kaen off his stool. "Let's finish this up before you go. I don't want Sulenda getting mad at me for shirking my duties."

The next hour was spent double-checking the number of students, instructors, staff counts, and everything Sulenda felt Kaen should know about the academy. His mind struggled to appreciate all the nuances and specifics regarding salaries and costs of housing all these people. Knowing he would eat through the entire forty gold promised by the lords had committed to this venture was staggering. Yet knowing they would hopefully have fifty students within a year, brought a sense of pride he wouldn't let go.

"Remember, our *friend* will be waiting with those antlers you wanted in a few hours at that clearing. He said not to be late."

"Oh, I won't be late." Hess laughed as he shoved Kaen toward the carriage waiting for him. "I have a full cow, slaughtered as a gift and already waiting in a cart outside of town. I need to hurry and get to him."

Kaen grinned and tapped his forehead. "I cannot begin to tell you how excited he is for this."

Smiling, Hess nodded and shooed Kaen into his ride. He felt Sulenda putting her hand around his waist as she waved at Kaen with her other.

"You sure this is the right decision?" she whispered. "It's like sending that boy into the wolf's den."

Hess nodded, waiting for the carriage door to close. "You know, if I thought you or me going with him would help, I would do it. We both know there is nothing we can do now."

Sulenda kissed Hess on his cheek before slapping his butt. "Well, get that cow delivered to whoever it is and hurry back. I want to make sure things are ready for tomorrow," she stated excitedly. "I still can't believe I am meeting King Aldric tomorrow. Me! A lowly inn owner!"

Hess spun around, drew her into an embrace, and stared into her eyes. "There is nothing lowly about you. That is why I love you."

Her lip quivered, and she bobbed her head at those words.

Standing on his tiptoes, he kissed her forehead and laughed. "I forgot how tall you are," he teased.

She just smiled and laid her head on his shoulder for a moment. "Go do what you need to do," she finally said as she broke their embrace.

Nodding, Hess winked at her and moved toward his waiting horse.

* * *

"Pammon, I need you to listen to me. I am going to tell you something, and you cannot tell Kaen what I tell you until the day you reach your quest location. Do you understand?"

Staring at him, Pammon's eyelids flickered and narrowed at Hess as he licked his snout.

"If you promise me you will not share what I say until that day, nod your head."

Pammon snorted at him. It was something akin to a growl, but Hess held his ground as he faced down a dragon now larger than the shed they had built in the woods back in Minoosh.

"We both want Kaen to be safe. Right?"

Pammon nodded slowly as his massive eyes took in everything Hess said and did.

Moving slowly forward, Hess put his hand on Pammon's snout and sighed when Pammon did not move away. "I love him. I know you love him too. This is why I have to do this the way I am. I made a promise and cannot break it," Hess explained as he scratched the scales below Pammon's eyes. "If you want to help me keep Kaen safe, promise me."

Pammon sat there a moment as Hess watched him. He knew Hess would not ask such a thing if it wasn't important. He didn't like keeping things from Kaen, but if Hess was willing to trust him, he knew it was for the right reasons.

Lifting his front talons slowly, he gently tapped it against Hess's heart and nodded his head.

"Good!" exclaimed Hess, joy sweeping across his face. "Now listen. Bad things will happen; you will be the only way we all survive.

Pammon sat there, torn. Hess's news of the invading armies of creatures had left a bad taste in his mouth, even after eating that delicious cow. He stayed motionless as Hess fastened the ropes and the bundles of arrows onto his back near where Kaen would sit. It was a smart move on Hess's part, proving how much Hess cared about Kaen.

"Now listen, if things go bad, you keep that promise to flee," Hess said again as he tightened another rope. "You two are more important than all of us. If something happens, you fly to the elven kingdom, Roccnari. They will take you in, and Elies will give you two the training you both need."

Snorting, Pammon slowly nodded where he knew Hess could see his acknowledgment. He would never allow Kaen to die if he could help it, even if he had to carry him in his talons while he flew.

It took every ounce of his being not to let his emotions flood through their connection, but thankfully, Kaen was enjoying himself at that girl's house. He took a deep breath and blew it out forcefully, causing Hess to glance at him as he dealt with the feelings of a woman trying to steal Kaen.

"I don't like it either," Hess proclaimed, believing Pammon was agreeing with Hess's last statement. "Now remember, try not to let these rub too much, as they might snap or fall apart. I have double tied and used more rope than is needed, but three hundred arrows are on each side of you. I pray that many is unnecessary, and I won't mention how hard it was to procure that many without bringing attention to it."

Hess moved back and examined his handiwork, watching as Pammon moved around again and tested his wings. Satisfied that they didn't shift too much or slide, Hess moved back to Pammon and held out his hand.

Coming forward, Pammon put the bottom of his head on Hess's hand and trilled.

Hess smiled and gave a long scratch along Pammon's neck scales before giving his neck a small hug. "I'm glad you two found each other," Hess declared as he moved back, wiping a tear from his eyes. "You two are perfect for each other. Thankfully, you both don't act like egglings anymore."

Pammon couldn't help but laugh, feeling the thrum in his body growing louder. Hess was right. They were perfect for each other. He was grateful for how Hess had helped both of them and knew it would be hard on Kaen when the time came to say goodbye for a while. As he sat looking at Hess and wishing he could tell him those things, something in the back of his head itched. He felt like he was being guided to do something to show his appreciation.

Eyes going wide, Pammon realized what he needed to do. Lifting his talons, he plunged one at the base of one of his side teeth, ignoring the pain as he pressed it until the tooth came free. Using his tongue, he brought it out of his mouth and clasped it carefully between his claws.

Hess was staring at him in shock. Pammon could see the confusion on Hess's face until he saw the tooth Pammon was holding.

Moving forward lightly on his three legs, he held out the tooth to Hess, who slowly came forward and took it from him.

As Hess stood there, holding the six-inch long tooth, Pammon moved closer and put his head against Hess's.

He could feel his mana building up, wanting to be used. He gave into it, allowing knowledge he had no idea of before to flow through him.

[Mark Complete - Hess Brumlin]

Hess's eyes went wide as he received a notification.

[You Have Been Marked by Pammon]

Glancing at the tooth in his hand, he saw it glow briefly before returning to its normal white color, blood, and roots still hanging from it.

Thank you for keeping Kaen safe and for trusting him to me.

Hess felt the sound in his head. He knew what it was, but he couldn't believe it. "Pa . . . Pammon? I can hear you?"

The thrum of Pammon's laughter echoed in the clearing as he nodded.

Yes. I just figured it out now. Somehow, because my desire to say thank you was so great, it came upon me. I didn't know it was even possible until now.

Hess held up the tooth and pointed at it, shaking his head in disbelief. "You can talk because of the tooth?"

I don't know everything yet. I know when we are close, and you have that, you can hear me. I also know where you are because you have my tooth. It would do nothing if someone else took it or you lost it. I am not sure I can do this too often, but you are worthy of this, Hess Brumlin. You are worthy of my thanks that I will never be able to repay.

Laughing as tears streamed down from his face, Hess smiled, put out his hand, and embraced Pammon.

"I cannot tell you thank you enough. I know it is not easy what I have asked, yet we will do what we must to protect our boy."

You are correct. Now, I know you need to return, and I need to go scout like you asked. I will tell Kaen the code words when I confirm what I find.

Scratching Pammon's neck one last time, Hess smiled and bobbed his head. "Be safe, Pammon."

Hess wanted to say more but found no words to add. He felt the tooth in his hand and gripped it tightly.

I will, and you be safe as well.

Pammon turned, preparing to take off but paused and looked back at Hess.

One last thing. Make sure that Kaen does not let this woman ensnare him. I am not ready to lose him to a woman.

Choking as he laughed, Hess covered his mouth until he regained his composure. "I feel the same way," Hess replied. "I'll do my best."

Nodding, Pammon launched himself upward as Hess kept an eye on the bundles of arrows. Thankfully, none of them fell off or slid down. Hopefully, the leather he had used to wrap the rope in specific areas, would prevent them from rubbing too much.

Looking at the tooth in his hand once more, Hess smiled and put it in a pouch on his hip. He then moved to where the two large antlers were waiting, knowing he needed to get home.

80

Meeting Lady Hurem

"I'm not sure I can call you that," Kaen answered, feeling his cheeks going red.

Bridgette and Ava laughed at Kaen's expense as they watched Kaen shift on his chair.

"If a lady tells you to call her by her first name, it would be considered rude not to," Ava chimed in as she moved a tray of treats closer to Kaen.

"I guess . . . " Kaen replied as he glanced at Ava's mother, still in disbelief that she barely looked above thirty-five. "If you insist, Lady Bridgette, I will honor your request."

Nodding, she picked up her cup of tea and drank it, keeping her eyes on him the entire time.

For the last few hours, they had sat in this *sitting* room, larger than the house he and Hess had shared in Minoosh. Pictures, decorations, ornate wallpaper, and more filled a room with just a few couches and this small table and chairs positioned right next to a set of massive windows that looked out over the inside city of Ebonmount.

"You will do fine tomorrow," Bridgette continued, "as long as you remember to keep your head clear and make no promises or commitments. Like we practiced, you must only commit to specific things. King Aldric will not do anything mischievous, as he is smitten with the story he expects you to tell him upon arriving. Hearing you tell it now, I have no doubt he will enjoy it as well."

Smiling the way he had been taught, Kaen nodded. He could not believe he had gained another point in his storytelling skill. He felt he had been tame when he had told it to Lady Bridgette. His shirt had stayed on, and he had not lain on the ground as he had during his previous renditions.

A servant popped in, walked over to where Lady Hurem was sitting, and whispered something into her ear. Kaen watched as her face never changed or revealed anything the servant had said.

"I need to deal with something related to business," she stated as she rose from her seat.

Kaen quickly jumped to his feet and moved around the table to assist with her chair. "Allow me," he said with a slight bow and smile.

"A quick learner. You will be fine," she stated, allowing Kaen to help with her chair. "Now, you two enjoy the snacks, and I will see you tomorrow, if I do not see you later today."

"Thank you for allowing me to visit your home. It is truly breathtaking, almost as breathtaking as your daughter is."

Ava's cheeks flushed, and Lady Bridgette laughed the way she always did when amused.

"Kaen Marshell, I heard you were quick with your tongue when it comes to women. I would hope for your sake that you make sure to always be truthful with it. Nothing is worse than a man gaining a reputation for leading women on and then leaving them after getting what they want."

The intense change in her gaze as she said those words conveyed her seriousness.

Nodding, Kaen smiled and gave a slight bow. "I mean every word I say."

"Good," she responded with a clap. "Now, you two enjoy yourselves. The life of one in our family is never dull."

"You did quite well," Ava whispered as they lounged on a couch, cuddled against each other. "My mother would typically not leave the room as she has done, with no servants to watch over me and a man. It appears she must like you."

Even though Ava was not looking at his face, Kaen grinned and felt her running her finger up and down the back of his hand.

"This is going to be a busy week, isn't it?" Kaen said.

"It is. I still cannot fathom how you have gained so much favor in this town," Ava admitted. "I was a bit intimidated when we danced, and you did what you did with me. As much as I wanted to stay, I knew if I didn't run away at that moment, I would be bound by whatever spell you must cast on all those you meet."

Chuckling, Kaen leaned over and kissed her head. "I will admit I cast no spell, and I am just as confused as to why everyone seems to want a piece of me. I'm just a backwoods kid who wants to be an adventurer."

Sitting up and turning to face Kaen, Ava shook her head as she playfully glared at him. "There is nothing *backwoods* about you, Kaen Marshell," she informed him in a tone he had heard her mother use that day. "You seem to draw people to you. Even if you are unaware of it, somehow you inspire and make others feel better simply by being in your presence. You might not realize it, but you had my mother acting in ways I have not seen in years."

Ava pointed a finger at him and wagged it in his face. "I have danced with many men at balls and other events, yet none swept me off my feet like you did that night. So before you downplay everything, know you are meant for something great, and I am willing to tell you I will always do what I can to help you succeed, if you desire it."

Reaching out, Kaen gently snagged her finger and pulled her hand close to him. "I would promise something, but I am afraid you might attempt to use your skill and bind me to it," he teased as he kissed her fingertip.

"Hmmm . . . " Ava muttered as she watched him lower her finger from his mouth. "That sounds like something we should try and do."

Leaning back a little, Kaen stretched his neck and glanced at her from the corner of his eyes.

"You want me to let you try and bind me to you?"

Bobbing her head side to side, she shrugged. "Not like that, you fool!" she exclaimed. "I would give you my word that I will not ask for anything and will release you immediately. It would be more to show you the dangers of it and how to caution you against it. We could devise a specific promise and not one that will allow me to abuse before I bind you to it."

"You have that skill? How is that possible?"

"I would prefer not to go into how it is acquired as it was unpleasant, but yes, I have it. As one in my family's position, it is required and will be used at some point."

"But you are an adventurer. How can you do both?"

Giggling a little, Ava smiled and pulled out her silver token that was nestled between her breasts. "This is only for a while. Eventually, I will leave the guild, keeping my contacts and relationships but also understanding why our family's potions are needed and how to use them best. This was a decision I made, one my father supported after I told him why I wanted to do it."

"Why did you want to do it?" Kaen asked as he saw the facade she sometimes wore falling away.

"Look at all this," Ava responded as she motioned around the room. "We have far more money than we need, and the potions we provide have more use in the hands of adventurers on the front lines. Why not find a way to help keep our kingdom safe? Especially after all the horrible things that have happened these past few weeks."

Kan grimaced as he saw Ava struggle with the last line. "There was nothing any of us could have done about that."

"Wasn't there?" she asked as she looked at Kaen. "Perhaps if my family had sold potions cheaper or donated some, they might have had the chance to keep fighting for a while longer and won."

Kaen reached out, lifting her chin gently from where she was staring down at her token. "If that is how you feel, then you can make that change when the time comes. You can make the difference you feel you need to."

Ava nodded and grabbed his hand, kissing his fingers and smiling. "Thank you," she whispered. "Now, let me help you see what you need to prepare yourself to defend against."

After discussing things for a while, Kaen finally had his promise, worded precisely how they both felt it should be. It sounded stupid, but he knew it would never be one he had to worry about breaking.

"I, Kaen Marshell, promise never to dump apple pudding on your head."

Smiling, Ava grabbed his hand.

His lifestone surged for a brief moment.

[Charm Resisted]
[Charm Resistance Skill Increased x6]

Kaen cocked his head, watching Ava's perplexed expression. "Something went wrong, didn't it?"

"Yes!" she exclaimed, glaring at him. "It said it failed! It never does that. Let's try it again."

Kaen nodded as he fought not to smile. "I, Kaen Marshell, promise never to dump apple pudding on your head."

Ava still had ahold of his hand and squeezed tightly as he finished those words.

Once more, his lifestone responded as it had before.

[Charm Resisted]
[Charm Resistance Skill Increased x3]
[Charm Resist Skill Evolved]

Shock overwhelmed Kaen as a chuckle escaped his mouth when he saw Ava's face turning red.

"You know it's failing, don't you!?"

"I do. I got a message, but I resisted it each time."

"Impossible!" she exclaimed, and she growled in frustration. "No one has ever resisted this, not even my father!"

"I don't know what to say," Kaen admitted, not wanting to share the truth that he had gained nine points in his charm resist. He would need to ask Hess about what it meant that it had evolved.

"Stay here! I need to figure out what is going on!"

Ava leaped up from where she was on the couch, ignoring her dress and how it did not appear very ladylike as she dashed across the room to one of the doors. She opened it and talked to the servant outside.

Once the door shut, she quickly moved back across the room, red-faced and a little more reserved than when she first had left his side.

"Is everything ok? You seem upset about this."

Plopping down on the couch next to him, she groaned. "You don't understand. This should not fail. Either something is wrong with my ability, or you are indeed something special."

"Peculiar," murmured Lady Bridgette as she watched Kaen. "It seems you are resisting every attempt I have tried, no matter how we word the promise."

Kaen nodded and shrugged slightly. He had gained four more points since they had attempted to bind him to various things.

"Do you know why neither of us can get it to work?" Ava asked, frustration and concern filling her voice.

"I do not, but I will talk to Lord Hurem in private tonight," Lady Bridgette replied, never taking her eyes off Kaen. "As for you, do not tell anyone about this, if you are smart. If what I imagine is true, you are a wild card that could potentially resist the king himself."

"Is that even possible?" Kaen gasped as he considered what that meant.

"Who is to say? Regardless, I think this would be a fine opportunity for us to end this visit for the day."

Ava started to speak before her mother's glance cut her off.

"It has nothing to do with either of you or something wrong happening. For now, Kaen needs to head back to prepare and rest for tomorrow," Lady Bridgette informed them both. "You also need to secure the supplies for your trip."

"You are questing?" Kaen asked.

"I am," Ava replied, trying not to groan at her mother's instructions. "I will be accompanying Adventurer Selah on a quest after tomorrow. I can learn many things from her and practice some of my skills."

"I'm glad to hear you will be in good hands," Kaen stated as relief washed over him. Knowing quests had been mislabeled in the previous weeks had left him not wanting her to take unnecessary risks.

"Until tomorrow then, Adventurer Kaen," Ava said with a curtsey and a wink. "I cannot wait to see what you wear when you meet the king."

Both women laughed when Kaen let out the groan he was unable to keep inside.

"Forgive my manners, but I'm more of a leather tunic and pants kind of guy."

The women nodded and smiled.

"That is what she likes about you. The way you look in leather," Lady Bridgette stated as Ava's face turned red again.

81

King Aldric

"My legs are getting tired of standing," Kaen whispered to Hess as he listened to what seemed like the fiftieth man inform the king about shipments, trades, and other stuff that could put someone to sleep. "I thought we were meeting the king, not listening to all this."

Hess chuckled and received an elbow from Sulenda, who never took her eyes off the king.

They were standing in a crowd of people on one side of the massive throne room with people who had come today to update the king on matters of the state.

"If we had a private audience, it would not look good for your first time. Do what you were told, and things will be fine."

Nodding, Kaen began zoning out again as he stared across the open space, locking eyes with Ava, who was on the other side behind her mother and father. She winked at him again, and he smiled, helping him drown out the noise of news he cared not for.

An elbow knocked him out of his daydream, causing him to glance up at Hess, who was motioning with his head for Kaen to move forward.

A man in an outrageous outfit, with a puffy feather on top of his hat and holding a staff of some sort, was looking at him.

"Adventurer Kaen, please follow me to present yourself to the king!"

Kaen bowed and moved behind the man as he walked toward the king, who had leaned forward on his throne.

Murmurs could be heard around as people motioned to him as he walked down the purple carpet that ran from one end of the hall to the other.

As they arrived at the end of the carpet, fifteen yards from the king, the man stepped to the side, motioning for Kaen to stop beside him.

"Your Highness! May I present to you Adventurer Kaen, slayer of goblins and orcs, and our newest silver adventurer!"

Kaen gave a deep bow, holding it like he had been told to.

"Arise Adventurer Kaen."

Kaen stood tall, surprised by the strength in the king's voice. It sounded like one who could crush rocks with just the very words from his mouth. He saw the king sitting on his stone throne, wearing armor that looked like it could stop anything sent at him. Even though it was a full plate, it seemed to move easily and not hinder the king. It shined like the sun, the gold plates radiating light. The king, with his black hair and brown eyes, had a face that looked aged but wise.

"Thank you for humoring your king and coming here today. I must admit I have been anxious to meet the one who slew six orcs on his first quest in order to rise to the rank of silver."

"Forgive me, Your Highness, but it was only five orcs," Kaen interrupted, causing a stir in the room and the man on his right to shift nervously.

The king smiled, unfazed by Kaen's interruption.

"I had heard it was six," he stated, glancing around the room. "Are you saying I was misinformed?"

"Forgive me again, Your Highness, but I only killed five myself. The sixth one you have been told about was a tier-three orc, and while I did deliver the killing blow, Luca, the silver token adventurer who gave his life to save Aubri and myself, did the damage that allowed me to survive and defeat the orc. Any honor for that one should be given to Luca and Aubri. The role I played was small at best."

King Aldric nodded as he leaned against one of the stone armrests. "Perhaps you would be willing to share the details of all the orcs and goblins you have killed so far? I have heard you have a knack for making it enjoyable to listen to."

Kaen saw the smile the king gave him with his request. "I would be honored to hopefully tell a story worthy of entertaining the king."

Taking a deep breath, Kaen closed his eyes briefly, honing his thoughts on one thing.

Protecting families.

His lifestone roared with heat. Smiling, he opened his eyes and his mouth.

Panting, Kaen stood there, his feet spread apart, spinning around the room as he enacted holding the head of the orc Luca had given his life to kill in his hand.

He gave a slight bow when he turned back and faced King Aldric. "And that, Your Highness, is the story of the five orcs I killed, and the one Luca sacrificed everything for so that Aubri and I might live."

He paused, his lifestone still burning in his chest.

[Story Telling Skill Increased x5]

King Aldric stood up and descended from his throne. As he did, guards shifted, and people throughout the hall held their breath, waiting to hear and see what the king would do.

As Aldric stood just a few feet from him, Kaen started to drop to his knee, and the king reached out with both hands, grabbing Kaen by the shoulders and lifting him back up.

He then spun him around and moved to Kaen's side. "Let it be known that no finer tale has been told in these halls in a long time," belted out Aldric. "Give this adventurer who has heart, skill with a bow, and honor, the applause he deserves!"

The hall erupted in applause, and the occasional whistle that Kaen knew was coming from Hess. King Aldric himself clapped his hands as he stood next to Kaen, encouraging the applause of the nobles and other leaders present.

"You have quite the gift, if I do say so," whispered Aldric above the noise. "If you were not an adventurer, I would offer to hire you to always tell stories here."

Kaen gave a slight bow and smiled.

After a moment, the king raised his hands, and the room became absolutely still. "After this fine tale, I doubt anyone would want to follow it. As such, I shall end today's gathering and thank you all who do what you do to keep our kingdom safe."

The man who had initially escorted Kaen up, quickly moved down the carpet, motioning for people to head to the room's exit.

As Kaen prepared to leave, he felt a hand on his shoulder.

"Stay with me a moment," Aldric said. "I have a few questions, if you don't mind answering them."

"I would be honored," Kaen replied. "Can I have my guardian and mentor stay with me? I know both of them, or perhaps at least one of them, would like to meet you."

Chucking, Aldric nodded as he motioned to where Sulenda and Hess were standing, waiting to see what would happen. Both of their faces lit up, and as they moved toward Kaen, the man who had escorted Kaen verified the king had given permission before allowing them to continue.

"Follow me if you would," Aldric said as he walked away. "I prefer somewhere a little more private."

"Thank you for this privilege," Sulenda gushed as she did a deep curtsy. "We are honored just to be able to meet you, let alone to have a private audience."

Aldric smiled and motioned for them to sit down. Once Sulenda sat in her chair, the men took their seats.

"Now, Kaen, let me say, you probably do not know this, but I had met your father a few times before, and you are the spitting image of him. I would be honest when I say the apple does not fall far from the tree."

Stunned at the knowledge that his father had met King Aldric a few times, Kaen wondered if the reason for the meeting was because of his own merit or because of his father.

"Adventurer Hess, I have known about you for a while, but it seemed you never wanted to visit me, from what I have gleaned. What changed this time?"

Glancing at Sulenda and her watchful eye, Hess smiled as he motioned to Kaen with his hand. "As his guardian for the last eight years, I wanted to ensure Kaen was not alone during such an important event. I'm not one for getting dressed up. A good ale and a hard chair are more my style."

King Aldric laughed and tapped the armrest with his fist a few times. "I appreciate the honesty. I wish I had the freedom to enjoy such simple things," he declared as he motioned to the men in the room with them. "Alas, I cannot even be alone with others due to concerns for my safety."

Hess chuckled and shook his head. "I doubt many people would assume that you have anything to fear from most. I have been told by Hoste just how formidable you could be."

Kaen sat in awe when a boyish grin flashed across King Adlric's face.

"Well, let's get down to business," Aldric suddenly declared as he motioned to a man off to the side. "I have heard of your desire to fund an academy, and Lord Hurem and a few others told me of their commitment to this cause. I want you to know I am excited to see such an endeavor, and I will support you, but it will be done behind the scenes."

"Behind the scenes?" Kaen asked.

"If I put my name on this, Kaen," explained Aldric, "it will no longer be your academy. It would be ours, and that is not what this kingdom needs. The adventurers' guild is part of and separate for a reason. I have no true power over it, nor do I want that responsibility. I know of the quests you often partake in and the kingdom and myself are grateful to all the adventurers who risk their lives for us."

The man whom the king had summoned handed a rolled-up paper to him.

"In this document is my commitment to you for lifestones which are currently in short supply."

Aldric leaned forward and handed the letter to Kaen, who stood up to collect his prize.

"Do not break the seal, but for now, hold onto it and use it to collect from my house when the time comes for your first twenty lifestones. I have some set aside just for you."

"Thank you," gushed Kaen as he spun the document in his hand, admiring the wax seal with the king's crest. "I will not forget such a gift as this."

Nodding, Aldric waved off Kaen's statement and leaned forward toward the three of them. "I know things look bleak right now. I spoke with Fiola and want you to understand we are doing everything possible to help." He paused, and a look of concern washed over his face. "I know you leave tomorrow and would caution you to be safe. Come back, and perhaps we can enjoy another chance to hear you share the tales of how you killed more creatures to protect the kingdom."

Kaen bowed and sat down on his chair.

"One last thing," Aldric said, as the man beside him pulled out a small box from behind him. "I have a gift. May it aid you in the coming battles, and may you never lose the honor you showed today in sharing the story of Luca and his sacrifice."

The servant walked over and opened the box. Inside was a simple leather belt that had leaves made of silver etched all over it.

Staring at it, Kaen hesitated to take the belt until he saw Hess nodding at him. His fingers slowly grasped the leather, and as he pulled the belt out, he could feel the magic it carried.

"That is a belt a friend of mine had a lifetime ago. It may not seem like much, but it offers two points to dexterity. Perhaps they will serve you in the coming days."

"I am honored and grateful for such a gift. I will wear it proudly and do what I can to honor your friend's name."

The servant closed the box and returned to King Aldric's side.

"If you will excuse me, I have a variety of other matters that I must attend to today, and if I do not take care of them, some of my servants," Aldric said as he motioned to the man behind him with his eyes, "will become impatient and make my life difficult."

King Aldric stood up, and as he did, the other three rose as well. "Adventurer Kaen, Hess, and Sulenda, it has been a pleasure. May the spirits watch over you and keep you safe."

The three of them bowed as the king left through a door on the side of the room. Once he was gone, one of the servants escorted them out of the king's keep and back to the courtyard outside it.

You seem in a good mood. Pammon suddenly spoke as Kaen rode his horse behind Sulenda and Hess. **What has you all excited?**

Running a finger over the belt, Kaen smiled.

I received a gift from King Aldric. I had not expected it, but it will help in our quest. What about you? I can tell you are flying, and you feel far away. What are you up to?

Different emotions, mixed and more, flooded their bond for a moment before fading.

I am on a mission for Hess. He asked me to scout where we were to make sure nothing had changed. You can tell him that I will have a full report later. You should also ask him about the conversation we had today. I think it surprised him to hear me.

WHAT?! Hess heard you?! How is that possible?

Kaen's emotions boiled over as he flooded the connection.

Relax, please! You are overly excited. I wanted to tell him thank you for protecting you and loving you the way he did. Somehow, I just knew how to do it. I cannot do it with everyone, but I marked him. He carries one of my teeth, and I know he is right next to you.

Amazed at what Pammon was telling him, Kaen had hundreds of questions to ask, but only one seemed important right now.

Can he hear you right now?

No, chuckled Pammon. **Only when we are close will it work. He still has to talk to me like you two talk, but he can hear me now.**

Kaen sighed as the joy that Pammon and Hess could share a little of what he felt erupted from him.

Thank you for doing that for him. It means a lot to both of us.

While you might call him your dad, I guess I would call him an uncle.

Laughing out loud, Kaen saw that Sulenda and Hess had turned and were looking at him.

"Sorry," Kaen said with a shrug. "Just thinking about today and how much I wished this belt would let me talk with others far away."

Hess's face never changed, but Kaen saw the twinkle in his eye as Hess tapped his temple.

"You're keeping your head in the clouds, son. Remember to keep your feet on the ground."

Grinning, Kaen nodded. "Wouldn't it be great if Hess could read your mind, Sulenda?"

Roaring in laughter, Sulenda shook her head emphatically. "Please no . . . There are not many worse things I could think of than for a man to read my mind."

The three of them laughed as they rode back to the inn. They had a few things to finish preparing for, and then it would be time to turn in. Tomorrow would be the day they went their separate ways.

82

The Secrets We Keep

Before they retired upstairs, Kaen and Hess sat in the office with Sulenda.

"I know you know I am nervous about tomorrow, so don't complain when I give you these things," Hess stated as he put the pouch with three potions in it back in Kaen's hand. "Stop fighting and just keep them. They are yours; perhaps one of your new squad mates will need it."

Kaen finally resigned to the fact that he would not win this argument and bobbed his head in appreciation, as he took the pouch from him.

"I still think it's a waste, but whatever," he muttered. "When did you say you are leaving?"

Sulenda shifted in her chair, and Kaen saw the look on her face.

"I leave in about five hours, and she is not excited about you not being there to protect me."

"That's a load of goblin shite, and you know it," Sulenda declared, glaring at him. "I'm just not happy with all this cloak-and-dagger stuff you don't want to share, and I know you are worried about Kaen more than you should be. He will be fine. If you believe he won't, we can strap his arse to that chair and not let him go."

"Woah . . . " Kaen said as he leaned back in his chair. "What is going on?"

Hess shot Sulenda a look, and she gave it right back.

"We are having a disagreement about something, and I won't bother you with it," growled Hess as he returned to his chair. "Did you have a message for me?"

I . . . Uh . . . " Kaen was surprised Hess had asked such a thing before Sulenda but figured it wouldn't matter. "Seven and one thousand five hundred."

Leaning back in his chair, Hess folded his arms before he let out a sigh. "Thank you. It is what I expected."

"What does that mean?" Sulenda asked Kaen as she turned her attention to him.

"Beats me," he responded with a shrug. "I was just told to pass that information on."

Growling a little, Sulenda glared at Hess again. "Actually, I need to go. I want to double-check some details on my group before I leave tomorrow."

Hess slowly stood up, trying to act natural, but Kaen knew something was wrong.

"Can I walk you a few blocks and ask a few more things regarding squad fighting?" inquired Kaen as he tapped his temple. "I want to make sure I have it all locked in here tight so I'm not the weakest link."

Hess nodded with a chuckle. "I have no doubt you won't be the weakest link, but sure, you can ask a few questions."

Both stood, and Kaen waved at Sulenda, who was watching them leave.

As the door shut, she wadded up a piece of paper and threw it across the room in frustration. "Blast that man!" she cursed as she leaned against her desk. "I swear I'll wring his neck if he doesn't come back to me . . . "

Glancing down at her desk, she saw wet marks on top of it, and realized she was crying over a fear she couldn't shake.

"What am I missing!?" Kaen demanded as they left the inn and started down the street. "Pammon won't tell me, but I can feel he is hiding something!"

Hess shrugged and kept his eyes ahead. "I can't say."

"Can't say or won't say?"

Hess stopped and turned and pulled out his gold token from his shirt. "I cannot say because of this," Hess answered, frustrated by a promise he knew he'd had to make. "If I could, I would share more, but I cannot! Just know I am doing everything possible to help you and the kingdom."

Glancing around the near-empty streets, Hess pulled Kaen close and gave him a hug. "Trust me and Pammon," he whispered as he squeezed Kaen. "We both will protect you above everything else. Tomorrow, do what you must do; when the time comes, you will know what must be done."

"When the time comes?" Kaen asked, pulling back and looking up at Hess.

Breaking the embrace, Hess nodded and ruffled Kaen's hair. "You're smart. Smarter than me and everyone else around you. Use that brain, and you will understand when the time comes," Hess declared as he smiled at Kaen. "Now go. Get some rest, prepare your mind, and make sure to bring as many arrows as you can."

Hess began to walk away, leaving Kaen looking at his back.

"Listen, Fiola, just trust what I say!" Hess proclaimed loudly as he pointed at the map they were looking at again. "One thousand five hundred is a small but accurate number. There are easily more there than this!"

Fiola was frustrated that Hess had somehow managed to acquire these numbers so quickly after she had spent so much time being secretive in collecting them. Two scouts had died before they could return, making the truth of what he was telling her now, harder to argue against.

"We have no other option," she declared as she adjusted the tokens at each mark on the map representing the squads descending upon those armies of creatures. "Look at what we have! The adventurers we lost have limited our ability to fight this battle!"

Fiola leaned back against the couch and let out a sigh. "I will be on the battlefield, personally assisting a group of squads. That is how grave this is."

Hess saw the look in her eyes and realized she was terrified. "How will you manage the guild hall if you are on the front line?"

Fiola held out her hand. Turning it over, she showed a gold coin with a *H* carved on top of it.

Fighting everything he had, Hess resisted snatching that coin from her.

"I'm sorry. I should never have made you do what you did. Take this coin, and if you can forgive me, I ask it now."

His hands trembled, knowing that the coin symbolized how she had screwed him over years ago, making him bind himself and preventing his relationship with Sulenda. He took a deep breath then slowly let it out. "Keep it for now. When we return from this event, you can give it to me then."

A small smile appeared as she withdrew her hand. The tremor in her arm betrayed the calm she tried to hide behind. "It is a deal," she replied, moving back to the map. "You will be here, two spots from where Kaen will be. I will be taking the far east camp. Selmah and her squad will be nearest to me. The others will all be manned by adventurers you might not know but who are all competent. I need you to press inward, if you succeed. Do not go to Kaen; the group next to you may need your help."

She pushed his tokens toward the *X* she was talking about. "You are going here because you can close that gap in less than four hours if everything goes well. If things go badly, this will be the first weak point, and you are my strongest warrior."

Pride that he did not want to admit he felt washed over him. For Fiola to say those words meant she believed them. She never complimented him on anything but his negative attitude and stubbornness.

"I will do what I can to help there. Anything else? I still need to finish a few small things before I leave in a few hours."

Shaking her head, Fiola stood up and held out her hand. "I wish you luck, Adventurer Hess Brumlin. May you be safe and return home to us, ready to keep helping Kaen become the man he is meant to be."

Caught off guard by her last words, Hess almost stumbled as he reached for her hand. He managed to shake it and smile before heading toward the door. He paused and asked a question he had meant to ask weeks ago but never had. "Why did you want to know his stats so badly? What is so important about them?"

"You really don't know, do you?" Fiola asked, reading Hess's body language.

"It must be obvious that I don't."

"Kaen is the son of two adventurer bloodlines," Fiola answered, never flinching. "From what I know about Hoste and Kaen's mother, I know now that he will be greater than any adventurer we have seen. Greater than even his father."

Frozen with his hand on the doorknob, Hess wracked his brain around what he knew about Madalyn, Kaen's mother. She wasn't an adventurer! She had always stayed home with Kaen until she suddenly passed away. Hoste had been fortunate to find Ruth, the one who married him after Madalyn died while Kaen was a baby.

"Madalyn wasn't an adventurer! She never left Kaen's side!" exclaimed Hess. "What makes you believe that she was one?"

"We adventured together long before Hoste met her and they fell in love," replied Fiola. "She died because she fought her commitment from a promise she had made. She would not abandon her son until the day her heart claimed her. It was why she suddenly died."

Hess struggled to stand, the doorknob the only thing keeping Hess on his feet. He had not known any of this! Hoste had never shared this, and now he felt like he was betraying Kaen for not running to him and telling him the truth.

"How can you do this to me? On the night before I leave?!" he shouted, eyes red with anger.

"Because, Hess," she admitted, "we both know I won't be returning, and Kaen needs to be told the truth."

"But . . . " Hess found his throat was dry, and words were failing him.

"From watching you and other adventurers, I have learned to be willing to risk everything for our kingdom. How can I not do the same now? Now begone and take care of the things you need to do."

Herb,

I have filled the box with all the knowledge I have to share. You will do a wonderful job as the new guild master, and I am grateful for your years of service and faithfulness.

This last letter has been sealed, and if you read it, you have solved the puzzle. No one but you can or must read this.

Kaen Marshell must stay alive at all cost, and you must make sure he does not repeat his father's mistake. He is the tenth generation on his father's side of adventurers and the eleventh line of his mother's. He is not aware of this yet, but in time, you must inform him so he knows why he is growing so fast. I have spent years dedicated to tracking down how far their family lines ran, and the truth is that often, most of them have grown up without parents.

If he sires a child, they will be even greater than him. I know it would be too much to ask, yet if you can find a way to make him see the value of a child and what it can do for the kingdom . . . no, the world, I would encourage him to do so.

He shared his stats with me, not knowing why I wanted to know them. I needed to verify what I believed was true. His quest was not fair, yet it was required for what I had intended to do. I regret deeply still, the loss of Luca.

Guide him, motivate him, and support him. He is the future of this kingdom.

I have faith in your ability to handle him as I have watched you handle Hess for all these years. The faith you put in the two when you enlisted their help with our recent problem shows me how wise you are.

Remember, pursue your own path. Do not follow the path I forged. You are better equipped to deal with people and manage them without breaking them like I have always done.

Lastly, forgive me for the way this took place. I know you will be angry, but it had to be done. There was no other way.

Guild Master

Fiola Da'Verna

Glancing at the paper once more, Fiona brushed her wand over it before adding one drop of Herb's blood she kept for just this thing. The text faded from the paper, leaving it looking as if nothing was there.

She sealed it in the safe box and glanced around her office one last time. She felt a single tear fall from her eye and prayed she would be remembered as one who knew the cost and willingly gave it to her guild and kingdom.

Hess slowly opened the door to Sulenda's room and saw her sitting in the chair reading a book and waiting for him.

"You are going to tell me what you are doing, Hess Brumlin, or do I need to beat it out of you?" she asked as she set the book on the table next to her.

"I'm saving the kingdom one last time," he replied with a soft smile. "I promise you on my life I will return, though. Not for Kaen, not for this kingdom, but for you."

As he strode toward her, she sprung out of her chair, not caring about her gown or how it flung around her, and ran across the room, almost tackling him as she wrapped her arms around him.

She started to sob gently on his shoulder, and he brushed her hair with his hand. "What is wrong? This isn't my first time leaving you for a quest."

She nodded and, after a moment, was finally able to speak. "I know," she whispered. "It is the first time, though, you leave for one knowing you will be a father."

Hess's heart stopped as what Sulenda said registered in his brain. He pulled away from her, holding her arms and looking into her eyes, and saw that she was telling the truth.

"A child? Of my own?" he gasped, excitement bursting from his eyes and face.

She nodded and smiled. "I didn't want to tell you, as I knew you had a lot on your mind, but something told me I needed to. You have to return to make sure you keep that promise and fight with everything."

Hess pulled her close, kissing her on the lips and not letting her go as her hands embraced him once more.

"On both your lives, I will return," Hess promised.

"You better, or I'll hunt you down and make you suffer," she joked.

83

The Road to Death

"Get your sorry arses moving," Gertrude shouted as they set out on the second day of their trip. "We must ensure we keep to the schedule Fiola gave us. I believe her words were something about shaving my beard off and using it as a whip on me."

"Bah, she wouldn't do that," Brazuc shouted from the back of the group. "She wouldn't want to scare every child who sees your ugly face!"

Without turning around, Gertrude held up her middle finger, and the group laughed as they urged their horses on.

Kaen knew they had a solid day of riding ahead of them before they would be close to where they were supposed to be.

You have been quiet lately. Are you sure everything is alright?

I will be fine, Pammon lied. **For now, focus, as I have scouted the group where you are headed, and it has grown. They have cleared more trees and set up a camp outside of the mountain now.**

Glancing at the caravan of adventurers behind him and Gertrude, Kaen wondered if it would be enough. Three sets of well-trained silver groups seemed like a lot until one considered the forces they were about to engage.

Any sight of a higher orc yet?

Not yet, but there are now two of the bigger ones. There are also more hunting squads in the forests, going deeper as they look for game. In a few days, they will most likely reach the place where you are planning on camping.

Grunting, Kaen got Gertrude's attention and moved his horse up next to hers. "How much information do you have on the number of orcs, goblins, and hobgoblins we are facing?" Kaen asked quietly.

Furling her eyebrows, Gertrude gave him an awful look. "Apparently not as much as you," she replied, seeing how anxious he was, something she knew Kaen was usually not. "What is it you know that I don't."

Glancing around, Kaen made sure no one was listening and told her what he knew and how many he expected.

"You cannot be serious," she exclaimed, trying to keep her voice down. "That many?"

Nodding, Kaen motioned to his saddle bags and the slew of arrows bound to his horse. "I am not sure how much the mages will be able to do, and I know they will have casters. If we take it to them, we will face a fortified group. If we don't, they will be able to attack us from a distance."

Gertrude rifled through a pack on the side of her horse pulling out a document, almost falling but quickly regaining her balance. "Stupid horse," she muttered as the horse jerked from her movement. "Take a look at this."

Kaen took the rolled-up document and read the report Gertrude had been given. Three or four days ago, the information in the document would have been right. Now, it was utterly wrong.

"It seems you either knew something ahead of time or like to prepare," Gertrude informed him as she watched him read the report. "I wondered why you were so adamant about bringing that many arrows, but now it makes sense."

"What is this?" Kaen asked, pointing at a spot on the map with an *X* further southwest along the mountain range.

"The *X* is another group facing what I assume is similar to ours." She shrugged. "We were supposed to go and assist them once we took care of our group, but now I wonder if we can even do that."

"Hairy dwarf balls!" Kaen suddenly cursed loudly, only realizing he had shouted when he saw how Gertrude was looking at him.

"What am I missing?" she asked, her voice sounding weaker than usual.

"That goat humping Hess!" he complained as he handed the paper to Gertrude. "He knew! He knew how many there were going to be, and I think there are several spots like this!"

Pammon! Did Hess make you scout out the rest of this bowl and check for other spots like ours?! Don't lie to me. Tell me the truth!

Relief and frustration came through their bond, and Kaen knew he was right.

Yes, and he made me promise not to tell you. If you figure it out, I can tell you what I know.

Why?! Why would you two do that? demanded Kaen, ignoring the look he was getting from Gertrude as he took his frustration out on Pammon.

Because you are the most important thing to both of us. If things go badly, I told him I would carry you off in my talons and fly you to safety. Do not think for a moment we did this because we wanted to keep you in the dark. He said if you knew, you would not have gone with the group you must go with. They will die without you.

"Are you ok, Kaen?" Gertrude asked, seeing his face turning red from his frustration.

Snorting as he nodded, Kaen grabbed his horse's reins a little tighter. "I need a minute to think. Sorry if I took any of this out on you."

He rode up ahead a few links, moving a bit away, and turned his attention back to Pammon.

What have the two of you done? What is going to happen?

I don't know all the details, but I believe he expects you to find me and fly with me at some point. I am carrying six hundred arrows he tied to me when we met in the woods. I believe he knows you must show us to everyone if we are going to win this fight.

Closing his eyes, Kaen fought the torrent of emotions that wanted to overcome him. Frustration, anger, joy, excitement, and more, demanded a turn to be felt and expressed. He had no time for all of this. They were riding into a death trap and had no other option but to hit it hard and fast.

I have a plan to help them all, but we need to finish ours quickly. Will you help me, even if it means we can no longer hide who we are?

A joy that Kaen had never felt before almost took him out of his saddle. Honor, pride, and contentment all flowed from Pammon before he said a word.

I have waited my whole life to announce that we are one. I will hide no longer, if you will allow it.

Kaen felt precisely the same way. He was done hiding, and he had a job to do.

"Listen, you fools," Hess shouted as they stopped for a quick break to water the horses at the stream they had finally reached. "It is a long and hard journey till we get where we must. The trees are thick, and we do not have time to waste! Tomorrow, we must be in position, and if we don't have horses to ride when this is done, it is better to lose them along the way and make it."

The men and women, dwarves and elves, nodded as Hess continued to give orders.

Fourteen . . . fourteen adventurers to fight a horde.

Hess reached down and felt the pouch at his hip. There were no extra potions to be saved for another day. He had one job, and he would make sure it went well. He couldn't risk not returning home and forcing *his* child to grow up as Kaen had.

"Selmah, tell me again, why don't we have mana potions?" Ava asked as they rode side by side. "The health potions are not easy to make, but I saw a record of a time when our family had made mana potions."

"Lots of reasons," Selmah replied, smiling at Ava. She remembered being young and having lots of questions about *why* things were the way they were.

"Your family does not have the recipe anymore, according to your father, and we no longer possess some of the ingredients. Rumor has it that dragons were required to sacrifice part of themselves to make those potions."

"Sacrifice?" gasped Ava. "Like they killed themselves?"

Shaking her head as she laughed, Selmah looked at the group of adventures ahead of them.

"No, but how many do you think want to line up to be cut and bled?"

"I would assume not many."

"Correct," she replied, bobbing her head. "Just like you and I, no one wants to bleed, and gold can only convince someone to endure so much before they choose to say no. Would you bleed for Kaen?"

Ava felt her cheeks turn red at that question, and she wondered what Selmah meant by it.

"Not like that, silly girl," Selmah stated, rolling her eyes. "Would you bleed so that he could have a potion that might help him a little?"

"I guess it would depend on how much was required, but yes, I believe I would."

"I figured, but what about the man up front, the one they call Fretzenk? Would you bleed for a random dwarf, knowing it wouldn't save his life?"

Tsking, Ava considered it. "I would probably not, unless convinced it was worth it."

"Exactly," answered Selmah. "How do you convince a dragon to bleed for someone they don't care about, especially if it doesn't even mean the person will necessarily live? The days when we were allies and they cared about us are no more. I have heard that somewhere in our world is a place still filled with dragons. The rumor claims that most never leave their land; they are tired of how men have treated them."

"I heard that story once," admitted Ava. "I guess we will never know."

A moment later, Ava pulled out a letter from between her robe and tunic. She had written it for Kaen but could not get it to him this morning. She hoped he would never get to read it.

"How bad is this?" Ava asked as she slipped the letter back where she had taken it. "I mean, what are our chances?"

Selmah winked and shook her head as she smiled. "I would not worry, my dear. I will make sure you return to that young man I know you are fond of. I have no doubt the intel we received is wrong, but we will do what we must to rid this Kingdom of this filth."

"Guild Master Fiola," the man shouted as he rode up behind her. "You do not need to lead the group! We have plenty of men and women who would be honored to be in front, reducing the risk of something happening to you!"

"Cory, how old am I?" Fiola asked without turning around.

The man gasped and opened his mouth but quickly closed it. "I'm sorry, Guild Master Fiola, but why does that matter?" he replied, wondering what was worse, guessing her age correctly or being way off.

"It matters because I'm old enough to know there is no risk today with me riding up front. I have things on my mind, and sitting in the middle of you all distracts me," she snapped.

Realizing what she had done, Fiola took a breath and let it out. She slowed her horse a little and smiled at the man whose face went white as he wondered what she would do to him.

"I'm sorry that was not fair of me. I should not have acted that way. I understand that you and the others are simply trying to protect me. I will ride in the middle, and you can take turns letting whoever wants to be up front do so."

Fiola narrowed her eyes a little as the man smiled, and her voice returned to her typical icy tone. "Just make sure they set the pace I have. We cannot be late!"

"Yes, ma'am!" the man shouted, and he turned around and waved his hands, summoning two warriors to move to the front.

Nodding to them as they passed her, Fiola wondered at the odd pair. An elven warrior riding next to a dwarven one. Part of her wished she had the twin sisters as her warriors. She let the thought go, knowing wishes were a foolish thing.

Instead, she prayed that the spirits would hear her prayers and that the fewest number of adventurers possible would die. Praying that none would, she knew, was a waste.

84

Hiding No More

"Go!" exclaimed Kaen as he motioned to the others to go ahead into the woods.

He had just taken out four packs of hobgoblins with a bit of help from the other archer in the group and a lot of guidance from Pammon.

There are just a few guards who are either half asleep or not really paying attention. The rest of the camp appears to be back inside, gathering for something. You have maybe an hour tops before more hunters are sent out.

How many did you count the last time you were overhead?

There are still close to seventy or so outside the cave. It has gotten wider as they have done work on it since the last time it appeared.

Cursing to himself, Kaen considered the problem with that. His squad had two barrels that would be used to collapse the entrance, but that might not work if the orcs had built supports inside the cave. Who knows how long it would take for the orcs to clear the cave-in? It also left the problem of where all the goblin and orcs were coming from.

I wish we had time to scout the other side of the mountain, but we will have to do that later. For now, just keep me informed.

"Your eyesight is far better than I can imagine," Gertrude stated as the rest of their squad moved up to him. "How you saw those two is . . . well it just proves how lucky we are to have you."

"Quit yer flirty," Rory whispered, "you know he has a woman."

The others chuckled, and Gertrude almost gave her beard a tug, but she had already tucked it inside her plate armor.

"Listen, we don't have time for this," Kaen interrupted before they got started again. "There are probably about fifty or seventy outside the cave. We need to take them out and get those two barrels in place and blow them. Once we start, goblin shite is going to hit the fan."

"We got your front," Brazuc informed him as he hefted his shield and regripped his hammer. "Stay behind us and do what you need to. We know your calls and will follow them."

Gertrude nodded, and Aila moved up next to Kaen.

"Listen, Kaen, I only have so many spells I can cast. I prefer fire, as that is my affinity. I'll focus on the big groups. You take down the big targets. Just watch for healers if you can," Aila said.

Grimacing, Kaen nodded, already familiar with what they could do. "Ok, the sun's coming up, and they are tired. They put in a long night, meaning the next group will be up soon. Let's do this."

Two on the right, both casters!

Kaen's lifestone had never stopped burning as he unleashed holy hell upon the creatures. The second Pammon spotted them, Kaen's eyes drifted, arrows already loaded and launched before he ever truly saw his target. Kaen was death to all who stood in his way, and within the first five minutes, he had unleashed over seventy arrows, taking out fifty-plus of the horde.

The other group is struggling with that orc! There is a healer nearby!

As Kaen let Pammon focus his vision, he noticed a fire erupt from a group charging at them. An explosion rocked the ground, blowing chunks of goblin and hobgoblin pieces as Aila struck down a pack of five.

Off in the distance, way out of his normal range, Kaen saw the hobgoblin healer, a shaman they were called, healing the orc who was badgering the second group, limiting their two warriors' abilities to keep their archer and caster safe.

I have no choice. I have to show it.

Do it before another one dies!

Power flooded Kaen's arrow. He felt his mana infusing the first arrow of this fight. It streaked across the ground, and when it impacted, the shaman turned the area into a circle of flame, as it had that day before. Nothing was left of the shaman other than a fine, burnt red mist.

"What the hell was that!" shouted Bruzac as he lifted his shield, deflecting a few arrows.

"You can cast bloody magic!?"

"Focus!" Kaen shouted back. "We don't have time for this! Aila, get those archers! There are three!"

As they turned their attention to the never-ending slaughter of goblins and orcs, a roar echoed across the grounds from inside the cave, just as a fireball leaped from Aila's hand.

"Frack!" cursed Gertrude, bashing the skull of a goblin twitching on the ground as they continued moving closer to the cave entrance. "That's a blood-cave troll! We can't handle that with our current group!"

I can't see it, but I heard it!

It's a cave troll! It's bad . . . really bad. Worse than that orc we fought.

Kaen saw that the third group was basically out. They had pulled back after their mage had been taken out by an arrow, and the other one had been hurt by a caster. One of their warriors had tried to make it to the second group and was cut down by the orc who, with no healer around, had just fallen.

Pammon, it's time!

Pure passion and fury flowed over Kaen as he took out two more hobgoblins, dashing toward them.

I will be there in just a moment.

"LISTEN!" Kaen yelled as he fired an arrow, taking out the last goblin in range. "ALL EYES ON ME!"

Everyone snapped their attention to him, even Gertrude and Brazuc, who kept their shield facing the tunnel.

"I need you to not freak out, but I have help coming in a moment. We can take out the troll, but I need you to stay calm and trust me, and do not attack anything but the orcs and goblins!"

"What in a goblin's arse are you talking about?!" shouted Gertrude as an arrow plinked off her shield. "There ain't be no one out here to help!"

Kaen stared at her, and she saw the look in his eyes. "Look to the sky, coming down the mountainside from the southwest. You will see our help soon!"

As he spoke, Kaen released a twin shot, taking out two more hobgoblins, coming in a pack of six who had rushed out of the tunnel with a group of at least twenty more behind them.

"Aila, cover that tunnel entrance with a wall of fire!" Kaen yelled.

Ignoring the caster as she began chanting, Kaen unleashed his multishot, dropping the four others who were hot on the heels of their fallen allies.

"Hurry, Aila!" Kaen shouted as a few more hobgoblins rushed from the opening. Five escaped before a wall of fire filled the mouth of the cave, causing horrible screams and sounds to echo from inside through the mountainside.

"Five seconds," Aila said with a grunt. "Four."

Nodding, Kaen fired arrow after arrow, dropping an empty quiver as he reached for one of the extras he had on his hip. "Arrows!" he belted out, causing Rory to dash close and refill the one he had just dropped with his reserves.

"One . . . " gasped Aila as the wall suddenly cut off, and the magical flames went out.

The mouth of the cave was forty yards away, and coming out of it was a creature as tall as the orc Kaen had faced. He was wearing almost no armor, but his skin was thick and a puke green color. It carried a massive tree trunk that was at least eight feet long and a good two feet thick.

"Kaen!" Brazuc yelled, "Where is this help?!"

Kaen could see Pammon falling quickly from the sky; he was streaking along the mountainside, but he was still a good twenty seconds out, and Kaen doubted they had that much time.

"Twenty seconds!" Kaen shouted as he began to move back some. "Fall back, stay in formation!"

As the squad scurried backward, the troll saw them and slammed his club into the ground. He roared in their direction, and smashed a few goblins who had attempted to skirt by him.

"We need to run!" Rory shouted as he saw that there were no goblins or orcs behind them. "We can make it!"

"HOLD!" Gertrude shouted at him. "Trust Kaen! We can't make it if we run!"

Kaen glanced at Aila and saw she was done. She could barely stand, and seeing her like that reminded him of how Luca looked before the orc killed him.

"No more!" Kaen muttered as his lifestone turned into a white-hot flame in his chest. He felt like he was glowing as the power raged through him. The arrow he had drawn burned white—not the red color it had been before—flew from his bow, and streaked across the distance, penetrating the troll's chest and exploding, sending chunks and fire all around it.

The troll roared in pain, patting its chest and body as flames erupted over it.

"Hairy dwarf balls," Rory uttered in shock, witnessing the power of what had just taken place.

Kaen stood there momentarily, smiling at what he had done, only to lose that smile as the troll moved out of the circle of fire, and its blackened and red body began to regenerate slowly.

"That's what makes them so bad!" yelled Gertrude as she held up her shield, preparing for a charge she knew was coming.

The troll swung its flaming club, smashing dead corpses and sending them flying toward the two dwarves. Brazuc was bowled over from the force of two goblins that struck his shield. Its eyes, black with blood seeping out of them, glared at Kaen as it roared again.

I'm here!

As the troll began to move forward, a bronze shape swooped down from the sky, a red and blue flame pouring from its mouth and engulfing the troll in it before it quickly flew back up into the sky, leaving all to stare in shock.

"A . . . a . . . Dragon!" Aila shouted first.

"We need to run!" Rory yelled.

"Can it, Rory!" Kaen ordered. "It's my dragon. Now stay and fight!"

All of them turned and looked at Kaen as he made the claim, none believing he could mean what he had said, and yet they saw Kaen not pausing, firing arrow after arrow at the troll.

Within ten seconds, the dragon reappeared and, this time, hovered over the burning troll, who was now on his knees, suffering the pain of a fire that would not go out. Roaring, Pammon announced himself and again breathed fire on the troll, causing it to roast alive. After a three-second burst of flame, Pammon flew to where the troll was and reached down with his back claws, grabbing its burning corpse and tearing it in half before depositing it in the fire again.

"Good work, Pammon!" Kaen shouted as he took down a few more goblins who were standing in shock at what they had just witnessed.

"Rally to the dragon!" Kaen shouted as he rushed toward Pammon, who moved off to the side and landed on the ground.

I think they are afraid of me. At least they did not attack me.

You were amazing! Keep the goblins from advancing, but don't breathe fire in the tunnel.

Kaen turned and saw the two men who were holding the barrels one hundred yards off, trembling in fear.

He waved at them and shouted for them to come, yet neither moved.

"Gertrude! Go get those barrels! Rory, heal Brazuc! Aila, go with Gertrude, I got this!"

Kaen's steady gaze and orders snapped them out of their fears, and they bobbed their heads and ran to obey his instructions.

Your harness is inside one of the containers on my right. Hess figured you would need it.

Laughing, Kaen nodded as he ran up next to Pammon, shooting arrows at any goblin foolish enough to poke its head out of the cave.

The second party had managed to clear their area during the confusion, and the four of them stood there in shock, watching Kaen engage a dragon who had come to their rescue. Around them were well over a hundred and fifty goblin and orc corpses.

BOOOM!

With the cave sealed from the barrels and Kaen's explosive shot, everyone stood back in shock and awe over Kaen and Pammon.

"I don't have time, as I need to go help the others, but, everyone, this is Pammon! He is my dragon!"

They glanced at Kaen, who was grinning like a fool.

"You have a dragon?" Brazuc asked, still confused from the hit that he had taken from the troll.

"Of course, you idiot," Gertrude announced, though she was obviously not completely sure herself.

"His name is Pammon, and he is safe. Another day, I will introduce you better, but I need to go!" shouted Kaen as he climbed onto Pammon's neck. "You guys recover, and then go to the next point! I'll fly there now and see if we can help!"

Kaen smiled when he saw the two loops Hess had made, perfect for his feet, with the rope he had tied the arrows on. Pammon helped him get the harness on, and as everyone watched, he was soon ready to go.

I think they would soil themselves if you roared, so don't do it.

Pammon thrummed and watched as they all backed away from him as the sound hit them.

I was considering that.

I know. I could feel you wanting to be mischievous. Now, thank you again, and let's go!

Pammon gave a slight roar after he had cleared the ground, thrumming as he saw the adventurers below back up in shock and awe.

You couldn't resist, could you?

No . . . no, I could not.

85

Adventurers Falling

"Fall back!" Hess shouted. "Fall back! To the trees!"

How did they know we were going to attack?

Hess was still struggling with how quickly the horde of creatures had responded as soon as they had been attacked. The moment they had charged, it was like every creature in the cave had surged at them.

As his group rushed toward the trees, Hess couldn't help but glance at the four dead bodies of the third group, knowing he couldn't help the last warrior who was now being slaughtered by half a dozen hobgoblins.

The second group was barely holding their own, and their healer was struggling to keep them up and fighting. Hundreds of arrow shards littered the ground around where they were retreating, broken from hitting Hess's shield.

What I wouldn't give for a real archer.

It wasn't their fault, and Hess knew it. The two archers in his group were not horrible, but they did not have a thirty, and their skills choices were not helping here. Headshot had been great for taking out the orcs, but the long-timer and the lack of multi-target shots turned this fight into a range battle they couldn't win. His single mage was out of mana already, which meant he was nothing more than a weak fighter with a staff.

I swear if I live, I'm going to kill Fiola.

As that thought ran through his mind, the fear of what he had just admitted rocked him. He had to survive! He had a child of his own coming, and he could not, *would not* allow it to grow up without him!

"To the trees!"

His group was running, and he smashed any creature foolish enough to get within range of his hammer. The shield was thankfully able to withstand the onslaught of arrows and the magical spells that had hit it. The few cuts and spots he was bleeding from were fine for now. If they could get to the trees, his healer could soon help him with those.

"Hess! Behind you!"

Glancing behind him as he ran, Hess saw what the archer had pointed out. Coming from the cave entrance was a tier-three orc with a pair of shamans behind him.

"RUN, you idiot!" Hess shouted again. "We have to get to the trees!"

Arrows rained down upon them, dozens bouncing off his shield. One got past it, hitting his chainmail and sending a stinger through his forearm, weakening his grip on his hammer for a moment.

Fifty yards more.

The last fifty yards were the worst. Every few yards required them to stop and raise their shields to prevent the arrow storm that fell upon them from striking them dead. Slowly, they made it to the tree line, fighting the creatures approaching them. The large orc shouted and bellowed orders, mocking them as it strode through its allies.

Perhaps he should have attacked earlier, but Fiola had called for them to wait till three hours after sunrise. It made sense, and yet they were being driven back.

"Can we make it if we flee?" called out his healer as they made it to the trees.

"No! They will run us down!" Hess shouted as he quickly pivoted, surprising a group of three goblins that was almost upon him as he swept his hammer in an arc. He dropped all three in one blow. "We fight in the trees! Form up! Protect the archer and call out targets!"

They began to slowly move as a group, using the trees to try and provide safety from arrows, knowing they would eventually be surrounded. The only advantage they had was the thickness of the tree growth that kept them from being attacked at once by fifty or more enemies. There was one spot they needed to get to, if they had any hope at all, but it was still a bit away.

"To your left!" Selmah shouted as she watched Ava burn down a group of hobgoblins with bows. "Good work!"

Wiping the sweat from her face, Ava nodded, impressed with Selmah's tactics. The ring of six warriors around the three mages and the archers behind them taking out the individual attackers was admirable. Selmah cast only when she deemed it worthwhile, but it was a sight to behold when she did.

Her single lightning attack had killed over twenty-five creatures in one go, arching through all of them and burning them instantly.

"The cave is close! Bring up the barrels!"

The archer behind Selmah responded to the order by whistling four times in a row. She glanced back and saw the two men tasked with bringing the kegs to the cave, dashing from the trees and toward their position.

As Ava turned her attention back to the cave opening, a fireball erupted from inside it, slamming into their front warriors, engulfing them in flames, and knocking them over ten feet from their position.

As the men slammed into the ground near them, Ava saw the shield she had cast flash and disappear.

"ORC MAGUS!" Selmah bellowed as she ran over to Ava and flung her backward.

Another fireball appeared from the cave opening, hitting a barrier that Selmah had erected just in time, sending flames running over the invisible.

Climbing to her feet, Ava saw more goblins and orcs rushing their position as the remaining two warriors tried to close the gap the Magus had created. Both were slightly injured but still alive, while the other four were not moving.

"Heal them!" Selmah ordered as she released a fireball into the cave's opening and watched it bounce off a shield similar to hers.

The healer rushed forward, chanting and glowing as a small light glowed around him.

"We need to move!" the warrior called out as he pointed at the edge of the mountainside with his weapon. "Take away that thing's line of sight and make it come out! Otherwise, we are dwarves in a barrel!"

"Sound the retreat to the barrel, men!" Selmah ordered. "Everyone shift right!"

The archer turned to whistle and, as he did, saw that the two men who were coming toward them were being chased by two hobgoblins who had appeared out of the woods. The men were losing ground, as the barrels they carried weighed them down.

"Selmah! The barrels!"

Selmah turned and saw the two hobgoblins who would be upon the two men quickly, and a curse slipped from her lips. "Shoot them, you idiot!"

All three archers turned and began loosing arrows at the hobgoblins. As the arrows reached the area they were aiming at, one of the hobgoblins managed to strike one of the men from behind, causing him to drop his barrel and fall to the ground, rolling on the rocky soil.

The other hobgoblin took two arrows, one in his shoulder and the other in his gut, falling to the ground injured but not yet out.

Ava focused her mind, summoned the arrow she had practiced with for so long, and prepared to let it go.

"NO!" Selmah shouted as the arrow flew at the hobgoblin about to butcher their allies. A shield shimmered a few yards in front of the hobgoblin, deflecting Selmah's spell and shooting into the air, allowing the goblin to skewer the man.

An explosion rocked an area behind Ava, and she felt herself pushed forward toward the trees. Ears ringing and covered in dirt, she groaned as she tried to stand up and saw both warriors gone and Selmah still in a massive crater devoid of dirt except for where she was. Their other mage was gone, evaporated, and one of their healers and archers was dead as well.

Another fireball moved toward their location, even bigger than the first, caught by a shield again, leaking fire all over its edges.

"You fool!" Selmah yelled as she started a wall of flame inside the cave, allowing her to see the Magus waving its hands and holding a talisman as it grinned at them. "You would have exploded those barrels! Now, all of you move right! Archers, take out that last hobgoblin!"

Ava wanted to apologize, yet she knew this was not the time to talk. Her mistake had cost them the lives of four adventurers because she had made Selmah drop her shield.

She saw the two archers firing arrows at the last hobgoblin, injuring it before finally finishing it off as they moved to follow Selmah and her shield.

Groaning, Ava stood up and dashed to get in position, casting a fireball at the cave entrance, watching it bounce harmlessly off the shield the orc magus had created.

"I'm sorry," Ava said, panting and leaning on the staff she had somehow managed to keep with her. "I forgot about the—"

"Focus," Selmah interrupted and snapped her fingers. "You two, keep the opening clear. Matthew, keep us healed. Ava, save your spells for when a large group comes."

Ava closed her mouth and nodded, moving back behind Selmah's position. Now, it was a waiting game.

The group had about seventy-five arrows left between the archers, and she was currently down to maybe four or five spells. She knew Selmah had more power and mana, but how much she was not certain. They could see the cave but could not see inside, which meant the Magus could not see them either.

The few orcs and goblins who had exited had died quickly due to the arrows, but she knew they would prepare defenses against that soon enough.

"Meditate, regain your mana, and be ready to act when I tell you to."

Ava saw the expression on Selmah's face. Things were bad, and it was obvious.

The Magus had not been expected, and as powerful as Selmah was, having to protect all of them limited what she could do. One-on-one, she could win, but protecting these fools would be her downfall. She wished she could meditate and try to regain as much mana as possible, but with no warriors, she had to be ready for anything.

"What are we going to do?" Ava asked, realizing how bleak things were going to turn. "Once nightfall comes, we will be at a major disadvantage."

Selmah weighed all their options. The odds of the Magus making a mistake were small. She could try and bring down a portion of the cave opening, but there was no guarantee it would work, and it would take a large amount of her mana to do it. The Magus could easily get his minions to clear it, and then they would be hot on their heels.

"Meditate for now," she repeated. "Let me consider our options. I need you to get as much mana back as possible right now."

Ava nodded, her eyes closed as she sat on the ground. Her thoughts were conflicted as she took deep breaths, trying to settle herself and clear her mind. All she could think about was her mistake and the lives she had cost.

I'll never get out of here . . . I'm going to die . . . Kaen . . .

Her heart hurt at the thought of knowing she would not see him again. No man had made her feel the way he had. She knew he cared about her, and it was not because of her title or power. He liked her for who she was. That was the first time she had ever met a man who saw her as she was and not as the daughter of Lord Hurem, heir to the family business.

He would like me even if I was just some poor adventurer with no family.

"Focus!" snapped Selmah. "Stop letting your mind wander and focus!"

Ava took a deep breath and held it as she cursed in her mind. Selmah could tell she was not meditating . . . just how powerful was she?

She wondered if Selmah was strong enough to save them from what awaited them in the cave.

86

Fiola's Stand

Dropping the wand which held no more charges, Fiola fished for the one she had strapped to her hip.

"HOLD THE LINE!" Corey shouted as a group of fifteen or more creatures rushed at them.

The four warriors held shields out, the middle two with spears pointed at the incoming group with Corey and the other warrior on the end waving their swords.

"Now!" shouted Fiola as her casters let lightning bolts stream from their fingers which arched through the attacking group causing them to thrash from the pain. "Arrows!"

The two archers behind her loosed arrow after arrow at the pack, killing and injuring even more of them as they stood defenseless. Only a few survived that combo, and the two warriors with spears stepped forward, finishing off the weakened attackers before falling back into position.

Fiola smiled as she held her wand ready. It had been a gift from her father long ago, and she had saved it, knowing the day would come that she could actually use it. Three charges. It had cost more money than most people could imagine. It was a treasure to their people, yet her father had given it to her because he said he knew she would be great.

Glancing across the mountainside, Fiola saw the other group with its six members holding back the advance of the monsters who tried to flank them. She had been unfair in the way she had made groups, but she knew she needed them. The two gold warriors would match almost anyone other than Hess in terms of durability. Their archers were both almost gold rank and had multi-shot skills. Their mage was smart, using mana only when required, a thought that momentarily reminded Fiola of Luca. The healer was the weakest link. Barely a silver, but that group would provide him protection and would not need as much healing as her group did.

This section of the mountain was the worst spot. It had been the first one reported and appeared to have been there the longest. There had initially been two hundred creatures outside the camp when she attacked. Her first two wands had frozen most of them, allowing her to unleash the one shot the other had provided. It had decimated almost three-fourths of them, allowing her group to get close and begin the real assault. Over one hundred gold in wands had been used. Kings would have married off children for them, and she had discarded their empty shells as if they were nothing more than twigs.

Even if I don't survive this, the cost will be worth it. She thought as she watched the creatures continue to pour out of the mouth of the cave that had been widened to a good forty feet or more. She could see the support beams they had braced it with.

"Barrier!" she called out.

A shimmering shield appeared over them as fifty-plus arrows rained down upon them from a pack of archers that had moved up the mountainside and out of their spell range. Corey was being a fantastic leader. His reputation as a skilled tactician was proving to be absolutely correct.

"Thirteen more!" shouted the mage behind her on her right informing him of how many more spells she had left.

"Fifteen!" called out the other mage.

"How close do we need to be for you to reach them?" asked Corey as he pointed at the archers spread out on the mountain.

"Fifty yards or less!"

Grumbling, Fiola twisted the bone wand in her hand. She knew it was foolish to waste all their mana on shields, and the hobgoblins also knew it. They were content raining arrows down till Fiola and her group ran out of mana.

"Get me within one hundred yards!" ordered Fiola as she calculated the distance.

Without hesitating, the warriors moved a little farther apart.

"On my go, everyone runs behind us!" Corey cried out.

Each of them prepared and waited as arrows flew over their heads at the orc or goblin approaching them.

"Go!" Corey shouted as he saw the archers losing their volley.

The warriors sprinted, knowing they could save a spell and get the distance Fiola needed if they moved fast. They dashed forward, cutting down and spearing those surprised to see them pressing the attack. The archers fired shots as they ran, not killing but injuring those in the group's path. One of the mages stopped, casting another lightning bolt before moving forward, barely getting out of the range of arrows that landed behind them, impaling the dirt and ground like a bunch of new shoots springing up.

"Twenty more yards! Keep moving!" Fiola drew a small amount of mana into the wand. It didn't take nearly as much as casting the real spell, and she would have more than enough mana once the wand was gone, to hold off anything that came for a while.

As they covered the needed distance, the warriors dispatched those injured from the lightning spell and formed up, holding their shields high once they hit the spot Corey knew they needed to reach. "Now!" he called out as another volley of arrows approached them.

Power flowed through her arm and into the bone wand. It vibrated and began to glow before unleashing a green bolt that flew toward the middle of the hobgoblin and archer line. As it hit the ground at the center of where they stood, massive vines and thorns erupted from the ground, grasping at anything close to them, impaling them, and tearing the hobgoblins apart.

The line began to break, but the vines kept growing and following them.

"Barrier!" Corey call out again.

The volley of arrows bounced off the barrier, as the group stood in the middle of corpses and burnt flesh. Everyone watched in horror and appreciation that Fiola's spell was not focused on them.

"What in an elf's tit is that?" asked one of the warriors who was holding a spear, forgetting exactly who was standing behind him.

"An elven weapon of old," replied Fiola as she scanned the area. "It is much worse against an army in the forest."

The man's head bobbed as he focused on an orc approaching them. The orc already had two arrows in him but seemed unfazed as it rushed the two warriors with spears. Both impaled it as it came, finding their spears stuck in its body.

"Disengage it!"

As one of the warriors backed up, pulling his spear out, an explosion rocked them, sending them both flying just as Fiola realized the orc had been wearing an explosive device of some sort on its back.

"Heal!" Corey shouted as he pinched the line closed, glancing at the two warriors, bleeding and lying on the ground, barely moving.

"Incoming!" Fiola shouted, pointing at a group of seven orcs running at them, all wearing the same *X-shaped* leather straps across their chests and coming from different directions.

When had those appeared?

Fiola knew she couldn't waste any more time. Three arrows formed next to her and zipped across the battleground, taking three of them in the chest and setting off a chain reaction of explosions, sending body parts and armor flying in all directions.

A fireball roared past her head, taking out another two as their bodies detonated.

Both archers fired and hit the same orc. It somehow shrugged an arrow in one of its eyes and the other in its chest as it shambled toward them.

"Protect Fiola!" shouted Corey as he ran forward, his shield raised and his sword out.

"Wait!" she began to shout, but it was too late. He had already closed the gap, and when he took the head off the orc, it erupted in a ball of flame and gore, catching the last orc near him and setting off his charge as well.

Corey was blown back toward the party. The other warrior raced to stand near him. Fiola ran forward and found that Corey's sword arm was gone from the shoulder, and his shield was broken in half, impaled into his body.

"You fool!" she hissed as she began to cast her healing spell on him.

He grunted and tried to shake his head as blood gurgled from his mouth. "Save it . . . my . . ."

When stopped talking, Fiola glanced at his chest and realized there was a piece of shield where his heart was.

Screaming, she stood up and looked at the mouth of the tunnel and saw two orcs coming out of it with another fifty or more minions ahead of them. They were only seventy yards away, as had also been the case with the one Luca had taken out.

Anger and frustration gripped Fiola's heart, and she held out her wand, channeling the power it required, and released the green bolt at the massive pack of goblins and orcs, smiling as she watched the watched the vines of the plant she had summoned once again tear through all the creatures as the vines raced toward the cave entrance.

"To the other group!" she ordered, pointing to where the group standing almost two hundred yards away. "We need to go now while we can!"

"What are our options?" asked Hozzut, the golden warrior she was standing behind. "Your spell took out a lot of them and has clogged up their tunnel, but I can hear them hacking it apart."

Fiola nodded and spat on the ground as she cursed her luck. Neither of the orcs had died from the spell, both retreating and feeding it with the lives of their minions. She hoped they had gotten injured at least, but here on this mountainside, there was not enough life in the ground for the plant to draw from. If she could have fought them in the woods, bundled up in a single pack, she could have wiped them all out in one blow.

Each member of the group drank quickly from the water pouch they carried, and a few were taking a small snack as the mages meditated on the ground behind them.

"We have to hold," Fiola stated, "and we need to press our chance. I know the three kegs we brought will not close that opening unless we get it deep inside. Doing that will be a death sentence, as I doubt anyone could escape in time."

"I will volunteer if that is what is required," Hozzut immediately answered. "You know I will give everything for the kingdom!"

Bobbing her head, Fiola smiled and touched the dwarf warrior's shoulder. "I will not ask it right now. If the time comes and you are our only option, then I know you will do what must be done. Just as I will do what must be done."

He looked at her and cocked his head. "Permission to speak freely?"

She chuckled and nodded.

"You seem different. Less . . . "

"Uptight? A bitch?" she asked, smiling.

"Your words, Guild Master Fiola, but yes," Hozzut answered, unable to hold the grin that felt unnatural when surrounded by so much death.

"I feel different," Fiola replied as she motioned to the carnage around them. "I had forgotten the true cost of being an adventurer, and I have a new respect for those who gladly face it, as you have. The kingdom and I are grateful for adventurers like all of you."

She turned and saw them all looking at her. "Even if I fail to make it through, I will know I stood by the bravest our adventurer's guild has ever produced."

She reached for the waterskin Hozzut held out to her, took a swig, and smiled. "This water tastes funny," she stated as she handed the skin back to him.

"That's because it ain't water," he replied, taking a long drink. "If I'm going to meet my ancestors, I want to be celebrating beforehand."

They laughed for a moment, but their attention quickly returned to the mouth of the cave where explosions started ringing out over and over from inside.

Hozzut pointed at the pieces of the giant thorn bush and vines erupting from the cave's mouth. "Looks like they found volunteers to help clear their way."

Sighing, Fiola nodded. It had happened quicker than she had hoped.

The last four minutes had been impossible to withstand, as a hundred-plus more orcs and goblins surged from the cave, rushing at them. Behind them stood three orcs, all tier-three. One magus and two warriors forced their horde at them, even when struck down by spells and weapons from afar.

"I'm out!" shouted the last of the four mages.

"Go," coughed out Fiola as she pointed to the group that had already made it into the trees. "Both of you go!"

"Sorry, Guild Master, but I won't leave you," argued Hozzut as he deflected an arrow and pushed against her back as they ran. "Even if you threaten me, I won't leave you alone to fight this fight."

Fiola nodded, not wasting breath to argue. She was almost out of mana and had only one trick left up her sleeve. Five hundred or more were dead on the other side. They were out of arrows, and only she could still fight, though barely. She still had one charge left of her wand.

"To the trees, get inside. I know a spot . . . we will end it there."

Grunting, Hozzut nodded as he ran behind her, protecting her backside as the others took off toward the horses as she had commanded.

Please be alive, Kaen. I pray it is not as bad where you are!

87

Time Runs Out

There!

Kaen pointed at the orc running after the group closest to them.

Pammon had made it in record time, turning a four-hour trip by foot into a fifteen-minute one as he flew only slightly off the ground. Speed was more important now than worrying about altitude, and they needed to be close for him to attack.

I will lay down a path of fire. You focus on the orc! I cannot dispatch him without risking hitting your fellow adventurers.

I got this. You do what you can!

Pammon roared before he reached the edge of the group of goblins and orcs streaming from the cave's mouth. Kaen could see far more orcs and goblins here than had been at his previous location. The adventurers looked to be down to two groups and were not doing well as the tier-three orc swung at them with a massive hunk of metal, cutting down its own minions when they got in his way.

As Pammon roared and began to breathe fire across the battleground, all of the orcs and goblins turned to see the source of the sound. The froze as they saw death upon them, flames igniting their skin and reducing them to ashes in mere seconds.

While the trail of fire swept from outside the cave toward the massive orc who had turned to see them coming at him, Kaen let his lifestone and the fire burning inside it take over. He felt both arrows between his fingers and the power of his magic flowing to the heads. This was the first time he had ever seen his lifestone do that. As they drew near and the orc roared at them, preparing to swing its weapon when they got close, Kaen watched as the red-tipped arrows left his bowstring, losing sight of them connecting as Pammon angled off to the side to avoid the orc and his attack.

The attack would never have happened, though, because both arrows struck simultaneously, blowing off the shoulder of the orc's arm that held its weapon high and the leg on the same side of its body. The orc tumbled to the ground, blood gushing from its wounds. An adventurer wasted no time, rushing forward and slamming its sword into the orc's throat.

[Archery Skill Increased]

A grinning Kaen was amazed at that message. Two points today. It seemed impossible to believe he was still gaining points.

You got another point, didn't you? Pammon asked as he circled once more for a status check.

Yes . . . I cannot believe it, but I did. We need to hurry up here and go find Hess!

The battle quickly changed directions as Kaen fired arrow after arrow at the group of monsters below. They began to break and run as Pammon occasionally swooped down, running his back claws through them, splitting them like someone stomping on a melon.

When the battle looked like the other two groups had it solidly in hand, Kaen had Pammon hover a little ways from them, allowing the groups to see him on the back of the dragon.

"FINISH THIS!" Kaen shouted as he pointed at the cave entrance.

As Pammon turned and flew away, the adventurers let out a shout and raised their weapons to the sky.

I think they figured out who we are.

Pammon began to thrum as he gained speed and altitude.

I'm just glad they didn't shoot at you or me if I am being honest.

I would have been fine.

Groaning, Kaen thumped Pammon's neck and urged him to fly faster.

Hess leaned against the tree; his breath was ragged as he yanked the arrow out of his shoulder. "Healing!" cried their healer.

Bobbing his head, Hess laughed as he glanced at the pack of advancing creatures. He had chosen this spot because of the tree line they had found when scouting. The twenty massive trees had grown in a circle, most of them bark to bark, all coming from a dead tree in the middle of them. His group had come through a ten-foot opening, but the rest of the trees provided a small amount of protection from behind. He and the last warrior were doing their best with their shields, blocking the arrows that came at them as other goblins and hobgoblins funneled into the enclosure of trees.

Hess's arm burned, having swung the hammer more times than he could remember today. Bodies of crushed enemies blocked the opening, and the goblins and orcs had to keep pulling them out of the way before coming again.

The worst was what he now heard coming through the wounds.

"Little man . . . little man . . . I'm coming for you, little man."

"Ignore it!" Hess shouted as he smashed in the head of an orc who got too close, blowing through its shield and into its skull.

"It speaks our language!" cried out the archer behind him. "How?!"

"Worry later, shoot more now! How many arrows do you have left?"

A few more goblins died before he heard the man stutter a response. "Less than twenty!"

"Goblin piss," Hess cursed as he blocked two arrows and slammed his shield into another creature on the other side of it, sending it flying back into its allies. "Save them for when I say!"

"I smell you, little man . . . I'm coming for you."

The laughter that came after those words caused even Hess to feel a trembling in his spirit.

He glanced at the warrior next to him and saw that the man was frozen in fear. "Snap out of it!" Hess bellowed as he pushed the man, saving his life from the sword a goblin was swinging.

The man snapped out of his fear and tried to get back into position, but Hess could see the piss running down his leg. The man's resist charm skill was too low . . .

I'm sorry, Sulenda . . . forgive me.

Hess knew this circle of trees that had grown from death would be his tomb.

Pammon suddenly shuddered, and Kaen could feel the change in him.

What's wrong?

It's Hess. Something is wrong. I can feel it.

Panic spread through Kaen as he heard Pammon.

What do you mean?! Wrong how?

I don't know, but I just know . . . he is marked for me. It's different than you, but something changed. Something bad.

Can you go faster?! Is that possible?

Pammon began flapping his wings more, straining and urging himself to go faster.

I need more power. I need your strength. It's there, but I can't seem to do it alone.

Closing his eyes, Kaen focused on Pammon. He could feel the strain in Pammon's wings and muscles as he beat against the wind, driving himself as fast as he could. Kaen began pouring his strength into him and felt Pammon go slightly faster.

I need more! Share your fire with me!

Realizing what Pammon wanted, Kaen focused on his lifestone. It had gone quiet as they flew, resting, as there had been no need for it. Kaen now knew it was necessary, knew it was needed. *Family . . . I cannot lose my family.*

The fire in his lifestone erupted in flames as it had earlier, filling him with power, and he felt it flow from him into Pammon through their bond.

Hold on!

Without hesitation, Kaen squeezed his legs against Pammon's neck and clenched the reins with all his strength.

[Activate Flight Burst]

The world shifted, or so it felt. The ground streaked past him so fast that it was impossible for Kaen to keep his eyes open as the wind rushed against his face. He pulled himself closer to Pammon's neck, trying to streamline himself as they raced over the treetops.

What is this?!

A skill . . . flight burst*!* Pammon slowly said, strain coming across as he spoke. **Need . . . to . . . focus.**

Just fly!

Kaen continued to feed his lifestone through their bond, feeling the strain it was putting on Pammon as they blazed across the sky.

[Flight Burst Expired]

Pammon was panting as his flying speed returned to normal.

I need a break before I can do that again, but we are close. Five minutes, maybe less!

That was unbelievable! How often can you do that?

For a couple moments Pammon remained silent. Kaen could feel him thinking and feeling something.

I could do it again right now, but I do not think I can sustain or withstand it. I am not sure I should have been able to do that yet. It feels like it's for later when I am older and bigger. My joints are hurting, and my whole body aches. It may take a few days for me to recover fully.

My lifestone . . . it let you do something you should not have been able to, like it did for me once.

Yes . . . We need to be careful with that. I don't want to injure myself and fall from the sky, hurting you in the process.

What about you? Wouldn't you get hurt?

Pammon started to thrum and then stopped; the pain of laughing was too much.

Don't push yourself. How far?

Soon, up ahead is a small clearing. I'm unsure how I will get into the clearing, but I can see it.

Staring across the treetops, Kaen spotted what Pammon was looking at off in the distance, but he could not see it at all like Pammon could. How Pammon managed to see as far as he did still amazed him.

Hess screamed in silence. No words came from his mouth, but he knew it would happen that way. His shield was gone, and his arm was missing from his elbow down, ripped off by the orc who was laughing as he ate the warrior he had been standing by. Hess's potion had stopped the bleeding, but it could not replace what was not there to fix.

"Tasty meat, so sweet and warm. I cannot wait to break you," taunted the orc as he watched Hess rise, a stump where his forearm once was. "Don't fight yet. I want to enjoy this before I crush you and suck the marrow from your bones."

Hess knew there were no options. He had nothing left to give. Both weapons were gone, and the rest of the orc's army was outside the opening, letting their leader enjoy the spoils of it all.

Glancing around the small grove, he saw the others pinned against the trees, dead and hanging from arrows.

HESS WE ARE ALMOST THERE!

Clutching his head with his right hand, Hess groaned. Pammon? Was that possible?

He fished through his pouch and pulled out the tooth, struggling to do so with just one hand.

Rough, sharp, and vibrating, he felt power coming through it.

"It's too late, Pammon," he whispered. "Save Kaen . . . Protect my unborn child."

Pammon roared so loudly, the treetops swayed as he passed over them. It echoed through the woods, vibrating off every tree.

Pammon, what is it? Kaen asked as he felt pain and rage like never before flood over Pammon.

Hess is dying, and he just told me Sulenda is pregnant!

88

Two Become One

Before Kaen could register those words, his lifestone engulfed him and Pammon both. Energy neither had experienced before filled each of them to the point their skin and scales seemed to tingle as air rushed over them.

Neither spoke as Kaen slammed a handful of arrows into his quiver with one hand before grabbing his knife and cutting the rope around one of his feet. Swapping hands, he cut the other and flung his knife over his shoulder, grabbing two more arrows and putting them in his mouth.

Go, I have you!

Pammon suddenly angled his wings, causing him to slow down, sending Kaen leaping up and running along his neck and jumping off his head toward the trees.

A beat of his wings and a slight change in his direction had him right behind Kaen, both claws gently caressing his body as he dove through the air.

Without hesitation, Kaen loaded both arrows into the bow, unaware of what his body was doing. He just knew his lifestone was controlling him to do what needed to be done.

Twenty seconds!

Hess leaned against the tree as he watched the orc toss the warrior's trunk aside like a piece of trash. He had eaten all of the appendages and the head, not trying to deal with the flesh inside the armor.

"Why?!" he shouted as the orc turned and smiled at him. "Why come and invade us?"

Pausing, the orc picked his teeth with his finger, flicking a warrior's finger from his teeth, and gave Hess a sinister grin. "The dragon man paid well," he answered, slowly walking along the edge of the trees. "We get this land. He gets the rest."

"Stioks?!" exclaimed Hess. "He made a deal with you?"

The orc laughed as he scraped his nails across the tree trunks, leaving massive gouges that looked like a wild cat had used it as a scratching post.

"Me? No . . . the king, yes," he answered, spitting on the ground as he slowly approached. "We are done hiding and dying. We come for you all."

A look of hate filled the orc's eyes as he glared at Hess. The orc stopped and turned and saw the goblins and shamans looking at them through the opening. They were making noise and licking their lips, wondering if there would be leftovers.

"Perhaps I should share . . . " he stated as he motioned to the others. "They are hun—"

Every lesser creature cowered and shrieked when the sound of the dragon's roar echoed through the woods and reached them. They glanced at the sky, trying to see what might be above them.

The orc glared at Hess and then turned his eyes upward as he spun around, trying to see why that sound had rang out. None could deny that it was the roar of a dragon, but none expected one to be here.

The grove got quiet as they all looked at the orc, wondering what to do. A few seconds later, he turned and looked at Hess and gave a shrug as he smiled. "It matters not."

Twenty seconds!

Hess's eyes went wide from shock. It was Pammon, and he was close if Hess could hear him.

The orc began to move toward him again; Hess knew he had to act fast.

"Wait!" he shouted, causing the orc to pause mid-stride, just about ten yards away. "If it's Stioks, he will want to talk to me! I know things he will want to know! Things about the Dragon Riders!"

A grin broke out on the orc's face, and he turned his head upward and laughed, letting the sound of his voice echo in the circle of trees. "He does not care about you," the orc replied as he slowly lifted his massive metal sword and pointed it at Hess. "What could a man like you offer him?"

As the orc opened his mouth, a shape appeared above the trees, blocking out the light. Two white tips were blazing beneath a bronze shape hanging in the sky.

"Kaen?" Hess muttered watching two lights streak down from the sky and realizing Kaen was hanging from Pammon's claws.

Power surged through him, an amount that almost made his body ache. Pammon had caught him as he jumped, holding him just right so he could still draw his bow without any impairment.

Neither was talking, yet they moved as one, completely focused on the same thing as Pammon began the descent, aiming for the small opening.

Kaen knew that Pammon would come to a stop right above the opening. He knew the second he was over the opening, he would fire.

The thought of Hess being a father to his own child and not being able to raise them, made his lifestone feel like a volcano, eating away at everything but his one purpose. *To save families.*

The moment came, and Pammon twisted his body, altered his wings, and froze midair above the opening of the trees.

Looking down, Kaen saw a massive orc, one that appeared even larger than the one he and Pammon had killed with Luca's help, just a few yards from Hess, holding his sword out at him. Time slowed as he saw the opening in the trees and the pack of goblins and orcs inside it. He let the arrows go, knowing nothing would prevent him from saving Hess.

The second he saw those two white points headed in his direction, Hess dove to the ground, trying to get as small as possible.

Doing so left him unable to see the orc, who stared at the lights coming at him until one struck him in his head, penetrating his skull and exploding in a dazzling, bright white burst of light that sent a shockwave that made the trees sway backward, creaking and cracking as if they were about to split and break.

The second arrow reached the horde that was unprepared for the power that erupted inside their midst. The next ten yards of creatures vaporized in a flash of light, as fire that burned pure turned them to ash before any of them could take a breath.

The trees around them were cut through and began to move and fall as they lost their base.

Faster than Kaen could watch his own hands move, two arrows fired from his bow, exploding on the side of the two falling trees, knocking them deep into the forest and onto more creatures trapped by the pressing of bodies who had been led there by the belief of a show and a free meal.

Need to . . .

I know, hold on.

Kaen pulled another arrow and launched it and three more into the darkness of the woods. Each exploded and erupted into flames, setting the trees on fire.

Pammon had barely a few feet on each side of his wings as they descended into the trees, branches falling as he lowered himself amidst the trees and their limbs. He knew it would be a tight fit both ways, but right then, power as he had never felt flowed through him. He knew that somehow it was supposed to be like this, that he and Kaen shared power and that it made them both better. Stronger and perhaps invincible.

* * *

Hess glanced up, looking at the sight above him.

Kaen was still suspended between Pammon's talons, firing arrow after arrow at those evil creatures that had torn apart all Hess's group.

Standing to his feet, Hess watched as Pammon finally deposited Kaen on the ground, and smiled as Kaen ran toward him, embracing him with both arms.

"Thank you," Hess whispered as Kaen squeezed him tighter than ever. "Thank you for coming for me."

"You idiot!" Kaen exclaimed as he cried against Hess's shoulder. "You cannot die on me! You cannot die on Sulenda or your child!"

Hess embraced Kaen and squeezed him back using his stub and good arm. "I had not planned on it going this way. I'm sorry, son."

Kaen nodded and moved back from Hess, looking at the stub of his arm. "Is that . . . "

"No, it's not. Now focus. We need to finish the mission. Can Pammon get both of us out of here?"

I can and don't forget I can talk with you now.

Hess nodded and moved to where Pammon was, gently rubbing his rump as Pammon gazed into the woods, watching for anyone foolish enough to brave the flames still burning.

"Thank you, Pammon, for everything. I would not be here without you," Hess said.

You are welcome. Now stop talking and climb on. We need to get out of here before the fire makes things worse.

"Let me help you," Kaen declared, providing a boost for Hess.

Growling, Hess reached for Pammon's neck and realized that without his hand, he couldn't get ahold of Pammon's neck.

"Fine, I'll take the gosh damn help," complained Hess as he waited for Kaen to give him a knee.

Hurry, you two, they are regrouping.

Riding front-to-back with Hess was not what Kaen had imagined at all. Pammon struggled to get them straight up out of the circle, but the two trees that had been knocked down provided just enough room for it to work.

Kaen's lifestone provided the strength for Pammon to carry them both far enough that they found the horses, still tied up, and set Hess down near them.

"I need to go and finish this before I check on the rest," Kaen said as he checked the arrows still on Pammon. "Hopefully, I can find the kegs quickly and take care of it before they return."

"You're going back?" Hess asked. "Why risk it?"

When Kaen turned and Hess saw the tears that were coming down his face, he ran to Kaen and embraced him.

"How could you?" Kaen demanded, as he cried. "You knew she was pregnant, and you still risked your life, knowing what I went through!"

Hess tried to pat him on the back, and felt his stub hitting Kaen's leather piece. He held it up and looked at it.

He let out a sigh, pushed Kaen back, and gave him a hard stare. "Someday, you will understand. It won't be today, but it is the same reason why you risk your life right now," Hess answered as he fought back his own tears. "Just like your father, just like me, someone must be willing to sacrifice their life so others can live."

Unable to speak, Kaen wiped the tears from his face with his arm and began to turn around.

Hess grabbed him with his only hand and held him in place.

"Do not forget why you are doing what you do. We all do this for the same reason."

He is right, and you know it. Do not hold it against him for doing the same thing you did. I have told you what you have also just told him. I will risk everything to save you because I do not want you to die either.

Kaen stood between the two of them, realizing they were right but unable to let go of the hurt that still ached. "Sacrifice . . . Being committed to something so much you are willing to sacrifice yourself," Kaen whispered as the idea took root in his brain.

"What was that?" Hess asked, hearing Kaen mumble.

Centering himself, Kaen took a deep breath and let it out as he turned to face Hess. "We are both committed to the task before us and willing to sacrifice ourselves for it. Every adventurer today came here knowing they might die. They were willing to do it because if we didn't put our lives on the line, everyone else's life would be at risk."

Kaen set his hand on Hess's arm and gave it a squeeze. "You have sacrificed enough. Go home and join Sulenda. Pammon and I will come to see you soon," Kaen declared as he walked toward Pammon. "I need to finish what we started, and I mean for them to know we will not run away."

Hess opened his mouth to speak but stopped when he saw Pammon shake his head at him.

Right before Kaen and Pammon took flight, Hess waved and made one last remark. "When you come to Ebonmount, I will be there to sing a tale greater than any bard has ever told. I will tell of the son and his dragon who saved his father so that his brother would not grow up alone."

Kaen smiled, and a thrum emanated from Pammon.

See you soon, Dad.

As Pammon leaped into the air, still thrumming, Hess chuckled, and then it turned into laughter so hard he fell to his knees crying. Tears flowed as he laughed. The truth was his heart was so full and grateful at that moment, Hess didn't know how to express it.

89

Hurt by the Ones We Help

Are you sure you can make it? Do we need to rest?

I will be fine. The orcs did not taste great, but they gave me the energy I lacked.

If you say so, just don't push yourself. I can feel your body hurting from how much you have exerted yourself. We both know I don't want to get injured because you fall from the sky.

Pammon grunted and snorted, sending a small shower of snot at Kaen, who, knowing when it was coming, had learned to dodge it.

As I said before, I will be fine. We are twenty minutes out from the next spot.

Kaen nodded and flattened himself against Pammon's neck. He hoped they were not too late.

Next time I tell you to let me carry the casks, do not argue. You are far better at defending and attacking while I do that. The only reason you lived was because they ran from me.

I wonder why that is . . . perhaps it's because you are a dragon, and I was just a guy carrying explosive kegs . . .

Pammon thrummed and continued beating his wings as they raced to the fourth spot he was aware of.

They had found the three kegs, and most of the goblins and orcs there had taken off when Pammon came into view, running into the cave or woods, whichever was closer. Kaen had carried two casks on his shoulders into the mouth of the cave, setting them down inside and blowing it from a charged shot.

Mana Check
Mana: 32/196

Ever realize you have no idea how to actually do something or how it works? I just realized I don't know how fast mana regenerates, and I have been using my explosive shot without any thought about this.

Pammon nodded, and Kaen felt a trickle of energy flowing through their bond into him.

Are you sharing your mana with me?

Yes. I cannot use any more since the skill I used is unavailable. I have one hundred and sixty left. How much do you have now?

Mana Check
Mana: 132/196

You gave me one hundred mana! I didn't know we could do that.

I didn't know I couldn't do that, replied Pammon with a thrum. **Perhaps that is why I could.**

We really need to find another Dragon Rider and learn from them. I'm tired of not knowing what we are missing out on.

Perhaps you are looking at it wrong, also. We might be able to do something they say is impossible. Which is better to have?

Mumbling to himself and glad that the wind carried it away, Kaen rubbed Pammon's neck with his hand as they flew. One day, they would figure out what they could really do.

It appears they have won. The cave is sealed, and I see at least six adventurers going through the dead bodies and ensuring they have killed them all.

So, angle for the next point. There are still three more left.

As Pammon angled slightly to the southeast, Kaen could feel Pammon's eyes still on the battle that had taken place miles away.

What is it you are looking at?

There are two large orcs like the one Hess faced. They are dead, but I wonder why there are two here. The number of dead is also more than the first two spots. I think I realize now that the farther east we go, the larger the groups are. I believe the ones that attacked Minoosh were from the farthest one. We were not supposed to have found them at all. I am guessing that doing so allowed your adventurers' guild to scout out here and find what they were not meant to find.

Kaen had not considered that, and now he felt exceedingly lucky that none of the larger orcs or other creatures had come to Minoosh. If they had, he knew the town would have been destroyed.

Then let's hurry. The sun is moving toward the mountains, and I don't want to do this at night when we can't see.

You . . . You can't see. I can see just fine at night.

Whatever. How long till the next camp?

I would say an hour or more. Stop talking, and let me focus on flying. Perhaps I can shave some time off it.

They need help! It appears it is a stalemate right now as there are adventurers on both sides of the cave entrance, yet no one is going in, and nothing is coming out. A large pile of dead bodies is blocking the entrance.

Tell me your plan. What do you think we should do?

Pammon's thoughts tingled against Kaen's brain. He wondered if it was because his lifestone was so intense when Hess was in danger that he could somehow *read* them, but right now, it was like he could only *feel* them again.

Do you want to go in hot and heavy, laying down a trail of fire?

Kaen's backside felt the laughter after his question. Pammon was obviously amused that Kaen could feel his thoughts.

Impressive, you felt that. I think it might be the best option. From what I see, that pile of corpses will prevent anyone from getting close and setting off their casks. The only way to fix that is to remove the pile and figure out what is inside, sending out more to die.

How much time do you have left on your flame?

Eight or nine seconds. I won't use it long. Three seconds should be plenty of time to come in and send it inside the cave. If I focus on it, I can cause it to go farther and spread less.

Weighing the options in his mind, Kaen realized he had not asked the question that was really on his mind.

Can you see the adventurers at all? Like what do they look like?

Perturbed at that question, Pammon snorted before replying.

Yes. Why ask such an ignorant question? I can see the beard on a dwarf and the way he has it twisted into a . . . . Wait . . . Is that another dwarf woman? How do you tell if they are a woman or not?

Laughing, Kaen thumped Pammon's side.

You have to look for female curves.

They are wearing plate armor . . . There are no curves!

I guess we will have to wait. For now, I'm trying to find a dark-haired human woman with green eyes wearing a robe. Do you see one of those anywhere?

Even if I did, I'm not sure I would tell you. You need to focus on the fight, not on some woman you barely know! Besides, we will be there in a minute, and I need to adjust the angle I am coming in from.

Suppressing what he wanted to say, Kaen gladly let his frustration drift through their bond, and he felt Pammon ignoring it.

As the battle area below came into view, Kaen saw hundreds of dead orcs and goblins, burnt and frozen and hacked to pieces. He picked out the corpse of an adventurer as Pammon glided across the clearing between the forest and mountains.

The fire inside Pammon began to grow, and he wondered, for a moment, if Kaen would feel it as he did. One of the adventuring parties saw him coming, and it appeared they were hunkering down behind the two warriors with shields.

I hope they don't attack us . . .

Pammon kept his path, knowing he wouldn't have a better chance than now. Inside the cave, he saw a massive group of orcs with goblins. They had not noticed him yet.

He felt Kaen rising on his back; an arrow was in his bow, and Pammon could feel the power inside him. He was going to shoot an arrow when he used his fire. Pride and joy filled him, knowing that Kaen was brighter than most, seeing the opportunity to do double the damage.

As Kaen got into range, his arrow soared ahead, flying into the cave where he was watching the orc leader. The arrow exploded inside, causing death and damage to those around it.

The last fifty meters approached, and Pammon began to open his mouth, letting the fire begin to rise up his throat.

Arrow! Kaen warned.

It was too late. Pammon ignored Kaen's warning. He would have to endure the arrow and finish the task at hand. Pain hit him in the side near his back leg as he reached the last twenty yards. He flared his wings, lurching to a stop and releasing the jet of fire stream from his mouth over the pile of corpses and into the cave.

He could see the monsters immediately dying in the flames, pressing against one other as they tried to run in the opposite direction, becoming wedged and stuck. The skin and armor melted off them as they turned to ash.

Cutting the flow of fire, Pammon took three giant beats of his wings to raise himself in the air and begin turning to move away from the mouth of the cave.

"STOP FIRING, YOU FOOLS!"

He heard Kaen shouting but moved on instinct, knowing he needed to flee until they knew he was not a threat. One day, perhaps they would not attack first, but for now, he would show mercy to the archer who had been foolish enough to shoot him.

Are you ok? Are you hurt?!

I am fine. It is still in me near my back leg, but it is not deep. It barely penetrated. I need to land and get you to pull it out.

I'm sorry that he fired, and I am going to beat his arse for it!

Kaen's frustration and anger were filling his senses.

Please let it go. Your anger is making me angry, and we don't want me to get angry.

Kaen grunted and Pammon felt the amount of frustration reduce some, but it was still there.

Fine . . . but I cannot promise I won't hit the guy.

I will allow that, Pammon replied as he landed on the ground a hundred yards from the nearest group.

"Where are the casks!?" shouted Kaen as he jumped off Pammon and began running to the group that had not shot at them.

They stared at him as he ran toward them, glancing back at Pammon and then back at Kaen.

When he was within thirty yards, he recognized the gold warrior woman he had seen the first day he entered the guild hall. She had a few bandages wrapped around her one arm, and her massive sword was missing.

"The casks! Where are they?" Kaen asked.

"How the bloody hell is a dragon here and helping you?!" yelled a dwarven guy who looked like their healer. "That's not possible!"

People are idiots.

Yes, they are. Some even shoot at you when it is obvious you are not attacking them.

Refusing to smile at Pammon's comment, Kaen, now just a few feet from the party, saw that all of them were wounded and barely standing.

"The casks. We need them now! Stop worrying about my dragon, who is here to help, and tell me where the casks are!"

The dwarf pointed at the other group, which had not yet moved.

"Of course they are," grumbled Kaen as he pointed at the gold token warrior. "You come with me and help me get the casks. Pammon will keep the enemies at bay, provided no one attacks him again."

"A dragon . . . a bloody goblin-licking dragon," cursed the dwarf as he stared at Kaen. "How the hell do you have a dragon?"

Frustrated, Kaen walked over to the dwarf, grabbed him by his robes, and lifted him off the ground. "Listen, I don't have time! There are still two more spots to check, and I need to go help. Now get your arses over there to help with the casks, or the dragon will be the least of your worries!"

Kaen let go of the robes, and the healer stumbled back, nearly falling on his butt. "Now go!" he ordered, running toward the other group.

Watch the cave, and tell me if you see something.

They are all hiding or burning right now. You are safe to move.

"I'm sorry! I didn't know!"

Kaen glared at the archer, who was holding his hands up as if he was surrendering. "I understand," he stated as he glared at the man, able to almost kill with his gaze. "Had you hurt him, I could not promise I wouldn't return the favor. Now stop pissing your pants, get those three casks, and follow me!"

Two warriors and the gold token warrior each picked up a cask and followed Kaen as he kept an eye on the flames.

Still clear? I need like ten or twelve seconds.

Let me help. Prepare them. I'm going to get loud.

Kaen chuckled as he ran and looked back at the three following him.

"Pammon is going to roar, so don't trip or fall when he does it. Right after, I will tell you when to toss those in and run."

They nodded and kept pace as Kaen turned back toward the entrance.

Seven coppers says the archer pisses his pants.

We both know he is going to. Perhaps I should see if I can make him do it more than once.

You're on!

90

Commitment Even Till Death

Ava felt the sweat that was running down her entire body. Her robe was soaked, and she had finished the last of her water hours ago. Everyone was reaching the point where they knew the moment would come when they would have to make their last stand.

"You all need to flee while you still can," Selmah declared as she meditated on the ground. "It's a fool's death unless the other side makes a grave mistake, and I don't believe that magus is a fool."

"We aren't leaving you," Ava replied without hesitation. "We didn't sign up to run away and abandon one of our own. The only way we go, is if we all go."

"You four know I can't . . . " Selmah paused as she felt the aura Matthew had cast end. "Forget it. You missed your chance, and now we must decide when to make our last stand. How many arrows?"

"Eighteen. We have scavenged all the ones we could. The goblin arrows won't work with our bows."

Standing, Selmah glanced at the four who were still with her. Two archers with maybe nine shots each, a healer with no more mana to heal, and an iron token mage who, while gifted, was out of her league in experience. That one mistake had cost them everything. She couldn't blame the poor girl. She had never been in a situation like this before. None of them had.

The last option she had was not one she wanted to take. She had enough power for the spell, but it would ultimately end her life.

It's been over forty years on this journey. Am I really willing to die for this?

"I'll take over. Rest if you still need it, or wait for my orders," Selmah stated as she walked past Ava. "Give me a few minutes to think."

"What are our odds?" one of the archers asked Matthew quietly.

"Almost non-existent," called out Selmah, not bothering to turn around. "We have two hours max before the sun disappears behind those mountains. Unless something changes, I will make one last stand. For now, you two archers trade shots. Make sure you hit. Ava, be ready if I call for you to take out a group. I need to conserve all the mana I can."

Pausing for a moment, Selmah let out a small sigh. "And, Matthew, please try and meditate. You may be the most important asset in the coming hours."

She heard Matthew's knees stop knocking together. She knew he was terrified and was actually surprised the man had not run away. The rocks grinded and scraped along the ground as, she assumed, the man sat down, trying to focus on clearing his thoughts to speed up his mana regeneration.

All she could do now was wait.

"Last arrow!!" the archer shouted before he let it loose. The sun was almost down, and the shadows were stretched along the mountain range and trees, sending long, dark, shadows everywhere.

"Ava, prepare to cast a firewall, and hold it as long as you can!" ordered Selmah as she moved toward the top of the cave entrance along the mountain. "When you see me wave, let it go, and the four of you run!"

Ava's heart was pounding. She knew things were bad, as the last twenty minutes had been a steady stream of anywhere from one to three goblins being sent out to die every so often. The Magus knew the group was weak and wanted to ensure they were still here. Her mana would be gone soon, and even with Matthew finally being able to cast one more buff to help with it, the constant fighting had taken its toll.

Her fear was the truth she knew. She would never see her parents again. She would never see Kaen again. Selmah's promise was not possible. No matter what that woman did, there was no way she would be able to prevent their deaths.

Kaen, I pray you are safe! Don't forget me . . .

Goblins began to move again, and she opened herself and created a wall of fire stretching into the cave. She knew it only went so far inside, but it had to buy time for Selmah to do whatever she would do.

Seconds felt like hours as the mana drained from her body, her heart pounding. The last little bit would soon be gone, and there was nothing she could do . . . she knew she would be dead in a few moments. Hopefully, it would be quick, even if she had to use her own weapon to end her own life, lest the monsters do the horrible things to her she had been warned about.

As the wall began to flicker and Selmah had still not given a signal to cut it yet, Ava cried, knowing her best wasn't good enough. Knowing she couldn't save all the people she wanted to save. That silly idea to help people with potions would never come about.

As those thoughts ravaged her mind, her lifestone did something she had only felt it do one other time in her life. It didn't just pulse gently as it had when she was first trained. No, it roared like it had that night on the floor with Kaen. When he danced with her, she gazed into his eyes and saw how he looked at her, how he smiled at her, how he laughed with her. It had surprised her and was the real reason she had run away that night. It had never beat that strong in her chest before, and now it did so again.

The wall of fire that had begun to flicker and fade surged again, roaring taller and wider and changing to a darker shade of orange and blue. She fell to her knees as she weakened, her lifestone draining her life for mana she did not have. Her body burned as her life powered a spell she could not hold, somehow knowing her need at that moment. Struggling to stay focused, she saw Selmah waving her hands.

She let the spell go and felt her strength return slightly.

"Are you ok?!" Matthew shouted as he stood beside her. She had not realized he had been there the whole time.

"No, but I will be," she gasped as she took the hand he offered and helped her to stand. "We need to run. I think I know what she is going to do."

Selmah felt her life draining. It had been over a decade since the last time she had needed to use her life for a spell, but there was no time to hold back now. A smile crossed her face when she saw the flames that Ava had summoned. Perhaps that girl would be strong enough in time. She had found a way to tap into her lifestone. She had the resolve to be willing to give everything when the moment was required.

The blue flames below were flickering, and soon they would be gone. Left to linger from the power embedded in them. It had been hot, standing right over the roof of the mouth of the cave, but the flames had not bothered her. She wouldn't be able to move once she cast this spell. She would have to fall and let the earth accept her and the power she would release.

Her hairs stood up on her skin. Even the hair on her head began to rise as all her mana filled the spell she was summoning.

Inferno.

The greatest fire spell she had learned, taking two centuries to figure out how to cast. It burned hotter than any other fire she knew, outside of dragon breath. Her body felt alive and yet weak as the power of her lifestone roared, draining her health and her strength, depositing into her enough power to kill everything forty yards around her. It could almost melt stone.

Smiling, she gazed ahead, looking out over the forest as the sun almost vanished behind the mountains. The beautiful colors of the sunset contrasted starkly with the death and destruction below.

All this was happening so fast. Seconds flew by, and yet movement over the trees caught her eye. Something large was moving fast.

Flying.

Flying toward her.

A dragon? Impossible! Elies?

No, it couldn't be him. They said he wouldn't come, and this was not large enough to be his dragon.

Her eyes focused as the power filled her. It was streaking across the sky. It would be here in less than a minute. Its bronze body was perfect as its wings flapped over the trees, the sun's light glistening off its scales.

The rider on its back . . .

"It can't be!" Selmah gasped as her body struggled to stay erect.

A dragon and a rider! Not the massive black dragon Juthom and not Tharnok.

Someone new!

Chills ran up her body, almost sending a wave of pain and ecstasy as she held the power inside her.

Generations! It had been forever since a new Dragon Rider had been found! How could this be?!

It was almost upon her.

Could it be a foe? An ally? If she cast her spell while it was in her range, she might kill it. If it was an ally, the consequences of her releasing her spell and killing them would be impossible to imagine. It might be the only chance the kingdom would have to take it out if it was a foe.

Think!

Less than ten seconds. It would be in range by then. Orcs and goblins were starting to stream out. None had noticed her yet. None had noticed the dragon either.

Why would a Dragon Rider be coming here? No enemy would bother coming, as none would expect them to fail. It had to be an ally!

Everything in her was burning. She tried to pull back the spell she had begun to cast. Some spell had to use the power she now held, and she couldn't do what she had planned. She couldn't risk killing this hope flying toward her like an arrow toward its mark.

She screamed as the pain of changing the spell tore through her. The fibers in her body that allowed the mana to flow bulged and ripped. As she screamed, she turned, sending forth a solid column of fire to the east, away from the mouth of the cave, and creating a pillar of fire flowing from her hands for a good seventy yards.

The orcs saw and gestured toward her. One of the hobgoblins shot an arrow at her, hitting her in the shoulder.

Tears ran down her face as she felt her life slipping away. She turned and heard a roar that felt like her eardrums were going to shatter and she watched a spout of flame leap forth and consume the orcs and goblins outside the cave before streaming into its mouth.

The rock below her felt hot, and she could smell burning, though she was unsure if it was her own skin or the creatures dying below. The pain was overtaking her, and she was beginning to black out when she felt herself being lifted.

Her eyes were heavy. It was so hard to focus as she glanced at the massive bronze belly of scales and saw a massive claw holding her carefully.

Ava was running when she heard a sound unlike anything she had ever heard before. It echoed off the rocks and the side of the mountain. She turned as she ran and saw a dragon appear from nowhere, spewing flames inside the mouth of the cave.

She tripped and fell over a rock as she looked backward and then stood up, turning around to see the dragon unleashing its fury upon the horde of creatures that were hellbent on killing her and the others.

Dazed, she realized someone was on the back of the dragon.

That's not possible! There are no Dragon Riders that small.

She gasped as she saw the dragon carefully pick up Selmah from the top of the cave entrance and then fly toward her.

Panic struck her as backed up and tripped over another rock, falling to her rear. She scooted across the ground and felt someone grab her shoulder. Glancing up, she saw Matthew had run back and was trying to help her.

"We need to go!" he exclaimed, jerking her to her feet.

"But they have Selmah!" she shouted as Matthew took off in a sprint. "They defeated the Magus!"

Matthew kept running, not wanting to risk it. Surviving the orcs and goblins was enough. A dragon was too much.

Ava watched as the dragon flew closer, amazed and enthralled at its bronze scales that shimmered in the dwindling light of the night. As she gazed at the dragon, its head moved to the side and she saw the rider on its back.

She saw him!

Her knees went weak, and she fell to the ground.

Kaen!

It wasn't possible, but it was him. There was no doubt. Her heart had skipped two beats the moment she recognized him.

She watched as the dragon gently laid Selmah on the ground and flew a few yards away before resting on the dusty ground.

Kaen hopped off and ran to Selmah, taking something from his pouch as he ran.

The dragon just looked at her, holding her eyes with its. Somehow, it felt like it was peering into her soul.

Turning her eyes back at Kaen, she saw Selmah now sitting up, no longer lifeless but still looking weary. Strength returned to Selmah's body, and Ava ran toward the two of them. Kaen turned and smile at her.

"Go," Selmah wheezed. "She is coming for you."

Smiling, Kaen nodded and, knowing Selmah was fine, turned and saw Ava running toward him.

She was a mess. Her hair was going in every direction, her clothes were matted against her body, and dirt was all over her face, hands, and robe, and yet she was just as beautiful as that night in her carriage.

Running to her, he smiled, and when she slowed down, he did not.

"Kaen . . . " she uttered before he embraced her and put his lips on hers, holding her close and feeling her return the kiss. Time seemed to stretch on until it was interrupted.

You need to let her breathe, or she will die.

Kaen felt a tinge of jealousy and humor coming through Pammon. The thrumming of his laughter let him know for certain it was more of a joke, as he broke the embrace with Ava, and they both took a deep breath.

"How? When?" Ava asked as she glanced at Kaen and then at the dragon behind him, who was turning his head to look at the area where the cave was.

"It's a long story," Kaen answered as he brushed her matted hair from her forehead. "You are safe now, and Pammon and I need to seal the cave. The rest of you need to head back to town. I have one last spot to visit."

As Kaen gave her a kiss on her forehead and began to turn, Ava grabbed his arm and pulled him back.

"Your dragon?!"

Chuckling, Kaen nodded. "Let me introduce you two, real quick," he stated as he pulled her along.

"Pammon, this is Ava. Ava, this is Pammon."

She is awfully skinny. Not even worth eating, Pammon declared as he gave a small snort and shook his head.

"Play nice, Pammon, or I won't give scratches for a long time," Kaen said as he winked at Ava, keeping Pammon's thoughts hidden from her. "Forgive him. He likes to protect me and keep him for himself. Perhaps if he is kind, he will let you touch his snout momentarily before we must go."

Ava glanced at Pammon, saw how he looked at her, then glanced back at Kaen. "Uh . . . are you sure? It doesn't appear he is interested in that."

Laughing, Kaen nodded, took her hand with his, and held it out.

Be nice. We don't have time for this, and stop acting like an eggling.

Pammon thrummed, and Ava started to move her hand back, but Kaen held it in place and smiled. "He is just laughing. He makes that noise when he laughs. You will get used to it, trust me."

I will do this for you, but she must prove herself worthy of you to me.

Thank you. I know it isn't easy, but it means a lot to me.

Pammon moved his head forward and slowly put his snout against Ava's hand, letting her feel his scales.

"See, he isn't that bad," joked Kaen as he took his hand off hers, letting her feel them all on her own. "Now scratch between the scales with your fingertips. He likes it."

Ava nodded and began to scratch a few small areas gently, and even though Pammon did try to fight it at first, he began to trill as she found a spot near the ridge that needed a good scratching.

Ava laughed and then pulled her hand back. "Thank you, Pammon. I will remember this always."

"Good," Kaen announced as he gave her a quick peck on the cheek and climbed onto Pammon's neck. "I need to go. Selmah, get them home safely."

Having forgotten all about her, Ava glanced over to where Selmah was and saw her standing with her mouth wide open in awe of what she was witnessing.

"Kaen Marshell . . . . Be safe, and thank you," replied Selmah, still shocked. She had known this boy was special, but this was beyond anything she had ever imagined.

Kaen nodded, and Pammon backed up before taking off.

Ava watched as Pammon reached where the kegs had been dropped and flew them over to the cave where the fire was almost out. He pitched them forward with his legs, and Kaen shot an arrow that collapsed the tunnel when the two collided inside.

"Amazing," Ava mumbled as Pammon and Kaen turned and flew off to the east.

Selmah moved to stand beside Ava and shook her head as she stared at the girl. "We are going to have a long talk about that boy and how special he will be," Selmah said before she turned and headed toward their horses.

91

Returning Home with a Dragon

They are all dead. Something is consuming life in the forest. I will not risk flying near it.

Kaen could make out the section Pammon was looking at between the vision he somehow gained from Pammon and the light of the moon that was now a fourth of the way in the sky.

The whole forest . . . it's like . . . is a mile of it gone?

I don't know what it was, but that spell killed everything and turned it all brown. And there is a vine down there that is still moving a little. We need to forget it and focus on the cave. It is the last one.

Patting Pammon's neck, Kaen felt it was too great of a risk to try and land and see if any of the adventurers were still alive. Whoever had been here had either unleashed a power he could not imagine, or something far worse was waiting for them at the cave they needed to seal.

It had taken an hour to find the three casks, and Kaen had shot over three hundred arrows from the sky, killing an army that had constantly been searching for them. He was content to have gained one more point of archery in the process, bringing it to thirty-three.

No creature or monster could be found beyond the lower-level orcs and hobgoblins. Whoever had cast that spell had to have died in the woods with it.

Faced with a foe they could not locate, the minions fled into the cave, and once the horde had been forced inside, Pammon finished off those foolish enough to stand close to the entrance with his last two seconds of fire.

Once that was complete, Pammon and Kaen fetched the casks and sealed the cave entrance, giving the kingdom a little time before any creatures still left alive could dig out.

If they wanted to.

I'm tired. Can we find somewhere to land and rest? It has been a long day, and every part of my body aches.

I am with you. Even though I did not do as much as you, it feels like every part of me has been beaten. You find a place, and we can sleep there.

The next morning, Kaen had his experience hunting with Pammon while flying.

He laughed and hollered as Pammon chased down animals and devoured them with ease. He even managed to score a shot that killed a deer. Pammon helped start a fire and used his talon to cut the deer since Kaen had tossed his knife like an idiot while flying.

They forgot about the worries of the previous day, knowing that in a few days, everything would change.

Thank you for being kind to Ava. I know it wasn't easy for you.

I still think you are too young to pursue a female. You need to wait a few years at least before considering siring an offspring.

Kaen's howl of laughter echoed off the trees as he scratched the scales under Pammon's wings.

Pammon's body shook as he tried to laugh and sigh at the same time, creating a humorous trilling and thrumming sound.

We both know I am not looking to have an eggling anytime soon.

You say that, but look at Hess. He and his woman have not been together long, and now she is pregnant.

Kaen winced as he thought about Hess riding home and showing up to Sulenda missing part of his arm. He knew she would be happy that he had returned. It still hurt to know Hess had hidden all this from him.

When we get back, I'm going to have to have a talk with Fiola. I'm pretty sure it was her who didn't let Hess tell me about all this.

You and Hess seem to have issues with her. Do I need to talk to her?

Pammon's thrum at his own joke drowned out Kaen's laughter as they reclined in the woods, enjoying the night fire and gazing up at the sky.

They took an extra day, enjoying a night by a stream, laughing, sleeping, and resting. They knew it would take the other groups two days to return, and it would be more complicated if they returned first.

Are you sure about this? I understand if you want to wait.

Sitting on Pammon, overlooking Ebonmount below, Kaen knew it was time. He watched the city moving like an ant hill, small dots traveling all over the streets, flowing between the buildings and bringing the city to life. It was almost mid-afternoon, and everyone would be up and about. There was no better time than now.

Yes. It is time. Head to the guild hall. I will direct you.

Pammon thrummed, and Kaen laughed as he felt the joy coming from Pammon at finally being announced to the kingdom. No longer would he have to hide by himself in the mountains or forest.

As they flew down toward the guild hall, Kaen watched as the walls around Ebonmount began to buzz with movement.

There are a lot of guards on the walls, and they are all moving to the edge. I see some weapons that look like they might be useful against a dragon. Are you sure this is still a good idea?

It is. That is why I tied that white shirt to my bow and will hold it up as we circle around nice and slow. You can always dodge if it looks like they will fire, and we can rethink this.

We will see how it goes.

What could have taken a minute or less to descend, stretched on as Pammon kept his distance, informing Kaen of the movements below and on the wall. Finally, after a few moments, what they had hoped for happened.

There is a white flag waving on the wall.

Kaen felt Pammon sigh in relief at the same time he did.

Fly to the wall, but be ready just in case. I doubt they will fire, but I will not risk you.

Nor I, you.

As they flew low and over the streets and buildings, Kaen could see the people in the city looking up at him. Gliding over the walls, Kaen swore he saw Gertrude waving the white flag on the wall as they drifted overhead.

Was that the dwarven woman from my group?

That was a woman? Why must they have a beard?

Seriously, Pammon, you knew she was a woman. Now tell me, was that really her?

It was, and it appeared she was happy to see both of us by the way she was waving that flag.

Once past the wall, Kaen saw the street leading to the guild hall with white flags stationed on every block, creating a path for them to take. The flags led to the courtyard before it, where a circle of flags marked off a section to the left of the building.

There! Land there!

You act like I don't know where they want us to go. Please relax some. I can tell you are excited, and I am trying to control my own excitement. So that you know, Hess is there.

Just seconds from the guild courtyard, Kaen strained his eyes, trying to look ahead as they flew past the shops

When there were less than two blocks away, Kaen could see Hess and Sulenda standing near the steps, waving at him. He couldn't see the look on Sulenda's face, but by the energy that powered Hess's waving Kaen felt Hess was more excited than Sulenda was.

After Pammon landed, everyone stayed back except Hess.

Kaen patted Pammon on the neck and scratched a scale before sliding off.

This is the moment of truth. Remember to behave.

You are no fun, replied Pammon as he snorted, causing a few people to back up a step.

"Kaen! Pammon!" Hess yelled as he ran past the white flags and crossed the distance in a flash.

Smiling, Kaen ran over and embraced Hess when he saw the look on his mentor's face.

"They are here for both of you," Hess declared as he waved his stump toward the crowd and drew Kaen toward Herb and the others. "The king himself is waiting inside and wants to have a private word with you."

Kaen stopped, causing Hess to move forward a few steps without him.

Crossing his arms, Kaen shook his head. "I will not leave Pammon. If the king or anyone else wishes to see me, it will be with Pammon in my presence. We both have earned that. Pammon even more so."

Hess bobbed his head slowly. "Well said, Kaen, well said. I think you are ready to meet the king after all."

Hess held up his hand, and everyone who had been whispering and murmuring became quiet. "Adventurers and citizens of Ebonmount. May I introduce to you Kaen and his dragon, Pammon! The dragon and his rider who saved our kingdom!"

Barely a moment passed before the crowd began shouting and clapping.

Herb strode forward when he realized Kaen would not leave the circle his dragon was in. "Congratulations, Kaen and Pammon!" Herb exclaimed, extending a hand to Kaen. "A job well done! We owe a debt to you both that we cannot repay."

Kaen smiled as he shook Herb's hand and glanced around the crowd. "Where is Fiola? Why isn't she here?"

Kaen knew the moment he saw how Herb's face change, that Fiola would never see him again. "That was her at the farthest cave to the southeast, wasn't it?" Kaen asked.

Tears fell from Herb's eyes as he nodded. "She would not ask anyone to do what she was unwilling to do. A mark of a true adventurer," Herb declared wiping the tears from his face. "She stayed behind so that those with her could live."

This Fiola woman did all that damage in the forest? She must have been a powerful adventurer.

Trying to catch his breath, Kaen nodded in understanding.

It would appear that she was stronger than most and could carry a burden many would never be willing to try.

As they stood there, lost in the moment of reverence for Fiola, a voice rang out over the crowd.

"KAEN!"

Kaen turned his head and saw Ava running past those who were trying to stand in her way. Her parents had tried to hold her back, but they had lost that fight.

"Ava!" Kaen shouted as he smiled at her and held his arms wide, waiting for her to reach him.

You're not going to run to her?

I told you I'm not leaving you. We are in this together.

Pammon thrummed as he laughed, causing people in the crowd to back up a little.

Do not ask me to give her a ride yet. I am not quite ready to meet that request.

Kaen laughed out loud, smiling as Ava reached him and flung herself into his arms.

Ava pulled him close, and the two shared a kiss without caring about who saw.

"I owe you more than this one for saving me," she whispered after they pulled apart, ignoring the cheers that came from the crowd.

"Well, I won't force you to give me anything you don't want. Just try to remember I'm a gentleman."

Ava laughed and nodded as she glanced at Pammon, who she saw was looking at her intently.

She moved to stand before Pammon and gave him a deep curtsey. "Thank you, Pammon, for saving my life. I owe much to you. Hess has informed me that you enjoy cows. Perhaps ten of them might help begin to settle the debt I owe?"

Pammon quickly moved forward until he was just a few feet from Ava, whose eyes had gone wide from the speed at which he had approached her. Pammon gave the best smile he could and moved his snout till it was just a foot from her face.

Tell her I would appreciate it if she scratched the same spot she did last time. I might get to like her, if she keeps offering me cows.

Kaen laughed so hard he coughed a few times and had to catch his breath. "He says he appreciates your gift and would like it if you scratch that ridge you found last time."

Grinning, Ava began running her fingernails along the spot Pammon wanted, and in moments, a trill reverberated around the square.

Herb snapped his fingers, and Kaen turned and saw adventurers who had been at the caves line up behind him, each carrying something in their arms. They wore smiles and did their best to hide the fear they might feel at approaching Pammon. Kaen noticed Selmah in front, holding a small box. Her hair had become completely white.

"Kaen, as gratitude for saving their lives, each adventurer has something for the two of you."

Kaen began to protest, but Herb held up his hand and stopped him. "You and Pammon risked your lives, flying across the kingdom to save us all. There is no greater honor than a small gift in a moment like this. To turn it down is to tell each of them their life is worth nothing. Would you want them to believe that?"

A soft smile formed on his lips and Kaen shook his head. "I would be honored to accept their gifts."

92

A Promotion

King Aldric stood quietly with his hands behind his back, gazing at Pammon and Kaen, who had moved to a training courtyard so no one could bother them.

"I'm a bit frustrated, but I also understand," he stated, never taking his gaze off Kaen. "You had a dragon and kept it a secret. A wise decision but also a risky one."

Tell me again, why do we have to listen to this nonsense? Why would we have revealed ourselves while you and I were still weak?

Kaen let the humor of what Pammon said wash back through their bond and tried to keep a straight face.

He is the king. He could summon Elies and Tharnok, which would be bad if we were on the wrong side of them.

Do you think they would honestly threaten us? From what I have gathered, we should be treated with honor, yet I have not gotten that feeling from this 'king' of yours.

"So I would like to know your thoughts on this matter," King Aldric said.

Kaen realized he had missed something in the conversation with Aldric while he had been talking with Pammon.

A thought struck Kaen, as he was doing his best to nod and act like he was considering his words. "What would you consider to be the wisest decision regarding that?"

King Aldric smiled and bobbed his head.

That was impressive. I had not . . .

Quiet, please, Pammon. I really need to listen.

Pammon tried to hold back the thrumming as he began to laugh. He could feel Kaen struggling with this as well.

"Staying here is something that would be helpful for our kingdom. I know you have the academy to think of, which will only grow in renown with what the two of you have accomplished. I could offer you two a place inside or outside the walls, but I believe you know as I do, that you are not ready to stay here. Would you agree you need to go and meet Elies and Tharnok and learn from them?"

"For a time, yes," answered Kaen. "I am not ready to leave just yet, as I need to deal with a few things that are here first. Perhaps in a month, at the latest, we would be ready to travel to Roccnari and meet with them. As for where we would want to stay while here, let me ask Pammon."

I am not ready to be cooped up behind some walls. I prefer the countryside where I can fly whenever I want and find game as I desire.

Smiling, Kaen motioned with his head at Pammon. "He would prefer someplace in the country where he can hunt and possibly have some land with cows for when the mood strikes him. Far enough away that most won't bother us but close enough to town that coming to see us isn't a day's journey."

The king snapped his fingers and summoned a servant who dashed forward. He whispered something to the man who then ran out of the courtyard.

"I will attend to that matter immediately and hopefully have something located within a day," the king announced as he motioned to another servant to come forward. "Your status puts me in a very difficult position if we speak frankly. I cannot influence you like I can others. You are a Dragon Rider, so my choices are to ally with you, have nothing to do with you, or fight you. Seeing the man you are and how your dragon has acted, I want to offer you an alliance. I do not expect you to be ready to put pen to paper, but in time, I would like to structure something that works for you and the kingdom."

Kaen began to speak, but King Aldric cut him off with a smile and a raised hand.

"No response is needed right now. Sleep on it. Enjoy even more renown with the people. Just know I pledge myself to you and Pammon to help you be the best protectors our kingdom has ever seen."

With that, King Aldric gave a slight bow and departed.

That was unexpected. I assumed he had a daughter and would want you to marry her.

Kaen elbowed Pammon, who smacked him with his wing, sending Kaen sprawling across the dirt floor as he thrummed.

One of these days . . .

Kaen smiled as he stood back up and dusted himself off. "Let's go find Hess."

Once Aldric had left, Kaen and Pammon moved to another area of the training grounds where they knew Hess was.

The second Pammon and Kaen entered through the massive doors leading to the other training grounds, Kaen was almost tackled when Sulenda rushed and bear-hugged him.

She was sobbing and crying, and he felt her tears on his cheek and forehead as she squeezed him, even lifting him off the ground for a moment. "I cannot thank you enough," she cried. "I owe you everything."

"Breathe . . . I need to breathe . . . "

Realizing she was hurting him, Sulenda dropped Kaen and stepped back, looking at him with bloodshot eyes. "I'm sorry," she gasped. "Hormones! I cannot control myself."

Taking a breath, he nodded and moved back, giving her a hug and feeling her return it a lot gentler this time. "I love him just as much as you do," Kaen told her as he broke the embrace. "Why, I have no idea, but I do."

Sulenda laughed, tears still falling, and nodded as Hess moved to her side. "Oh, and Pammon!" she exclaimed, turning and holding her hand to Hess.

Hess placed a tied-off bag that was about a foot in length into her hand. "I have something for you, Pammon," Sulenda stated as she bowed low and moved slowly toward him. "Hess told me you enjoyed these back in Minoosh." Stopping a few yards from Pammon, she opened the bag, dumped a pile of blood cubes on the dirt floor, and backed away.

Pammon moved quickly forward and sniffed them before using his tongue to deposit them into his mouth. He trilled and bowed his head at her before lying down on the ground.

Tell her thank you.

"He says thank you," Kaen and Hess said simultaneously.

They chuckled and saw Pammon was smiling, having done that on purpose.

"You can hear him!" Sulenda gasped as she slapped Hess's shoulder. "I didn't believe you when you said you could!"

Massaging the shoulder that was missing part of his arm, Hess bobbed his head and shrugged. "Only when he is close. I'm unsure of the range, but I must be near him."

Suddenly, Sulenda's face turned red, and she pivoted on her heel, looking at Kaen as if she would rip his head off. "How could you keep Pammon a secret! Didn't you trust me?!" she yelled, waving her hands in the air. "I would have done anything for you two! I would not have told anyone. I would have . . . "

She broke into tears again, letting Hess pull her close and stroke her hair.

Kaen grimaced as he glanced at Hess, who tried motioning with his eyebrows at Sulenda.

"I'm sorry," she said as she lifted her face from his shoulder. "It's the hormones."

"Yeah . . . it's ok," Kaen replied, taking a step back. "I need to talk with Herb anyway. He wanted to see me before I left today. You two going to be ok?"

"We will be fine. You two go have fun dealing with Herb. You might find him more difficult to deal with now that he is in charge."

Sucking wind in through his teeth, Kaen bobbed his head and began to walk back toward the training grounds they had just left.

"You'll be back for dinner! Right?" called out Sulenda.

"I wouldn't miss it!" Kaen answered, waving goodbye without turning around.

We need to get out of here before she cries again . . .

Pammon followed Kaen back through the massive doors, his whole body shaking and thrumming as he moved.

They could both hear Sulenda crying as they walked away.

Herb and Kaen sat on chairs surrounding the small wooden table their cups rested on.

"Words cannot describe how proud I know your dad would be," Herb stated as he rotated his cup with his fingers. "I knew him well enough to know he never expected anything less."

Herb paused and glanced over at Pammon, who appeared to be dozing after the meat Herb had waiting for him now rest in his belly.

"Perhaps he might have expected a little less," he joked as he pointed at Pammon. "Regardless, you and I need to have an important talk."

"It's not any more trophies or gifts, is it?"

Herb just smiled and shook his head. "It is the last thing I can do as guild master of this adventurers hall before you are no longer allowed to be part of it."

"What?" Kaen asked, sitting up in his chair. "Why is that?"

"It is the rules or has been, I should say, since long before this place ever was. Dragon Riders are a different sect of the world. Kingdoms and kings will try to lure you with promises of wealth and power. Adventurers' guilds are supposed to be neutral. We rarely get involved in kingdom matters outside of quests and things like this last few days. As such, you cannot do both, and I doubt you are willing to walk away from Pammon."

Watching Pammon as he snoozed, Kaen knew that he was listening to every word they said. The truth of what Herb told him was hard to swallow.

"King Aldric already made an offer, of sorts. I guess I can understand what you are saying."

"He did not make an official one because I asked him to wait. I need you to be able to do something first, and I cannot do that if you are no longer part of us. I only have two or three days to complete this, and I want you to know I have only learned a few things recently. Things about your father and your mother."

Kaen's hands betrayed him as they knocked over his cup, and Kaen turned sharply to face Herb.

"What about my mother?" His tone was heavy and dripped with concern about something Herb might know.

"Are you sure you want to hear this now or do you want to wait till tomorrow? I know it has been a long day."

Kaen rose from his chair, stood before Herb, and held his hands out, confused that he would even ask that. "You're telling me there is a secret about my mother, and you expect me to walk away and wait till tomorrow? Are you insane?"

Herb never lost his composure as he shook his head. "You are right. You have proven you can handle difficult things. Sit, and let's talk."

For the third time, Kaen read the paper that Fiola had written for Herb. His face was expressionless as he tried to comprehend all of that information.

Herb sat watching him, waiting till he knew Kaen was ready to talk.

"Why would you let me read this? Some of this does not seem like something Fiola wanted me to know."

"Because I want you to know I am not playing you," answered Herb placing his cup on the table. "Everyone is going to try and play you from now on. You will be the greatest thing in this kingdom. What you believe is coming next is nowhere close to how it will really be."

"Why aren't you going to try and use me?" asked Kaen as he handed the letter back to Herb. "Is your goal to tell me you aren't and then try another way?"

Herb chuckled as he took the letter, folded it, and put it into his vest. "That is a perspective some might consider, but I am not. I . . . " he paused as he talked and rubbed his fingers against his chin. "We, the kingdom, and every adventurer alive from this mission, owe you too much to play that game. Because of that, I will not dishonor those who died or live. I will pledge myself always to be honest and explain my actions. To do so will require a few things, one of which you and your dragon Pammon will not like."

At the mention of his name, Pammon's head lifted, and his eyelids, which had been closed, revealed two sparkling eyes peering at Herb.

"You will need to come with me to the vault inside."

"I thought I couldn't go in there if I wasn't at least a gold adventurer."

Rising from his chair, Herb nodded, put his hand into his pocket, and pulled something out.

"You are correct," he answered as he held out his hand. Turning over his closed hand, he showed a platinum token with Kaen's name stamped on it. "My last act I can do for you is give you the rank you have earned."

As Kaen sat in shock, he watched Herb reach into his other pocket with his other hand and hold something out.

"I believe Pammon has earned this as well."

A trill rose from Pammon when he saw a matching platinum token with a dragon stamped on it.

93

Truth In a Vault

As Herb led him through the guild hall's back rooms and doors, avoiding the main areas where others might be gathered, Kaen ran his fingers over both tokens he now wore.

I cannot believe they made us both platinum adventurers.

We should have been made much higher. After all, we did save the kingdom.

Pammon was laughing, and Kaen smiled as he felt him through their bond. It was still overwhelming to know and see his name on a token he had never believed he would ever bear it. Sure, every adventurer dreamed of reaching these ranks, but somehow, he had done it in just a few months.

Lost in his thoughts, he almost bumped into Herb when the man suddenly stopped before a door.

"In here is the vault. I will go with you the first time. After you are inside, I will allow you to be alone in your father's vault," Herb informed Kaen as he swiped his hand over an invisible rune on the door. "I have no idea what all is in there, but Hess has told me that most of it is locked even to him. Perhaps you will be able to access it all."

The door shifted and creaked before it slid backward a foot and then slid to the side. Kaen noticed it was a solid metal door thicker than the length of his forearm. Steps led down behind it.

"That is . . . impressive."

Herb bobbed his head and laughed and began descending the stairs. After Kaen passed through the door and started down the steps, Herb held his hand over a section of the wall, and another rune lit up. The door behind him returned to its original position, locking them inside the vault.

* * *

For what felt like a good twenty minutes, stairs twisted and turned, and they were presented with the occasional door that required Herb to unlock and open it. Finally, Herb stopped outside a door that looked like every other one they had passed, and grinned.

"This is your father's vault. If you would please place your hand on the handle."

Nerves suddenly overwhelmed Kaen as he realized that this was a moment he had not considered being at for years. On the other side of the door were things he could only imagine about his father but that he never knew.

Kaen grabbed the silver handle and felt it go cold. Suddenly, a sharp pain pricked his palm. He tried to pull his hand from the handle, but it would not let him go. Three seconds later, there was a popping noise from the door, and it began to creak as his hand finally released the handle.

Kaen looked at his hand and saw a small, barely noticeable prick and a small drop of blood.

"The door is locked to just you, your father, and Hess," explained Herb as they waited for the door to open up on its own. "Anyone else who keeps trying to get it to open will not enjoy the pain that grows each time they fail."

"It gets worse?"

"It can even kill someone foolish enough to keep trying," he answered as he pointed at the opening. "Go inside. I'll wait out here."

"You sure you don't want to come in?"

Licking his lips, Herb sighed and shook his head. "I am honestly tempted to say yes and see what is in there. Many of us have often laid wagers about the contents," he stated as the temptation he faced was evident by how he peered into the open doorway. "I believe, however, you need to see it on your own the first time and decide if you want to invite someone in. On another day, I can walk you through how to permit it."

"Thank you for being honest."

Nodding, Herb moved down the hallway to where a chair Kaen had not noticed was. "I'll be here until you return."

Taking a deep breath, Kaen strode through the doorway, feeling a chill wash over him as he moved through the room's threshold.

What is it like?

Hold on, and I will tell you!

Once he was past the main door, a small hallway of only five feet led to a small wooden door. As Kaen turned the handle, he heard the sound of the first door moving and closing, sealing him inside. Small light globes lit up, and as the door shut behind him, Kaen opened the wooden door, gasping as the door swung open.

A solid stone room made from bricks that reminded him of the ones that covered the buildings of Ebonmount, lined the floors and walls. All over the room, rows of meticulously organized weapons and items assaulted his sight, and a twelve-foot ceiling had multiple light orbs casting a warmth over the space. The room was easily the size of Hess's house in Minoosh,

Spears ran half the length of one wall until replaced by swords, each held up by a pair of metal rings. Shields, maces, clubs, bows, axes, and more lined the other walls of the room. Each one was slightly different, yet none seemed out of place. Small bookshelves lined the wall on his left, each filled with books of all shapes and sizes.

Rolled-up paper tubes filled a bookshelf that seemed almost squished between weapons. A row of glass cases on a wooden table ran along the left side of the room. Each case was filled with rings and necklaces. One case had no glass top, and when Kaen inspected it, he saw a single ring missing from one of the case's twelve spots. There was a small piece of paper under each ring, and when he touched it, words appeared.

Blood Ring - Constitution increase

He lifted his hand and glanced at the blood ring he wore. A smile crossed his face. He wanted to touch all the rings' papers, but there was still too much to see.

Kaen turned to the other side of the room and saw a chair in a corner with a table and an assortment of bottles and other containers that appeared to have liquid in them. If he had to guess, they were filled with alcohol, and as much as he wanted to sample one, lessons learned the hard way told him right now was not the time.

As his eyes swept the right side of the room, he saw a small box on a desk all by itself against the wall. The way the box looked reminded him of the one he had seen Sulenda use multiple times to keep her private things. It was at least three times the size of Sulenda's but, by all other appearances, was exactly alike.

Walking toward it, Kaen noticed the rug on the floor. It felt soft and somehow relaxing as he traversed it, making him wonder if it had enchantment that made him feel this way or if it was knowing he was somewhere his dad must have come to relax and unwind.

He stood next to the desk and pulled out the small wooden chair that was under it. Sitting down, he gazed at the box and noticed a quill lying next to it, just like the one Sulenda had used. He hesitated as he reached for it.

Are you ok? I'm still waiting for you to tell me what you see.

It is a room filled with weapons, books, rings, and more. Things my dad felt the need to bring here. It looks like he even sat here and relaxed. Right now, I'm looking at a desk with a box that I hope to open.

I'm here if you need me. Take your time and learn about your father. Most will never get the chance you have right now.

Resting both hands on the desk, Kaen took a deep breath and let it out.

A small prayer that this would work left his lips as he picked up the quill and pierced his finger. A drop of blood formed, and he placed it on the top part of the box, as he had seen Sulenda do, then waited and watched.

Nothing happened, and just as he resigned himself that it wasn't going to work, a small sound came from the inside of the box.

A drawer the width of his thumb emerged from the bottom, revealing a few sheets of paper. As he pulled the stack out, the words on the top sheet caught his eye.

Hello, Son.

Kaen set the papers down on the desk and felt his chest throbbing. He was sobbing, and he couldn't help it. Leaning back so that the tears might not ruin the letters, he turned sideways and bawled. As he did, he felt a peace of some sort coming through his bond with Pammon. It could only be described as the feeling he had when they slept through the night together, and Pammon wrapped his wing around him.

Thank you, Pammon, for more than you know.

As I said, I will always be here. Do you need to talk about what happened, or do you just need a moment?

The hug is plenty. Thank you again for it.

Wiping his eyes and nose, which was extremely runny, Kaen took a few deep breaths and returned to the stack of papers. It was time to know whatever his dad wanted him to know.

Hello, Son.

I know the only way you are reading this is if I have died on my last mission and you made it to the rank of gold token! Congratulations on such a huge achievement, and I know that you and Hess have worked hard for this. I wish I were there to tell you how proud I am of you. Perhaps you will forgive me as you read these few pages I wrote.

Know, I have written this letter countless times. Words never seemed right, and every time, I threw them away. This one won't be perfect, but time is short. I must leave soon on the most dangerous quest I have ever undertaken. As such, I will talk about it first before dealing with other things you must learn.

I was asked to take on a quest no others would touch. A man has gotten stronger and is causing havoc in the Kingdom of Luthaelia. He is an evil man, bent on using dark magic and trying to find a way to grow in power. His name is Stioks, and he was once a Mithril adventurer. While I am not officially one, I am not worried about my ability to fight him. Rumor has it he has made a pact with a black dragon and is attempting to find a dragon's egg and become a Dragon Rider. We cannot allow this, or our kingdom and world will fall into darkness unseen for thousands of years.

This task is dangerous. Was dangerous . . . and obviously, I failed. I know you might wonder why I would risk it. Why would I consider this, knowing you would grow up without me?

First, it has to be attempted. I cannot stand by and watch evil take hold of our kingdom. One thing drives me more than anything, and that is to protect others. Too many sit idly by, content to grow rich or old, not caring for those who suffer from their lack of action.

The guild offered me a reward regardless of the outcome, if I took on this quest. You were given a rare lifestone. Occasionally in a generation or two, a lifestone is crafted that is usually kept for the children of kings. They knew I was searching for one, bartering for one, offering my soul for one, because you will thrive with one. As such, Fiola secured it, and the cost was unbearable. Certain death, but you are worth it. It is worth it.

She knows more than I wish she did, but I have no doubt she has pestered you with endless questions and requests. If she asks to know your stats, do not share them with her at all!

Kaen paused and chuckled as he read that last line.

"If only I had known that wisdom beforehand, Dad," he muttered.

She tried to get me to share mine as part of this deal, but I would not bend or break. Eventually, she relented. You remember that moment I gave you your lifestone, I am sure. The power it gave you. She gave me a few more months with you after that, before I had to set out on the quest. I want you to know I cherished every one of those days.

I will share with you what she wanted. Guard these numbers with your life. I am sitting here in a shirt, pants, and boots with no items. What I have acquired is only a fraction of what you are capable of.

Kaen's eyes felt like saucers as he stared at what he read next.

94

Words Sometimes Cut

My stats are as follows
Hoste Marshell - Adult
Age - 53
HP - 820/820
MP - 330/330
STR - 37
CON - 41
DEX - 36
INT - 33
WIS - 35

Kaen could not believe his father had acquired those stats with no items. Everything he had heard about him from Hess and others had to be true.

I know your numbers must be close to mine if you are gold, as the work needed to earn that rank will require you to spend a lot of time training. I won't share my skills, as it would take pages to write, but know that I hold a thirty in over ten skills and have two at forty. I have trained countless days, sought out the best teachers, and put in as much work as possible daily because I need to be the best to protect others.

Your lifestone will allow you to grow, if you do the same. Go move rocks, carry tree trunks, run through the woods, dodging items thrown at you, read my books here, and learn from others. Consider it a blessing that what you can learn and experience is far greater to what most adventurers will ever hope to achieve. People will flock to you, they will desire to be around you and help you. It may surprise you, but it is because the lifestone you have is meant for kings. I don't know everything about them, but I knew my life was worth getting you one.

Allow my sacrifice to mean something.

Ignore that last line. I know that you deserve more than that. I am sorry I left you. I wish I hadn't, but I wanted you to be the best there was because I saw potential in you.

Your mother saw that same potential.

The sheet ended, and Kaen slowly turned it over, looking at the next sheet.

Your mother, your birth mother, Madalyn Marshell, died when you were two.

Kaen's heart froze. Ruth had not been his real mother? That wasn't possible! All of his memories till the day she passed had been with her, until the time Hess had taken him from the couple who watched him when his dad was adventuring. This couldn't be.

Ruth was not your birth mom, but she loved you like you were her own. She comforted me and loved you and me after your mother died. She had been the servant who helped care for you as your mother grew sicker.

Madalyn was from an adventurer family in Luthaelia. She came here to get away from the kingdom and her family. This next part is as important as your lifestone. Pay attention, even though I am certain you are upset.

I am the fourteenth adventurer in our family tree. For fourteen generations, there has always been at least one or more children born from two parents who were adventurers. We have not advertised it because of what it means. We grow faster and stronger, and our lifestones allow us to be better than the rest. The longer the line, the more powerful it becomes. I would have been much stronger if I'd owned a lifestone like yours when I was your age.

Your mother was a twelfth-generation adventurer. Her family was not happy when she left. They were even more upset when she returned pregnant after we had married in secret. She mistakenly made a promise to her father, and he bent his will and bound her to a horrible promise, making her choose between you and me, or them. I told her to stay with them, but she would not stay because they would try to control you if she had. She left, fighting the bond and its call, until the day it stole her life from her. For over two years, she fought it because she knew you were worth it.

Do not seek them out, as they are the reason for her death.

It hurt when Ruth died from the pandemic that swept our kingdom. It hurts now as I write this, knowing had I been home, she would have survived, but like a fool, I was away, chasing my cause instead of being with you.

I am sorry about that. I cannot make up lost time, but I have a few small gifts to give as you continue your adventurer career.

I hope the bow is treating you well. I remember the day I needed your blood, and you so bravely allowed it. It was hard, but you were terrific. I want you to know I had it constructed just for you. If you manage to reach a forty in the archery skill, it will unlock a new bonus. Yes, I could tell you. No, I won't. I want you to want it bad enough to train for it. Just know it will be worth the work.

Your armor is better than most of the armor I have in my vault. The weapons will be usable, and I provided a list at the bottom of these pages with the ones I think will be best for you. Do not train with just a bow. Realize that each situation may require a different weapon. Seek out trainers for everything, and master all that you can.

There are plenty of rings to choose from, as well as necklaces here. Most are only a two bonus to a stat, yet ten rings with two strength each can do a lot, especially if you make it to sixty for a stat. I would assume Hess has taught you those things by now.

I feel like I should give you some fatherly advice, but the truth is I wasn't there when you needed me, and I realize this more as I write these words. I kept secrets I now know I should not have. I imagine you sitting here, tearing these pages up and lighting them on fire because of how angry you are with me for all this. I wouldn't blame you. I am angry at myself.

So I will end with this. I am going to walk out this door, lock my vault, and attempt the impossible. I pray you never read this letter. I pray that I will return to you, and we will have lived our lives to the fullest. That I get to watch you grow up, pass your test, achieve the impossible, and one day find someone you love, the way I did. I hope I am able to see the child you have and tell them horrible stories about things you did as a child and send them home after feeding them countless sweet treats.

Yet as I write this, I know the truth is, you are most likely reading this. So pretend I am there, watching you succeed and looking down from wherever the spirits take us when we die, cheering for you. Let Hess be the one who watches you grow and cheers at your success. Give him a hard time when he cries at your wedding or when he plays with the child I one day pray you have.

Find something worth living for and live life completely. Do not take risks unless you know the world requires it and have weighed the cost of sitting idly by and doing nothing with your life.

I love you, Kaen. Never doubt that, and forgive me if you do.

Your Father.

Kaen left the paper there on the desk and stood up. He felt empty at that moment. His life felt like a lie. His heart ached, and he couldn't understand why his father had never told him the truth.

All those years, he cried after Ruth died. He had memories of her as a baby because she had been there. He tried to remember his birth mother's appearance but couldn't. That knowledge stung even worse. There had been no picture of her. No painting. It was like the woman was gone from his mind and his life forever.

I do not know how to help, Pammon suddenly said as Kaen resisted the urge to rip everything off the walls and smash all the things in the room. **I can feel your heart is like a raging storm, twisting and turning in every direction. What did you learn?**

I learned my whole life is a lie . . . everything I thought I knew, isn't true. My mother was not really my mom, but instead my birth mother's servant, and she raised me when my mom, Madalyn, died. My dad never told me. Hess never told me.

My dad wrote words about how great I would be because of how he threw his life away on a quest he knew was hopeless. He wanted me to have this crazy lifestone and to be great, when all I wanted was my father.

Kaen paused for a moment, walked over to the large soft chair in the corner, and grabbed a bottle off the table next to it. He held it up to his face and then threw it against the wall, sending liquid and glass all over it and the floor.

Snorting, he flopped down in the chair, frustrated that even doing that had not helped with how he was feeling.

Hess will probably tell me he knew about the quest and was 'bound' by his lifestone not to share. That is goblin shite, and I know it. Fiola knew about my dad and my lifestone, so she had that stupid quest to begin with. She knew about my stats and wanted to know them so badly she risked my life and the others. She let Luca die for that knowledge!

Kaen leaned his head against the chair, closed his eyes, and rubbed them with his fingers.

I'm lost. Everything I thought was important seems broken and a lie. I'm not sure what to do.

Kaen sat silently in his chair, waiting for Pammon to speak.

Am I a lie? Am I broken?

Groaning, Kaen dropped his hands to his lap.

No! You know that is not what I meant!

Do I? You are whining like an eggling who cannot eat the chicken they want. You got everything you had hoped for, but now you complain about it. I am sorry your father lied to you. I am sorry your mother died and you never knew her. Yet we would not have met if those things had not taken place. We would not be bonded. So tell me now, do you wish those things were reversed, or do you believe having me in your life is better?

Many times in Kaen's life, he felt pain in his chest from words he had spoken or things he had done. None of them compared to this moment right now. It felt worse than back in Minoosh when he had been pierced through his chest by the arrow.

You know I would rather have you, he responded sheepishly.

Do I?! You complain about things you cannot change and make it sound like I am nothing! You forget how we both risked our lives for something you told me you believe in! I believed in you, so I risked my life for your cause! Would you toss me away as quickly as you do your beliefs?

Kaen felt the fire and passion in the questions Pammon kept launching at him. He was angry, and he was right to be angry.

I'm sorry, Pammon . . . I'm sorry for being a fool, for acting like an eggling. You are the greatest thing in my life; I forgot that just now. Please forgive me, if you would.

Silence stretched on for what seemed an eternity before Pammon finally spoke.

I know your kind struggles with feelings and other things that make you do foolish things. There are many days I wished I could have met my mother. There were so many times as I slept alone in the woods because I could not come into the city with you, that I would have given so much to have her take me under her wing and hold me close. Never, though, would I have traded any of that if it meant not having you.

Kaen could feel Pammon's gaze through the layers of dirt, stone, and whatever else was between them. He knew that Pammon was staring at his soul.

Being bonded is more than just being a friend. You are a part of me in an impossible way to describe to you. If you die, I will die. I will not be the dragon I am now. I would most likely go mad and need to be put down, as I would unleash all the hurt on everything around me. There is only room for one thing in my heart, in my soul right now: you. In time, I know it will change, and I will desire a mate like you do right now, but as I said before, that is many years from now.

Know I will forgive you for many things. I know you will forgive me for when I make a mistake. Just promise me that you will never desire anything more than me.

Emotions and feelings wrestled inside Kaen. There was a battle for his heart and soul, and he knew it. It was as if Pammon's request had put something in motion, and he had to respond. There were no maybes or possiblys that would work. He either had to choose Pammon completely and promise that now, or forever lose what they had.

The knowledge of that hurt because, for a moment, he had to consider what Pammon said. Nothing, no one, could ever be more important. He might have to let Hess, Ava, or even his own child, if he ever had one, die over Pammon.

The truth hit even harder when Kaen realized that if the moment came, he might have to die in order for Pammon to live.

Kaen's resolve solidified, and with imaginary hands, he grabbed the two forces fighting against each other, tore off his own selfish desires and wants, and pulled the part that was Pammon only, to his chest.

I choose you over everything else, including myself.

[Bond Complete]

Kaen's body began to thrash in the chair like one having an epileptic seizure. He felt Pammon thrashing too. His being was torn apart on the inside for a few seconds, and in a single breath, it stopped. He felt different, and he knew Pammon was, too.

We are one now, as it was always meant to be until death.

95

Figuring Out Life Together

After spending a while talking with Pammon, making up and figuring things out, Kaen knew it was time to go. He found the rings listed as dexterity and put six on his empty fingers, watching as the rings shrunk to fit each of them. His pinky and thumb looked weird with small bands around them, but the added twelve dexterity seemed impossible to imagine. He was closing in on sixty.

When he left the room and entered the hallway, he found Herb standing across from the door. "Were you waiting here this whole time?"

"No," Herb answered as he waited for Kaen to step across the threshold. "Once the door began to move, I got up and came over. Find everything you needed?"

Kaen saw Herb glance at his fingers and the assortment of jewelry he now sported. "Perhaps I should put these away until I actually need them," Kaen muttered as he began taking them off.

"It does look like you are preparing for battle. Anything change from what you found inside?"

Kaen grimaced as the door shut behind him, knowing he had to speak truthfully about what he had learned.

Herb tapped his finger against his chin as Kaen finished sharing everything he had learned about his father and mother's bloodline.

"So what are your plans now?" asked Herb, seemingly ignoring everything Kaen had just told him. "That is the real question. What are *you* going to do with this knowledge?"

Kaen sighed and leaned against the wall in the hallway. "I need to train, and I need to get stronger. I have some questions I know I need to ask about this

Stioks guy and," Kaen paused as he saw Herb's reaction to hearing the name, "I'm assuming that grimace isn't a good thing."

Herb shook his head and bit his lip as he grunted. "That name has been the bane of our kingdom and others for a decade or more. You have no idea how bad he is. Elies almost lost to him, and Stioks is not a true Dragon Rider. If he manages to get a dragon egg and bond with it . . . " Herb's eyes went wide as he realized what he was saying. "Your dragon, how did you get his egg?!"

"It had to be the reason Stioks invaded Elies's territory," muttered Herb as he paced the hallway once Kaen finished telling him about how they had found Pammon. "We know that he has three females he is trying to breed, but there used to be four. She must have been the one no one has seen since they moved into their new keep."

"What does that mean?" asked Kaen as he considered how that might change things for them. "That Pammon's mother somehow escaped and brought him here?"

Herb nodded as he turned around in the hall and kept pacing while he thought.

Pammon, do you remember anything about a man named Stioks?

Hatred and anger flowed through their bond, and Kaen felt confused by it, as it came not from Pammon but something else.

That name . . . it angers me, and yet I know nothing about them. It is like something inside me despises it and wishes to end that person's life. What are you not telling me?

I just found out from Herb that your mother may have been a captive of his, and she escaped from him, bringing you here. Herb thinks Stioks meant for you to be his dragon.

That same rage pulsed again through the bond, and Kaen could tell Pammon was getting worked up.

If that is true, then I look forward to the day I can bring revenge on that man.

Not you, we. He is the one who killed my father. The quest he died trying to accomplish.

Pammon's rage exploded, and Kaen felt his lifestone pulse in response to it. Whatever he felt was so real and deep that it resonated inside the soul he knew they shared.

Calm down, please. It hurts, Kaen informed Pammon as he grabbed his chest and squeezed his eyes shut.

Pammon relaxed some, letting the rage slowly begin to flow from him. Kaen's lifestone went back to being quiet.

It responded to me? To my anger?

It felt like it did. It never did that before . . . do you think it was the new bond that we formed?

Perhaps, but I am sorry for causing you pain. I will try to control my rage better next time.

You are fine. I know what it is like to be angry and upset. We will figure it out in time and find a way to deal with this man.

"Kaen?"

"Sorry," Kaen blurted out as he focused, and Herb, standing a few feet from him, glanced up at Kaen's blank face. "I was talking to Pammon. That name upsets him for some reason, so I would guess that you are right. His mother may have been the captive dragon, but we don't know for certain."

"Incredible. Being able to communicate with your dragon even down here behind all these wards."

Realizing he was not focused on what was important, Herb motioned for Kaen to follow him. "We need to get out of here, and you need to get back to your dragon. There are things I must take care of, and you are going to need to rest and be prepared for the coming weeks and months. Things are going to get hard for a while to come."

Kaen nodded as he followed Herb and the small man's quick pace.

I don't like it. Something feels off about all this. What are the odds that your dad died at the hands of the man who enslaved my mother?

Kaen rubbed Pammon's neck as they stood alone in the training grounds, except for two people on the far end watching them.

It's not good, and I'm certain Hess will have some thoughts about all of it. My real question is, what do you want to do tonight? We can camp in the fields or the forest, but I must check in with Hess first.

Fancy a flight into town? I mean, how bad could things get if we landed in the streets?

Groaning, Kaen began climbing onto the spot on Pammon he always sat in.

I could ask if someone I know not too far from the inn, if he would let you stay at his place. It is walled off, and I would join you at night. You could still land in the street near the inn after I get permission and cause all the problems I know you want to.

Pammon began to thrum as he leaped into the air.

You know me too well.

"I must say, it is an honor you would consider this," Bren told Kaen as he bowed before Pammon. "I wish you had warned me, though, of your visit since a few of my students may require a few days before they will return."

Laughing, Kaen nodded as he rubbed the underside of Pammon's head.

"Well, let me introduce you to Pammon. Pammon, this is Master Bren, the one who trains me in one-handed weapons and shields."

Pammon gave a slight nod of the head before lying on the ground and watching them.

"It is an honor, again." Bren smiled as he watched them both. "I would say your timing is impeccable, and I am sure you have seen the ones glancing from the doorway every few seconds who would love to come and say hi."

"I thought that was Phillip and Frederick. I would be delighted to introduce them to Pammon and say hi myself."

Pammon snorted and groaned.

Be nice. These two are special to me. If you aren't, I might have to hurry up and have one of my own.

I may need to tap you harder next time to ensure that is impossible.

Turning around, Kaen leaped onto Pammon's neck and wrestled with him while Bren fetched the two boys.

"KAEN!" the boys shouted as they ran, apparently unafraid of the dragon who was larger than all the wagons or horses they had ever seen in town.

When the boys got close, Kaen stopped wrestling with Pammon, got on one knee, and smiled at the two of them. "How are you two boys doing? Training hard, I hear!"

They snapped to attention and nodded.

"Yes sir," replied Phillip as he stared at Pammon, who was moving his head closer to Kaen.

"Good. Now, how would you two like to meet my friend Pammon?"

"Can . . . can we?" Frederick asked as his eyes went wide. "Can we ride him?"

Pammon snorted and shook his head, causing both boys to back up a step.

"He's just messing with you two. Sadly, you can't ride him, as he isn't a pet. He can hear you, but if you want, hold out your hands like this and remain still, and he might let you feel his snout."

Kaen turned and held his hand out, and Pammon glared at him as he moved his head forward till they touched.

I feel like some trick animal working for scraps.

I know . . . I'm sorry, but this means the world to these two; they are my first students for the school I'm starting. Imagine how this one small thing will help keep them committed to being the adventures this kingdom needs.

Pammon grunted and saw both boys trembling as they stood shoulder to shoulder with their hands out. He slowly moved his head till his snout was just inches from them.

"Put your hands on his scales. Feel how hard they are and scratch them a little. He likes it," Kaen informed them.

Both boys took a half step, and Kaen heard a slight sigh when their hands touched Pammon's scales. They laughed and then began scratching the scales with their fingers until a trill rose from Pammon's throat.

They yelped and backed up, causing Pammon and Kaen to both laugh.

"That noise is a sound he makes when he likes it. You can try again. Remember, be brave and overcome your fears; you might find something worthwhile like meeting a dragon."

Both boys grinned and rushed back, putting their hands on Pammon's snout again, scratching with greater intensity until Pammon once again trilled for them both.

They laughed as they scratched, each claiming to be the better one at it.

Kaen just smiled as he scratched Pammon's neck, content to find joy in a few boys having fun.

"Do you have any idea what you have done?!" Eltina exclaimed as she pulled Kaen behind the bar.

"Uh . . . I tried to make sure he didn't scare off too many people when he landed in the street."

Smacking her forehead with her hand, she shook her head and grabbed Kaen by the shirt, bringing his eyes near hers.

"You have made work harder on me, boy! That stunt is going to fill this place with people waiting to see if you will return on a dragon giving them a chance to see him! I'll be packed for days! For weeks! Hairy elf chests, maybe even months!" she shouted as she let go of his shirt and glanced over the bar. "Look! They are already streaming in! Hoping to talk to you and get a chance to see your dragon in person!"

"I'm . . . sorry?"

"Bah," scoffed Eltina as she moved to her block on the bar. "Go back to the office where those two are. One day, I'll get my revenge, don't you worry!"

Bewildered, Kaen stood tall and had started to walk away when he felt arms wrap around his midsection.

He glanced down, and Eltina was letting go, moving back to her spot again, wiping a rare tear from her eye.

He opened his mouth to ask her why but closed it, content to accept her affection however it came.

"I'm sorry about earlier today. Hormones are worse in the morning and afternoon," Sulenda explained after they had all sat down. "Right now, I am fine, but I was a little overwhelmed, and it took over."

"You are fine," Kaen answered as he watched her relax at his words. "I am just glad we all made it back."

"As am I, boy, as I am," Hess stated as he held up his stub. "I'm content to be back, even if it's not in one piece."

Sulenda snorted and bobbed her head. "That joke is getting older by the day."

"So tell me, son." Hess said. "Why are you here? I know you love us, but I also know you have thousands of things on your plate."

Kaen nodded and told them both what he learned from Herb and from his father's vault.

"Hairy dwarf balls, Kaen. I'm sorry. I didn't even know," Hess finally stated. "How did you process all of that?"

"It wasn't easy, but Pammon and I are fine. Right now, I need to know what you think. How could my father and Pammon's mother be connected?"

"Fate? I have no idea, boy. That philosophical goblin shite isn't for me. I don't believe in futures beyond what one makes. Ask someone who believes in that nonsense, and then try to live, *waiting* for that special one to come."

Sighing, Kaen accepted that answer. It was easier than considering the alternative; multiple parents would die so that a human and a dragon could be bound.

"What are you going to do now?" asked Sulenda. "You can't stay here, as much as I would love to have you at the inn."

"I know, and I appreciate that. I'll stay with Pammon tonight at Master Bren's place, and then tomorrow, the king is supposed to have a place for us in the countryside. Somewhere with privacy and, hopefully, cows for Pammon."

"And what about the girl?" Hess asked as he raised an eyebrow. "Her father is chomping at the bit to get you two married after discovering how you saved her. Even more so with the news of you being a Dragon Rider."

"I don't know," he declared, shrugging slightly. "I like her. A lot. Right now, though, I need to focus on getting stronger. I need to learn to unlock this."

Kaen was tapping his lifestone. "Something tells me it's going to get worse before it gets better. A lot worse. We still need to deal with the invading army and—"

"You don't need to deal with that," announced Hess. "The king has committed a few forces to help with that now that the adventurers' guild succeeded due to you. There are other adventurers coming from other kingdoms to help with the loss. Things are changing, and you need to focus on you and Pammon."

Hess rose from his chair, moved to where Kaen was, and offered him a hand. His only hand.

"Give me a hug and go spend the night with Pammon. Tomorrow, go where the king finds you a place, and spend a few days figuring out what you want. Once you do, then find me. I'm not going anywhere."

Kaen grasped the hand and stood up, embracing Hess in a hug. "You know I can never repay you," Kaen told him as he looked up at the man who had raised him.

Hess laughed and waved his stump in Kaen's face. "I believe you have paid me back in full," he joked. "I'm just glad it didn't cost me a leg too!"

Laughing, Kaen punched Hess in the gut and acted like he was going to tackle him.

"If you two break anything in here, I'll beat both of you," growled Sulenda as she smiled at them. "Now hug and make up. This momma is tired."

"Oh, I forgot! I have something for your child." Kaen walked to the desk, pulled a pouch out, and set it on top. "Whatever your child decides to be, there is a ring for each stat."

Surprised, Sulenda grabbed the pouch and poured out the contents on the desk. Six different rings spilled out and came to rest before her.

"This is too much!" she exclaimed.

"Not for my little brother or sister, it isn't!"

96

Elies and Thurnok

Sweat poured down his back as Kaen took a breath. He glanced at the field behind him and the rows he had plowed. Sure, an ox would have been a smart choice, but he was taking Hoste's advice. He had already gained one point of strength and constitution over the last day after beginning this task.

Seems there should be an easier way to get stronger, but do what you must.

You're one to talk. I think I have seen you eat four cows in the last two days. You should be flying more.

The king told us to do what we want, and right now, I want to rest. My body finally doesn't hurt anymore, and I feel full. I am growing, and I need more food to keep it up. You, on the other hand, could use a little more food.

Kaen laughed as he took a drink from the waterskin he had on his hip. He had been eating like Pammon, consuming food like crazy. All this work and exercise was making him eat like never before. Thankfully, the king had given him a few servants to help around the house and with the chores.

Finished with his break, he grabbed the ropes and looped them over his shoulders, armpit, and arms. He still had ten more acres to break up.

It seems we are about to have a visitor.

Letting the rope go slack, Kaen glanced in the direction he knew Pammon was looking. There was a horse approaching in a gallop across the fields and headed straight toward them.

What kind of visitor? One of the servants?

No. This one is not one I recognize. He is wearing the king's crest, though. A young man, perhaps a few years older than you.

Kaen stretched his arms and shoulders as the ropes fell to the ground, noticing the red marks from where the thick ropes had bitten into his skin. They healed quickly enough, and it was good training, Bren had said, to learn to endure constant pain.

Moving closer to Pammon, he knew the rider was still minutes away, even at that pace.

I'm going to call this done for the day. I might be up for a trip into town if you are interested in it.

Can I scare the locals again?

Would it matter if I said no?

Kaen could hear the thrumming even as far away as he was. Pammon enjoyed that part of visiting the city way too much.

"Sir Kaen!" the man shouted as he leaped from his horse and covered the last fifty yards on foot.

This wasn't the first time King Aldric had sent a messenger, and the first few learned the hard way that horses do not like riding up near a dragon.

"A letter!"

Kaen nodded, and the young man stopped, bent over, and held out the tube of paper for him.

Kaen broke the wax seal, and his gut clenched when he read the words on the page.

Kaen,

News has reached me. Elies and Tharnok will arrive here in two days.
King *Aldric*

Sighing, Kaen glanced at the messenger who was watching him. "Tell King Aldric I appreciate this. Inform him that I plan on staying here for a few days."

When the man realized Kaen was done, he bowed and took off running toward his horse again.

It appears Elies is on his way. They will be here in two days.

What do you want to do?

Kaen laughed when he looked at Pammon and saw the way he was watching him.

We both knew someday this would happen. There is nowhere to run, and I am not a coward.

Well, we have two days to do whatever we want. Any ideas?

This was not at all what I had in mind.

Pammon's displeasure felt like sandpaper across his skin. Kaen ignored it, instead focusing on the two boys tied to his waist who were laughing and holding their arms out as they flew above the city.

How can you be so upset about this idea? They are having the time of their life. Sulenda has informed me that since our first visit, the number of people wanting to be part of the academy has grown. In the first year, she will be full and expects to have well over two hundred potential students by the second year.

And yet, it will take many years to replace all the adventurers lost in the last month.

Kaen smiled and ignored the moody dragon, laughing with the boys as the wind rushed across their faces.

Pammon trilled with delight as both boys attacked the underside of his neck as he lay on his back in Bren's courtyard.

Chuckling, Kaen knew Pammon had a soft heart for these two as much as he pretended to hate giving into their demands. They constantly told Pammon that he was the greatest dragon ever, thus inflating his ego even more.

"I would never have imagined this," Bren stated as he watched the two boys playing with Pammon. "I guess I shouldn't be surprised by how you improved so fast. It makes sense now."

"I would not have kept it a secret except for the fact we both know I was not ready."

"You still aren't *ready*, but you are getting closer. Done slacking off and ready to keep training?"

"Always!" Kaen declared as he moved to get a sword and a shield from the rack. With Pammon here and knowing what he could do, he had already brought his sword up to an eighteen and his shield to a twenty-four. It seemed Hoste had been right after all. He had a lot more potential than he realized.

"You smell like the backside of someone's arse," Ava informed him as she wrinkled her nose. "Did you bathe at all while you were gone?"

Kaen laughed and rushed forward, pretending to hug her before stopping at the last minute and just kissing her on the cheek. "I'm sorry, but some of us have training to complete. Perhaps you might need to practice a little more yourself."

Rolling her eyes, Ava strode over to Pammon. "Is he always this much trouble," she asked.

Pammon nodded his head before resting it on the ground again.

"Kaen told me you managed to eat four cows already. I will have to make sure I get a few more for you. I can't let you starve."

A little drool dripped from the corner of Pammon's mouth, and Kaen groaned.

She isn't too bad. Perhaps this is her dowry for you. A lifetime of cows.

Who knew the way to your heart was through food?

I remember someone making me wait to eat when I was young.

Chuckling, Kaen joined Ava as she watched Pammon.

"He says you might have found the way to his heart. Only one thousand more cows, and he says you can earn my hand."

Ava blushed and she looked at Kaen before turning to Pammon. "I was willing to go as high as nine hundred, but I'm not sure you're worth one thousand," she said, sighing.

Pammon's thrumming reverberated off the ground as Kaen groaned. It was almost unbearable as he laughed so hard and so long it seemed to shake their bodies.

"It appears he thinks you are funny after all."

"Oh, I had no doubt. Funny and smart. My two best qualities."

"Yes," Kaen mocked her, "your two best qualities."

I can see them . . . I don't know how to say this other than Tharnok is massive.

Glancing up into the sky, Kaen could see the two of them coming toward them. Pammon was right. For them to be that far away and Kaen still able to see them, meant Tharnok was massive compared to Pammon.

You appear nervous. Should I be concerned?

No. It is just . . . If we tried to run, I realize now that we would not get far at all.

Kaen felt the same way. No matter what he wanted, the next few moments of his life were out of his control.

Elies stood on the ground, watching them. Kaen had been impressed with many things about Elies and Tharnok, but the saddle and harness the man had on his dragon were what had his attention at the moment. He could see how one of those would provide much more assistance than his current rope and leather system.

Kaen could feel the other dragon staring at him and Pammon. Tharnok was at least five times larger than Pammon. His head was almost the size of Pammon's body.

"I will say, I am impressed," Elies said as he closed the final ten yards that stood between him and Kaen. "You do not tremble like most when we stand before them, and both Tharnok and I can feel the link between the two of you. You have achieved something not done in over a hundred years."

"I'm glad we could impress you, but I'm not sure what you are talking about," Kaen admitted. He knew the only reason he was not trembling in fear was because he had no other option. "What have we achieved?"

"You two are bonded completely. That does not happen for a long time, and yet here you two are, bonded, and your dragon is not even a year old."

"Pammon. His name is Pammon."

Elies smiled.

Kaen could see the scars on his face. A patch of burnt skin ran up his neck on one side before hiding under his chest piece.

"We like that you will not allow one to treat Pammon as anything other than an equal. Another fine quality." He paused as Tharnok moved his head forward. A growl came from him.

Enough with the banter. You two will follow us back to our home. There is no time for discussion.

Kaen and Pammon both flinched as the voice of Tharnok wracked their minds. It was so powerful, it almost made Kaen want to fall to his knees. Power and pressure assaulted them both, and Kaen was barely able to resist it. Pammon felt as if he was about to give in to the command.

I . . . can't . . . fight him.

Kaen sent his strength to Pammon, helping him to stay put while using everything he had just to remain standing. "Why should we do that?" he finally asked as he gritted his teeth.

Impossible! How can you resist my command?!

Tharnok's head bobbed as he leaned forward even more, extending his neck toward them as his massive eyes gazed at them.

Elies started laughing. Kaen saw that he was thoroughly amused at whatever had just transpired.

"The rumors we heard do not do you two justice," Elies informed them as he kept smiling. "Neither one of you should have been able to resist that. The force he just used would send kings to their knees. I cannot remember the last time someone has resisted him."

Kaen started to speak but Elies held up his hand, glancing at Tharnok.

They are talking to each other.

I know! How did you resist that? I would have given in, but your strength carried me. It felt like a mountain was crushing me for a moment.

I don't know. I'm just grateful it worked.

A cough broke them from their time together.

"It appears we both are out of practice dealing with others with dragons. If you would permit me, I will ask you to join us instead of ordering you to."

Kaen could see that Elies was serious, and he felt like Tharnok was still upset that whatever he had attempted had not worked.

"Can I ask why we need to come?"

Elies nodded and slowly peeled up his shirt, revealing his stomach and chest, which looked to be rotting.

Kaen could not hold back the look of horror, and Elies was silent as he lowered his shirt.

"I am dying, Kaen. Stioks and his dragon did this to me, and I probably only have a few years left. What would have taken over ten years to teach you and Pammon, I must try to accomplish in just a few."

"Dying? What about potions? I have some that seem to heal anything," Kaen asked as he began to move toward their estate.

"It won't work," Elies called out. "Nothing will. I have tried it all. Only my bond with Tharnok has held it off. After a while, even he will not be able to keep me alive. When news that I have fallen reaches Stioks's ears, there will need to be a trained Dragon Rider to make him think twice about pursuing his path."

Kaen saw the battle-worn face, which had seen more than he could imagine, change. The light in his eyes dimmed, and a concerned expression replaced the calm demeanor Elies had been wearing this entire time.

"I'm afraid if you also do not follow me, he may come here to remove the threat he will realize you are," he admitted, frowning. "He will most likely offer you women, wealth, and lands, but in the end, I would expect he would kill you the moment he was close."

Kaen knew it was true. Pammon had told him already this would be an outcome. Before seeing Tharnok with his own eyes, he believed they could fight or escape Stioks and Juthom. That belief and hope were now shattered.

"When will we need to leave?" Kaen asked as he glanced back at Pammon, who was moving toward him.

We need to go.

What? Why?

You and I need to go for lots of reasons, but you need to go because it's time. It's time for you to learn what you need to know. It's time to accept what you are still struggling with; your father, Hoste. You're upset about his commitment to his belief, and you are not as committed to yours as you believe you are.

What? I am committed! Look at what I have been doing the last few days! Training and working.

Yes. Your body has been, but your heart has not. You could have used your lifestone while you plowed that field, but you didn't. You wanted to do it on your own. I had hoped you might work through this, but now we are fighting for your life and mine. You have lost your way. If you do not find it, Elies and Tharnok might die. I might die.

Kaen winced, and he knew Pammon was right. He needed to let it go.

How will going fix this? What about Hess and Sulenda and their baby?

You are asking questions you already know the answer to.

Kaen felt no anger or frustration through his bond with Pammon. He was upset, and his emotions were twisted, but Pammon wasn't. He was thinking clearly.

How can you protect them if we stay here? You have spent more time playing than training. I understand you need some release and want to be around those you love, but will that protect them against what is coming?

Kaen sighed and shook his head.

I guess . . . I guess I hoped I would have more time here, with you and with them.

Kaen felt Pammon's snout pushing against him. A gentle bit of pressure as Pammon waited for him to put his hand on his head.

Look at the two of them. See how old they are and the time they have had together. If we want that, we must go. We must learn what we have talked about for a while. There is no other way if you genuinely mean to protect this kingdom.

Kaen nodded. Pammon was right, and he knew it.

"We will follow you," Kaen stated, though it almost sounded like a whisper. "I will go collect my stuff."

Kaen had not realized how few worldly goods he owned. A beat-up leather tunic, a few new pairs of clothes to replace the ones he had worn the threads out of, a bow, and some jewelry. Beyond that, nothing in the house he stayed in was his. Seeing everything fit inside a single backpack almost made leaving easier.

It had been like this when they had left Minoosh. Nothing but the clothes on their backs. He had owned even less then. Now, he had a pouch full of rings and gold in his pockets. Clothes fine enough to meet a king were tucked away in the bottom of his pack. Who knew what kind of attire he would need there?

Four letters had been written and turned in to the servants.

One letter was for Hess, telling him what he was doing and why. It wasn't an easy decision to leave without saying goodbye in person, but no good would come from that meeting. He had shared his feelings in words. It had been hard, for a moment, till he was honest with himself. Hess would always be the man he considered his dad.

The second letter was for Sulenda, giving her complete control over the school until he could return down the road and help. He planned on returning occasionally, but too much would need to be done, and he wasn't sure how often he would be able to make it, at first.

There was also a letter for Herb, short but sweet, telling him thank you and explaining Kaen's plan. It was the easiest letter he'd written, since Herb already knew what was coming.

The last letter was for Ava and had been rewritten three times.

He promised her more letters in the coming months and said he would try to visit if he could. For now, he had to do this, if he was going to protect this kingdom. Words describing how he felt for her seemed hollow and empty. He had considered making Pammon take him to see her, but that would have been unwise, and he knew it. If she would wait, he would too.

Cinching up his pack, he glanced around the bedroom he had barely slept in for a few nights.

It was time to go.

You ready?

The moment he asked that question, Kaen knew Pammon's answer.

I have been ready since the day we bonded. It is time we learn what this is all about.

Smiling, Kaen adjusted his bow on his back and as he felt the magic flow through it, he had one more thought.

Simple Status Check
Kaen Marshell - Adolescent
Age - 17
HP - 126/126 (25%)
MP - 250/250 (25%)
STR - 25 + 0 (25%)
CON - 25 + 4 (25%)
DEX - 26 + 6 (25%)
INT - 19 + 0 (25%)
WIS - 16 + 0 (25%)
Blessings:
Dragonbound Complete - 25% current bonus to all stats

That smile grew as Kaen knew his stats would increase in the coming days. Soon, he would be able to defend everyone he could.

It really is a fantastic sight.

Kaen agreed with Pammon as they flew high over Ebonmount and prepared to go above the mountains that surrounded it.

From up here, it was almost impossible to make out much of anything. Below was the place that had been his home for the last few months. Looking ahead, he saw Tharnok and Elies leading them toward where they would train and live. In the kingdom of Roccnari.

Epilogue

He looked at his hands and realized how much blood dripped from them. His own laughter sounded off as he heard it echo through the room.

Lifting his eyes from the corpse at his feet, he saw the orcs who had come with their leader cowering. None of them had ever seen a fraction of his power.

You should not have done that. You are letting your emotions and temper undo everything we have done. This is not what you promised me.

Turning on his heels, Stioks glared at Juthom, who lounged on the stone floor yards away, glaring at the orcs in the room.

They failed! After years of working and planning, they failed to uphold their promise! I would almost fly out here with you and burn them to the ground!

Then what? We lose our allies who want nothing more than to help you destroy a kingdom? It was not their fault that a Dragon Rider appeared and undid our plans. You and I both know where the blame for that lies.

Screaming in rage, Stioks turned back around and picked up the heart he had ripped from the Magus's body. The foolish orc had felt like it could talk to him like an equal; that it could lay blame on his shoulders for their failures.

That mistake was why the Magus's eyes were still open from where he had pounced on it and pulled it's beating heart from its chest.

He held the heart in his hand and then slammed it on the ground, sending a spray of blood and chunks of flesh flying. "Listen to me," he growled as he glared at the orcs who had lost all the bravery they so often claimed to be proud of. "You will return and tell your *king* that I expect him to uphold his part of the bargain. He does not want us to come there personally and explain the need for this."

They all nodded and grunted. Even though they were all taller and appeared stronger, they were nothing when compared to him, and they knew it.

"Now go!" he ordered, pointing to the door they had come through.

The ten orcs ran, almost tripping over each other, fleeing for safety behind the special entrance he had built for them.

After they left, the room was deathly quiet for a while before Stioks finally spoke. "I would carve Indyn into pieces, if given that chance again," he declared with a growl as he walked toward his black throne. "You are right. The blame lies on me."

Juthom said nothing but watched as Stioks walked toward him and the throne he felt he must sit on. His burnt face was leaking blood, from the behavior he had just displayed. That kind of exertion always left him bleeding.

We were both mistaken to believe we could break her. She was too old and too proud. That she had managed to do what she did, reminds me of what I sometimes miss about my kind.

Plopping onto his throne, Stioks laced his fingers together and closed his eyes. "Have you considered my other idea? Is there a chance at all?"

I have, and I still believe it is foolish. You would risk leaving your throne empty for weeks, flying across the great waters and hoping that the dragons there would not tear us both in half, all while trying to convince them to give you an egg! We are committed to this path we are on, and that plan would only guarantee our death.

Stioks's eye began to twitch. Even closed, the pain in his face was excruciating. His one eye felt on fire every moment he breathed.

"Why . . . why can't those other three females conceive? They give themselves to you every moment, and yet nothing happens."

They are young. I warned you that most dragons do not pursue a mate until they are over a hundred years old. After 'capturing' Indyn, we both realized finding younger ones who could be persuaded versus broken was better. We have time.

Resisting the desire to touch his eye, knowing it would feel good for that brief moment before it seared with even greater pain, Stioks shook his head in disagreement.

"Time is not what we have. The longer this takes, the older I get. Soon, this will all be for naught if I cannot bond with a hatchling," he stated as he finally opened his eyes, and a few drops of blood flowed out. "Elies should die soon, but how long will that take? Will this new Dragon Rider pose a threat before that happens?"

The throne room echoed as Juthom laughed; his huge body shook, and the thrum it gave off seemed to assault the air around him.

It takes decades for a Dragon Rider to learn what they need to know. Trust me. We have time.

Acknowledgments

I owe so much to countless people for helping me along this journey! Simply put, thank you to the authors who poured into me, encouraging me and giving me advice as I learned to write. Every day, I get better because of the help you give.

Thank you to Madix, Miles, Kae, Rachasudd, Haylock, Host, Timewalk, Luca, Mizarcaph, Serhmy, Andykay, BabaVadar, Zuesified, SavingThrow, JTB and countless other authors. May your words always inspire others and create joy for those who read them.

About the Author

Shawn Wilson is the author of the Last Dragon Rider series, originally released on Royal Road. Movies, shows, books, and more provide inspiration for his stories. Wilson is a father of six and enjoys spending time with his wife and kids.

DISCOVER
STORIES UNBOUND

PodiumAudio.com

Milton Keynes UK
Ingram Content Group UK Ltd.
UKHW010632290424
441924UK00001B/208